A Dictionary of English Synonyms

英文同義字典

劉 毅 主編

這是一本學英文必備的工具書。

背同義字有助於寫作。

背同義字可以快速增加單字。

修編序

　　字彙的使用是一門藝術，同義字在這門藝術中扮演了極重要的角色。本書的目的，即是為您提供最常用的同義字資料，以強化您的用字能力。

　　平日當我們在說話或寫作時，往往需要重複表達相同的意念。此時，說話或文章的內容會不會變得枯燥而累贅，就完全要看是否能夠活用同義字了。例如，要在作文中強調某事是 necessary「必要的」，但是若重複使用此字，所寫的文章必然會變得十分單調。此時，便可查閱本書而知與 necessary 同義的還有 required、essential、needed、compelling、imperative 等字，將這些字交替使用，文章就會變得十分活潑而有力。

　　本書經過精心編排，特別為每個字都注上詳細的 KK 音標。因此，除了是一本不可或缺的工具書之外，更可幫助您擴大字彙範圍。透過同義字群的方式來記憶單字，是增加字彙最迅速而有效的方法，因為按照字義將單字分門別類，日後只要再看到其中的一個，就能夠迅速地聯想出其它同義的字，如此經常練習，就能夠確保字彙不會遺忘了。

　　本書還有一大特色，就是將與單字意義相同的成語都一併列出。例如在 abolish「廢除」一字下，就列出了同義成語 put an end to、wipe out、do away with 等，以便讀者將單字與成語交替使用，使文章或說話的內容更加生動活潑。

　　本書的內容不限任何階層，不論是各級學生，或一般社會人士，都可隨時置於案頭，作為參考或自修之用，並從而領略出同義字之妙。希望本書能在您手中發揮最大的功效。

　　「英文同義字典」的修編，是一項大的工程，蘇淑玲小姐花了一年的時間重新打字，由李冠勳老師負責總校，張怡萱小姐協助，黃淑貞小姐負責版面設計，白雪嬌小姐負責美編，非常感謝他們的努力。全書雖經審慎校對，疏漏之處恐所難免，誠盼各界先進不吝指正。

編者　謹識

背同義字是學英文的新方法

全世界的人學英文，方法都錯了，大家不會說、不會聽、不會寫，是最佳的證明。先有語言才有語法，先有文字，才有文法。人類為了學習英文，想要抄近路，把平常所講的話變成規則，把字分成形容詞、名詞、動詞等，忽略那些沒辦法用文法歸納的句子，所以英文學不好。例如：Consider the greater good. 如果照文法解釋累死了，consider 是完全及物動詞還是不完全及物動詞？good 是否為受詞補語？這句話應該當成慣用句來看，意思是「要考慮大家的利益。」（= *Consider what is best for everyone.*）再如：Always put "the team" first. 意思是 "There's no 'I' in team." 你看這兩句話中的 "team"，一個加 the，另一個不加 the，難道用到句子時還要想文法不成？！

背句子是最好的方法，背了自然會寫、自然會說。句子一定要短，用同義字串連。我們最新研發的「一口氣背同義字」，是以一個劇情、9個句子，背出 100 多個同義字，也是 100 多個可用的句子，例如：

How to Be a True Leader
（如何成為一個真正的領導者）

1. **Be noble**. （人格要高尚。）
2. Be brave. （要勇敢。）
3. Be willing to risk failure. （要願意冒失敗的風險。）
4. **Be selfless**. （要無私。）
5. Be human. （要有人性。）
6. Always put "the team" first. （總是把「團隊」放在第一位。）
7. **Lead by example**. （要以身作則。）
8. Commit yourself to excellence. （要盡全力做到最好。）
9. Inspire people to believe in themselves.
   （要激勵人們相信自己的力量。）

這九句話精心編排，很容易背，從 noble 的同義字裡面，找出可以用在 Be noble. 句子中的重要 12 個字：worthy, trustworthy, upright, righteous, virtuous, honest, just, moral, ethical, conscientious, principled, high-minded, aboveboard。只要背了 Be noble. 這句話，你就會說：Be worthy.、Be trustworthy. 等。

可用這九句話寫出短篇作文：

How to Be a Leader

What does it take to be a leader? *For openers*, you must be noble and brave. Be willing to risk failure. *Furthermore*, you must be selfless. Be human, and always put "the team" first.

Most important of all, you should lead by example. Actions speak louder than words. Be a model for others to follow. *To be sure*, you should work harder than anyone else. *All in all*, commit yourself to excellence. True leaders inspire people to believe in themselves.

如何成為領導者

領導者必須具備什麼條件？首先，你必須人格要高尚，而且要勇敢，要願意冒會失敗的風險。此外，你必須要無私。要有人情味，而且總是把「團隊」放在第一位。

最重要的是，你應該要以身作則。行動勝於言辭。要當個能讓人效法的典範。當然，你應該要比任何人更努力。總之，要努力做到最好。真正的領導者會激勵別人，相信自己的力量。

可用同義字和同義句寫出長篇作文：

How to Be a Leader

What does it take to be a leader? *First of all,* you must be noble, worthy, and trustworthy. You should let people know you are an upright, righteous, and just person. *No doubt*, you are virtuous, honest, and honorable. Being moral, ethical, and conscientious is important, *too*. Whatever you do has to be principled, high-minded, and aboveboard.

Second, to be a leader, you must be brave, bold, and courageous. Be fearless, unafraid, and adventurous. When you are faced with difficulties, you should always be daring, unshrinking, and valiant. *Third*, you must be willing to risk failure. You must be ready, prepared, and eager for more challenges. Be inclined and keen to take chances. A brave man is happy, pleased, and content in the face of adversity.

Fourth, a true leader must be selfless, unselfish, and self-sacrificing. People like to follow a big-hearted, open-handed, and devoted person. A charitable, benevolent, and philanthropic man wins everything. *Fifth*, to err is human. A good leader should be humane and natural. He should be kind and compassionate to everyone. He should also be mortal, understandable, and approachable.

In addition, if you want to be a leader, remember that there is no "I" in team. Always put "the team" first. A leader not only believes in teamwork but also tries hard to be a team player. He has to consider the greater good. *In other words*, he has to consider the benefit of all people and decide what's best for everyone. *What's more*, actions speak louder than words. Example is better than precept. A leader should lead by example. He needs to practice what he preaches and be a model for others to follow.

Most important of all, you must commit yourself to excellence, dedicate yourself to your cause, and be devoted to achieving perfection. Keep striving to be the best. *All in all*, you should keep in mind that a good leader can inspire people to believe in themselves. You should make every effort to motivate and encourage others, and persuade them to improve themselves. A successful leader will have a positive influence on those around him.

本書使用方法

1. 各字按字母順序排列，用黑體字。各頁上方標出該頁的起迄單字，以便查閱。

2. 各字採其最清晰常用的解釋。若有兩種或以上的不同解釋，則分別列出各解釋的同義字。如：

   fruit〔 frut 〕*n.* ①果實　②成果

   ① = *plant product*

   ② = yield〔 jild 〕

   　 = result〔 rɪˈzʌlt 〕

3. 有些字有不同的詞性，且意思不同，表示法如下：

   gear〔 gɪr 〕① *v.* 裝備　② *n.* 齒輪

   ① = equip〔 ɪˈkwɪp 〕

   　 = furnish〔 ˈfɝnɪʃ 〕

   　 = outfit〔 ˈaʊtˌfɪt 〕

   　 = rig〔 rɪg 〕

   ② = wheel〔 hwil 〕

4. 與單字意義相同的片語以斜體字表示。

快速增加單字法

——如何背同義字

　　人類的瞬時記憶力是有限的，例如一串數字 781293478 不易記住。但是若採用分段式的記憶，即 781,293,478，就很容易背下來。背同義字也可採用同樣的方法。例如下列同義字，您可試著以分組的方式記下來。

---

unhappy *adj.* 〔ʌnˋhæpɪ〕

$\begin{cases} = \text{sad} 〔\text{sæd}〕 \\ = \text{blue} 〔\text{blu}〕 \end{cases}$

$\begin{cases} = \text{discontented} 〔\text{ˏdɪskənˋtɛntɪd}〕 \\ = \text{displeased} 〔\text{dɪsˋplizd}〕 \end{cases}$

$\begin{cases} = \text{dejected} 〔\text{dɪˋdʒɛktɪd}〕 \\ = \text{depressed} 〔\text{dɪˋprɛst}〕 \\ = \text{melancholy} 〔\text{ˋmɛlənˏkɑlɪ}〕 \end{cases}$

$\begin{cases} = \text{sorrowful} 〔\text{ˋsɑrofəl}〕 \\ = \text{uncheerful} 〔\text{ʌnˋtʃɪrfəl}〕 \\ = \text{wistful} 〔\text{ˋwɪstfəl}〕 \end{cases}$

A

abandon 〔 ə'bændən 〕 *v.* 放棄；
捨棄

= cede 〔 sid 〕
= desert 〔 dɪ'zɜt 〕
= discard 〔 dɪs'kard 〕
= discontinue 〔 ,dɪskən'tɪnju 〕
= evacuate 〔 ɪ'vækju,et 〕
= forgo 〔 fɔr'go 〕
= forsake 〔 fə'sek 〕
= leave 〔 liv 〕
= quit 〔 kwɪt 〕
= relinquish 〔 rɪ'lɪŋkwɪʃ 〕
= surrender 〔 sə'rɛndə 〕
= waive 〔 wev 〕
= withdraw 〔 wɪð'drɔ , wɪθ- 〕
= yield 〔 jild 〕
= *give up*

abase 〔 ə'bes 〕 *v.* 降低；貶抑

= debase 〔 dɪ'bes 〕
= degrade 〔 dɪ'gred 〕
= demean 〔 dɪ'min 〕
= demote 〔 dɪ'mot 〕
= humble 〔 'hʌmbḷ 〕
= lower 〔 'loə 〕
= reduce 〔 rɪ'djus 〕
= *bring down*

abashed 〔 ə'bæʃt 〕 *adj.* 羞愧的；
困惑的；侷促不安的

= ashamed 〔 ə'ʃemd 〕
= bewildered 〔 bɪ'wɪldəd 〕
= confused 〔 kən'fjuzd 〕
= confounded 〔 kɑn'faʊndɪd ,
  kən- 〕
= embarrassed 〔 ɪm'bærəst 〕
= humble 〔 'hʌmbḷ 〕
= humiliated 〔 hju'mɪlɪ,etɪd 〕
= mortified 〔 'mɔrtə,faɪd 〕

abate 〔 ə'bet 〕 *v.* ①減少；降低
②清除；廢止

① = alleviate 〔 ə'livɪ,et 〕
= decrease 〔 dɪ'kris 〕
= lessen 〔 'lɛsṇ 〕
= moderate 〔 'mɑdə,ret 〕
= reduce 〔 rɪ'djus 〕
= subside 〔 səb'saɪd 〕
= weaken 〔 'wikən 〕
② = stop 〔 stɑp 〕
= *do away with*
= *put an end to*

abbey 〔 'æbɪ 〕 *n.* 修道院

= cloisters 〔 'klɔɪstəz 〕
= convent 〔 'kɑnvɛnt 〕
= friary 〔 'fraɪərɪ 〕
= monastery 〔 'mɑnəs,tɛrɪ 〕
= nunnery 〔 'nʌnərɪ 〕
= priory 〔 'praɪərɪ 〕

abbot 〔 'æbət 〕 *n.* 方丈；住持

= friar 〔 'fraɪə 〕
= monk 〔 mʌŋk 〕

abbreviate 〔 ə'brivɪ,et 〕 *v.*
縮短；縮寫

= abridge 〔 ə'brɪdʒ 〕
= compress 〔 kəm'prɛs 〕
= condense 〔 kən'dɛns 〕
= contract 〔 kən'trækt 〕

A

= curtail (kɜ'tel)
= cut (kʌt)
= reduce (rɪ'djus)
= shorten ('ʃɔrtn̩)

abdicate ('æbdə,ket) *v.* 放棄

= abandon (ə'bændən)
= abjure (əb'dʒʊr , æb-)
= quit (kwɪt)
= relinquish (rɪ'lɪŋkwɪʃ)
= renounce (rɪ'naʊns)
= resign (rɪ'zaɪn)
= surrender (sə'rɛndɚ)
= vacate ('veket)
= yield (jild)
= *give up*

abdomen (æb'domən , 'æbdəmən) *n.* 腹部

= stomach ('stʌmək)
= belly ('bɛlɪ)
= paunch (pɔntʃ)

abhor (əb'hɔr , æb-) *v.* 憎恨；厭惡

= abominate (ə'bɑmə,net)
= detest (dɪ'tɛst)
= despise (dɪ'spaɪz)
= dislike (dɪs'laɪk)
= loathe (loð)

abide (ə'baɪd) *v.* ①忍受 ②居住 ③遵守

① = accept (ək'sɛpt)
= bear (bɛr)

= endure (ɪn'djur)
= stand (stænd)
= tolerate ('tɑlə,ret)
= *put up with*
② = dwell (dwɛl)
= live (lɪv)
= lodge (lɑdʒ)
= reside (rɪ'zaɪd)
= stay (ste)
③ = comply (kəm'plaɪ) (with)
= follow ('fɑlo)
= obey (ə'be , o'be)
= observe (əb'zɝv)

ability (ə'bɪlətɪ) *n.* 能力

= aptitude ('æptə,tjud)
= capability (,kepə'bɪlətɪ)
= capacity (kə'pæsətɪ)
= competence ('kɑmpətəns)
= faculty ('fækl̩tɪ)
= knack (næk)
= power ('paʊɚ)
= skill (skɪl)
= talent ('tælənt)

abject ('æbdʒɛkt) *adj.* ①可憐的 ②卑鄙的

① = miserable ('mɪzərəbl̩)
= pitiable ('pɪtɪəbl̩)
= wretched ('rɛtʃɪd)
② = base (bes)
= contemptible (kən'tɛmptəbl̩)
= degraded (dɪ'gredɪd)
= dishonorable (dɪs'ɑnərəbl̩)
= low (lo)
= mean (min)

able (ˈebl̩) *adj.* 能幹的；有能力的

= adept (əˈdɛpt)
= competent (ˈkɑmpətənt)
= efficient (ɪˈfɪʃənt , ə-)
= gifted (ˈgɪftɪd)
= qualified (ˈkwɑləˌfaɪd)
= skillful (ˈskɪlfəl)
= talented (ˈtæləntɪd)

abnormal (æbˈnɔrmḷ) *adj.*
異常的；變態的

= anomalous (əˈnɑmələs)
= eccentric (ɪkˈsɛntrɪk , ɛk-)
= extraordinary (ɪkˈstrɔrdn̩ˌɛrɪ)
= irregular (ɪˈrɛgjələ)
= monstrous (ˈmɑnstrəs)
= odd (ɑd)
= unnatural (ʌnˈnætʃərəl)

aboard (əˈbord , əˈbɔrd) *adv.* 在船上（飛機上；火車上；汽車上）

= on board
= on (*or into*) *a ship, airplane, train or bus*

abode (əˈbod) *n.* 住所

= domicile (ˈdɑməsaɪl , -sḷ)
= dwelling (ˈdwɛlɪŋ)
= habitation (ˌhæbəˈteʃən)
= home (hom)
= house (haʊs)
= lodging (ˈlɑdʒɪŋ)
= quarters (ˈkwɔrtəz)
= residence (ˈrɛzədəns)

abolish (əˈbɑlɪʃ) *v.* 廢除

= abrogate (ˈæbrəˌget)
= cancel (ˈkænsḷ)
= destroy (dɪˈstrɔɪ)
= eliminate (ɪˈlɪməˌnet)
= exterminate (ɪkˈstɝməˌnet)
= rescind (rɪˈsɪnd)
= *do away with*
= *put an end to*
= *wipe out*

abominable (əˈbɑmnəbḷ , -mən-) *adj.* 可惡的；可厭的

= abhorrent (əbˈhɔrənt)
= atrocious (əˈtroʃəs)
= detestable (dɪˈtɛstəbḷ)
= disgusting (dɪsˈgʌstɪŋ)
= hateful (ˈhetfəl)
= horrible (ˈhɑrəbḷ)
= nauseous (ˈnɔʒəs , -zɪəs)
= obnoxious (əbˈnɑkʃəs)

abound (əˈbaʊnd) *v.* 充滿；富於

= flourish (ˈflɝɪʃ)
= overflow (ˌovəˈflo)
= swarm (swɔrm)
= swell (swɛl)
= teem (tim)
= *be plentiful*

about (əˈbaʊt) ① *prep.* 關於
② *prep.* 將要   ③ *prep.* 四周
④ *adv.* 將近

① = concerning (kənˈsɝnɪŋ)
= on (ɑn)
= regarding (rɪˈgardɪŋ)

A

② = *ready to*
   = *on the point of*
③ = around (ə'raʊnd)
   = surrounding (sə'raʊndɪŋ)
④ = almost ('ɔl,most , ɔl'most)
   = approximately (ə'prɑksəmɪtlɪ)
   = nearly ('nɪrlɪ)
   = *close to*

above (ə'bʌv) ① *prep.* 在～之上
② *adv.* 在上方

① = on (ɑn)
   = over ('ovɚ)
   = upon (ə'pɑn)
   = *on top of*
② = aloft (ə'lɔft)
   = overhead ('ovɚ'hɛd)
   = up (ʌp)

abreast (ə'brɛst) *adv.* 並肩

   = alongside (ə'lɔŋ'saɪd)
   = beside (bɪ'saɪd)
   = *shoulder to shoulder*
   = *side by side*

abridge (ə'brɪdʒ) *v.* 縮短；削減

   = abbreviate (ə'brivɪ,et)
   = compress (kəm'prɛs)
   = condense (kən'dɛns)
   = contract (kən'trækt)
   = curtail (kɝ'tel , kɚ-)
   = cut (kʌt)
   = decrease (dɪ'kris)
   = lessen ('lɛsn̩)
   = reduce (rɪ'djus)
   = shorten ('ʃɔrtn̩)

abroad (ə'brɔd) *adv.* 在國外

   = overseas ('ovɚ'siz)
   = *in foreign lands*
   = *out of the country*

abrupt (ə'brʌpt) *adj.* ①突然的
②粗魯的

① = hasty ('hestɪ)
   = sudden ('sʌdn̩)
   = unexpected (,ʌnɪk'spɛktɪd)
② = brusque (brʌsk , brusk)
   = curt (kɝt)
   = rough (rʌf)
   = rude (rud)
   = short (ʃɔrt)

abscess ('æb,sɛs) *n.* 膿瘡

   = ulcer ('ʌlsɚ)
   = boil (bɔɪl)

absent ('æbsn̩t) *adj.* ①缺席的
②茫然的；不關心的

① = away (ə'we)
   = lacking ('lækɪŋ)
   = truant ('truənt)
   = unavailable (,ʌnə'veləbl̩)
   = *not present*
② = inattentive (,ɪnə'tɛntɪv)
   = unaware (,ʌnə'wɛr)
   = unheeding (ʌn'hidɪŋ)

absolute ('æbsə,lut) *adj.* 完全的

   = complete (kəm'plit)
   = entire (ɪn'taɪr)
   = perfect ('pɝfɪkt)
   = pure (pjʊr)

= sheer〔ʃɪr〕
= thorough〔'θɝo〕
= total〔'totḷ〕

absolve〔æb'salv , əb-〕*v.*
赦免；解除

= acquit〔ə'kwɪt〕
= clear〔klɪr〕
= discharge〔dɪs'tʃardʒ〕
= excuse〔ɪk'skjuz〕
= exonerate〔ɪg'zanəˌret〕
= forgive〔fə'gɪv〕
= free〔fri〕
= pardon〔'pardṇ〕

absorb〔əb'sɔrb〕*v.* ①吸收
②全神貫注

① = assimilate〔ə'sɪmḷˌet〕
= incorporate〔ɪn'kɔrpəˌret〕
= receive〔rɪ'siv〕
= *soak up*
= *suck in*
= *take in*
② = engage〔ɪn'gedʒ〕
= engross〔ɪn'gros〕
= preoccupy〔pri'akjəˌpaɪ〕

abstain〔əb'sten , æb-〕*v.* 戒絕

= avoid〔ə'vɔɪd〕
= forbear〔fɔr'bɛr , fə- , -'bær〕
= refrain〔rɪ'fren〕
= refuse〔rɪ'fjuz〕
= shun〔ʃʌn〕
= withhold〔wɪð'hold , wɪθ-〕
= *give up*
= *keep from*

abstract〔*adj.* æb'strækt ,
'æbstrækt , *n.* 'æbstrækt ,
v. æb'strækt〕① *adj.* 抽象的；
深奧的 ② *n.* 摘要 ③ *v.* 抽出

① = abstruse〔æb'strus , əb-〕
= profound〔prə'faund〕
= subtle〔'sʌtḷ〕
= *not concrete*
② = epitome〔ɪ'pɪtəmɪ〕
= essence〔'ɛsṇs〕
= outline〔'autˌlaɪn〕
= summary〔'sʌmərɪ〕
= synopsis〔sɪ'napsɪs〕
③ = extract〔ɪk'strækt〕
= remove〔rɪ'muv〕
= *take away*
= *take out*

absurd〔əb'sɝd〕*adj.* 荒謬的；
可笑的

= foolish〔'fulɪʃ〕
= irrational〔ɪ'ræʃənḷ〕
= laughable〔'læfəbḷ〕
= ludicrous〔'ludɪkrəs , 'lɪu-〕
= ridiculous〔rɪ'dɪkjələs〕

abundant〔ə'bʌndənt〕*adj.*
豐富的；充足的

= ample〔'æmpḷ〕
= bounteous〔'bauntɪəs〕
= bountiful〔'bauntəfəl〕
= full〔ful〕
= overflowing〔ˌovə'floɪŋ〕
= plentiful〔'plɛntɪfəl〕
= profuse〔prə'fjus〕
= rich〔rɪtʃ〕

A

abuse〔ə'bjuz〕v. ①濫用
②虐待　③辱罵

①= misuse〔mɪs'juz〕
　= misapply〔,mɪsə'plaɪ〕
②= damage〔'dæmɪdʒ〕
　= injure〔'ɪndʒɚ〕
　= mistreat〔mɪs'trit〕
③= curse〔kɝs〕
　= insult〔ɪn'sʌlt〕
　= malign〔mə'laɪn〕
　= scold〔skold〕

academy〔ə'kækəmɪ〕n. 學院

　= college〔'kɑlɪdʒ〕
　= school〔skul〕
　= *educational institution*

accelerate〔æk'sɛlə,ret〕v.
加速

　= expedite〔'ɛkspɪ,daɪt〕
　= hasten〔'hesn̩〕
　= hurry〔'hɝɪ〕
　= quicken〔'kwɪkən〕
　= *speed up*

accent〔'æksɛnt〕① v. 加重；
強調　② n. 重音　③ n. 音調

①= accentuate〔æk'sɛntʃu,et , ək-〕
　= emphasize〔'ɛmfə,saɪz〕
　= stress〔strɛs〕
②= emphasis〔'ɛmfəsɪs〕
　= stress〔strɛs〕
③= articulation〔ɑr,tɪkjə'leʃən〕
　= inflection〔ɪn'flɛkʃən〕
　= pronunciation〔prə,nʌnsɪ'eʃən〕
　= tone〔ton〕

accept〔ək'sɛpt , æk-〕v. ①接受
②同意

①= gain〔gen〕
　= obtain〔əb'ten〕
　= receive〔rɪ'siv〕
　= take〔tek〕
②= adopt〔ə'dɑpt〕
　= agree〔ə'gri〕
　= approve〔ə'pruv〕
　= believe〔bɪ'liv〕
　= consent〔kən'sɛnt〕

access〔'æksɛs〕n. 方法；接觸

　= approach〔ə'protʃ〕
　= avenue〔'ævə,nju〕
　= entering〔'ɛntɚɪŋ〕
　= gateway〔'get,we〕
　= passage〔'pæsɪdʒ〕
　= path〔pæθ , pɑθ〕

accessory〔ək'sɛsərɪ〕n. ①附件
②從犯

①= addition〔ə'dɪʃən〕
　= adjunct〔'ædʒʌŋkt〕
　= appendage〔ə'pɛndɪdʒ〕
　= attachment〔ə'tætʃmənt〕
　= extra〔'ɛkstrə〕
　= supplement〔'sʌpləmənt〕
②= accomplice〔ə'kɑmplɪs〕
　= assistance〔ə'sɪstənt〕
　= confederate〔kən'fɛdərɪt〕
　= helper〔'hɛlpɚ〕

accident〔'æksədənt〕n. 意外

　= casualty〔'kæʒuəltɪ〕
　= chance〔tʃæns〕

= injury（'ɪndʒərɪ）

= misfortune（mɪs'fɔrtʃən）

= mishap（'mɪs,hæp , mɪs'hæp）

accidental（,æksə'dɛntl̩）*adj.*
偶然的；無意中的

= adventitious（,ædvɛn'tɪʃəs , ,ædvən-）

= casual（'kæʒuəl）

= chance（tʃæns）

= haphazard（,hæp'hæzəd）

= inadvertent（,ɪnəd'vɝtn̩t）

= incidental（,ɪnsə'dɛntl̩）

= random（'rændəm）

= unexpected（,ʌnɪk'spɛktɪd）

= unforeseen（,ʌnfor'sin）

= unintentional（,ʌnɪn'tɛnʃənl̩）

acclaim（ə'klem）*v.* 歡呼

= applaud（ə'plɔd）

= approve（ə'pruv）

= celebrate（'sɛlə,bret）

= cheer（tʃɪr）

= clap（klæp）

= hail（hel）

accommodate（ə'kamə,det）*v.*
①容納 ②幫助；供應 ③適應

①= board（bord , bɔrd）

= house（haus）

= lodge（ladʒ）

= *put up*

②= aid（ed）

= help（hɛlp）

= oblige（ə'blaɪdʒ）

= provide（prə'vaɪd）

= supply（sə'plaɪ）

③= accustom（ə'kʌstəm）

= adapt（ə'dæpt）

= adjust（ə'dʒʌst）

= conform（kən'fɔrm）

= fit（fɪt）

= suit（sut , sɪut , sjut）

accomplice（ə'kamplɪs）*n.*
同謀者；共犯

= abettor（ə'bɛtə）

= accessory（æk'sɛsərɪ）

= confederate（ken'fɛdərɪt）

= partner（'partnə）

accomplish（ə'kamplɪʃ）*v.* 實現

= achieve（ə'tʃiv）

= attain（ə'ten）

= complete（kəm'plit）

= do（du）

= effect（ə'fɛkt , ɪ- , ɛ-）

= finish（'fɪnɪʃ）

= fulfil（fʊl'fɪl）

= perform（pə'fɔrm）

= realize（'riə,laɪz , rɪə-）

= *carry out*

accord（ə'kɔrd）*n. v.* 一致；相同
v. = agree（ə'gri）

= assent（ə'sɛnt）

= concur（kən'kɝ）

= conform（kən'fɔrm）

= harmonize（'harmə,naɪz）

= match（mætʃ）

n. = accordance（ə'kɔrdn̩s）

= agreement（ə'grimənt）

A

= concurrence (kən'kʒəns)

= correspondence
(,kɔrə'spandəns)

= harmony ('harmənɪ)

account (ə'kaʊnt) *n.* ①報告；
記事 ②理由；原因

① = description (dɪ'skrɪpʃən)

= information (,ɪnfə'meʃən)

= narrative ('nærətɪv)

= report (rɪ'port)

= statement ('stetmənt)

= story ('storɪ)

= tale (tel)

② = cause (kɔz)

= consideration (kən,sɪdə'reʃən)

= reason ('rizn̩)

= regard (rɪ'gard)

accumulate (ə'kjumjə,let) *v.*
積聚

= amass (ə'mæs)

= collect (kə'lɛkt)

= gather ('gæðə)

= increase (ɪn'kris)

= store (stor , stɔr)

= *build up*

= *pile up*

accurate ('ækjərɪt) *adj.* 正確的

= correct (kə'rɛkt)

= exact (ɪg'zækt)

= precise (prɪ'saɪs)

= right (raɪt)

accuse (ə'kjuz) *v.* 控告

= allege (ə'lɛdʒ)

= blame (blem)

= censure ('sɛnʃə)

= charge (tʃardʒ)

= denounce (dɪ'naʊns)

= impeach (ɪm'pitʃ)

= indict (ɪn'daɪt)

accustom (ə'kʌstəm) *v.* 使習慣

= acclimatize (ə'klaɪmə,taɪz)

= acquaint (ə'kwent)

= adapt (ə'dæpt)

= familiarize (fə'mɪljə,raɪz)

= habituate (hə'bɪtʃʊ,et)

= *make used to*

ache (ek) *n.* 疼痛；苦痛

= hurt (hʒt)

= pain (pen)

= soreness ('sornɪs , 'sor-)

= suffering ('sʌfrɪŋ , 'sʌfərɪŋ)

= throb (θrab)

achieve (ə'tʃiv) *v.* 實現；完成

= accomplish (ə'kamplɪʃ)

= complete (kəm'plit)

= do (du)

= finish ('fɪnɪʃ)

= fulfil (fʊl'fɪl)

= perform (pə'fɔrm)

= reach (ritʃ)

= realize ('riə,laɪz)

= win (wɪn)

acknowledge (ək'nalɪdʒ) *v.*
承認

= accede〔æk'sid〕

= accept〔ək'sɛpt〕

= admit〔əd'mɪt〕

= concede〔kən'sid〕

= confess〔kən'fɛs〕

= grant〔grænt〕

= recognize〔'rɛkəgˌnaɪz〕

= *make known*

acme〔'ækmɪ , 'ækmi〕*n.* 頂點

= apex〔'epɛks〕

= crown〔kraʊn〕

= culmination〔ˌkʌlmə'neʃən〕

= peak〔pik〕

= pinnacle〔'pɪnəkl̩ , -ɪkl̩〕

= summit〔'sʌmɪt〕

= top〔tɑp〕

= zenith〔'zinɪθ , (英)'zɛnɪθ〕

acquaint〔ə'kwent〕*v.* 告知；
使熟識

= advise〔əd'vaɪz〕

= disclose〔dɪs'kloz〕

= enlighten〔ɪn'laɪtn̩〕

= familiarize〔fə'mɪljəˌraɪz〕

= inform〔ɪn'fɔrm〕

= notify〔'notəfaɪ〕

= reveal〔rɪ'vil〕

= tell〔tɛl〕

= *let know*

= *make familiar with*

acquiesce〔ˌækwɪ'ɛs〕*v.* 默許；
默認

= agree〔ə'gri〕

= accede〔æk'sid〕

= assent〔ə'sɛnt〕

= comply〔kəm'plaɪ〕

= concur〔kən'kɝ〕

= consent〔kən'sɛnt〕

= submit〔səb'mɪt〕

= *go along with*

acquire〔əˌkwaɪr〕*v.* 獲得

= earn〔ɝn〕

= find〔faɪnd〕

= gain〔gen〕

= get〔gɛt〕

= obtain〔əb'ten〕

= secure〔sɪ'kjʊr〕

= *come by*

acquit〔ə'kwɪt〕*v.* 宣告無罪

= absolve〔æb'salv〕

= cleanse〔klɛnz〕

= clear〔klɪr〕

= discharge〔dɪs'tʃɑrdʒ〕

= exculpate〔'ɛkskʌlˌpet ,
ɪk'skʌlpet〕

= excuse〔ɪk'skjuz〕

= exonerate〔ɪg'zanəˌret〕

= free〔fri〕

= pardon〔'pɑrdn̩〕

= vindicate〔'vɪndəˌket〕

acrid〔'ækrɪd〕*adj.* 辛辣的；
尖刻的

= acid〔'æsɪd〕

= biting〔'baɪtɪŋ〕

= bitter〔'bɪtɚ〕

= caustic〔'kɔstɪk〕

= harsh〔hɑrʃ〕

A

= pungent（'pʌndʒənt）
= sharp（ʃɑrp）
= stinging（'stɪŋɪŋ）

acrobat（'ækrə,bæt）n. 表演特技者

= gymnast（'dʒɪmnæst）
= tumbler（'tʌmblə）

act（ækt）① v. 行動；起作用 ② v. 假裝 ③ n. 法案

① = behave（bɪ'hev）
= do（du）
= function（'fʌŋkʃən）
= perform（pə'fɔrm）
= work（wɜk）
② = assume（ə'sjum）
= feign（fen）
= pretend（prɪ'tɛnd）
③ = bill（bɪl）
= law（lɔ）

action（'ækʃən）n. ①行為 ②戰鬥

① = behavior（bɪ'hevjə）
= performance（pə'fɔrməns）
= work（wɜk）
② = battle（'bætḷ）
= clash（klæʃ）
= combat（'kɑmbæt , 'kʌm-）
= fight（faɪt）

active（'æktɪv）adj. 活躍的

= animated（'æmə,metɪd）
= dynamic（daɪ'næmɪk）
= energetic（,ɛnə'dʒɛtɪk）
= lively（'laɪvlɪ）

= spirited（'spɪrɪtɪd）
= vigorous（'vɪgərəs）
= vivacious（vaɪ'veʃəs , vɪ-）
= on the go

activity（æk'tɪvətɪ）n. 活動

= action（'ækʃən）
= exercise（'ɛksə,saɪz）
= motion（'moʃən）
= movement（'muvmənt）
= work（wɜk）

actor（'æktə）n. 演員

= entertainer（,ɛntə'tenə）
= performer（pə'fɔrmə）
= player（'pleə）
= trouper（'trupə）
= dramatic artist

actual（'æktʃuəl）adj. 實際的；真實的

= authentic（ɔ'θɛntɪk）
= factual（'fæktʃuəl）
= genuine（'dʒɛnjuɪn）
= real（'riəl , rɪl , 'rɪəl）
= true（tru）
= truthful（'truθfəl）

acute（ə'kjut）adj. 銳利的；敏銳的

= astute（ə'stjut）
= clever（'klɛvə）
= discerning（dɪ'zɜnɪŋ , dɪ's3nɪŋ）
= incisive（ɪn'saɪsɪv）
= keen（kin）
= piercing（'pɪrsɪŋ）
= sharp（ʃɑrp）

= shrewd〔ʃrud〕
= smart〔smɑrt〕

adamant〔'ædə,mænt〕*adj.*
不屈服的

= determined〔dɪ'tɜmɪnd〕
= firm〔fɜm〕
= inflexible〔ɪn'flɛksəbḷ〕
= obstinate〔'ɑbstənɪt〕
= resolute〔'rɛzə,lut , 'rɛzḷ,jut〕
= stubborn〔'stʌbən〕
= unrelenting〔,ʌnrɪ'lɛntɪŋ〕
= unyielding〔ʌn'jildɪŋ〕

adapt〔ə'dæpt〕*v.* 改變；使適合

= accommodate〔ə'kɑmə,det〕
= adjust〔ə'dʒʌst〕
= alter〔'ɔltə〕
= change〔tʃendʒ〕
= modify〔'mɑdə,faɪ〕
= vary〔'vɛrɪ〕
= *make fit*
= *make suitable*

add〔æd〕*v.* 加起來

= augment〔ɔg'mɛnt〕
= increase〔ɪn'kris〕
= join〔dʒɔɪn〕
= total〔'totḷ〕
= unite〔ju'naɪt〕
= *put together*
= *sum up*

address〔*n.* ə'drɛs , 'ædrɛs ,
v. ə'drɛs〕① *n.* 演講 ② *n.* 地址
③ *v.* 演說

① = discourse〔'dɪskors , dɪ'skors〕
= lecture〔'lɛktʃə〕
= oration〔o'reʃən , ɔ'reʃən〕
= speech〔spitʃ〕
= talk〔tɔk〕
② = abode〔ə'bod〕
= dwelling〔'dwɛlɪŋ〕
= house〔haʊs〕
= residence〔'rɛzədəns〕
③ = lecture〔'lɛktʃə〕
= orate〔'oret , 'ɔret , o'ret〕
= speak〔spik〕
= talk〔tɔk〕
= *give a speech*
= *give a talk*

adept〔ə'dɛpt , 'æ-〕*adj.* 熟練的

= adroit〔ə'drɔɪt〕
= dexterous〔'dɛkstrəs〕
= expert〔'ɛkspɜt , ɪks'pɜt〕
= masterful〔'mæstəfəl〕
= proficient〔prə'fɪʃənt〕
= skillful〔'skɪlfəl〕

adequate〔'ædəkwɪt〕*adj.*
足夠的；適當的

= enough〔ə'nʌf , ɪ'nʌf〕
= fair〔fɛr〕
= satisfactory〔,sætɪs'fæktərɪ〕
= sufficient〔sə'fɪʃənt〕
= suitable〔'sutəbḷ , 'sɪu- , 'sju-〕

adhere〔əd'hɪr , æd-〕*v.* ①附著
②堅持

① = attach〔ə'tætʃ〕
= cleave〔kliv〕

A

= cling〔klɪŋ〕
= cohere〔ko'hɪr〕
= fix〔fɪks〕
= glue〔glu〕
= stick〔stɪk〕
② = abide〔ə'baɪd〕
= cling〔klɪŋ〕
= maintain〔men'ten , mən'ten〕
= *hold closely to*

adjacent〔ə'dʒesn̩t〕*adj.* 鄰接的

= adjoining〔ə'dʒɔɪnɪŋ〕
= bordering〔'bɔrdəɪŋ〕
= close〔kloz〕
= contiguous〔kən'tɪgjuəs〕
= near〔nɪr〕
= neighboring〔'nebərɪŋ〕
= touching〔'tʌtʃɪŋ〕
= *next to*

adjoin〔ə'dʒɔɪn〕*v.* 鄰接

= border〔'bɔrdə〕
= connect〔kə'nɛkt〕
= neighbor〔'nebə〕
= touch〔tʌtʃ〕
= *be close to*
= *be next to*
= *be side by side*

adjourn〔ə'dʒɝn〕*v.* 延期

= defer〔dɪ'fɝ〕
= delay〔dɪ'le〕
= discontinue〔,dɪskən'tɪnju〕
= postpone〔post'pon〕
= recess〔rɪ'sɛs〕
= suspend〔sə'spɛnd〕
= *put off*

adjust〔ə'dʒʌst〕*v.* 調節；調整

= adapt〔ə'dæpt〕
= alter〔'ɔltə〕
= arrange〔ə'rendʒ〕
= modify〔'madə,faɪ〕
= *make fit*
= *make suitable*

administer〔əd'mɪnəstə〕*v.*
①管理　②實施；執行

① = conduct〔kən'dʌkt〕
= control〔kən'trol〕
= direct〔də'rɛkt , daɪ-〕
= govern〔'gʌvən〕
= manage〔'mænɪdʒ〕
= rule〔rul〕
= supervise〔,supə'vaɪz〕
② = apply〔ə'plaɪ〕
= contribute〔kən'trɪbjut〕
= execute〔'ɛksɪ,kjut〕
= perform〔pə'fɔrm〕
= *put into operation*

admirable〔'ædmərəbl̩〕*adj.*
優良的

= commendable〔kə'mɛndəbl̩〕
= deserving〔dɪ'zɝvɪŋ〕
= estimable〔'ɛstəməbl̩〕
= excellent〔'ɛksələnt〕
= fine〔faɪn〕
= laudable〔'lɔdəbl̩〕
= praiseworthy〔'prez,wɝðɪ〕

admit〔əd'mɪt〕*v.* ①承認
②許入

① = acknowledge〔ək'nɑlɪdʒ〕

= consent〔kən'sɛnt〕

= confess〔kən'fɛs〕

② = receive〔rɪ'siv〕

= *allow to enter*

= *let in*

admonition〔,ædmə'nɪʃən〕*n.*
警告

= advice〔əd'vaɪs〕

= caution〔'kɔʃən〕

= remonstrance〔rɪ'mɑnstrəns〕

= reproach〔rɪ'protʃ〕

= tip〔tɪp〕

= warning〔'wɔrnɪŋ〕

ado〔ə'du〕*n.* 騷擾

= bother〔'bɑðə〕

= commotion〔kə'moʃən〕

= confusion〔kən'fjuʒən〕

= disturbance〔dɪ'stɜbəns〕

= excitement〔ɪk'saɪtmənt〕

= fuss〔fʌs〕

= stir〔stɜ〕

= to-do〔tə'du〕

= trouble〔'trʌbl̩〕

adopt〔ə'dɑpt〕*v.* 採納

= accept〔ək'sɛpt, æk-〕

= assume〔ə'sjum〕

= choose〔tʃus〕

= embrace〔ɪm'bres〕

= *take to oneself*

adore〔ə'dor, ə'dɔr〕*v.* 崇拜

= admire〔əd'maɪr〕

= cherish〔'tʃɛrɪʃ〕

= esteem〔ə'stim〕

= idolize〔'aɪdl̩,aɪz〕

= revere〔rɪ'vɪr〕

= worship〔'wɜʃəp〕

= *love and respect*

adorn〔ə'dɔrn〕*v.* 裝飾

= beautify〔'bjutə,faɪ〕

= decorate〔'dɛkə,ret〕

= embellish〔ɪm'bɛlɪʃ〕

= garnish〔'gɑrnɪʃ〕

= ornament〔'ɔrnə,mɛnt〕

= trim〔trɪm〕

adroit〔ə'drɔɪt〕*adj.* 熟練的

= adept〔ə'dɛpt, 'ædɛpt〕

= apt〔æpt〕

= clever〔'klɛvə〕

= expert〔'ɛkspɜt, ɪks'pɜt〕

= ingenious〔ɪn'dʒinjəs〕

= nimble〔'nɪmbl̩〕

= proficient〔prə'fɪʃənt〕

= skillful〔'skɪlfəl〕

adult〔ə'dʌlt〕*adj.* 成熟的

= developed〔dɪ'vɛləpt〕

= grown-up〔'gron'ʌp〕

= mature〔mə'tjur, -'tʃur〕

= ripe〔raɪp〕

= *full grown*

= *of age*

advance〔əd'væns〕*v.* 前進

= proceed〔prə'sid〕

= progress〔prə'grɛs〕

= promote〔prə'mot〕

A

= *go ahead*
= *move forward*

advantage (əd'væntɪdʒ) *n.*
利益；優點

= asset ('æsɛt)
= benefit ('bɛnəfɪt)
= gain (gen)
= interest ('ɪntrɪst , 'ɪntərɪst)
= profit ('prɑfɪt)
= *upper hand*

adventure (əd'vɛntʃɚ) *n.*
奇遇；冒險

= enterprise ('ɛntɚ,praɪz)
= experience (ɪk'spɪrɪəns)
= exploit ('ɛksplɔɪt , ɪk-)
= hazard ('hæzɚd)
= incident ('ɪnsədənt)
= occurrence (ə'kʒəns)
= risk (rɪsk)
= venture ('vɛntʃɚ)

adverse (əd'vʒs , 'æd-) *adj.*
敵對的；不利的

= antagonistic (æn,tægə'nɪstɪk)
= contrary ('kɑntrɛrɪ)
= disadvantage (,dɪsəd'væntɪdʒ)
= harmful ('hɑrmfəl)
= hostile ('hɑstɪl)
= opposing (ə'pozɪŋ)
= opposite ('ɑpəzɪt)
= unfavorable (ʌn'fevrəbl)
= unfriendly (ʌn'frɛndlɪ)

adversity (əd'vʒsətɪ) *n.* 災禍

= affliction (ə'flɪkʃən)
= calamity (kə'læmətɪ)
= catastrophe (kə'tæstrəfɪ)
= disaster (dɪz'æstɚ)
= distress (dɪ'strɛs)
= hardship ('hɑrdʃɪp)
= misery ('mɪzərɪ)
= misfortune (mɪs'fɔrtʃən)
= mishap ('mɪs,hæp , mɪs'hæp)
= trouble ('trʌbl)

advertise ('ædvɚ,taɪz , ,ædvɚ't-)
v. 通知

= announce (ə'naʊns)
= declare (dɪ'klɛr)
= inform (ɪn'fɔrm)
= notify ('notə,faɪ)

advice (əd'vaɪs) *n.* 忠告

= admonition (,ædmə'nɪʃən)
= counsel ('kaʊnsl)
= direction (də'rɛkʃən , daɪ-)
= instruction (ɪn'strʌkʃən)
= recommendation
  (,rɛkəmɛn'deʃən)
= suggestion (sə'dʒɛstʃən ,
  səg'dʒ-)

advocate ('ædvə,ket) *v.* 提倡；
辯護

= defend (dɪ'fɛnd)
= favor ('fevɚ)
= plead (plid)
= promote (prə'mot)
= propose (prə'poz)
= support (sə'port , -'pɔrt)

A

= uphold〔ʌp'hold〕
= *speak for*

affable〔'æfəbḷ〕*adj.* 和藹可親的

= amiable〔'emɪəbḷ〕
= approachable〔ə'protʃəbḷ〕
= benign〔bɪ'naɪn〕
= courteous〔'kɜtɪəs〕
= friendly〔'frɛndlɪ〕
= genial〔'dʒinjəl〕
= gracious〔'greʃəs〕
= kindly〔'kaɪndlɪ〕
= pleasant〔'plɛznt〕
= sociable〔'soʃəbḷ〕
= warm〔wɔrm〕

affair〔ə'fɛr〕*n.* 事件

= activity〔æk'tɪvətɪ〕
= business〔'bɪznɪs〕
= concern〔kən'sɜn〕
= event〔ɪ'vɛnt〕
= happening〔'hæpənɪŋ〕
= incident〔'ɪnsədənt〕
= matter〔'mætɚ〕
= occurence〔ə'kɜəns〕

affect〔ə'fɛkt〕*v.* ①影響
②假裝

① = influence〔'ɪnfluəns〕
= sway〔swe〕
= *act on*
= *have an effect*
= *have an impact on*
② = assume〔ə'sum , ə'sjum〕
= imitate〔'ɪmə,tet〕
= pretend〔prɪ'tɛnd〕

= simulate〔'sɪmjə,let〕

affection〔ə'fɛkʃən〕*n.* 愛；情愛

= amity〔'æmətɪ〕
= care〔kɛr〕
= fondness〔'fɑndnɪs〕
= liking〔'laɪkɪŋ〕
= love〔lʌv〕

affiliate〔ə'fɪlɪ,et〕*v.* 使有關連；
聯合

= ally〔ə'laɪ〕
= associate〔ə'soʃɪ,et〕
= connect〔kə'nɛkt〕
= incorporate〔ɪn'kɔrpə,ret〕
= join〔dʒɔɪn〕
= unite〔ju'naɪt〕

affirm〔ə'fɜm〕*v.* 斷言

= assert〔ə'sɜt〕
= avow〔ə'vau〕
= certify〔'sɜtə,faɪ〕
= confirm〔kən'fɜm〕
= declare〔dɪ'klɛr〕
= pronounce〔prə'nauns〕
= ratify〔'rætə,faɪ〕
= state〔stet〕

afflict〔ə'flɪkt〕*v.* 使痛苦

= beset〔bɪ'sɛt〕
= distress〔dɪ'strɛs〕
= grieve〔griv〕
= plague〔pleg〕
= torment〔tɔr'mɛnt〕
= trouble〔'trʌbḷ〕
= wound〔wund〕

A

affluent ('æfluənt) *adj.* 富裕的；
豐富的

= abundant (ə'bʌndənt)
= ample ('æmpl̩)
= bountiful ('bauntəfəl)
= plentiful ('plɛntɪfəl)
= rich (rɪtʃ)
= wealthy ('wɛlθɪ)
= well-off ('wɛl'ɔf)
= well-to-do ('wɛltə'du)

afford (ə'ford , ə'fɔrd) *v.*
①足以承擔　②供給

① = bear (bɛr)
= sustain (sə'sten)
② = furnish ('fɝnɪʃ)
= give (gɪv)
= offer ('ɔfə , 'afə)
= provide (prə'vaɪd)
= supply (sə'plaɪ)
= yield (jild)

affront (ə'frʌnt) *n.* 冒犯；
公然侮辱

= indignity (ɪn'dɪgnətɪ)
= insult ('ɪnsʌlt)
= offense (ə'fɛns)
= provocation (,pravə'keʃən)

afraid (ə'fred) *adj.* 害怕的

= cowardly ('kauədlɪ)
= fearful ('fɪrfəl)
= frightened ('fraɪtn̩d)
= intimidated (ɪn'tɪmə,det)
= scared (skɛrd)
= timid ('tɪmɪd)

after ('æftə) *adv.* 隨後

= afterward ('æftəwəd)
= following ('faloɪŋ)
= later ('letə)
= subsequently ('sʌbsəkwəntlɪ)
= thereafter (ðɛr'æftə)

again (ə'gɛn , ə'gen) *adv.* ①再
②此外

① = afresh (ə'frɛʃ)
= anew (ə'nju , ə'nu)
= repeatedly (rɪ'pitɪdlɪ)
= *another time*
= *once more*
② = also ('ɔlso)
= besides (bɪ'saɪdz)
= furthermore ('fɝðə,mor)
= *in addition*
= *on the other hand*

against (ə'genst , ə'gɛnst) *prep.*
反對

= counter ('kauntə) (to)
= versus ('vɝsəs)
= *hostile to*
= *in contrast to*
= *in opposition to*

age (edʒ) ① *n.* 時代
② *v.* 成熟；變老

① = epoch ('ɛpək)
= era ('ɪrə , 'irə)
= period ('pɪrɪəd)
= span (spæn)
= time (taɪm)
② = mature (mə'tʃur , -'tʃjur)

A

= ripen（'raɪpən）

= *grow old*

agency（'edʒənsɪ）*n.* 代理

  = bureau（'bjʊro）

  = department（dɪ'pɑrtmənt）

  = management（'mænɪdʒmənt）

  = office（'ɔfɪs , 'ɑ- ）

  = operation（ˌɑpə'reʃən）

  = organization（ˌɔrgənə'zeʃən）

agent（'edʒənt）*n.* ①代理人
②動作者

① = deputy（'dɛpjətɪ）

  = envoy（'ɛnvɔɪ）

  = representative（ˌrɛprɪ'zɛntətɪv）

② = actor（'æktɚ）

  = doer（'duɚ）

  = executor（ɪg'zɛkjətɚ）

  = operator（'ɑpəˌretɚ）

  = performer（pɚ'fɔrmɚ）

  = worker（'wɝkɚ）

aggravate（'ægrəˌvet）*v.*
①使惡化　②激怒

① = exacerbate（ɪg'zæsɚˌbet ,
   ɪk'sæ- ）

  = intensify（ɪn'tɛnsəˌfaɪ）

  = worsen（'wɝsn̩）

  = *make worse*

② = annoy（ə'nɔɪ）

  = exasperate（ɪg'zæspɚˌret）

  = infuriate（ɪn'fjʊrɪˌet）

  = irritate（'ɪrəˌtet）

  = provoke（prə'vok）

  = vex（vɛks）

aggregate（'ægrɪˌget）*v.* 聚集；
合計

  = accumulate（ə'kjumjəˌlet）

  = amass（ə'mæs）

  = assemble（ə'sɛmbl̩）

  = pile（paɪl）

  = total（'totl̩）

  = *add up to*

  = *amount to*

  = *sum up*

aggression（ə'grɛʃən）*n.*
侵略；攻擊

  = assault（ə'sɔlt）

  = attack（ə'tæk）

  = invasion（ɪn'veʒən）

  = offense（ə'fɛns）

  = raid（red）

aggressive（ə'grɛsɪv）*adj.*
①侵略的；攻擊的　②積極的

① = belligerent（bə'lɪdʒərənt）

  = combative（kəm'bætɪv ,
   'kɑmbə- ）

  = hostile（'hɑstl̩ , 'hɑstɪl ,
   'hɑstaɪl ）

  = militant（'mɪlətənt）

  = offensive（ə'fɛnsɪv）

  = quarrelsome（'kwɔrəlsəm ,
   'kwɑr- ）

② = assertive（ə'sɝtɪv）

  = dynamic（daɪ'næmɪk）

  = energetic（ˌɛnɚ'dʒɛtɪk）

  = enterprising（'ɛntɚˌpraɪzɪŋ）

  = pushing（'pʊʃɪŋ）

  = pushy（'pʊʃɪ）

A

aghast (ə'gæst , ə'gɑst) *adj.*
吃驚的

= amazed (ə'mezd)

= astonished (ə'stɑnɪʃt)

= astounded (ə'staundɪd)

= awed (ɔd)

= flabbergasted ('flæbɚ,gæstɪd)

= shocked (ʃɑkt)

= startled ('stɑrtl̩d)

= stunned ('stʌnd)

= thunderstruck ('θʌndɚ,strʌk)

agile ('ædʒəl , -aɪl) *adj.* 機敏的

= alert (ə'lɜt)

= brisk (brɪsk)

= clever ('klɛvɚ)

= fast (fæst , fɑst)

= lively ('laɪvlɪ)

= nimble ('nɪmbl̩)

= quick (kwɪk)

= spry (spraɪ)

= swift (swɪft)

agitate ('ædʒə,tet) *v.* 擾亂；煽動

= disturb (dɪ'stɜb)

= excite (ɪk'saɪt)

= incite (ɪn'saɪt)

= inflame (ɪn'flem)

= instigate ('ɪnstə,get)

= provoke (prə'vok)

= upset (ʌp'sɛt)

= *stir up*

agony ('ægənɪ) *n.* 痛苦

= affliction (ə'flɪkʃən)

= anguish ('æŋgwɪʃ)

= distress (dɪ'strɛs)

= grief (grif)

= heartache ('hɑrt,ek)

= pain (pen)

= suffering ('sʌfrɪŋ , 'sʌfɚ-)

= torment ('tɔrmɛnt)

= torture ('tɔrtʃɚ)

= woe (wo)

agree (ə'gri) *v.* 同意

= accept (ək'sɛpt , æk-)

= assent (ə'sɛnt)

= approve (ə'pruv)

= comply (kəm'plaɪ)

= consent (kən'sɛnt)

= *see eye to eye*

agreement (ə'grimənt) *n.*
①同意　②協議；契約

① = accord (ə'kɔrd)

= approval (ə'pruvl̩)

= compliance (kəm'plaɪəns)

= concord ('kɑnkɔrd , 'kɑŋ-)

= harmony ('hɑrmənɪ)

② = bargain ('bɑrgɪn)

= contract ('kɑntrækt)

= deal (dil)

= pact (pækt)

= treaty ('tritɪ)

= understanding (,ʌndɚ'stændɪŋ)

agriculture ('ægrɪ,kʌltʃɚ) *n.*
農業

= cultivation (,kʌltə'veʃən)

= farming ('fɑrmɪŋ)

= husbandry ('hʌzbəndrɪ)

ahead (ə'hɛd) *adv.* 在前面

  = before (bɪ'for , -'fɔr)

  = forward ('fɔrwəd)

  = leading ('lidɪŋ)

  = winning ('wɪnɪŋ)

  = *in advance*

  = *in front*

aid (ed) *n.* ①幫助　②幫助者

①= assistance (ə'sɪstəns)

  = benefit ('bɛnəfɪt)

  = help (hɛlp)

  = relief (rɪ'lif)

  = service ('sɜvɪs)

②= assistant (ə'sɪstənt)

  = helper ('hɛlpə)

  = supporter (sə'portə , sə'pɔrtə)

ailment ('elmənt) *n.* 生病

  = complaint (kəm'plent)

  = disease (dɪ'ziz)

  = distemper (dɪs'tɛmpə)

  = illness ('ɪlnɪs)

  = indisposition (ˌɪndɪspə'zɪʃən)

  = sickness ('sɪknɪs)

aim (em) ① *v.* 瞄準；對準
② *n.* 目標

①= direct (də'rɛkt , daɪ-)

  = point (pɔɪnt)

②= end (ɛnd)

  = goal (gol)

  = intention (ɪn'tɛnʃən)

  = objective (əb'dʒɛktɪv)

  = purpose ('pɜpəs)

  = target ('tɑrgɪt)

airy ('ɛrɪ) *adj.* 快活的；輕快的

  = animated ('ænəˌmetɪd)

  = gay (ge)

  = happy ('hæpɪ)

  = high-spirited ('haɪ'spɪrɪtɪd)

aisle (aɪl) *n.* 走廊；走道

  = corridor ('kɔrədə , -ˌdor , 'kɑr-)

  = lane (len)

  = passage ('pæsɪdʒ)

  = passageway ('pæsɪdʒˌwe)

  = path (pæθ)

ajar (ə'dʒɑr) *adj.* , *adv.* 半開地

  = agape (ə'gep , ə'gæp)

  = *slightly open*

akin (ə'kɪn) *adj.* 類似的

  = alike (ə'laɪk)

  = analogous (ə'næləgəs)

  = related (rɪ'letɪd)

  = similar ('sɪmələ)

alarm (ə'lɑrm) *v.* ①使驚慌
②警告

①= frighten ('fraɪtn̩)

  = panic ('pænɪk)

  = startle ('stɑrtl̩)

  = terrify ('tɛrəˌfaɪ)

  = unnerve (ʌn'nɜv)

②= alert (ə'lɜt)

  = warn ('wɔrn)

alcoholic (ˌælkə'hɔlɪk , -'hɑlɪk)
n. 酒鬼

  = boozer ('buzə)

A

= drunkard ('drʌŋkəd)
= inebriate (ɪn'ibrɪɪt)
= soak (sok)
= sot (sat)
= tippler ('tɪplə)

alert (ə'lɝt) *adj.* 留心的；
機警的；靈活的
= attentive (ə'tɛntɪv)
= careful ('kɛrfəl)
= heedful ('hidfəl)
= lively ('laɪvlɪ)
= nimble ('nɪmbḷ)
= prompt (prampt)
= ready ('rɛdɪ)
= wary ('wɛrɪ)
= watchful ('watʃfəl)
= wide-awake ('waɪdə'wek)
= *on one's toes*
= *on the lookout*

alibi ('ælə,baɪ) *n.* 託辭
= excuse (ɪk'skjus)
= pretext ('pritɛkst)
= reason ('rizn̩)

alien ('elɪən , 'eljən) *adj.*
①不同的；外國的　②外國人
① = exotic (ɪg'zɑtɪk)
= foreign ('fɔrɪn)
= strange (strendʒ)
= unfamiliar (ʌnfə'mɪljə)
= *not native*
② = foreigner ('fɔrɪnə)
= outsider ('aut'saɪdə)
= stranger ('strendʒə)

allay (ə'le) *v.* 緩和
= alleviate (ə'livɪ,et)
= calm (kɑm)
= ease (iz)
= lessen ('lɛsn̩)
= moderate ('madə,ret)
= pacify ('pæsə,faɪ)
= quiet ('kwaɪət)
= relieve (rɪ'liv)

allege (ə'lɛdʒ) *v.* 宣稱
= assert (ə'sɝt)
= claim (klem)
= declare (dɪ'klɛr)
= profess (prə'fɛs)
= state (stet)

allegiance (ə'lidʒəns) *n.* 忠誠
= devotion (dɪ'voʃən)
= faithfulness ('feθfəlnɪs)
= fidelity (faɪ'dɛlətɪ , fə-)
= homage ('hamɪdʒ)
= loyalty ('lɔɪəltɪ , 'lɔj-)

alley ('ælɪ) *n.* 巷；弄
= lane (len)
= passage ('pæsɪdʒ)
= passageway ('pæsɪdʒ,we)
= path (pæθ)

alliance (ə'laɪəns) *n.* 聯盟
= agreement (ə'grimənt)
= association (ə,sosɪ'eʃən ,
  ə,soʃ-)
= coalition (,koə'lɪʃən)
= federation (,fɛdə're ʃən)

= league〔lig〕
= pact〔pækt〕
= partnership〔'pɑrtnəʃɪp〕
= treaty〔'tritɪ〕
= union〔'junjən〕

allot〔ə'lɑt〕*v.* 分配

= allocate〔'æləˌket , 'ælo-〕
= apportion〔ə'porʃən , ə'por-〕
= assign〔ə'saɪn〕
= budget〔'bʌdʒɪt〕
= distribute〔dɪ'strɪbjut〕
= divide〔də'vaɪd〕
= share〔ʃɛr〕

allow〔ə'laʊ〕*v.* ①允許　②承認

① = grant〔grænt〕
= let〔lɛt〕
= permit〔pɚ'mɪt〕
② = acknowledge〔ək'nɑlɪdʒ〕
= admit〔əd'mɪt〕
= concede〔kən'sid〕

allowance〔ə'laʊns〕*n.* 分配

= allotment〔ə'lɑtmənt〕
= grant〔grænt〕
= portion〔'porʃən , 'por-〕
= ration〔'ræʃən , 're-〕

allude〔ə'lud , ə'lɪud〕*v.* 暗指；
提及

= hint〔hɪnt〕
= imply〔ɪm'plaɪ〕
= mention〔'mɛnʃən〕
= refer〔rɪ'fɝ〕

= suggest〔səg'dʒɛst , sə'dʒɛst〕

allure〔ə'lɪur , ə'lur〕*v.* 誘惑

= attract〔ə'trækt〕
= captivate〔'kæptəˌvet〕
= charm〔tʃɑrm〕
= coax〔koks〕
= enchant〔ɪn'tʃænt〕
= entice〔ɪn'taɪs〕
= lure〔lur〕
= seduce〔sɪ'dus , -'djus〕
= tempt〔tɛmpt〕

almighty〔ɔl'maɪtɪ〕*adj.* 萬能的

= all-powerful〔əl'paʊəfəl〕
= divine〔də'vaɪn〕
= omnipotent〔ɑm'nɪpətənt〕
= supreme〔sə'prim〕

almost〔'ɔlˌmost , ɔl'-〕*adv.* 幾乎

= approximately〔ə'nʌf , ɪ'nʌf〕
= nearly〔'nɪrlɪ〕
= *close to*
= *just about*

alms〔ɑmz〕*n.* 施捨；救濟

= charity〔'tʃærətɪ〕
= contribution〔ˌkɑntrə'bjuʃən〕
= dole〔dol〕
= donation〔do'neʃən〕

aloft〔ə'lɔft〕*adv.* 在上面

= above〔ə'bʌv〕
= overhead〔'ovɚ'hɛd〕
= *on high*

A

alone ﹝ ə'lon ﹞ *adj.* 單獨的

= isolated ﹝'aɪsḷˌetɪd ﹞

= lonely ﹝'lonlɪ ﹞

= sole ﹝ sol ﹞

= solitary ﹝'sɑləˌtɛrɪ ﹞

= unaccompanied

﹝ˌʌnə'kʌmpənɪd ﹞

= *by oneself*

aloof ﹝ ə'luf ﹞ ① *adj.* 冷漠的；疏遠的　② *adv.* 遠離；躲開

① = cool ﹝ kul ﹞

= distant ﹝'dɪstənt ﹞

= indifferent ﹝ ɪn'dɪfrənt ,

-fərənt ﹞

= remote ﹝ rɪ'mot ﹞

= reserved ﹝ rɪ'zɜvd ﹞

= standoffish ﹝ stænd'ɔfɪʃ ﹞

= unsociable ﹝ ʌn'soʃəbḷ ﹞

② = apart ﹝ ə'pɑrt ﹞

= away ﹝ ə'we ﹞

= *at a distance*

also ﹝'ɔlso ﹞ *adv.* 並且

= besides ﹝ bɪ'saɪdz ﹞

= too ﹝ tu ﹞

= *as well*

= *in addition*

alter ﹝'ɔltɚ ﹞ *v.* 改變

= change ﹝ tʃendʒ ﹞

= diversify ﹝ də'vɜsəˌfaɪ , daɪ- ﹞

= modify ﹝'mɑdəˌfaɪ ﹞

= shift ﹝ ʃɪft ﹞

= vary ﹝'vɛrɪ ﹞

= *make different*

alternate ﹝'ɔltɚˌnet ﹞ *v.* 交替

= interchange ﹝ˌɪntɚ'tʃendʒ ﹞

= substitute ﹝'sʌbstəˌtut , -ˌtjut ﹞

= switch ﹝ swɪtʃ ﹞

= *take turns*

alternative ﹝ ɔl'tɜnətɪv , æl- ﹞
n. 二者選一；供選擇的東西

= choice ﹝ tʃɔɪs ﹞

= option ﹝'ɑpʃən ﹞

= replacement ﹝ rɪ'plesmənt ﹞

= substitute ﹝'sʌbstəˌtut , -ˌtjut ﹞

altogether ﹝ˌɔltə'gɛðɚ ﹞ *adv.*
總共

= total ﹝'totḷ ﹞

= completely ﹝ kəm'plitlɪ ﹞

= entirely ﹝ ɪn'taɪrlɪ ﹞

= wholly ﹝'holɪ , 'hollɪ ﹞

= thoroughly ﹝'θɜolɪ ﹞

= collectively ﹝ kə'lɛktɪvlɪ ﹞

= all ﹝ ɔl ﹞

always ﹝'ɔlwɪz , -wez ﹞ *adv.* 總是

= continually ﹝ kən'tɪnjuəlɪ ﹞

= forever ﹝ fɚ'ɛvɚ ﹞

= invariably ﹝ ɪn'vɛrɪəblɪ ﹞

= *at all times*

amass ﹝ ə'mæs ﹞ *v.* 積聚

= accumulate ﹝ ə'kjumjəˌlet ﹞

= assemble ﹝ ə'sɛmbḷ ﹞

= collect ﹝ kə'lɛkt ﹞

= compile ﹝ kəm'paɪl ﹞

= gather ﹝'gæðɚ ﹞

= pile ﹝ paɪl ﹞

A

= *heap up*
= *store up*

amateur (ˈæmə‚tʃʊr , -‚tur) *n.*
業餘者

= beginner (bɪˈgɪnə)
= nonprofessional
  (‚nɑnprəˈfɛʃənḷ)

amaze (əˈmez) *v.* 使吃驚

= astonish (əˈstɑnɪʃ)
= astound (əˈstaʊnd)
= bewilder (bɪˈwɪldə)
= flabbergast (ˈflæbə‚gæst)
= shock (ʃɑk)
= surprise (səˈpraɪz)

ambiguous (æmˈbɪgjʊəs) *adj.*
含糊的；曖昧的

= equivocal (ɪˈkwɪvəkḷ)
= indefinite (ɪnˈdɛfənɪt)
= uncertain (ʌnˈsɝtn̩)
= undecided (‚ʌndɪˈsaɪdɪd)
= vague (veg)

ambitious (æmˈbɪʃəs) *adj.*
有野心的

= aspiring (əsˈpaɪrɪŋ)
= desirous (dɪˈzaɪrəs)
= eager (ˈigə)
= enterprising (ˈɛntə‚praɪzɪŋ)
= intent (ɪnˈtɛnt)
= striving (ˈstraɪvɪŋ)
= zealous (ˈzɛləs)

amble (ˈæmbḷ) *v.* 徐行

= saunter (ˈsɔntə , ˈsɑn-)
= stroll (strol)
= *walk slowly*

ambush (ˈæmbʊʃ) ① *v.* 偷襲
② *n.* 埋伏處

① = bushwhack (ˈbʊʃ‚hwæk)
  = *lie in wait*
② = ambuscade (‚æmbəsˈked)
  = cover (ˈkʌvə)
  = trap (træp)
  = *hiding place*

amend (əˈmɛnd) *v.* 改良；修正

= better (ˈbɛtə)
= change (tʃendʒ)
= correct (kəˈrɛkt)
= improve (ɪmˈpruv)
= mend (mɛnd)
= modify (ˈmɑdə‚faɪ)
= rectify (ˈrɛktə‚faɪ)
= revise (rɪˈvaɪz)

ammunition (‚æmjəˈnɪʃən) *n.*
彈藥

= ammo (ˈæmo)
= bomb (bɑm)
= bullet (ˈbʊlɪt)
= powder (ˈpaʊdə)
= shells (ʃɛlz)
= shot (ʃɑt)

among (əˈmʌŋ) *prep.* 在…之中

= amid (əˈmɪd)
= with (wɪð)
= *included in*
= *in the middle*

A

amount〔ə'maʊnt〕*n.* 總額

= aggregate〔'ægrɪˌget, -ˌgɪt〕
= quantity〔'kwɑntətɪ〕
= sum〔sʌm〕
= total〔'totl̩〕
= whole〔hol, hʊl〕

ample〔'æmpl̩〕*adj.* 充足的

= abundant〔ə'bʌndənt〕
= copious〔'kopɪəs〕
= enough〔ə'nʌf, ɪ-〕
= expansive〔ɪk'spænsɪv〕
= full〔fʊl〕
= large〔lɑrdʒ〕
= plenty〔'plɛntɪ〕
= sufficient〔sə'fɪʃənt〕

amplify〔'æmpləˌfaɪ〕*v.* 放大；
加強

= enlarge〔ɪn'lɑrdʒ〕
= expand〔ɪk'spænd〕
= intensify〔ɪn'tɛnsəˌfaɪ〕
= magnify〔'mægnəˌfaɪ〕
= strengthen〔'strɛŋkθən,
'strɛŋθ-〕
= swell〔swɛl〕

amuse〔ə'mjuz〕*v.* 娛樂

= delight〔dɪ'laɪt〕
= divert〔də'vɜt, daɪ-〕
= entertain〔ˌɛntə'ten〕
= recreate〔ˌrikrɪ'et〕
= tickle〔'tɪkl̩〕

analyze〔'ænl̩ˌaɪz〕*v.* ①分析；
審察 ②分解

① = assay〔ə'se, 'æse〕
= estimate〔'ɛstəˌmet〕
= evaluate〔ɪ'væljuˌet〕
= interprete〔ɪn'tɜprɪt〕
= test〔tɛst〕
② = dissect〔dɪ'sɛkt〕
= divide〔də'vaɪd〕
= separate〔'sɛpəˌret〕
= *break down*

ancestor〔'ænsɛstə〕*n.* 祖先

= forebear〔'forˌbɛr, for-〕
= forefather〔'forˌfɑðə, 'for-〕
= forerunner〔'forˌrʌnə〕
= precursor〔prɪ'kɜsə〕
= predecessor〔ˌprɛdɪ'sɛsə,
'prɛdɪˌs-〕

anchor〔'æŋkə〕① *v.* 固定
② *n.* 錨

① = attach〔ə'tætʃ〕
= fasten〔'fæsn̩, 'fɑ-〕
= fix〔fɪks〕
② = grapnel〔'græpnəl〕
= kedge〔kɛdʒ〕
= *ship hook*

ancient〔'enʃənt〕*adj.* 古代的

= aged〔'edʒɪd〕
= antique〔æn'tik〕
= archaic〔ɑr'keɪk〕
= hoary〔'horɪ, 'hɔrɪ〕
= old〔old〕

anecdote〔'ænɪkˌdot〕*n.* 軼事

= narrative〔'nærətɪv〕

= sketch〔skɛtʃ〕
= story〔'stɔrɪ〕
= tale〔tel〕
= yarn〔jɑrn〕

angelic〔æn'dʒɛlɪk〕*adj.* 天使般的；天堂的
= godly〔'gɑdlɪ〕
= good〔gʊd〕
= heavenly〔'hɛvənlɪ〕
= innocent〔'ɪnəsn̩t〕
= lovely〔'lʌvlɪ〕
= pure〔pjʊr〕
= saintly〔'sentlɪ〕
= virtuous〔'vɜtʃʊəs〕

anger〔'æŋgɚ〕*n.* 憤怒
= annoyance〔ə'nɔɪəns〕
= fury〔'fjʊrɪ〕
= ire〔aɪr〕
= irritation〔,ɪrə'teʃən〕
= outrage〔'aʊt,redʒ〕
= rage〔redʒ〕
= resentment〔rɪ'zɛntmənt〕
= wrath〔ræθ〕

anguish〔'æŋgwɪʃ〕*n.* 痛苦
= agony〔'ægənɪ〕
= distress〔dɪ'strɛs〕
= grief〔grif〕
= heartache〔'hɑrt,ek〕
= pain〔pen〕
= suffering〔'sʌfrɪŋ , 'sʌfərɪŋ〕
= torment〔'tɔrmɛnt〕
= torture〔'tɔrtʃɚ〕
= woe〔wo〕

animal〔'ænəml̩〕*n.* 獸
= beast〔bist〕
= *brute creature*

animated〔'ænə,metɪd〕*adj.* 活潑的
= active〔'æktɪv〕
= chipper〔'tʃɪpɚ〕
= dynamic〔daɪ'næmɪk〕
= energetic〔,ɛnɚ'dʒɛtɪk〕
= gay〔ge〕
= lively〔'laɪvlɪ〕
= snappy〔'snæpɪ〕
= spry〔spraɪ〕
= vigorous〔'vɪgərəs〕
= vivacious〔vaɪ'veʃəs , vɪ-〕

animosity〔,ænə'mɑsətɪ〕*n.* 仇恨
= acrimony〔'ækrə,monɪ〕
= bitterness〔'bɪtɚnɪs〕
= dislike〔dɪs'laɪk〕
= hatred〔'hetrɪd〕
= rancor〔'ræŋkɚ〕
= *ill will*

annex〔*v.* ə'nɛks , *n.* 'ænɛks〕
① *v.* 附加 ② *n.* 附件
① = add〔æd〕
= affix〔ə'fɪks〕
= attach〔ə'tætʃ〕
= join〔dʒɔɪn〕
= unite〔jʊ'naɪt〕
② = accessory〔æk'sɛsərɪ〕
= addition〔ə'dɪʃən〕
= *something joined*

A

annihilate (ə'naɪə,let) v. 消滅

= abolish (ə'balɪʃ)
= demolish (dɪ'malɪʃ)
= destroy (dɪ'strɔɪ)
= eliminate (ɪ'lɪmə,net)
= exterminate (ɪk'stɝmə,net)
= end (ɛnd)
= *wipe out*

announce (ə'nauns) v. 發表

= broadcast ('brɔd,kæst)
= declare (dɪ'klɛr)
= notify ('notə,faɪ)
= proclaim (pro'klem)
= report (rɪ'port)
= state (stet)
= tell (tɛl)
= *make known*

annoy (ə'nɔɪ) v. 使生氣

= anger ('æŋgɚ)
= disturb (dɪ'stɝb)
= exasperate (ɪg'zæspə,ret)
= irritate ('ɪrə,tet)
= pester ('pɛstɚ)
= tease (tiz)
= vex (vɛks)
= *make angry*

anoint (ə'nɔɪnt) v. 塗油

= grease (gris)
= oil (ɔɪl)

answer ('ænsɚ) v. 回答

= reply (rɪ'plaɪ)
= respond (rɪ'spɑnd)

antagonize (æn'tægə,naɪz) v.
反對；敵對

= counteract (,kauntɚ'ækt)
= cross (krɔs)
= oppose (ə'poz)
= *go against*

anthology (æn'θalədʒɪ) n.
詩集；文選

= analects ('ænə,lɛkts)
= collection (kə'lɛkʃən)
= garland ('garlənd)
= miscellany ('mɪsḷ,ɛnɪ)

anticipate (æn'tɪsə,pet) v.
期望

= await (ə'wet)
= expect (ɪk'spɛkt)
= *hope for*
= *look forward to*

antics ('æntɪks) n. 戲謔

= capers ('kepɚz)
= escapades ('ɛskə,pedz ,
    ,ɛskə'pedz)
= frolics ('fralɪks)
= mischief ('mɪstʃɪf)
= pranks (præŋks)
= tricks (trɪks)

antipathy (æn'tɪpəθɪ) n. 憎惡

= aversion (ə'vɝʒən , -ʃən)
= disgust (dɪs'gʌst)
= dislike (dɪs'laɪk)
= enmity ('ɛnmətɪ)
= hatred ('hetrɪd)

antique〔æn'tɪk〕*adj.* 古代的；
古老的

   = aged〔'edʒɪd〕
   = ancient〔'enʃənt〕
   = archaic〔ɑr'ke·ɪk〕
   = old〔old〕

antithesis〔æn'tɪθəsɪs〕*n.*
正相反；對比

   = contrast〔'kɑntræst〕
   = opposition〔ˌɑpə'zɪʃən〕

anxiety〔æŋ'zaɪətɪ〕*n.* 憂慮；
不安

   = apprehension〔ˌæprɪ'hɛnʃən〕
   = care〔kɛr〕
   = concern〔kən'sɜn〕
   = worry〔'wɜɪ〕

anxious〔'æŋkʃəs，æŋʃəs〕*adj.*
①不安的 ②渴望的

①= apprehensive〔ˌæprɪ'hɛnsɪv〕
   = concerned〔kən'sɜnd〕
   = fearful〔'fɪrfəl〕
   = restless〔'rɛstlɪs〕
   = troubled〔'trʌbḷd〕
   = uneasy〔ʌn'izɪ〕
②= desirous〔dɪ'zaɪrəs〕
   = eager〔'igɚ〕
   = keen〔kin〕
   = yearning〔'jɜnɪŋ〕

apartment〔ə'pɑrtmənt〕*n.*
公寓

   = flat〔flæt〕
   = rooms〔rumz〕

   = suite〔swit〕

apathetic〔ˌæpə'θɛtɪk〕*adj.*
冷淡的；無動於衷的

   = cold〔kold〕
   = emotionless〔ɪ'moʃənlɪs〕
   = impassive〔ɪm'pæsɪv〕
   = indifferent〔ɪn'dɪfrənt，-fərənt〕
   = unconcerned〔ˌʌnkən'sɜnd〕
   = unmoved〔ʌn'muvd〕

apathy〔'æpəθɪ〕*n.* 冷淡；
漠不關心

   = coldness〔'koldnɪs〕
   = indifference〔ɪn'dɪfrəns，
    -'dɪfər-〕
   = lethargy〔'lɛθɚdʒɪ〕
   = unconcern〔ˌʌnkən'sɜn〕

aperture〔'æpɚtʃɚ〕*n.* 孔；隙

   = crack〔kræk〕
   = gap〔gæp〕
   = hole〔hol〕
   = opening〔'opənɪŋ，'opnɪŋ〕
   = rift〔rɪft〕

apex〔'epɛks〕*n.* 最高點；頂點

   = acme〔'ækmɪ，'ækmi〕
   = climax〔'klaɪmæks〕
   = crown〔kraʊn〕
   = peak〔pik〕
   = pinnacle〔'pɪnəkḷ〕
   = summit〔'sʌmɪt〕
   = tip〔tɪp〕
   = top〔tɑp〕
   = zenith〔'zinɪθ，(英)'zɛnɪθ〕

A

apologize (əˈpaləˌdʒaɪz) *v.*
道歉

= *ask forgiveness*
= *beg pardon*
= *express regret*
= *offer an excuse*

apostate (əˈpastet) *n.* 脫黨者；
背教者；變節者

= backslider (ˈbækˌslaɪdɚ)
= deserter (dɪˈsɝtɚ)
= renegade (ˈrɛnɪˌged)
= traitor (ˈtretɚ)
= turncoat (ˈtɝnˌkot)

appalling (əˈpɔlɪŋ) *adj.* 恐怖的

= awful (ˈɔful)
= daunting (ˈdɔntɪŋ)
= dismaying (dɪsˈmeɪŋ)
= dreadful (ˈdrɛdfəl)
= horrible (ˈhɔrəbl̩ , ˈhɑr-)
= shocking (ˈʃakɪŋ)
= terrible (ˈtɛrəbl̩)

apparatus (ˌæpəˈretəs ,
-ˈrætəs) *n.* 儀器；裝置

= equipment (ɪˈkwɪpmənt)
= gear (gɪr)
= implement (ˈɪmpləmənt)
= machine (məˈʃin)
= tackle (ˈtækl̩)

apparel (əˈpærəl) *n.* 衣服；
服飾

= attire (əˈtaɪr)
= clothing (ˈkloðɪŋ)

= costume (ˈkastum , -tjum)
= dress (drɛs)
= garb (garb)
= garments (ˈgarmənts)

apparent (əˈpærənt , əˈpɛr-)
adj. ①顯然的　②表面的

① = clear (klɪr)
= evident (ˈɛvədənt)
= manifest (ˈmænəˌfɛst)
= obvious (ˈabvɪəs)
= overt (ˈovɝt)
= plain (plen)
② = ostensible (asˈtɛnsəbl̩)
= seeming (ˈsimɪŋ)
= superficial (ˌsupɚˈfɪʃəl)

apparition (ˌæpəˈrɪʃən) *n.* 幽靈

= ghost (gost)
= phantom (ˈfæntəm)
= specter (ˈspɛktɚ)
= spirit (ˈspɪrɪt)

appeal (əˈpil) *v.* 懇求

= ask (æsk)
= beg (bɛg)
= beseech (bɪˈsitʃ)
= entreat (ɪnˈtrit)
= implore (ɪmˈplor , -ˈplɔr)
= petition (pəˈtɪʃən)
= plead (plid)

appear (əˈpɪr) *v.* ①似乎；顯得
②出現

① = look (luk)
= seem (sim)

② = emerge (ɪ'mɝdʒ)
  = materialize (mə'tɪrɪəl,aɪz)
  = show (ʃo)
  = *be present*
  = *come into view*
  = *crop up*

appease (ə'piz) *v.* 使平靜；
使緩和

  = allay (ə'le)
  = alleviate (ə'livɪ,et)
  = calm (kɑm)
  = ease (iz)
  = lessen ('lɛsn̩)
  = pacify ('pæsə,faɪ)
  = placate ('pleket)
  = quiet ('kwaɪət)
  = relieve (rɪ'liv)
  = satisfy ('sætɪs,faɪ)
  = soothe (suð)

appendage (ə'pɛndɪdʒ) *n.*
附屬物

  = accessory (æk'sɛsərɪ)
  = addition (ə'dɪʃən)
  = adjunct ('ædʒʌŋkt)
  = attachment (ə'tætʃmənt)
  = supplement ('sʌpləmənt)

appetite ('æpə,taɪt) *n.* 欲望；
渴望

  = craving ('krevɪŋ)
  = desire (dɪ'zaɪr)
  = hunger ('hʌŋgɚ)
  = yearning ('jɝnɪŋ)
  = zeal (zil)

appetizing ('æpə,taɪzɪŋ) *adj.*
開胃的；促進食慾的

  = delicious (dɪ'lɪʃəs)
  = palatable ('pælətəbl̩)
  = savory ('sevərɪ)
  = tasty ('testɪ)

applaud (ə'plɔd) *v.* 贊許；喝采

  = acclaim (ə'klem)
  = approve (ə'pruv)
  = cheer (tʃɪr)
  = clap (klæp)
  = compliment ('kɑmpləmənt)
  = hail (hel)
  = laud (lɔd)
  = praise (prez)

appliance (ə'plaɪəns) *n.* 用具

  = apparatus (,æpə'rætəs , -'retəs)
  = device (dɪ'vaɪs)
  = implement ('ɪmpləmənt)
  = instrument ('ɪnstrəmənt)
  = machine (mə'ʃin)
  = tool (tul)
  = utensil (ju'tɛnsl̩)

apply (ə'plaɪ) *v.* ①塗；敷
②應用 ③請求；申請

① = anoint (ə'nɔɪnt)
  = place (ples)
  = *cover with*
  = *put on*
  = *spread on*
② = exercise ('ɛksɚ,saɪz)
  = use (juz)
  = *bring into play*

A

= *carry out*

③ = ask (æsk)

= petition (pə'tɪʃən)

= request (rɪ'kwɛst)

appoint (ə'pɔɪnt) *v.* 任命；派

= assign (ə'saɪn)

= choose (tʃuz)

= commission (kə'mɪʃən)

= delegate ('dɛlə,get)

= elect (ɪ'lɛkt , ə'lɛkt)

= name (nem)

= nominate ('nɑmə,net)

appreciate (ə'priʃɪ,et) *v.*
①重視；賞識　②感激

① = admire (əd'maɪr)

= enjoy (ɪn'dʒɔɪ)

= esteem (ə'stim)

= prize (praɪz)

= respect (rɪ'spɛkt)

= value ('vælju)

= *think highly of*

② = *be grateful*

= *be obliged*

= *be thankful*

apprehend (,æprɪ'hɛnd) *v.*
①憂慮　②捕捉　③明瞭

① = dread (drɛd)

= fear (fɪr)

= *be afraid of*

② = arrest (ə'rɛst)

= capture ('kæptʃə)

= pinch (pɪntʃ)

= seize (siz)

= *take prisoner*

③ = comprehend (,kɑmprɪ'hɛnd)

= grasp (græsp)

= know (no)

= perceive (pə'siv)

= see (si)

= understand (,ʌndə'stænd)

apprehensive (,æprɪ'hɛnsɪv)
adj. 憂慮的

= afraid (ə'fred)

= anxious ('æŋkʃəs , 'æŋʃəs)

= bothered ('bɑðəd)

= concerned (kən'sɝnd)

= fearful ('fɪrfəl)

= perturbed (pə'tɝbd)

= troubled ('trʌbḷd)

= uneasy (ʌn'izɪ)

= worried ('wɝɪd)

apprentice (ə'prɛntɪs) *n.*
初學者；學徒

= beginner (bɪ'gɪnə)

= learner ('lɝnə)

= novice ('nɑvɪs)

= probationer (pro'beʃənə)

= pupil ('pjupḷ)

= student ('stjudṇt)

= tyro ('taɪro)

approach (ə'protʃ) ① *v.* 行近；
接近　② *v.* 進行　③ *n.* 通路

① = advance (əd'væns)

= *come near*

= *move forward*

② = begin (bɪ'gɪn)

= undertake (ˌʌndə'tek)
= *make a start*
= *set about*
③ = access ('æksɛs)
= entrance ('ɛntrəns)
= passage ('pæsɪdʒ)

appropriate (*adj.* ə'proprɪɪt ,
v. ə'proprɪˌet) ① *adj.* 適當的
② *v.* 分配

① = becoming (bɪ'kʌmɪŋ)
= fitting ('fɪtɪŋ)
= proper ('prɑpə)
= suitable ('sutəbḷ , 'sju-)
② = allocate ('æləˌket , 'ælo-)
= allot (ə'lɑt)
= apportion (ə'porʃən , ə'pɔr-)
= assign (ə'saɪn)
= budget ('bʌdʒɪt)
= distribute (dɪs'trɪbjut)
= divide (də'vaɪd)
= share (ʃɛr , ʃær)

approve (ə'pruv) *v.* ①贊同；
贊許 ②批准

① = admire (əd'maɪr)
= appreciate (ə'priʃɪˌet)
= like (laɪk)
= praise (prez)
= *think highly of*
② = accept (ək'sɛpt , æk-)
= assent (ə'sɛnt)
= endorse (ɪn'dɔrs)
= ratify ('rætəˌfaɪ)
= O.K. ('o'ke)

approximate (ə'prɑksəmɪt)
adj. 大概的；大致的

= close (klos)
= near (nɪr)
= rough (rʌf)

apt (æpt) *adj.* ①適當的；合宜的
②傾向；易於 ③敏捷的；聰明的

① = appropriate (ə'proprɪɪt)
= fitting ('fɪtɪŋ)
= proper ('prɑpə)
= suitable ('sutəbḷ , 'sju-)
② = inclined (ɪn'klaɪnd)
= likely ('laɪklɪ)
= prone (pron)
③ = astute (ə'stjut , ə'stut)
= bright (braɪt)
= clever ('klɛvə)
= sharp (ʃɑrp)
= smart (smɑrt)

aqueduct ('ækwɪˌdʌkt) *n.* 水道；
溝渠

= canal (kə'næl)
= gully ('gʌlɪ)
= waterway ('wɔtəˌwe)

arbitrary ('ɑrbəˌtrɛrɪ) *adj.*
武斷的

= capricious (kə'prɪʃəs)
= subjective (səb'dʒɛktɪv)
= unreasonable (ʌn'riznəbḷ ,
-zņəbḷ)
= willful ('wɪlfəl)

A

arbitrate (ˈɑrbəˌtret) v. 仲裁

  = intervene (ˌɪntəˈvin)
  = mediate (ˈmidɪˌet)
  = negotiate (nɪˈgoʃɪˌet)
  = referee (ˌrɛfəˈri)
  = settle (ˈsɛtl̩)
  = umpire (ˈʌmpaɪr)

architecture (ˈɑrkəˌtɛktʃɚ) n.
建築;建築物

  = building (ˈbɪldɪŋ)
  = construction (kənˈstrʌkʃən)
  = design (dɪˈzaɪn)
  = framework (ˈfremˌwɝk)
  = structure (ˈstrʌktʃɚ)

ardent (ˈɑrdn̩t) adj. 熱心的;
熱情的

  = eager (ˈigɚ)
  = earnest (ˈɝnɪst , -əst)
  = enthusiastic (ɪnˌθjuzɪˈæstɪk ,
    -ˌθuz-)
  = fervent (ˈfɝvənt)
  = passionate (ˈpæʃənɪt)
  = warm (wɔrm)
  = zealous (ˈzɛləs)

arduous (ˈɑrdʒuəs) adj. 費力的

  = difficult (ˈdɪfəˌkʌlt , ˈdɪfəkəlt)
  = hard (hɑrd)
  = laborious (ləˈborɪəs)
  = onerous (ˈɑnərəs)
  = strenuous (ˈstrɛnjuəs)
  = wearisome (ˈwɪrɪsəm)

area (ˈɛrɪə , ˈerɪə) n. ①地域
②範圍

  ① = district (ˈdɪstrɪkt)
  = neighborhood (ˈnebɚˌhʊd)
  = region (ˈridʒən)
  = section (ˈsɛkʃen)
  = space (spes)
  = territory (ˈtɛrəˌtorɪ , ˈtɛrəˌtɔrɪ)
  = tract (trækt)
  = zone (zon)
  ② = expanse (ɪkˈspæns)
  = extent (ɪkˈstɛnt)
  = range (rendʒ)
  = scope (skop)
  = size (saɪz)

argue (ˈɑrgju) v. ①爭論;辯論
②說服;勸告

  ① = bicker (ˈbɪkɚ)
  = debate (dɪˈbet)
  = dispute (dɪˈspjut)
  = object (ˈɑbdʒɪkt)
  = reason (ˈrizn̩)
  ② = convince (kənˈvɪns)
  = persuade (pɚˈswed)
  = talk into

arid (ˈærɪd) adj. ①乾燥的
②死板的

  ① = dry (draɪ)
  = parched (pɑrtʃt)
  = waterless (ˈwɔtɚlɪs , ˈwɑtɚ-)
  ② = dull (dʌl)
  = flat (flæt)
  = uninteresting (ʌnˈɪntərɪstɪŋ)
  = stuffy (ˈstʌfɪ)
  = unimaginative
    (ˌʌnɪˈmædʒɪnətɪv)

aristocrat 〔 ə'rɪstə,kræt ,
'ærɪstə- 〕 *n.* 貴族

  = noble 〔'nobḷ 〕

  = patrician 〔 pə'trɪʃən 〕

arm 〔 ɑrm 〕 ① *n.* 手臂
② *n. pl.* 武器   ③ *v.* 武裝

① = *upper limb*

② = weapons 〔'wɛpənz 〕

③ = equip 〔 ɪ'kwɪp 〕

  = fortify 〔'fɔrtə,faɪ 〕

  = provide 〔 prə'vaɪd 〕

armistice 〔'ɑrməstɪs 〕 *n.* 休戰

  = cease-fire 〔'sis,faɪr 〕

  = lull 〔 lʌl 〕

  = peace 〔 pis 〕

  = respite 〔'rɛspɪt 〕

  = truce 〔 trus 〕

army 〔'ɑrmɪ 〕 *n.* 軍隊

  = forces 〔'forsɪz , 'fɔrsɪz 〕

  = legion 〔'lidʒən 〕

  = military 〔'mɪlə,tɛrɪ 〕

  = militia 〔 mə'lɪʃə 〕

  = soldiers 〔'soldʒəz 〕

  = troops 〔 trups 〕

aroma 〔 ə'romə 〕 *n.* 香氣；芳香

  = fragrance 〔'fregrəns 〕

  = odor 〔'odə 〕

  = perfume 〔'pɜfjum , pə'fjum 〕

  = scent 〔 sɛnt 〕

  = smell 〔 smɛl 〕

arouse 〔 ə'raʊz 〕 *v.* 喚起

  = agitate 〔'ædʒə,tet 〕

  = awaken 〔 ə'wekən 〕

  = excite 〔 ɪk'saɪt 〕

  = foment 〔 fo'mɛnt 〕

  = inflame 〔 ɪn'flem 〕

  = kindle 〔'kɪndḷ 〕

  = move 〔 muv 〕

  = provoke 〔 prə'vok 〕

  = rouse 〔 raʊz 〕

  = spur 〔 spɜ 〕

  = stimulate 〔'stɪmjə,let 〕

  = stir 〔 stɜ 〕

arrange 〔 ə'rendʒ 〕 *v.* 配置；
整理

  = array 〔 ə're 〕

  = catalog 〔'kætḷ,ɔg , -,ɑg 〕

  = classify 〔'klæsə,faɪ 〕

  = dispose 〔 dɪ'spoz 〕

  = file 〔 faɪl 〕

  = form 〔 fɔrm 〕

  = organize 〔'ɔrgən,aɪz 〕

  = place 〔 ples 〕

  = settle 〔'sɛtḷ 〕

  = systematize 〔'sɪstəmə,taɪz 〕

  = *line up*

  = *put in order*

array 〔 ə're 〕 ① *v.* 展示；部署
② *n.* 排列   ③ *v.* 盛裝

① = arrange 〔 ə'rendʒ 〕

  = display 〔 dɪ'sple 〕

  = dispose 〔 dɪ'spoz 〕

  = order 〔'ɔrdə 〕

② = arrangement 〔 ə'rendʒmənt 〕

  = display 〔 dɪ'sple 〕

A

= exhibition (ˌɛksə'bɪʃən)
= order ('ɔrdə)
③ = adorn (ə'dɔrn)
= attire (ə'taɪr)
= dress (drɛs)

arrest (ə'rɛst) v. ①停止；阻擋
②逮捕
① = check (tʃɛk)
= halt (hɔlt)
= hinder ('hɪndə)
= retard (rɪ'tɑrd)
= stop (stɑp)
② = apprehend (ˌæprɪ'hɛnd)
= capture ('kæptʃə)
= catch (kætʃ)
= pinch (pɪntʃ)
= seize (siz)
= *take prisoner*

arrive (ə'raɪv) v. 到達
= come (kʌm)
= reach (ritʃ)
= attain (ə'ten)
= *come to*
= *get to*

arrogant ('ærəgənt) adj.
傲慢的
= cavalier (ˌkævə'lɪr)
= contemptuous
   (kəm'tɛmptʃuəs)
= disdainful (dɪs'denfəl , dɪz-)
= haughty ('hɔtɪ)
= insolent ('ɪnsələnt)
= proud (praʊd)

art (ɑrt) n. ①藝術；藝品
②技術
① = design (dɪ'zaɪn)
= masterpiece ('mæstə,pis)
= work (wɜk)
② = craft (kræft)
= knack (næk)
= skill (skɪl)
= technique (tɛk'nik)

artery ('ɑrtərɪ) n. ①動脈
②孔道
① = vein (ven)
= vessel ('vɛsl̩)
② = channel ('tʃænl̩)
= aqueduct ('ækwɪ,dʌkt)

artful ('ɑrtfəl) adj. 狡詐的；
技巧的；機敏的
= clever ('klɛvə)
= crafty ('kræftɪ)
= cunning ('kʌnɪŋ)
= deceitful (dɪ'sitfəl)
= intriguing (ɪn'trigɪŋ)
= shrewd (ʃrud)
= skillful ('skɪlfəl)
= sly (slaɪ)

article ('ɑrtɪkl̩) n. ①文章
②物品
① = composition (ˌkɑmpə'zɪʃən)
= essay ('ɛsɪ , 'ɛse)
= piece (pis)
= report (rɪ'port , -'pɔrt)
= story ('storɪ , 'stɔrɪ)
= treatise ('tritɪs)

② = item ('aɪtəm)
  = object ('abdʒɪkt)
  = thing (θɪŋ)

artifice ('artəfɪs) *n.* 詭計；策略

  = device (dɪ'vaɪs)
  = ruse (ruz)
  = scheme (skim)
  = stratagem ('strætədʒəm)
  = tactic ('tæktɪk)
  = trick (trɪk)

artificial (,artə'fɪʃəl) *adj.* 人造的；仿造的

  = counterfeit ('kaʊntəfɪt)
  = fake (fek)
  = false (fɔls)
  = feigned (fend)
  = imitation (,ɪmə'teʃən)
  = man-made ('mæn,med)
  = pretended (prɪ'tɛndɪd)
  = synthetic (sɪn'θɛtɪk)

artisan ('artəsn̩) *n.* 技工

  = craftsman ('kræftsmən)
  = mechanic (mə'kænɪk)
  = technician (tɛk'nɪʃən)
  = workman ('wɜkmən)

artless ('artlɪs) *adj.* ①笨拙的 ②自然的

① = clumsy ('klʌmzɪ)
  = incompetent (ɪn'kampətəns)
  = unskilled (ʌn'skɪld)
② = natural ('nætʃərəl)
  = plain (plen)

  = pure (pjʊr)
  = simple ('sɪmpl̩)

ascend (ə'sɛnd) *v.* 上升

  = climb (klaɪm)
  = mount (maʊnt)
  = rise (raɪz)
  = *go up*

ascertain (,æsə'ten) *v.* 發現；確定

  = determine (dɪ'tɜmɪn)
  = discover (dɪ'skʌvə)
  = establish (ə'stæblɪʃ)
  = learn (lɜn)
  = *find out*

ascribe (ə'skraɪb) *v.* 歸於

  = accredit (ə'krɛdɪt)
  = assign (ə'saɪn)
  = attribute (ə'trɪbjut)
  = impute (ɪm'pjut)

ashamed (ə'ʃemd) *adj.* 羞恥的

  = abashed (ə'bæʃt)
  = embarrassed (ɪm'bærəst)
  = humiliated (hju'mɪlɪ,etɪd)
  = mortified ('mɔrtɪ,faɪd)

ask (æsk) *v.* ①詢問；調查 ②請求；要求

① = question ('kwɛstʃən)
  = inquire (ɪn'kwaɪr)
  = query ('kwɪrɪ)
② = request (rɪ'kwɛst)

A

= beg〔bɛg〕
= demand〔dɪ'mænd〕
= solicit〔sə'lɪsɪt〕

askance〔ə'skæns〕*adv.* ①斜地
②懷疑地；不贊許地

① = awry〔ə'raɪ〕
= obliquely〔ə'blɪklɪ〕
= sideways〔'saɪd,wez〕
② = disapprovingly〔,dɪsə'pruvɪŋlɪ〕
= skeptically〔'skɛptɪkl̩ɪ〕
= suspiciously〔sə'spɪʃəslɪ〕

askew〔ə'skju〕*adj.* 斜的；歪的

= awry〔ə'raɪ〕
= crooked〔'krʊkɪd〕
= oblique〔ə'blik〕
= *to one side*

aspect〔'æspɛkt〕*n.* ①外觀
②觀點

① = appearance〔ə'pɪrəns〕
= look〔lʊk〕
= view〔vju〕
② = facet〔'fæsɪt〕
= prospect〔'praspɛkt〕
= *point of view*

aspire〔ə'spaɪr〕*v.* 熱望

= aim〔em〕
= crave〔krev〕
= desire〔dɪ'zaɪr〕
= long〔lɔŋ, lɑŋ〕
= seek〔sik〕
= strive〔straɪv〕
= *be ambitious*

ass〔æs〕① *n.* 驢 ② *adj.* 笨拙的

① = burro〔'bɝo, 'buro〕
= donkey〔'dɑŋkɪ〕
② = dunce〔dʌns〕
= fool〔ful〕
= silly〔'sɪlɪ〕
= simpleton〔'sɪmpl̩tən〕
= stupid〔'stjupɪd〕

assail〔ə'sel〕*v.* 攻擊

= assault〔ə'sɔlt〕
= attack〔ə'tæk〕

assassinate〔ə'sæsn̩,et〕*v.*
暗殺；行刺

= kill〔kɪl〕
= murder〔'mɝdɚ〕
= purge〔pɝdʒ〕

assault〔ə'sɔlt〕*n.* 攻擊

= attack〔ə'tæk〕
= charge〔tʃɑrdʒ〕
= invasion〔ɪn'veʒən〕
= offense〔ə'fɛns〕
= onslaught〔'ɑn,slɔt, 'ɔn-〕

assemble〔ə'sɛmbl̩〕*v.* 聚集；
集會

= cluster〔'klʌstɚ〕
= collect〔kə'lɛkt〕
= congregate〔'kɑŋgrɪ,get〕
= crowd〔kraʊd〕
= gather〔'gæðɚ〕
= group〔grup〕
= meet〔mit〕
= *come together*

assent (ə'sɛnt) *v.* 同意

= accept (ək'sɛpt , æk-)

= agree (ə'gri)

= allow (ə'lau)

= approve (ə'pruv)

= comply (kəm'plaɪ)

= consent (kən'sɛnt)

= permit (pə'mɪt)

assert (ə'sɜt) *v.* 確說；斷言

= affirm (ə'fɜm)

= avow (ə'vau)

= claim (klem)

= declare (dɪ'klɛr , -'klær)

= pronounce (prə'nauns)

= state (stet)

= *insist on*

assets ('æsɛts) *n. pl.* 有價值的東西；資產

= capital ('kæpətḷ)

= estate (ə'stet)

= funds (fʌndz)

= possessions (pə'zɛʃənz)

= property ('prapətɪ)

= resources (rɪ'sorsɪz)

= valuables ('væljuəbḷz)

= wealth (wɛlθ)

assign (ə'saɪn) *v.* ①指定 ②分配

① = appoint (ə'pɔɪnt)

= choose (tʃuz)

= delegate ('dɛləgɪt)

= elect (ɪ'lɛkt , ə'lɛkt)

= name (nem)

② = allocate ('ælə,ket , 'ælo-)

= allot (ə'lat)

= apportion (ə'porʃən , ə'pɔr-)

= distribute (dɪ'strɪbjut)

= *give out*

assimilate (ə'sɪml,et) *v.* 吸收；消化

= absorb (əb'sorb , æb- , -'z-)

= digest (də'dʒɛst , daɪ'dʒɛst)

= *soak up*

= *take in*

assist (ə'sɪst) *v.* 幫助

= aid (ed)

= help (hɛlp)

= support (sə'port , -'pɔrt)

= *give a hand*

associate (*v.* ə'soʃɪ,et , *n.* ə'soʃɪɪt) ① *v.* 聯合 ② *n.* 同夥

① = ally (ə'laɪ)

= combine (kəm'baɪn)

= connect (kə'nɛkt)

= join (dʒɔɪn)

= link (lɪŋk)

= unite (ju'naɪt)

② = ally ('ælaɪ)

= companion (kəm'pænjən)

= comrade ('kamræd , 'kamrɪd)

= friend (frɛnd)

= mate (met)

= partner ('partnə)

assort (ə'sort) *v.* 分類

= arrange (ə'rendʒ)

= categorize ('kætəgə,raɪz)

= classify ('klæsə,faɪ)

= group (grup)

= sort (sɔrt)

assuage (ə'swedʒ) v. 緩和

= allay (ə'le)

= alleviate (ə'livɪ,et)

= calm (kɑm)

= ease (iz)

= lessen ('lɛsn̩)

= moderate ('mɑdə,ret)

= pacify ('pæsə,faɪ)

= quiet ('kwaɪət)

= relieve (rɪ'liv)

= soothe (suð)

assume (ə'sum , ə'sjum) v.
①假定　②假裝

① = believe (bə'liv , bɪ'liv)

= guess (gɛs)

= presume (prɪ'zum , -'zjum)

= suppose (sə'poz)

= suspect (sə'spɛkt)

= think (θɪŋk)

= understand (,ʌndə'stænd)

= *take for granted*

② = adopt (ə'dɑpt)

= affect (ə'fɛkt)

= *put on*

assure (ə'ʃur) v. 保證

= guarantee (,gærən'ti)

= promise ('prɑmɪs)

= pledge (plɛdʒ)

= swear (swɛr)

astonish (ə'stɑnɪʃ) v. 使驚訝

= amaze (ə'mez)

= astound (ə'staund)

= surprise (sə'praɪz , sə-)

astound (ə'staund) v. 使驚訝

= amaze (ə'mez)

= astonish (ə'stɑnɪʃ)

= stun (stʌn)

= surprise (sə'praɪz , sə-)

asunder (ə'sʌndə) adj.
星散的；分開的

= apart (ə'pɑrt)

= separate ('sɛpərɪt , -prɪt)

= divided (də'vaɪdɪd)

asylum (ə'saɪləm) n. ①庇護所
②精神病院

① = haven ('hevən)

= refuge ('rɛfjudʒ)

= shelter ('ʃɛltə)

② = madhouse ('mæd,haus)

= *mental hospital*

athletic (æθ'lɛtɪk) adj. 活潑的；
健壯的

= able-bodied ('ebl̩'bɑdɪd)

= active ('æktɪv)

= brawny ('brɔnɪ)

= gymnastic (dʒɪm'næstɪk)

= muscular ('mʌskjələ)

= sporting ('sportɪŋ , 'spɔr-)

= strong (strɔŋ)

= well-built ('wɛl'bɪlt)

= robust (ro'bʌst)

atone (ə'ton) v. 補償

= repay (rɪ'pe)
= compensate ('kɑmpən,set)
= *make amends for*
= *make up for*

atrocious (ə'troʃəs) *adj.*
殘忍的；惡劣的

= brutal ('brutḷ)
= cruel ('kruəl)
= hideous ('hɪdɪəs)
= horrible ('hɔrəbḷ , 'hɑr-)
= inhuman (ɪn'hjumən)
= ruthless ('ruθlɪs)
= savage ('sævɪdʒ)
= terrible ('tɛrəbḷ)
= vile (vaɪl)
= wicked ('wɪkɪd)
= wretched ('rɛtʃɪd)

attach (ə'tætʃ) v. 附著；連接

= add (æd)
= affix (ə'fɪks)
= append (ə'pɛnd)
= connect (kə'nɛkt)
= fasten ('fæsṇ , 'fɑsṇ)
= join (dʒɔɪn)
= link (lɪŋk)
= unite (ju'naɪt)
= *put together*

attack (ə'tæk) n. 攻擊

= assault (ə'sɔlt)
= bombardment (bɑm'bɑrdmənt)
= charge (tʃɑrdʒ)
= drive (draɪv)

= invasion (ɪn've‍ʒən)
= offense (ə'fɛns)
= onslaught ('ɑn,slɔt)
= raid (red)
= siege (sidʒ)
= strike (straɪk)

attain (ə'ten) v. ①到達
②實現

① = arrive (ə'raɪv)
= come (kʌm)
= reach (ritʃ)
= *get to*
② = achieve (ə'tʃiv)
= complete (kəm'plit)
= finish ('fɪnɪʃ)
= fulfill (fʊl'fɪl)
= gain (gen)
= obtain (əb'ten)
= realize ('riə,laɪz)
= secure (sɪ'kjur)
= accomplish (ə'kɑmplɪʃ)

attempt (ə'tɛmpt) v. 嘗試；
努力

= try (traɪ)
= endeavor (ɪn'dɛvɚ)
= essay (ə'se , ɛ'se)
= *make an effort*

attend (ə'tɛnd) v. ①出席
②照顧 ③陪伴；隨至

① = visit ('vɪzɪt)
= *be present*
= *go to*
② = serve (sɝv)

A

= nurse (nɜs)
= *care for*
= *look after*
= *minister to*
③ = accompany (ə'kʌmpənɪ)
= escort (ɪ'skɔrt)
= follow ('falo)

attention (ə'tɛnʃən) *n.* ①專心
②禮貌

① = attentiveness (ə'tɛntɪvnɪs)
= care (kɛr)
= concern (kən'sɜn)
= concentration (,kɑnsɛn'treʃən)
= consideration (kən,sɪdə'reʃən)
= heed (hid)
= intentness (ɪn'tɛntnɪs)
= thoughtfulness ('θɔtfəlnɪs)
② = courtesy ('kɜtəsɪ)
= politeness (pə'laɪtnɪs)

attest (ə'tɛst) *v.* 證實;證明

= certify ('sɜtə,faɪ)
= swear (swɛr)
= testify ('tɛstə,faɪ)
= vouch (vautʃ)
= *bear witness*
= *give proof*
= *give evidence*

attic ('ætɪk) *n.* 閣樓

= cockloft ('kɑk,lɔft)
= garret ('gærɪt)
= loft (lɔft)

attire (ə'taɪr) *v.* 盛裝

= apparel (ə'pil)
= array (ə're)
= clothe (kloð)
= dress (drɛs)
= garb (gɑrb)

attitude ('ætə,tjud) *n.* 態度;
觀點

= opinion (ə'pɪnjən)
= position (pə'zɪʃən)
= posture ('pastʃɚ)
= stance (stæns)
= standpoint ('stænd,pɔɪnt)
= viewpoint ('vju,pɔɪnt)

attract (ə'trækt) *v.* 吸引

= allure (ə'lur)
= captivate ('kæptə,vet)
= charm (tʃɑrm)
= draw (drɔ)
= entice (ɪn'taɪs)
= fascinate ('fæsn̩,et)
= interest ('ɪnt(ə)rɪst)
= lure (lur)
= pull (pul)
= seduce (sɪ'djus)
= tempt (tɛmpt)

attractive (ə'træktɪv) *adj.*
有誘惑力的

= alluring (ə'lurɪŋ)
= charming ('tʃɑrmɪŋ)
= engaging (ɪn'gedʒɪŋ)
= interesting ('ɪntrɪstɪŋ)
= seductive (sɪ'dʌktɪv)
= winning ('wɪnɪŋ)

attribute (*v.* ə'trɪbjut ,
n. 'ætrə,bjut) ① *v.* 歸於 ② *n.* 性質

① = apply (ə'plaɪ)
= ascribe (ə'skraɪb)
= assign (ə'saɪn)
= credit ('krɛdɪt)
= impute (ɪm'pjut)

② = characteristic (,kærɪktə'rɪstɪk)
= feature ('fitʃ⋅)
= nature ('netʃ⋅)
= property ('prɑpətɪ)
= quality ('kwɑlətɪ)
= trait (tret)

audacious (ɔ'deʃəs) *adj.*
無禮的；大膽的

= arrogant ('ærəgənt)
= bold (bold)
= brave (brev)
= cavalier (,kævə'lɪr)
= courageous (kə'redʒəs)
= daring ('dɛrɪŋ , 'dærɪŋ)
= foolhardy ('ful,hɑrdɪ)
= haughty ('hɔtɪ)
= insolent ('ɪnsələnt)

audible ('ɔdəbḷ) *adj.* 聽得見的

= clear (klɪr)
= distinct (dɪ'stɪŋkt)
= hearable ('hɪrəbḷ)
= perceptive (pɚ'sɛptɪv)

augment (ɔg'mɛnt) *v.* 增大

= broaden ('brɔdṇ)
= enlarge (ɪn'lɑrdʒ)
= expand (ɪk'spænd)

= extend (ɪk'stɛnd)
= increase (ɪn'kris)
= magnify ('mægnə,faɪ)
= raise (rez)

auspicious (ɔ'spɪʃəs) *adj.*
幸運的

= favorable ('fevrəbḷ , 'fevərəbḷ)
= fortunate ('fɔrtʃənɪt)
= lucky ('lʌkɪ)
= promising ('prɑmɪsɪŋ)
= propitious (prə'pɪʃəs)
= timely ('taɪmlɪ)

austere (ɔ'stɪr) *adj.* 苛刻的

= harsh (hɑrʃ)
= rigorous ('rɪgərəs)
= severe (sə'vɪr)
= stern (stɜn)
= strict (strɪkt)

authentic (ɔ'θɛntɪk) *adj.* 真正的

= actual ('æktʃuəl)
= authoritative (ə'θɔrə,tetɪv)
= factual ('fæktʃuəl)
= genuine ('dʒɛnjuɪn)
= legitimate (lɪ'dʒɪtəmɪt)
= real ('riəl , ril , 'rɪəl)
= reliable (rɪ'laɪəbḷ)
= true (tru)
= trustworthy ('trʌst,wɜðɪ)

authoritative (ə'θɔrə,tetɪv)
adj. 有權威的

= commanding (kə'mændɪŋ)
= decisive (dɪ'saɪsɪv)

= official (ə'fɪʃəl)
= powerful ('pauɚfəl)

authorize ('ɔθə,raɪz) v. 授權；認可

= assign (ə'saɪn)
= commission (kə'mɪʃən)
= empower (ɪm'pauɚ)
= enable (ɪn'ebl̩)
= *give authority*
= *give power to*

autocrat ('ɔtə,kræt) n. 專制君主

= despot ('dɛspat)
= dictator ('dɪktetɚ , dɪk'tetɚ)
= monarch ('manɚk)
= ruler ('rulɚ)
= tyrant ('taɪrənt)

autograph ('ɔtə,græf) n. 簽名；手稿

= holograph ('halə,græf)
= manuscript ('mænjə,skrɪpt)
= signature ('sɪgnətʃɚ)

automatic (,ɔtə'mætɪk) adj. 自動的

= mechanical (mə'kænɪkl̩)
= self-acting ('sɛlf'æktɪŋ)
= self-working ('sɛlf'wɜkɪŋ)

auxiliary (ɔg'zɪljərɪ) adj. 協助的

= accessory (æk'sɛsərɪ)
= aiding ('edɪŋ)
= assisting (ə'sɪstɪŋ)

= helping ('hɛlpɪŋ)
= subsidiary (səb'sɪdɪ,ɛrɪ)

avail (ə'vel) n. 利益；用處

= advantage (əd'væntɪdʒ)
= benefit ('bɛnəfɪt)
= help (hɛlp)
= profit ('prafɪt)
= service ('sɜvɪs)
= use (jus)
= value ('vælju)
= worth (wɜθ)

available (ə'veləbl̩) adj. 可用的

= handy ('hændɪ)
= convenient (kən'vinjənt)
= obtainable (əb'tenəbl̩)
= ready ('rɛdɪ)
= *at hand*

avarice ('ævərɪs , 'ævrɪs) n. 貪婪

= covetousness ('kʌvɪtəsnɪs)
= desire (dɪ'zaɪr)
= greed (grid)
= voracity (vɔ'ræsətɪ)

average ('ævrɪdʒ , 'ævərɪdʒ) adj. ①普通的 ②平均的

① = common ('kamən)
= fair (fɛr)
= ordinary ('ɔrdn̩,ɛrɪ , 'ɔrdnɛrɪ)
= passable ('pæsəbl̩)
= usual ('juʒuəl)
② = medium ('midɪəm)
= mean (min)
= middle ('mɪdl̩)

A

averse (ə'vɝs) *adj.* 不願意的；反對的

= against (ə'gɛnst)
= forced (forst , fɔrst)
= involuntary (ɪn'vɑlən,tɛrɪ)
= loath (loθ)
= opposed (ə'pozd)
= reluctant (rɪ'lʌktənt)
= unwilling (ʌn'wɪlɪŋ)

aversion (ə'vɝʒen , -ʃən) *n.* 嫌惡

= antipathy (æn'tɪpəθɪ)
= disgust (dɪs'gʌst)
= hatred ('hetrɪd)
= loathing ('loθɪŋ)
= *strong dislike*

avert (ə'vɝt) *v.* ①避免；防止 ②移轉

① = prevent (prɪ'vɛnt)
= thwart (θwɔrt)
= avoid (ə'vɔɪd)
= *keep off*
② = *turn away*
= *turn aside*

avid ('ævɪd) *adj.* 貪婪的；渴望

= covetous ('kʌvɪtəs)
= eager ('igɚ)
= greedy ('gridɪ)
= keen (kin)
= voracious (vo'reʃəs)

avocation (,ævə'keʃən , ,ævo-) *n.* 嗜好；副業

= hobby ('hɑbɪ)
= sideline ('saɪd,laɪn)
= *minor occupation*

avoid (ə'vɔɪd) *v.* 逃避

= avert (ə'vɝt)
= elude (ɪ'lud)
= evade (ɪ'ved)
= refrain (rɪ'fren)
= shun (ʃʌn)
= sidestep ('saɪd,stɛp)
= *keep away from*

award (ə'wɔrd) *n.* 獎賞

= gift (gɪft)
= grant (grænt)
= medal ('mɛdl̩)
= prize (praɪz)
= trophy ('trofɪ)

aware (ə'wɛr) *adj.* 知道的

= cognizant ('kɑgnɪzənt , 'kɑnɪ-)
= conscious ('kɑnʃəs)
= informed (ɪn'fɔrmd)
= knowing ('noɪŋ)
= realizing ('riə,laɪzɪŋ , 'riə-)

awe (ɔ) *n.* 敬畏

= respect (rɪ'spɛkt)
= surprise (sə'praɪz)
= dread (drɛd)
= astonishment (ə'stɑnɪʃmənt)
= alarm (ə'lɑrm)
= fear (fɪr)
= wonder ('wʌndɚ)

A

awful ('ɔfʊl , 'ɔfḷ) *adj.* 可怕的

= dreadful ('drɛdfəl)
= fearful ('fɪrfəl)
= ghastly ('gæstlɪ)
= gruesome ('grusəm)
= horrible ('hɑrəbḷ)
= terrible ('tɛrəbḷ)
= unpleasant (ʌn'plɛzṇt)

awkward ('ɔkwəd) *adj.*
①笨拙的　②不便的；麻煩的

① = clumsy ('klʌmzɪ)
= ungainly (ʌn'genlɪ)
= ungraceful (ʌn'gresfəl)
= *all thumbs*
② = cumbersome ('kʌmbəsəm)
= inconvenient (,ɪnkən'vinjənt)
= troublesome ('trʌbḷsəm)

awry (ə'raɪ) *adj.* ①歪曲的
②錯誤的

① = askew (ə'skju)
= crooked ('krʊkɪd)
= twisted ('twɪstɪd)
② = disorderly (dɪs'ɔrdəlɪ)
= mistaken (mə'stekən)
= wrong (rɔŋ)

B

babble ('bæbḷ) *v.* 言語含糊；
嘮叨；多嘴

= chatter ('tʃætə)
= gabble ('gæbḷ)
= prattle ('prætḷ)
= gossip ('gɑsɪp)

= *baby talk*

background ('bæk,graʊnd) *n.*
①背景　②經驗；知識

① = environment (ɪn'vaɪrənmənt)
= setting ('sɛtɪŋ)
② = experience (ɪk'spɪrɪəns)
= knowledge ('nɑlɪdʒ)
= practice ('præktɪs)
= training ('trenɪŋ)

backslide ('bæk,slaɪd) *v.* 墮落；
退步

= lapse (læps)
= regress (rɪ'grɛs)
= *go wrong*
= *fall from grace*

bad (bæd) *v.* 壞的；不良的

= evil ('ivḷ)
= poor (pʊr)
= unfavorable (ʌn'fevrəbḷ)
= wrong (rɔŋ)

badge (bædʒ) *n.* 標記；徽章

= emblem ('ɛmbləm)

badger ('bædʒə) ① *v.* 困擾
② *n.* 獾

① = annoy (ə'nɔɪ)
= bait (bet)
= bother ('bɑðə)
= harass ('hærəs , hə'ræs)
= nag (næg)
= pester ('pɛstə)
= tease (tiz)

= torment〔ˋtɔrˏmɛnt〕
② = *small hairy animal*

baffle〔ˋbæfḷ〕*v.* 使困惑
= confuse〔kənˋfjuz〕
= puzzle〔ˋpʌzḷ〕
= perplex〔pəˋplɛks〕
= confound〔kɑnˋfaʊnd, kən-〕
= mystify〔ˋmɪstəˏfaɪ〕
= bewilder〔bɪˋwɪldɚ〕

bait〔bet〕*v.* ①困擾 ②誘惑
① = badger〔ˋbædʒɚ〕
② = lure〔lʊr〕
= tempt〔tɛmpt〕
= seduce〔sɪˋdjus〕

balance〔ˋbæləns〕① *n.* 天平
② *n.* 平衡 ③ *v.* 權衡
① = scale〔skel〕
② = equilibrium〔ˏikwəˋlɪbrɪəm〕
= steadiness〔ˋstɛdɪnɪs〕
= stability〔stəˋbɪlətɪ〕
③ = assess〔əˋsɛs〕
= weigh〔we〕
= deliberate〔dɪˋlɪbəˏret〕
= evaluate〔ɪˋvæljʊˏet〕

bald〔bɔld〕*adj.* 光禿的
= bare〔bɛr〕
= hairless〔ˋhɛrlɪs〕
= naked〔ˋnekɪd〕
= nude〔njud〕
= uncovered〔ʌnˋkʌvɚd〕

baleful〔ˋbelfəl〕*adj.* 有害的

= harmful〔ˋhɑrmfəl〕
= hurtful〔ˋhɝtfəl〕
= injurious〔ɪnˋdʒʊrɪəs〕

balk〔bɔk〕*v.* 停止；中斷；
拒絕繼續
= discontinue〔ˏdɪskənˋtɪnju〕
= rebel〔rɪˋbɛl〕
= stop〔stɑp〕

ballad〔ˋbæləd〕*n.* 民謠
= chantey〔ˋtʃæntɪ〕
= ditty〔ˋdɪtɪ〕
= song〔sɔŋ〕

ballot〔ˋbælət〕*n.* 選票
= choice〔tʃɔɪs〕
= poll〔pol〕
= vote〔vot〕

balmy〔ˋbɑmɪ〕*adj.* 溫柔的；
芳香的
= mild〔maɪld〕
= soft〔sɔft〕
= gentle〔ˋdʒɛntḷ〕
= fragrant〔ˋfregrənt〕

ban〔bæn〕*v.* 禁止
= bar〔bɑr〕
= block〔blɑk〕
= exclude〔ɪkˋsklud〕
= forbid〔fɚˋbɪd〕
= obstruct〔əbˋstrʌkt〕
= outlaw〔ˋaʊtˏlɔ〕
= prohibit〔proˋhɪbɪt〕
= *shut out*

B

bandit ('bændɪt) *n.* 強盜；土匪

= brigand ('brɪgənd)
= gangster ('gæŋstɚ)
= highwayman ('haɪ,wemən)
= outlaw ('aʊt,lɔ)
= robber ('rɑbɚ)
= thief (θif)

bang (bæŋ) *v.* 重擊

= batter ('bætɚ)
= hit (hɪt)
= pound (paʊnd)
= slam (slæm)
= strike (straɪk)

banish ('bænɪʃ) *v.* 驅逐

= deport (dɪ'port , -'pɔrt)
= dismiss (dɪs'mɪs)
= exile ('ɛgzaɪl , 'ɛksaɪl)
= expel (ɪk'spɛl)
= outlaw ('aʊt,lɔ)
= *force away*
= *drive away*

bank (bæŋk) *n.* ①堤；岸
②銀行 ③一列

① = shore (ʃor , ʃɔr)
② = storehouse ('storhaʊs)
= storage ('storɪdʒ)
③ = series ('sɪriz)
= string (strɪŋ)
= row (ro)

banquet ('bæŋkwɪt) *n.* 宴會

= feast (fist)

= regale (rɪ'gel)
= *formal dinner*

banter ('bæntɚ) *v.* 嘲弄

= jest (dʒɛst)
= joke (dʒok)
= tease (tiz)

bar (bɑr) ① *v.* 禁止
② *n.* 棒狀物 ③ *n.* 律師業
④ *n.* 酒店 ⑤ *n.* 五線譜上之縱線

① = ban (bæn)
② = pole (pol)
= rod (rɑd)
= stick (stɪk)
= rail (rel)
③ = court (kort)
= *legal profession*
= *body of lawyers*
④ = saloon (sə'lun)
= tavern ('tævɚn)
= counter ('kaʊntɚ)
= pub (pʌb)
⑤ = *music staff*

barbarian (bɑr'bɛrɪən) *adj.*
野蠻的

= brutal ('brutl̩)
= coarse (kors , kɔrs)
= cruel ('kruəl)
= primitive ('prɪmətɪv)
= savage ('sævɪdʒ)
= uncivilized (ʌn'sɪvl̩,aɪzd)
= uncouth (ʌn'kuθ)
= uncultured (ʌn'kʌltʃɚd)

bare〔bɛr〕*adj.* 赤裸的

= bald〔bɔld〕

= naked〔'nekɪd〕

= nude〔njud〕

= unclothed〔ʌn'kloðd〕

barely〔'bɛrlɪ〕*adv.* 幾乎不能；
僅僅

= scarcely〔'skɛrslɪ〕

= hardly〔'hardlɪ〕

= just〔dʒʌst〕

= only〔'onlɪ〕

bargain〔'bargɪn〕*n.* ①協議；
交易 ② *n.* 廉價買的東西

① = agreement〔ə'grimənt〕

= contract〔'kantrækt〕

= deal〔dil〕

= negotiation〔nɪ,goʃɪ'eʃən〕

= transaction〔træns'ækʃən,
trænz'ækʃən〕

② = discount〔'dɪskaunt〕

= *good buy*

= *good deal*

barren〔'bærən〕*adj.* 不生產的；
不孕的

= childless〔'tʃaɪldlɪs〕

= infertile〔ɪn'fɜtḷ〕

= sterile〔'stɛrəl〕

= unproductive〔ʌnprə'dʌktɪv〕

barricade〔,bærə'ked, 'bærə,ked〕
① *n.* 障礙物 ② *v.* 阻礙

① = barrier〔'bærɪɚ〕

② = block〔blak〕

= fortify〔'fɔrtə,faɪ〕

= obstruct〔əb'strʌkt〕

barrier〔'bærɪɚ〕*n.* 障礙物

= barricade〔,bærə'ked, 'bærə,ked〕

= blockade〔bla'ked〕

= fortification〔,fɔrtəfə'keʃən〕

= obstacle〔'abstəkḷ〕

barter〔'bartɚ〕*v.* 以物易物

= trade〔tred〕

= deal〔dil〕

= swap〔swap, swɔp〕

= exchange〔ɪks'tʃendʒ〕

base〔bes〕① *v.* 設立
② *adj.* 卑鄙的；低級的
③ *n.* 基礎 ④ *n.* 基地

① = build〔bɪld〕

= establish〔ə'stæblɪʃ〕

= found〔faund〕

= set〔sɛt〕

= settle〔'sɛtḷ〕

② = debased〔de'best〕

= inferior〔ɪn'fɪrɪɚ〕

= low〔lo〕

= mean〔min〕

③ = bottom〔'batəm〕

= foundation〔faun'deʃən〕

= groundwork〔'graund,wɝk〕

④ = headquarters〔'hɛd'kwɔrtɚz〕

= station〔'steʃən〕

bashful〔'bæʃfəl〕*adj.* 害羞的

= coy〔kɔɪ〕

= diffident〔'dɪfədənt〕

B

= shy (ʃaɪ)
= timid ('tɪmɪd)

basic ('besɪk) *adj.* 基本的

= elementary (ˌɛlə'mɛntərɪ)
= essential (ə'sɛnʃəl)
= fundamental (ˌfʌndə'mɛntḷ)
= primary ('praɪˌmɛrɪ)
= underlying ('ʌndəˌlaɪɪŋ)

bat (bæt) *v.* 擊；打

= bang (bæŋ)
= clout (klaʊt)
= crack (kræk)
= hit (hɪt)
= knock (nɑk)
= strike (straɪk)

bathe (beð) *v.* 浸於；洗

= cleanse (klɛnz)
= rinse (rɪns)
= wash (wɑʃ)
= soak (sok)
= immerse (ɪ'mɜs)
= drench (drɛntʃ)
= *pour over*

batter ('bætə) ① *v.* 重擊
② *n.* 糊狀混合物　③ *n.* 打擊手

① = beat (bit)
= pound (paʊnd)
= smash (smæʃ)
= thrash (θræʃ)
② = mixture ('mɪkstʃə)
③ = *baseball player*

battery ('bætərɪ) *n.* 一組相連
之東西

= series ('sɪriz)
= set (sɛt)
= suite (swit)

battle ('bætḷ) *n.* 戰鬥

= combat ('kɑmbæt , 'kʌm-)
= conflict ('kɑnflɪkt)
= contest ('kɑntɛst)
= fight (faɪt)
= struggle ('strʌgḷ)
= war (wɔr)

bauble ('bɔbḷ) *n.* 玩具

= plaything ('pleˌθɪŋ)
= toy (tɔɪ)
= trinket ('trɪŋkɪt)

bawl (bɔl) *v.* 大喊；號叫

= bellow ('bɛlo)
= cry (kraɪ)
= howl (haʊl)
= shout (ʃaʊt)
= sob (sɑb)
= yell (jɛl)

beach (bitʃ) *n.* 海濱

= shore (ʃor , ʃɔr)
= seaside ('siˌsaɪd)
= coast (kost)
= waterfront ('wɔtəˌfrʌnt)

beacon ('bikən) *n.* ①信號；
烽火　②燈塔

① = flare (flɛr)

= signal（'sɪgn̩）
② = lighthouse（'laɪt,haʊs）
= watchtower（'wɑtʃ,taʊɚ）

beam（bim）① v. 放光
② n. 屋樑

① = gleam（glim）
= glow（glo）
= shine（ʃaɪn）
② = joist（dʒɔɪst）
= shaft（ʃæft）
= timber（'tɪmbɚ）

bear（bɛr）v. ①承載；負擔
②忍受　③生產

① = carry（'kærɪ）
= convey（kən've）
= transport（træns'port）
= hold（hold）
= withstand（wɪθ'stænd , wɪð-）
= support（sə'port , -'port）
② = endure（ɪn'djʊr）
= tolerate（'tɑlə,ret）
③ = produce（prə'djus）
= yield（jild）

bearing（'bɛrɪŋ , 'bær-）v.
①態度　②關係　③方向

① = air（ɛr）
= attitude（'ætətjud）
= manner（'mænɚ）
② = connection（kə'nɛkʃən）
= reference（'rɛfərəns）
= relation（rɪ'leʃən）
③ = course（kors , kɔrs）
= direction（də'rɛkʃən , daɪ-）

= trend（trɛnd）
= way（we）

beast（bist）v. 動物；獸類

= animal（'ænəm̩l）
= creature（'kritʃɚ）
= brute（brut）

beat（bit）① v. 打　② v. 攪拌
③ n. 拍子　④ v. 打敗

① = bat（bæt）
② = mix（mɪks）
= stir（stɝ）
③ = accent（'æksɛnt）
= rhythm（'rɪðəm）
④ = conquer（'kɑŋkɚ）
= defeat（dɪ'fit）
= overcome（,ovɚ'kʌm）
= surpass（sɚ'pæs）
= outdo（,aʊt'du）

beautiful（'bjutəfəl）adj. 美麗的

= attractive（ə'træktɪv）
= handsome（'hænsəm）
= lovely（'lʌvlɪ）
= pretty（'prɪtɪ）

beckon（'bɛkən）v. 打手勢

= gesture（'dʒɛstʃɚ）
= motion（'moʃən）
= signal（'sɪgn̩l）
= summon（'sʌmən）

bedlam（'bɛdləm）n. ①喧擾
②瘋人院

① = confusion（kən'fjuʒən）

B

= racket ('rækɪt)

= rumpus ('rʌmpəs)

= tumult ('tumʌlt , tju-)

= turmoil ('tɜmɔɪl)

= uproar ('ʌp,ror , -,rɔr)

② = asylum (ə'saɪləm)

bedraggled (bɪ'dræɡl̩d) *adj.*
邋遢的

= dirty ('dɜtɪ)

= messy ('mɛsɪ)

= shabby ('ʃæbɪ)

= sloppy ('slɑpɪ)

= untidy (ʌn'taɪdɪ)

= *wet and limp*

beefy ('bifɪ) *adj.* 強壯的

= muscular ('mʌskjələ)

= solid ('sɑlɪd)

= stocky ('stɑkɪ)

= strong (strɔŋ)

= sturdy ('stɜdɪ)

before (bɪ'for , bɪ'fɔr) *adv.*
以前；曾經

= ahead (ə'hɛd)

= earlier ('ɜlɪə)

= formerly ('fɔrməlɪ)

= previously ('privɪəslɪ)

= prior ('praɪə)

= *in advance*

beg (bɛɡ) *v.* 懇求

= appeal (ə'pil)

= beseech (bɪ'sitʃ)

= entreat (ɪn'trit)

= implore (ɪm'plor , -'plɔr)

= plead (plid)

begin (bɪ'ɡɪn) *v.* 開始

= commence (kə'mɛns)

= initiate (ɪ'nɪʃɪ,et)

= start (stɑrt)

= *take off*

beguile (bɪ'ɡaɪl) *v.* ①欺騙
②消遣

① = bamboozle (bæm'buzl̩)

= cheat (tʃit)

= deceive (dɪ'siv)

= delude (dɪ'lud)

= dupe (djup , dup)

= trick (trɪk)

② = amuse (ə'mjuz)

= charm (tʃɑrm)

= divert (daɪ'vɜt)

= entertain (,ɛntə'ten)

behalf (bɪ'hæf) *n.* 利益

= advantage (əd'væntɪdʒ)

= benefit ('bɛnəfɪt)

= good (ɡud)

= interest ('ɪntərɪst , 'ɪntrɪst)

= welfare ('wɛl,fɛr)

behavior (bɪ'hevɪə) *n.* 行爲；
態度

= action ('ækʃən)

= conduct ('kɑndʌkt)

= manner ('mænə)

behest (bɪ'hɛst) *n.* 吩咐

= bidding (ˈbɪdɪŋ)

= command (kəˈmænd)

= order (ˈɔrdɚ)

behind (bɪˈhaɪnd) ① *prep.* 在後 ② *adv.* 落後地

① = after (ˈæftɚ)

= following (ˈfɑləwɪŋ)

= *in back of*

= *later than*

② = rearward (ˈrɪrwɚd)

= aft (aft)

= backward (ˈbækwɚd)

behold (bɪˈhold) *v.* 看

= look (lʊk)

= observe (əbˈzɝv)

= see (si)

= sight (saɪt)

= view (vju)

= watch (watʃ)

belated (bɪˈletɪd) *adj.* 誤期的

= delayed (dɪˈled)

= late (let)

= overdue (ˌovɚˈdju)

= tardy (ˈtardɪ)

= *behind time*

belie (bɪˈlaɪ) *v.* ①使人誤會；掩飾 ②辜負

① = conceal (kənˈsil)

= disguise (dɪsˈgaɪz)

= falsify (ˈfɔlsəˌfaɪ)

= mislead (mɪsˈlid)

= misrepresent (ˌmɪsrɛprɪˈzɛnt)

② = disappoint (ˌdɪsəˈpɔɪnt)

believe (bəˈliv, bɪ-) *v.* 相信；認爲

= suppose (səˈpoz)

= surmise (sɚˈmaɪz)

= think (θɪŋk)

= trust (trʌst)

belittle (bɪˈlɪtḷ) *v.* 輕視

= disparage (dɪˈspærɪdʒ)

= minimize (ˈmɪnəˌmaɪz)

= scorn (skɔrn)

= underestimate (ˌʌndɚˈɛstəˌmet)

= underrate (ˌʌndɚˈret)

= *run down*

belligerent (bəˈlɪdʒərənt) *adj.* 好戰的

= aggressive (əˈgrɛsɪv)

= bellicose (ˈbɛləˌkos)

= combative (kəmˈbætɪv, ˈkambətɪv)

= hostile (ˈhastḷ, hastˈaɪl)

= militant (ˈmɪlətənt)

= warlike (ˈwɔrˌlaɪk)

bellow (ˈbɛlo) *v.* 吼叫

= bawl (bɔl)

belly (ˈbɛlɪ) *n.* 腹；胃

= abdomen (æbˈdomən, ˈæbdəmən)

= stomach (ˈstʌmək)

B

belongings ﹝ bɪ'lɔŋɪŋz ﹞ *n. pl.*
財產

= property ﹝'prɑpətɪ ﹞

= possessions ﹝ pə'zɛʃənz ﹞

below ﹝ bə'lo ﹞ ① *prep.* 在…之
下；不及 ② *adv.* 在下面

① = beneath ﹝ bɪ'niθ ﹞

= under ﹝'ʌndɚ ﹞

② = less ﹝ lɛs ﹞

= lower ﹝'loɚ ﹞

= subordinate ﹝ sə'bɔrdn̩ɪt ﹞

= underneath ﹝ˌʌndɚ'niθ ﹞

bend ﹝ bɛnd ﹞ *v.* ①彎 ②鞠躬
③屈服

① = curve ﹝ kɝv ﹞

= turn ﹝ tɝn ﹞

= twist ﹝ twɪst ﹞

② = bow ﹝ baʊ ﹞

= stoop ﹝ stup ﹞

③ = shape ﹝ ʃep ﹞

= submit ﹝ səb'mɪt ﹞

= yield ﹝ jild ﹞

beneath ﹝ bɪ'niθ ﹞ *prep.* 在…之下

= below ﹝ bə'lo ﹞

benediction ﹝ˌbɛnə'dɪkʃən ﹞ *n.*
祝福

= blessing ﹝'blɛsɪŋ ﹞

= commendation ﹝ˌkɑmən'deʃən ﹞

= prayer ﹝ prɛr , prær ﹞

= thankfulness ﹝'θæŋkfəlnɪs ﹞

beneficial ﹝ˌbɛnə'fɪʃəl ﹞ *adj.*
有益的

= advantageous ﹝ˌædvən'tedʒəs ﹞

= favorable ﹝'fevrəbl̩ ﹞

= helpful ﹝'hɛlpfəl ﹞

= profitable ﹝'prɑfɪtəbl̩ ﹞

= salutary ﹝'sæljəˌtɛrɪ ﹞

= useful ﹝'jusfəl ﹞

benefit ﹝'bɛnəfɪt ﹞ *n.* 利益

= advantage ﹝ əd'væntɪdʒ ﹞

= boon ﹝ bun ﹞

= gain ﹝ gen ﹞

= interest ﹝'ɪntrɪst ﹞

= profit ﹝'prɑfɪt ﹞

benevolence ﹝ bə'nɛvələns ﹞ *n.*
仁慈

= charity ﹝'tʃærətɪ ﹞

= compassion ﹝ kəm'pæʃən ﹞

= generosity ﹝ˌdʒɛnə'rɑsətɪ ﹞

= humanity ﹝ hju'mænətɪ ﹞

= kindness ﹝'kaɪndnɪs ﹞

= *good will*

benign ﹝ bɪ'naɪn ﹞ *adj.* 親切的

= affable ﹝'æfəbl̩ ﹞

= friendly ﹝'frɛndlɪ ﹞

= genial ﹝'dʒinjəl ﹞

= kind ﹝ kaɪnd ﹞

= sympathetic ﹝ˌsɪmpə'θɛtɪk ﹞

bent ﹝ bɛnt ﹞ ① *adj.* 彎曲的
② *n.* 傾向

① = curved ﹝ kɝvɪd ﹞

= twisted ('twɪstɪd)

② = inclination (,ɪnklə'neʃən)

= tendency ('tɛndənsɪ)

= nature ('netʃɚ)

= propensity (prə'pɛnsətɪ)

berate (bɪ'ret) *v.* 痛罵

= chide (tʃaɪd)

= reproach (rɪ'protʃ)

= scold (skold)

= *yell at*

beseech (bɪ'sitʃ) *v.* 懇求

= beg (bɛg)

beset (bɪ'sɛt) *v.* 圍攻

= besiege (bɪ'sidʒ)

besides (bɪ'saɪdz) *adv.* 且；又

= also ('ɔlso)

= further ('fɝðɚ)

= moreover (mor'ovɚ , mɔr-)

= too (tu)

= *as well*

= *in addition*

= *what's more*

besiege (bɪ'sidʒ) *v.* 圍攻

= assault (ə'sɔlt)

= attack (ə'tæk)

= beleaguer (bɪ'ligɚ)

= invest (ɪn'vɛst)

= raid (red)

= siege (sidʒ)

bespeak (bɪ'spik) *v.* ①預約 ②表示

① = reserve (rɪ'zɝv)

= engage (ɪn'gedʒ)

② = show (ʃo)

= express (ɪk'sprɛs)

= indicate ('ɪndə,ket)

= signify ('sɪgnə,faɪ)

best (bɛst) *adj.* 最佳的

= choice (tʃɔɪs)

= prime (praɪm)

= select (sə'lɛkt)

bestial ('bɛstʃəl , 'bɛstɪl) *adj.* 野蠻的

= beastly ('bistlɪ)

= brutal ('brutl̩)

= cruel ('kruəl)

= savage ('sævɪdʒ)

bestow (bɪ'sto) *v.* 贈給

= award (ə'wɔrd)

= donate ('donet)

= give (gɪv)

= grant (grænt)

bet (bɛt) *v.* 打賭

= gamble ('gæmbl̩)

= wager ('wedʒɚ)

betray (bɪ'tre) *v.* ①出賣 ②顯示

① = deceive (dɪ'siv)

= trick (trɪk)

B

B

= *sell out*

② = expose (ɪksˈpoz)

= reveal (rɪˈvil)

= uncover (ʌnˈkʌvə)

= unmask (ʌnˈmæsk)

betrothal (bɪˈtroθəl , -ˈtroðəl)
n. 訂婚；婚約

= engagement (ɪnˈgedʒmənt)

= *marriage contract*

better (ˈbɛtə) *adj.* 較好的

= improved (ɪmˈpruvd)

= finer (ˈfaɪnə)

= preferable (ˈprɛfrəbļ , ˈprɛfərə-)

= superior (səˈpɪrɪə , su-)

between (bəˈtwin) *prep.*
在…之間

= amidst (əˈmɪdst)

= among (əˈmʌŋ)

= betwixt (bəˈtwɪkst)

beware (bɪˈwɛr) *v.* 小心

= heed (hid)

= mind (maɪnd)

= *be careful*

= *guard against*

= *look out*

= *look sharp*

= *take care*

= *watch out*

bewilder (bɪˈwɪldə) *v.* 使迷惑

= baffle (ˈbæfļ)

= confound (kɑnˈfaʊnd , kən-)

= confuse (kənˈfjuz)

= perplex (pəˈplɛks)

= puzzle (ˈpʌzļ)

bewitch (bɪˈwɪtʃ) *v.* ①蠱惑；
施法術於　②令人著迷

① = hex (hɛks)

= spellbind (ˈspɛlˌbaɪnd)

= *put under a spell*

② = beguile (bɪˈgaɪl)

= charm (tʃɑrm)

= enchant (ɪnˈtʃænt)

= fascinate (ˈfæsṇˌet)

beyond (bɪˈjɑnd) *prep.* 超過

= above (əˈbʌv)

= farther (ˈfɑrðə)

= over (ˈovə)

= past (pæst)

bias (ˈbaɪəs) ① *adj.* 傾斜的；
對角的　② *n.* 偏見

① = diagonal (daɪˈægənļ)

= oblique (əˈblik)

= slanting (ˈslæntɪŋ)

② = bigotry (ˈbɪgətrɪ)

= partiality (ˌpɑrʃɪˈælətɪ)

= predilection (ˌpridɪˈlɛkʃən)

= prejudice (ˈprɛdʒədɪs)

bid (bɪd) *v.* 命令；請求

= ask (æsk)

= command (kəˈmænd)

= direct (dəˈrɛkt , daɪ-)

= instruct (ɪnˈstrʌkt)

= invite (ɪnˈvaɪt)

B

= order（'ɔrdɚ）

= require（rɪ'kwaɪr）

big（bɪg）*adj.* ①大的　②重要的

① = considerable（kən'sɪdərəbl̩）

= enormous（ɪ'nɔrməs）

= gigantic（dʒaɪ'gæntɪk）

= grand（grænd）

= great（gret）

= huge（hjudʒ）

= large（lardʒ）

= massive（'mæsɪv）

② = important（ɪm'pɔrtn̩t）

= weighty（'wetɪ）

bind（baɪnd）*v.* ①綁（束）縛　②使負義務

① = fasten（'fæsn̩）

= restrain（rɪ'stren）

= tie（taɪ）

② = obligate（ə'blaɪdʒ）

= require（rɪ'kwaɪr）

birth（bɝθ）*n.* ①起源　②初期

① = beginning（bɪ'gɪnɪŋ）

= genesis（'dʒɛnəsɪs）

= inception（ɪn'sɛpʃən）

= origin（'ɔrədʒɪn , 'ar-）

② = infancy（'ɪnfənsɪ）

bit（bɪt）*n.* ①少許　②約束

① = jot（dʒat）

= morsel（'mɔrsl̩）

= piece（pis）

= *small amount*

② = check（tʃɛk）

= restraint（rɪ'strent）

bite（baɪt）*v.* 咬

= nip（nɪp）

= gnaw（nɔ）

= *cut with teeth*

biting（'baɪtɪŋ）*adj.* 銳利的；諷刺的

= cutting（'kʌtɪŋ）

= harsh（harʃ）

= pungent（'pʌndʒənt）

= sarcastic（sar'kæstɪk）

= sharp（ʃarp）

bitter（'bɪtɚ）*adj.* ①苦味的　②尖酸的

① = distasteful（dɪs'testfəl）

= unpleasant（ʌn'plɛznt）

② = acrid（'ækrɪd）

= stinging（'stɪŋɪŋ）

blade（bled）*n.* 刀；劍

= knife（naɪf）

= sword（sord , sɔrd）

blame（blem）*v.* 歸咎；控告

= accuse（ə'kjuz）

= censure（'sɛnʃɚ）

= charge（tʃardʒ）

= condemn（kən'dɛm）

= denounce（dɪ'naʊns）

= indict（ɪn'daɪt）

= reproach（rɪ'protʃ）

= reprove（rɪ'pruv）

B

blameless ('blemlɪs) *adj.* 無過失的

= faultless ('fɔltlɪs)
= innocent ('ɪnəsn̩t)

bland (blænd) *adj.* ①溫和的 ②無味的

① = agreeable (ə'griəbl̩)
= gentle ('dʒɛntl̩)
= mild (maɪld)
= smooth (smuð)
② = boring ('borɪŋ)
= dull (dʌl)
= insipid (ɪn'sɪpɪd)
= tasteless ('testlɪs)

blank (blæŋk) *adj.* 空的

= empty ('ɛmptɪ)
= vacant ('vekənt)
= void (vɔɪd)

blast (blæst) *n.* 爆炸

= blowup ('blo,ʌp)
= burst (bɝst)
= discharge (dɪs'tʃardʒ)
= explosion (ɪk'sploʒən)

blaze (blez) *n.* ①火焰 ②刻痕

① = fire (faɪr)
= flame (flem)
= flare (flɛr)
② = marking ('markɪŋ)
= notch (natʃ)

bleak (blik) *adj.* ①荒涼的 ②陰鬱的

① = bare (bɛr)
= barren ('bærən)
= chilly ('tʃɪlɪ)
= desolate ('dɛslɪt)
② = dismal ('dɪzml̩)
= dreary ('drɪrɪ)
= gloomy ('glumɪ)

bleed (blid) *v.* ①流血 ②悲痛

① = *lose blood*
② = ache (ek)
= grieve (griv)
= sorrow ('saro)

blemish ('blɛmɪʃ) ① *n.* 污點 ② *v.* 損傷

① = defect (dɪ'fɛkt , 'difɛkt)
= flaw (flɔ)
= scar (skar)
= stain (sten)
② = damage ('dæmɪdʒ)
= impair (ɪm'pɛr)
= injure ('ɪndʒɚ)

blend (blɛnd) *v.* 混合

= combine (kəm'baɪn)
= fuse (fjuz)
= merge (mɝdʒ)
= mingle ('mɪŋgl̩)
= mix (mɪks)

bless (blɛs) *v.* 祝福；感謝

= glorify ('glorə,faɪ , 'glɔr-)
= praise (prez)
= thank (θæŋk)

blight ﹝ blaɪt ﹞① v. 毀壞
② n. 植物病害

① = decay ﹝ dɪ'ke ﹞
　 = destroy ﹝ dɪ'strɔɪ ﹞
　 = ruin ﹝ 'ruɪn ﹞
　 = wither ﹝ 'wɪðɚ ﹞
② = disease ﹝ dɪ'ziz ﹞
　 = pestilence ﹝ 'pɛstələns ﹞

blind ﹝ blaɪnd ﹞ adj. ①盲的
②無知的

① = sightless ﹝ 'saɪtlɪs ﹞
　 = visionless ﹝ 'vɪʒənlɪs ﹞
② = ignorant ﹝ 'ɪgnərənt ﹞
　 = stupid ﹝ 'stjupɪd ﹞
　 = *without judgment*
　 = *without thought*

bliss ﹝ blɪs ﹞ n. 極大的幸福

　 = delight ﹝ dɪ'laɪt ﹞
　 = ecstasy ﹝ 'ɛkstəsɪ ﹞
　 = happiness ﹝ 'hæpɪnɪs ﹞
　 = joy ﹝ dʒɔɪ ﹞
　 = rapture ﹝ 'ræptʃɚ ﹞

blithe ﹝ blaɪð ﹞ adj. 快樂的；
無憂無慮的

　 = breezy ﹝ 'brizɪ ﹞
　 = carefree ﹝ 'kɛrfri ﹞
　 = cheerful ﹝ 'tʃɪrfəl ﹞
　 = gay ﹝ ge ﹞
　 = happy ﹝ 'hæpɪ ﹞
　 = lighthearted ﹝ ˌlaɪt'hɑrtɪd ﹞
　 = merry ﹝ 'mɛrɪ ﹞
　 = mirthful ﹝ 'mɝθfəl ﹞

bloat ﹝ blot ﹞ v. 膨脹

　 = balloon ﹝ bə'lun ﹞
　 = inflate ﹝ ɪn'flet ﹞
　 = swell ﹝ swɛl ﹞
　 = *puff up*

blob ﹝ blɑb ﹞ n. 一滴

　 = bubble ﹝ 'bʌbl̩ ﹞
　 = drop ﹝ drɑp ﹞
　 = droplet ﹝ 'drɑplɪt ﹞

block ﹝ blɑk ﹞ ① v. 阻礙
② n. 塊

① = clog ﹝ klɑg , klɔg ﹞
　 = hinder ﹝ 'hɪndɚ ﹞
　 = impede ﹝ ɪm'pid ﹞
　 = obstruct ﹝ əb'strʌkt ﹞
② = lump ﹝ lʌmp ﹞
　 = mass ﹝ mæs ﹞
　 = solid ﹝ 'sɑlɪd ﹞

blockade ﹝ blɑ'ked ﹞ n. 障礙物

　 = barricade ﹝ ˌbærə'ked , 'bærəˌked ﹞
　 = barrier ﹝ 'barɪɚ ﹞
　 = hindrance ﹝ 'hɪndrəns ﹞
　 = obstruction ﹝ əb'strʌkʃən ﹞

bloodthirsty ﹝ 'blʌdˌθɝstɪ ﹞ adj.
殘忍的

　 = bloody ﹝ 'blʌdɪ ﹞
　 = brutal ﹝ 'brutl̩ ﹞
　 = cruel ﹝ 'kruəl ﹞
　 = murderous ﹝ 'mɝdərəs ﹞

bloom ﹝ blum ﹞ v. 繁榮；開花

　 = blossom ﹝ 'blɑsəm ﹞

B

B

= flourish ('flɜɪʃ)
= flower ('flauɚ)
= prosper ('prɑspɚ)
= thrive (θraɪv)

blossom ('blɑsəm) v. 繁榮；
開花

= bloom (blum)
= develop (dɪ'vɛləp)
= flower ('flauɚ)

blot (blɑt) ① n. 污點
② v. 抹去

① = spot (spɑt)
= stain (sten)
② = erase (ɪ'res)
= obliterate (ə'blɪtə,ret)
= *wipe out*

blow (blo) ① v. 吹 ② n. 打擊

① = pipe (paɪp)
= puff (pʌf)
= trumpet ('trʌmpɪt)
② = knock (nɑk)
= punch (pʌntʃ)
= rap (ræp)
= stroke (strok)
= whack (hwæk)

blowout ('blo,aut) n. 爆炸

= blast (blæst)
= burst (bɜst)
= explosion (ɪk'sploʒən)

bluff (blʌf) ① v. 虛張聲勢
② n. 懸崖

① = deceive (dɪ'siv)
= delude (dɪ'lud)
= trick (trɪk)
② = bank (bæŋk)
= precipice ('prɛsəpɪs)
= *steep cliff*

blunder ('blʌndɚ) v. 做錯

= err (ɜ)
= flounder ('flaundɚ)
= mistake (mə'stek)
= stumble ('stʌmbl̩)

blunt (blʌnt) adj. ①鈍的
②坦白的

① = dull (dʌl)
= unsharpened (ʌn'ʃɑrpənd)
② = candid ('kændɪd)
= direct (də'rɛkt , daɪ-)
= forthright ('forθ,raɪt)
= frank (fræŋk)
= outspoken (aut'spokən)
= straightforward (,stret'forwɚd)

blur (blɜ) v. 玷污；使模糊

= cloud (klaud)
= dim (dɪm)
= smear (smɪr)

board (bord , bɔrd) ① v. 登車
(船) ② n. 董事會 ③ n. 板
④ n. 膳食

① = embark (ɪm'bɑrk)
= mount (maunt)
= *get on*
② = cabinet ('kæbənɪt)

= committee〔kə'mɪtɪ〕

③ = plank〔plæŋk〕

= timber〔'tɪmbə〕

④ = food〔fud〕

= meals〔milz〕

boast〔bost〕v. 自誇

= brag〔bræg〕

= *pat oneself on the back*

= *puff up*

body〔'bɑdɪ〕n. ①實體 ②主體 ③團體

① = solidity〔sə'lɪdɪtɪ〕

= substance〔'sʌbstəns〕

② = bulk〔bʌlk〕

= mass〔mæs〕

= *the main part*

③ = crowd〔kraʊd〕

= group〔grup〕

= mob〔mɑb〕

= throng〔θrɔŋ〕

boil〔bɔɪl〕① v. 發怒 ② v. 沸騰；煮 ③ n. 癤

① = fume〔fjum〕

= rage〔redʒ〕

= seethe〔sið〕

② = bubble〔'bʌbḷ〕

= cook〔kʊk〕

③ = pimple〔'pɪmpḷ〕

= swelling〔'swɛlɪŋ〕

boisterous〔'bɔɪstərəs〕adj. 喧鬧的；激烈的

= clamorous〔'klæmərəs〕

= noisy〔'nɔɪzɪ〕

= rowdy〔'raʊdɪ〕

= violent〔'vaɪələnt〕

= vociferous〔vo'sɪfərəs〕

bold〔bold〕adj. 魯莽的；自大的

= arrogant〔'ærəgənt〕

= audacious〔ɔ'deʃəs〕

= brazen〔'brezṇ〕

= defiant〔dɪ'faɪənt〕

= haughty〔'hɔtɪ〕

= impudent〔'ɪmpjədənt〕

= insolent〔'ɪnsələnt〕

= rude〔rud〕

= saucy〔'sɔsɪ〕

bolt〔bolt〕① v. 逃走 ② n. 門栓

① = flee〔fli〕

= *break away*

= *take flight*

② = fastener〔'fæsṇə〕

= lock〔lɑk〕

bombard〔bɑm'bɑrd〕v. 攻擊

= assail〔ə'sel〕

= assault〔ə'sɔlt〕

= attack〔ə'tæk〕

= *fire upon*

= *open fire*

bonus〔'bonəs〕n. 紅利

= dividend〔'dɪvə,dɛnd〕

= extra〔'ɛkstrə〕

= premium〔'primɪəm〕

B

B

boom ﹝ bum ﹞① *v.* 提高
② *v.* 發隆隆聲 ③ *n.* 桿

① = advance ﹝ əd'væns ﹞
= flourish ﹝ 'flɝıʃ ﹞
= gain ﹝ gen ﹞
= grow ﹝ gro ﹞
= increase ﹝ ın'kris ﹞
= progress ﹝ prə'grɛs ﹞
= swell ﹝ swɛl ﹞
= thrive ﹝ θraɪv ﹞
② = roar ﹝ ror , rɔr ﹞
= rumble ﹝ 'rʌmbl̩ ﹞
= thunder ﹝ 'θʌndɚ ﹞
③ = beam ﹝ bim ﹞
= pole ﹝ pol ﹞

boon ﹝ bun ﹞① *n.* 恩賜
② *adj.* 愉快的

① = blessing ﹝ 'blɛsıŋ ﹞
= gift ﹝ gıft ﹞
= godsend ﹝ 'gɑd,sɛnd ﹞
= windfall ﹝ 'wınd,fɔl ﹞
② = jolly ﹝ 'dʒɑlı ﹞
= jovial ﹝ 'dʒovıəl ﹞
= merry ﹝ 'mɛrı ﹞
= pleasant ﹝ 'plɛznt ﹞

boost ﹝ bust ﹞ *v.* 提高
= elevate ﹝ 'ɛlə,vet ﹞
= hoist ﹝ hɔıst ﹞
= lift ﹝ lıft ﹞
= promote ﹝ prə'mot ﹞
= raise ﹝ rez ﹞

boot ﹝ but ﹞① *v.* 踢 ② *n.* 靴
① = kick ﹝ kık ﹞
② = shoe ﹝ ʃu ﹞

bootless ﹝ 'butlıs ﹞ *adj.* 無用的
= fruitless ﹝ 'frutlıs ﹞
= useless ﹝ 'juslıs ﹞
= vain ﹝ ven ﹞

booty ﹝ 'butı ﹞ *n.* 擄獲物
= loot ﹝ lut ﹞
= plunder ﹝ 'plʌndɚ ﹞
= prize ﹝ praɪz ﹞
= *stolen goods*

border ﹝ 'bɔrdɚ ﹞ *n.* 邊緣
= brim ﹝ brım ﹞
= margin ﹝ 'mɑrdʒın ﹞
= rim ﹝ rım ﹞
= skirt ﹝ skɝt ﹞

bore ﹝ bor , bɔr ﹞ *v.* ①穿孔
②使厭煩

① = drill ﹝ drıl ﹞
= pierce ﹝ pırs ﹞
= puncture ﹝ 'pʌnktʃɚ ﹞
② = fatigue ﹝ fə'tig ﹞
= irk ﹝ ɝk ﹞
= *make weary*

boring ﹝ borıŋ ﹞ *adj.* 令人厭煩的
= dull ﹝ dʌl ﹞
= tedious ﹝ 'tidıəs ﹞
= uninteresting ﹝ ʌn'ınt(ə)rıstıŋ ﹞
= wearisome ﹝ 'wırısəm ﹞

born ﹝ bɔrn ﹞ *adj.* 天生的
= gifted ﹝ 'gıftıd ﹞
= natural ﹝ 'nætʃərəl ﹞

borrow ('bɑro) v. 借；挪用
  = appropriate (ə'propri,et)
  = copy ('kɑpɪ)
  = take (tek)

boss (bɔs) ① v. 管理
② n. 上司
① = direct (də'rɛkt , daɪ-)
  = manage ('mænɪdʒ)
  = oversee ('ovə'si)
  = supervise ('supə,vaɪz)
② = director (də'rɛktə)
  = manager ('mænɪdʒə)
  = overseer ('ovə,siə)
  = supervisor (,supə'vaɪzə)

bother ('bɑðə) v. 打擾
  = fuss (fʌs)
  = pester ('pɛstə)
  = upset (ʌp'sɛt)
  = vex (vɛks)
  = worry ('wʒɪ)

bottom ('bɑtəm) n. 基礎；底部
  = base (bes)
  = foundation (faun'deʃən)
  = groundwork ('graund,wʒk)
  = *lowest part*

bound (baund) ① n. 界限
② v. 彈回   ③ adj. 前往的
④ adj. 必然的
① = boundary ('baundərɪ , 'baundrɪ)
  = limit ('lɪmɪt)
② = jump (dʒʌmp)
  = leap (lip)

  = *spring back*
③ = going ('goɪŋ)
  = *on the way*
④ = certain ('sʒtn)
  = sure (ʃur)

boundary ('baundərɪ ,
'baundrɪ) n. 境界線
  = barrier ('bærɪə)
  = border ('bɔrdə)
  = bound (baund)
  = frontier ('frʌntɪr)
  = limit ('lɪmɪt)

boundless ('baundlɪs) adj.
無限的
  = endless ('ɛndlɪs)
  = infinite ('ɪnfənɪt)
  = unlimited (ʌn'lɪmɪtɪd)

bountiful ('bauntəfəl) adj.
大方的；豐富的
  = abundant (ə'bʌndənt)
  = ample ('æmpl̩)
  = bounteous ('bauntɪəs)
  = fertile ('fʒtl̩)
  = generous ('dʒɛnərəs , 'dʒɛnrəs)
  = liberal ('lɪbərəl)
  = plentiful ('plɛntɪfəl)

bout (baut) n. ①比賽
②一回合
① = battle ('bætl̩)
  = competition (,kɑmpə'tɪʃən)
  = contest ('kɑntɛst)
  = match (mætʃ)

B

= test (tɛst)
= trial ('traɪəl)
② = period ('pɪrɪəd)
= round (raʊnd)
= spell (spɛl)
= turn (tɝn)

bow (baʊ) v. 鞠躬
= bend (bɛnd)
= stoop (stup)

box (bɑks) ① v. 打   ② n. 盒
① = fight (faɪt)
= hit (hɪt)
= punch (pʌntʃ)
② = carton ('kɑrtn̩)
= container (kən'tenɚ)
= crate (kret)

boy (bɔɪ) n. 男孩
= buddy ('bʌdɪ)
= fellow ('fɛlo)
= lad (læd)
= youngster ('jʌŋstɚ)
= youth (juθ)

boycott ('bɔɪ͵kɑt) v. 杯葛；
聯合抵制
= ban (bæn)
= blackball ('blæk͵bɔl)
= embargo (ɪm'bɑrgo)
= prohibit (prə'hɪbɪt)
= revolt (rɪ'volt)

boyish ('bɔɪɪʃ) adj. 孩子氣的

= childish ('tʃaɪldɪʃ)
= immature (͵ɪmə'tjʊr)
= innocent ('ɪnəsn̩t)
= juvenile ('dʒuvənl̩ , -͵naɪl)

brace (bres) ① v. 支撐
② n. 支撐物
① = bolster ('bolstɚ)
= buttress ('bʌtrɪs)
= strengthen ('strɛŋθən ,
'strɛŋkθən)
= support (sə'port , -'pɔrt)
② = prop (prɑp)
= a support

bracket ('brækɪt)
① v. 相提並論   ② n. 托架
① = couple ('kʌpl̩)
= enclose (ɪn'kloz)
= join (dʒɔɪn)
= relate (rɪ'let)
② = brace (bres)
= support (sə'port , -'pɔrt)

brag (bræg) v. 自誇
= boast (bost)
= trumpet ('trʌmpɪt)
= vaunt (vɔnt)
= pat oneself on the back

brake (brek) v. 煞車
= check (tʃɛk)
= decelerate (di'sɛlə͵ret)
= stop (stɑp)
= slow down

B

brainless ('brenlıs) *adj.* 無知的

= foolish ('fulıʃ)

= mindless ('maɪndlıs)

= stupid ('stupɪd)

= thoughtless ('θɔtlıs)

branch (bræntʃ) ① *v.* 分枝
② *n.* 樹枝

① = diverge (daɪ'vɜdʒ)

= divide (də'vaɪd)

= fork (fɔrk)

② = sprig (sprɪg)

= *part of a tree*

brand (brænd) ① *v.* 烙印
② *n.* 種類

① = label ('lebḷ)

= mark (mɑrk)

= stamp (stæmp)

② = class (klæs)

= kind (kaɪnd)

= sort (sɔrt)

= type (taɪp)

brave (brev) *adj.* 勇敢的

= bold (bold)

= courageous (kə'redʒəs)

= daring ('dɛrɪŋ)

= fearless ('fɪrlıs)

= heroic (hɪ'ro·ɪk)

brawl (brɔl) *n.* 爭吵

= dispute (dı'spjut)

= fracas ('frekəs)

= quarrel ('kwɔrəl , 'kwɑr-)

= racket ('rækıt)

brawn (brɔn) *n.* 肌肉；臂力

= muscle ('mʌsḷ)

= strength (strɛŋθ , strɛŋkθ)

brazen ('brezn̩) *adj.* 厚臉皮的

= audacious (ɔ'deʃəs)

= immodest (ı'mɑdɪst)

= shameless ('ʃemlıs)

= unabashed (ˌʌnə'bæʃt)

breach (britʃ) *n.* 違反；裂口

= break (brek)

= quarrel ('kwɔrəl , 'kwɑr-)

= gap (gæp)

= falling-out ('fɔlıŋ'aʊt)

break (brek) ① *v.* 打破
② *n.* 違反　③ *n.* 中斷

① = crack (kræk)

= fracture ('fræktʃə)

= rupture ('rʌptʃə)

= smash (smæʃ)

② = transgression (træns'grɛʃən)

= violation (ˌvaɪə'leʃən)

③ = interruption (ˌıntə'rʌpʃən)

= interval ('ıntəvḷ)

= letup ('lɛtˌʌp)

= pause (pɔz)

= rest (rɛst)

breed (brid) *v.* 養育

= cultivate ('kʌltəˌvet)

= foster ('fɑstə , 'fɔstə)

= nourish ('nɜ̩ʃ)

= nurture ('nɜtʃə)

= raise (rez)

= *bring up*

B

breezy ('brizɪ) *adj.* 快活的

= brisk (brɪsk)

= carefree ('kɛrfri)

= cheerful ('tʃɪrfəl)

= jolly ('dʒɑlɪ)

= lively ('laɪvlɪ)

= spirited ('spɪrɪtɪd)

= spry (spraɪ)

brevity ('brɛvətɪ) *n.* 簡潔

= briefness ('brifnɪs)

= concision (kən'saɪsnɪs)

= shortness ('ʃɔrtnɪs)

brew (bru) *v.* ①企圖　②調理

① = plan (plæn)

= plot (plɑt)

= scheme (skim)

② = boil (bɔɪl)

= cook (kʊk)

= stew (stju)

bribe (braɪb) *v.* 賄賂

= *buy off*

bridle ('braɪdḷ) ① *v.* 束縛

② *n.* 馬勒

① = check (tʃɛk)

= control (kən'trol)

= restrain (rɪ'stren)

= *hold back*

② = harness ('hɑrnɪs)

brief (brif) *adj.* 簡短的

= concise (kən'saɪs)

= curt (kɜt)

= short (ʃɔrt)

= terse (tɜs)

brigand ('brɪgənd) *n.* 盜賊

= bandit ('bændɪt)

= robber ('rɑbɚ)

= thief (θif)

bright (braɪt) *adj.* ①光亮的
②聰明的　③快活的

① = glowing ('gloɪŋ)

= radiant ('redjənt)

= shining ('ʃaɪnɪŋ)

② = brilliant ('brɪljənt)

= intelligent (ɪn'tɛlədʒənt)

= smart (smɑrt)

③ = cheerful ('tʃɪrfəl)

= lively ('laɪvlɪ)

= pleasant ('plɛznt)

brilliant ('brɪljənt) *adj.*
①輝煌的　②聰明的

① = bright (braɪt)

= radiant ('redjənt)

= shining ('ʃaɪnɪŋ)

= sparkling ('sparklɪŋ , -kḷɪŋ)

② = brainy ('brenɪ)

= clever ('klɛvɚ)

= intelligent (ɪn'tɛlədʒənt)

= smart (smɑrt)

brisk (brɪsk) *adj.* 活潑有朝氣的

= active ('æktɪv)

= breezy ('brizɪ)

= energetic (ˌɛnɚ'dʒɛtɪk)

B

= jolly ('dʒɑlɪ)
= lively ('laɪvlɪ)
= quick (kwɪk)
= spirited ('spɪrɪtɪd)
= spry (spraɪ)

brittle ('brɪtḷ) *adj.* 易碎的

= breakable ('brekəbḷ)
= crisp (krɪsp)
= fragile ('frædʒəl , -dʒaɪl)
= frail (frel)

broad (brɔd) *adj.* 廣闊的

= expansive (ɪk'spænsɪv)
= roomy ('rumɪ)
= spacious ('speʃəs)
= wide (waɪd)

broadcast ('brɔd,kæst) *v.* 廣播

= advertise ('ædvɚ,taɪz)
= announce (ə'naʊns)
= circulate ('sɝkjə,let)
= promulgate (prə'mʌl,get)
= publish ('pʌblɪʃ)

broken ('brokən) *adj.* 破的

= demolished (dɪ'mɑlɪʃɪd)
= fractured ('fræktʃɚd)
= shattered ('ʃætɚd)

brood (brud) ① *v.* 沈思
② *n.* 同母的子女

① = consider (kən'sɪdɚ)
= contemplate ('kɑntəm,plet)
= meditate ('mɛdə,tet)
= ponder ('pɑndɚ)

= reflect (rɪ'flɛkt)
② = family ('fæməlɪ)
= offspring ('ɔf,sprɪŋ)

brotherhood ('brʌðɚ,hʊd) *n.* 兄弟關係

= comradeship ('kɑmræd,ʃɪp)
= fellowship ('fɛlo,ʃɪp)
= fraternity (frə'tɝnətɪ)
= friendliness ('frɛndlɪnɪs)
= kinship ('kɪnʃɪp)

browse (braʊz) *v.* ①瀏覽
②吃飼料

① = scan (skæn)
= skim (skɪm)
② = feed (fid)
= graze (grez)

bruise (bruz) *v.* 打傷

= hurt (hɝt)
= injure ('ɪndʒɚ)
= wound (waʊnd)

brush (brʌʃ) ① *v.* 拂拭
② *n.* 灌木

① = clean (klin)
= sweep (swip)
= wipe (waɪp)
② = bushes ('bʊʃɪz)
= shrubs (ʃrʌbz)

brusque (brʌsk , brʊsk) *adj.* 唐突的

= abrupt (ə'brʌpt , æb'rʌpt)
= curt (kɝt)

B

= discourteous (dɪs'kɝtɪəs)

= impolite (ˌɪmpə'laɪt)

= unmannerly (ʌn'mænə˞li)

brutal ('brutḷ) *adj.* 野蠻的

= barbarian (bɑr'bɛrɪən , -'bær-)

= brutish ('brutɪʃ)

= cruel ('kruəl)

= savage ('sævɪdʒ)

buccaneer (ˌbʌkə'nɪr) *n.* 海盜

= pirate ('paɪrət , 'paɪrɪt)

= *sea robber*

buck (bʌk) ① *v.* 跳躍 ② *n.* 雄性之動物

① = jump (dʒʌmp)

= leap (lip)

= spring (sprɪŋ)

= vault (vɔlt)

② = *male animal*

buckle ('bʌkḷ) *v.* ①扣住 ②彎曲；起皺

① = clasp (klæsp)

= fasten ('fæsn̩)

= hook (hʊk)

= secure (sɪ'kjʊr)

② = bend (bɛnd)

= distort (dɪs'tɔrt)

= wrinkle ('rɪŋkḷ)

bud (bʌd) ① *v.* 發芽 ② *n.* 芽

① = burgeon ('bɝdʒən)

= germinate ('dʒɝməˌnet)

= sprout (spraʊt)

② = burgeon ('bɝdʒən)

= germ (dʒɝm)

= sprout (spraʊt)

= *baby plant*

buddy ('bʌdɪ) *n.* 同伴

= chum (tʃʌm)

= companion (kəm'pænjən)

= comrade ('kɑmræd , -rɪd)

= friend (frɛnd)

= mate (met)

= pal (pæl)

budge (bʌdʒ) *v.* 移動

= move (muv)

= stir (stɝ)

budget ('bʌdʒɪt) *n.* 預算

= allocation (ˌælə'keʃən)

= allowance (ə'laʊəns)

= ration ('ræʃən , 'reʃən)

buff (bʌf) *v.* 磨光

= burnish ('bɝnɪʃ)

= polish ('pɑlɪʃ)

buffet ('bʌfɪt) *v.* 打擊

= bat (bæt)

= batter ('bætə˞)

= beat (bit)

= blow (blo)

= hit (hɪt)

= knock (nɑk)

= slap (slæp)

= strike (straɪk)

B

build 〔 bɪld 〕 v. 建造

= construct 〔 kən'strʌkt 〕
= create 〔 krɪ'et 〕
= make 〔 mek 〕

bulk 〔 bʌlk 〕 n. 巨大；大部分

= lump 〔 lʌmp 〕
= mass 〔 mæs 〕
= majority 〔 mə'dʒɔrətɪ , -'dʒɑr- 〕

bulletin 〔 'bʊlətn̩ , -tɪn 〕 n. 公報

= message 〔 'mɛsɪdʒ 〕
= circular 〔 'sɝkjələ 〕
= news 〔 njuz , nuz 〕
= statement 〔 'stetmənt 〕
= flash 〔 flæʃ 〕
= newsletter 〔 'njuz,lɛtə 〕

bully 〔 'bʊlɪ 〕 v. 困擾

= tease 〔 tiz 〕
= pester 〔 'pɛstə 〕
= annoy 〔 ə'nɔɪ 〕
= badger 〔 'bædʒə 〕
= torment 〔 tɔr'mɛnt 〕
= bother 〔 'bɑðə 〕
= harass 〔 'hærəs , hə'ræs 〕

bump 〔 bʌmp 〕 v. 撞擊

= hit 〔 hɪt 〕
= shake 〔 ʃek 〕
= push 〔 pʊʃ 〕
= collide 〔 kə'laɪd 〕

bunch 〔 bʌntʃ 〕 n. 一束

= cluster 〔 'klʌstə 〕
= group 〔 grup 〕
= set 〔 sɛt 〕
= batch 〔 bætʃ 〕

bundle 〔 'bʌndl̩ 〕 n. 一捆

= parcel 〔 'pɑrsl̩ 〕
= package 〔 'pækɪdʒ 〕
= bale 〔 bel 〕
= packet 〔 'pækɪt 〕

bungle 〔 'bʌŋgl̩ 〕 v. 搞壞

= botch 〔 bɑtʃ 〕
= tumble 〔 'tʌmbl̩ 〕
= blunder 〔 'blʌndə 〕

buoyant 〔 'bɔɪənt , 'bujənt 〕 n.
①浮的 ②快樂的

① = light 〔 laɪt 〕
= elastic 〔 ɪ'læstɪk , ə- 〕
= floating 〔 'flotɪŋ 〕
= springy 〔 'sprɪŋɪ 〕
② = cheerful 〔 'tʃɪrfəl 〕
= lighthearted 〔 ,laɪt'hɑrtɪd 〕
= carefree 〔 'kɛr,fri 〕

burden 〔 'bɝdn̩ 〕 n. 負擔

= load 〔 lod 〕
= charge 〔 tʃɑrdʒ 〕
= task 〔 tæsk 〕
= *hard work*

burglar 〔 'bɝglə 〕 n. 竊盜

= robber 〔 'rɑbə 〕
= thief 〔 θif 〕
= housebreaker 〔 'haʊs,brekə 〕

burly (ˈbɜlɪ) *adj.* 強壯的

= strong (strɔŋ)

= sturdy (ˈstɜdɪ)

= brawny (ˈbrɔnɪ)

burn (bɜn) *n.* 烈火

= blaze (blez)

= fire (faɪr)

= flame (flem)

= flare (flɛr)

burnish (ˈbɜnɪʃ) *v.* 磨光

= shine (ʃaɪn)

= wax (wæks)

= rub (rʌb)

= polish (ˈpalɪʃ)

= buff (bʌf)

burrow (ˈbɜo) *n.* ①鑽洞
②尋找

① = dig (dɪg)

= tunnel (ˈtʌnḷ)

= excavate (ˈɛkskə‚vet)

② = search (sɜtʃ)

= seek (sik)

= hunt (hʌnt)

burst (bɜst) *v.* 爆發

= break (brek)

= rupture (ˈrʌptʃɚ)

= explode (ɪkˈsplod)

bury (ˈbɛrɪ) *v.* 埋；隱藏

= cover (ˈkʌvɚ)

= conceal (kənˈsil)

= immerse (ɪˈmɜs)

= hide (haɪd)

= cache (kæʃ)

business (ˈbɪznɪs) *n.* 職業

= work (wɜk)

= occupation (‚akjəˈpeʃən)

= affair (əˈfɛr)

= job (dʒab)

= trade (tred)

= profession (prəˈfɛʃən)

bustle (ˈbʌsḷ) *n.* 緊張而喧擾的
活動

= commotion (kəˈmoʃən)

= excitement (ɪkˈsaɪtmənt)

= hubbub (ˈhʌbʌb)

= noise (nɔɪz)

= activity (ækˈtɪvətɪ)

= flurry (ˈflɜɪ)

= action (ˈækʃən)

= trouble (ˈtrʌbḷ)

= fuss (fʌs)

= stir (stɜ)

= to-do (təˈdu)

busy (ˈbɪzɪ) *adj.* 忙碌的

= working (ˈwɜkɪŋ)

= active (ˈæktɪv)

= occupied (ˈakjəpaɪd)

= engaged (ɪnˈgedʒd)

= *on the job*

busybody (ˈbɪzɪ‚badɪ) *n.* 多嘴者

= meddler (ˈmɛdlɚ)

= tattletale (ˈtætḷ‚tel)

= gossip (ˈgasəp)

= kibitzer (ˈkɪbɪtsɚ)

button 〔'bʌtn̩〕v. 扣上

  = fasten 〔'fæsn̩〕

  = clasp 〔klæsp〕

  = hook 〔hʊk〕

  = close 〔kloz〕

buxom 〔'bʌksəm〕adj. ①豐滿的 ②健美活潑的

①= plump 〔plʌmp〕

②= cheerful 〔'tʃɪrfəl〕

  = healthy 〔'hɛlθɪ〕

  = merry 〔'mɛrɪ〕

  = jolly 〔'dʒɑlɪ〕

buy 〔baɪ〕v. 買

  = shop 〔ʃɑp〕

  = market 〔'mɑrkɪt〕

  = purchase 〔'pɝtʃəs〕

by 〔baɪ, bə〕prep. 在⋯旁

  = near 〔nɪr〕

  = beside 〔bɪ'saɪd〕

  = at 〔æt, ət〕

byway 〔'baɪ,we〕n. 旁徑

  = path 〔pæθ〕

  = passage 〔'pæsɪdʒ〕

  = detour 〔'ditʊr, dɪ'tʊr〕

  = *back street*

C

cab 〔kæb〕n. 出租汽車

  = taxi 〔'tæksɪ〕

  = coach 〔kotʃ〕

  = carriage 〔'kærɪdʒ〕

  = car 〔kɑr〕

cabin 〔'kæbɪn〕n. 小屋

  = hut 〔hʌt〕

  = cottage 〔'kɑtɪdʒ〕

  = bungalow 〔'bʌŋgə,lo〕

  = house 〔haʊs〕

cable 〔'kebl̩〕n. ①電報　②電機

①= telegraph 〔'tɛlə,græf〕

  = wire 〔waɪr〕

②= cord 〔kɔrd〕

  = wire 〔waɪr〕

  = rope 〔rop〕

cache 〔kæʃ〕v. 隱藏

  = bury 〔'bɛrɪ〕

  = conceal 〔kən'sil〕

  = store 〔stor, stɔr〕

  = hide 〔haɪd〕

  = cover 〔'kʌvɚ〕

cackle 〔'kækl̩〕v. 喋喋而談

  = prattle 〔'prætl̩〕

  = babble 〔'bæbl̩〕

  = chatter 〔'tʃætɚ〕

  = *laugh shrilly*

cafeteria 〔,kæfə'tɪrɪəl〕 n. 自助餐店

  = cafe 〔kə'fe, kæ'fe〕

  = diner 〔'daɪnɚ〕

  = restaurant 〔'rɛstərənt, -,rɑnt〕

  = *snack bar*

C

calamity (kəˈlæmətɪ) *n.* ①不幸
②災難

① = misfortune (mɪsˈfɔrtʃən)
  = mishap (ˈmɪsˌhæp , mɪsˈhæp)
  = accident (ˈæksədənt)
② = disaster (dɪzˈæstə)
  = tragedy (ˈtrædʒədɪ)
  = catastrophe (kəˈtæstrəfɪ)

calculate (ˈkælkjəˌlet) *v.*
①計算 ②考慮

① = count (kaʊnt)
  = figure (ˈfɪgjə , ˈfɪgə)
  = compute (kəmˈpjut)
  = estimate (ˈɛstəˌmet)
  = reckon (ˈrɛkən)
② = think (θɪŋk)
  = suppose (səˈpoz)
  = plan (plæn)
  = reason (ˈrizn̩)

call (kɔl) *v.* ①叫喊 ②要求；
打電話

① = cry (kraɪ)
  = shout (ʃaʊt)
  = yell (jɛl)
② = speak (spik)
  = ask (æsk)
  = command (kəˈmænd)
  = invite (ɪnˈvaɪt)
  = telephone (ˈtɛləˌfon)

calling (ˈkɔlɪŋ) *n.* 職業

  = profession (prəˈfɛʃən)
  = occupation (ˌɑkjəˈpeʃən)
  = trade (tred)

  = vocation (voˈkeʃən)

callous (ˈkæləs) *adj.* 堅硬的；
無情的

  = hard (hɑrd)
  = unfeeling (ʌnˈfilɪŋ)
  = insensitive (ɪnˈsɛnsətɪv)
  = heartless (ˈhɑrtlɪs)
  = cold (kold)

calm (kɑm) *adj.* 安靜的

  = quiet (ˈkwaɪət)
  = still (stɪl)
  = tranquil (ˈtrænkwɪl , ˈtræŋ-)
  = serene (səˈrin)
  = peaceful (ˈpisfəl)

camouflage (ˈkæməˌflɑʒ) *v.*
偽裝

  = disguise (dɪsˈgaɪz)
  = masquerade (ˌmæskəˈred)

campaign (kæmˈpen) *n.* (爲了
特定目地的) 運動

  = drive (draɪv)
  = cause (kɔz)
  = movement (ˈmuvmənt)
  = crusade (kruˈsed)

can (kæn) *n.* 罐頭

  = container (kənˈtenə)
  = tin (tɪn)
  = receptacle (rɪˈsɛptəkl̩ , -tɪkl̩)

canal (kəˈnæl) *n.* 運河；管道

  = gully (ˈgʌlɪ)

= duct〔dʌkt〕
= tube〔tjub , tub〕
= aqueduct〔'ækwɪ,dʌkt〕
= waterway〔'wɔtə,we〕

cancel〔'kænsḷ〕*v.* 取消

= erase〔ɪ'res〕
= repeal〔rɪ'pil〕
= obliterate〔ə'blɪtə,ret〕
= *wipe out*

candid〔'kændɪd〕*adj.* 坦白的

= sincere〔sɪn'sɪr〕
= blunt〔blʌnt〕
= outspoken〔,aut'spokən〕
= direct〔də'rɛkt , daɪ- 〕
= frank〔fræŋk〕
= straightforward〔,stret'fɔrwəd〕

candidate〔'kændə,det , -dɪt〕*n.*
候選人；申請者

= seeker〔'sikə〕
= nominee〔,namə'ni〕
= applicant〔'æpləkənt〕

candor〔'kændə〕*n.* 坦白；誠意

= fairness〔'fɛrnɪs〕
= sincerity〔sɪn'sɛrətɪ〕
= frankness〔'fræŋknɪs〕

canine〔'kenaɪn〕*n.* 狗

= dog〔dɔg〕
= pooch〔putʃ〕
= puppy〔'pʌpɪ〕

canny〔'kænɪ〕*adj.* ①狡詐的
②謹慎的

① = shrewd〔ʃrud〕
= artful〔'artfəl〕
= skillful〔'skɪlfəl〕
= crafty〔'kræftɪ〕
= cunning〔'kʌnɪŋ〕
= clever〔'klɛvə〕
② = cautious〔'kɔʃəs〕
= careful〔'kɛrfəl〕
= prudent〔'prudṇt〕

canopy〔'kænəpɪ〕*n.* 罩蓋

= cover〔'kʌvə〕
= awning〔'ɔnɪŋ〕
= shelter〔'ʃɛltə〕
= screen〔skrin〕

cantankerous〔kæn'tæŋkərəs〕
adj. 脾氣壞的

= cross〔krɔs〕
= mean〔min〕
= irritable〔'ɪrətəbḷ〕
= cranky〔'kræŋkɪ〕
= quarrelsome〔'kwɔrəlsəm ,
'kwar- 〕

cap〔kæp〕① *n.* 蓋子
② *v.* 比⋯更好

① = cover〔'kʌvə〕
= top〔tap〕
= crown〔kraun〕
= lid〔lɪd〕
② = excel〔ɪk'sɛl〕
= beat〔bit〕

C

capability (‚kepə'bɪlətɪ) *n.* 能力

  = ability (ə'bɪlətɪ)
  = skill (skɪl)
  = power ('pauɚ)
  = fitness ('fɪtnɪs)
  = talent ('tælənt)
  = capacity (kə'pæsətɪ)
  = efficiency (ə'fɪʃənsɪ , ɪ-)
  = competency ('kampətənsɪ)

capacity (kə'pæsətɪ) *n.* ①容量
②能力　③地位；職責

  ① = size (saɪz)
  = volume ('valjəm)
  = content ('kantɛnt , kən'tɛnt)
  ② = intelligence (ɪn'tɛlədʒəns)
  = mentality (mɛn'tælətɪ)
  = power ('pauɚ)
  = fitness ('fɪtnɪs)
  ③ = position (pə'zɪʃən)
  = role (rol)
  = duty ('djutɪ)
  = function ('fʌŋkʃən)

caper ('kepɚ)① *v.* 跳躍
② *n.* 嬉戲

  ① = leap (lip)
  = jump (dʒʌmp)
  = hop (hap)
  = skip (skɪp)
  = romp (ramp)
  = cavort (kə'vort)
  ② = frolic ('fralɪk)
  = play (ple)
  = antic ('æntɪk)
  = trick (trɪk)

  = prank (præŋk)

capital ('kæpətḷ) ① *adj.* 主要的
② *n.* 資本　③ *n.* 首都
④ *n.* 大寫字母

  ① = important (ɪm'portn̩t)
  = leading ('lidɪŋ)
  = top (tap)
  = chief (tʃif)
  ② = money ('mʌnɪ)
  = funds (fʌndz)
  = stock (stak)
  ③ = city ('sɪtɪ)
  = *government seat*
  ④ = *large letter*

caprice (kə'pris) *n.* 突發的奇想

  = whim (hwɪm)
  = fancy ('fænsɪ)
  = fad (fæd)
  = *unreasonable desire*

capsize (kæp'saɪz) *v.* 傾覆

  = upset (ʌp'sɛt)
  = overthrow (‚ovɚ'θro)
  = overturn (‚ovɚ'tɜn)
  = *tip over*

caption ('kæpʃən) *n.* 標題

  = title ('taɪtḷ)
  = heading ('hɛdɪŋ)
  = headline ('hɛd‚laɪn)

captivate ('kæptə‚vet) *v.* 迷惑

  = delight (dɪ'laɪt)
  = bewitch (bɪ'wɪtʃ)

= charm〔tʃɑrm〕
= fascinate〔'fæsn̩‚et〕

capture〔'kæptʃɚ〕*v.* 逮捕
= apprehend〔‚æprɪ'hɛnd〕
= seize〔siz〕
= arrest〔ə'rɛst〕
= imprison〔ɪm'prɪzn̩〕

car〔kɑr〕*n.* 汽車
= vehicle〔'viɪkl̩‚'viəkl̩〕
= automobile〔'ɔtəmə‚bil‚ ‚ɔtə'mobil〕

caravan〔'kærə‚væn〕*n.*
①旅行隊 ②大篷車

① = group〔grup〕
= parade〔pə'red〕
= procession〔prə'sɛʃen‚pro-〕
② = wagon〔'wægən〕
= van〔væn〕

carcass〔'kɑrkəs〕*n.* 動物的屍體
= body〔'bɑdɪ〕
= *animal corpse*

care〔kɛr〕*n.* ①小心 ②照顧
① = thought〔θɔt〕
= worry〔'wɝɪ〕
= concern〔kən'sɝn〕
= attention〔ə'tɛnʃən〕
② = protection〔prə'tɛkʃən〕
= charge〔tʃɑrdʒ〕
= custody〔'kʌstədɪ〕
= keeping〔'kipɪŋ〕

= supervision〔‚supɚ'vɪʒən〕

career〔kə'rɪr〕*n.* 職業
= vocation〔vo'keʃən〕
= trade〔tred〕
= calling〔'kɔlɪŋ〕
= profession〔prə'fɛʃən〕
= occupation〔‚ɑkjə'peʃən〕

carefree〔'kɛr‚fri〕*adj.* 快活的
= happy〔'hæpɪ〕
= jolly〔'dʒɑlɪ〕
= breezy〔'brizɪ〕
= lively〔'laɪvlɪ〕
= gay〔ge〕
= active〔'æktɪv〕
= spirited〔'spɪrɪtɪd〕
= spry〔spraɪ〕
= energetic〔‚ɛnɚ'dʒɛtɪk〕
= lighthearted〔'laɪt'hɑrtɪd〕

careful〔'kɛrfəl〕*adj.* 謹慎的
= watchful〔'watʃfəl〕
= prudent〔'prudn̩t〕
= cautious〔'kɔʃəs〕

careless〔'kɛrlɪs〕*adj.* 疏忽的
= reckless〔'rɛklɪs〕
= sloppy〔'slɑpɪ〕
= slovenly〔'slʌvənlɪ〕

caress〔kə'rɛs〕*v.* 撫摸
= pet〔pɛt〕
= stroke〔strok〕
= touch〔tʌtʃ〕
= fondle〔'fɑndl̩〕

C

cargo ('kɑrgo) *n.* (船、機載之) 貨物

= load (lod)
= freight (fret)
= shipment ('ʃɪpmənt)

carnival ('kɑrnəvḷ) *n.* 展覽會；狂歡節

= fair (fɛr)
= fete (fet)
= jamboree (,dʒæmbə'ri)
= festival ('fɛstəvḷ)

carol ('kærəl) *n.* 歌謠

= song (sɔŋ)
= hymn (hɪm)
= ballad ('bæləd)

carp (kɑrp) ① *v.* 吹毛求疵 ② *n.* 鯉魚

① = complain (kəm'plen)
= pick (pɪk)
= *find fault*
= *tear to pieces*
② = *fresh-water fish*

carpet ('kɑrpɪt) *n.* 地毯

= rug (rʌg)
= mat (mæt)
= *floor covering*

carriage ('kærɪdʒ) *n.* ①運輸 ②姿態

① = vehicle ('viɪkḷ , 'viəkḷ)
= conveyance (kən'veəns)
② = posture ('pɑstʃə)

= position (pə'zɪʃən)
= bearing ('bɛrɪŋ)

carry ('kærɪ) *v.* 攜帶

= hold (hold)
= take (tek)
= transport (træns'port , -'port)

carve (kɑrv) *n.* 切割

= cut (kʌt)
= slice (slaɪs)

case (kes) *n.* ①情況 ②盒子 ③案子

① = condition (kən'dɪʃən)
= state (stet)
= circumstance ('sɝkəmstəns)
② = covering ('kʌvərɪŋ)
= box (bɑks)
= receptacle (rɪ'sɛptəkḷ)
③ = lawsuit ('lɔ,sut , -,sjut)
= *legal action*

cash (kæʃ) *n.* 現金

= money ('mʌnɪ)
= currency ('kɝənsɪ)

casket ('kæskɪt) *n.* 小箱

= box (bɑks)
= coffin ('kɔfɪn)
= crate (kret)

cast (kæst) ① *v.* 擲 ② *v.* 鑄成 ③ *n.* 演員陣容 ④ *n.* 種類 ⑤ *n.* 色度

① = throw (θro)

= fling (flɪŋ)
= pitch (pɪtʃ)
= toss (tɔs)
② = mold (mold)
= form (fɔrm)
= shape (ʃep)
③ = company ('kʌmpənɪ)
= troupe (trup)
= actors ('æktəz)
④ = sort (sɔrt)
= kind (kaɪnd)
= type (taɪp)
= variety (və'raɪətɪ)
⑤ = color ('kʌlə)
= tint (tɪnt)
= shade (ʃed)

castle ('kæsḷ) *n.* 城堡

= palace ('pælɪs , -əs)
= mansion ('mænʃən)
= chateau (ʃæ'to)

casual ('kæʒʊəl , 'kæʒʊl) *adj.*
偶然的

= accidental (,æksə'dɛntḷ)
= chance (tʃæns)
= informal (ɪn'fɔrmḷ)
= unexpected (,ʌnɪk'spɛktɪd)
= natural ('nætʃərəl , 'nætʃrəl)

casualty ('kæʒʊəltɪ) *n.* 意外；
災禍

= fluke (fluk)
= mishap ('mɪs,hæp , mɪs'hæp)
= injury ('ɪndʒərɪ)
= accident ('æksədənt)

= misfortune (mɪs'fɔrtʃən)

catalog ('kætḷ,ɔg) ① *v.* 編目
② *n.* 目錄

① = list (lɪst)
= classify ('klæsə,faɪ)
= record (rɪ'kɔrd)
= group (grup)
= sort (sɔrt)
② = file (faɪl)

catastrophe (kə'tæstrəfɪ) *n.*
災難

= calamity (kə'læmətɪ)
= accident ('æksədənt)
= misfortune (mɪs'fɔrtʃən)
= tragedy ('trædʒədɪ)
= disaster (dɪz'æstə)

catch (kætʃ) *v.* ①逮捕 ②當場
發現

① = take (tek)
= seize (siz)
= arrest (ə'rɛst)
= capture ('kæptʃə)
= apprehend (,æprɪ'hɛnd)
② = surprise (sə'praɪz , sə-)
= discover (dɪs'kʌvə)

catchy ('kætʃɪ) *adj.* ①吸引人的
②詭詐的

① = attractive (ə'træktɪv)
② = tricky ('trɪkɪ)
= deceptive (dɪ'sɛptɪv)
= misleading (mɪs'lidɪŋ)

C

cater ('ketɚ) v. ①嬌養　②提供服務

① = pamper ('pæmpɚ)
= indulge (ɪn'dʌldʒ)
= coddle ('kadḷ)
= spoil (spɔɪl)
= oblige (ə'blaɪdʒ)
② = serve (sɝv)
= provide (prə'vaɪd)

cause (kɔz) n. 動機；原由

= motive ('motɪv)
= reason ('rizn̩)
= basis ('besɪs)
= interest ('ɪntərɪst , 'ɪntrɪst)
= grounds (graundz)

caution ('kɔʃən) v. 警告；勸告

= tip (tɪp)
= advise (əd'vaɪz)
= alert (ə'lɝt)
= warn (wɔrn)
= remind (rɪ'maɪnd)
= admonish (əd'manɪʃ , æd-)

cavalcade (ˌkævḷ'ked) n. 一隊人馬

= parade (pə'red)
= column ('kaləm)
= procession (prə'sɛʃen , pro-)

cavalier (ˌkævə'lɪr)

① adj. 傲慢的　② n. 騎士；豪俠

① = haughty ('hɔtɪ)
= insolent ('ɪnsələnt)
= arrogant ('ærəgənt)

= contemptuous (kən'tɛmptʃuəs)
② = knight (naɪt)
= escort ('ɛskɔrt)
= gentleman ('dʒɛntḷmən)
= horseman ('hɔrsmən)

cave (kev) n. 洞穴

= lair (lɛr , lær)
= shelter ('ʃɛltɚ)
= den (dɛn)
= cavern ('kævən)

cavity ('kævətɪ) n. 洞

= pit (pɪt)
= crater ('kretɚ)
= hole (hol)

cavort (kə'vɔrt) v. 跳躍

= romp (ramp)
= skip (skɪp)
= leap (lip)
= caper ('kepɚ)
= hop (hap)
= jump (dʒʌmp)
= frolic ('fralɪk)
= prance about

cease (sis) v. 停止

= stop (stap)
= end (ɛnd)
= quit (kwɪt)
= halt (hɔlt)
= discontinue (ˌdɪskən'tɪnju)

cede (sid) v. 讓步

= yield (jild)

= relinquish (rɪ'lɪŋkwɪʃ)
= surrender (sə'rɛndə)
= *give up*

celebrate ('sɛlə,bret) *n.* ①表揚
②慶祝　③讚揚

① = proclaim (pro'klem)
② = observe (əb'zɝv)
= commemorate (kə'mɛmə,ret)
= revel ('rɛvḷ)
= *make merry*
③ = praise (prez)

celebrity (sə'lɛbrətɪ) *n.* 名人

= notable ('notəbḷ)
= somebody ('sʌm,bɑdɪ , -,bʌdɪ ,
-bədɪ)
= *well-known person*

celestial (sə'lɛstʃəl) *adj.* 天國的

= heavenly ('hɛvṇlɪ)
= divine (də'vaɪn)
= godly ('gɑdlɪ)
= angelic (æn'dʒɛlɪk)

cement (sə'mɛnt) *v.* 使強固

= weld (wɛld)
= fasten ('fæsṇ)
= solidify (sə'lɪdə,faɪ)
= secure (sɪ'kjur)

cemetery ('sɛmə,tɛrɪ) *n.* 墓地

= graveyard ('grev,jɑrd)
= *burial ground*

censure ('sɛnʃə) *v.* 責難

= blame (blem)
= reproach (rɪ'protʃ)
= denounce (dɪ'nauns)
= criticize ('krɪtə,saɪz)
= condemn (kən'dɛm)

center ('sɛntə) *n.* 中心

= middle ('mɪdḷ)
= heart (hɑrt)
= core (kor , kɔr)
= nucleus ('njuklɪəs , 'nu-)

central ('sɛntrəl) *adj.* 主要的

= main (men)
= chief (tʃif)
= leading ('lidɪŋ)
= principal ('prɪnsəpḷ)

ceremonious (,sɛrə'monɪəs)
adj. ①儀式的　②有禮貌的

① = formal ('fɔrmḷ)
= ritualistic (,rɪtʃuəl'ɪstɪk)
= stately ('stetlɪ)
= pompous ('pampəs)
② = courteous ('kɝtɪəs)
= polite (pə'laɪt)
= gracious ('greʃəs)

certain ('sɝtṇ) *adj.* ①確定的
②某

① = sure (ʃur)
= positive ('pɑzətɪv)
= definite ('dɛfənɪt)
② = some ('sʌm , səm)
= special ('spɛʃəl)
= particular (pə'tɪkjələ)

C

certify ('sɝtə,faɪ) *v.* 保證

= confirm (kən'fɝm)

= guarantee (,gærən'ti)

= vouch (vautʃ)

= affirm (ə'fɝm)

= testify ('tɛstə,faɪ)

cessation (sɛ'seʃən) *n.* 停止

= end (ɛnd)

= close (kloz)

= discontinuation
(,dɪskən,tɪnju'eʃən)

chafe (tʃef) *v.* ①擦熱　②激怒

① = rub (rʌb)

= heat (hit)

= warm (wɔrm)

② = anger ('æŋgɚ)

= annoy (ə'nɔɪ)

= irritate ('ɪrə,tet)

= vex (vɛks)

= disturb (dɪ'stɝb)

chagrin (ʃə'grɪn) *n.* 懊惱

= mortification (,mɔrtəfə'keʃən)

= humiliation (hju,mɪlɪ'eʃən)

= embarrassment
(ɪm'bærəsmənt)

= disappointment
(,dɪsə'pɔɪntmənt)

chain (tʃen) *v.* 束縛

= bind (baɪnd)

= restrain (rɪ'stren)

= fasten ('fæsn̩)

= shackle ('ʃækl̩)

chair (tʃɛr) *n.* 座位

= seat (sit)

= bench (bɛntʃ)

chairman ('tʃɛrmən) *n.* 主席

= speaker ('spikɚ)

= *presiding officer*

challenge ('tʃælɪndʒ) *n.* 懷疑；
反對

= confront (kən'frʌnt)

= question ('kwɛstʃən)

= defy (dɪ'faɪ)

= dispute (dɪ'spjut)

= doubt (daut)

= dare (dɛr)

chamber ('tʃembɚ) *n.* 房間

= room (rum)

= compartment (kəm'partmənt)

champion ('tʃæmpɪən) *n.*
①冠軍　②擁護者

① = winner ('wɪnɚ)

= victor ('vɪktɚ)

= choice (tʃɔɪs)

= best (bɛst)

= select (sə'lɛkt)

= conqueror ('kaŋkərɚ)

② = defender (dɪ'fɛndɚ)

= protector (prə'tɛktɚ)

= upholder (ʌp'holdɚ)

= advocate ('ædvəkɪt , -,ket)

chance 〔 tʃæns 〕 *n.* ①機會
②可能性　③運氣

① = opportunity 〔ˌɑpəˈtjunətɪ 〕
　= opening 〔ˈopənɪŋ 〕
　= occasion 〔 əˈkeʒən 〕
② = possibility 〔ˌpɑsəˈbɪlətɪ 〕
　= probability 〔ˌprɑbəˈbɪlətɪ 〕
　= prospect 〔ˈprɑspɛkt 〕
　= likelihood 〔ˈlaɪklɪˌhʊd 〕
③ = fate 〔 fet 〕
　= luck 〔 lʌk 〕
　= lot 〔 lɑt 〕

change 〔 tʃendʒ 〕 ① *v.* 變更
② *n.* 零錢

① = alter 〔ˈɔltɚ 〕
　= vary 〔ˈvɛrɪ 〕
　= deviate 〔ˈdivɪˌet 〕
　= substitute 〔ˈsʌbstəˌtjut 〕
　= replace 〔 rɪˈples 〕
② = cash 〔 kæʃ 〕
　= money 〔ˈmʌnɪ 〕
　= coins 〔 kɔɪnz 〕

channel 〔ˈtʃænl̩ 〕 *n.* ①海峽；
水道　②頻道

① = waterway 〔ˈwɔtɚˌwe 〕
　= passageway 〔ˈpæsɪdʒˌwe 〕
　= strait 〔 stret 〕
　= corridor 〔ˈkɔrədɚ , -ˌdɔr , ˈkɑr- 〕
　= artery 〔ˈɑrtərɪ 〕
② = *TV station*

chant 〔 tʃænt 〕 *n.* 歌謠

　= song 〔 sɔŋ , sɑŋ 〕
　= psalm 〔 sɑm 〕

　= prayer 〔 prɛr , prær 〕
　= ballad 〔ˈbæləd 〕

chaos 〔ˈkeɑs 〕 *n.* 混亂

　= muddle 〔ˈmʌdl̩ 〕
　= disorder 〔 dɪsˈɔrdɚ 〕
　= confusion 〔 kənˈfjuʒən 〕
　= mix-up 〔ˈmɪksˌʌp 〕

chap 〔 tʃæp 〕 ① *v.* (使) 裂開；
變粗糙　② *n.* 傢伙

① = crack 〔 kræk 〕
　= break 〔 brek 〕
　= split 〔 splɪt 〕
　= *become rough*
② = fellow 〔ˈfɛlo 〕
　= man 〔 mæn 〕
　= boy 〔 bɔɪ 〕

chapter 〔ˈtʃæptɚ 〕 *n.* 章；部分

　= section 〔ˈsɛkʃən 〕
　= part 〔 pɑrt 〕
　= division 〔 dəˈvɪʒən 〕

char 〔 tʃɑr 〕 *v.* 燒焦

　= burn 〔 bɝn 〕
　= scorch 〔 skɔrtʃ 〕
　= sear 〔 sɪr 〕
　= singe 〔 sɪndʒ 〕

character 〔ˈkærɪktɚ , -ək- 〕 *n.*
①本性　②角色　③文字
④古怪的人

① = nature 〔ˈnetʃɚ 〕
　= makeup 〔ˈmekˌʌp 〕
　= disposition 〔ˌdɪspəˈzɪʃən 〕

C

= temperament ('tɛmprəmənt ,
  -pərə-)
= constitution (,kɑnstə'tjuʃən)
② = actor ('æktə)
= player ('pleə)
= performer (pə'fɔrmə)
③ = letter ('lɛtə)
= sign (saɪn)
= symbol ('sɪmbḷ)
④ = eccentric (ɪk'sɛntrɪk , ɛk-)

characterize ('kærɪktə,raɪz) v.
描寫

= picture ('pɪktʃə)
= describe (dɪ'skraɪb)
= distinguish (dɪ'stɪŋwɪʃ)
= portray (por'tre , pɔr-)
= represent (,rɛprɪ'zɛnt)
= depict (dɪ'pɪkt)

charge (tʃɑrdʒ) v. ①裝載
②委以責任   ③責備   ④索價
⑤攻擊

① = load (lod)
= fill (fɪl)
= stuff (stʌf)
② = order ('ɔrdə)
= command (kə'mænd)
= direct (də'rɛkt , daɪ-)
= bid (bɪd)
③ = accuse (ə'kjuz)
= blame (blem)
= complain (kəm'plen)
= denounce (dɪ'naʊns)
= impeach (,ɪm'pitʃ)
= indict (ɪn'daɪt)

④ = rate (ret)
= *ask as a price*
⑤ = attack (ə'tæk)
= *rush at*

charitable ('tʃærətəbḷ) adj.
仁慈慷慨的

= generous ('dʒɛnərəs)
= kindly ('kaɪndlɪ)
= giving ('gɪvɪŋ)
= big-hearted ('bɪg,hɑrtɪd)

charming ('tʃɑrmɪŋ) adj.
迷人的

= enchanting (ɪn'tʃæntɪŋ)
= alluring (ə'ljurɪŋ)
= pleasing ('plizɪŋ)
= delightful (dɪ'laɪtfəl)
= fascinating ('fæsṇ,etɪŋ)
= appealing (ə'pilɪŋ)

charter ('tʃɑrtə) ① v. 租
② n. 許可證

① = hire (haɪr)
= lease (lis)
= rent (rɛnt)
② = treaty ('tritɪ)
= alliance (ə'laɪəns)

chase (tʃes) v. ①追   ②驅逐

① = follow ('fɑlo)
= pursue (pə'su)
= *run after*
② = repulse (rɪ'pʌls)
= reject (rɪ'dʒɛkt)
= *drive away*

chaste〔tʃest〕*adj.* 貞潔的

  = pure〔pjʊr〕
  = clean〔klin〕
  = virtuous〔'vɝtʃʊəs〕
  = modest〔'mɑdɪst〕
  = decent〔'dɪ'sɛnt〕

chasten〔'tʃesn̩〕*v.* 懲戒

  = restrain〔rɪ'stren〕
  = punish〔'pʌnɪʃ〕
  = chastise〔tʃæs'taɪz〕
  = discipline〔'dɪsəplɪn〕

chastise〔tʃæs'taɪz〕*v.* 責罰

  = chasten〔'tʃesn̩〕
  = punish〔'pʌnɪʃ〕
  = restrain〔rɪ'stren〕
  = discipline〔'dɪsəplɪn〕

chat〔tʃæt〕*v.* 閒談

  = gossip〔'gɑsəp〕
  = talk〔tɔk〕
  = converse〔kən'vɝs〕

chatter〔'tʃætɚ〕*v.* ①喋喋不休 ②顫動

①= babble〔'bæbl̩〕
  = talk〔tɔk〕
  = prattle〔'prætl̩〕
  = gabble〔'gæbl̩〕
②= shiver〔'ʃɪvɚ〕
  = rattle〔'rætl̩〕
  = chill〔tʃɪl〕
  = quiver〔'kwɪvɚ〕

cheap〔tʃip〕① *adj.* 便宜的 ② *adj.* 普通的 ③ *n.* 供應豐富

①= inexpensive〔ˌɪnɪk'spɛnsɪv〕
  = low-priced〔'lo'praɪst〕
②= common〔'kɑmən〕
③= abundance〔ə'bʌndəns〕

cheat〔tʃit〕*v.* 欺騙

  = defraud〔dɪ'frɔd〕
  = swindle〔'swɪndl̩〕
  = beguile〔bɪ'gaɪl〕
  = trick〔trɪk〕
  = dupe〔djup , dup〕
  = deceive〔dɪ'siv〕
  = bamboozle〔bæm'buzl̩〕

check〔tʃɛk〕① *v.* 抑制 ② *v.* 核對 ③ *n.* 支票

①= stop〔stɑp〕
  = control〔kən'trol〕
  = restrain〔rɪ'stren〕
  = curb〔kɝb〕
②= prove〔pruv〕
  = mark〔mɑrk〕
  = verify〔'vɛrəˌfaɪ〕
③= bill〔bɪl〕
  = money〔'mʌnɪ〕
  = certificate〔sə'tɪfəkɪt〕

checkup〔'tʃɛkˌʌp〕*n.* 健康檢查

  = *physical examination*

cheer〔tʃɪr〕① *v.* 使愉快 ② *n.* 愉快

①= comfort〔'kʌmfɚt〕
  = gladden〔'glædn̩〕
  = praise〔prez〕
②= hope〔hop〕

C

= gladness ('glædnɪs)
= happiness ('hæpɪnɪs)
= *good spirits*

cherish ('tʃɛrɪʃ) v. 珍愛
= adore (ə'dor , ə'dɔr)
= worship ('wɝʃəp)
= treasure ('trɛʒə)
= protect (prə'tɛkt)
= *hold dear*

chest (tʃɛst) n. ①箱子；化粧台
②胸
① = box (baks)
= locker ('lakə)
= dresser ('drɛsə)
= safe (sef)
② = breast (brɛst)
= thorax ('θoræks)

chew (tʃu) v. 咀嚼
= bite (baɪt)
= grind (graɪnd)
= munch (mʌntʃ)
= nibble ('nɪbḷ)

chicken-hearted
('tʃɪkɪn 'hartɪd) adj. 膽小的
= cowardly ('kaʊədlɪ)
= timid ('tɪmɪd)
= lily-livered ('lɪlɪ'lɪvəd)

chide (tʃaɪd) v. 斥責
= reproach (rɪ'protʃ)
= blame (blem)
= scold (skold)

= lecture ('lɛktʃə)
= reprimand ('rɛprə,mænd)

chief (tʃif) n. 領袖
= leader ('lidə)
= head (hɛd)
= authority (ə'θɔrətɪ)

chiefly ('tʃiflɪ) adv. 主要地
= mainly ('menlɪ)
= mostly ('mostlɪ)
= especially (ə'spɛʃəlɪ)
= *above all*

child (tʃaɪld) n. 小孩
= youngster ('jʌŋstə)
= baby ('bebɪ)
= tot (tat)
= youth (juθ)
= juvenile ('dʒuvənḷ , -,naɪl)
= offspring ('ɔf,sprɪŋ , 'af-)
= *young boy or girl*

chilly ('tʃɪlɪ) adj. 寒冷的
= cold (kold)
= cool (kul)
= brisk (brɪsk)
= nippy ('nɪpɪ)
= wintery ('wɪntərɪ)
= snappy ('snæpɪ)

chime (tʃaɪm) v. ① (鐘) 鳴
②使和諧
① = ring (rɪŋ)
= jingle ('dʒɪŋgḷ)
= peal (pil)

② = agree〔ə'gri〕
　= harmonize〔'hɑrmə,naɪz〕

chip〔tʃɪp〕① v. 切爲碎片
② n. 碎片

① = break〔brek〕
　= crack〔kræk〕
② = piece〔pis〕
　= bit〔bɪt〕
　= crumb〔krʌm〕

chisel〔'tʃɪzl̩〕① v. 刻
② v. 銘記　③ n. 鑿子

① = make〔mek〕
　= sculpture〔'skʌlptʃɚ〕
　= carve〔kɑrv〕
② = engrave〔ɪn'grev〕
　= inscribe〔ɪn'skraɪb〕
③ = tool〔tul〕
　= point〔pɔɪnt〕

chivalrous〔'ʃɪvl̩rəs〕adj.
有武士風度的

　= courteous〔'kɝtɪəs〕
　= gallant〔'gælənt〕
　= knightly〔'naɪtlɪ〕
　= polite〔pə'laɪt〕
　= noble〔'nobl̩〕

choice〔tʃɔɪs〕n. ①選擇
②精選物

① = selection〔sə'lɛkʃən〕
　= preference〔'prɛfərəns〕
　= pick〔pɪk〕
　= decision〔dɪ'sɪʒən〕
　= option〔'ɑpʃən〕

　= alternative〔æl'tɝnətɪv〕
② = best〔bɛst〕
　= cream〔krim〕

choke〔tʃok〕v. 使窒息

　= smother〔'smʌðɚ〕
　= suffocate〔'sʌfə,ket〕
　= muffle〔'mʌfl̩〕
　= strangle〔'stræŋgl̩〕

chop〔tʃɑp〕v. 砍斷

　= cut〔kʌt〕
　= cleave〔kliv〕
　= sever〔'sɛvɚ〕

chore〔tʃor , tʃɔr〕n. 零工；工作

　= task〔tæsk〕
　= job〔dʒɑb〕
　= work〔wɝk〕
　= duty〔'djutɪ〕
　= function〔'fʌŋkʃən〕
　= assignment〔ə'saɪnmənt〕

chorus〔'korəs〕n. ①合唱隊
②詩節

① = choir〔kwaɪr〕
　= group〔grup〕
　= unison〔'junəsn̩ , 'junəzn̩〕
② = verse〔vɝs〕
　= stanza〔'stænzə〕
　= refrain〔rɪ'fren〕

chronic〔'krɑnɪk〕adj. 長期的

　= constant〔'kɑnstənt〕
　= established〔ə'stæblɪʃt〕
　= fixed〔fɪkst〕

= lasting ('læstɪŋ , 'lɑs-)
= set (sɛt)
= continuing (kən'tɪnjuɪŋ)

chronicle ('krɑnɪkl̩) n. 編年史

= history ('hɪstrɪ , 'hɪstərɪ)
= story ('storɪ)
= account (ə'kaʊnt)
= journal ('dʒɝnl̩)
= narrative ('nærətɪv)

chubby ('tʃʌbɪ) adj. 豐滿的

= plump (plʌmp)
= round (raʊnd)
= stout (staʊt)
= tubby ('tʌbɪ)
= fat (fæt)
= fleshy ('flɛʃɪ)
= corpulent ('kɔrpjələnt)
= pudgy ('pʌdʒɪ)
= stocky ('stɑkɪ)
= chunky ('tʃʌŋkɪ)

chuck (tʃʌk) v. ①輕拍　②投擲

①= pat (pæt)
= tap (tæp)
= flick (flɪk)
②= throw (θro)
= pitch (pɪtʃ)
= fling (flɪŋ)
= toss (tɔs)

chuckle ('tʃʌkl̩) v. 輕笑

= laugh (læf , lɑf)
= giggle ('gɪgl̩)
= titter ('tɪtɚ)

chum (tʃʌm) n. 密友

= friend (frɛnd)
= mate (met)
= buddy ('bʌdɪ)
= pal (pæl)
= companion (kəm'pænjən)
= partner ('pɑrtnɚ)
= comrade ('kɑmræd , 'kɑmrɪd)

chunk (tʃʌŋk) n. 大量

= lump (lʌmp)
= wad (wɑd)
= bulk (bʌlk)
= mass (mæs)

cinch (sɪntʃ) v. 緊握

= grip (grɪp)
= bind (baɪnd)
= hold (hold)
= wrap (ræp)
= tie (taɪ)
= fasten ('fæsn̩)

circulate ('sɝkjə,let) v. 流通；傳布

= publish ('pʌblɪʃ)
= broadcast ('brɔd,kæst)
= distribute (dɪ'strɪbjut)
= scatter ('skætɚ)
= *go around*

circumstance ('sɝkəm,stæns) n. 情況

= condition (kən'dɪʃən)
= situation (,sɪtʃu'eʃən)
= state (stet)

citadel ('sɪtədḷ , -ˌdɛl) *n.* 城堡

= fortress ('fɔrtrɪs)

= stronghold ('strɔŋˌhold)

citation (saɪ'teʃən , sɪ-) *n.*
①褒獎 ②傳票 ③引文

① = decoration (ˌdɛkə'reʃən)

= medal ('mɛdḷ)

= *honorable mention*

② = subpoena (sə'pinə , səb-)

= summons ('sʌmənz)

③ = quotation (kwo'teʃən)

cite (saɪt) *v.* 引證；提及

= quote (kwot)

= name (nem)

= refer (rɪ'fɝ)

= mention ('mɛnʃən)

= illustrate ('ɪləstret)

citizen ('sɪtəzn̩) *n.* 居民

= inhabitant (ɪn'hæbətənt)

= occupant ('ɑkjəpənt)

= resident ('rɛzədənt)

city ('sɪtɪ) *n.* 大城市

= metropolis (mə'trɑpḷɪs)

= municipality (ˌmjunɪsə'pælətɪ)

civil ('sɪvḷ) *adj.* ①平民的
②有禮貌的

① = public ('pʌblɪk)

= common ('kɑmən)

= social ('soʃəl)

② = ceremonious (ˌsɛrə'monɪəs)

= courteous ('kɝtɪəs)

= polite (pə'laɪt)

civilization (ˌsɪvḷə'zeʃən) *n.*
文明

= culture ('kʌltʃɚ)

clad (klæd) *adj.* 穿上衣服的

= clothed (kloðd)

= dressed (drɛst)

= attired (ə'taɪrd)

claim (klem) ① *v.* 要求
② *n.* 要求的權利

① = demand (dɪ'mænd)

= require (rɪ'kwaɪr)

② = right (raɪt)

= due (dju)

= interest ('ɪntərɪst , 'ɪntrɪst)

= title ('taɪtḷ)

clammy ('klæmɪ) *adj.* 冷而濕的

= sweaty ('swɛtɪ)

= *cold and damp*

clamor ('klæmɚ) *v.* 大聲要求
或責難

= demand (dɪ'mænd)

= complain (kəm'plen)

= *cry out*

clamp (klæmp) *v.* 使附著固定

= fasten ('fæsn̩)

= clasp (klæsp)

= brace (bres)

C

clan ﹝ klæn ﹞ *n.* 朋黨團體、家族
  = group ﹝ grup ﹞
  = crowd ﹝ kraud ﹞
  = clique ﹝ klɪk , klik ﹞
  = tribe ﹝ traɪb ﹞
  = folk ﹝ fok ﹞
  = family ﹝ 'fæməlɪ ﹞

clap ﹝ klæp ﹞ *n.* 擊；鼓掌
  = strike ﹝ straɪk ﹞
  = bang ﹝ bæŋ ﹞
  = applaud ﹝ ə'plɔd ﹞

clarify ﹝ 'klærə,faɪ ﹞ *v.* 使清楚；
清楚說明
  = explain ﹝ ɪk'splen ﹞
  = refine ﹝ rɪ'faɪn ﹞
  = simplify ﹝ 'sɪmplə,faɪ ﹞
  = *make clear*

clash ﹝ klæʃ ﹞ *v.* ①衝突；意見
不合　②撞擊
① = contradict ﹝ ,kɑntrə'dɪkt ﹞
  = oppose ﹝ ə'poz ﹞
  = disagree ﹝ ,dɪsə'gri ﹞
  = differ ﹝ 'dɪfə ﹞
  = conflict ﹝ kən'flɪkt ﹞
② = collide ﹝ kə'laɪd ﹞
  = bump ﹝ bʌmp ﹞
  = bang ﹝ bæŋ ﹞
  = hit ﹝ hɪt ﹞

clasp ﹝ klæsp ﹞ *v.* 緊握；扣住
  = grasp ﹝ græsp ﹞
  = buckle ﹝ 'bʌkl ﹞
  = fasten ﹝ 'fæsn ﹞

  = hook ﹝ huk ﹞
  = clip ﹝ klɪp ﹞

class ﹝ klæs , klɑs ﹞ *n.* ①等級
②種類
① = rank ﹝ ræŋk ﹞
  = grade ﹝ gred ﹞
  = quality ﹝ 'kwɑlətɪ ﹞
② = group ﹝ grup ﹞
  = category ﹝ 'kætə,gorɪ ﹞
  = division ﹝ də'vɪʒən ﹞

classify ﹝ 'klæsə,faɪ ﹞ *v.* 分類
  = organize ﹝ 'ɔrgən,aɪz ﹞
  = group ﹝ grup ﹞
  = categorize ﹝ 'kætəgə,raɪz ﹞
  = sort ﹝ sɔrt ﹞

clatter ﹝ 'klætə ﹞ *n.* 喧鬧嘈雜聲
  = noise ﹝ nɔɪz ﹞
  = rattle ﹝ 'rætl ﹞
  = racket ﹝ 'rækɪt ﹞
  = din ﹝ dɪn ﹞

clean ﹝ klin ﹞ *v.* 使清潔
  = cleanse ﹝ klɛnz ﹞
  = purify ﹝ 'pjurə,faɪ ﹞
  = wash ﹝ wɑʃ , wɔʃ ﹞
  = tidy ﹝ 'taɪdɪ ﹞

clear ﹝ klɪr ﹞ *n.* ①除去　②澄清
③使清潔
① = remove ﹝ rɪ'muv ﹞
  = eliminate ﹝ ɪ'lɪmə,net ﹞
  = *get rid of*
② = free ﹝ fri ﹞

= acquit〔ə'kwɪt〕
③ = clean〔klin〕
= cleanse〔klɛnz〕
= purify〔'pjʊrə,faɪ〕
= wash〔waʃ , wɔʃ〕
= tidy〔'taɪdɪ〕

cleavage〔'klivɪdʒ〕*n.* 分裂

= split〔splɪt〕
= division〔də'vɪʒən〕
= break〔brek〕

cleft〔klɛft〕*n.* 裂縫；空間

= space〔spes〕
= opening〔'opənɪŋ〕
= crack〔kræk〕
= crevice〔'krɛvɪs〕
= notch〔natʃ〕
= indentation〔,ɪndɛn'teʃən〕

clemency〔'klɛmənsɪ〕*n.* 憐憫；
同情；和善

= mercy〔'mɝsɪ〕
= pity〔'pɪtɪ〕
= sympathy〔'sɪmpəθɪ〕
= compassion〔kəm'pæʃən〕
= lenience〔'linɪəns , 'linjəns〕
= mildness〔'maɪldnɪs〕

clench〔'klɛntʃ〕*v.* 緊握

= grasp〔græsp〕
= grip〔grɪp〕
= clutch〔klʌtʃ〕
= hold〔hold〕

clever〔'klɛvɚ〕*adj.* 巧妙的；
聰明的

= skillful〔'skɪlfəl〕
= cunning〔'kʌnɪŋ〕
= bright〔braɪt〕
= smart〔smɑrt〕
= alert〔ə'lɝt〕
= intelligent〔ɪn'tɛlədʒənt〕

client〔'klaɪənt〕*n.* 顧客

= customer〔'kʌstəmɚ〕
= prospect〔'praspɛkt〕
= patron〔'petrən〕

climate〔'klaɪmɪt〕*n.* 氣候

= weather〔'wɛðɚ〕
= elements〔'ɛləmənts〕
= *atmospheric conditions*

climax〔'klaɪmæks〕*n.* ①極點；
結果 ②轉捩點

① = result〔rɪ'zʌlt〕
= end〔ɛnd〕
= conclusion〔kən'kluʒən〕
② = *turning point*

climb〔klaɪm〕*v.* 攀登

= mount〔maʊnt〕
= ascend〔ə'sɛnd〕
= rise〔raɪz〕

clinch〔klɪntʃ〕*v.* ①緊握；扭住
②確定

① = seize〔siz〕
= grip〔grɪp〕
= cinch〔sɪntʃ〕
= bind〔baɪnd〕
= hold〔hold〕

C

= wrap〔 ræp 〕

= tie〔 taɪ 〕

= fasten〔'fæsn̩ 〕

② = establish〔 ə'stæblɪʃ 〕

= insure〔 ɪn'ʃʊr 〕

= *make certain*

cling〔 klɪŋ 〕 *v.* 緊握;堅持

= hold〔 hold 〕

= grasp〔 græsp 〕

= adhere〔 əd'hɪr , æd- 〕

= stick〔 stɪk 〕

clip〔 klɪp 〕① *v.* 修剪 ② *v.* 夾住 ③ *n.* 速度

① = cut〔 kʌt 〕

= shear〔 ʃɪr 〕

= crop〔 krɑp 〕

② = fasten〔'fæsn̩ 〕

= attach〔 ə'tætʃ 〕

③ = pace〔 pes 〕

clique〔 klɪk , klik 〕 *n.* 團體; 部落

= set〔 sɛt 〕

= clan〔 klæn 〕

= group〔 grup 〕

= crowd〔 kraʊd 〕

= folk〔 fok 〕

= family〔'fæməlɪ 〕

cloak〔 klok 〕 *v.* ①掩飾 ②穿衣

① = hide〔 haɪd 〕

= conceal〔 kən'sil 〕

= cover〔'kʌvɚ 〕

= protect〔 prə'tɛkt 〕

② = robe〔 rob 〕

= wrap〔 ræp 〕

= coat〔 kot 〕

clod〔 klɑd 〕 *n.* ①一塊 ②粗鄙之人;愚人

① = lump〔 lʌmp 〕

= hunk〔 hʌŋk 〕

= chunk〔 tʃʌŋk 〕

② = oaf〔 of 〕

= lout〔 laʊt 〕

= *stupid person*

clog〔 klɑg , klɔg 〕 *v.* 阻礙;填塞

= stuff〔 stʌf 〕

= block〔 blɑk 〕

= obstruct〔 əb'strʌkt 〕

= choke〔 tʃok 〕

1. **close**〔 kloz 〕 *v.* ①關 ②結束

① = shut〔 ʃʌt 〕

= fasten〔'fæsn̩ 〕

= lock〔 lɑk 〕

② = end〔 ɛnd 〕

= finish〔'fɪnɪʃ 〕

= stop〔 stɑp 〕

= conclude〔 kən'klud 〕

= terminate〔'tɝmə,net 〕

2. **close**〔 klos 〕 *adj.* ①接近的 ②窒悶的

① = near〔 nɪr 〕

= approaching〔 ə'protʃɪŋ 〕

= imminent〔'ɪmənənt 〕

② = stuffy〔'stʌfɪ 〕

= airless〔'ɛrlɪs 〕

= stifling (ˈstaɪflɪŋ)
= suffocating (ˈsʌfə͵ketɪŋ)

clothe (kloð) *v.* 穿衣

= dress (drɛs)
= cover (ˈkʌvɚ)
= wrap (ræp)
= attire (əˈtaɪr)

cloudy (ˈklaʊdɪ) *adj.* 不明朗的；憂鬱的

= dark (dɑrk)
= unclear (ʌnˈklɪr)
= overcast (ˈovɚ͵kæst)
= gloomy (ˈglumɪ)
= dismal (ˈdɪzml̩)

clout (klaʊt) *v.* 敲；打

= rap (ræp)
= hit (hɪt)
= bat (bæt)
= knock (nɑk)
= strike (straɪk)

clown (klaʊn) ① *v.* 愚弄
② *n.* 丑角

① = fool (ful)
= play (ple)
② = comic (ˈkɑmɪk)
= performer (pɚˈfɔrmɚ)
= prankster (ˈpræŋkstɚ)

club (klʌb) ① *v.* 打擊　② *n.* 棒
③ *n.* 團體

① = beat (bit)
= strike (straɪk)

= blow (blo)
= bat (bæt)
= knock (nɑk)
② = bat (bæt)
= stick (stɪk)
③ = group (grup)
= society (səˈsaɪətɪ)
= clique (klik , klɪk)

clue (klu) *n.* 線索

= hint (hɪnt)
= evidence (ˈɛvədəns)
= proof (pruf)
= sign (saɪn)
= key (ki)
= lead (lid)

clump (klʌmp) *n.* 塊；團

= cluster (ˈklʌstɚ)
= lump (lʌmp)

clumsy (ˈklʌmzɪ) *adj.* 笨拙的

= awkward (ˈɔkwɚd)
= ungraceful (ʌnˈgresfəl)
= ungainly (ʌnˈgenlɪ)
= cumbersome (ˈkʌmbɚsəm)

cluster (ˈklʌstɚ) *n.* 團；一批

= bunch (bʌntʃ)
= group (grup)
= set (sɛt)
= batch (bætʃ)

clutch (klʌtʃ) *v.* 緊握

= cling (klɪŋ)
= hold (hold)

C

= grasp〔græsp〕
= adhere〔əd'hɪr〕
= stick〔stɪk〕

clutter〔'klʌtə〕*n.* ①廢物
②混亂

① = rubbish〔'rʌbɪʃ〕
= trash〔træʃ〕
= debris〔də'bri , 'debri〕
② = confusion〔kən'fjuʒən〕
= disorder〔dɪs'ɔrdə〕
= jumble〔'dʒʌmbḷ〕

coach〔kotʃ〕① *v.* 做教練
② *n.* 輤車

① = train〔tren〕
= teach〔titʃ〕
= tutor〔'tutə , 'tjutə〕
② = carriage〔'kærɪdʒ〕
= car〔kɑr〕

coagulate〔ko'ægjə,let〕*v.*
使凝結

= thicken〔'θɪkən〕
= clot〔klɑt〕
= set〔sɛt〕

coarse〔kors , kɔrs〕*adj.*
①粗的；不平的 ②劣等的
③粗鄙的

① = rough〔rʌf〕
= choppy〔'tʃɑpɪ〕
= bumpy〔'bʌmpɪ〕
② = common〔'kɑmən〕
= poor〔pur〕
= inferior〔ɪn'fɪrɪə〕
③ = crude〔krud〕

= vulgar〔'vʌlgə〕

coast〔kost〕① *v.* 溜下；滑行
② *n.* 海岸

① = slide〔slaɪd〕
= glide〔glaɪd〕
= ride〔raɪd〕
② = seashore〔'si,ʃor , -,ʃɔr〕
= seaside〔'si,saɪd〕
= waterfront〔'watə,frʌnt〕
= beach〔bitʃ〕

coat〔kot〕*n.* 外衣

= wrap〔ræp〕
= cloak〔klok〕
= robe〔rob〕

coax〔koks〕*v.* 勸誘；影響

= persuade〔pə'swed〕
= influence〔'ɪnfluəns〕
= urge〔ɝdʒ〕
= pressure〔'prɛʃə〕
= push〔puʃ〕

cocky〔'kɑkɪ〕*adj.* 自負的

= conceited〔kən'sitɪd〕
= impudent〔'ɪmpjədənt〕
= swaggering〔'swægəɪŋ〕
= saucy〔'sɔsɪ〕

coddle〔'kɑdḷ〕*v.* 溺愛；縱容

= pamper〔'pæmpə〕
= spoil〔spɔɪl〕
= oblige〔ə'blaɪdʒ〕
= indulge〔ɪn'dʌldʒ〕
= *cater to*

code (kod) *n.* 法規;章程;信號

= laws (lɔz)
= rules (rulz)
= arrangement (ə'rendʒmənt)
= system ('sɪstəm)
= signal ('sɪgn̩)

coerce (ko'ɝs) *v.* 強迫

= compel (kəm'pɛl)
= force (fɔrs , fors)

coin (kɔɪn) ① *v.* 創造 ② *n.* 錢
① = invent (ɪn'vɛnt)
= devise (dɪ'vaɪz)
= originate (ə'rɪdʒə,net)
= *make up*
② = money ('mʌnɪ)
= silver ('sɪlvɚ)

collapse (kə'læps) *v.* 崩潰;
失敗

= fail (fel)
= crash (kræʃ)
= topple ('tɑp̩)
= *break down*

collar ('kɑlɚ) ① *v.* 捉住
② *n.* 衣領
① = seize (siz)
= nab (næb)
= capture ('kæptʃɚ)
② = neckband ('nɛk,bænd)

colleague ('kɑlig) *n.* 同事

= associate (ə'soʃɪɪt)

= buddy ('bʌdɪ)
= friend (frɛnd)
= companion (kəm'pænjən)
= partner ('pɑrtnɚ)
= comrade ('kɑmræd , 'kɑmrɪd)

collect (kə'lɛkt) *v.* 收集

= assemble (ə'sɛmb̩)
= gather ('gæðɚ)
= accumulate (ə'kjumjə,let)
= *store up*

collide (kə'laɪd) *v.* 衝突;碰撞

= conflict (kən'flɪkt)
= bump (bʌmp)
= clash (klæʃ)
= bang (bæŋ)

colony ('kɑlənɪ) *n.* 殖民地;
群聚

= settlement ('sɛt̩mənt)
= community (kə'mjunətɪ)

colorful ('kʌlɚfəl) *adj.* 生動的;
富有色彩的

= vivid ('vɪvɪd)
= picturesque (,pɪktʃə'rɛsk)
= bright (braɪt)
= gay (ge)
= rich (rɪtʃ)

colorless ('kʌlɚlɪs) *adj.* 無趣的

= dull (dʌl)
= uninteresting (ʌn'ɪntərɪstɪŋ)
= flat (flæt)
= dreary ('drɪrɪ)

colossal ﹙kə'lasḷ﹚ *adj.* 巨大的

= huge ﹙hjudʒ﹚
= gigantic ﹙dʒaɪ'gæntɪk﹚
= vast ﹙væst﹚
= enormous ﹙ɪ'nɔrməs﹚
= immense ﹙ɪ'mɛns﹚
= mammoth ﹙'mæməθ﹚

column ﹙'kaləm﹚ *n.* ①部分 ②柱子；石碑

① = division ﹙də'vɪʒən﹚
= section ﹙'sɛkʃən﹚
= part ﹙part﹚
② = tower ﹙'taʊɚ﹚
= pillar ﹙'pɪlɚ﹚
= cylinder ﹙'sɪlɪndɚ﹚
= monument ﹙'manjəmənt﹚

combat ﹙'kambæt , 'kʌmbæt﹚ *n.* 格鬥

= battle ﹙'bætḷ﹚
= struggle ﹙'strʌgḷ﹚
= fight ﹙faɪt﹚
= contest ﹙'kantɛst﹚
= conflict ﹙'kanflɪkt﹚
= war ﹙wɔr﹚

combine ﹙kəm'baɪn﹚ *v.* 聯合； 混合

= join ﹙dʒɔɪn﹚
= unite ﹙ju'naɪt﹚
= mix ﹙mɪks﹚
= connect ﹙kə'nɛkt﹚
= couple ﹙'kʌpḷ﹚
= blend ﹙blɛnd﹚
= fuse ﹙fjuz﹚

combustible ﹙kəm'bʌstəbḷ﹚ *adj.* 易燃的

= flammable ﹙'flæməbḷ﹚
= burnable ﹙'bɜnəbḷ﹚
= fiery ﹙'faɪrɪ , 'faɪərɪ﹚

comedian ﹙kə'midɪən﹚ *n.* 喜劇 演員

= comic ﹙'kamɪk﹚
= gagman ﹙'gæg,mæn﹚
= funnyman ﹙'fʌnɪ,mæn﹚

comely ﹙'kʌmlɪ﹚ *adj.* 漂亮的； 令人愉快的

= attractive ﹙ə'træktɪv﹚
= fair ﹙fɛr﹚
= pleasing ﹙'plizɪŋ﹚
= personable ﹙'pɜsṇəbḷ﹚
= good-looking ﹙'gʊd 'lʊkɪŋ﹚

comfort ﹙'kʌmfɚt﹚ *v.* 使舒適； 安慰

= console ﹙kən'sol﹚
= ease ﹙iz﹚
= assure ﹙ə'ʃʊr﹚
= relieve ﹙rɪ'liv﹚
= cheer ﹙tʃɪr﹚
= gladden ﹙'glædən﹚

comical ﹙'kamɪkḷ﹚ *adj.* 詼諧的； 可笑的

= amusing ﹙ə'mjuzɪŋ﹚
= funny ﹙'fʌnɪ﹚
= humorous ﹙'hjumərəs , 'ju-﹚

commemorate (kə'mɛmə,ret)
v. 慶祝;表揚

= honor ('ɑnə)
= celebrate ('sɛlə,bret)
= observe (əb'zɜv)
= proclaim (pro'klem)

command (kə'mænd)
① *v.* 指揮　② *n.* 控制
① = bid (bɪd)
= order ('ɔdə)
= direct (də'rɛkt , daɪ-)
= instruct (ɪn'strʌkt)
= enjoin (ɪn'dʒɔɪn)
② = power ('pauə)
= control (kən'trol)

commence (kə'mɛns) *v.* 開始

= begin (bɪ'gɪn)
= start (start)
= *take off*
= *fire away*

commend (kə'mɛnd) *v.* ①稱讚
②委託
① = praise (prez)
= compliment ('kɑmpləmənt)
= approve (ə'pruv)
② = commit (kə'mɪt)
= assign (ə'saɪn)
= trust (trʌst)

comment ('kɑmɛnt) *v.* 評論;
註釋
= remark (rɪ'mark)
= note (not)

= observe (əb'zɜv)
= mention ('mɛnʃən)

commerce ('kɑmɜs) *n.* 貿易

= trade (tred)
= business ('bɪznɪs)
= dealings ('dilɪŋz)

commit (kə'mɪt) *v.* ①委託
②做
① = entrust (ɪn'trʌst)
= promise ('prɑmɪs)
= pledge (plɛdʒ)
② = perform (pə'fɔrm)
= do (du)

committee (kə'mɪtɪ) *n.* 委員會

= council ('kaunsḷ)
= group (grup)
= delegation (,dɛlə'geʃən)

commodious (kə'modɪəs) *adj.*
寬敞舒適的
= roomy ('rumɪ)
= spacious ('speʃəs)
= comfortable ('kʌmfətəbḷ)

commodity (kə'mɑdətɪ) *n.*
貨物
= product ('prɑdəkt , -dʌkt)
= ware (wɛr)
= article ('artɪkḷ)

common ('kɑmən) *adj.*
①公有的　②普通的　③劣等的
① = public ('pʌblɪk)

C

C

= general ('dʒɛnərəl)
② = usual ('juʒʊəl)
= familiar (fə'mɪljɚ)
= ordinary ('ɔrdn̩ˌɛrɪ , 'ɔrdnɛrɪ)
= everyday ('ɛvrɪ'de)
③ = low (lo)
= crude (krud)
= coarse (kors , kɔrs)
= vulgar ('vʌlgɚ)
= poor (pʊr)
= inferior (ɪn'fɪrɪɚ)

commotion (kə'moʃən) n.
暴動；騷動

= disturbance (dɪ'stɝbəns)
= tumult ('tjumʌlt)
= confusion (kən'fjuʒən)
= rumpus ('rʌmpəs)
= ado (ə'du)
= action ('ækʃən)
= stir (stɝ)
= fuss (fʌs)
= trouble ('trʌbl̩)
= excitement (ɪk'saɪtmənt)
= row (raʊ)
= hubbub ('hʌbʌb)
= to-do (tə'du)

communicable (kə'mjunɪkəbl̩)
adj. 可傳染的

= contagious (kən'tedʒəs)
= catching ('kætʃɪŋ)
= transferable (træns'fɝəbl̩)
= infectious (ɪn'fɛkʃəs)

communicate (kə'mjunəˌket)
v. 聯絡

= inform (ɪn'fɔrm)
= tell (tɛl)
= enlighten (ɪn'laɪtn̩)
= report (rɪ'port)
= convey (kən've)

community (kə'mjunətɪ) n.
①同住一地的民眾 ②共享

① = society (sə'saɪətɪ)
= people ('pipl̩)
= colony ('kɑlənɪ)
= district ('dɪstrɪkt)
= town (taʊn)
② = ownership together

commute (kə'mjut) v. ①變換
②定期往返於兩地間

① = exchange (ɪks'tʃendʒ)
= substitute ('sʌbstəˌtjut)
= replace (rɪ'ples)
= switch (swɪtʃ)
② = travel ('trævl̩)
= move (muv)

compact (adj. kəm'pækt ,
n. 'kɑmpækt) ① adj. 簡明的
② n. 協定

① = concise (kən'saɪs)
= short (ʃɔrt)
= brief (brif)
② = agreement (ə'grimənt)
= contract ('kɑntrækt)
= pact (pækt)
= understanding (ˌʌndɚ'stændɪŋ)
= concord ('kɑnkɔrd , 'kɑŋ-)
= bargain ('bɑrgɪn)

= treaty ('tritɪ)

= alliance (ə'laɪəns)

= deal (dil)

companion (kəm'pænjən) *n.*
同伴

= partner ('portnɚ)

= accompanist (ə'kʌmpənɪst)

= buddy ('bʌdɪ)

= friend (frɛnd)

= pal (pæl)

= chum (tʃʌm)

= comrade ('kɑmræd , 'kɑmrɪd)

company ('kʌmpənɪ) *n.*
①一群人；團體 ②公司 ③賓客

① = group (grup)

= association (ə,sosɪ'eʃən ,
ə,soʃɪ'eʃən)

② = business ('bɪznɪs)

= firm (fɜm)

= enterprise ('ɛntɚ,praɪz)

③ = guest (gɛst)

= visitors ('vɪzɪtɚz)

= companions (kəm'pænjənz)

compare (kəm'pɛr) *v.* 比較

= match (mætʃ)

= liken ('laɪkən)

= contrast (kən'træst)

= measure ('mɛʒɚ)

compassion (kəm'pæʃən) *n.*
憐憫

= clemency ('klɛmənsɪ)

= mercy ('mɝsɪ)

= pity ('pɪtɪ)

= sympathy ('sɪmpəθɪ)

= leniency ('linɪənsɪ , 'linjənsɪ)

= mildness ('maɪldnɪs)

compatible (kəm'pætəbḷ) *adj.*
能共處的

= agreeing (ə'griɪŋ)

= harmonious (hɑr'monɪəs)

compel (kəm'pɛl) *v.* 強迫

= force (fors , fɔrs)

= make (mek)

= require (rɪ'kwaɪr)

compensate ('kɑmpən,set) *v.*
報酬；賠償

= pay (pe)

= reward (rɪ'wɔrd)

= balance ('bæləns)

= *atone for*

= *make up for*

compete (kəm'pit) *v.* 競爭

= rival ('raɪvḷ)

= *vie with*

competent ('kɑmpətənt) *adj.*
能勝任的

= effective (ə'fɛktɪv)

= able ('ebḷ)

= adequate ('ædəkwɪt)

= capable ('kepəbḷ)

= qualified ('kwɑlə,faɪd)

= fit (fɪt)

C

compile 〔 kəm'paɪl 〕 v. 聚積

= gather 〔'gæðɚ 〕
= collect 〔 kə'lɛkt 〕
= assemble 〔 ə'sɛmbl̩ 〕
= accumulate 〔 ə'kjumjə,let 〕
= *store up*

complacent 〔 kəm'plesn̩t 〕 adj.
自滿的

= contented 〔 kən'tɛntɪd 〕
= self-satisfied 〔'sɛlf'sætɪs,faɪd 〕

complain 〔 kəm'plen 〕 v. 抱怨

= grumble 〔'grʌmbl̩ 〕
= squawk 〔 skwɔk 〕
= *find fault*

complement 〔'kampləmənt 〕 v.
補充

= supply 〔 sə'plaɪ 〕
= supplement 〔'sʌplə,mɛnt 〕

complete 〔 kəm'plit 〕 ① v. 完成
② adj. 完整的

① = finish 〔'fɪnɪʃ 〕
= conclude 〔 kən'klud 〕
= terminate 〔'tɝmə,net 〕
= end 〔 ɛnd 〕
= *clean up*
= *wind up*
= *close up*
② = whole 〔 hol 〕
= entire 〔 ɪn'taɪr 〕
= thorough 〔'θɝo 〕

complex 〔 adj. kəm'plɛks ,
n. 'kamplɛks 〕 ① adj. 混雜的
② n. 成見

① = complicated 〔'kamplə,ketɪd 〕
= confused 〔 kən'fjuzd 〕
= involved 〔 ɪn'valvd 〕
= mixed 〔 mɪkst 〕
② = prejudice 〔'prɛdʒədɪs 〕
= bias 〔'baɪəs 〕
= leaning 〔'linɪŋ 〕
= inclination 〔,ɪnklə'neʃən 〕

complexion 〔 kəm'plɛkʃən 〕 n.
臉色

= appearance 〔 ə'pɪrəns 〕
= look 〔 lʊk 〕
= color 〔'kʌlɚ 〕
= pigment 〔'pɪgmənt 〕

complicate 〔'kamplə,ket 〕 v.
使複雜

= confuse 〔 kən'fjuz 〕
= confound 〔 kan'faʊnd , kən- 〕
= involve 〔 ɪn'valv 〕
= *mix up*

compliment 〔'kampləmənt 〕 v.
稱讚；恭維

= commend 〔 kə'mɛnd 〕
= flatter 〔'flætɚ 〕
= praise 〔 prez 〕
= congratulate 〔 kən'grætʃə,let 〕

comply 〔 kəm'plaɪ 〕 v. 同意

= conform 〔 kən'fɔrm 〕

C

= agree (ə'gri)

= assent (ə'sɛnt)

= submit (sʌb'mɪt)

= obey (ə'be , o'be)

compose (kəm'poz) v. ①創作；組成 ②使安靜

① = devise (dɪ'vaɪz)

= construct (kən'strʌkt)

= build (bɪld)

= create (krɪ'et)

= make (mek)

= *make up*

= *put together*

② = calm (kɑm)

= pacify ('pæsə,faɪ)

= soothe (suð)

= quiet ('kwaɪət)

composition (,kɑmpə'zɪʃən) n. ①著作；作品 ②混合物

① = writing ('raɪtɪŋ)

= work (wɜk)

= paper ('pepə)

= document ('dɑkjəmənt)

= script (skrɪpt)

② = composite (kəm'pɑzɪt)

= combination (,kɑmbə'neʃən)

= mixture ('mɪkstʃə)

= blend (blɛnd)

composure (kəm'poʒə) n. 鎮靜

= calmness ('kɑmnɪs)

= quiet ('kwaɪət)

= peace (pis)

= rest (rɛst)

= serenity (sə'rɛnətɪ)

= self-control (,sɛlfkən'trol)

= tranquility (træn'kwɪlətɪ , træŋ-)

comprehend (,kɑmprɪ'hɛnd) v. ①了解 ②包括

① = understand (,ʌndə'stænd)

= realize ('rɪə,laɪz , 'rɪə-)

= know (no)

② = include (ɪn'klud)

= contain (kən'ten)

= cover ('kʌvə)

compress (kəm'prɛs) v. 緊壓；鎮壓

= squeeze (skwiz)

= press (prɛs)

= reduce (rɪ'djus)

= condense (kən'dɛns)

= concentrate ('kɑnsn̩,tret)

= crush (krʌʃ)

comprise (kəm'praɪz) v. 包括

= include (ɪn'klud)

= contain (kən'ten)

= involve (ɪn'valv)

= *consist of*

compromise ('kɑmprə,maɪz) v. 妥協

= settle ('sɛtl̩)

= yield (jild)

= concede (kən'sid)

= adjust (ə'dʒʌst)

= *meet halfway*

compulsory ﹝kəm'pʌlsərɪ﹞ *adj.*
強迫的；必修的

= compelled﹝kəm'pɛld﹞
= required﹝rɪ'kwaɪrd﹞
= necessary﹝'nɛsə,sɛrɪ﹞

compute ﹝kəm'pjut﹞ *v.* 計算

= calculate﹝'kælkjə,let﹞
= count﹝kaunt﹞
= figure﹝'fɪgɚ, 'fɪgjɚ﹞
= estimate﹝'ɛstə,met﹞
= reckon﹝'rɛkən﹞
= *sum up*

comrade ﹝'kɑmræd, 'kɑmrɪd﹞
n. 同伴

= buddy﹝'bʌdɪ﹞
= friend﹝frɛnd﹞
= pal﹝pæl﹞
= companion﹝kəm'pænjən﹞
= partner﹝'pɑrtnɚ﹞
= chum﹝tʃʌm﹞

conceal ﹝kən'sil﹞ *v.* 隱藏

= hide﹝haɪd﹞
= cover﹝'kʌvɚ﹞
= cloak﹝klok﹞
= camouflage﹝'kæmə,flɑʒ﹞
= veil﹝vel﹞

concede ﹝kən'sid﹞ *v.* 承認

= admit﹝əd'mɪt﹞
= allow﹝ə'lau﹞
= grant﹝grænt﹞
= confess﹝kən'fɛs﹞

conceited ﹝kən'sitɪd﹞ *adj.*
自負的

= vain﹝ven﹞
= boastful﹝'bost,fəl﹞
= proud﹝praud﹞
= cocky﹝'kɑkɪ﹞
= saucy﹝'sɔsɪ﹞

conceivable ﹝kən'sivəbḷ﹞ *adj.*
可想像的

= vain﹝ven﹞
= imaginable﹝ɪ'mædʒɪnəbḷ﹞
= thinkable﹝'θɪŋkəbḷ﹞
= possible﹝'pɑsəbḷ﹞
= likely﹝'laɪklɪ﹞
= plausible﹝'plɔzəbḷ﹞

concentrate ﹝'kɑnsṇ,tret,
-sɛn-﹞ *v.* ①集中；專心 ②濃縮

① = focus﹝'fokəs﹞
= think *about*
② = strengthen﹝'strɛŋθən﹞
= intensify﹝ɪn'tɛnsə,faɪ﹞
= *make stronger*

concept ﹝'kɑnsɛpt﹞ *n.* 觀念

= thought﹝θɔt﹞
= notion﹝'noʃən﹞
= idea﹝aɪ'diə, -'dɪə﹞
= opinion﹝ə'pɪnjən﹞

concern ﹝kən'sɝn﹞ ① *v.* 有關
② *n.* 公司

① = interest﹝'ɪntrɪst﹞
= affect﹝ə'fɛkt﹞
= trouble﹝'trʌbḷ﹞

= involve (ɪn'vɑlv)

② = business ('bɪznɪz)
= company ('kʌmpənɪ)
= firm (fɝm)
= enterprise ('ɛntɚ,praɪz)

concert ('kɑnsɝt) *n.* ①音樂會
②和諧

① = music ('mjuzɪk)
= recital (rɪ'saɪtḷ)
② = agreement (ə'grimənt)
= harmony ('hɑrmənɪ)
= unison ('junəsn̩ , 'junəzn̩)
= teamwork ('tim,wɝk)

conciliate (kən'sɪlɪ,et) *v.*
安慰;調解

= soothe (suð)
= allay (ə'le)
= quiet ('kwaɪət)
= calm (kɑm)
= pacify ('pæsə,faɪ)
= moderate ('mɑdə,ret)
= restrain (rɪ'stren)
= alleviate (ə'livɪ,et)

concise (kən'saɪs) *adj.* 簡明的

= brief (brif)
= short (ʃɔrt)
= terse (tɝs)
= curt (kɝt)

conclude (kən'klud) *v.* ①結束
②推斷;結論

① = close (kloz)
= end (ɛnd)

= finish ('fɪnɪʃ)
= stop (stɑp)
= terminate ('tɝmə,net)
② = reason ('rizn̩)
= suppose (sə'poz)
= assume (ə'sjum)
= presume (prɪ'zum)
= infer (ɪn'fɝ)
= gather ('gæðɚ)

concoct (kɑn'kɑkt , kən-) *v.*
編造

= make (mek)
= invent (ɪn'vɛnt)
= prepare (prɪ'pɛr)
= devise (dɪ'vaɪz)
= create (krɪ'et)
= manufacture (,mænjə'fæktʃɚ)

concord ('kɑnkɔrd , 'kɑŋ-) *n.*
和諧

= peace (pis)
= harmony ('hɑrmənɪ)
= agreement (ə'grimənt)

concrete ('kɑnkrit)
① *adj.* 具體的 ② *n.* 混凝土

① = real (ril , 'riəl , 'rɪəl)
= solid ('sɑlɪd)
= substantial (sʌb'stænʃəl)
= tangible ('tændʒəbḷ)
② = cement (sə'mɛnt)
= pavement ('pevmənt)

concur (kən'kɝ) *v.* 同意;協力

= agree (ə'gri)
= cooperate (ko'ɑpə,ret)

C

concussion (kən'kʌʃən) *n.* 衝擊;腦震盪

= shock (ʃɑk)
= *head injury*

condemn (kən'dɛm) *v.* 反對; 責難

= disapprove (ˌdɪsə'pruv)
= doom (dum)
= censure ('sɛnʃɚ)
= blame (blem)
= reproach (rɪ'protʃ)
= denounce (dɪ'nauns)
= criticize ('krɪtəˌsaɪz)

condense (kən'dɛns) *v.* 壓縮; 使聚集

= compress (kəm'prɛs)
= squeeze (skwiz)
= reduce (rɪ'djus)
= concentrate ('kɑnsn̩ˌtret)

condition (kən'dɪʃən) *n.* ①情況 ②條件

① = circumstance ('sɝkəmˌstæns)
= situation (ˌsɪtʃu'eʃən)
= state (stet)
② = provision (prə'vɪʒən)
= specification (ˌspɛsəfə'keʃən)

conduct (*v.* kən'dʌkt , *n.* 'kɑndʌkt) ① *v.* 處理;指引 ② *n.* 行為

① = manage ('mænɪdʒ)
= direct (də'rɛkt , daɪ-)
= guide (gaɪd)

= lead (lid)
② = behavior (bɪ'hevjɚ)
= action ('ækʃən)
= manner ('mænɚ)

confederation (kənˌfɛdə'reʃən) *n.* 同盟

= league (lig)
= alliance (ə'laɪəns)
= association (əˌsosɪ'eʃən , əˌsoʃɪ'eʃən)
= union ('junjən)

confer (kən'fɝ) *v.* 商議

= consult (kən'sʌlt)
= discuss (dɪ'skʌs)
= *talk over*

confess (kən'fɛs) *v.* 承認

= admit (əd'mɪt)
= acknowledge (ək'nɑlɪdʒ)
= consent (kən'sɛnt)

confide (kən'faɪd) *v.* 信賴

= rely (rɪ'laɪ)
= depend (dɪ'pɛnd)
= disclose (dɪs'kloz)
= *trust in*
= *tell a secret*

confident ('kɑnfədənt) *adj.* 確信的

= certain ('sɝtn̩)
= sure (ʃur)
= convinced (kən'vɪnst)
= believing (bɪ'livɪŋ)

confidential (ˌkɑnfəˈdɛnʃəl)
adj. 秘密的

  = secret (ˈsikrɪt)
  = unpublishable (ʌnˈpʌblɪˌʃəbḷ)
  = *off the record*

confine (kənˈfaɪn) *v.* 限制；
監禁

  = enclose (ɪnˈkloz)
  = surround (səˈraʊnd)
  = contain (kənˈten)
  = restrain (rɪˈstren)
  = imprison (ɪmˈprɪzṇ)
  = *keep in*
  = *coop up*

confirm (kənˈfɝm) *v.* 證實；
確定

  = establish (əˈstæblɪʃ)
  = verify (ˈvɛrəˌfaɪ)
  = substantiate (səbˈstænʃɪˌet)
  = prove (pruv)
  = O.K. (ˈoˈke)

confiscate (ˈkɑnfɪsˌket) *v.* 充公

  = seize (siz)
  = take (tek)

conflagration (ˌkɑnfləˈgreʃən)
n. 火災

  = fire (faɪr)
  = blaze (blez)

conflict (*v.* kənˈflɪkt ,
n. ˈkɑnflɪkt) ① *v.* 衝突　② *n.* 爭鬥
① = clash (klæʃ)

  = oppose (əˈpoz)
  = disagree (ˌdɪsəˈgri)
  = differ (ˈdɪfə)
② = fight (faɪt)
  = struggle (ˈstrʌgḷ)
  = opposition (ˌɑpəˈzɪʃən)
  = contest (ˈkɑntɛst)
  = battle (ˈbætḷ)

conform (kənˈfɔrm) *n.* 遵從

  = comply (kəmˈplaɪ)
  = agree (əˈgri)
  = assent (əˈsɛnt)
  = submit (səbˈmɪt)
  = obey (əˈbe)

confound (kɑnˈfaʊnd , kən-) *v.*
使混淆

  = confuse (kənˈfjuz)
  = perplex (pəˈplɛks)
  = baffle (ˈbæfḷ)
  = puzzle (ˈpʌzḷ)
  = mystify (ˈmɪstəˌfaɪ)
  = bewilder (bɪˈwɪldə)
  = stump (stʌmp)

confront (kənˈfrʌnt) *v.* 面對；
使相對

  = oppose (əˈpoz)
  = face (fes)
  = encounter (ɪnˈkaʊntə)
  = *meet squarely*

confuse (kənˈfjuz) *v.* 使混淆

  = complicate (ˈkɑmpləˌket)
  = mistake (məˈstek)

C

C

= muddle ('mʌdḷ)
= jumble ('dʒʌmbḷ)
= *mix up*

congeal (kən'dʒil) *v.* 使凝結

= freeze (friz)
= thicken ('θɪkən)
= stiffen ('stɪfən)
= clot (klɑt)
= solidify (sə'lɪdə,faɪ)

congenial (kən'dʒinjəl) *adj.* 志氣相投的

= agreeable (ə'griəbḷ)
= pleasing ('plizɪŋ)
= compatible (kəm'pætəbḷ)
= harmonious (hɑr'moniəs)
= like-minded ('laɪk 'maɪndɪd)

congested (kən'dʒɛstɪd) *adj.* 擁塞的

= overcrowded (,ovə'kraʊdɪd)
= overloaded (,ovə'lodɪd)
= stuffed (stʌft)
= full (fʊl)

congratulate (kən'grætʃə,let) *v.* 祝賀

= bless (blɛs)
= compliment ('kɑmpləmənt)
= flatter ('flætə)
= commend (kə'mɛnd)
= praise (prez)

congregate ('kɑŋgrɪ,get) *v.* 聚集

= crowd (kraʊd)
= mass (mæs)
= gather ('gæðə)
= meet (mit)
= assemble (ə'sɛmbḷ)

conjecture (kən'dʒɛktʃə) *v.* 推測

= guess (gɛs)
= suppose (sə'poz)

conjure ('kʌndʒə , 'kɑn-) *v.* 懇求

= entreat (ɪn'trit)
= appeal (ə'pil)
= plead (plid)
= implore (ɪm'plor , ɪm'plɔr)

connect (kə'nɛkt) *v.* 連結

= join (dʒɔɪn)
= unite (ju'naɪt)
= combine (kəm'baɪn)
= link (lɪŋk)
= attach (ə'tætʃ)

conquer ('kɑŋkə) *v.* 征服

= overtake (,ovə'tek)
= vanquish ('væŋkwɪʃ)
= defeat (dɪ'fit)
= crush (krʌʃ)
= win (wɪn)
= triumph ('traɪəmf)

conscientious (,kɑnʃɪ'ɛnʃəs) *adj.* 從良心的；盡責的

= exacting (ɪg'zæktɪŋ)

= particular〔pəˈtɪkjələ〕
= faithful〔ˈfeθfəl〕
= scrupulous〔ˈskrupjələs〕

conscious〔ˈkɑnʃəs〕*adj.*
①有意識的 ②知覺的

① = alive〔əˈlaɪv〕
= awake〔əˈwek〕
② = knowing〔ˈnoɪŋ〕
= realizing〔ˈriəˌlaɪzɪŋ, ˈrɪə-〕
= sensitive〔ˈsɛnsətɪv〕
= sensible〔ˈsɛnsəbḷ〕
= aware〔əˈwɛr〕
= cognizant〔ˈkɑgnɪzənt, ˈkɑnɪ-〕

consecutive〔kənˈsɛkjətɪv〕*adj.*
連續的

= following〔ˈfɑləwɪŋ〕
= successive〔səkˈsɛsɪv〕
= continuous〔kənˈtɪnjuəs〕

consent〔kənˈsɛnt〕*v.* 同意

= permit〔pəˈmɪt〕
= agree〔əˈgri〕
= assent〔əˈsɛnt〕
= accept〔əkˈsɛpt〕
= comply〔kəmˈplaɪ〕
= *approve of*

consequently〔ˈkɑnsəˌkwɛntlɪ〕
adv. 因此

= therefore〔ˈðɛrˌfor, -ˌfɔr〕
= accordingly〔əˈkɔrdɪŋlɪ〕
= hence〔hɛns〕
= *as a result*

conservative〔kənˈsɝvətɪv〕
adj. 保守的

= cautious〔ˈkɔʃəs〕
= unextreme〔ʌnˌɪkˈstrim〕
= protective〔prəˈtɛktɪv〕
= *opposed to change*

conserve〔kənˈsɝv〕*v.* 保存

= preserve〔prɪˈzɝv〕
= save〔sev〕
= keep〔kip〕
= guard〔gɑrd〕
= protect〔prəˈtɛkt〕
= maintain〔menˈten, mənˈten〕

consider〔kənˈsɪdə〕*v.* ①考慮
②為…著想

① = think〔θɪŋk〕
= study〔ˈstʌdɪ〕
= ponder〔ˈpɑndə〕
= reflect〔rɪˈflɛkt〕
= contemplate〔ˈkɑntəmˌplet〕
= deliberate〔dɪˈlɪbəˌret〕
② = regard〔rɪˈgɑrd〕
= *look upon*
= *think of*

considerable〔kənˈsɪdərəbḷ〕
adj. 重要的

= important〔ɪmˈpɔrtṇt〕
= much〔mʌtʃ〕
= great〔gret〕
= significant〔sɪgˈnɪfəkənt〕
= powerful〔ˈpauəfəl〕

considerate ﹝ kən'sɪdərɪt , -'sɪdrɪt ﹞ *adj.* 體貼的

= thoughtful ﹝'θɔtfəl ﹞
= kind ﹝ kaɪnd ﹞
= sympathetic ﹝ˏsɪmpə'θɛtɪk ﹞
= *mindful of others*

consign ﹝ kən'saɪn ﹞ *v.* 移交

= deliver ﹝ dɪ'lɪvə ﹞
= transfer ﹝ træns'fɝ ﹞
= entrust ﹝ ɪn'trʌst ﹞
= send ﹝ sɛnd ﹞
= convey ﹝ kən've ﹞
= *hand over*

consist ﹝ kən'sɪst ﹞ *v.* 組成；包括

= comprise ﹝ kəm'praɪz ﹞
= include ﹝ ɪn'klud ﹞
= *be made up*

consistency ﹝ kən'sɪstənsɪ ﹞ *n.* ①堅實 ②一致

① = firmness ﹝'fɝmnɪs ﹞
= stiffness ﹝'stɪfnɪs ﹞
② = steadiness ﹝'stɛdɪnɪs ﹞
= uniformity ﹝ˏjunə'fɔrmətɪ ﹞

console ﹝ kən'sol ﹞ *v.* 安慰

= comfort ﹝'kʌmfət ﹞
= cheer ﹝ tʃɪr ﹞
= solace ﹝'salɪs , -əs ﹞
= sympathize ﹝'sɪmpəˏθaɪz ﹞

consolidate ﹝ kən'saləˏdet ﹞ *v.* 結合

= unite ﹝ ju'naɪt ﹞

= combine ﹝ kəm'baɪn ﹞
= condense ﹝ kən'dɛns ﹞
= concentrate ﹝'kansnˏtret ﹞
= merge ﹝ mɝdʒ ﹞
= compress ﹝ kəm'prɛs ﹞
= squeeze ﹝ skwiz ﹞
= reduce ﹝ rɪ'djus ﹞

consort ﹝'kansɔrt ﹞ *n.* ①配偶 ②同伴

① = spouse ﹝ spauz ﹞
= mate ﹝ met ﹞
= *husband or wife*
② = associate ﹝ ə'soʃɪɪt ﹞
= companion ﹝ kəm'pænjən ﹞
= buddy ﹝'bʌdɪ ﹞
= friend ﹝ frɛnd ﹞
= pal ﹝ pæl ﹞
= partner ﹝'partnə ﹞
= comrade ﹝'kamræd , 'kamrɪd ﹞

conspicuous ﹝ kən'spɪkjuəs ﹞ *adj.* 顯而易見的

= noticeable ﹝'notɪsəbl̩ ﹞
= distinct ﹝ dɪ'stɪŋkt ﹞
= clear ﹝ klɪr ﹞
= obvious ﹝'abvɪəs ﹞
= prominent ﹝'pramənənt ﹞
= outstanding ﹝ aut'stændɪŋ ﹞

conspire ﹝ kən'spaɪr ﹞ *v.* 圖謀

= plot ﹝ plat ﹞
= scheme ﹝ skim ﹞

constantly ﹝'kanstəntlɪ ﹞ *adv.* 時常地

= always ﹝'ɔlwez , 'ɔlwɪz ﹞

= often ('ɔfən , 'ɔftən)

= continual (kən'tɪnjʊəl)

= *without stopping*

consternation (ˌkɑnstə'neʃən)

n. 驚愕

= dismay (dɪs'me)

= alarm (ə'lɑrm)

= terror ('tɛrə)

= fright (fraɪt)

= dread (drɛd)

constitute ('kɑnstəˌtjut) *v.* 組成

= organize ('ɔrgənˌaɪz)

= form (fɔrm)

= establish (ə'stæblɪʃ)

= compose (kəm'poz)

= *set up*

constrain (kən'stren) *v.* 強迫

= force (fɔrs , fors)

= compel (kəm'pɛl)

= urge (ɝdʒ)

= press (prɛs)

constrict (kən'strɪkt) *v.* 壓縮

= contract (kən'trækt)

= compress (kəm'prɛs)

= squeeze (skwiz)

= press (prɛs)

= crush (krʌʃ)

construct (kən'strʌkt) *v.*
製造;設立

= manufacture (ˌmænjə'fæktʃə)

= form (fɔrm)

= build (bɪld)

= make (mek)

= create (krɪ'et)

constructive (kən'strʌktɪv)

adj. 建設性的

= helpful ('hɛlpfəl)

= useful ('jusfəl)

= worthwhile ('wɝθ'hwaɪl)

construe (kən'stru) *v.* 解釋;
推斷

= explain (ɪk'splen)

= interpret (ɪn'tɝprɪt)

= infer (ɪn'fɝ)

consult (kən'sʌlt) *v.* 商議

= confer (kən'fɝ)

= discuss (dɪ'skʌs)

= *talk over*

consume (kən'sum , -'sjum) *v.*
①耗盡 ②浪費

① = spend (spɛnd)

= *use up*

= *eat up*

= *drink up*

② = waste (west)

= destroy (dɪ'strɔɪ)

= exhaust (ɪg'zɔst)

contact ('kɑntækt) *v.* 接觸;
聯繫

= touch (tʌtʃ)

= connect (kə'nɛkt)

= reach (ritʃ)

C

= join (dʒɔɪn)
= approach (ə'protʃ)

contagious (kən'tedʒəs) *adj.*
易感染的；蔓延的

= catching ('kætʃɪŋ)
= spreading ('sprɛdɪŋ)
= infectious (ɪn'fɛkʃəs)
= epidemic (ˌɛpə'dɛmɪk)

contain (kən'ten) *v.* ①包含
②容忍

① = hold (hold)
= include (ɪn'klud)
= comprise (kəm'praɪz)
= involve (ɪn'valv)
= *consist of*
② = control (kən'trol)
= restrain (rɪs'tren)
= curb (kɜb)

contaminate (kən'tæməˌnet)
v. 污染

= pollute (pə'lut)
= corrupt (kə'rʌpt)
= defile (dɪ'faɪl)
= infect (ɪn'fɛkt)

contemplate ('kantəmˌplet) *v.*
①考慮 ②打算

① = consider (kən'sɪdə)
= think (θɪŋk)
= study ('stʌdɪ)
= ponder ('pandə)
= reflect (rɪ'flɛkt)
= deliberate (dɪ'lɪbəˌret)

② = plan (plæn)
= intend (ɪn'tɛnd)
= expect (ɪk'spɛkt)

contemptible (kən'tɛmptəbḷ)
adj. 可鄙的

= mean (min)
= atrocious (ə'troʃəs)
= wicked ('wɪkɪd)
= cruel ('kruəl)
= brutal ('brutḷ)
= ruthless ('ruθlɪs)
= terrible ('tɛrəbḷ)
= horrible ('harəbḷ)
= dreadful ('drɛdfəl)
= awful ('ɔful , 'ɔfḷ)
= vile (vaɪl)
= wretched ('rɛtʃɪd)

contend (kən'tɛnd) *v.* 爭鬥；
爭論

= fight (faɪt)
= struggle ('strʌgḷ)
= argue ('argju)
= quarrel ('kwɔrəl , 'kwar-)

contented (kən'tɛntɪd) *adj.*
滿足的

= satisfied ('sætɪsˌfaɪd)
= pleased (plizd)
= delighted (dɪ'laɪtɪd)

contest (*v.* kən'tɛst , *n.* 'kantɛst)
① *v.* 爭鬥；爭論 ② *n.* 比賽

① = contend (kən'tɛnd)
= fight (faɪt)

= struggle ('strʌgl̩)
= argue ('argju)
= quarrel ('kwɔrəl , 'kwar-)
② = game (gem)
= sport (spɔrt , sport)
= tournament ('tɜnəmənt , 'tʊr-)

continue (kən'tɪnju) v. 繼續

= last (læst , lɑst)
= endure (ɪn'djʊr)
= persist (pɚ'zɪst , -'sɪst)
= *go on*
= *keep on*

contortion (kən'tɔrʃən) n.
扭歪；彎曲

= twist (twɪst)
= distortion (dɪs'tɔrʃən)
= crookedness ('krʊkɪdnɪs)

contour ('kantʊr) n. 外形；輪廓

= outline ('aut͵laɪn)
= profile ('profaɪl)
= form (fɔrm)

contraband ('kantrə͵bænd)
adj. 違法的；違禁的

= prohibited (pro'hɪbɪtɪd)
= forbidden (fɚ'bɪdn̩)
= illegal (ɪ'ligl̩)
= smuggled ('smʌgl̩d)
= outlawed ('aut͵lɔd)

1. **contract** (v. kən'trækt ,
n. 'kantrækt) ① v. 形成；沾染
② n. 合約

① = form (fɔrm)
= start (start)
= *enter into*
② = agreement (ə'grimənt)
= pact (pækt)
= understanding (͵ʌndɚ'stændɪŋ)
= bargain ('bargɪn)
= treaty ('tritɪ)
= alliance (ə'laɪəns)
= deal (dil)

2. **contract** (kən'trækt) v. 收縮

= shrink (ʃrɪŋk)
= reduce (rɪ'djus)
= compress (kəm'prɛs)

contradict (͵kantrə'dɪkt) v.
反駁；否認

= deny (dɪ'naɪ)
= oppose (ə'poz)
= dispute (dɪ'spjut)

contrary ('kantrɛrɪ) adj.
反對的；相反的

= opposed (ə'pozd)
= opposite ('apəzɪt)
= different ('dɪfərənt)
= clashing ('klæʃɪŋ)
= conflicting (kən'flɪktɪŋ)

contrast (kən'træst) v. 對比

= compare (kəm'pɛr)
= match (mætʃ)
= liken ('laɪkən)
= measure ('mɛʒɚ)

C

contribute (kən'trɪbjut) v.
捐助；貢獻

= give (gɪv)
= donate ('donet)
= participate (pə'tɪsə,pet , par-)
= provide (prə'vaɪd)

contrite ('kɑntraɪt , kɑn'traɪt)
adj. 後悔的

= regretful (rɪ'grɛtfḷ)
= sorry ('sɔrɪ , 'sarɪ)
= penitent ('pɛnətənt)

contrive (kən'traɪv) v. 發明；
計畫

= invent (ɪn'vɛnt)
= scheme (skim)
= plan (plæn)
= plot (plɑt)
= devise (dɪ'vaɪs)
= conspire (kən'spaɪr)

control (kən'trol) v. ①指揮
②約束

① = command (kə'mænd)
= influence ('ɪnfluəns)
= master ('mæstɚ , 'mɑstɚ)
② = restrain (rɪ'stren)
= check (tʃɛk)
= contain (kən'ten)
= curb (kɝb)

controversy ('kɑntrə,vɝsɪ) n.
爭論

= dispute (dɪ'spjut)
= argument ('ɑrgjəmənt)

= quarrel ('kwɔrəl , 'kwar-)

convalesce (,kɑnvə'lɛs) v. 病癒

= recover (rɪ'kʌvɚ)
= rally ('rælɪ)
= heal (hil)
= recuperate (rɪ'kjupə,ret)
= improve (ɪm'pruv)

convene (kən'vin) v. 集合

= gather ('gæðɚ)
= meet (mit)
= assemble (ə'sɛmbḷ)

convenient (kən'vinjənt) adj.
方便的；易得的

= handy ('hændɪ)
= suitable ('sutəbḷ , 'sju-)
= timely ('taɪmlɪ)
= nearby ('nɪr,baɪ)

conventional (kən'vɛnʃənḷ)
adj. 傳統的；習慣的

= customary ('kʌstəm,ɛrɪ)
= usual ('juʒuəl)
= traditional (trə'dɪʃənḷ)
= accepted (ək'sɛptɪd , æk-)
= established (ə'stæblɪʃt)
= formal ('fɔrmḷ)

converse (kən'vɝs) v. 談話

= talk (tɔk)
= discuss (dɪ'skʌs)
= *speak with*
= *communicate with*

convert ﹝kən'vɜt﹞ v. 改變

  = change ﹝tʃendʒ﹞
  = transform ﹝træns'fɔrm﹞

convey ﹝kən've﹞ v. ①運輸
②通知 ③傳遞

① = carry ﹝'kærɪ﹞
  = transport ﹝træns'port﹞
  = take ﹝tek﹞
② = communicate ﹝kə'mjunə,ket﹞
  = inform ﹝ɪn'fɔrm﹞
  = tell ﹝tɛl﹞
  = enlighten ﹝ɪn'laɪtn̩﹞
  = report ﹝rɪ'port﹞
③ = transfer ﹝træns'fɝ﹞
  = consign ﹝kən'saɪn﹞
  = entrust ﹝ɪn'trʌst﹞
  = send ﹝sɛnd﹞
  = deliver ﹝dɪ'lɪvɚ﹞
  = *hand over*

convict ﹝kən'vɪkt﹞ v. 判定有罪

  = condemn ﹝kən'dɛm﹞
  = doom ﹝dum﹞
  = sentence ﹝'sɛntəns﹞

convince ﹝kən'vɪns﹞ v. 使相信；
說服

  = persuade ﹝pɚ'swed﹞
  = assure ﹝ə'ʃur﹞
  = promise ﹝'pramɪs﹞
  = guarantee ﹝,gærən'ti﹞
  = pledge ﹝plɛdʒ﹞
  = *make certain*

convoy ﹝kən'vɔɪ﹞ v. 護衛；護送

  = accompany ﹝ə'kʌmpənɪ﹞
  = escort ﹝ɪ'skɔrt﹞
  = protect ﹝prə'tɛkt﹞
  = conduct ﹝kən'dʌkt﹞
  = guide ﹝gaɪd﹞
  = lead ﹝lid﹞

convulsion ﹝kən'vʌlʃən﹞ n.
震動；騷動

  = fit ﹝fɪt﹞
  = tantrum ﹝'tæntrəm﹞
  = seizure ﹝'siʒɚ﹞
  = spasm ﹝'spæzəm﹞
  = attack ﹝ə'tæk﹞

cook ﹝kʊk﹞ v. 烹調

  = prepare ﹝prɪ'pɛr﹞

cool ﹝kul﹞ adj. ①微冷的
②冷靜的

① = chilly ﹝'tʃɪlɪ﹞
  = fresh ﹝frɛʃ﹞
② = calm ﹝kɑm﹞
  = unexcited ﹝,ʌnɪk'saɪtɪd﹞

cooperate ﹝ko'apə,ret﹞ v. 合作

  = assist ﹝ə'sɪst﹞
  = collaborate ﹝kə'læbə,ret﹞
  = *work together*

coordinate ﹝ko'ɔrdn̩,et﹞ v.
協調

  = arrange ﹝ə'rendʒ﹞
  = organize ﹝'ɔrgən,aɪz﹞
  = harmonize ﹝'hɑrmə,naɪz﹞

cope (kop) *v.* 對付

  = struggle ('strʌgḷ)
  = face (fes)
  = *put up*

copious ('kopɪəs) *adj.* 豐富的

  = plentiful ('plɛntɪfəl)
  = abundant (ə'bʌndənt)
  = ample ('æmpḷ)

copy ('kapɪ) *v.* 摹倣；複製

  = imitate ('ɪmə,tet)
  = repeat (rɪ'pit)
  = duplicate ('djuplə,ket)
  = reproduce (,riprə'djus)

cordial ('kɔrdʒəl) *adj.* 熱誠的

  = sincere (sɪn'sɪr)
  = hearty ('hartɪ)
  = warm (wɔrm)
  = friendly ('frɛndlɪ)
  = hospitable ('haspɪtəbḷ)

corporation (,kɔrpə'reʃən) *n.*
公司

  = industry ('ɪndəstrɪ)
  = company ('kʌmpənɪ)
  = business ('bɪznɪz)
  = firm (fɜm)
  = enterprise ('ɛntɚ,praɪz)

corpulent ('kɔrpjələnt) *adj.*
肥大的

  = fat (fæt)
  = stout (staut)

  = chubby ('tʃʌbɪ)
  = plump (plʌmp)
  = round (raund)
  = fleshy ('flɛʃɪ)
  = pudgy ('pʌdʒɪ)
  = stocky ('stakɪ)
  = tubby ('tʌbɪ)
  = chunky ('tʃʌŋkɪ)

corral (kə'ræl) *v.* 圍捕

  = surround (sə'raund)
  = capture ('kæptʃɚ)
  = herd (hɜd)
  = enclose (ɪn'kloz)
  = *hem in*
  = *round up*
  = *fence in*

correct (kə'rɛkt) ① *v.* 改正
② *adj.* 正確的

  ① = mark (mark)
  = change (tʃendʒ)
  = remedy ('rɛmədɪ)
  = adjust (ə'dʒʌst)
  ② = true (tru)
  = right (raɪt)
  = proper ('prapɚ)
  = accurate ('ækjərɪt)

correspond (,kɔrə'spand) *v.*
①通信 ②調和

  ① = write (raɪt)
  = *communicate with*
  ② = agree (ə'gri)
  = harmonize ('harmə,naɪz)
  = resemble (rɪ'zɛmbḷ)

corridor ('kɔrədə , -,dɔr , 'kɑr-) *n.* 走廊

= hallway ('hɔl,we)
= passageway ('pæsɪdʒ,we)
= aisle (aɪl)

corroborate (kə'rɑbə,ret) *v.* 證實

= confirm (kən'fɝm)
= establish (ə'stæblɪʃ)
= verify ('vɛrɪ,faɪ)
= substantiate (səb'stænʃɪ,et)
= prove (pruv)
= O.K. ('o'ke)

corrode (kə'rod) *v.* 腐蝕；損害

= deteriorate (dɪ'tɪrɪə,ret)
= rot (rɑt)
= rust (rʌst)
= *eat away*

corrupt (kə'rʌpt) *adj.* 腐敗的；敗德的

= wicked ('wɪkɪd)
= evil ('ivl)
= rotten ('rɑtn)
= dishonest (dɪs'ɑnɪst)
= crooked ('krukɪd)
= shady ('ʃedɪ)

cost (kɔst) *n.* ①價值 ②損失

①= price (praɪs)
= charge (tʃɑrdʒ)
= rate (tet)
= amount (ə'maunt)

②= loss (lɔs)
= sacrifice ('sækrə,faɪs , -,faɪz)
= expense (ɪk'spɛns)

costume (kɑs'tjum) *v.* 著裝

= outfit ('aut,fɪt)
= dress (drɛs)
= equip (ɪ'kwɪp)
= fit (fɪt)
= suit (sut , sjut)

council ('kaunsl) *n.* 會議；顧問委員會

= conference ('kɑnfərəns)
= assembly (ə'sɛmblɪ)
= committee (kə'mɪtɪ)
= group (grup)
= delegation (,dɛlə'geʃən)

counsel ('kaunsl) *v.* 商議；勸告

= advise (əd'vaɪz)
= recommend (,rɛkə'mɛnd)
= instruct (ɪn'srʌkt)
= suggest (səg'dʒɛst , sə'dʒɛst)
= confer (kən'fɝ)

count (kaunt) *v.* ①計算 ②依賴 ③以為

①= add (æd)
= total ('totl)
= number ('nʌmbə)
②= depend (dɪ'pɛnd)
= rely (rɪ'laɪ)
③= consider (kən'sɪdə)
= regard (rɪ'gɑrd)
= judge (dʒʌdʒ)

countenance (ˈkaʊntənəns) *n.* 面容

= appearance (əˈpɪrəns)

= expression (ɪkˈsprɛʃən)

= face (fes)

= looks (lʊks)

counteract (ˌkaʊntɚˈækt) *v.* ①抵消 ②抵制；反對

① = offset (ɔfˈsɛt , ɑf-)

= balance (ˈbæləns)

= neutralize (ˈnjutrəlˌaɪz)

② = oppose (əˈpoz)

= contradict (ˌkɑntrəˈdɪkt)

= cross (krɔs)

= *act against*

counterfeit (ˈkaʊntɚfɪt) *adj.* 假冒的

= copied (ˈkɑpɪd)

= imitative (ˈɪmətətɪv)

= fake (fek)

= artificial (ˌɑrtəˈfɪʃəl)

countersign (ˈkaʊntɚˌsaɪn) *n.* 口令

= password (ˈpæsˌwɝd , ˈpɑs-)

= watchword (ˈwɑtʃˌwɝd)

= *secret signal*

countless (ˈkaʊntlɪs) *adj.* 無數的

= many (ˈmɛnɪ)

= endless (ˈɛndlɪs)

= unlimited (ʌnˈlɪmɪtɪd)

= innumerable (ɪˈnjumərəbl̩)

country (ˈkʌntrɪ) *n.* 國土

= land (lænd)

= region (ˈridʒən)

= nation (ˈneʃən)

= territory (ˈtɛrəˌtorɪ , -ˌtɔrɪ)

couple (ˈkʌpl̩) *v.* 連結；結合

= join (dʒɔɪn)

= pair (pɛr , pær)

= team (tim)

courage (ˈkɝɪdʒ) *n.* 勇氣

= bravery (ˈbrevərɪ)

= boldness (ˈboldnɪs)

= valor (ˈvælɚ)

= gallantry (ˈgæləntrɪ)

courier (ˈkʊrɪɚ , ˈkɝɪɚ) *n.* 信差

= messenger (ˈmɛsn̩dʒɚ)

= runner (ˈrʌnɚ)

course (kors , kɔrs) *n.* 路線；方向

= direction (dəˈrɛkʃən , daɪ-)

= line (laɪn)

= way (we)

= track (trækt)

= channel (ˈtʃænl̩)

court (kort , kɔrt) ① *v.* 求愛 ② *n.* 庭院 ③ *n.* 場 ④ *n.* 法庭

① = please (pliz)

= pursue (pɚˈsu)

= woo (wu)

② = yard (jɑrd)

= enclosure (ɪnˈkloʒɚ)

③ = playground（'pleɪˌgraʊnd）
  = field（fild）
④ = tribunal（trɪ'bjunḷ, traɪ- ）

courteous（'kɝtɪəs）*adj.*
殷勤的；有禮貌的

  = polite（pə'laɪt）
  = civil（'sɪvḷ）
  = gracious（'greʃəs）
  = obliging（ə'blaɪdʒɪŋ）
  = respectful（rɪ'spɛktfəl）

courtly（'kortlɪ, 'kɔrt- ）*adj.*
優雅的；有禮貌的

  = elegant（'ɛləgənt）
  = courteous（'kɝtɪəs）
  = polite（pə'laɪt）
  = civil（'sɪvḷ）
  = gracious（'greʃəs）
  = obliging（ə'blaɪdʒɪŋ）
  = respectful（rɪ'spɛktfəl）

covenant（'kʌvənənt,
'kʌvnənt）*n.* 合約

  = agreement（ə'grimənt）
  = pact（pækt）
  = contract（'kɑntrækt）
  = understanding（ˌʌndə'stændɪŋ）
  = bargain（'bɑrgɪn）
  = treaty（'tritɪ）
  = alliance（ə'laɪəns）
  = concord（'kɑŋkɔrd, 'kɑn- ）

cover（'kʌvɚ）*v.* ①掩藏
②包含

① = hide（haɪd）

  = protect（prə'tɛkt）
  = shelter（'ʃɛltɚ）
  = conceal（kən'sil）
② = include（ɪn'klud）
  = comprise（kəm'praɪz）
  = contain（kən'ten）
  = involve（ɪn'vɑlv）
  = *consist of*

covert（'kʌvɚt）① *adj.* 隱密的
② *n.* 掩蔽處

① = secret（'sikrɪt）
  = hidden（'hɪdṇ）
  = disguised（dɪs'gaɪzd）
  = covered（'kʌvɚd）
  = veiled（veld）
  = concealed（kən'sild）
② = shelter（'ʃɛltɚ）
  = hideaway（'haɪdəˌwe）
  = refuge（'rɛfjudʒ）
  = *hiding place*

covet（'kʌvɪt）*v.* 貪求；妄圖

  = desire（dɪ'zaɪr）
  = crave（krev）
  = lust（lʌst）
  = want（wɑnt, wɔnt）
  = envy（'ɛnvɪ）

coward（'kaʊɚd）*n.* 膽怯的人

  = weakling（'wiklɪŋ）

cower（'kaʊɚ）*v.* 畏縮

  = crouch（kraʊtʃ）
  = squat（skwɑt）
  = cringe（krɪndʒ）

coy (kɔɪ) *adj.* 害羞的

= shy (ʃaɪ)

= modest ('madɪst)

= bashful ('bæʃfəl)

= timid ('tɪmɪd)

= demure (dɪ'mjʊr)

cozy ('kozɪ) *adj.* 安適的

= comfortable ('kʌmfɚtəbḷ)

= snug (snʌg)

= relaxing (rɪ'læksɪŋ)

= homey ('homɪ)

crack (kræk) *n.* ①裂縫
②重擊;響聲

① = break (brek)

= split (splɪt)

= gap (gæp)

= slit (slɪt)

② = blow (blo)

= shot (ʃat)

= bang (bæŋ)

= noise (nɔɪz)

crack-up ('kræk,ʌp) *n.* ①撞碎
②崩潰

① = crash (kræʃ)

= smash (smæʃ)

② = collapse (kə'læps)

= breakdown ('brek,daʊn)

cradle ('kredḷ) ① *v.* 抱持
② *n.* 搖籃

① = support (sə'port , -'pɔrt)

= hold (hold)

= carry ('kærɪ)

② = rocker ('rakɚ)

= bed (bɛd)

craft (kræft , kraft) *n.* 技巧;
手藝

= skill (skɪl)

= trade (tred)

= art (art)

= handicraft ('hændɪ,kræft)

crafty ('kræftɪ , 'kraftɪ) *adj.*
狡猾的

= sly (slaɪ)

= scheming ('skimɪŋ)

= calculating ('kælkjə,letɪŋ)

= plotting ('platɪŋ)

= cunning ('kʌnɪŋ)

cram (kræm) *v.* 塡塞

= stuff (stʌf)

= fill (fɪl)

= load (lod)

= pack (pæk)

= gorge (gɔrdʒ)

= saturate ('sætʃə,ret)

cramp (kræmp) ① *v.* 約束
② *n.* 抽痛

① = confine (kən'faɪn)

= limit ('lɪmɪt)

= restrict (rɪ'strɪk)

= *box in*

② = pain (pen)

= twinge (twɪndʒ)

cranky ('kræŋkɪ) *adj.* 壞脾氣的

= cross〔 krɔs 〕
= irritable〔'ɪrətəbḷ 〕
= churlish〔'tʃɜlɪʃ 〕

crash〔 kræʃ 〕*v.* 撞碎

= strike〔 straɪk 〕
= shatter〔'ʃætə 〕
= break〔 brek 〕
= smash〔 smæʃ 〕

crate〔 kret 〕*n.* 箱子

= box〔 bɑks 〕
= container〔 kən'tenə 〕

crave〔 krev 〕*v.* 渴望

= covet〔'kʌvɪt 〕
= desire〔 dɪ'zaɪr 〕
= lust〔 lʌst 〕
= want〔 wɑnt , wɔnt 〕
= envy〔'ɛnvɪ 〕

crazy〔'krezɪ 〕*adj.* 發狂的

= insane〔 ɪn'sen 〕
= mad〔 mæd 〕
= lunatic〔'lunə,tɪk 〕
= daft〔 dæft 〕
= unbalanced〔 ʌn'bælənst 〕

crease〔 kris 〕*v.* 使皺摺

= ridge〔 rɪdʒ 〕
= wrinkle〔'rɪŋkḷ 〕
= crinkle〔'krɪŋkḷ 〕

create〔 krɪ'et 〕*v.* ①創造
②導致
① = make〔 mek 〕

= form〔 fɔrm 〕
= invent〔 ɪn'vɛnt 〕
= originate〔 ə'rɪdʒə,net 〕
= manufacture〔,mænjə'fæktʃə 〕
② = cause〔 kɔz 〕
= produce〔 prə'djus 〕
= *bring about*

credit〔'krɛdɪt 〕*n.* 信任；光榮

= belief〔 bɪ'lif 〕
= trust〔 trʌst 〕
= faith〔 feθ 〕
= honor〔'ɑnə 〕

credulous〔'krɛdʒələs 〕*adj.*
輕信的

= undoubting〔 ʌn'daʊtɪŋ 〕
= believing〔 bɪ'livɪŋ 〕
= trusting〔'trʌstɪŋ 〕
= gullible〔'gʌləbḷ 〕

crest〔 krɛst 〕*n.* ①裝飾；徽章
②動物的毛　③頂

① = decoration〔,dɛkə'reʃən 〕
= insignia〔 ɪn'sɪgnɪə 〕
② = tuft〔 tʌft 〕
= plume〔 plum 〕
③ = peak〔 pik 〕
= ridge〔 rɪdʒ 〕
= summit〔'sʌmɪt 〕
= top〔 tɑp 〕
= crown〔 kraʊn 〕

crestfallen〔'krɛst,fɔlən 〕*adj.*
沮喪的

= dejected〔 dɪ'dʒɛktɪd 〕

= depressed (dɪ'prɛst)
= discouraged (dɪs'kɝɪdʒd)
= downcast ('daʊn,kæst)

crevice ('krɛvɪs) *n.* 裂縫

= cleft (klɛft)
= rift (rɪft)
= gap (gæp)
= break (brek)

crew (kru) *n.* 一群；一組

= staff (stæf , stɑf)
= force (fors , fɔrs)
= gang (gæŋ)

crime (kraɪm) *n.* 罪行

= wrongdoing ('rɔŋ'duɪŋ)
= sin (sɪn)
= vice (vaɪs)
= evil ('ivl)

cringe (krɪndʒ) *v.* 畏縮

= crouch (kraʊtʃ)
= cower ('kaʊɚ)
= squat (skwɑt)

crinkle ('krɪŋkl̩) *v.* 使皺褶

= wrinkle ('rɪŋkl̩)
= ripple ('rɪpl̩)
= crease (kris)

cripple ('krɪpl̩) *v.* 使損傷；
使成殘廢

= damage ('dæmɪdʒ)
= weaken ('wikən)
= disable (dɪs'ebl̩)

= injure ('ɪndʒɚ)

crisis ('kraɪsɪs) *n.* 緊要關頭；
轉捩點

= emergency (ɪ'mɝdʒənsɪ)
= *critical point*
= *crucial period*
= *turning point*

crisp (krɪsp) *adj.* ①脆而易碎的
②新鮮的

① = brittle ('brɪtl̩)
= fragile ('frædʒəl , -aɪl)
= frail (frel)
= breakable ('brekəbl̩)
② = fresh (frɛʃ)
= sharp (ʃɑp)
= clear (klɪr)
= bracing ('bresɪŋ)

critical ('krɪtɪkl̩) *adj.* ①批評的
②危急的

① = disapproving (,dɪsə'pruvɪŋ)
= faultfinding ('fɔlt,faɪndɪŋ)
② = crucial ('kruʃəl)
= decisive (dɪ'saɪsɪv)
= urgent ('ɝdʒənt)
= pressing ('prɛsɪŋ)

crony ('kronɪ) *n.* 密友

= pal (pæl)
= friend (frɛnd)
= buddy ('bʌdɪ)
= companion (kəm'pænjən)
= partner ('pɑrtnɚ)
= comrade ('kɑmræd , 'kɑmrɪd)

= chum〔tʃʌm〕

crook〔krʊk〕① v. 彎曲
② n. 騙子；惡棍

① = hook〔hʊk〕
= bend〔bɛnd〕
= curve〔kɜv〕
② = criminal〔'krɪmənḷ〕
= gangster〔'gæŋstə〕
= lawbreaker〔'lɔ,brekə〕
= thief〔θif〕

croon〔krun〕v. 輕哼；低唱

= hum〔hʌm〕
= sing〔sɪŋ〕
= vocalize〔'vokḷ,aɪz〕

crop〔krɑp〕① v. 修剪
② n. 收成；收穫

① = cut〔kʌt〕
= clip〔klɪp〕
= shear〔ʃɪr〕
② = produce〔'prɑdjus〕
= growth〔groθ〕
= yield〔jild〕
= harvest〔'hɑrvɪst〕

cross〔krɔs〕① v. 橫過
② v. 使交配 ③ v. 反對
④ adj. 易怒的

① = pass〔pæs , pɑs〕
= *step over*
② = mate〔met〕
= interbreed〔,ɪntə'brid〕
③ = oppose〔ə'poz〕
= *go against*

④ = cranky〔'kræŋkɪ〕
= irritable〔'ɪrətəbḷ〕
= churlish〔'tʃɜlɪʃ〕

crouch〔kraʊtʃ〕v. 畏縮；蹲伏

= cower〔'kaʊə〕
= squat〔skwɑt〕
= cringe〔krɪndʒ〕

crowd〔kraʊd〕n. 群眾

= group〔grup〕
= mass〔mæs〕
= throng〔θrɔŋ〕
= mob〔bɑb〕

crown〔kraʊn〕① v. 加冕
② n. 頭 ③ n. 頂端 ④ n. 冠

① = honor〔'ɑnə〕
= reward〔rɪ'wɔrd〕
= glorify〔'glorə,faɪ , 'glɔr-〕
= decorate〔'dɛkə,ret〕
② = head〔hɛd〕
③ = crest〔krɛst〕
= peak〔pik〕
= ridge〔rɪdʒ〕
= summit〔'sʌmɪt〕
= top〔tɑp〕
④ = tiara〔taɪ'ɛrə , tɪ'ɑrə〕
= *head ornament*

crucial〔'kruʃəl〕adj. 決定性的；
迫急的

= important〔ɪm'pɔrtṇt〕
= critical〔'krɪtɪkḷ〕
= urgent〔'ɜdʒənt〕
= decisive〔dɪ'saɪsɪv〕
= pressing〔'prɛsɪŋ〕

C

crucify ('krusə,faɪ) v. 折磨

= torture ('tɔrtʃə)

= torment (tɔr'mɛnt)

= punish ('pʌnɪʃ)

= execute ('ɛksɪ,kjut)

crude (krud) adj. 粗的；未提煉的；生的

= rough (rʌf)

= unrefined (,ʌnrɪ'faɪnd)

= raw (rɔ)

= vulgar ('vʌlgə)

cruel ('kruəl) adj. 殘忍的

= mean (min)

= heartless ('hartlɪs)

= ruthless ('ruθlɪs)

= brutal ('brutl̩)

crumble ('krʌmbl̩) v. 弄碎

= disintegrate (dɪs'ɪntə,gret)

= *break up*

crumple ('krʌmpl̩) v. 壓皺

= crush (krʌʃ)

= crinkle ('krɪŋkl̩)

= wrinkle ('rɪŋkl̩)

= crease (kris)

= ripple ('rɪpl̩)

crusade (kru'sed) n. (為某目的的)運動

= cause (kɔz)

= movement ('muvmənt)

= drive (draɪv)

= campaign (kæm'pen)

crush (krʌʃ) v. ①征服 ②壓榨；減縮

① = subdue (səb'dju)

= conquer ('kaŋkə , 'kɔŋkə)

② = compress (kəm'prɛs)

= squeeze (skwiz)

= press (prɛs)

= reduce (rɪ'djus)

crutch (krʌtʃ) n. 支持

= support (sə'port , -'pɔrt)

= prop (prap)

= brace (bres)

cry (kraɪ) v. 哭泣；大聲喊叫

= wail (wel)

= sob (sab)

= weep (wip)

= bawl (bɔl)

cuddle ('krdl̩) v. 擁抱

= snuggle ('snʌgl̩)

= nestle ('nɛsl̩)

= fondle ('fandl̩)

cudgel ('kʌdʒəl) v. 以棍棒打

= beat (bit)

= club (klʌb)

= whip (hwɪp)

cue (kju) n. 暗示

= hint (hɪnt)

= signal ('sɪgnl̩)

= clue (klu)

= key (ki)

= lead (lid)

cull〔kʌl〕*v.* 選擇

= select〔sə'lɛkt〕
= separate〔'sɛpə,ret〕
= *pick out*

culminate〔'kʌlmə,net〕*v.*
結束；達於高潮

= top〔tap〕
= crown〔kraʊn〕
= end〔ɛnd〕
= terminate〔'tɝmə,net〕

culpable〔'kʌlpəbḷ〕*adj.* 該受譴
責的

= guilty〔'gɪltɪ〕
= faulty〔'fɔltɪ〕
= blamable〔'blem, əbḷ〕

culprit〔'kʌlprɪt〕*n.* 犯罪者

= offender〔ə'fɛndə〕
= sinner〔'sɪnə〕
= wrongdoer〔'rɔŋ'duə , 'rɔŋ,duə〕

cultivate〔'kʌltə,vet〕*v.* 培養

= condition〔kən'dɪʃən〕
= prepare〔prɪ'pɛr〕
= develop〔dɪ'vɛləp〕
= train〔tren〕
= improve〔ɪm'pruv〕

cultured〔'kʌltʃəd〕*adj.*
有修養的

= refined〔rɪ'faɪnd〕
= learned〔'lɝnɪd〕
= polished〔'palɪʃt〕
= well-bred〔'wɛl 'brɛd〕

cumbersome〔'kʌmbəsəm〕*adj.*
笨拙的；累贅的

= clumsy〔'klʌmzɪ〕
= bulky〔'bʌlkɪ〕
= awkward〔'ɔkwəd〕
= unmanageable〔ʌn'mænɪdʒəbḷ〕
= burdensome〔'bɝdṇsəm〕
= troublesome〔'trʌbḷsəm〕

cunning〔'kʌnɪŋ〕*adj.* 狡猾的；
熟練的

= skillful〔'skɪlfəl〕
= clever〔'klɛvə〕
= crafty〔'kræftɪ , 'kraftɪ〕
= sly〔slaɪ〕
= scheming〔'skimɪŋ〕
= calculating〔'kælkjə,letɪŋ〕
= plotting〔'platɪŋ〕

curb〔kɝb〕① *v.* 抑制
② *n.* 路的邊欄

① = check〔tʃɛk〕
= stop〔stap〕
= control〔kən'trol〕
= restrain〔rɪ'stren〕
② = pavement〔'pevmənt〕

cure〔kjʊr〕*v.* 治療；痊癒

= restore〔rɪ'stor , -'stɔr〕
= remedy〔'rɛmədɪ〕
= heal〔hil〕

curious〔'kjʊrɪəs〕*adj.* ①奇怪的
②好奇的

① = strange〔strendʒ〕
= odd〔ad〕

= unusual（ ʌn'juʒʊəl ）

= queer（ kwɪr ）

= peculiar（ pɪ'kjuljə ）

② = inquisitive（ ɪn'kwɪzətɪv ）

currency（'kɝənsɪ ）*n.* 錢幣

= money（'mʌnɪ ）

= cash（ kæʃ ）

= *legal tender*

current（ kɝənt ）① *n.* 水流
② *adj.* 現在的

① = flow（ flo ）

= stream（ strim ）

② = prevalent（'prɛvələnt ）

= present（'prɛznt ）

= happening（'hæpənɪŋ ）

curse（ kɝs ）① *v.* 詛咒
② *n.* 禍因

① = swear（ swɛr ）

② = affliction（ ə'flɪkʃən ）

= trouble（'trʌbl̩ ）

= burden（'bɝdn̩ ）

curt（ kɝt ）*adj.* 唐突的

= abrupt（ ə'brʌpt ）

= sudden（'sʌdn̩ ）

= short（ ʃɔrt ）

= unexpected（ˌʌnɪk'spɛktɪd ）

curtail（ kɝ'tel , kə- ）*v.* 縮短；
縮減

= shorten（'ʃɔrtn̩ ）

= abbreviate（ ə'brivɪˌet ）

= condense（ kən'dɛns ）

= abridge（ ə'brɪdʒ ）

= contract（ kən'trækt ）

= reduce（ rɪ'djus ）

= cut（ kʌt ）

= compress（ kəm'prɛs ）

curve（ kɝv ）*v.* 使彎曲

= bend（ bɛnd ）

= turn（ tɝn ）

= wind（ waɪnd ）

= twist（ twɪst ）

= curl（ kɝl ）

cushion（'kʊʃən ）① *v.* 裝置墊褥
於⋯ ② *n.* 墊子

① = soften（'sɔfən ）

= support（ sə'port , sə'pɔrt ）

② = pillow（'pɪlo ）

custodian（ kʌs'todɪən ）*n.*
管理員；監護人

= guardian（'gɑrdɪən ）

= keeper（'kipə ）

= caretaker（'kɛrˌtekə ）

custom（'kʌstəm ）*n.* 習慣

= tradition（ trə'dɪʃən ）

= use（ jus ）

= habit（'hæbɪt ）

= practice（'præktɪs ）

= way（ we ）

= manner（'mænə ）

cut（ kʌt ）*v.* ①減縮 ②切開

① = reduce（ rɪ'djus ）

= contract（ kən'trækt ）

= abbreviate〔ə'brivɪˌet〕
= shorten〔'ʃɔrtn̩〕
= curtail〔kɝ'tel , kə-〕
= condense〔kən'dɛns〕
= abridge〔ə'brɪdʒ〕
= compress〔kəm'prɛs〕
② = sever〔'sɛvɚ〕
= split〔splɪt〕

cute〔kjut〕*adj.* ①可愛的
②狡黠的

① = pretty〔'prɪtɪ〕
= dainty〔'dentɪ〕
② = clever〔'klɛvɚ〕
= shrewd〔ʃrud〕
= smart〔smɑrt〕
= cunning〔'kʌnɪŋ〕

cycle〔'saɪkl̩〕*n.* 循環

= series〔'sɪrɪz , 'sirɪz〕
= circle〔'sɝkl̩〕

D

dab〔dæb〕*v.* 輕拍；塗敷

= pat〔pæt〕
= smear〔smɪr〕
= coat〔kot〕

dabble〔'dæbl̩〕*v.* 戲水

= splash〔splæʃ〕
= splatter〔'splætɚ〕
= putter〔'pʌtɚ〕
= toy〔tɔɪ〕
= fiddle〔'fɪdl̩〕

daft〔dæft , dɑft〕*adj.* ①愚笨的
②癲狂的

① = silly〔'sɪlɪ〕
= foolish〔'fulɪʃ〕
② = crazy〔'krezɪ〕
= insane〔ɪn'sen〕

daily〔'delɪ〕*adv.* 每日

= regularly〔'rɛgjələlɪ〕
= *day by day*

dainty〔'dentɪ〕*adj.* 嬌美的

= fresh〔frɛʃ〕
= delicate〔'dɛləkət , -kɪt〕
= small〔smɔl〕
= pretty〔'prɪtɪ〕
= cute〔kjut〕

dally〔'dælɪ〕*v.* 荒廢；蹉跎

= loiter〔'lɔɪtɚ〕
= dawdle〔'dɔdl̩〕
= lag〔læg〕
= linger〔'lɪŋgɚ〕
= delay〔dɪ'le〕

damage〔'dæmɪdʒ〕*v.* 傷害

= harm〔hɑrm〕
= hurt〔hɝt〕
= impair〔ɪm'pɛr〕
= spoil〔spɔɪl〕
= ruin〔'ruɪn〕
= upset〔ʌp'sɛt〕

dame〔dem〕*n.* 婦女

= lady〔'ledɪ〕
= woman〔'wumən〕

damn (dæm) *v.* 咒罵；貶責

= condemn (kən'dɛm)

= doom (dum)

= denounce (dı'naʊns)

= censure ('sɛnʃə)

= curse (kɜs)

D

dampen ('dæmpən) *v.* ①使潮濕 ②使沮喪 ③使沉悶

① = moisten ('mɔɪsn̩)

= wet (wet)

= sprinkle ('sprıŋkl̩)

② = depress (dı'prɛs)

= discourage (dıs'kɜɪdʒ)

③ = muffle ('mʌfl̩)

= mute (mjut)

= dull (dʌl)

= deaden ('dɛdn̩)

= smother ('smʌðə)

= suppress (sə'prɛs)

dangerous ('dendʒərəs) *adj.* 危險的

= unsafe (ʌn'sef)

= hazardous ('hæzədəs)

= risky ('rıskı)

= perilous ('pɛrələs)

= chancy ('tʃænsı , 'tʃan-)

dangle ('dæŋgl̩) *v.* 懸垂

= hang (hæŋ)

= droop ('drup)

= sag (sæg)

= swing (swıŋ)

= flap (sæg)

dank (dæŋk) *adj.* 陰濕的

= wet (wet)

= moist (mɔıst)

= damp (dæmp)

= humid ('hjumıd)

= muggy ('mʌgı)

dapper (dæpə) *adj.* 漂亮整潔的

= neat (nit)

= trim (trım)

= smart (smart)

= chic (ʃik)

= natty ('nætı)

= sporty ('sportı , 'spɔrtı)

= dressy ('drɛsı)

= swanky ('swæŋkı)

= well-dressed ('wɛl'drɛst)

daring ('dɛrıŋ) *adj.* 勇敢的；大膽的

= bold (bold)

= fearless ('fırlıs)

= audacious (ɔ'deʃəs)

= foolhardy ('ful,hardı)

= adventurous (əd'vɛntʃərəs)

dark (dark) *adj.* ①黑暗的；朦朧的 ②憂鬱的 ③隱秘的

① = black (blæk)

= obscure (əb'skjur)

② = gloomy ('glumı)

= dismal ('dızml̩)

= somber ('sambə)

= solemn ('saləm)

= grave (grev)

= dreary ('drırı , 'drirı)

③ = hidden ('hɪdn̩)
  = secret ('sikrɪt)
  = concealed (kən'sild)
  = obscured (əb'skjʊrd)

darling ('darlɪŋ) *adj.* 親愛的
  = beloved (bɪ'lʌvd , bɪ'lʌvɪd)
  = dear (dɪr)
  = precious ('prɛʃəs)
  = adored (ə'dord , ə'dɔrd)
  = cherished ('tʃɛrɪʃt)

darn (darn) *v.* 補綴;縫補
  = mend (mɛnd)
  = repair (rɪ'pɛr)
  = fix (fiks)
  = *patch up*

dart (dart) *v.* ①衝 ②投射
① = dash (dæʃ)
  = rush (rʌʃ)
  = scurry ('skɝɪ)
  = scoot (skut)
  = hurry ('hɝɪ)
② = throw (θro)
  = fling (flɪŋ)
  = toss (tɔs)
  = cast (kæst , kast)

dash (dæʃ) ① *v.* 猛進
② *n.* 少量
① = hurry ('hɝɪ)
  = rush (rʌʃ)
  = dart (dart)
  = scamper ('skæmpɚ)
  = hasten ('hesn̩)

② = drop (drɑp)
  = trace (tres)
  = touch (tʌtʃ)
  = pinch (pɪntʃ)

data ('detə , 'dætə , 'datə) *n. pl.*
資料
  = facts (fækts)
  = information (ˌɪnfɚ'meʃən)
  = evidence ('ɛvədəns)
  = proof (pruf)
  = grounds (graʊndz)

date (det) *n.* ①日期 ②約會
③棗子
① = time (taɪm)
  = day (de)
② = appointment (ə'pɔɪntmənt)
  = engagement (ɪn'gedʒmənt)
③ = fruit (frut)

daub (dɔb) *v.* ①塗 ②弄污
③亂塗
① = grease (griz)
  = lubricate ('lubrɪˌket)
  = coat (kot)
  = cover ('kʌvɚ)
② = soil (sɔɪl)
  = dirty ('dɝtɪ)
  = stain (sten)
  = spot (spat)
  = smear (smɪr)
  = tarnish ('tarnɪʃ)
③ = scribble ('skrɪbl̩)
  = scrawl (skrɔl)
  = *paint badly*

daunt ﹝ dɔnt , dɑnt ﹞ v. ①恐嚇；
使失去勇氣

  = frighten ﹙'fraɪtn̩ ﹚
  = discourage ﹙ dɪs'kɝɪdʒ ﹚
  = deter ﹙ dɪ'tɝ ﹚
  = dishearten ﹙ dɪs'hɑrtn̩ ﹚

dauntless ﹙'dɔntlɪs , 'dɑnt- ﹚ adj.
大膽的

  = brave ﹙ brev ﹚
  = fearless ﹙'fɪrlɪs ﹚
  = unafraid ﹙ˌʌnə'fred ﹚

dawdle ﹙'dɔdl̩ ﹚ v. 怠惰

  = idle ﹙'aɪdl̩ ﹚
  = loiter ﹙'lɔɪtɚ ﹚
  = linger ﹙'lɪŋgɚ ﹚
  = delay ﹙ dɪ'le ﹚
  = tarry ﹙'tærɪ ﹚
  = dillydally ﹙'dɪlɪˌdælɪ ﹚

dawn ﹙ dɔn ﹚ n. ①破曉 ②開始

  ① = daybreak ﹙'deˌbrek ﹚
    = sunrise ﹙'sʌnˌraɪz ﹚
  ② = beginning ﹙ bɪ'gɪnɪŋ ﹚
    = start ﹙ stɑrt ﹚
    = commencement
      ﹙ kə'mɛnsmənt ﹚
    = outset ﹙'aʊtˌsɛt ﹚

daze ﹙ dez ﹚ v. 使惶恐

  = confuse ﹙ kən'fjuz ﹚
  = bewilder ﹙ bɪ'wɪldɚ ﹚
  = muddle ﹙'mʌdl̩ ﹚
  = upset ﹙ ʌp'sɛt ﹚

  = ruffle ﹙'rʌfl̩ ﹚

dazzle ﹙'dæzl̩ ﹚ v. 閃耀；使目眩

  = shine ﹙ ʃaɪn ﹚
  = glow ﹙ glo ﹚
  = flash ﹙ flæʃ ﹚
  = glaze ﹙ glez ﹚
  = glare ﹙ glɛr ﹚
  = blind ﹙ blaɪnd ﹚

dead ﹙ dɛd ﹚ adj. ①無生命的
②晦暗的

  ① = lifeless ﹙'laɪflɪs ﹚
    = deceased ﹙ dɪ'sist ﹚
    = gone ﹙ gɔn ﹚
  ② = dull ﹙ dʌl ﹚
    = inactive ﹙ ɪn'æktɪv ﹚
    = flat ﹙ flæt ﹚
    = dreary ﹙'drɪrɪ , 'drirɪ ﹚

deal ﹙ dil ﹚ ① v. 分配 ② v. 交易
③ v. 行為 ④ n. 協議

  ① = allot ﹙ ə'lɑt ﹚
    = grant ﹙ grænt ﹚
    = give ﹙ gɪv ﹚
  ② = trade ﹙ tred ﹚
    = buy ﹙ baɪ ﹚
    = sell ﹙ sɛl ﹚
  ③ = act ﹙ ækt ﹚
    = behave ﹙ bɪ'hev ﹚
  ④ = bargain ﹙'bɑrgɪn ﹚
    = compact ﹙'kɑmpækt ﹚
    = agreement ﹙ ə'grimənt ﹚
    = understanding ﹙ˌʌndɚ'stændɪŋ ﹚
    = transaction ﹙ træns'ækʃən ,
      trænz'ækʃən ﹚

dear ﹝ dır ﹞ *adj.* ①寶貴的
②昂貴的

① = precious ﹝ 'prɛʃəs ﹞
  = darling ﹝ 'darlıŋ ﹞
  = beloved ﹝ bı'lʌvd , bı'lʌvɪd ﹞
  = adored ﹝ ə'dord , ə'dɔrd ﹞
  = admired ﹝ əd'maırd ﹞
  = idolized ﹝ 'aıdḷ,aızd ﹞
② = expensive ﹝ ık'spɛnsıv ﹞
  = costly ﹝ 'kɔstlı ﹞
  = high-priced ﹝ 'haı'praıst ﹞

dearth ﹝ dɜr ﹞ *n.* 缺乏

  = lack ﹝ læk ﹞
  = scarcity ﹝ 'skɛrsətı ﹞
  = shortage ﹝ 'ʃɔrtıdʒ ﹞

debase ﹝ dı'bes ﹞ *v.* 貶低

  = lower ﹝ 'loə ﹞
  = discredit ﹝ dıs'krɛdıt ﹞
  = degrade ﹝ dı'gred ﹞
  = demote ﹝ dı'mot ﹞
  = abase ﹝ ə'bes ﹞
  = *run down*

debate ﹝ dı'bet ﹞ *v.* 討論

  = discuss ﹝ dı'skʌs ﹞
  = argue ﹝ 'argju ﹞
  = reason ﹝ 'rizn̩ ﹞
  = dispute ﹝ dı'spjut ﹞

debris ﹝ də'bri , 'debri ﹞ *n.* 垃圾

  = ruins ﹝ 'ruınz ﹞
  = rubbish ﹝ 'rʌbıʃ ﹞
  = trash ﹝ træʃ ﹞
  = scrap ﹝ skræp ﹞

  = litter ﹝ 'lıtə ﹞
  = residue ﹝ 'rɛzə,dju , -,du ﹞
  = junk ﹝ dʒʌŋk ﹞

debt ﹝ dɛt ﹞ *n.* 債務

  = obligation ﹝,ablə'geʃən ﹞
  = *amount due*

decay ﹝ dı'ke ﹞ *v.* 腐敗

  = rot ﹝ rat ﹞
  = spoil ﹝ spɔıl ﹞
  = crumble ﹝ 'krʌmbḷ ﹞
  = disintegrate ﹝ dıs'ıntə,gret ﹞

decease ﹝ dı'sis ﹞ *v.* 死

  = die ﹝ daı ﹞
  = perish ﹝ 'pɛrıʃ ﹞
  = depart ﹝ dı'part ﹞
  = expire ﹝ ık'spaır ﹞

deceive ﹝ dı'siv ﹞ *v.* 欺騙

  = beguile ﹝ bı'gaıl ﹞
  = trick ﹝ trık ﹞
  = hoax ﹝ hoks ﹞
  = dupe ﹝ djup , dup ﹞
  = betray ﹝ bı'tre ﹞
  = mislead ﹝ mıs'lid ﹞
  = lie ﹝ laı ﹞

decent ﹝ 'disn̩t ﹞ *adj.* ①正當的
②合適的

① = respectable ﹝ rı'spɛktəbḷ ﹞
  = proper ﹝ 'prapə ﹞
  = correct ﹝ kə'rɛkt ﹞
  = right ﹝ raıt ﹞
② = adequate ﹝ 'ædəkwıt ﹞

D

= suitable〔'sutəbḷ , 'sju-〕

= fit〔fɪt〕

= *good enough*

decide〔dɪ'saɪd〕*v.* 決定

= settle〔'sɛtḷ〕

= determine〔dɪ'tɜmɪn〕

= resolve〔rɪ'zɑlv〕

= judge〔dʒʌdʒ〕

decipher〔dɪ'saɪfə〕*v.* 釋明；
解（謎）

= solve〔sɑlv〕

= explain〔ɪk'splen〕

= *figure out*

declare〔dɪ'klɛr〕*v.* 斷言；宣稱

= state〔stet〕

= assert〔ə'sɜt〕

= announce〔ə'naʊns〕

= affirm〔ə'fɜm〕

= say〔se〕

= pronounce〔prə'naʊns〕

decline〔dɪ'klaɪn〕① *v.* 拒絕
② *v.* 降低；減弱　③ *n.* 傾斜

① = refuse〔rɪ'fjuz〕

= reject〔rɪ'dʒɛkt〕

② = sink〔sɪŋk〕

= fail〔fel〕

= fall〔fɔl〕

= weaken〔'wikən〕

= *run down*

③ = slope〔slop〕

= descent〔dɪ'sɛnt〕

= slant〔slænt〕

= hill〔hɪl〕

decompose〔ˌdikəm'poz〕*v.*
腐爛

= decay〔dɪ'ke〕

= rot〔rɑt〕

= crumble〔'krʌmbḷ〕

= disintegrate〔dɪs'ɪntəˌgret〕

decorate〔'dɛkəˌret〕*v.* 裝飾

= adorn〔ə'dɔrn〕

= trim〔trɪm〕

= beautify〔'bjutəˌfaɪ〕

= alleviate〔ə'liviˌet〕

= *fix up*

decorum〔dɪ'korəm〕*n.* 禮節

= decency〔'disṇsɪ〕

= etiquette〔'ɛtɪˌkɛt〕

= manners〔'mænəz〕

= formality〔fɔr'mælətɪ〕

= *social graces*

decoy〔dɪ'kɔɪ〕*n.* 餌

= bait〔bet〕

= lure〔lʊr〕

decrease〔dɪ'kris〕*v.* 減少

= lessen〔'lɛsṇ〕

= diminish〔də'mɪnɪʃ〕

= reduce〔rɪ'djus〕

= curtail〔kɜ'tel , kə-〕

= cut〔kʌt〕

= shorten〔'ʃɔrtṇ〕

= compress〔kəm'prɛs〕

decree〔dɪ'kri〕*v.* 命令

= pronounce〔prə'naʊns〕

D

= order ('ɔrdə)

= rule (rul)

= command (kə'mænd)

= dictate ('dɪktet , dɪk'tet)

= *pass judgment*

dedicate ('dɛdə,ket) v. 奉獻

= inscribe (ɪn'skraɪb)

= devote (dɪ'vot)

= address (ə'drɛs)

= assign (ə'saɪn)

deduct (dɪ'dʌkt) v. 減除

= subtract (səb'trækt)

= remove (rɪ'muv)

= withdraw (wɪð'drɔ , wɪθ-)

= discount (dɪs'kaʊnt)

= *take away*

deed (did) n. ①行為　②契據

① = act (ækt)

= action ('ækʃən)

= performance (pə'fɔrməns)

= doing ('duɪŋ)

② = contract ('kɑntrækt)

= policy ('pɑləsɪ)

deem (dim) v. 認為

= think (θɪŋk)

= believe (bɪ'liv)

= consider (kən'sɪdə)

= judge (dʒʌdʒ)

= regard (rɪ'gɑrd)

= suppose (sə'poz)

= assume (ə'sjum)

deface (dɪ'fes) v. 傷毀

= mar (mɑr)

= blemish ('blɛmɪʃ)

= disfigure (dɪs'fɪgjə)

= deform (dɪ'fɔrm)

defeat (dɪ'fit) v. 擊敗

= overcome (,ovə'kʌm)

= win (wɪn)

= triumph ('traɪəmf)

defect (dɪ'fɛkt , 'difɛkt) n. 缺失

= fault (fɔlt)

= flaw (flɔ)

= weakness ('wiknɪs)

= failing ('felɪŋ)

= shortcoming ('ʃɔrt,kʌmɪŋ)

= blemish ('blɛmɪʃ)

= imperfection (,ɪmpə'fɛkʃən)

= deficiency (dɪ'fɪʃənsɪ)

defend (dɪ'fɛnd) v. 保護

= protect (prə'tɛkt)

= safeguard ('sef,gɑrd)

= shield (ʃild)

= support (sə'port , -'pɔrt)

defenseless (dɪ'fɛnslɪs) adj.
不能保衛自己的

= helpless ('hɛlplɪs)

= unprotected (,ʌnprə'tɛktɪd)

defer (dɪ'fɝ) v. ①延緩　②順從

① = delay (dɪ'le)

= postpone (post'pon)

= *put off*

② = yield〔jild〕

　= submit〔səb'mɪt〕

　= respect〔rɪ'spɛkt〕

　= accept〔ək'sɛpt , æk-〕

　= acknowledge〔ək'nɑlɪdʒ〕

　= *bow to*

deficient〔dɪ'fɪʃənt〕*adj.* 不足的

= lacking〔'lækɪŋ〕

= incomplete〔,ɪnkəm'plit〕

= wanting〔'wɑntɪŋ , 'wɔntɪŋ〕

= needing〔'nidɪŋ〕

= missing〔'mɪsɪŋ〕

defile〔dɪ'faɪl〕*v.* ①弄髒
②列隊行進

① = dirty〔'dɝtɪ〕

　= pollute〔pə'lut〕

　= contaminate〔kən'tæmə,net〕

② = march〔mɑrtʃ〕

　= parade〔pə'red〕

　= file〔faɪl〕

define〔dɪ'faɪn〕*v.* ①闡釋
②立界限

① = explain〔ɪk'splen〕

　= describe〔dɪ'skraɪb〕

　= clarify〔'klærə,faɪ〕

② = fix〔fɪks〕

　= set〔sɛt〕

　= establish〔ə'stæblɪʃ〕

　= outline〔'aut,laɪn〕

definite〔'dɛfənɪt〕*adj.* 明白的

= clear〔klɪr〕

= precise〔prɪ'saɪs〕

= distinct〔dɪ'stɪŋkt〕

= plain〔plen〕

= obvious〔'ɑbvɪəs〕

= evident〔'ɛvədənt〕

= exact〔ɪg'zækt〕

= clear-cut〔'klɪr'kʌt〕

deform〔dɪ'fɔrm〕*v.* 使變形

= disfigure〔dɪs'fɪgjə〕

= blemish〔'blɛmɪʃ〕

= mar〔mɑr〕

= spoil〔spɔɪl〕

= *make ugly*

defraud〔dɪ'frɔd〕*v.* 欺詐

= cheat〔tʃit〕

= swindle〔'swɪndḷ〕

= gyp〔dʒɪp〕

deft〔dɛft〕*adj.* 敏捷的；熟練

= skillful〔'skɪlfəl〕

= nimble〔'nɪmbḷ〕

= clever〔'klɛvə〕

= adept〔ə'dɛpt〕

= expert〔'ɛkspɝt〕

= proficient〔prə'fɪʃənt〕

= apt〔æpt〕

= handy〔'hændɪ〕

= ingenious〔ɪn'dʒinjəs〕

defy〔dɪ'faɪ〕*v.* 反抗

= resist〔rɪ'zɪst〕

= confront〔kən'frʌnt〕

= challenge〔'tʃælɪndʒ〕

= disobey〔,dɪsə'be〕

D

= ignore〔ɪg'nor , -'nɔr〕
= disregard〔ˌdɪsrɪ'gɑrd〕

degrade〔dɪ'gred〕*v.* 降低

= demote〔dɪ'mot〕
= reduce〔rɪ'djus〕
= lower〔'loɚ〕
= downgrade〔'daʊnˌgred〕

degree〔dɪ'gri〕*n.* ①等級
②頭銜

①= step〔stɛp〕
= grade〔gred〕
= notch〔nɑtʃ〕
= amount〔ə'maʊnt〕
= extent〔ɪk'stɛnt〕
= measure〔'mɛʒɚ〕
= period〔'pɪrɪəd〕
②= rank〔ræŋk〕
= title〔'taɪtl̩〕
= honor〔'ɑnɚ〕

deign〔den〕*v.* 屈尊

= stoop〔stup〕
= yield〔jild〕
= concede〔kən'sid〕
= *lower oneself*
= *give in*

deity〔'diətɪ〕*adj.* 神

= divinity〔də'vɪnətɪ〕
= god〔dɑd〕

dejected〔dɪ'dʒɛktɪd〕*adj.*
沮喪的

= sad〔sæd〕

= depressed〔dɪ'prɛst〕
= discouraged〔dɪs'kɝɪdʒd〕
= downcast〔'daʊnˌkæst〕
= disheartened〔dɪs'hɑrtn̩d〕
= despondent〔dɪ'spɑndənt〕
= blue〔blu〕

delay〔dɪ'le〕*v.* 延緩

= detain〔dɪ'ten〕
= postpone〔post'pon〕
= *put off*
= *hold up*

delegate〔'dɛləˌget〕① *v.* 授權
② *n.* 代表

①= assign〔ə'saɪn〕
= authorize〔'ɔθəˌraɪz〕
= entrust〔ɪn'trʌst〕
= appoint〔ə'pɔɪnt〕
= charge〔tʃɑrdʒ〕
②= representative〔ˌrɛprɪ'zɛntətɪv〕
= envoy〔'ɛnvɔɪ〕
= agent〔'edʒənt〕
= deputy〔'dɛpjətɪ〕

deliberate〔*v.* dɪ'lɪbəˌret ,
adj. dɪ'lɪbərɪt〕① *v.* 考慮
② *adj.* 不慌不忙的

①= ponder〔'pɑndɚ〕
= consider〔kən'sɪdɚ〕
= study〔'stʌdɪ〕
= meditate〔'mɛdəˌtet〕
= reflect〔rɪ'flɛkt〕
= *think over*
= *mull over*
②= slow〔slo〕

= leisurely ('liʒəlɪ , 'lɛʒəlɪ)
= easy ('izɪ)
= unhurried (ʌn'hɝɪd)

delicate ('dɛləkət , -kɪt) *adj.*
精緻的;脆弱的

= mild (maɪld)
= soft (sɔft)
= fine (faɪn)
= dainty ('dentɪ)
= frail (frel)
= light (laɪt)
= fragile ('frædʒəl)
= sensitive ('sɛnsətɪv)
= tender ('tɛndɚ)

delicious (dɪ'lɪʃəs) *adj.* 美味的

= tasty ('testɪ)
= savory ('sevərɪ , 'sevrɪ)
= luscious ('lʌʃəs)

delightful (dɪ'laɪtfəl) *adj.*
歡樂的

= pleasant ('plɛznt)
= lovely ('lʌvlɪ)
= charming ('tʃɑrmɪŋ)
= appealing (ə'pilɪŋ)
= pleasing ('plizɪŋ)

delirious (dɪ'lɪrɪəs) *adj.* 精神
錯亂的

= giddy ('gɪdɪ)
= raving ('revɪŋ)
= frantic ('fræntɪk)
= mad (mæd)
= violent ('vaɪələnt)

= hysterical (hɪs'tɛrɪkl̩)

deliver (dɪ'lɪvɚ) *v.* ①遞送
②發言 ③釋放

① = transfer (træns'fɝ)
= pass (pæs , pɑs)
= consign (kən'saɪn)
= give (gɪv)
= *hand over*
② = say (se)
= voice (vɔɪs)
= express (ɪk'sprɛs)
= communicate (kə'mjunə,ket)
= recite (rɪ'saɪt)
= relate (rɪ'let)
③ = free (fri)
= rescue ('rɛskju)
= release (rɪ'lis)
= liberate ('lɪbə,ret)

delude (dɪ'lud) *v.* 欺騙

= mislead (mɪs'lid)
= deceive (dɪ'siv)
= beguile (bɪ'gaɪl)
= hoax (hoks)
= dupe (djup , dup)
= fool (ful)
= betray (bɪ'tre)

deluge ('dɛljudʒ) ① *v.* 泛濫
② *n.* 豪雨;洪水

① = flood (flʌd)
= overflow (,ovɚ'flo)
= overwhelm (,ovɚ'hwɛlm)
= *run over*
② = rain (ren)

= flood〔flʌd〕
= torrent〔'tɔrənt , 'tar- 〕
= storm〔stɔrm〕

delve〔dɛlv〕v. 掘;挖

= search〔sɝtʃ〕
= dig〔dɪg〕
= scoop〔skup〕
= hunt〔hʌnt〕
= look〔lʊk〕
= explore〔ɪk'splor , -'splɔr〕

demand〔dɪ'mænd〕v. ①要求 ②需要

① = ask〔æsk〕
= inquire〔ɪn'kwaɪr〕
= *want to know*
② = require〔rɪ'kwaɪr〕
= need〔nid〕
= want〔wɑnt , wɔnt〕
= *call for*

demeanor〔dɪ'minɚ〕n. 行為

= behavior〔bɪ'hevjɚ〕
= manner〔'mænɚ〕
= conduct〔'kɑndʌkt〕
= way〔we〕
= actions〔'ækʃənz〕

demolish〔dɪ'mɑlɪʃ〕v. 毀壞

= destroy〔dɪ'strɔɪ〕
= wreck〔rɛk〕
= dismantle〔dɪs'mæntl̩〕
= shatter〔'ʃætɚ〕
= *tear apart*

demon〔'dimən〕n. 惡魔

= devil〔'dɛvl̩〕
= fiend〔find〕
= monster〔'mɑnstɚ〕
= ogre〔'ogɚ〕
= *evil spirit*

demonstrate〔'dɛmən,stret〕v. 示範

= display〔dɪ'sple〕
= show〔ʃo〕
= illustrate〔'ɪləstret , ɪ'lʌs- 〕
= clarify〔'klærə,faɪ〕

demote〔dɪ'mot〕v. 降低

= degrade〔dɪ'gred〕
= reduce〔rɪ'djus〕
= lower〔'loɚ〕

demure〔dɪ'mjʊr〕adj. 害羞的

= coy〔kɔɪ〕
= timid〔'tɪmɪd〕
= bashful〔'bæʃfəl〕
= prim〔prɪm〕
= overmodest〔'ovɚ'mɑdɪst〕

denomination
〔dɪ,nɑmə'neʃən〕n. 宗派;名稱

= group〔grup〕
= sect〔sɛkt〕
= class〔klæs , klɑs〕
= kind〔kaɪnd〕
= brand〔brænd〕
= sort〔sɔrt〕
= name〔nem〕

D

denote (dɪ'not) *v.* 表示

= indicate ('ɪndə,ket)

= mean (min)

= say (se)

= signify ('sɪgnə,faɪ)

= imply (ɪm'plaɪ)

= show (ʃo)

= mark (mɑrk)

= express (ɪk'sprɛs)

denounce (dɪ'naʊns) *v.* 告發；當眾指責

= blame (blem)

= censure ('sɛnʃɚ)

= reproach (rɪ'protʃ)

= condemn (kən'dɛm)

= accuse (ə'kjuz)

= charge (tʃɑrdʒ)

= indict (ɪn'daɪt)

= damn (dæm)

dense (dɛns) *adj.* ①濃密的 ②愚蠢的

① = crowded ('kraʊdɪd)

= packed (pækt)

= compact (kəm'pækt)

= thick (θɪk)

= heavy ('hɛvɪ)

= close (klos)

= solid ('sɑlɪd)

= compressed (kəm'prɛst)

② = stupid ('stjupɪd)

= dull (dʌl)

dent (dɛnt) *n.* 凹痕

= pit (pɪt)

= notch (nɑtʃ)

= nick (nɪk)

= impress ('ɪmprɛs)

deny (dɪ'naɪ) *v.* 否認

= refute (rɪ'fjut)

= contradict (,kɑntrə'dɪkt)

= dispute (dɪ'spjut)

= renounce (rɪ'naʊns)

= reject (rɪ'dʒɛkt)

depart (dɪ'pɑrt) *v.* ①離去 ②死

① = leave (liv)

= exit ('ɛgzɪt , 'ɛksɪt)

= *go away*

② = die (daɪ)

= decease (dɪ'sis)

= perish ('pɛrɪʃ)

= *pass away*

depend (dɪ'pɛnd) *v.* 信賴

= rely (rɪ'laɪ)

= trust (trʌst)

= confide (kən'faɪd)

depict (dɪ'pɪkt) *v.* 描寫

= represent (,rɛprɪ'zɛnt)

= portray (por'tre , por-)

= describe (dɪ'skraɪb)

= picture ('pɪktʃɚ)

= illustrate ('ɪləstret , ɪ'lʌs-)

= characterize ('kærɪktə,raɪz)

deplore (dɪ'plor) *v.* 深悔

= regret (rɪ'grɛt)

deportment ﹝ dɪˈportmənt ﹞ *n.*
行為

　= behavior ﹝ bɪˈhevjɚ ﹞
　= conduct ﹝ ˈkɑndʌkt ﹞
　= manners ﹝ ˈmænɚz ﹞
　= action ﹝ ˈækʃən ﹞

deposit ﹝ dɪˈpɑzɪt ﹞ *v.* ①放下
②抵押

　① = lay ﹝ le ﹞
　= place ﹝ ples ﹞
　= leave ﹝ liv ﹞
　= store ﹝ stor , stɔr ﹞
　= *put down*
　② = pledge ﹝ plɛdʒ ﹞
　= stake ﹝ stek ﹞

depot ﹝ ˈdipo , ˈdɛpo ﹞ *n.* ①車站
②庫房

　① = station ﹝ ˈsteʃən ﹞
　= stand ﹝ stænd ﹞
　= post ﹝ post ﹞
　② = storehouse ﹝ ˈstorˌhaʊs , ˈstɔr- ﹞
　= depository ﹝ dɪˈpɑzəˌtorɪ ,
　　-ˌtɔrɪ ﹞
　= warehouse ﹝ ˈwɛrˌhaʊs ﹞

depress ﹝ dɪˈprɛs ﹞ *v.* ①使沮喪
②降低　③減弱

　① = sadden ﹝ ˈsædn̩ ﹞
　= deject ﹝ dɪˈdʒɛkt ﹞
　= discourage ﹝ dɪsˈkɝɪdʒ ﹞
　= dishearten ﹝ dɪsˈhɑrtn̩ ﹞

　② = lower ﹝ ˈloɚ ﹞
　= sink ﹝ sɪŋk ﹞
　= raise ﹝ rez ﹞
　③ = weaken ﹝ ˈwikən ﹞
　= reduce ﹝ rɪˈdjus ﹞
　= lessen ﹝ ˈlɛsn̩ ﹞

deprive ﹝ dɪˈpraɪv ﹞ *v.* 奪去

　= *take away*
　= *take from*

deputy ﹝ ˈdɛpjətɪ ﹞ *n.* 代理人

　= agent ﹝ ˈedʒənt ﹞
　= representative ﹝ ˌrɛprɪˈzɛntətɪv ﹞
　= delegate ﹝ ˈdɛləˌget ﹞

deride ﹝ dɪˈraɪd ﹞ *v.* 嘲笑

　= ridicule ﹝ ˈrɪdɪkjul ﹞
　= *laugh at*
　= *make fun of*

derive ﹝ dəˈraɪv ﹞ *v.* 得到

　= get ﹝ gɛt ﹞
　= obtain ﹝ əbˈten ﹞
　= acquire ﹝ əˈkwaɪr ﹞
　= gain ﹝ gen ﹞
　= secure ﹝ sɪˈkjur ﹞
　= receive ﹝ rɪˈsiv ﹞

derogatory ﹝ dɪˈrɑgəˌtorɪ ,
-ˌtɔrɪ ﹞ *adj.* 誹謗的

　= belittling ﹝ bɪˈlɪtl̩ɪŋ ﹞
　= unfavorable ﹝ ʌnˈfevrəbl̩ ﹞
　= slanderous ﹝ ˈslændərəs ﹞
　= malign ﹝ məˈlaɪn ﹞

D

descend (dɪ'sɛnd) v. 下降

= decline (dɪ'klaɪn)

= fall (fɔl)

= drop (drɑp)

= plunge (plʌndʒ)

descendant (dɪ'sɛndənt) n. 後裔

= child (tʃaɪld)

= offspring ('ɔf,sprɪŋ , 'af-)

describe (dɪ'skraɪb) v. 描寫

= define (dɪ'faɪn)

= characterize ('kærɪktə,raɪz)

= portray (por'tre , pɔr-)

= picture ('pɪktʃə)

= depict (dɪ'pɪkt)

= represent (,rɛprɪ'zɛnt)

= paint (pent)

= tell (tɛl)

desert (dɪ'zɝt) v. 放棄

= leave (liv)

= forsake (fə'sek)

= abandon (ə'bændən)

deserve (dɪ'zɝv) v. 應得

= merit ('mɛrɪt)

= earn (ɝn)

= *be worthy of*

design (dɪ'zaɪn) v. ①設計
②計劃

① = sketch (skɛtʃ)

= draw (drɔ)

= paint (pent)

= picture ('pɪktʃə)

= portray (por'tre , pɔr-)

= depict (dɪ'pɪkt)

② = intend (ɪn'tɛnd)

= plan (plæn)

= propose (prə'poz)

designate ('dɛzɪg,net) v. ①指示
②指名

① = show (ʃo)

= indicate ('ɪndə,ket)

= specify ('spɛsə,faɪ)

= *point out*

② = name (nem)

= nominate ('namə,net)

= appoint (ə'pɔɪnt)

desire (dɪ'zaɪr) v. 意欲

= wish (wɪʃ)

= want (want , wɔnt)

= fancy ('fænsɪ)

= lust (lʌst)

desist (dɪ'zɪst) v. 停止

= stop (stap)

= cease (sis)

= end (ɛnd)

= halt (hɔlt)

= discontinue (,dɪskən'tɪnju)

= abandon (ə'bændən)

desolate ('dɛslɪt) adj. ①荒涼的
②凄涼的

① = empty ('ɛmptɪ)

= vacant ('vekənt)

= void (vɔɪd)

= barren ('bærən)
② = gloomy ('glumɪ)
= dismal ('dɪzml̩)
= dreary ('drɪrɪ , 'drɪrɪ)

despair (dɪ'spɛr) v. 失望
= lose hope
= give up

desperate ('dɛspərɪt) adj.
不顧一切的；猛烈的
= frantic ('fræntɪk)
= wild (waɪld)
= reckless ('rɛklɪs)
= mad (mæd)

despise (dɪ'spaɪz) v. 輕視
= hate (het)
= scorn (skɔrn)
= loathe (loð)
= disdain (dɪs'den)

despoil (dɪ'spɔɪl) v. 奪取
= rob (rab)
= plunder ('plʌndə)
= loot (lut)

despondent (dɪ'spandənt) adj.
沮喪的
= depressed (dɪ'prɛst)
= dejected (dɪ'dʒɛktɪd)
= downhearted ('daʊn'hartɪd)
= downcast ('daʊn,kæst)
= discouraged (dɪs'kɝɪdʒd)

despot ('dɛspət , -pat) n. 暴君

= ruler ('rulə)
= tyrant ('taɪrənt)
= dictator (dɪk'tetə)
= oppressor (ə'prɛsə)
= slave driver

destination (,dɛstə'neʃən) n.
①目的 ②注定
① = end (ɛnd)
= goal (gol)
= objective (əb'dʒɛktɪv)
② = lot (lat)
= fortune ('fɔrtʃən)
= fate (fet)

destitute ('dɛstə,tjut , -,tut) adj.
窮困的
= poor (pʊr)
= penniless ('pɛnɪlɪs)
= bankrupt ('bæŋkrʌpt)
= down-and-out ('daʊnən'aʊt ,
'daʊnənd'aʊt)

destroy (dɪ'strɔɪ) v. ①毀壞
②消滅
① = spoil (spɔɪl)
= ruin ('rʊɪn)
= wreck (rɛk)
= devastate ('dɛvəs,tet)
② = kill (kɪl)
= slay (sle)
= exterminate (ɪk'stɝmə,net)
= finish ('fɪnɪʃ)

detach (dɪ'tætʃ) v. ①分開
②派遣
① = separate ('sɛpə,ret)

D

= unfasten (ʌn'fæsn̩)

= disconnect (,dɪskə'nɛkt)

② = assign (ə'saɪn)

= delegate ('dɛlə,get)

= draft (dræft)

detail ('ditel , dɪ'tel) ① v. 詳述
② v. 選派　③ n. 細節

① = itemize ('aɪtəm,aɪz)

= elaborate (ɪ'læbə,ret)

= *dwell on*

= *tell fully*

② = commission (kə'mɪʃən)

= assign (ə'saɪn)

= delegate ('dɛlə,get)

③ = part (part)

= portion ('porʃən , 'pɔr-)

= fraction ('frækʃən)

= division (də'vɪʒən)

= segment ('sɛgmənt)

= fragment ('frægmənt)

detain (dɪ'ten) v. 阻止

= delay (dɪ'le)

= retard (rɪ'tard)

= *hold up*

= *slow up*

detect (dɪ'tɛkt) v. 發現

= discover (dɪ'skʌvə)

= spy (spaɪ)

= recognize ('rɛkəg,naɪz)

= perceive (pə'siv)

= catch (kætʃ)

deter (dɪ'tɝ) v. 阻礙

= discourage (dɪs'kɝɪdʒ)

= hinder ('hɪndə)

= prevent (prɪ'vɛnt)

= prohibit (pro'hɪbɪt)

determined (dɪ'tɝmɪnd) *adj.*
有決心的

= firm (fɝm)

= sure (ʃur)

= convinced (kən'vɪnst)

= resolute ('rɛzə,lut)

= resolved (rɪ'zalvd)

= serious ('sɪrɪəs)

detest (dɪ'tɛst) v. 憎惡

= hate (het)

= dislike (dɪs'laɪk)

= loathe (loð)

= abhor (eb'hɔr , æb-)

= despise (dɪ'spaɪz)

= scorn (skɔrn)

dethrone (dɪ'θron , di-) v.
罷免

= remove (rɪ'muv)

= dismiss (dɪs'mɪs)

= overthrow (,ovə'θro)

detour ('ditur , dɪ'tur) v. 繞道
而行

= shift (ʃɪft)

= bypass ('baɪ,pæs)

= *go around*

devastate ('dɛvəs,tet) v. 毀壞

= destroy (dɪ'strɔɪ)

= ruin ('ruɪn)
= wreck (rɛk)

develop (dɪ'vɛləp) v. ①發展 ②進化

① = grow (gro)
= flourish ('flɜɪʃ)
= mature (mə'tjʊr , -'tʊr)
② = progress (prə'grɛs)
= advance (əd'væns)

device (dɪ'vaɪs) n. ①裝置 ②策略

① = machine (mə'ʃin)
= apparatus (,æpə'retəs , ,æpə'rætəs)
= tool (tul)
= instrument ('ɪnstrəmənt)
= implement ('ɪmpləmənt)
② = plan (plæn)
= scheme (skim)
= trick (trɪk)

devil ('dɛvḷ) n. 惡魔

= demon ('dimən)
= fiend (find)
= ogre ('ogə)
= monster ('mɑnstə)

devise (dɪ'vaɪz) v. 設計

= plan (plæn)
= invent (ɪn'vɛnt)
= contrive (kən'traɪv)
= arrange (ə'rendʒ)
= create (krɪ'et)
= *make up*

devoid (dɪ'vɔɪd) adj. 空的

= empty ('ɛmpti)
= vacant ('vekənt)
= bare (bɛr)
= blank (blæŋk)

devote (dɪ'vot) v. 奉獻

= dedicate ('dɛdə,ket)
= assign (ə'saɪn)
= apply (ə'plaɪ)

devotion (dɪ'voʃən) n. ①摯愛 ②忠誠

① = affection (ə'fɛkʃən)
= love (lʌv)
= fondness ('fɑndnɪs)
= liking ('laɪkɪŋ)
② = loyalty ('lɔɪəltɪ)
= dedication (,dɛdə'keʃən)

devour (dɪ'vaʊr) v. ①吃 ②破壞

① = eat (it)
= consume (kən'sum , -'sjum)
= swallow ('swɑlo)
② = waste (west)
= destroy (dɪ'strɔɪ)
= ruin ('ruɪn)

devout (dɪ'vaʊt) adj. ①虔誠的 ②熱誠的

① = religious (rɪ'lɪdʒəs)
= pious ('paɪəs)
② = earnest ('ɜnɪst , -əst)
= sincere (sɪn'sɪr)
= hearty ('hɑrtɪ)

D

= devoted〔dɪ'votɪd〕

= serious〔'sɪrɪəs〕

= zealous〔'zɛləs〕

dexterity〔ˌdɛks'tɛrətɪ〕 n. 靈敏

= skill〔skɪl〕

= cleverness〔'klɛvənɪs〕

= competence〔'kampətəns〕

diagnose〔ˌdaɪəg'nos , -'noz〕 v. 分析

= interpret〔ɪn'tɝprɪt〕

= gather〔'gæðɚ〕

= deduce〔dɪ'djus , -'dus〕

= analyze〔'ænḷˌaɪz〕

diagram〔'daɪəˌgræm〕 v. 圖示

= draw〔drɔ〕

= sketch〔skɛtʃ〕

= portray〔por'tre , pɔr-〕

= design〔dɪ'zaɪn〕

= depict〔dɪ'pɪkt〕

dial〔'daɪəl〕 v. 撥電話；收聽

= call〔kɔl〕

= ring〔rɪŋ〕

= *tune in*

dialogue〔'daɪəˌlɔg〕 n. 對話

= conversation〔ˌkanvə'seʃən〕

= talk〔tɔk〕

= speech〔spitʃ〕

= words〔wɝds〕

diary〔'daɪərɪ〕 n. 日記

= memo〔'mɛmo〕

= journal〔'dʒɝnḷ〕

= account〔ə'kaʊnt〕

= chronicle〔'kranɪkḷ〕

= *record book*

dice〔daɪs〕 ① v. 切成小方塊 ② n. 骰子

① = cube〔kjub〕

= cut〔kʌt〕

② = cubes〔kjubz〕

dictate〔'dɪktet , dɪk'tet〕 v. ①命令　②要求

① = order〔'ɔrdɚ〕

= demand〔dɪ'mænd〕

= direct〔də'rɛkt , daɪ-〕

= instruct〔ɪn'strʌkt〕

= rule〔rul〕

= charge〔tʃardʒ〕

② = advise〔əd'vaɪz〕

= recommend〔ˌrɛkə'mɛnd〕

= suggest〔sə'dʒɛst , səg'dʒɛst〕

die〔daɪ〕 v. 死

= decease〔dɪ'sis〕

= perish〔'pɛrɪʃ〕

= expire〔ɪk'spaɪr〕

= *pass away*

different〔'dɪfərənt〕 adj. 不同的

= unlike〔ʌn'laɪk〕

= distinct〔dɪ'stɪŋkt〕

= opposite〔'apəzɪt〕

= contrary〔'kantrɛrɪ〕

= reverse〔rɪ'vɝs〕

= dissimilar〔dɪ'sɪmələ , dɪs'sɪ-〕

D

= varied ('vɛrɪd)

= assorted (ə'sɔrtɪd)

difficult ('dɪfə,kʌlt , 'dɪfəkəlt)
adj. 困難的

= hard (hɑrd)

= rough (rʌf)

= rugged ('rʌgɪd)

= arduous ('ɑrdʒʊəs)

dig (dɪg) *v.* 掘；挖

= scoop (skup)

= excavate ('ɛkskə,vet)

= gouge (gaʊdʒ)

= tunnel ('tʌnl̩)

digest (də'dʒɛst , daɪ'dʒɛst) *v.*
①消化　②了解

① = absorb (əb'sɔrb)

② = understand (,ʌndə'stænd)

= comprehend (,kɑmprɪ'hɛnd)

= grasp (græsp)

= *catch on*

digit ('dɪdʒɪt) *n.* ①數目　②手指
或足趾

① = number ('nʌmbə)

= numeral ('njumərəl)

= figure ('fɪgjə , 'fɪgə)

② = *finger or toe*

dignified ('dɪgnə,faɪd) *adj.*
高貴的

= noble ('nobl̩)

= worthy ('wɜðɪ)

= stately ('stetlɪ)

= majestic (mə'dʒɛstɪk)

= grand (grænd)

dilapidated (də'læpə,detɪd)
adj. 毀壞的

= decayed (dɪ'ked)

= ruined ('ruɪnd)

= battered ('bætəd)

= broken-down ('brokən'daʊn)

= run-down ('rʌn'daʊn , -,daʊn)

dilate (daɪ'let , dɪ-) *v.* 擴大

= expand (ɪk'spænd)

= enlarge (ɪn'lɑrdʒ)

= widen ('waɪdn̩)

= broaden ('brɔdn̩)

= magnify ('mægnə,faɪ)

= increase (ɪn'kris)

diligent ('dɪlədʒənt) *adj.* 勤勞的

= industrious (ɪn'dʌstrɪəs)

= energetic (,ɛnə'dʒɛtɪk)

= hard-working ('hɑrd'wɜkɪŋ)

dillydally ('dɪlɪ,dælɪ) *v.* 遊蕩

= loiter ('lɔɪtə)

= delay (dɪ'le)

= tarry ('tærɪ)

= linger ('lɪŋgə)

= dawdle ('dɔdl̩)

dilute (dɪ'lut , daɪ'lut) *v.* 變弱

= weaken ('wikən)

= reduce (rɪ'djus)

= thin (θɪn)

= cut (kʌt)

= *water down*

D

dim (dɪm) *adj.* 微暗的

= faint (fent)

= weak (wik)

= pale (pel)

= indistinct (ˌɪndɪ'stɪŋkt)

= vague (veg)

= darkish ('dɑrkɪʃ)

dimension (də'mɛnʃən) *n.* 大小

= measurement ('mɛʒəmənt)

= size (saɪz)

= expanse (ɪk'spæns)

= proportions (prə'porʃənz, -'pɔr-)

diminish (də'mɪnɪʃ) *v.* 減少

= decrease (dɪ'kris , ˌdi'kris)

= reduce (rɪ'djus)

= lessen ('lɛsn̩)

= curtail (kɜ'tel , kə-)

= cut (kʌt)

din (dɪn) *n.* 喧聲

= noise (nɔɪz)

= racket ('rækɪt)

= clamor ('klæmə)

= uproar ('ʌp,ror , -,rɔr)

= tumult ('tjumʌlt)

dine (daɪn) *v.* ①用餐 ②供養

① = eat (it)

= sup (sʌp)

② = feed (fid)

= nourish ('nɝɪʃ)

dingy ('dɪndʒɪ) *adj.* 骯髒的

= dirty ('dɝtɪ)

= dull (dʌl)

= grimy ('graɪmɪ)

= dark (dɑrk)

= gray (gre)

dip (dɪp) *v.* 浸水

= sink (sɪŋk)

= ladle ('ledl̩)

= immerse (ɪ'mɝs)

= dunk (dʌŋk)

diplomat ('dɪplə,mæt) *n.* 外交家

= politician (ˌpɑlə'tɪʃən)

= envoy ('ɛnvɔɪ)

= ambassador (æm'bæsədə)

= emissary ('ɛmə,sɛrɪ)

= *a tactful person*

dire (daɪr) *adj.* 可怕的

= bad (bæd)

= terrible ('tɛrəbl̩)

= dreadful ('drɛdfəl)

= horrible ('hɑrəbl̩)

= awful ('ɔful , -fl̩)

= wretched ('rɛtʃɪd)

= disastrous (dɪz'æstrəs , -'as-)

= tragic ('trædʒɪk)

= black (blæk)

direct (də'rɛkt , daɪ-) *v.* ①管理 ②命令 ③指引 ④書寫

① = manage ('mænɪdʒ)

= control (kən'trol)

= conduct (kən'dʌkt)

= handle（'hændḷ）
= head（hɛd）
= govern（'gʌvən）
= rule（rul）
= regulate（'rɛgjə‚let）
② = order（'ɔrdə）
= command（kə'mænd）
= dictate（'dɪktet，dɪk'tet）
= instruct（ɪn'strʌkt）
= charge（tʃɑrdʒ）
③ = show（ʃo）
= point（pɔɪnt）
= aim（em）
④ = address（ə'drɛs）
= inscribe（ɪn'skraɪb）

dirty（'dɝtɪ）*adj.* 骯髒的

= grimy（'graɪmɪ）
= soiled（sɔɪld）
= muddy（'mʌdɪ）
= untidy（ʌn'taɪdɪ）
= dingy（'dɪndʒɪ）
= messy（'mɛsɪ）
= sloppy（'slɑpɪ）

disable（dɪs'ebḷ）*v.* 使殘廢；
使無能力

= cripple（'krɪpḷ）
= weaken（'krɪpḷ）
= *make useless*
= *put out of order*

disadvantage（‚dɪsəd'væntɪdʒ）
n. 缺點；不便

= drawback（'drɔ‚bæk）
= handicap（'hændɪ‚kæp）

= liability（‚laɪə'bɪlətɪ）
= inconvenience（‚ɪnkən'vinjəns）

disagree（‚dɪsə'gri）*v.* 不合

= differ（'dɪfə）
= quarrel（'kwɔrəl，'kwɑr-）
= conflict（kən'flɪkt）
= dispute（dɪ'spjut）

disappear（‚dɪsə'pɪr）*v.* 消失

= vanish（'vænɪʃ）
= *go away*
= *fade out*

disappoint（‚dɪsə'pɔɪnt）*v.*
使失望

= dissatisfy（dɪs'sætɪs‚faɪ）
= displease（dɪs'pliz）
= *let down*

disapprove（‚dɪsə'pruv）*v.*
不贊成

= disfavor（dɪs'fevə）
= oppose（ə'poz）
= frown *upon*
= *object to*

disarm（dɪs'ɑrm，dɪz-）*v.*
解除…的武裝

= demilitarize（di'mɪlətə‚raɪz）
= paralyze（'pærə‚laɪz）
= *make powerless*

disaster（dɪz'æstə）*n.* 災禍

= casualty（'kæʒʊəltɪ）
= calamity（kə'læmətɪ）

D

= misfortune (mɪs'fɔrtʃən)
= mishap ('mɪs,hæp , mɪs'hæp)
= catastrophe (kə'tæstrəfɪ)
= tragedy ('trædʒədɪ)
= accident ('æksədənt)

disband (dɪs'bænd) v. 解散

= separate ('sɛpə,ret , -pret)
= scatter ('skætə)
= disperse (dɪ'spɜs)
= split (splɪt)
= dismiss (dɪs'mɪs)
= dissolve (dɪ'zɑlv)
= *break up*

discard (dɪs'kɑrd) v. 拋棄

= reject (rɪ'dʒɛkt)
= scrap (skræp)
= *throw away*
= *get rid of*
= *dispose of*
= *cast off*

discern (dɪ'zɜn , -'sɜn) v.
目睹；認識

= see (si)
= behold (bɪ'hold)
= observe (əb'zɜv)
= view (vju)
= perceive (pə'siv)
= recognize ('rɛkəg,naɪz)
= know (no)
= realize ('rɪə,laɪz , 'rɪə-)
= understand (,ʌndə'stænd)
= detect (dɪ'tɛkt)
= spot (spɑt)
= spy (spaɪ)

discharge (dɪs'tʃɑrdʒ) v. 卸貨；
發射

= unload (ʌn'lod)
= release (rɪ'lis)
= dismiss (dɪs'mɪs)
= expel (ɪk'spɛl)
= dump (dʌmp)
= fire (faɪr)
= *let go*

disciple (dɪ'saɪpl̩) n. 信徒

= believer (bɪ'livə)
= follower ('faloə)
= convert ('kɑnvɜt)

discipline ('dɪsəplɪn) v. ①訓練
②懲罰

① = train (tren)
= drill (drɪl)
= exercise ('ɛksə,saɪz)
= practice ('præktɪs)
= prepare (prɪ'pɛr)
= condition (kən'dɪʃən)
= groom (grum)
② = punish ('pʌnɪʃ)
= chastise (tʃæs'taɪz)
= correct (kə'rɛkt)
= penalize ('pinl̩,aɪz , 'pɛnl̩-)

disclaim (dɪs'klem) v. 否認

= deny (dɪ'naɪ)
= refuse (rɪ'fjuz)
= withhold (wɪð'hold , wɪθ-)
= reject (rɪ'dʒɛkt)

disclose (dɪs'kloz) v. 揭發

= uncover (ʌn'kʌvə)

= open ('opən)
= reveal (rɪ'vil)
= show (ʃo)
= expose (ɪk'spoz)
= unmask (ʌn'mæsk)

discolor (dɪs'kʌlə) v. 使褪色

= fade (fed)
= dull (dʌl)
= tarnish ('tɑrnɪʃ)
= bleach (blitʃ)

discomfort (dɪs'kʌmfət) v. 使不舒服

= distress (dɪ'strɛs)
= trouble ('trʌbl)
= bother ('bɑðə)
= disturb (dɪ'stɝb)
= perturb (pə'tɝb)
= upset (ʌp'sɛt)

discord ('dɪskɔrd) n. ①爭論 ②雜音

① = disagreement (,dɪsə'grimənt)
= difference (,dɪfərəns)
= dispute (dɪ'spjut)
= conflict ('kɑnflɪkt)
= friction ('frɪkʃən)
② = noise (nɔɪz)
= racket ('rækɪt)
= din (dɪn)
= clamor ('klæmə)

discount ('dɪskaʊnt , dɪs'kaʊnt) v. ①減少 ②考慮

① = deduct (dɪ'dʌkt)
= subtract (səb'trækt)

= remove (rɪ'muv)
② = consider (kən'sɪdə)
= *allow for*
= *take into account*

discourage (dɪs'kɝɪdʒ) v. 阻止

= deter (dɪ'tɝ)
= prevent (prɪ'vɛnt)
= hinder ('hɪndə)
= disapprove (,dɪsə'pruv)
= deject (dɪ'dʒɛkt)
= daunt (dɔnt , dɑnt)
= *keep from*

discourse (dɪ'skors) v. 演講

= talk (tɔk)
= converse (kən'vɝs)
= lecture ('lɛktʃə)
= preach (pritʃ)
= expound (ɪk'spaʊnd)
= address (ə'drɛs)

discover (dɪ'skʌvə) v. 發現

= reveal (rɪ'vil)
= learn (lɝn)
= observe (əb'zɝv)
= see (si)
= notice ('notɪs)
= perceive (pə'siv)
= find (faɪnd)
= disclose (dɪs'kloz)
= expose (ɪk'spoz)

discredit (dɪs'krɛdɪt) v. ①懷疑 ②使丟臉

① = doubt (daʊt)
= disbelieve (,dɪsbə'liv)

D

D

② = disgrace (dɪs'gres)

= dishonor (dɪs'ɑnɚ)

= shame (ʃem)

= humiliate (hju'mɪlɪ,et)

discreet (dɪ'skrit) *adj.* 小心的

= careful ('kɛrfəl)

= prudent ('prudn̩t)

= considerate (kən'sɪdərɪt)

= thoughtful ('θɔtfəl)

= cautious ('kɔʃəs)

discriminate (dɪ'skrɪmə,net)
v. 分別

= separate ('sɛpə,ret , -prɛt)

= segregate ('sɛgrɪ,get)

= distinguish (dɪ'stɪŋgwɪʃ)

= *set apart*

discuss (dɪ'skʌs) *v.* 討論

= debate (dɪ'bet)

= reason ('rizn̩)

= consider (kən'sɪdɚ)

= confer (kən'fɝ)

= *talk over*

disdain (dɪs'den) *v.* 輕視

= scorn (skɔrn)

= despise (dɪ'spaɪz)

= reject (rɪ'dʒɛkt)

= spurn (spɝn)

disease (dɪ'ziz) *n.* 疾病

= sickness ('sɪknɪs)

= illness ('ɪlnɪs)

= ailment ('elmənt)

= malady ('mælədɪ)

= infirmity (ɪn'fɝmətɪ)

disfigure (dɪs'fɪgjɚ) *v.* 毀壞

= deform (dɪ'fɔrm)

= deface (dɪ'fes)

= blemish ('blɛmɪʃ)

= mar (mar)

= injure ('ɪndʒɚ)

= scar (skar)

= spoil (spɔɪl)

disgrace (dɪs'gres) *v.* 使丟臉

= shame (ʃem)

= dishonor (dɪs'ɑnɚ)

= discredit (dɪs'krɛdɪt)

= humiliate (hju'mɪlɪ,et)

= embarrass (ɪm'bærəs)

disguise (dɪs'gaɪz) *v.* 偽裝

= conceal (kən'sil)

= hide (haɪd)

= cover ('kʌvɚ)

= camouflage ('kæmə,flɑʒ)

= misrepresent (,mɪsrɛprɪ'zɛnt)

disgust (dɪs'gʌst) *v.* 使厭惡

= sicken ('sɪkən)

= offend (ə'fɛnd)

= repel (rɪ'pɛl)

= revolt (rɪ'volt)

= nauseate ('nɔzɪ,et , -zɪ,et)

dish (dɪʃ) ① *v.* 盛於盤中
② *n.* 碟；盤

① = give (gɪv)

= serve〔sɝv〕

② = receptacle〔rɪ'sɛptəkḷ〕

= container〔kən'tenɚ〕

dishearten〔dɪs'hɑrtṇ〕v. 使沮喪

= discourage〔dɪs'kɝɪdʒ〕

= depress〔dɪ'prɛs〕

= sadden〔'sædṇ〕

= deject〔dɪ'dʒɛkt〕

disheveled〔dɪ'ʃɛvḷd, -əld〕adj. 凌亂的

= rumpled〔'rʌmpḷd〕

= mussed〔mʌst〕

= untidy〔ʌn'taɪdɪ〕

= sloppy〔'slɑpɪ〕

disintegrate〔dɪs'ɪntə,gret〕v. 分裂

= separate〔'sɛpə,ret, -pret〕

= decompose〔,dikəm'poz〕

= crumble〔'krʌmbḷ〕

= decay〔dɪ'ke〕

= rot〔rɑt〕

= break up

dismal〔'dɪzmḷ〕adj. 陰沉的

= dark〔dɑrk〕

= gloomy〔'glumɪ〕

= dreary〔'drɪrɪ, 'drirɪ〕

= miserable〔'mɪzərəbḷ, 'mɪzrə-〕

= bleak〔blik〕

= depressing〔dɪ'prɛsɪŋ〕

dismantle〔dɪs'mæntḷ〕v. 拆除

= disassemble〔,dɪsə'sɛmbḷ〕

= demolish〔dɪ'mɑlɪʃ〕

= wreck〔rɛk〕

= take apart

dismay〔dɪs'me〕v. 使驚慌

= bewilder〔bɪ'wɪldɚ〕

= disturb〔dɪ'stɝb〕

= embarrass〔ɪm'bærəs〕

= bother〔'bɑðɚ〕

= confuse〔kən'fjuz〕

= alarm〔ə'lɑrm〕

= frighten〔'fraɪtṇ〕

dismiss〔dɪs'mɪs〕v. 解散

= discharge〔dɪs'tʃɑrdʒ〕

= expel〔ɪk'spɛl〕

= send away

dispatch〔dɪ'spætʃ〕v. ①派遣 ②匆匆做完

① = send〔sɛnd〕

= transmit〔træns'mɪt〕

= forward〔'fɔrwɚd〕

= discharge〔dɪs'tʃɑrdʒ〕

② = hurry〔'hɝɪ〕

= hasten〔'hesṇ〕

= speed〔spid〕

= rush〔rʌʃ〕

dispel〔dɪ'spɛl〕v. 驅散

= scatter〔'skætɚ〕

= disperse〔dɪ'spɝs〕

= drive away

dispense〔dɪ'spɛns〕v. 分配

= distribute〔dɪ'strɪbjut〕

= issue ('ɪʃʊ , 'ɪʃju)

= allot (ə'lɑt)

= grant (grænt)

= *give out*

= *deal out*

= *dole out*

= *mete out*

disperse (dɪ'spɝs) v. 解散

= scatter ('skætɚ)

= distribute (dɪ'strɪbjut)

= spread (sprɛd)

display (dɪ'sple) v. 展示

= demonstrate ('dɛmən,stret)

= illustrate ('ɪləstret , ɪ'lʌstret)

= exhibit (ɪg'zɪbɪt)

= parade (pə'red)

= flaunt (flɔnt)

disposal (dɪ'spozḷ) n. ①清理 ②陳列

① = removal (rɪ'muvḷ)

= elimination (ɪ,lɪmə'neʃən)

= release (rɪ'lis)

② = arrangement (ə'rendʒmənt)

= settlement ('sɛtḷmənt)

= adjustment (ə'dʒʌstmənt)

= administration (əd,mɪnə'streʃən)

disposition (,dɪspə'zɪʃən) n. ①性情 ②排列

① = nature ('netʃɚ)

= temperament ('tɛmprəmənt , -pərə-)

= character ('kærɪktɚ , -ək-)

= inclination (,ɪnklə'neʃən)

② = arrangement (ə'rendʒmənt)

= settlement ('sɛtḷmənt)

= order ('ɔrdɚ)

= adjustment (ə'dʒʌstmənt)

= administration (əd,mɪnə'streʃən)

dispute (dɪ'spjut) v. 爭論

= argue ('ɑrgju)

= debate (dɪ'bet)

= quarrel ('kwɔrəl , 'kwɑr-)

= oppose (ə'poz)

= resist (rɪ'zɪst)

= fight (faɪt)

= bicker ('bɪkɚ)

= contest (kən'tɛst)

dissect (dɪ'sɛkt) v. 分析

= cut (kʌt)

= examine (ɪg'zæmɪn)

= analyze ('ænḷ,aɪz)

dissent (dɪ'sɛnt) v. 不同意

= disagree (,dɪsə'gri)

= differ ('dɪfɚ)

= *take exception*

dissipate ('dɪsə,pet) v. ①驅散 ②浪費

① = scatter ('skætɚ)

= spread (sprɛd)

= dispel (dɪ'spɛl)

= disperse (dɪ'spɝs)

② = squander ('skwɑndɚ)

= waste〔west〕

= *spend foolishly*

dissolve〔dɪ'zɑlv〕*v.* ①溶解 ②消滅

① = melt〔mɛlt〕

= liquefy〔'lɪkwə,faɪ〕

② = cease〔sis〕

= end〔ɛnd〕

= fade〔fed〕

= disappear〔,dɪsə'pɪr〕

= *pass away*

dissuade〔dɪ'swed〕*v.* 勸阻

= discourage〔dɪs'kɜrɪdʒ〕

= *talk out of*

distance〔'dɪstəns〕*n.* ①距離 ②遠

① = space〔spes〕

= length〔lɛŋkθ, lɛŋθ〕

= extent〔ɪk'stɛnt〕

= reach〔ritʃ〕

② = remoteness〔rɪ'motnɪs〕

distend〔dɪ'stɛnd〕*v.* 擴張

= expand〔ɪk'spænd〕

= swell〔swɛl〕

= stretch〔strɛtʃ〕

= widen〔'waɪdn̩〕

= enlarge〔ɪn'lɑrdʒ〕

= magnify〔'mægnə,faɪ〕

= increase〔ɪn'kris〕

= bulge〔bʌldʒ〕

= *blow out*

distinct〔dɪ'stɪŋkt〕*adj.* ①不同的 ②清楚的

① = different〔'dɪfərənt〕

= dissimilar〔dɪ'sɪmələ, dɪs'sɪ-〕

= diverse〔də'vɜs, daɪ-〕

= separate〔'sɛpərɪt, -prɪt〕

② = clear〔klɪr〕

= plain〔plen〕

= obvious〔'ɑbvɪəs〕

= precise〔prɪ'saɪs〕

= exact〔ɪg'zækt〕

= definite〔'dɛfənɪt〕

= unmistakable〔,ʌnmə'stekəbl̩〕

= clear-cut〔'klɪr'kʌt〕

distinguish〔dɪ'stɪŋgwɪʃ〕*v.* ①辨識 ②使揚名

① = define〔dɪ'faɪn〕

= see〔si〕

= detect〔dɪ'tɛkt〕

= *tell apart*

② = honor〔'ɑnə〕

= dignify〔'dɪgnə,faɪ〕

= *make famous*

distinguished〔dɪ'stɪŋgwɪʃt〕 *adj.* 著名的

= important〔ɪm'pɔrtn̩t〕

= great〔gret〕

= outstanding〔aut'stændɪŋ〕

= famous〔'feməs〕

= well-known〔'wɛl'non〕

= noted〔'notɪd〕

= popular〔'pɑpjələ〕

= celebrated〔'sɛləbretɪd〕

= honored〔'ɑnəd〕

distort (dɪs'tɔrt) v. 曲解

= twist (twɪst)

= contort (kən'tɔrt)

= misrepresent (,mɪsrɛprɪ'zɛnt)

= falsify ('fɔlsə,faɪ)

distract (dɪ'strækt) v. 擾亂

= divert (də'vɜt , daɪ-)

= confuse (kən'fjuz)

= disturb (dɪ'stɜb)

distress (dɪ'strɛs) v. 使痛苦

= pain (pen)

= hurt (hɜt)

= afflict (ə'flɪkt)

= torment (tɔr'mɛnt)

= torture ('tɔrtʃə)

= agonize ('ægə,naɪz)

= trouble ('trʌbl)

= bother ('baðə)

= disturb (dɪ'stɜb)

= upset (ʌp'sɛt)

distribute (dɪ'strɪbjut) v. 分配

= scatter ('skætə)

= disperse (dɪ'spɜs)

= spread (sprɛd)

= dispense (dɪ'spɛns)

= allot (ə'lat)

= *dole out*

= *mete out*

district ('dɪstrɪkt) n. 地區

= region ('ridʒən)

= area ('ɛrɪə , 'erɪə)

= zone (zon)

= territory ('tɛrə,torɪ , -,tɔrɪ)

= place (ples)

= section ('sɛkʃən)

= neighborhood ('nebə,hud)

disturb (dɪ'stɜb) v. ①煩惱
②擾亂

① = annoy (ə'nɔɪ)

= irk (ɜk)

= vex (vɛks)

= bother ('baðə)

= irritate ('ɪrə,tet)

② = trouble ('trʌbl)

= perturb (pə'tɜb)

= concern (kən'sɜn)

= agitate ('ædʒə,tet)

= upset (ʌp'sɛt)

= excite (ɪk'saɪt)

= alarm (ə'larm)

dive (daɪv) v. 跳入

= plunge (plʌndʒ)

= drop (drap)

= fall (fɔl)

diverse (də'vɜs , daɪ-) adj.
①不同的　②多樣的

① = different ('dɪfərənt)

= unlike (ʌn'laɪk)

= distinct (dɪ'stɪŋkt)

② = various ('vɛrɪəs)

= several ('sɛvərəl)

divert (də'vɜt , daɪ-) v. ①擾亂
②娛樂

① = distract (dɪ'strækt)

= detract (dɪ'trækt)
= confuse (kən'fjuz)
② = amuse (ə'mjuz)
= entertain (ˌɛntə'ten)
= delight (dɪ'laɪt)
= tickle ('tɪkḷ)

divide (də'vaɪd) v. 分開

= separate ('sɛpəˌret , -prɪt)
= portion ('porʃən , 'pɔr-)
= partition (par'tɪʃən , pə-)
= split (splɪt)
= share (ʃɛr)
= sort (sɔrt)

divine (də'vaɪn) ① adj. 神聖的
② adj. 極好的 ③ v. 預言

① = heavenly ('hɛvənlɪ)
= sacred ('sekrɪd)
= holy ('holɪ)
② = superb (su'pɝb , sə-)
= delightful (dɪ'laɪtfəl)
= excellent ('ɛksḷənt)
= great (gret)
= beautiful ('bjutəfəl)
③ = foretell (for'tɛl , fɔr-)
= predict (prɪ'dɪkt)
= guess (gɛs)
= forecast (for'kæst)
= prophesy ('prɑfəˌsaɪ)
= anticipate (æn'tɪsəˌpet)

divorce (də'vors , '-vɔrs) v.
分開

= separate ('sɛpəˌret , -prɪt)
= disjoin (dɪs'dʒɔɪn)

= divide (də'vaɪd)
= disconnect (ˌdɪskə'nɛkt)

divulge (də'vʌldʒ) v. 宣佈

= reveal (rɪ'vil)
= tell (tɛl)
= publish ('pʌblɪʃ)
= broadcast ('brɔdˌkæst)
= circulate ('sɝkjəˌlet)
= *let out*
= *come out with*
= *make known*

dizzy ('dɪzɪ) adj. 暈眩的

= giddy ('gɪdɪ)
= staggering ('stægərɪŋ)
= spinning ('spɪnɪŋ)
= unsteady (ʌn'stɛdɪ)
= confused (kən'fjuzd)

do (du) v. 實行

= perform (pə'fɔrm)
= act (ækt)
= behave (bɪ'hev)
= produce (prə'djus)

docile ('dɑsḷ , 'dɑsɪl) adj. 溫順的

= obedient (ə'bidɪənt)
= willing ('wɪlɪŋ)
= receptive (rɪ'sɛptɪv)
= responsive (rɪ'spɑnsɪv)
= yielding ('jildɪŋ)
= gentle ('dʒɛntḷ)
= tame (tem)
= mild (maɪld)

D

dock (dɑk) v. ①固定 ②剪短

① = anchor ('æŋkə)
  = moor (mur)
  = tie (taɪ)
② = clip (klɪp)
  = *cut off*

doctor ('dɑktə) ① v. 醫治
② n. 醫生

① = treat (trit)
  = remedy ('rɛmədɪ)
  = heal (hil)
  = cure (kjur)
② = physician (fə'zɪʃən)
  = medic ('mɛdɪk)

doctrine ('dɑktrɪn) n. 教條

  = belief (bɪ'lif)
  = teachings ('titʃɪŋz)
  = creed (krid)

document ('dɑkjəmənt) n. 文書

  = writing ('raɪtɪŋ)
  = paper ('pepə)
  = certificate (sə'tɪfəkɪt)
  = statements ('stetmənts)

dodge (dɑdʒ) v. 閃避

  = avoid (ə'vɔɪd)
  = duck (dʌk)
  = recoil (rɪ'kɔɪl)

doff (dɔf) v. 脫去

  = remove (rɪ'muv)
  = undo (ʌn'du)
  = *take off*

dogged ('dɔgɪd) adj. 頑強的

  = stubborn ('stʌbən)
  = willful ('wɪlfəl)
  = headstrong ('hɛd,strɔŋ)
  = obstinate ('ɑbstənɪt)

doldrums ('dɑldrəmz) n. pl.
消沉

  = blues (bluz)
  = gloom (glum)
  = *low spirits*

dole (dol) v. 分配

  = give (gɪv)
  = donate ('donet)
  = allot (ə'lɑt)
  = dispense (dɪ'spɛns)
  = grant (grænt)
  = *deal out*
  = *mete out*

doleful ('dolfəl) adj. 陰鬱的

  = sad (sæd)
  = mournful ('mornfḷ , 'mɔrnfḷ)
  = dreary ('drɪrɪ , 'drirɪ)
  = dismal ('dɪzmḷ)

dolt (dolt) n. 傻瓜

  = dunce (dʌns)
  = blockhead ('blɑk,hɛd)
  = numskull ('nʌm,skʌl)

domain (do'men) n. 領地

  = sphere (sfɪr)
  = realm (rɛlm)
  = province ('prɑvɪns)

= field〔fild〕

= property〔'prɑpətɪ〕

domestic〔də'mɛstɪk〕

① *adj.* 家庭的 ② *adj.* 馴良的

③ *n.* 僕人

① = household〔'haʊs,hold〕

= family〔'fæməlɪ〕

= internal〔ɪn'tɜnḷ〕

② = tame〔tem〕

③ = servant〔'sɜvənt〕

= maid〔med〕

dominate〔'dɑmə,net〕 *v.* 統治

= control〔kən'trol〕

= rule〔rul〕

= command〔kə'mænd〕

= lead〔lid〕

domineering〔,dɑmə'nɪrɪŋ〕 *adj.*

跋扈的

= arrogant〔'ærəgənt〕

= overbearing〔,ovə'bɛrɪŋ〕

= bossy〔'bɔsɪ〕

= high-handed〔'haɪ'hændɪd〕

dominion〔də'mɪnjən〕 *n.*

①控制 ②領土

① = rule〔rul〕

= control〔kən'trol〕

= command〔kə'mænd〕

= power〔'paʊə〕

= hold〔hold〕

= grasp〔græsp〕

② = lands〔lændz〕

= sphere〔sfɪr〕

= country〔'kʌntrɪ〕

= domain〔do'men〕

don〔dɑn〕 *v.* 穿

= wear〔wɛr〕

= *put on*

= *slip on*

= *dress in*

donate〔'donet〕 *v.* 贈與

= give〔gɪv〕

= contribute〔kən'trɪbjut〕

= present〔prɪ'zɛnt〕

= bestow〔bɪ'sto〕

= award〔ə'wɔrd〕

= allot〔ə'lɑt〕

= grant〔grænt〕

done〔dʌn〕 *adj.* 已完成的

= finished〔'fɪnɪʃt〕

= complete〔kəm'plit〕

= ended〔'ɛndɪd〕

= concluded〔kən'kludɪd〕

= terminated〔'tɜmə,netɪd〕

= over〔'ovə〕

= *wound up*

= *through with*

donkey〔'dɑŋkɪ〕 *n.* ①頑強的人

②驢

① = dolt〔dolt〕

= blockhead〔'blɑk,hɛd〕

= *stubborn person*

② = ass〔æs〕

= mule〔mjul〕

= burro〔'bɜo , 'buro〕

doom ﹝ dum ﹞ v. 判罪

= condemn ﹝ kən'dεm ﹞

= damn ﹝ dæm ﹞

= censure ﹝ 'sεnʃə ﹞

= convict ﹝ kən'vɪkt ﹞

= sentence ﹝ 'sεntəns ﹞

dormant ﹝ 'dɔrmənt ﹞ adj. 休眠的

= sleeping ﹝ 'slipɪŋ ﹞

= inactive ﹝ ɪn'æktɪv ﹞

dose ﹝ dos ﹞ n. 量

= amount ﹝ ə'maʊnt ﹞

= quantity ﹝ 'kwɑntətɪ ﹞

= portion ﹝ 'porʃən , 'por- ﹞

double ﹝ 'dʌbḷ ﹞ ① n. 副本
② v. 摺 ③ adj. 加倍的

① = duplicate ﹝ 'djupləkɪt ﹞

= copy ﹝ 'kɑpɪ ﹞

② = fold ﹝ fold ﹞

= turn *over*

③ = twofold ﹝ 'tu'fold ﹞

= *twice as much*

doubt ﹝ daʊt ﹞ v. 懷疑

= mistrust ﹝ mɪs'trʌst ﹞

= suspect ﹝ sə'spεkt ﹞

= question ﹝ 'kwεstʃən ﹞

= challenge ﹝ 'tʃælɪndʒ ﹞

= dispute ﹝ dɪ'spjut ﹞

douse ﹝ daʊs ﹞ v. ①浸 ②熄滅

① = dip ﹝ dɪp ﹞

= immerse ﹝ ɪ'mɝs ﹞

= dunk ﹝ dʌŋk ﹞

② = extinguish ﹝ ɪk'stɪŋgwɪʃ ﹞

= quench ﹝ kwεntʃ ﹞

dowdy ﹝ 'daʊdɪ ﹞ adj. 不整潔的

= shabby ﹝ 'ʃæbɪ ﹞

= untidy ﹝ ʌn'taɪdɪ ﹞

= messy ﹝ 'mεsɪ ﹞

= mussy ﹝ 'mʌsɪ ﹞

= sloppy ﹝ 'slɑpɪ ﹞

= seedy ﹝ 'sidɪ ﹞

downcast ﹝ 'daʊn,kæst ﹞ adj.
憂鬱的

= dejected ﹝ dɪ'dʒεktɪd ﹞

= sad ﹝ sæd ﹞

= discouraged ﹝ dɪs'kɝɪdʒd ﹞

= disheartened ﹝ dɪs'hɑrtṇd ﹞

= depressed ﹝ dɪ'prεst ﹞

= gloomy ﹝ 'glumɪ ﹞

= melancholy ﹝ 'mεlən,kɑlɪ ﹞

= glum ﹝ glʌm ﹞

downfall ﹝ 'daʊn,fɔl ﹞ n. ①敗亡
②落下（雨）

① = ruin ﹝ 'ruɪn ﹞

= failure ﹝ 'feljə ﹞

= defeat ﹝ dɪ'fit ﹞

= upset ﹝ ʌp'sεt ﹞

= overthrow ﹝ ,ovə'θro ﹞

② = rainstorm ﹝ 'ren,stɔrm ﹞

= cloudburst ﹝ 'klaʊd,bɝst ﹞

= flood ﹝ flʌd ﹞

= downpour ﹝ 'daʊn,por , -,pɔr ﹞

downhearted ﹝ 'daʊn,hɑrtɪd ﹞
adj. 沮喪的

= discouraged ﹝ dɪs'kɝɪdʒd ﹞

= dejected〔dɪ'dʒɛktɪd〕
= depressed〔dɪ'prɛst〕
= downcast〔'daʊn,kæst〕
= sad〔sæd〕
= glum〔glʌm〕
= melancholy〔'mɛlən,kɑlɪ〕

downpour〔'daʊn,por , -,pɔr , -,pʊr〕*n.* 大雨

= rainstorm〔'ren,stɔrm〕
= cloudburst〔'klaʊd,bɝst〕
= flood〔flʌd〕
= downfall〔'daʊn,fɔl〕

downright〔'daʊn,raɪt〕*adj.* 完全的

= thorough〔'θɝo , -ə〕
= complete〔kəm'plit〕
= plain〔plen〕
= positive〔'pɑzətɪv〕
= utter〔'ʌtɚ〕
= absolute〔'æbsə,lut〕
= entire〔ɪn'taɪr〕
= total〔'totḷ〕

dowry〔'daʊrɪ〕*n.* ①嫁妝 ②天才

① = settlement〔'sɛtḷmənt〕
= endowment〔ɪn'daʊmənt〕
② = talent〔'tælənt〕
= gift〔gɪft〕
= ability〔ə'bɪlətɪ〕
= genius〔'dʒinjəs〕

drab〔dræb〕*adj.* 單調的

= dull〔dʌl〕

= unattractive〔,ʌnə'træktɪv〕
= flat〔flæt〕
= lifeless〔'laɪflɪs〕

draft〔dræft〕*n.* ①氣流 ②草稿 ③徵募兵士 ④匯票

① = wind〔wɪnd〕
= air〔ɛr〕
② = sketch〔skɛtʃ〕
= drawing〔'drɔɪŋ〕
= outline〔'aʊt,laɪn〕
= *rough copy*
③ = enlistment〔ɪn'lɪstmənt , ɛn-〕
= enrollment〔ɪn'rolmənt〕
= induction〔ɪn'dʌkʃən〕
= recruitment〔rɪ'krutmənt〕
= call-up〔'kɔl,ʌp〕
④ = note〔not〕
= bill〔bɪl〕
= check〔tʃɛk〕

drag〔dræg〕*v.* ①拖曳 ②延遲

① = pull〔pʊl〕
= heave〔hiv〕
= haul〔hɔl〕
= draw〔drɔ〕
= tug〔tʌg〕
= tow〔to〕
② = crawl〔krɔl〕
= creep〔krip〕
= tarry〔'tærɪ〕
= lag〔læg〕
= dillydally〔'dɪlɪ,dælɪ〕
= delay〔dɪ'le〕
= *linger on*

D

drain (dren) *v.* ①流盡 ②耗盡

① = dry (draɪ)
= empty ('ɛmptɪ)
= *draw off*

② = deprive (dɪ'praɪv)
= filter ('fɪltɚ)
= use (juz)
= spend (spɛnd)
= exhaust (ɪg'zɔst)

dramatize ('dræmə,taɪz) *v.*
編為戲劇

= stage (stedʒ)
= produce (prə'djus)
= present (prɪ'zɛnt)
= feature ('fitʃɚ)
= *put on*

drape (drep) *v.* 懸掛

= cover ('kʌvɚ)
= hang (hæŋ)
= flow (flo)

drastic ('dræstɪk) *adj.* 激烈的

= extreme (ɪk'strim)
= severe (sə'vɪr)
= intense (ɪn'tɛns)
= rough (rʌf)
= violent ('vaɪələnt)
= fierce (fɪrs)
= tough (tʌf)

draw (drɔ) *v.* ①拖曳 ②吸引
③設計 ④使和局

① = pull (pʊl)
= drag (dræg)

= haul (hɔl)

② = attract (ə'trækt)
= lure (lʊr)
= magnetize ('mægnə,taɪz)
= interest ('ɪntərɪst , 'ɪntrɪst)

③ = sketch (skɛtʃ)
= portray (por'tre , pɔr-)
= picture ('pɪktʃɚ)
= design (dɪ'zaɪn)

④ = tie (taɪ)
= equal ('ikwəl)
= match (mætʃ)

drawback ('drɔ,bæk) *n.* 缺點；
障礙

= disadvantage (,dɪsəd'væntɪdʒ)
= handicap ('hændɪ,kæp)
= fault (fɔlt)
= obstacle ('ɑbstəkl̩)
= objection (əb'dʒɛkʃən)
= failing ('felɪŋ)
= shortcoming ('ʃɔrt,kʌmɪŋ)
= flaw (flɔ)
= catch (kætʃ)

dread (drɛd) *v.* 害怕

= fear (fɪr)
= *be afraid*

dreadful ('drɛdfəl) *adj.* 可怕的

= bad (bæd)
= terrible ('tɛrəbl̩)
= awful ('ɔful , 'ɔfl̩)
= unpleasant (ʌn'plɛznt)
= horrible ('hɑrəbl̩)
= vile (vaɪl)

= wretched ('rɛtʃɪd)
= detestable (dɪ'tɛstəbl̩)
= ghastly ('gæstlɪ , 'gɑst-)

dream (drim) v. 夢想

= imagine (ɪ'mædʒɪn)
= vision ('vɪʒən)
= muse (mjuz)

dreary ('drɪrɪ , 'drirɪ) adj.
憂鬱的

= gloomy ('glumɪ)
= dull (dʌl)
= dismal ('dɪzml̩)
= somber ('sɑmbɚ)
= depressing (dɪ'prɛsɪŋ)
= disheartening (dɪs'hɑrtn̩ɪŋ)
= discouraging (dɪs'kɝɪdʒɪŋ)

dredge (drɛdʒ) v. 挖取

= dig (dɪg)
= excavate ('ɛkskə,vet)
= scoop (skup)
= *pick up*

drench (drɛntʃ) v. 浸濕

= soak (sok)
= wet (wɛt)
= saturate ('sætʃə,ret)
= flood (flʌd)

dress (drɛs) v. 裝飾

= clothe (kloð)
= adorn (ə'dɔrn)
= decorate ('dɛkə,ret)
= attire (ə'taɪr)
= outfit ('aut,fɪt)

dressing ('drɛsɪŋ) n. ①繃帶
②調味品

① = medicine ('mɛdəsn̩)
= bandage ('bændɪdʒ)
② = sauce (sɔs)
= seasoning ('siznɪŋ)

dribble ('drɪbl̩) v. 滴下

= drip (drɪp)
= trickle ('trɪkl̩)
= leak (lik)

drift (drɪft) v. 漫遊

= wander ('wɑndɚ)
= roam (rom)
= stray (stre)
= meander (mɪ'ændɚ)
= ramble ('ræmbl̩)
= float (flot)
= cruise (kruz)
= glide (glaɪd)

drill (drɪl) ① v. 訓練 ② n. 鑽

① = practice ('præktɪs)
= instruct (ɪn'strʌkt)
= teach (titʃ)
= train (tren)
= exercise ('ɛksɚ,saɪz)
= prepare (prɪ'pɛr)
= condition (kən'dɪʃən)
= discipline ('dɪsəplɪn)
② = tool (tul)

drink (drɪŋk) v. 飲

= swallow ('swɑlo)
= sip (sɪp)
= guzzle ('gʌzl̩)

D

drive (draɪv) *v.* ①駕駛 ②驅使

① = steer (stɪr)
= ride (raɪd)
= handle ('hændḷ)
= operate ('ɑpə,ret)
= work (wɜk)
= run (rʌn)
= conduct (kən'dʌkt)
= manage ('mænɪdʒ)

② = move (muv)
= thrust (θrʌst)
= compel (kəm'pɛl)
= force (fors , fɔrs)
= make (mek)
= impel (ɪm'pɛl)

drizzle ('drɪzḷ) *n.* 雨

= rain (ren)
= shower ('ʃaʊɚ)
= sprinkle ('sprɪŋkḷ)

droll (drol) *adj.* 有趣的

= amusing (ə'mjuzɪŋ)
= humorous ('hjumərəs , 'ju-)
= laughable ('læfəbḷ , 'lɑf-)
= funny ('fʌnɪ)
= witty ('wɪtɪ)

drone (dron) *n.* ①嗡嗡聲
②雄蜂 ③遊民

① = hum (hʌm)
= buzz (bʌz)
② = *male bee*
③ = loafer ('lofɚ)
= nonworker (nɑn'wɜkɚ)
= unemployed (,ʌnɪm'plɔɪd)

= idler ('aɪdlɚ)

drool (drul) *v.* 流口水

= salivate ('sælə,vet)
= dribble ('drɪbḷ)
= trickle ('trɪkḷ)

droop (drup) *v.* ①低垂 ②變弱
③消沉

① = hang (hæŋ)
= dangle ('dæŋgḷ)
= drag (dræg)
② = weaken ('wikən)
= sink (sɪŋk)
= fade (fed)
= fail (fel)
= decline (dɪ'klaɪn)
③ = despond (dɪ'spɑnd)
= despair (dɪ'spɛr)
= *lose heart*
= *give up*

drop (drɑp) ① *v.* 落下
② *v.* 終止 ③ *v.* 放棄 ④ *n.* 少量

① = fall (fɔl)
= dive (daɪv)
= plunge (plʌndʒ)
= descend (dɪ'sɛnd)
② = end (ɛnd)
= cease (sis)
= stop (stɑp)
③ = dismiss (dɪs'mɪs)
= abandon (ə'bændən)
= *let go*
= *give up*
④ = *hardly anything*
= *small amount*

drown ﹝ draʊn ﹞ v. 溺死

= submerge ﹝ səb'mɝdʒ ﹞

= sink ﹝ sɪŋk ﹞

= immerse ﹝ ɪ'mɝs ﹞

= inundate ﹝ 'ɪnʌn,det , ɪn'ʌndet ﹞

drowsy ﹝ 'draʊzɪ ﹞ adj. 昏昏欲睡的

= sleepy ﹝ 'slipɪ ﹞

= dreamy ﹝ 'drimɪ ﹞

= heavy-eyed ﹝ 'hɛvɪ'aɪd ﹞

drudge ﹝ drʌdʒ ﹞ v. 做苦工

= plod ﹝ plɑd ﹞

= *work away*

drug ﹝ drʌg ﹞ ① v. 使麻醉 ② n. 麻醉藥

① = numb ﹝ nʌm ﹞

= deaden ﹝ 'dɛdn̩ ﹞

= *put to sleep*

= *knock out*

② = medicine ﹝ 'mɛdəsn̩ ﹞

= potion ﹝ 'poʃən ﹞

= narcotic ﹝ nɑr'kɑtɪk ﹞

drum ﹝ drʌm ﹞ ① v. 擊 ② v. 反覆進言 ③ n. 鼓

① = beat ﹝ bit ﹞

= tap ﹝ tæp ﹞

= strike ﹝ straɪk ﹞

= pound ﹝ paʊnd ﹞

② = repeat ﹝ rɪ'pit ﹞

= drill ﹝ drɪl ﹞

= reiterate ﹝ ri'ɪtə,ret ﹞

③ = *musical instrument*

drunk ﹝ drʌŋk ﹞ adj. 醉的

= intoxicated ﹝ ɪn'tɑksə,ketɪd ﹞

= tipsy ﹝ 'tɪpsɪ ﹞

= dizzy ﹝ 'dɪzɪ ﹞

dry ﹝ draɪ ﹞ adj. 乾燥的

= waterless ﹝ 'wɔtə.lɪs , 'wɑt- ﹞

= arid ﹝ 'ærɪd ﹞

= parched ﹝ pɑrtʃt ﹞

= thirsty ﹝ 'θɝstɪ ﹞

dual ﹝ 'djuəl , 'duəl ﹞ adj. 雙重的

= twofold ﹝ 'tu'fold ﹞

= double ﹝ 'dʌbl̩ ﹞

= duplicate ﹝ 'djupləkɪt ﹞

dub ﹝ dʌb ﹞ v. 授以稱號

= name ﹝ nem ﹞

= call ﹝ kɔl ﹞

= title ﹝ 'taɪtl̩ ﹞

= label ﹝ 'lebl̩ ﹞

= tag ﹝ tæg ﹞

= christen ﹝ 'krɪsn̩ ﹞

dubious ﹝ 'djubɪəs , 'du- ﹞ adj. 懷疑的

= doubtful ﹝ 'daʊtfəl ﹞

= uncertain ﹝ ʌn'sɝtn̩ ﹞

= questionable ﹝ 'kwɛstʃənəbl̩ ﹞

duck ﹝ dʌk ﹞ ① v. 沒入水中 ② v. 閃避 ③ n. 鴨

① = plunge ﹝ plʌndʒ ﹞

= dip ﹝ dɪp ﹞

= submerge ﹝ səb'mɝdʒ ﹞

= sink ﹝ sɪŋk ﹞

D

D

= immerse〔ɪˈmɝs〕

= dunk〔dʌŋk〕

② = sidestep〔ˈsaɪdˌstɛp〕

③ = *web-footed bird*

due〔dju〕*adj.* ①適當的
②到期的

① = proper〔ˈprɑpɚ〕

= rightful〔ˈraɪtfəl〕

= fitting〔ˈfɪtɪŋ〕

= just〔dʒʌst〕

= fair〔fɛr〕

= square〔skwɛr〕

= equitable〔ˈɛkwɪtəbḷ〕

② = owed〔od〕

duel〔ˈdjuəl〕*v.* 決鬥

= fight〔faɪt〕

= contest〔kənˈtɛst〕

= contend〔kənˈtɛnd〕

= struggle〔ˈstrʌgḷ〕

dull〔dʌl〕*adj.* ①鈍的 ②晦暗的
③笨的 ④無趣的 ⑤不活潑的

① = blunt〔blʌnt〕

= unsharp〔ʌnˈʃɑrp〕

② = gray〔gre〕

= dingy〔ˈdɪndʒɪ〕

= dreary〔ˈdrɪrɪ, ˈdrirɪ〕

③ = stupid〔ˈstjupɪd〕

= slow〔slo〕

④ = boring〔ˈborɪŋ, ˈbɔrɪŋ〕

= uninteresting〔ʌnˈɪnt(ə)rɪstɪŋ〕

= dry〔draɪ〕

= flat〔flæt〕

⑤ = slow〔slo〕

= inactive〔ɪnˈæktɪv〕

= sluggish〔ˈslʌgɪʃ〕

dumb〔dʌm〕*adj.* ①沈默的
②笨的

① = silent〔ˈsaɪlənt〕

= mute〔mjut〕

= speechless〔ˈspitʃlɪs〕

② = stupid〔ˈstjupɪd〕

= dull〔dʌl〕

= dense〔dɛns〕

dummy〔ˈdʌmɪ〕*n.* ①人像模型
②笨人

① = imitation〔ˌɪməˈteʃən〕

= copy〔ˈkɑpɪ〕

= model〔ˈmɑdḷ〕

= figure〔ˈfɪgjɚ, ˈfɪgɚ〕

= doll〔dɑl, dɔl〕

= fake〔fek〕

② = dolt〔dolt〕

= dunce〔dʌns〕

dump〔dʌmp〕*v.* 卸下

= empty〔ˈɛmptɪ〕

= unload〔ʌnˈlod〕

= discharge〔dɪsˈtʃɑrdʒ〕

= discard〔dɪsˈkɑrd〕

= scrap〔skræp〕

= *throw away*

dunce〔dʌns〕*n.* 笨蛋

= dolt〔dolt〕

= dummy〔ˈdʌmɪ〕

= fool〔ful〕

dupe (djup , dup) *v.* 欺騙

= deceive (dɪ'siv)

= trick (trɪk)

= beguile (bɪ'gaɪl)

= betray (bɪ'tre)

= hoax (hoks)

= bamboozle (bæm'buzl)

duplicate ('djuplə,ket) *v.* 複製

= copy ('kapɪ)

= repeat (rɪ'pit)

= reproduce (,riprə'djus)

= double ('dʌbl)

durable ('djurəbl) *adj.* 耐久的

= longlasting ('lɔŋ'læstɪŋ , 'laŋ-)

= enduring (ɪn'djurɪŋ)

= permanent ('pɜmənənt)

= endless ('ɛndlɪs)

= sturdy ('stɜdɪ)

= solid ('salɪd)

= strong (strɔŋ)

duration (djʊ'reʃən) *n.* 持續時間

= time (taɪm)

= period ('pɪrɪəd)

= term (tɜm)

dusk (dʌsk) *n.* ①傍晚 ②昏暗

① = sundown ('sʌn,daʊn)

= sunset ('sʌn,sɛt)

= twilight ('twaɪ,laɪt)

= evening ('ivnɪŋ)

= nightfall ('naɪt,fɔl)

② = shade (ʃed)

= dark (dark)

= gloom (glum)

dust (dʌst) ① *v.* 拂去灰塵
② *v.* 撒 ③ *n.* 砂

① = clean (klin)

= *wipe off*

② = sprinkle ('sprɪŋkl)

= powder ('paʊdɚ)

③ = *fine powder*

duty ('djutɪ) *n.* ①任務 ②稅

① = task (tæsk , tɑsk)

= work (wɜk)

= job (dʒab)

= chore (tʃor , tʃɔr)

= assignment (ə'saɪnmənt)

= charge (tʃardʒ)

= function ('fʌŋkʃən)

= obligation (,ablə'geʃən)

= responsibility
(rɪ,spansə'bɪlətɪ)

② = tax (tæks)

= toll (tol)

= tariff ('tærɪf)

dwarf (dwɔrf) *n.* 矮人

= midget ('mɪdʒɪt)

= runt (rʌnt)

= shrimp (ʃrɪmp)

dwell (dwɛl) *v.* 居住

= live (lɪv)

= reside (rɪ'zaɪd)

= inhabit (ɪn'hæbɪt)

= occupy ('akjə,paɪ)

D

dwindle ('dwɪndl̩) v. 減少

= shrink (ʃrɪŋk)

= decrease (dɪ'kris)

= diminish (də'mɪnɪʃ)

= lessen ('lɛsn̩)

= decline (dɪ'klaɪn)

= subside (səb'saɪd)

= *waste away*

dye (daɪ) n. 染料

= color ('kʌlɚ)

= stain (sten)

= tint (tɪnt)

dynamic (daɪ'næmɪk) adj.
精力充沛的

= active ('æktɪv)

= energetic (ˌɛnɚ'dʒɛtɪk)

= forceful ('forsfəl , 'fɔrs-)

= strong (strɔŋ)

= lively ('laɪvlɪ)

= animated ('ænəˌmetɪd)

= spirited ('spɪrɪtɪd)

E

eager ('igɚ) adj. 渴望的;
急切的

= wanting ('wɑntɪŋ , 'wɔntɪŋ)

= wishing ('wɪʃɪŋ)

= desirous (dɪ'zaɪrəs)

= anxious ('æŋkʃəs , 'æŋʃəs)

= keen (kin)

= ready ('rɛdɪ)

= willing ('wɪlɪŋ)

early ('ʒlɪ) adv. ①早
②很久以前

① = beforetime (bɪ'forˌtaɪm)

= *in advance*

② = back (bæk)

= *long ago*

= *in the past*

earn (ʒn) v. 獲得

= get (gɛt)

= gain (gen)

= obtain (əb'ten)

= require (rɪ'kwaɪr)

= secure (sɪ'kjur)

= make (mek)

= deserve (dɪ'zʒv)

= merit ('mɛrɪt)

= *be in line for*

earnest ('ʒnɪst , -əst) adj. 熱誠的

= determined (dɪ'tʒmɪnd)

= sincere (sɪn'sɪr)

= serious ('sɪrɪəs)

= decided (dɪ'saɪdɪd)

= resolute ('rɛzəˌlut)

= devoted (dɪ'votɪd)

earth (ʒθ) n. ①地球
②泥土;地

① = world (wʒld)

= globe (glob)

② = ground (graʊnd)

= dirt (dʒt)

= soil (sɔɪl)

= land (lænd)

= sod (sɑd)

ease〔 iz 〕 *v.* ①減輕　②使容易

① = relieve 〔 rɪ'liv 〕
　= reduce 〔 rɪ'djus 〕
　= soothe 〔 suð 〕
　= allay 〔 ə'le 〕
　= comfort 〔 'kʌmfət 〕
　= lighten 〔 'laɪtn̩ 〕
　= relax 〔 rɪ'læks 〕
　= loosen 〔 'lusn̩ 〕
② = help 〔 hɛlp 〕
　= aid 〔 ed 〕
　= facilitate 〔 fə'sɪlə,tet 〕

easy 〔 'izɪ 〕 *adj.* ①容易的
②舒適的　③不嚴的
④從容自如的

① = simple 〔 'sɪmpl̩ 〕
　= effortless 〔 'ɛfətlɪs 〕
　= plain 〔 plen 〕
　= *not hard*
② = comfortable 〔 'kʌmfətəbl̩ 〕
　= restful 〔 'rɛstfəl 〕
　= relaxing 〔 rɪ'læksɪŋ 〕
　= cozy 〔 'kozɪ 〕
　= snug 〔 snʌg 〕
③ = kindly 〔 'kaɪndlɪ 〕
　= mild 〔 maɪld 〕
　= gentle 〔 'dʒɛntl̩ 〕
　= lenient 〔 'linɪənt , 'linjənt 〕
④ = pleasant 〔 'plɛznt 〕
　= smooth 〔 smuð 〕
　= natural 〔 'nætʃərəl 〕
　= informal 〔 ɪn'fɔrml̩ 〕

eat 〔 it 〕 *v.* ①吃　②侵蝕

① = dine 〔 daɪn 〕

　= consume 〔 kən'sum , '-sjum 〕
　= chew 〔 tʃu 〕
　= swallow 〔 'swɑlo 〕
② = corrode 〔 kə'rod 〕
　= erode 〔 ɪ'rod 〕
　= *waste away*

ebb 〔 ɛb 〕 *v.* 衰弱

　= decrease 〔 dɪ'kris 〕
　= diminish 〔 də'mɪnɪʃ 〕
　= lessen 〔 'lɛsn̩ 〕
　= decline 〔 dɪ'klaɪn 〕
　= subside 〔 səb'saɪd 〕
　= recede 〔 rɪ'sid 〕
　= retreat 〔 rɪ'trit 〕
　= withdraw 〔 wɪð'drɔ , wɪθ- 〕

eccentric 〔 ɪk'sɛntrɪk 〕 *adj.*
古怪的

　= unusual 〔 ʌn'juʒʊəl 〕
　= peculiar 〔 pɪ'kjulɪə 〕
　= odd 〔 ɑd 〕
　= abnormal 〔 æb'nɔrml̩ 〕
　= irregular 〔 ɪ'rɛgjələ 〕
　= queer 〔 kwɪr 〕

echo 〔 'ɛko 〕 *v.* 附和；模仿

　= repeat 〔 rɪ'pit 〕
　= duplicate 〔 'djuplə,ket 〕
　= imitate 〔 'ɪmə,tet 〕

eclipse 〔 ɪ'klɪps 〕 *v.* 遮掩

　= hide 〔 haɪd 〕
　= conceal 〔 kən'sil 〕
　= cover 〔 'kʌvə 〕
　= screen 〔 skrin 〕

= veil (vel)
= obscure (əb'skjʊr)
= darken ('dɑrkən)
= shadow ('ʃædo)
= overcast ('ovɚ͵kæst , ͵ovɚ'kæst)

economy (ɪ'kɑnəmɪ , i-) *n.* 節約

= thrift (θrɪft)
= frugality (fru'gælətɪ)
= saving ('sevɪŋ)

ecstasy ('ɛkstəsɪ) *n.* 狂喜

= joy (dʒɔɪ)
= rapture ('ræptʃɚ)
= happiness ('hæpɪnɪs)
= delight (dɪ'laɪt)
= glee (gli)
= elation (ɪ'leʃən)

edge (ɛdʒ) *n.* 邊緣

= border ('bɔrdɚ)
= bound (baʊnd)
= fringe (frɪndʒ)

edict ('idɪkt) *n.* 敕令；命令

= decree (dɪ'kri)
= order ('ɔrdɚ)
= law (lɔ)
= ruling ('rulɪŋ)
= proclamation (͵prɑklə'meʃən)

edifice ('ɛdəfɪs) *n.* 大廈

= building ('bɪldɪŋ)
= structure ('strʌktʃɚ)
= construction (kən'strʌkʃən)
= establishment (ə'stæblɪʃmənt)

edit ('ɛdɪt) *v.* 修正

= correct (kə'rɛkt)
= check (tʃɛk)
= rewrite (ri'raɪt)
= revise (rɪ'vaɪz)
= amend (ə'mɛnd)

educate ('ɛdʒə͵ket , -dʒʊ-) *v.* 培育

= teach (titʃ)
= instruct (ɪn'strʌkt)
= school (skul)
= train (tren)
= tutor ('tutɚ , 'tju-)
= enlighten (ɪn'laɪtn̩)
= direct (də'rɛkt , daɪ-)
= guide (gaɪd)
= show (ʃo)

eerie ('ɪrɪ , 'irɪ) *adj.* 怪誕的

= strange (strendʒ)
= weird (wɪrd)
= spooky ('spukɪ)
= deathlike ('dɛθ͵laɪk)
= ghastly ('gæstlɪ , 'gɑst-)
= ghostly ('gostlɪ)

efface (ɪ'fes , ɛ-) *v.* 消除

= erase (ɪ'res)
= destroy (dɪ'strɔɪ)
= obliterate (ə'blɪtə͵ret)
= *rub out*

effect (ə'fɛkt , ɪ- , ɛ-) *v.* 產生（效果）

= cause (kɔz)

= influence ('ɪnfluəns)
= produce (prə'djus)
= perform (pɚ'fɔrm)
= evoke (ɪ'vok)
= determine (dɪ'tɜmɪn)
= achieve (ə'tʃiv)
= make (mek)
= accomplish (ə'kɑmplɪʃ)
= execute ('ɛksɪ,kjut)
= complete (kəm'plit)

efficacy ('ɛfəkəsɪ) *n.* 功能

= ability (ə'bɪlətɪ)
= capacity (kə'pæsətɪ)
= competence ('kɑmpətəns)
= proficiency (prə'fɪʃənsɪ)

effort ('ɛfɚt) *n.* 努力

= attempt (ə'tɛmpt)
= try (traɪ)
= endeavor (ɪn'dɛvɚ)
= undertaking (,ʌndɚ'tekɪŋ)
= fling (flɪŋ)

egg (ɛg) ① *n.* 卵 ② *v.* 煽動

① = ovum ('ovəm)
= embryo ('ɛmbrɪ,o)
② = urge (ɜdʒ)
= stir (stɜ)
= agitate ('ædʒə,tet)
= incite (ɪn'saɪt)
= provoke (prə'vok)
= arouse (ə'raʊz)

eject (ɪ'dʒɛkt , i-) *v.* 逐出

= remove (rɪ'muv)

= eliminate (ɪ'lɪmə,net)
= expel (ɪk'spɛl)
= oust (aʊst)
= *drive out*

elaborate (ɪ'læbə,ret) *v.* 詳述；
用心做

= develop (dɪ'vɛləp)
= detail ('ditel , dɪ'tel)
= *dwell on*
= *work out*

elapse (ɪ'læps) *v.* (光陰) 逝去

= pass (pæs , pɑs)
= expire (ɪk'spaɪr)
= *run out*
= *slip away*

elastic (ɪ'læstɪk)
① *adj.* 有彈性的　② *n.* 橡皮筋

① = flexible ('flɛksəbl̩)
= pliable ('plaɪəbl̩)
= yielding ('jildɪŋ)
= adaptable (ə'dæptəbl̩)
② = *rubber band*

elated (ɪ'letɪd) *adj.* 興高采烈的

= overjoyed (,ovɚ'dʒɔɪd)
= enchanted (ɪn'tʃæntɪd)
= delighted (dɪ'laɪtɪd)
= jubilant ('dʒublənt)
= rejoicing (rɪ'dʒɔɪsɪŋ)

elder ('ɛldɚ) *adj.* 年長的

= older ('oldɚ)
= senior ('sinjɚ)

E

elect (ɪ'lɛkt , ə-) v. 選擇

= choose (tʃuz)

= pick (pɪk)

= select (sə'lɛkt)

= appoint (ə'pɔɪnt)

= *vote for*

electrify (ɪ'lɛktrə,faɪ , ə-) v.
①帶電;感電 ②震駭

① = charge (tʃɑrdʒ)

= generate ('dʒɛnə,ret)

= shock (ʃɑk)

② = excite (ɪk'saɪt)

= thrill (θrɪl)

= jolt (dʒolt)

= agitate ('ædʒə,tet)

= stir (stɜ)

= ruffle ('rʌfḷ)

= shake (ʃek)

= upset (ʌp'sɛt)

elegant ('ɛləgənt) adj. 優雅的

= refined (rɪ'faɪnd)

= superior (sə'pɪrɪə , su-)

= tasteful ('testfəl)

= polished ('pɑlɪʃt)

= cultured ('kʌltʃəd)

= fine (faɪn)

elementary (,ɛlə'mɛntərɪ) adj.
基本的

= fundamental (,fʌndə'mɛntḷ)

= basic ('besɪk)

= primary ('praɪ,mɛrɪ , -mərɪ)

= essential (ə'sɛnʃəl)

= simple ('sɪmpḷ)

= beginning (bɪ'gɪnɪŋ)

= introductory (,ɪntrə'dʌktərɪ)

= initial (ɪ'nɪʃəl)

= underlying ('ʌndə,laɪɪŋ)

elevate ('ɛlə,vet) v. 提高

= lift (lɪft)

= raise (rez)

= boost (bust)

elf (ɛlf) n. 小精靈

= devil ('dɛvḷ)

= imp (ɪmp)

= fairy ('fɛrɪ)

= mischief-maker
('mɪstʃɪf,mekə)

elicit (ɪ'lɪsɪt) v. 引出

= summon ('sʌmən)

= secure (sɪ'kjur)

= *draw forth*

= *get from*

eligible ('ɛlɪdʒəbḷ) adj. 合格的

= qualified ('kwɑlə,faɪd)

= fit (fɪt)

= desirable (dɪ'zaɪrəbḷ)

= suitable ('sutəbḷ , 'sju-)

eliminate (ɪ'lɪmə,net) v. 除去

= remove (rɪ'muv)

= discard (dɪs'kɑrd)

= reject (rɪ'dʒɛkt)

= exclude (ɪk'sklud)

= *throw out*

= *get rid of*

= *dispose of*

elongate ﹝ ɪ'lɔŋget ﹞ v. 延伸

= lengthen ﹝ 'lɛŋkθən , 'lɛŋθ- ﹞

= extend ﹝ ɪk'stɛnd ﹞

= stretch ﹝ strɛtʃ ﹞

= prolong ﹝ prə'lɔŋ , -'laŋ ﹞

elope ﹝ ɪ'lop ﹞ v. 逃亡

= flee ﹝ fli ﹞

= run ﹝ rʌn ﹞

= escape ﹝ ə'skep , ɪ- , ɛ- ﹞

eloquent ﹝ 'ɛləkwənt ﹞ adj. 雄辯的

= fluent ﹝ 'fluənt ﹞

= meaningful ﹝ 'minɪŋfəl ﹞

= expressive ﹝ ɪk'sprɛsɪv ﹞

= well-spoken ﹝ 'wɛl'spokən ﹞

else ﹝ ɛls ﹞ adj. 其他的

= other ﹝ 'ʌðə ﹞

= different ﹝ 'dɪfərənt ﹞

= instead ﹝ ɪn'stɛd ﹞

= another ﹝ ə'nʌðə ﹞

elude ﹝ ɪ'lud , ɪ'ljud ﹞ v. 躲避

= avoid ﹝ ə'vɔɪd ﹞

= escape ﹝ ə'skep , ɪ- , ɛ- ﹞

= evade ﹝ ɪ'ved ﹞

= miss ﹝ mɪs ﹞

= dodge ﹝ dadʒ ﹞

emaciated ﹝ ɪ'meʃɪ,etɪd ﹞ adj. 瘦弱的

= thin ﹝ θɪn ﹞

= undernourished ﹝ ,ʌndə'nɝɪʃt ﹞

= wasted ﹝ 'westɪd ﹞

= starved ﹝ 'starvd ﹞

= haggard ﹝ 'hægəd ﹞

emancipate ﹝ ɪ'mænsə,pet ﹞ v. 解放

= free ﹝ fri ﹞

= release ﹝ rɪ'lis ﹞

= liberate ﹝ 'lɪbə,ret ﹞

= deliver ﹝ dɪ'lɪvə ﹞

= rescue ﹝ 'rɛskju ﹞

= save ﹝ sev ﹞

embalm ﹝ ɪm'bam ﹞ v. 保存

= preserve ﹝ prɪ'zɝv ﹞

= keep ﹝ kip ﹞

embankment ﹝ ɪm'bæŋkmənt ﹞ n. 堤防

= bank ﹝ bæŋk ﹞

= buttress ﹝ 'bʌtrɪs ﹞

= shore ﹝ ʃor , ʃɔr ﹞

= barrier ﹝ 'bærɪə ﹞

= dam ﹝ dæm ﹞

= fortification ﹝ ,fɔrtəfə'keʃən ﹞

embark ﹝ ɪm'bark ﹞ v. 上車 ; 出發

= depart ﹝ dɪ'part ﹞

= start ﹝ start ﹞

= board ﹝ bord , bɔrd ﹞

embarrass ﹝ ɪm'bærəs ﹞ v. 困窘

= fluster ﹝ 'flʌstə ﹞

= confuse ﹝ kən'fjuz ﹞

= bewilder ﹝ bɪ'wɪldə ﹞

= humiliate ﹝ hju'mɪlɪ,et ﹞

E

E

= shame (ʃem)

= mortify ('mɔrtə,faɪ)

embed (ɪm'bɛd) *v.* 埋入；插入

= enclose (ɪn'kloz)

= fix (fɪks)

= root (rut)

= plant (plænt)

= lodge (lɑdʒ)

= wedge (wɛdʒ)

= inset (ɪn'sɛt)

= inlay (ɪn'le)

embezzle (ɪm'bɛzl̩) *v.* 盜用

= steal (stil)

= thieve (θiv)

= take (tek)

= rob (rɑb)

embitter (ɪm'bɪtɚ) *v.* 激怒

= anger ('æŋgɚ)

= provoke (prə'vok)

= incense (ɪn'sɛns)

= arouse (ə'raʊz)

= inflame (ɪn'flem)

= alienate ('eljən,et)

= antagonize (æn'tægə,naɪz)

= *set against*

emblem ('ɛmbləm) *n.* 象徵

= symbol ('sɪmbl̩)

= sign (saɪn)

= token ('tokən)

= badge (bædʒ)

= mark (mɑrk)

embody (ɪm'bɑdɪ) *v.* 編入

= include (ɪn'klud)

= comprise (kəm'praɪz)

= contain (kən'ten)

= cover ('kʌvɚ)

= embrace (ɪm'bres)

= incorporate (ɪn'kɔrpə,ret)

= *take in*

embrace (ɪm'bres) *v.* ①擁抱 ②包含 ③接受

① = grasp (græsp)

= hug (hʌg)

= clasp (klæsp)

= enfold (ɪn'fold)

= press (prɛs)

= hold (hold)

= clutch (klʌtʃ)

② = include (ɪn'klud)

= contain (kən'ten)

= comprise (kəm'praɪz)

= cover ('kʌvɚ)

= involve (ɪn'vɑlv)

③ = accept (ək'sɛpt , æk-)

= adopt (ə'dɑpt)

= *take up*

embroider (ɪm'brɔɪdɚ) *v.* ①潤飾 ②舖張

① = stitch (stɪtʃ)

= decorate ('dɛkə,ret)

= ornament ('ɔrnə,mɛnt)

= adorn (ə'dɔrn)

= trim (trɪm)

= embellish (ɪm'bɛlɪʃ)

② = exaggerate (ɪg'zædʒə,ret)

= overstate (,ovə'stet)
= overdo (,ovə'du)
= stretch (strɛtʃ)
= magnify ('mægnə,faɪ)

emerge (ɪ'mɝdʒ) v. 出現

= appear (ə'pɪr)
= *come out*
= *come into view*

emergency (ɪ'mɝdʒənsɪ) n.
緊急

= crisis ('kraɪsɪs)
= danger ('dendʒə)
= period ('pɪrɪəd)
= pinch (pɪntʃ)

emigrate ('ɛmə,gret) v. 移居

= leave (liv)
= migrate ('maɪgret)

eminent ('ɛmənənt) adj.
聞名的；卓越的

= high (haɪ)
= great (gret)
= prominent ('pramənənt)
= noble ('nobl̩)
= distinguished (dɪ'stɪŋgwɪʃt)
= superior (sə'pɪrɪə, su-)
= important (ɪm'pɔrtn̩t)
= outstanding ('aʊt'stændɪŋ)
= famous ('feməs)

emissary ('ɛmə,sɛrɪ) n. 密使

= delegate ('dɛlə,get)

= messenger ('mɛsn̩dʒə)
= envoy ('ɛnvɔɪ)
= agent ('edʒənt)
= diplomat ('dɪplə,mæt)
= minister ('mɪnɪstə)
= ambassador (æm'bæsədə)
= spy (spaɪ)

emit (ɪ'mɪt) v. 放射

= discharge (dɪs'tʃardʒ)
= ooze (uz)
= *give off*
= *send out*

emotion (ɪ'moʃən) n. 情感

= feeling ('filɪŋ)
= sentiment ('sɛntəmənt)
= sensitivity (,sɛnsə'tɪvətɪ)
= excitement (ɪk'saɪtmənt)

emphasis ('ɛmfəsɪs) n. 強調

= stress (strɛs)
= importance (ɪm'pɔrtn̩s)
= accent ('æksɛnt)
= insistence (ɪn'sɪstəns)

employ (ɪm'plɔɪ) v. 僱用

= hire (haɪr)
= engage (ɪn'gedʒ)
= contract (kən'trækt)
= sign (saɪn)
= retain (rɪ'ten)
= occupy ('akjə,paɪ)
= busy ('bɪzɪ)
= use (juz)

E

empower (ɪm'pauɚ) v.
使能夠；授權

= permit (pɚ'mɪt)
= enable (ɪn'ebḷ)
= authorize ('ɔθə,raɪz)
= sanction ('sæŋkʃən)
= license ('laɪsn̩s)
= warrant ('wɔrənt , 'warənt)
= commission (kə'mɪʃən)
= delegate ('dɛlə,get)
= assign (ə'saɪn)
= entrust (ɪn'trʌst)
= *take in*

empty ('ɛmptɪ) ① v. 使空
② v. 流出 ③ adj. 空的

① = discharge (dɪs'tʃardʒ)
= eliminate (ɪ'lɪmə,net)
= evacuate (ɪ'vækju,et)
= *let out*
② = drain (dren)
= *run out*
= *flow out*
③ = vacant ('vekənt)
= void (vɔɪd)
= barren ('bærən)
= blank (blæŋk)
= hollow ('halo)

emulate ('ɛmjə,let) v. 與…競爭

= imitate ('ɪmə,tet)
= follow ('falo)
= copy ('kapɪ)
= rival ('raɪvḷ)
= *vie with*
= *compete with*

enable (ɪn'ebḷ) v. 使能夠；准許

= empower (ɪm'pauɚ)
= qualify ('kwalə,faɪ)
= authorize ('ɔθə,raɪz)
= sanction ('sæŋkʃən)
= license ('laɪsn̩s)

enact (ɪn'ækt) v. ①通過
②扮演

① = pass (pæs , pas)
= legislate ('lɛdʒɪs,let)
② = portray (por'tre , pɔr-)
= represent (,rɛprɪ'zɛnt)
= perform (pɚ'fɔrm)
= stage (stedʒ)
= *act out*

enchant (ɪn'tʃænt) v. 使入迷

= delight (dɪ'laɪt)
= charm (tʃarm)
= thrill (θrɪl)
= enthrall (ɪn'θrɔl)
= titillate ('tɪtḷ,et)
= fascinate ('fæsn̩,et)
= captivate ('kæptə,vet)

encircle (ɪn'sɝkḷ) v. 包圍

= include (ɪn'klud)
= comprise (kəm'praɪz)
= enclose (ɪn'kloz)
= surround (sə'raund)
= encompass (ɪn'kʌmpəs)
= bound (baund)

enclose (ɪn'kloz) v. 圍繞

= surround (sə'raund)

E

= fence〔fɛns〕

= contain〔kən'ten〕

= include〔ɪn'klud〕

= encircle〔ɪn's3kl̩〕

= envelop〔ɪn'vɛləp〕

= *shut in*

encompass〔ɪn'kʌmpəs〕*v.*
包圍

= encircle〔ɪn's3kl̩〕

= include〔ɪn'klud〕

= surround〔sə'raʊnd〕

= enclose〔ɪn'kloz〕

encore〔'ɑŋkɔr , 'ɑn-〕① *int.* 再
② *n.* 要求再演

① = again〔ə'gɛn , ə'gen〕

② = repetition〔ˌrɛpɪ'tɪʃən〕

= *curtain call*

encounter〔ɪn'kaʊntɚ〕*v.*
①遭遇　②迎戰

① = meet〔mit〕

= come *across*

② = battle〔'bætl̩〕

= confront〔kən'frʌnt〕

= collide〔kə'laɪd〕

= oppose〔ə'poz〕

encourage〔ɪn'k3ɪdʒ〕*v.* 鼓勵

= support〔sə'port , -'pɔrt〕

= urge〔3dʒ〕

= invite〔ɪn'vaɪt〕

= promote〔prə'mot〕

= sponsor〔'spɑnsɚ〕

= cheer〔tʃɪr〕

= inspire〔ɪn'spaɪr〕

encroach〔ɪn'krotʃ〕*v.* 侵佔

= intrude〔ɪn'trud〕

= interfere〔ˌɪntɚ'fɪr〕

= infringe〔ɪn'frɪndʒ〕

= trespass〔'trɛspəs〕

= *break in*

encumber〔ɪn'kʌmbɚ , ɛn-〕*v.*
妨礙

= burden〔'b3dn̩〕

= load〔lod〕

= hamper〔'hæmpɚ〕

= *weigh down*

= *saddle with*

E

end〔ɛnd〕*v.* 結束

= finish〔'fɪnɪʃ〕

= stop〔stɑp〕

= terminate〔't3məˌnet〕

= close〔kloz〕

= conclude〔kən'klud〕

= cease〔sis〕

= quit〔kwɪt〕

= discontinue〔ˌdɪskən'tɪnju〕

= halt〔hɔlt〕

= result〔rɪ'zʌlt〕

= complete〔kəm'plit〕

= *wind up*

= *clean up*

endanger〔ɪn'dendʒɚ , ɛn-〕*v.*
危及

= risk〔rɪsk〕

= imperil〔ɪm'pɛrəl〕

= jeopardize ('dʒɛpəd,aɪz)
= hazard ('hæzəd)

endear (ɪn'dɪr , ɛn-) v. 使親密

= charm (tʃɑrm)
= captivate ('kæptə,vet)
= allure (ə'lɪʊr , -'lʊr)

endeavor (ɪn'dɛvə) v. 努力

= try (traɪ)
= effort ('ɛfət)
= strive (straɪv)
= attempt (ə'tɛmpt)
= labor ('lebə)
= struggle ('strʌgḷ)

endless ('ɛndlɪs) adj. 不停的

= continuous (kən'tɪnjʊəs)
= constant ('kɑnstənt)
= ceaseless ('sislɪs)
= incessant (ɪn'sɛsṇt)
= uninterrupted (,ʌnɪntə'rʌptɪd)
= nonstop ('nɑn'stɑp)
= eternal (ɪ't3nḷ)
= infinite ('ɪnfənɪt)
= perpetual (pə'pɛtʃʊəl)
= everlasting (,ɛvə'læstɪŋ)

endorse (ɪn'dɔrs , ɛn-) v. 簽名；
支持

= sign (saɪn)
= approve (ə'pruv)
= support (sə'port , -'pɔrt)
= accept (ək'sɛpt , æk-)
= ratify ('rætə,faɪ)
= certify ('s3tə,faɪ)

= confirm (kən'f3m)
= O.K. ('o'ke)
= validate ('vælə,det)
= pass (pæs , pɑs)

endow (ɪn'daʊ) v. 賦與

= give (gɪv)
= invest (ɪn'vɛst)
= bequeath (bɪ'kwið)
= provide (prə'vaɪd)
= supply (sə'plaɪ)
= furnish ('f3nɪʃ)
= contribute (kən'trɪbjut)

endure (ɪn'djʊr) v. ①持久
②忍受

① = last (læst , lɑst)
= continue (kən'tɪnju)
= persist (pə'zɪst , -'sɪst)
= remain (rɪ'men)
= stay (ste)
② = stand (stænd)
= undergo (,ʌndə'go)
= bear (bɛr)
= experience (ɪk'spɪrɪəns)
= feel (fil)
= suffer ('sʌfə)
= tolerate ('tɑlə,ret)

enemy ('ɛnəmɪ) n. 敵人

= opponent (ə'ponənt)
= foe (fo)
= opposition (,ɑpə'zɪʃən)

energy ('ɛnədʒɪ) n. 力量

= force (fors , fɔrs)

= strength〔 strɛŋθ , strɛŋkθ 〕
= vigor〔'vɪgɚ 〕
= potency〔'potn̩sɪ 〕
= vim〔 vɪm 〕
= drive〔 draɪv 〕
= might〔 maɪt 〕
= power〔'pauɚ 〕
= vitality〔 vaɪ'tælətɪ 〕
= stamina〔'stæmənə 〕

enfold〔 ɪn'fold 〕 v. 圍繞

= embrace〔 ɪm'bres 〕
= clasp〔 klæsp 〕
= wrap〔 ræp 〕
= hug〔 hʌg 〕
= surround〔 sə'raʊnd 〕
= envelop〔 ɪn'vɛləp 〕

enforce〔 ɪn'fors 〕 v. 強迫

= compel〔 kəm'pɛl 〕
= force〔 fors , fɔrs 〕
= make〔 mek 〕
= oblige〔 ə'blaɪdʒ 〕
= drive〔 draɪv 〕
= execute〔'ɛksɪ,kjut 〕

engage〔 ɪn'gedʒ 〕 v. ①佔去 ②僱 ③允諾

① = involve〔 ɪn'vɑlv 〕
= entangle〔 ɪn'tæŋgl̩ , ɛn- 〕
= absorb〔 əb'sɔrb 〕
= engross〔 ɪn'gros , ɛn- 〕
= occupy〔'ɑkjə,paɪ 〕
= hold〔 hold 〕
= grip〔 grɪp 〕
② = employ〔 ɪm'plɔɪ 〕

= busy〔'bɪzɪ 〕
= hire〔 haɪr 〕
= *contract for*
③ = promise〔'prɑmɪs 〕
= agree〔 ə'gri 〕

engaging〔 ɪn'gedʒɪŋ , ɛn- 〕 *adj.* 迷人的

= interesting〔'ɪnt(ə)rɪstɪŋ 〕
= absorbing〔 əb'sɔrbɪŋ 〕
= fascinating〔'fæsn̩,etɪŋ 〕
= engrossing〔 ɛn'grosɪŋ 〕
= enthralling〔 ɪn'θrɔlɪŋ 〕
= spellbinding〔'spɛl,baɪndɪŋ 〕
= charming〔'tʃɑrmɪŋ 〕
= enchanting〔 ɪn'tʃæntɪŋ 〕
= captivating〔'kæptə,vetɪŋ 〕
= appealing〔 ə'pilɪŋ 〕
= tempting〔'tɛmptɪŋ 〕
= enticing〔 ɪn'taɪsɪŋ , ɛn- 〕
= delightful〔 dɪ'laɪtfəl 〕
= lovely〔'lʌvlɪ 〕
= exquisite〔'ɛkskwɪzɪt , ɪk's- 〕

engender〔 ɪn'dʒɛndɚ , ɛn- 〕 v. 產生

= cause〔 kɔz 〕
= produce〔 prə'djus 〕
= develop〔 dɪ'vɛləp 〕
= generate〔'dʒɛnə,ret 〕
= breed〔 brid 〕

engineer〔,ɛndʒə'nɪr 〕 v. 監督

= guide〔 gaɪd 〕
= manage〔'mænɪdʒ 〕
= direct〔 də'rɛkt , daɪ- 〕

= regulate ('rɛgjə,let)

= conduct (kən'dʌkt)

= run (rʌn)

= lead (lid)

= maneuver (mə'nuvɚ)

engrave (ɪn'grev) v. 雕刻

= carve (karv)

= cut (kʌt)

= fix (fɪks)

= print (prɪnt)

= inscribe (ɪn'skraɪb)

= stamp (stæmp)

= sketch (skɛtʃ)

= impress (ɪm'prɛs)

engross (ɪn'gros , ɛn-) v. 使專心

= occupy ('akjə,paɪ)

= absorb (əb'sɔrb)

= engage (ɪn'gedʒ)

= fascinate ('fæsn̩,et)

= enthrall (ɪn'θrɔl)

engulf (ɪn'gʌlf , ɛn-) v. 吞噬

= swallow ('swalo)

= devour (dɪ'vaʊr)

= flood (flʌd)

= inundate ('ɪnʌn,det , ɪn'ʌndet)

enhance (ɪn'hæns) v. 提高

= improve (ɪm'pruv)

= better ('bɛtɚ)

= enrich (ɪn'rɪtʃ)

= uplift (ʌp'lɪft)

enigma (ɪ'nɪgmə) n. 謎

= riddle ('rɪdl̩)

= puzzle ('pʌzl̩)

= mystery ('mɪstrɪ , 'mɪstərɪ)

= problem ('prabləm)

= stumper ('stʌmpɚ)

enjoy (ɪn'dʒɔɪ) v. 享受

= like (laɪk)

= appreciate (ə'priʃɪ,et)

= savor ('sevɚ)

= relish ('rɛlɪʃ)

enlarge (ɪn'lardʒ) v. 擴充

= increase (ɪn'kris)

= expand (ɪk'spænd)

= broaden ('brɔdn̩)

= magnify ('mægnə,faɪ)

enlighten (ɪn'laɪtn̩) v. 啓迪

= clarify ('klærə,faɪ)

= inform (ɪn'fɔrm)

= instruct (ɪn'strʌkt)

= illuminate (ɪ'lumə,net , ɪ'lju-)

= explain (ɪk'splen)

= simplify ('sɪmplə,faɪ)

= acquaint (ə'kwent)

= teach (titʃ)

= educate ('ɛdʒə,ket , -dʒu-)

enlist (ɪn'lɪst) v. ①入伍
②使參加

① = join (dʒɔɪn)

= enroll (ɪn'rol)

= *sign up*

② = induce (ɪn'djus)

= prompt (prampt)

= move〔muv〕
= influence〔'ɪnfluəns〕
= sway〔swe〕
= persuade〔pɚ'swed〕

enliven〔ɪn'laɪvən , ɛn-〕*v.*
使活潑

= stimulate〔'stɪmjə,let〕
= inspire〔ɪn'spaɪr〕
= cheer〔tʃɪr〕
= brighten〔'braɪtn̩〕

enmity〔'ɛnmətɪ〕*n.* 敵意

= hate〔het〕
= dislike〔dɪs'laɪk〕
= loathing〔'loðɪŋ〕
= unfriendliness〔ʌn'frɛndlɪnɪs〕

enormous〔ɪ'nɔrməs〕*adj.*
極大的

= large〔lɑrdʒ〕
= great〔gret〕
= vast〔væst , vɑst〕
= immense〔ɪ'mɛns〕
= huge〔hjudʒ〕
= colossal〔kə'lɑsl̩〕
= giant〔'dʒaɪənt〕

enough〔ə'nʌf , ɪ'nʌf〕*adj.*
足夠的

= sufficient〔sə'fɪʃənt〕
= ample〔'æmpl̩〕
= plenty〔'plɛntɪ〕
= satisfactory〔,sætɪs'fæktərɪ〕
= adequate〔'ædəkwɪt〕

enrage〔ɪn'redʒ , ɛn-〕*v.* 激怒

= madden〔'mædn̩〕
= infuriate〔ɪn'fjʊrɪ,et〕
= anger〔'æŋgɚ〕
= inflame〔ɪn'flem〕
= provoke〔prə'vok〕

enrich〔ɪn'rɪtʃ〕*v.* 使富足

= improve〔ɪm'pruv〕
= enhance〔ɪn'hæns〕
= better〔'bɛtɚ〕
= uplift〔ʌp'lɪft〕

enroll〔ɪn'rol〕*v.* ①登記
②列入

① = list〔lɪst〕
= register〔'rɛdʒɪstɚ〕
= write〔raɪt〕
= record〔rɪ'kɔrd〕
= join〔dʒɔɪn〕
② = enlist〔ɪn'lɪst〕
= draft〔dræft〕
= induct〔ɪn'dʌkt〕
= recruit〔rɪ'krut〕

enshrine〔ɪn'ʃraɪn , ɛn-〕*v.* 埋

= entomb〔ɪn'tum , ɛn-〕
= inter〔ɪn'tɝ〕
= bury〔'bɛrɪ〕

ensign〔'ɛnsaɪn , 'ɛnsn̩〕*n.*
①旗幟 ②海軍少尉

① = flag〔flæg〕
= banner〔'bænɚ〕
= pennant〔'pɛnənt〕
= standard〔'stændɚd〕

E

= colors ('kʌlɚz)
② = officer ('ɔfəsɚ , 'af-)

enslave (ɪn'slev , ɛn-) v. 奴役

= subject ('sʌbdʒɪkt)
= capture ('kæptʃɚ)
= *hold down*

ensue (ɛn'su , ɛn'sju) v.
因而發生

= follow ('falo)
= succeed (sək'sid)
= result (rɪ'zʌlt)

ensure (ɪn'ʃur) v. ①保證
②保護

① = assure (ə'ʃur)
= guarantee (͵gærən'ti)
= *make certain*
② = protect (prə'tɛkt)
= guard (gard)
= defend (dɪ'fɛnd)
= shelter ('ʃɛltɚ)
= cover ('kʌvɚ)
= shield (ʃild)
= screen (skrin)

entangle (ɪn'tæŋgḷ , ɛn-) v.
使複雜

= involve (ɪn'valv)
= complicate ('kamplə͵ket)
= confuse (kən'fjuz)
= trap (træp)
= snare (snɛr)

enter ('ɛntɚ) v. 參加

= join (dʒɔɪn)
= *go into*
= *set foot in*

enterprise ('ɛntɚ͵praɪz) n.
事業；進取心

= ambition (æm'bɪʃən)
= project ('pradʒɛkt)
= endeavor (ɪn'dɛvɚ)
= undertaking (͵ʌndɚ'tekɪŋ)
= business ('bɪznɪs)
= venture ('vɛntʃɚ)
= deed (did)
= exploit ('ɛksplɔɪt , ɪk'splɔɪt)
= achievement (ə'tʃivmənt)
= adventure (əd'vɛntʃɚ)

entertain (͵ɛntɚ'ten) v.
①使娛樂　②考慮

① = amuse (ə'mjuz)
= delight (dɪ'laɪt)
= interest ('ɪntərɪst , 'ɪntrɪst)
= excite (ɪk'saɪt)
= fascinate ('fæsn͵et)
= give *a party*
② = consider (kən'sɪdɚ)
= contemplate ('kantəm͵plet)
= *have in mind*

enthrall (ɪn'θrɔl) v. 迷惑

= fascinate ('fæsn͵et)
= charm (tʃarm)
= captivate ('kæptə͵vet)
= intrigue (ɪn'trig)
= enchant (ɪn'tʃænt)
= delight (dɪ'laɪt)

= titillate ('tɪtl̩,et)
= thrill (θrɪl)

enthrone (ɪn'θron) *v.* 尊崇；
使就任

= crown (kraʊn)
= glorify ('glorə,faɪ , 'glɔr-)
= exalt (ɪg'zɔlt)
= install (ɪn'stɔl)
= instate (ɪn'stet)
= inaugurate (ɪn'ɔgjə,ret)

enthusiastic (ɪn,θjuzɪ'æstɪk)
adj. 熱心的

= interested ('ɪntərɪstɪd)
= attracted (ə'træktɪd)
= eager ('igɚ)
= *keen about*

entice (ɪn'taɪs , ɛn-) *v.* 誘惑

= attract (ə'trækt)
= tempt (tɛmpt)
= lure (lʊr)
= seduce (sɪ'djus)

entirely (ɪn'taɪrlɪ) *adv.* 全部地

= wholly ('holɪ , 'hollɪ)
= fully ('fʊlɪ)
= altogether (,ɔltə'gɛθɚ)
= completely (kəm'plitlɪ)
= thoroughly ('θɝolɪ , -əlɪ)
= totally ('totl̩ɪ)
= exclusively (ɪk'sklusɪvlɪ , ɛk-)
= solely ('sollɪ)

entitle (ɪn'taɪtl̩) *v.* ①定名稱
②授權

① = name (nem)
= call (kɔl)
= designate ('dɛzɪg,net)
= tag (tæg)
= label ('lebl̩)
= title ('taɪtl̩)
= identify (aɪ'dɛntə,faɪ)
② = authorize ('ɔθə,raɪz)
= empower (ɪm'paʊɚ)
= enable (ɪn'ebl̩)
= license ('laɪsn̩s)

entrance (ɪn'træns , ɛn- ,
-'trɑns) *v.* ①使狂喜 ②使昏迷

① = fascinate ('fæsn̩,et)
= charm (tʃɑrm)
= intrigue (ɪn'trig)
= enthrall (ɪn'θrɔl)
= enchant (ɪn'tʃænt)
= delight (dɪ'laɪt)
= thrill (θrɪl)
② = hypnotize ('hɪpnə,taɪz)
= spellbind ('spɛl,baɪnd)

entreat (ɪn'trit) *v.* 懇求

= beg (bɛg)
= ask (æsk)
= implore (ɪm'plor , -'plɔr)
= plead (plid)

entrust (ɪn'trʌst) *v.* 委託

= delegate ('dɛlə,get)
= assign (ə'saɪn)
= charge (tʃɑrdʒ)
= commission (kə'mɪʃən)

E

E

enumerate (ɪ'njumə,ret) v. 列舉

= list (lɪst)
= count (kaʊnt)
= tally ('tælɪ)
= number ('nʌmbə)

enunciate (ɪ'nʌnsɪ,et , -ʃɪ-) v. 發音;宣告

= speak (spik)
= pronounce (prə'naʊns)
= announce (ə'naʊns)
= state (stet)
= express (ɪk'sprɛs)

envelop (ɪn'vɛləp) v. 包裝

= wrap (ræp)
= cover ('kʌvə)
= embrace (ɪm'bres)
= surround (sə'raʊnd)
= encompass (ɪn'kʌmpəs , ɛn-)
= hide (haɪd)
= conceal (kən'sil)

environment (ɪn'vaɪrənmənt) n. 環境

= surroundings (sə'raʊndɪŋz)
= neighborhood ('nebə,hʊd)
= vicinity (və'sɪnətɪ)
= setting ('sɛtɪŋ)

envoy ('ɛnvɔɪ) n. 使者

= messenger ('mɛsn̩dʒə)
= delegate ('dɛlə,get)
= agent ('edʒənt)
= diplomat ('dɪplə,mæt)

envy ('ɛnvɪ) v. 羨慕

= covet ('kʌvɪt)
= be jealous of

epidemic (,ɛpə'dɛmɪk) adj. 傳染性的

= widespread ('waɪd'sprɛd)
= prevalent ('prɛvələnt)
= contagious (kən'tedʒəs)
= infectious (ɪn'fɛkʃəs)
= catching ('kætʃɪŋ)

episode ('ɛpə,sod , -,zod) n. 插曲

= occurrence (ə'kɝəns)
= happening ('hæpənɪŋ)
= experience (ɪk'spɪrɪəns)
= event (ɪ'vɛnt)
= incident ('ɪnsədənt)
= affair (ə'fɛr)

epoch ('ɛpək) n. 紀元

= era ('ɪrə , 'irə)
= period ('pɪrɪəd)
= age (edʒ)

equal ('ikwəl) v. 比得上;不亞於

= match (mætʃ)
= rival ('raɪvl̩)
= tie (taɪ)
= parallel ('pærə,lɛl)

equilibrium (,ikwə'lɪbrɪəm) n. 平衡

= balance ('bæləns)
= stability (stə'bɪlətɪ)

= firmness ('fɜmnɪs)

= soundness ('saʊndnɪs)

= steadiness ('stɛdɪnɪs)

equip (ɪ'kwɪp) *v.* 裝備

= provide (prə'vaɪd)

= furnish ('fɜnɪʃ)

= fit (fɪt)

= prepare (prɪ'pɛr)

= rig (rɪg)

= costume (kɑ'stjum)

equitable ('ɛkwɪtəbḷ) *adj.*
公平的

= fair (fɛr)

= just (dʒʌst)

= square (skwɛr)

= even ('ivən)

= rightful ('raɪtfəl)

= due (dju)

= fit (fɪt)

= proper ('prɑpɚ)

equivalent (ɪ'kwɪvələnt) *n.*
相等物

= equal ('ikwəl)

= match (mætʃ)

= like (laɪk)

= rival ('raɪvḷ)

= substitute ('sʌbstə,tjut)

= replacement (rɪ'plesmənt)

era ('ɪrə , 'irə) *n.* 紀元

= epoch ('ɛpək)

= period ('pɪrɪəd)

= age (edʒ)

eradicate (ɪ'rædɪ,ket) *v.* 根除

= eliminate (ɪ'lɪmə,net)

= remove (rɪ'muv)

= exterminate (ɪk'stɜmə,net)

= *get rid of*

erase (ɪ'res) *v.* 抹去

= cancel ('kænsḷ)

= obliterate (ə'blɪtə,ret)

= *wipe out*

= *cross off*

erect (ɪ'rɛkt) ① *v.* 建立
② *adj.* 直立的

① = build (bɪld)

= construct (kən'strʌkt)

= *make rise*

② = upright ('ʌp,raɪt)

= vertical ('vɜtɪk)

= straight (stret)

erode (ɪ'rod) *v.* 腐蝕

= disintegrate (dɪs'ɪntə,gret)

= corrode (kə'rod)

= rust (rʌst)

= *break up*

= *wear away*

err (ɜ) *v.* 犯錯

= misjudge (mɪs'dʒʌdʒ)

= slip (slɪp)

= sin (sɪn)

= *go wrong*

errand ('ɛrənd) *n.* 工作

= task (tæsk , tɑsk)

= job (dʒɑb)

= chore (tʃor , tʃɔr)

= assignment (ə'saɪnmənt)

= duty ('djutɪ)

= exercise ('ɛksəˌsaɪz)

errant ('ɛrənt) *adj.* 漂泊的

= wandering ('wɑndərɪŋ)

= roving ('rovɪŋ)

= roaming ('romɪŋ)

= rambling ('ræmblɪŋ)

= meandering (mɪ'ændrɪŋ)

= drifting ('drɪftɪŋ)

= straying ('streɪŋ)

= vagrant ('vegrənt)

erratic (ə'rætɪk) *adj.* 不穩定的

= uncertain (ʌn'sɝtn̩)

= irregular (ɪ'rɛgjələ)

= queer (kwɪr)

= abnormal (æb'nɔrml̩)

= unusual (ʌn'juʒuəl)

= changeable ('tʃendʒəbl̩)

= unstable (ʌn'stebl̩)

erroneous (ə'ronɪəs , ɛ-) *adj.* 錯誤的

= mistaken (mə'stekən)

= incorrect (ˌɪnkə'rɛkt)

= untrue (ʌn'tru)

= wrong (rɔŋ)

= false (fɔls)

erupt (ɪ'rʌpt) *v.* 迸出

= vomit ('vɑmɪt)

= discharge (dɪs'tʃɑrdʒ)

= *burst forth*

= *pour out*

escape (ə'skep , ɪ- , ɛ-) *v.* 逃脫

= evade (ɪ'ved)

= flee (fli)

= *get away*

escort (ɪ'skɔrt) *v.* 護送

= accompany (ə'kʌmpənɪ)

= conduct (kən'dʌkt)

= guide (gaɪd)

= lead (lid)

= usher ('ʌʃə)

= attend (ə'tɛnd)

= squire (skwaɪr)

= chaperon ('ʃæpəˌron)

especially (ə'spɛʃəlɪ) *adv.* 特別地

= particularly (pə'tɪkjələlɪ)

= principally ('prɪnsəplɪ)

= chiefly ('tʃiflɪ)

= mainly ('menlɪ)

= mostly ('mostlɪ)

= primarily ('praɪˌmɛrəlɪ)

espionage ('ɛspɪənɪdʒ , ə'spaɪənɪdʒ , ˌɛspɪə'nɑʒ) *n.* 間諜活動

= spying ('spaɪɪŋ)

essay (*v.* ə'se , ɛ'se , *n.* 'ɛsɪ , 'ɛse)
① *v.* 嘗試　② *n.* 文章

① = try (traɪ)

= attempt (ə'tɛmpt)

= test〔tɛst〕
= experiment〔ɪk'spɛrəmənt〕
= undertake〔ˌʌndə'tek〕
② = composition〔ˌkɑmpə'zɪʃən〕
= article〔'ɑrtɪkḷ〕
= study〔'stʌdɪ〕
= paper〔'pepə〕
= thesis〔'θisɪs〕

essence〔'ɛsṇs〕 n. ①本質
②香水

① = meaning〔'minɪŋ〕
= significance〔sɪg'nɪfəkəns〕
= substance〔'sʌbstəns〕
② = perfume〔'pɝfjum〕
= scent〔sɛnt〕
= smell〔smɛl〕
= odor〔'odə〕
= fragrance〔'fregrəns〕

essential〔ə'sɛnʃəl〕 adj.
基本的；重要的

= needed〔'nidɪd〕
= necessary〔'nɛsəˌsɛrɪ〕
= important〔ɪm'pɔrtṇt〕
= vital〔'vaɪtḷ〕
= fundamental〔ˌfʌndə'mɛntḷ〕
= required〔rɪ'kwaɪrd〕
= basic〔'besɪk〕

establish〔ə'stæblɪʃ〕 v. ①建立
②證實

① = fix〔fɪks〕
= set〔sɛt〕
= settle〔'sɛtḷ〕
= found〔faund〕

= organize〔'ɔrgənˌaɪz〕
② = prove〔pruv〕
= demonstrate〔'dɛmənˌstret〕
= show〔ʃo〕

estate〔ə'stet〕 n. 財產

= property〔'prɑpətɪ〕
= land〔lænd〕

esteem〔ə'stim〕 v. ①認為
②重視

① = think〔θɪŋk〕
= consider〔kən'sɪdə〕
= judge〔dʒʌdʒ〕
= regard〔rɪ'gɑrd〕
② = prize〔praɪz〕
= value〔'vælju〕
= appreciate〔ə'priʃɪˌet〕
= treasure〔'trɛʒə〕
= *rate highly*

estimate〔'ɛstəˌmet〕 v. 評估

= judge〔dʒʌdʒ〕
= calculate〔'kælkjəˌlet〕
= evaluate〔ɪ'væljuˌet〕
= rate〔ret〕
= value〔'vælju〕
= figure〔'fɪgə〕
= compute〔kəm'pjut〕
= gauge〔gedʒ〕

etch〔ɛtʃ〕 v. 刻畫

= engrave〔ɪn'grev〕
= imprint〔ɪm'prɪnt〕
= stamp〔stæmp〕
= impress〔ɪm'prɛs〕

E

eternal (ɪˈtɜnḷ) *adj.* 永恒的

= always (ˈɔlwez , ˈɔlwɪz)

= forever (fəˈɛvə)

= endless (ˈɛndlɪs)

= perpetual (pəˈpɛtʃuəl)

= everlasting (ˌɛvəˈlæstɪŋ)

= permanent (ˈpɜmənənt)

= infinite (ˈɪnfənɪt)

= continual (kənˈtɪnjuəl)

= constant (ˈkɑnstənt)

= ceaseless (ˈsislɪs)

ethereal (ɪˈθɪrɪəl) *adj.* 輕的

= light (laɪt)

= airy (ˈɛrɪ)

= delicate (ˈdɛləkət , -kɪt)

etiquette (ˈɛtɪ.kɛt) *n.* 禮節

= manners (ˈmænəz)

= formalities (fɔrˈmælətɪz)

= *social code*

evacuate (ɪˈvækju.et) *v.* 撤離

= leave (liv)

= withdraw (wðˈdrɔ , wɪθ-)

= remove (rɪˈmuv)

= depart (dɪˈpɑrt)

= quit (kwɪt)

= empty (ˈɛmptɪ)

= abandon (əˈbændən)

= vacate (ˈveket)

evade (ɪˈved) *v.* 逃避

= avoid (əˈvɔɪd)

= escape (əˈskep , ɪ- , ɛ-)

= miss (mɪs)

= bypass (ˈbaɪ.pæs)

evaporate (ɪˈvæpə.ret) *v.*
使消失

= vanish (ˈvænɪʃ)

= disappear (ˌdɪsəˈpɪr)

= *fade away*

even (ˈivən) ① *adj.* 平的
② *adj.* 相等的 ③ *adv.* 更

①= level (ˈlɛvḷ)

= flat (flæt)

= smooth (smuð)

②= same (sem)

= uniform (ˈjunə.fɔrm)

= equal (ˈikwəl)

= identical (aɪˈdɛntɪkḷ)

③= still (stɪḷ)

= yet (jɛt)

evening (ˈivnɪŋ) *n.* 晚間

= nightfall (ˈnaɪt.fɔl)

= sunset (ˈsʌn.sɛt)

= sundown (ˈsʌn.daʊn)

event (ɪˈvɛnt) *n.* 事件

= happening (ˈhæpənɪŋ)

= occurrence (əˈkɝəns)

= incident (ˈɪnsədənt)

= episode (ˈɛpə.sod , -.zod)

= experience (ɪkˈspɪrɪəns)

eventually (ɪˈvɛntʃuəlɪ) *adv.*
最後地

= finally (ˈfaɪnḷɪ)

= ultimately (ˈʌltəmɪtlɪ)

= *in time*

everlasting (ˌɛvɚ'læstɪŋ) *adj.*
永久的

= perpetual (pɚ'pɛtʃuəl)
= permanent ('pɝmənənt)
= eternal (ɪ'tɝnl̩)
= infinite ('ɪnfənɪt)
= endless ('ɛndlɪs)
= continual (kən'tɪnjuəl)
= constant ('kɑnstənt)
= ceaseless ('sislɪs)

evermore (ˌɛvɚ'mor , -'mɔr)
adv. 永久地

= forever (fɚ'ɛvɚ)
= always ('ɔlwez , 'ɔlwɪz)

every ('ɛvrɪ) *adj.* 所有的

= each (itʃ)
= all (ɔl)

evict (ɪ'vɪkt) *v.* 逐出

= expel (ɪk'spɛl)
= oust (aust)
= *turn out*

evidence ('ɛvədəns) *n.* 證據

= facts (fækts)
= proof (pruf)
= grounds (graundz)
= data ('detə , 'dætə , 'datə)
= indication (ˌɪndə'keʃən)
= sign (saɪn)
= clue (klu)

evident ('ɛvədənt) *adj.* 明白的

= clear (klɪr)

= plain (plen)
= apparent (ə'pærənt , ə'pɛrənt)
= obvious ('ɑbvɪəs)
= clear-cut ('klɪr'kʌt)

evil ('ivl̩) *adj.* 邪惡的

= bad (bæd)
= wrong (rɔŋ)
= sinful ('sɪnful , -fəl)
= wicked ('wɪkɪd)

evoke (ɪ'vok) *v.* 引起

= summon ('sʌmən)
= induce (ɪn'djus)
= prompt (prɑmpt)
= *bring forth*

evolve (ɪ'vɑlv) *v.* 發展

= unfold (ʌn'fold)
= develop (dɪ'vɛləp)
= grow (gro)
= progress (prə'grɛs)
= advance (əd'væns)

exact (ɪg'zækt) *adj.* 準確的

= detailed (dɪ'teld)
= precise (prɪ'saɪs)
= correct (kə'rɛkt)
= accurate ('ækjərɪt)

exaggerate (ɪg'zædʒəˌret) *v.*
誇大

= overstate (ˌovɚ'stet)
= stretch (strɛtʃ)
= overdo (ˌovɚ'du)
= magnify ('mægnəˌfaɪ)
= enlarge (ɪn'lardʒ)

E

exalt (ɪɡ'zɔlt) v. 讚揚

= honor ('ɑnɚ)

= praise (prez)

= laud (lɔd)

= extol (ɪk'stɑl , -'stol , ɛk-)

= glorify ('ɡlorə,faɪ , 'ɡlɔr-)

= compliment ('kɑmpləmənt)

= elevate ('ɛlə,vet)

examine (ɪɡ'zæmɪn) v. ①調查
②考試

① = inspect (ɪn'spɛkt)

= observe (əb'zɝv)

= study ('stʌdɪ)

= consider (kən'sɪdɚ)

= review (rɪ'vju)

= analyze ('ænl̩aɪz)

② = test (tɛst)

= question ('kwɛstʃən)

= quiz (kwɪz)

example (ɪɡ'zæmpl̩) n. ①樣本
②例題

① = sample ('sæmpl̩)

= model ('mɑdl̩)

= pattern ('pætɚn)

= representative (,rɛprɪ'zɛntətɪv)

= symbol ('sɪmbl̩)

= type (taɪp)

② = *arithmetic problem*

exasperate (ɛɡ'zæspə,ret ,
ɪɡ-) v. 激怒

= irritate ('ɪrə,tet)

= aggravate ('æɡrə,vet)

= annoy (ə'nɔɪ)

= anger ('æŋɡɚ)

= infuriate (ɪn'fjʊrɪ,et)

= madden ('mædn̩)

excavate ('ɛkskə,vet) v. 挖空

= dig (dɪɡ)

= scoop (skup)

= unearth (ʌn'ɝθ)

= burrow ('bɝo)

= *pull up*

exceed (ɪk'sid) v. 越過

= surpass (sɚ'pæs , -'pɑs)

= better ('bɛtɚ)

= excel (ɪk'sɛl)

= top (tɑp)

= cap (kæp)

= beat (bit)

excel (ɪk'sɛl) v. 勝過

= surpass (sɚ'pæs , -'pɑs)

= better ('bɛtɚ)

= top (tɑp)

= cap (kæp)

= beat (bit)

= exceed (ɪk'sid)

except (ɪk'sɛpt) prep.
①除…之外 ② v. 拒絕

① = excluding (ɪk'skludɪŋ)

= omitting (o'mɪtɪŋ , ə-)

= barring ('bɑrɪŋ)

= besides (bɪ'saɪdz)

= save (sev)

= *aside from*

= *leaving out*

= *outside of*

② = reject〔rɪ'dʒɛkt〕

= exclude〔ɪk'sklud〕

= deny〔dɪ'naɪ〕

exceptional〔ɪk'sɛpʃənḷ〕*adj.*
特別的

= unusual〔ʌn'juʒʊəl〕

= extraordinary〔ɪk'strɔrdn̩ˌɛrɪ〕

= remarkable〔rɪ'mɑrkəbḷ〕

= notable〔'notəbḷ〕

= outstanding〔'aʊt'stændɪŋ〕

excess〔ɪk'sɛs〕*adj.* 額外的；
超過的

= additional〔ə'dɪʃənḷ〕

= extra〔'ɛkstrə〕

= surplus〔'sɝplʌs〕

= remaining〔rɪ'menɪŋ〕

= *left over*

exchange〔ɪks'tʃendʒ〕*v.* 交換

= change〔tʃendʒ〕

= substitute〔'sʌbstəˌtjut〕

= switch〔swɪtʃ〕

= trade〔tred〕

= swap〔swɑp , swɔp〕

excite〔ɪk'saɪt〕*v.* 鼓舞

= arouse〔ə'raʊz〕

= stir〔stɝ〕

= stimulate〔'stɪmjəˌlet〕

= provoke〔prə'vok〕

= incite〔ɪn'saɪt〕

= move〔muv〕

= affect〔ə'fɛkt〕

exclaim〔ɪk'sklem〕*v.* 呼喊

= clamor〔'klæmɚ〕

= shout〔ʃaʊt〕

= *cry out*

exclude〔ɪk'sklud〕*v.* 拒絕

= bar〔bɑr〕

= outlaw〔'aʊtˌlɔ〕

= reject〔rɪ'dʒɛkt〕

= forbid〔fɚ'bɪd〕

= prohibit〔pro'hɪbɪt〕

= *shut out*

= *keep out*

excursion〔ɪk'skɝʒən , -ʃən〕*n.*
旅行

= trip〔trɪp〕

= journey〔'dʒɝnɪ〕

= outing〔'aʊtɪŋ〕

= tour〔tʊr〕

excuse〔*v.* ɪk'skjuz , *n.* ɪk'skjus〕
① *v.* 原諒 ② *n.* 理由

① = pardon〔'pɑrdn̩〕

= forgive〔fɚ'gɪv〕

= absolve〔æb'sɑlv , əb- , -'zɑlv〕

② = reason〔'rizn̩〕

= alibi〔'æləˌbaɪ〕

execute〔'ɛksɪˌkjut〕*v.* ①實現
②處死

① = do〔du〕

= perform〔pɚ'fɔrm〕

= complete〔kəm'plit〕

= accomplish〔ə'kɑmplɪʃ〕

= *carry out*

E

= *put into effect*

② = kill (kɪl)

= *put to death*

executive (ɪg'zɛkjʊtɪv) *adj.*
執行的

= directing (də'rɛktɪŋ , daɪ-)

= managing ('mænɪdʒɪŋ)

= administrative
(əd'mɪnə,stretɪv)

exemplify (ɪg'zɛmplə,faɪ , ɛg-)
v. 例示

= illustrate ('ɪləstret , ɪ'lʌs-)

= demonstrate ('dɛmən,stret)

= show (ʃo)

exempt (ɪg'zɛmpt , ɛg-) *v.*
使免除

= free (fri)

= release (rɪ'lis)

= excuse (ɪk'skjuz)

= except (ɪk'sɛpt)

= *let off*

exercise ('ɛksɚ,saɪz) *v.* 運動

= practice ('præktɪs)

= use (juz)

= train (tren)

= drill (drɪl)

= prepare (prɪ'pɛr)

= condition (kən'dɪʃən)

= perform (pɚ'fɔrm)

exert (ɪg'zɝt) *v.* 運用

= use (juz)

= employ (ɪm'plɔɪ)

= utilize ('jutḷ,aɪz)

= *put forth*

exhale (ɛks'hel , ɪg'zel) *v.* 發出

= blow (blo)

= expel (ɪk'spɛl)

= *breathe out*

= *give off*

exhaust (ɪg'zɔst , ɛg-) *v.* ①耗盡
②使疲憊

① = empty ('ɛmptɪ)

= drain (dren)

= consume (kən'sum , -'sjum)

= finish ('fɪnɪʃ)

= spend (spɛnd)

= *use up*

② = tire (taɪr)

= fatigue (fə'tig)

= *wear out*

= *knock out*

exhibit (ɪg'zɪbɪt) *v.* 顯示

= show (ʃo)

= demonstrate ('dɛmən,stret)

= display (dɪ'sple)

= present (prɪ'zɛnt)

= flaunt (flɔnt)

exhilarate (ɪg'zɪlə,ret , ɛg-) *v.*
使高興

= cheer (tʃɪr)

= gladden ('glædṇ)

= enliven (ɪn'laɪvən , ɛn-)

= encourage (ɪn'kɝɪdʒ)

= inspire (ɪn'spaɪr)
= stimulate ('stɪmjə,let)
= refresh (rɪ'frɛʃ)
= excite (ɪk'saɪt)

exhort (ɪg'zɔrt , ɛg-) v. 勸告

= urge (ɝdʒ)
= advise (əd'vaɪz)
= press (prɛs)
= coax (koks)
= prompt (prɑmpt)

exile ('ɛgzaɪl , 'ɛksaɪl) v. 放逐

= banish ('bænɪʃ)
= expel (ɪk'spɛl)
= deport (dɪ'port , -'port)
= ban (bæn)
= exclude (ɪk'sklud)
= *cast out*

exist (ɪg'zɪst) v. ①存在 ②發生

① = be (bi)
= live (lɪv)
② = occur (ə'kɝ)
= prevail (prɪ'vel)
= stand (stænd)

exit ('ɛgzɪt , 'ɛksɪt) v. 離去

= depart (dɪ'part)
= leave (liv)
= *go out*

exodus ('ɛksədəs) n. 離去

= departure (dɪ'partʃɚ)
= leaving ('livɪŋ)
= going ('goɪŋ)
= parting ('partɪŋ)

= exit ('ɛgzɪt , 'ɛksɪt)

exorbitant (ɪg'zɔrbətənt) adj.
過度的

= excessive (ɪk'sɛsɪv)
= unreasonable (ʌn'riznəbl̩)
= outrageous (aʊt'redʒəs)
= overpriced (,ovɚ'praɪst)

exotic (ɪg'zɑtɪk) adj. ①外來的
②華麗的

① = foreign ('fɔrɪn , 'fɑrɪn)
= strange (strendʒ)
② = colorful ('kʌləfəl)
= bright (braɪt)
= rich (rɪtʃ)
= vivid ('vɪvɪd)
= gay (ge)

expand (ɪk'spænd) v. 擴張

= spread (sprɛd)
= swell (swɛl)
= unfold (ʌn'fold)
= grow (gro)
= enlarge (ɪn'lardʒ)
= extend (ɪk'stɛnd)
= broaden ('brɔdn̩)
= increase (ɪn'kris)
= magnify ('mægnə,faɪ)

expect (ɪk'spɛkt) v. 期待

= anticipate (æn'tɪsə,pet)
= await (ə'wet)
= think (θɪŋk)
= suppose (sə'poz)
= hope (hop)
= *look for*

E

expedient (ɪk'spidɪənt) *adj.*
有利的；適當的

= useful ('jusfəl)
= helpful ('hɛlpfəl)
= fitting ('fɪtɪŋ)
= desirable (dɪ'zaɪrəbḷ)
= appropriate (ə'proprɪɪt)
= wise (waɪz)
= sensible ('sɛnsəbḷ)

expedition (ˌɛkspɪ'dɪʃən) *n.*
①遠征　②迅速

① = journey ('dʒɝnɪ)
= trip (trɪp)
= trek (trɛk)
= pilgrimage ('pɪlgrəmɪdʒ)
② = speed (spid)
= promptness ('prɑmptnəs)
= swiftness ('swɪftnɪs)
= haste (hest)
= hurry ('hɝɪ)

expel (ɪk'spɛl) *v.* 逐出

= remove (rɪ'muv)
= eliminate (ɪ'lɪmə,net)
= eject (ɪ'dʒɛkt , i-)
= dismiss (dɪs'mɪs)
= discharge (dɪs'tʃɑrdʒ)
= oust (aʊst)
= banish ('bænɪʃ)
= outlaw ('aʊt,lɔ)
= *get rid of*
= *dispose of*

expend (ɪk'spɛnd) *v.* 花費

= spend (spɛnd)

= consume (kən'sum , -'sjum)
= exhaust (ɪg'zɔst , ɛg-)
= waste (west)
= *use up*

expensive (ɪk'spɛnsɪv) *adj.*
昂貴的

= costly ('kɔstlɪ)
= dear (dɪr)
= high-priced ('haɪ'praɪst)

experience (ɪk'spɪrɪəns) *n.*
①經歷　②感受　③知識

① = happening ('hæpənɪŋ)
= occurrence (ə'kɝəns)
= incident ('ɪnsədənt)
= episode ('ɛpə,sod , -,zod)
= adventure (əd'vɛntʃɚ)
② = sensation (sɛn'seʃən)
= feeling ('filɪŋ)
= emotion (ɪ'moʃən)
③ = practice ('præktɪs)
= knowledge ('nɑlɪdʒ)
= know-how ('no,haʊ)

experiment (ɪk'spɛrəmənt) *v.*
試驗

= try (traɪ)
= test (tɛst)
= prove (pruv)
= verify ('vɛrə,faɪ)

expert (ɪk'spɝt , 'ɛkspɝt) *adj.*
熟練的

= skillful ('skɪlfəl)
= adept (ə'dɛpt)

= apt (æpt)

= handy ('hændı)

= clever ('klɛvɚ)

= proficient (prə'fıʃənt)

= ingenious (ın'dʒinjəs)

= masterful ('mæstɚfəl , 'mɑs-)

expire (ık'spaır) v. 終止

= end (ɛnd)

= cease (sis)

= perish ('pɛrıʃ)

= die (daı)

= vanish ('vænıʃ)

= disappear (‚dısə'pır)

= *pass away*

explain (ık'splen) v. 解釋

= solve (sɑlv)

= answer ('ænsɚ)

= clarify ('klærə‚faı)

= simplify ('sımplə‚faı)

= illustrate ('ıləstret , ı'lʌs-)

= show (ʃo)

= demonstrate ('dɛmən‚stret)

explicit (ık'splısıt) adj. 明白的

= clear (klır)

= distinct (dı'stıŋkt)

= definite ('dɛfənıt)

= direct (də'rɛkt , daı-)

= candid ('kændıd)

= express (ık'sprɛs)

= positive ('pɑzətıv)

= unmistakable (‚ʌnmə'stekəbḷ)

explode (ık'splod) v. 爆炸

= burst (bɝst)

= erupt (ı'rʌpt)

= *blow up*

exploit (v. ık'sploıt , n. 'ɛksploıt , ık'sploıt) ① v. 利用 ② n. 功蹟

① = *use unfairly*

= *take advantage of*

② = deed (did)

= feat (fit)

= adventure (əd'vɛntʃɚ)

= *bold act*

explore (ık'splor , '-splɔr) v. 探測

= search (sɝtʃ)

= hunt (hʌnt)

= look (lʊk)

= research (rı'sɝtʃ , 'risɝtʃ)

= examine (ıg'zæmın)

= investigate (ın'vɛstə‚get)

= probe (prob)

= *delve into*

export (ıks'port , 'ɛksport) v. 出口

= ship (ʃıp)

= *send abroad*

expose (ık'spoz) v. 暴露

= open ('opən)

= uncover (ʌn'kʌvɚ)

= show (ʃo)

= display (dı'sple)

= reveal (rı'vil)

= disclose (dıs'kloz)

= unmask (ʌn'mæsk)

E

expound (ɪk'spaʊnd) v. 解釋

= explain (ɪk'splen)
= clarify ('klærə,faɪ)
= illuminate (ɪ'lumə,net , ɪ'lju-)
= demonstrate ('dɛmən,stret)
= teach (titʃ)
= lecture ('lɛktʃɚ)
= present (prɪ'zɛnt)

E

express (ɪk'sprɛs) ① v. 表示
② v. 代表　③ v. 運送
④ adj. 快速的

① = say (se)
= voice (vɔɪs)
= present (prɪ'zɛnt)
= tell (tɛl)
= describe (dɪ'skraɪb)
② = show (ʃo)
= indicate ('ɪndə,ket)
= imply (ɪm'plaɪ)
③ = send (sɛnd)
= dispatch (dɪ'spætʃ)
= ship (ʃɪp)
④ = fast (fæst , fɑst)
= quick (kwɪk)
= speedy ('spidɪ)
= rapid ('ræpɪd)
= swift (swɪft)

expressly (ɪk'sprɛslɪ , ɛk-) adv.
明白地

= plainly ('plenlɪ)
= definitely ('dɛfənɪtlɪ)

expulsion (ɪk'spʌlʃən) n. 逐出

= removal (rɪ'muvl̩)

= ejection (ɪ'dʒɛkʃən , i-)
= elimination (ɪ,lɪmə'neʃən)
= discharge (dɪs'tʃɑrdʒ)

exquisite (ɪk'skwɪzɪt ,
'ɛkskwɪzɪt) adj. ①精美的
②靈敏的

① = lovely ('lʌvlɪ)
= delicate ('dɛləkət , -kɪt)
= beautiful ('bjutəfəl)
= superb (su'pɝb , sə-)
= magnificent (mæg'nɪfəsn̩t)
= marvelous ('mɑrvl̩əs)
= wonderful ('wʌndɚfəl)
= delightful (dɪ'laɪtʃəl)
= charming ('tʃɑrmɪŋ)
= appealing (ə'pilɪŋ)
= enchanting (ɪn'tʃæntɪŋ)
= heavenly ('hɛvənlɪ)
= attractive (ə'træktɪv)
② = sharp (ʃɑrp)
= intense (ɪn'tɛns)
= acute (ə'kjut)

extend (ɪk'stɛnd) v. ①伸展
②給

① = stretch (strɛtʃ)
= lengthen ('lɛŋkθən , 'lɛŋθ-)
= increase (ɪn'kris)
= enlarge (ɪn'lɑrdʒ)
= expand (ɪk'spænd)
= broaden ('brɔdn̩)
= magnify ('mægnə,faɪ)
= *reach out*
② = give (gɪv)
= grant (grænt)

= donate ('donet)
= present (pri'zɛnt)
= allot (ə'lɑt)
= contribute (kən'trɪbjʊt)
= supply (sə'plaɪ)
= provide (prə'vaɪd)
= furnish ('fɜnɪʃ)

exterior (ɪk'stɪrɪə) *adj.* 外部的

= outside ('aʊt'saɪd , aʊt'saɪd)
= outer ('aʊtə)
= external (ɪk'stɜnḷ)
= surface ('sɜfɪs)

exterminate (ɪk'stɜmə,net) *v.* 消滅

= destroy (dɪ'strɔɪ)
= eliminate (ɪ'lɪmə,net)
= kill (kɪl)
= *get rid of*
= *dispose of*
= *wipe out*

external (ɪk'stɜnḷ) *adj.* 外部的

= outside ('aʊt'saɪd , aʊt'saɪd)
= outer ('aʊtə)
= exterior (ɪk'stɪrɪə)
= surface ('sɜfɪs)

extinct (ɪk'stɪŋkt) *adj.* 絕種的

= dead (dɛd)
= gone (gɔn)
= past (pæst , pɑst)
= obsolete ('ɑbsə,lit)

extinguish (ɪk'stɪŋgwɪʃ) *v.* 撲滅

= smother ('smʌðə)
= quench (kwɛntʃ)
= suppress (sə'prɛs)
= crush (krʌʃ)
= *put out*

extol (ɪk'stɑl , -'stol , ɛk-) *v.* 頌揚

= praise (prez)
= glorify ('glorə,faɪ , 'glɔr-)
= laud (lɔd)
= compliment ('kɑmpləmənt)
= exalt (ɪg'zɔlt)

extra ('ɛkstrə) *adj.* 額外的

= additional (ə'dɪʃənḷ)
= surplus ('sɜplʌs)
= supplementary (,sʌplə'mɛntərɪ)
= more (mor)
= spare (spɛr)

extraordinary (ɪk'strɔrdṇ,ɛrɪ) *adj.* 特別的

= special ('spɛʃəl)
= unusual (ʌn'juʒʊəl)
= remarkable (rɪ'mɑrkəbḷ)
= exceptional (ɪk'sɛpʃənḷ)
= wonderful ('wʌndəfəl)
= marvelous ('mɑrvḷəs)
= noteworthy ('not,wɜðɪ)
= memorable ('mɛmərəbḷ)

extravagant (ɪk'strævəgənt) *adj.* 過度的

= extreme (ɪk'strim)
= excessive (ɪk'sɛsɪv)

E

= overdone ('ovɚ'dʌn)
= exaggerated (ɪg'zædʒɚ,retɪd)
= unreasonable (ʌn'riznəbḷ)
= luxurious (lʌg'ʒʊrɪəs , lʌk'ʃʊr-)
= grand (grænd)

extreme (ɪk'strim) *adj.*
①極端的　②最後的

① = extravagant (ɪk'strævəgənt)
= excessive (ɪk'sɛsɪv)
= exaggerated (ɪg'zædʒɚ,retɪd)
= overdone ('ovɚ'dʌn)
= drastic ('dræstɪk)
= radical ('rædɪkḷ)
② = final ('faɪnḷ)
= last (læst , lɑst)
= conclusive (kən'klusɪv)
= endmost ('ɛnd,most , 'ɛn,most)
= terminal ('tɝmənḷ)

extricate ('ɛkstrɪ,ket) *v.* 解救

= release (rɪ'lis)
= free (fri)
= liberate ('lɪbɚ,ret)
= rescue ('rɛskju)
= clear (klɪr)

exult (ɪg'zʌlt , ɛg-) *v.* 狂歡

= rejoice (rɪ'dʒɔɪs)
= delight (dɪ'laɪt)
= *be glad*

eye (aɪ) *v.* 看

= look (lʊk)
= glance (glæns , glɑns)
= watch (watʃ)

= observe (əb'zɝv)
= regard (rɪ'gard)
= view (vju)
= inspect (ɪn'spɛkt)
= stare (stɛr)

F

fable ('febḷ) *n.* 寓言

= story ('storɪ)
= legend ('lɛdʒənd)
= myth (mɪθ)
= fiction ('fɪkʃən)
= *fairy tale*

fabric ('fæbrɪk) *n.* 織物

= cloth (klɔθ)
= textile ('tɛkstaɪl , -tḷ , -tɪl)
= goods (gʊdz)
= material (mə'tɪrɪəl)

fabulous ('fæbjələs) *adj.*
驚人的

= unbelievable (,ʌnbɪ'livəbḷ)
= amazing (ə'mezɪŋ)
= remarkable (rɪ'markəbḷ)
= striking ('straɪkɪŋ)
= notable ('notəbḷ)
= marvelous ('marvḷəs)

facade (fə'sad , fæ'sad) *n.* 正面

= front (frʌnt)
= face (fes)

face (fes) ① *v.* 面對　② *n.* 面容
③ *n.* 表情

① = confront (kən'frʌnt)
  = oppose (ə'poz)
  = meet (mit)
  = encounter (ɪn'kaʊntə)
  = brave (brev)
② = features ('fitʃəz)
  = looks (lʊks)
  = countenance ('kaʊntənəns)
③ = look (lʊk)
  = expression (ɪk'sprɛʃən)

facet ('fæsɪt) *n.* 一面

  = side (saɪd)
  = aspect ('æspɛkt)
  = view (vju)
  = phase (fez)

facilitate (fə'sɪlə,tet) *v.* 使容易

  = ease (iz)
  = help (hɛlp)
  = assist (ə'sɪst)
  = speed (spid)
  = *smooth the way*

fact (fækt) *n.* 事實

  = detail ('ditel , dɪ'tel)
  = item ('aɪtəm)
  = point (pɔɪnt)
  = truth (truθ)
  = certainty ('sɜtn̩tɪ)
  = evidence ('ɛvədəns)
  = data ('detə , 'dætə , 'dɑtə)
  = clue (klu)

factory ('fæktrɪ , -tərɪ) *n.* 工廠

  = plant (plænt)

  = works (wɜks)

faculty ('fækl̩tɪ) *n.* ①才能
②全體教員；專業人員

① = talent ('tælənt)
  = gift (gɪft)
  = power ('paʊə)
  = ability (ə'bɪlətɪ)
  = capacity (kə'pæsətɪ)
  = qualification (,kwɑləfə'keʃən)
  = aptitude ('æptə,tjud , -tud)
② = teachers ('titʃəz)
  = staff (stæf , stɑf)

fad (fæd) *n.* 時尚

  = fashion ('fæʃən)
  = craze (krez)
  = rage (redʒ)

fade (fed) *v.* ①褪色　②衰退

① = dim (dɪm)
  = pale (pel)
  = dull (dʌl)
  = bleach (blitʃ)
  = lose *color*
② = weaken ('wikən)
  = sink (sɪŋk)
  = fail (fel)
  = droop (drup)
  = decline (dɪ'klaɪn)

fag (fæg) *v.* 使疲倦

  = tire (taɪr)
  = fatigue (fə'tig)
  = weary ('wɪrɪ)
  = exhaust (ɪg'zɔst , ɛg-)

F

fail 〔 fel 〕 *v.* ①失敗 ②忽略 ③衰退

① = flunk 〔 flʌŋk 〕
   = *be unsuccessful*
   = *lose out*
② = neglect 〔 nɪ'glɛkt 〕
   = *fall short*
③ = weaken 〔 'wikən 〕
   = fade 〔 fed 〕
   = decline 〔 dɪ'klaɪn 〕

faint 〔 fent 〕 ① *v.* 昏倒
② *adj.* 無力的

① = swoon 〔 swun 〕
   = weaken 〔 'wikən 〕
   = *black out*
   = *keel over*
② = weak 〔 wik 〕
   = dim 〔 dɪm 〕
   = pale 〔 pel 〕
   = indistinct 〔 ˌɪndɪ'stɪŋkt 〕
   = vague 〔 veg 〕
   = hazy 〔 'hezɪ 〕
   = blurred 〔 blɜd 〕

fair 〔 fɛr 〕 ① *adj.* 白的
② *adj.* 美好的 ③ *adj.* 尚可的
④ *adj.* 正直的 ⑤ *n.* 市集

① = light 〔 laɪt 〕
   = pale 〔 pel 〕
   = whitish 〔 'hwaɪtɪʃ 〕
② = clear 〔 klɪr 〕
   = sunny 〔 'sʌnɪ 〕
   = bright 〔 braɪt 〕
   = pleasant 〔 'plɛznt 〕
③ = average 〔 'ævərɪdʒ 〕

   = mediocre 〔 'midɪˌokɚ, ˌmidɪ'okɚ 〕
④ = honest 〔 'ɑnɪst 〕
   = just 〔 dʒʌst 〕
   = square 〔 skwɛr 〕
   = right 〔 raɪt 〕
   = impartial 〔 ɪm'parʃəl 〕
⑤ = festival 〔 'fɛstəvḷ 〕
   = fete 〔 fet 〕
   = affair 〔 ə'fɛr 〕
   = bazaar 〔 bə'zar 〕
   = exposition 〔 ˌɛkspə'zɪʃən 〕
   = market 〔 'markɪt 〕

fairy 〔 'fɛrɪ 〕 *n.* 小仙子

   = sprite 〔 spraɪt 〕
   = elf 〔 ɛlf 〕
   = goblin 〔 'gablɪn 〕
   = pixie 〔 'pɪksɪ 〕
   = sylph 〔 sɪlf 〕

faith 〔 feθ 〕 *n.* ①信仰 ②宗教

① = trust 〔 trʌst 〕
   = belief 〔 bə'lif, bɪ- 〕
   = confidence 〔 'kanfədəns 〕
   = hope 〔 hop 〕
② = religion 〔 rɪ'lɪdʒən 〕
   = teaching 〔 'titʃɪŋ 〕

fake 〔 fek 〕 ① *v.* 佯裝
② *adj.* 偽造的

① = pretend 〔 prɪ'tɛnd 〕
   = deceive 〔 dɪ'siv 〕
   = falsify 〔 'fɔlsəˌfaɪ 〕
   = disguise 〔 dɪs'gaɪz 〕
   = distort 〔 dɪs'tɔrt 〕
   = feign 〔 fen 〕

F

② = false (fɔls)
  = mock (mɑk)
  = imitative ('ɪmətətɪv)
  = artificial (,ɑrtə'fɪʃəl)
  = fraudulent ('frɔdʒələnt)
  = make-believe ('mekbə,liv)
  = counterfeit ('kaʊntəfɪt)

fall (fɔl) ① v. 落下　② v. 衰弱
③ v. 毀壞　④ n. 秋天　⑤ n. 假髮
① = drop (drɑp)
  = plunge (plʌndʒ)
  = descend (dɪ'sɛnd)
  = tumble ('tʌmbl̩)
② = lapse (læps)
  = slip (slɪp)
③ = ruin ('ruɪn)
  = destroy (dɪ'strɔɪ)
  = defeat (dɪ'fit)
  = overthrow (,ovə'θro)
④ = autumn ('ɔtəm)
⑤ = wig (wɪg)
  = hairpiece ('hɛr,pis)

fallow ('fælo) adj. 休耕的
  = unprepared (,ʌnprɪ'pɛrd)
  = uncultivated (ʌn'kʌltə,vetɪd)
  = idle ('aɪdl̩)
  = unproductive (,ʌnprə'dʌktɪv)

false (fɔls) adj. ①錯的
②虛偽的　③代用的
① = untrue (ʌn'tru)
  = incorrect (,ɪnkə'rɛkt)
  = lying ('laɪŋ)
  = wrong (rɔŋ)

② = deceitful (dɪ'sitfəl)
  = disloyal (dɪs'lɔɪəl)
  = two-faced ('tu'fest)
③ = artificial (,ɑrtə'fɪʃəl)
  = fake (fek)
  = counterfeit ('kaʊntəfɪt)
  = mock (mɑk)
  = imitative ('ɪmətətɪv)

falter ('fɔltə) v. 遲疑；躊躇
  = hesitate ('hɛzə,tet)
  = stumble ('stʌmbl̩)
  = stagger ('stægə)
  = waver ('wevə)
  = flounder ('flaʊndə)

fame (fem) n. 聲譽
  = reputation (,rɛpjə'teʃən)
  = name (nem)
  = renown (rɪ'naʊn)
  = glory ('glorɪ , 'glɔrɪ)
  = popularity (,pɑpjə'lærətɪ)
  = notoriety (,notə'raɪətɪ)

familiar (fə'mɪljə) adj.
①熟悉的　②親密的　③通曉的
① = popular ('pɑpjələ)
  = well-known ('wɛl'non)
② = friendly ('frɛndlɪ)
  = close (klos)
  = personal ('pɜsn̩l)
  = intimate ('ɪntəmɪt)
③ = knowledgeable ('nɑlɪdʒəbl̩)
  = well acquainted
  = informed in
  = versed in

F

family ('fæməlɪ) *n.* 家族

= group (grup)
= household ('haus,hold , -,old)
= kin (kɪn)
= relatives ('rɛlətɪvz)
= folks (foks)

famine ('fæmɪn) *n.* 缺乏；飢荒

= starvation (star'veʃən)
= lack (læk)
= need (nid)
= want (wɑnt , wɔnt)
= shortage ('ʃɔrtɪdʒ)
= deficiency (dɪ'fɪʃənsɪ)
= absence ('æbsns)

famish ('fæmɪʃ) *v.* 饑餓

= hunger ('hʌŋgɚ)
= starve (starv)

fan (fæn) ① *v.* 鼓動 ② *n.* 風扇
③ *n.* 狂熱者

① = stir (stɝ)
= arouse (ə'rauz)
= whip (hwɪp)
= stimulate ('stɪmjə,let)
= spread (sprɛd)
= flare (flɛr)
② = blower ('bloɚ)
③ = admirer (əd'maɪrɚ)
= follower ('faloɚ)
= devotee (,dɛvə'ti)
= fancier ('fænsɪɚ)

fancy ('fænsɪ) ① *v.* 想像
② *v.* 喜好 ③ *adj.* 精緻的

① = imagine (ɪ'mædʒɪn)
= visualize ('vɪʒuə,laɪz)
= picture ('pɪktʃɚ)
= dream (drim)
= suppose (sə'poz)
= think (θɪŋk)
② = like (laɪk)
= love (lʌv)
= *care for*
③ = elaborate (ɪ'læbərɪt)
= ornate (ɔr'net)
= flowery ('flaurɪ , 'flauərɪ)
= fussy ('fʌsɪ)
= frilly ('frɪlɪ)

fang (fæŋ) *n.* 尖牙

= tooth (tuθ)
= tusk (tʌsk)

fantastic (fæn'tæstɪk) *adj.*
奇異的

= odd (ɑd)
= unreal (ʌn'riəl , 'ʌnril)
= strange (strendʒ)
= wild (waɪld)
= unusual (ʌn'juʒuəl)
= incredible (ɪn'krɛdəbl)
= outrageous (aut'redʒəs)

fantasy ('fæntəsɪ , -zɪ) *n.*
①幻想 ②傳說

① = imagination (ɪ,mædʒə'neʃən)
= vision ('vɪʒən)
= illusion (ɪ'ljuʒən)
= fancy ('fænsɪ)
② = fiction ('fɪkʃən)

F

= myth〔mɪθ〕
= fable〔'febḷ〕
= legend〔'lɛdʒənd〕
= story〔'storɪ〕
= *fairy tale*

far〔fɑr〕*adj.* ①遠的　②大大的

① = distant〔'dɪstənt〕
= remote〔rɪ'mot〕
= removed〔rɪ'muvd〕
② = much〔mʌtʃ〕
= *a great deal*

fare〔fɛr〕① *v.* 吃　② *v.* 進展
③ *n.* 車費　④ *n.* 旅客

① = eat〔it〕
= *be fed*
② = prosper〔'prɑspɚ〕
= progress〔prə'grɛs〕
= thrive〔θraɪv〕
= *get on*
③ = charge〔tʃɑrdʒ〕
= toll〔tol〕
= fee〔fi〕
④ = passenger〔'pæsṇdʒɚ〕

farewell〔ˌfɛr'wɛl〕① *v.* 再會
② *adj.* 告別的

① = cheerio〔'tʃɪrɪˌo〕
= good-bye〔gud'baɪ〕
= *good luck*
= *good day*
= *so long*
= *see you later*
② = departing〔dɪ'pɑrtɪŋ〕
= leaving〔'livɪŋ〕

= parting〔'pɑrtɪŋ〕
= *taking leave*

farm〔fɑrm〕① *v.* 種植
② *v.* 承包　③ *n.* 農場

① = cultivate〔'kʌltəˌvet〕
= grow〔gro〕
= raise〔rez〕
= ranch〔ræntʃ〕
= harvest〔'hɑrvɪst〕
② = hire〔haɪr〕
= let〔lɛt〕
= rent〔rɛnt〕
= lease〔lis〕
= charter〔'tʃɑrtɚ〕
③ = plantation〔plæn'teʃən〕
= ranch〔ræntʃ〕
= homestead〔'homˌstɛd〕

far-reaching〔'fɑr'ritʃɪŋ〕*adj.*
遠大的；深遠的

= broad〔brɔd〕
= extensive〔ɪk'stɛnsɪv〕
= sweeping〔'swipɪŋ〕
= widespread〔'waɪdˌsprɛd〕

fascinate〔'fæsṇˌet〕*v.* 使著迷

= interest〔'ɪntərɪst , 'ɪntrɪst〕
= excite〔ɪk'saɪt〕
= attract〔ə'trækt〕
= enthrall〔ɪn'θrɔl〕
= captivate〔'kæptəˌvet〕
= charm〔tʃɑrm〕
= intrigue〔ɪn'trig〕
= enchant〔ɪn'tʃænt〕
= thrill〔θrɪl〕
= delight〔dɪ'laɪt〕

F

fashion ('fæʃən) ① v. 做成
② n. 時尚

① = make (mek)
= shape (ʃep)
= form (fɔrm)
= create (krɪ'et)
= mold (mold)
② = style (staɪl)
= mode (mod)
= vogue (vog)
= custom ('kʌstəm)

fast (fæst , fɑst) ① v. 禁食
② adj. 快的　③ adj. 牢固的

① = starve (starv)
= go hungry
② = speedy ('spidɪ)
= swift (swɪft)
= rapid ('ræpɪd)
= quick (kwɪk)
= hasty ('hestɪ)
③ = firm (fɝm)
= stable ('stebḷ)
= sure (ʃur)
= dependable (dɪ'pɛndəbḷ)
= solid ('salɪd)
= steady ('stɛdɪ)

fasten ('fæsn̩ , 'fɑsn̩) v. 綁住；
固定

= tie (taɪ)
= lock (lak)
= attach (ə'tætʃ)
= secure (sɪ'kjur)
= close (kloz)
= bind (baɪnd)

= connect (kə'nɛkt)

fastidious (fæs'tɪdɪəs) adj.
苛求的

= particular (pə'tɪkjələ , pə-)
= selective (sə'lɛktɪv)
= critical ('krɪtɪkḷ)
= choosy ('tʃuzɪ)

fat (fæt) ① adj. 肥胖的
② n. 脂肪

① = stout (staʊt)
= fleshy ('flɛʃɪ)
= plump (plʌmp)
= chubby ('tʃʌbɪ)
= tubby ('tʌbɪ)
= chunky ('tʃʌŋkɪ)
② = oil (ɔɪl)
= lubrication (,lubrɪ'keʃən)
= grease (gris)

fatal ('fetḷ) adj. ①致命的
②重大的

① = deadly ('dɛdlɪ)
= destructive (dɪ'strʌktɪv)
= killing ('kɪlɪŋ)
= mortal ('mɔrtḷ)
= disastrous (dɪz'æstrəs , -'as-)
② = important (ɪm'pɔrtn̩t)
= fateful ('fetfəl)
= serious ('sɪrɪəs)
= significant (sɪg'nɪfəkənt)

fate (fet) n. 命運

= fortune ('fɔrtʃən)
= destiny ('dɛstənɪ)

= lot〔lɑt〕
= custom〔'kʌstəm〕

father〔'fɑðɚ〕① v. 創始
② n. 教士　③ n. 父親

① = originate〔ə'rɪdʒə,net〕
= cause〔kɔz〕
= produce〔prə'djus〕
= breed〔brid〕
= bring *about*

② = priest〔prist〕

③ = daddy〔'dædɪ〕
= sire〔saɪr〕
= *male parent*

fathom〔'fæðəm〕 v. ①洞悉
②測量

① = understand〔,ʌndɚ'stænd〕
= follow〔'fɑlo〕
= grasp〔græsp〕
= comprehend〔,kɑmprɪ'hɛnd〕

② = measure〔'mɛʒɚ〕
= gauge〔gedʒ〕

fatigue〔fə'tig〕v. 使疲乏

= tire〔taɪr〕
= exhaust〔ɪg'zɔst , ɛg-〕
= *wear out*

fault〔fɔlt〕n. 過錯

= mistake〔mə'stek〕
= error〔'ɛrɚ〕
= defect〔dɪ'fɛkt , 'difɛkt〕
= flaw〔flɔ〕
= shortcoming〔'ʃɔrt,kʌmɪŋ〕
= wrongdoing〔'rɔŋ,duɪŋ〕

= misdeed〔mɪs'did〕
= catch〔kætʃ〕

favor〔'fevɚ〕① v. 偏好
② v. 相似　③ n. 善意

① = prefer〔prɪ'fɝ〕
= approve〔ə'pruv〕
= *like better*

② = resemble〔rɪ'zɛmbḷ〕
= *look like*

③ = kindness〔'kaɪndnɪs〕
= service〔'sɝvɪs〕
= benefit〔'bɛnəfɪt〕
= courtesy〔'kɝtəsɪ〕
= *good deed*

favorite〔'fevərɪt〕 adj. 最喜愛的

= choice〔tʃɔɪs〕
= cherished〔'tʃɛrɪʃt〕
= prized〔'praɪzd〕
= beloved〔bɪ'lʌvd , -vɪd〕
= precious〔'prɛʃəs〕
= pet〔pɛt〕
= adored〔ə'dord , ə'dɔrd〕
= treasured〔'trɛʒɚd〕

fealty〔'fiəltɪ , 'filtɪ〕n. 忠貞

= loyalty〔'lɔɪəltɪ , 'lɔj-〕
= faithfulness〔'feθfəlnəs〕
= allegiance〔ə'lidʒəns〕
= devotion〔dɪ'voʃən〕
= faith〔feθ〕
= attachment〔ə'tætʃmənt〕

fear〔fɪr〕v. 恐懼

= dread〔drɛd〕
= *be afraid*

F

feasible ('fizəbḷ) *adj.* 可能的

= possible ('pasəbḷ)
= practical ('præktɪkḷ)
= workable ('wɜkəbḷ)
= attainable (ə'tenəbḷ)

feast (fist) ① *v.* 享受
② *n.* 宴會

① = enjoy (ɪn'dʒɔɪ)
= like (laɪk)
= love (lʌv)
= appreciate (ə'priʃɪ,et)
= *delight in*
= *rejoice in*
② = banquet ('bæŋkwɪt)
= treat (trit)
= feed (fid)
= spread (sprɛd)

feat (fit) *n.* 功績

= deed (did)
= act (ækt)
= action ('ækʃən)
= exploit ('ɛksplɔɪt)
= achievement (ə'tʃivmənt)
= accomplishment
  (ə'kamplɪʃmənt)
= stunt (stʌnt)

feature ('fitʃə) ① *v.* 以…為特色
② *n.* 特性

① = show (ʃo)
= headline ('hɛd,laɪn)
= star (star)
② = part (part)
= characteristic (,kærɪktə'rɪstɪk)

= trait (tret)
= mark (mark)

fee (fi) *n.* 費用

= charge (tʃardʒ)
= dues (djuz)
= toll (tol)
= fare (fɛr)

feeble ('fibḷ) *adj.* 微弱的

= weak (wik)
= powerless ('pauə-lɪs)
= frail (frel)

feed (fid) *v.* ①供給 ②吃飯

① = nourish ('nɜɪʃ)
= supply (sə'plaɪ)
= nurture ('nɜtʃə)
② = eat (it)
= dine (daɪn)

feel (fil) *v.* ①觸試 ②感覺是
③知覺

① = touch (tʌtʃ)
= finger ('fɪŋgə)
= handle ('hændḷ)
② = be (bi)
= seem (sim)
= look (luk)
= appear (ə'pɪr)
③ = experience (ɪk'spɪrɪəns)
= know (no)
= encounter (ɪn'kauntə)
= meet (mit)
= undergo (,ʌndə'go)
= endure (ɪn'djur)

= suffer ('sʌfɚ)

= sense (sɛns)

feign (fen) v. 假裝

= pretend (prɪ'tɛnd)

= fake (fek)

= act (ækt)

= bluff (blʌf)

= assume (ə'sjum)

= affect (ə'fɛkt)

= play (ple)

felicity (fə'lɪsətɪ) n. ①幸福
②幸運

① = happiness ('hæpɪnɪs)

= bliss (blɪs)

= gladness ('glædnɪs)

= delight (dɪ'laɪt)

= joy (dʒɔɪ)

= cheer (tʃɪr)

= glee (gli)

= enchantment (ɪn'tʃæntmənt)

② = blessing ('blɛsɪŋ)

= luck (lʌk)

= *good fortune*

fellow ('fɛlo) n. ①人 ②同伴

① = lad (læd)

= boy (bɔɪ)

= man (mæn)

= chap (tʃæp)

= guy (gaɪ)

② = companion (kəm'pænjən)

= mate (met)

= partner ('partnɚ)

= comrade ('kamræd , 'kamrɪd)

= associate (ə'soʃɪɪt)

= counterpart ('kaʊntɚ,part)

female ('fimel) adj. 女性的

= ladylike ('ledɪ,laɪk)

= womanly ('wʊmənlɪ)

= feminine ('fɛmənɪn)

fen (fɛn) n. 沼澤

= marsh (marʃ)

= swamp (swamp)

fence (fɛns) v. ①圍以柵欄
②鬥劍 ③作黑市買賣

① = enclose (ɪn'kloz)

= wall (wɔl)

= fortify ('fɔrtə,faɪ)

= blockade (bla'ked)

② = fight (faɪt)

= joust (dʒʌst , dʒaʊst)

= duel ('djuəl)

③ = bootleg ('but,lɛg)

= black-market ('blæk'markɪt)

= *sell illegally*

ferment (fɚ'mɛnt) v. ①發酵
②激動

① = sour (saʊr)

= change *chemically*

② = excite (ɪk'saɪt)

= agitate ('ædʒə,tet)

= disturb (dɪ'stɚb)

= stir (stɚ)

= trouble ('trʌbḷ)

= ruffle ('rʌfḷ)

= provoke (prə'vok)

F

ferocious (fə'roʃəs) *adj.* 殘忍的

= fierce (fɪrs)

= savage ('sævɪdʒ)

= vicious ('vɪʃəs)

= brutal ('brutl̩)

= wild (waɪld)

= cruel ('kruəl)

= ruthless ('ruθlɪs)

= bloodthirsty ('blʌd,θɜstɪ)

ferret ('fɛrɪt) ① *v.* 搜索

② *n.* 白鼬

① = hunt (hʌnt)

= search (sɜtʃ)

② = weasel ('wizl̩)

ferry ('fɛrɪ) ① *v.* 運輸

② *n.* 渡船

① = carry ('kærɪ)

= transport (træns'port)

= haul (hɔl)

= cart (kɑrt)

② = boat (bot)

fertile ('fɜtl̩) *adj.* 多產的

= productive (prə'dʌktɪv)

= fruitful ('frutfəl)

= enriched (ɪn'rɪtʃt)

= abundant (ə'bʌndənt)

= creative (krɪ'etɪv)

fervent ('fɜvənt) *adj.* 熱誠的

= sincere (sɪn'sɪr)

= devoted (dɪ'votɪd)

= ardent ('ɑrdn̩t)

= zealous ('zɛləs)

= passionate ('pæʃənɪt)

= intense (ɪn'tɛns)

= enthusiastic (ɪn,θjuzɪ'æstɪk)

festive ('fɛstɪv) *adj.* 快樂的

= merry ('mɛrɪ)

= gay (ge)

= jolly ('dʒɑlɪ)

= jovial ('dʒovɪəl)

= joyous ('dʒɔɪəs)

= gala ('gelə , 'gælə , 'gɑlə)

fetch (fɛtʃ) *v.* 取來

= bring (brɪŋ)

= *go to get*

fetching ('fɛtʃɪŋ) *adj.* 誘惑的

= enchanting (ɪn'tʃæntɪŋ)

= appealing (ə'pilɪŋ)

= interesting ('ɪntərɪstɪŋ , 'ɪntrɪ-)

= enticing (ɪn'taɪsɪŋ , ɛn-)

= alluring (ə'lurɪŋ)

= fascinating ('fæsn̩,etɪŋ)

= captivating ('kæptə,vetɪŋ)

= delightful (dɪ'laɪtfəl)

= exquisite ('ɛkskwɪzɪt , ɪk'skwɪzɪt)

= lovely ('lʌvlɪ)

= inviting (ɪn'vaɪtɪŋ-)

fete (fet) *n.* 慶祝

= festival ('fɛstəvl̩)

= party ('pɑrtɪ)

= *gala affair*

fetter ('fɛtɚ) *v.* 束縛

= bind〔baɪnd〕
= tie〔taɪ〕
= chain〔tʃen〕
= shackle〔'ʃækl̩〕
= restrain〔rɪ'stren〕

feud〔fjud〕 *n.* 仇恨

= quarrel〔'kwɔrəl , 'kwɑr-〕
= dispute〔dɪ'spjut〕
= controversy〔'kɑntrə,vɜsɪ〕
= fight〔faɪt〕
= squabble〔'skwɑbl̩〕
= bitterness〔'bɪtənɪs〕
= animosity〔,ænə'mɑsətɪ〕

fever〔'fivɚ〕 *n.* 發燒

= heat〔hit〕
= flush〔flʌʃ〕
= sickness〔'sɪknɪs〕
= *high body temperature*

few〔fju〕 *adj.* 很少的

= *not many*
= *small number*
= *very little*

fib〔fɪb〕 *n.* 小謊

= lie〔laɪ〕
= falsehood〔'fɔls,hʊd〕
= untruth〔ʌn'truθ〕
= tale〔tel〕
= story〔'storɪ〕
= yarn〔jɑrn〕

fickle〔'fɪkl̩〕 *adj.* 多變的

= changing〔'tʃendʒɪŋ〕

= unstable〔ʌn'stebl̩〕
= flighty〔'flaɪtɪ〕
= uncertain〔ʌn'sɜtn̩〕
= unreliable〔,ʌnrɪ'laɪəbl̩〕
= unfaithful〔ʌn'feθfəl〕
= *not constant*

fiction〔'fɪkʃən〕 *n.* 虛構

= fantasy〔'fæntəsɪ , 'fæntəzɪ〕
= untruth〔ʌn'truθ〕
= invention〔ɪn'vɛnʃən〕
= legend〔'lɛdʒənd〕
= myth〔mɪθ〕
= fable〔'febl̩〕
= *fairy tale*

fidelity〔faɪ'dɛlətɪ , fə-〕 *n.*
①忠貞　②精確

① = loyalty〔'lɔɪəltɪ , 'lɔj-〕
= faithfulness〔'feθfəlnəs〕
= allegiance〔ə'lidʒəns〕
= devotion〔dɪ'voʃen〕
= faith〔feθ〕
= attachment〔ə'tætʃmənt〕
= fealty〔'fiəltɪ〕
② = accuracy〔'ækjərəsɪ〕
= exactness〔ɪg'zæktnɪs〕
= precision〔prɪ'sɪʒən〕
= correctness〔kə'rɛktnəs〕

fidget〔'fɪdʒɪt〕 *v.* 坐立不安

= fuss〔fʌs〕
= twitch〔twɪtʃ〕
= jerk〔dʒɜk〕
= wriggle〔'rɪgl̩〕
= squirm〔skwɜm〕

F

= twist (twɪst)

= wiggle ('wɪgl̩)

field (fild) *n.* ①田野 ②領域

① = land (lænd)

= space (spes)

= region ('ridʒən)

= tract (trækt)

= plot (plɑt)

= ground (graʊnd)

= pasture ('pæstʃə , 'pɑs-)

② = sphere (sfɪr)

= range (rendʒ)

= realm (rɛlm)

= area ('ɛrɪə , 'erɪə)

fiend (find) *n.* ①惡魔
②耽於某種嗜好者

① = devil ('dɛvl̩)

= monster ('mɑnstə)

= demon ('dimən)

= ogre ('ogə)

② = addict ('ædɪkt)

fierce (fɪrs) *adj.* 兇猛的

= savage ('sævɪdʒ)

= raging ('redʒɪŋ)

= wild (waɪld)

= violent ('vaɪələnt)

= vicious ('vɪʃəs)

= brutal ('brutl̩)

= ferocious (fə'roʃəs)

= cruel ('kruəl)

fiery ('faɪrɪ , 'faɪərɪ) *adj.*
①燃燒的 ②激昂的

① = hot (hɑt)

= burning ('bɜnɪŋ)

= flaming ('flemɪŋ)

② = aroused (ə'raʊzd)

= excited (ɪk'saɪtɪd)

= violent ('vaɪələnt)

= heated ('hitɪd)

= ardent ('ɑrdn̩t)

= feverish ('fivərɪʃ)

= fervent ('fɜvənt)

fiesta (fɪ'ɛstə) *n.* 假日

= festival ('fɛstəvl̩)

= holiday ('hɑlə,de)

= festivity (fɛs'tɪvətɪ)

= fete (fet)

fight (faɪt) *v.* 戰鬥

= quarrel ('kwɔrəl , 'kwɑr-)

= struggle ('strʌgl̩)

= combat ('kɑmbæt , 'kʌm-)

= contest (kən'tɛst)

= battle ('bætl̩)

= contend (kən'tɛnd)

= oppose (ə'poz)

= attack (ə'tæk)

= row (raʊ)

figure ('fɪgjə , 'fɪgə) *n.* ①數字
②價目 ③形體 ④人物 ⑤圖解

① = symbol ('sɪmbl̩)

= number ('nʌmbr)

= numeral ('njumərəl)

= digit ('dɪdʒɪt)

② = price (praɪs)

= cost (kɔst)

= charge〔tʃɑrdʒ〕
= amount〔əˈmaʊnt〕
③ = shape〔ʃep〕
= form〔fɔrm〕
= physique〔fɪˈzik〕
= build〔bɪld〕
= structure〔ˈstrʌktʃɚ〕
④ = person〔ˈpɝsn̩〕
= individual〔ˌɪndəˈvɪdʒʊəl〕
⑤ = picture〔ˈpɪktʃɚ〕
= drawing〔ˈdrɔɪŋ〕
= diagram〔ˈdaɪəˌgræm〕
= illustration〔ˌɪləsˈtreʃən,
   ɪˌlʌsˈtreʃən〕
= design〔dɪˈzaɪn〕
= pattern〔ˈpætən〕
= outline〔ˈaʊtˌlaɪn〕
= chart〔tʃɑrt〕
= sketch〔skɛtʃ〕

file〔faɪl〕v. ①歸檔　②行進
③銼平

① = sort〔sɔrt〕
= classify〔ˈklæsəˌfaɪ〕
= group〔grup〕
= categorize〔ˈkætəgəˌraɪz〕
= catalog〔ˈkætl̩ˌɔg〕
= store〔stor, stɔr〕
② = march〔mɑrtʃ〕
= parade〔pəˈred〕
③ = smooth〔smuð〕
= grind〔graɪnd〕
= sand〔sænd〕
= sharpen〔ˈʃɑrpən〕
= edge〔ɛdʒ〕

fill〔fɪl〕v. ①填　②供應

① = load〔lod〕
= pack〔pæk〕
= stuff〔stʌf〕
= cram〔kræm〕
② = supply〔səˈplaɪ〕
= provide〔prəˈvaɪd〕
= furnish〔ˈfɝnɪʃ〕

filly〔ˈfɪlɪ〕n. 母駒

= mare〔mɛr〕
= *female colt*

film〔fɪlm〕① v. 攝影
② n. 薄膜

① = photograph〔ˈfotəˌgræf〕
= take *a picture*
② = coat〔kot〕
= coating〔ˈkotɪŋ〕
= layer〔ˈleɚ〕
= covering〔ˈkʌvərɪŋ〕

filter〔ˈfɪltɚ〕v. 濾過

= strain〔stren〕
= percolate〔ˈpɝkəˌlet〕
= screen〔skrin〕
= sift〔sɪft〕
= refine〔rɪˈfaɪn〕
= purify〔ˈpjʊrəˌfaɪ〕
= cleanse〔klɛnz〕
= drain〔dren〕
= separate〔ˈsɛpəˌret〕

filth〔fɪlθ〕n. 污物

= dirt〔dɝt〕
= much〔mʌtʃ〕
= rot〔rat〕
= *foul matter*

F

final (ˈfaɪn̩) *adj.* 最後的

= last (læst , lɑst)

= deciding (dɪˈsaɪdɪŋ)

= closing (ˈklozɪŋ)

= terminal (ˈtɜmən̩)

= conclusive (kənˈklusɪv)

final (fɪˈnɑlɪ) *n.* 結局

= end (ɛnd)

= finish (ˈfɪnɪʃ)

= conclusion (kənˈkluʒən)

= termination (ˌtɜməˈneʃən)

finance (fəˈnæns , ˈfaɪnæns) *v.*
供給經費

= sponsor (ˈspɑnsɚ)

= back (bæk)

= support (səˈport , -ˈpɔrt)

= aid (ed)

= assist (əˈsɪst)

= subsidize (ˈsʌbsəˌdaɪz)

= stake (stek)

find (faɪnd) *v.* ①發現 ②得知
③判定

① = discover (dɪˈskʌvɚ)

= disclose (dɪsˈkloz)

= *come upon*

② = learn (lɜn)

= get (gɛt)

= gather (ˈgæðɚ)

= *gain knowledge*

③ = decide (dɪˈsaɪd)

= declare (dɪˈklɛr)

= determine (dɪˈtɜmɪn)

fine (faɪn) ① *v.* 罰金
② *adj.* 微小的 ③ *adj.* 優雅的
④ *adj.* 優秀的

① = penalize (ˈpin̩ˌaɪz , ˈpɛn̩-)

= tax (tæks)

= charge (tʃɑrdʒ)

② = delicate (ˈdɛləkət , -kɪt)

= minute (məˈnjut , maɪ-)

③ = refined (rɪˈfaɪnd)

= tasteful (ˈtestfəl)

= polished (ˈpɑlɪʃt)

④ = excellent (ˈɛkslənt)

= good (gʊd)

= nice (naɪs)

= splendid (ˈsplɛndɪd)

finery (ˈfaɪnərɪ) *n.* 華麗的衣服

= clothes (kloz , kloðr)

= frillery (ˈfrɪlərɪ)

= ornaments (ˈɔrnəmənts)

finger (ˈfɪŋgɚ) ① *v.* 摸
② *n.* 手指

① = touch (tʌtʃ)

= handle (ˈhændl̩)

= feel (fil)

= manipulate (məˈnɪpjəˌlet)

② = digit (ˈdɪdʒɪt)

finish (ˈfɪnɪʃ) *v.* ①結束
②使完美

① = end (ɛnd)

= complete (kəmˈplit)

= close (kloz)

= terminate (ˈtɜməˌnet)

= conclude (kənˈklud)

= stop (stɑp)

= cease (sis)

② = perfect (pə'fɪkt)

= polish ('pɑlɪʃ)

= refine (rɪ'faɪn)

fire (faɪr) *v.* ①點燃 ②解職
③激動 ④放鎗

① = ignite (ɪg'naɪt)

= heat (hit)

= kindle ('kɪndl̩)

② = dismiss (dɪs'mɪs)

= discharge (dɪs'tʃɑrdʒ)

= expel (ɪk'spɛl)

= release (rɪ'lis)

= *lay off*

③ = arouse (ə'raʊz)

= excite (ɪk'saɪt)

= inflame (ɪn'flem)

= stir (stɝ)

= provoke (prə'vok)

= agitate ('ædʒə,tet)

④ = shoot (ʃut)

= discharge (dɪs'tʃɑrdʒ)

= blast (blæst)

firearms ('faɪr,ɑrmz) *n. pl.* 槍砲

= guns (gʌnz)

= artillery (ɑr'tɪlərɪ)

= ammunition (,æmjə'nɪʃən)

firebrand ('faɪr,brænd) *n.*
①火把 ②煽動者

① = lighter ('laɪtə)

② = troublemaker ('trʌbl̩,mekə)

= agitator ('ædʒə,tetə)

= provoker (prə'vokə)

= instigator ('ɪnstə,getə)

= rabble-rouser ('ræbl̩,raʊzə)

firm (fɝm) ① *adj.* 堅固的
② *n.* 公司

① = solid ('sɑlɪd)

= fixed (fɪkst)

= secure (sɪ'kjʊr)

= unyielding (ʌn'jildɪŋ)

= inflexible (ɪn'flɛksəbl̩)

= stationary ('steʃən,ɛrɪ)

= immovable (ɪ'muvəbl̩ ,
ɪm'muv-)

= rigid ('rɪdʒɪd)

② = company ('kʌmpənɪ)

= business ('bɪznɪs)

= enterprise ('ɛntə,praɪz)

fist (fɝst) ① *adj.* 首要的
② *adj.* 最先的 ③ *adv.* 寧願

① = principal ('prɪnsəpl̩)

= main (men)

= chief (tʃif)

= leading ('lidɪŋ)

= primary ('praɪ,mɛrɪ , -mərɪ)

= dominant ('dɑmənənt)

② = beginning (bɪ'gɪnɪŋ)

= foremost ('for,most , 'fɔr-)

= before (bɪ'for , bɪ'fɔr)

= ahead (ə'hɛd)

= *in front*

③ = rather ('ræθə , 'rɑðə)

= sooner ('sunə)

= preferably ('prɛfərəblɪ)

fissure ('fɪʃɚ) *n.* 裂縫

= split (splɪt)
= crack (kræk)
= opening ('opənɪŋ)
= break (brek)
= crevice ('krɛvɪs)
= gap (gæp)

fit (fɪt) ① *v.* 適合
② *adj.* 適當的   ③ *adj.* 健康的
④ *n.* 一陣

① = suit (sut , sjut)
= adapt (ə'dæpt)
= adjust (ə'dʒʌst)
② = proper ('prɑpɚ)
= right (raɪt)
= suitable ('sutəbl̩ , 'sjutəbl̩)
= qualified ('kwɑlə,faɪd)
③ = strong (strɔŋ)
= healthy ('hɛlθɪ)
= well (wɛl)
④ = attack (ə'tæk)
= seizure ('siʒɚ)
= spell (spɛl)
= spasm ('spæzəm)
= convulsion (kən'vʌlʃən)
= frenzy ('frɛnzɪ)
= rage (redʒ)

fitful ('fɪtfəl) *adj.* 斷續的

= irregular (ɪ'rɛgjəlɚ)
= sporadic (spo'rædɪk , spɔ-)
= choppy ('tʃɑpɪ)
= disconnected (,dɪskə'nɛktɪd)
= broken ('brokən)

fix (fɪks) ① *v.* 修理   ② *v.* 固定
③ *n.* 困境

① = mend (mɛnd)
= repair (rɪ'pɛr)
= adjust (ə'dʒʌst)
= regulate ('rɛgjə,let)
= doctor ('dɑktɚ)
② = settle ('sɛtl̩)
= establish (ə'stæblɪʃ)
= stabilize ('stebl̩,aɪz)
= solidify (sə'lɪdə,faɪ)
③ = dilemma (də'lɛmə , daɪ-)
= quandary ('kwɑndrɪ ,
'kwɑndərɪ)

fixture ('fɪkstʃɚ) *n.* 裝置物

= appliance (ə'plaɪəns)
= attachment (ə'tætʃmənt)
= accessory (æk'sɛsərɪ)

flag (flæg) ① *v.* 作信號
② *v.* 衰退   ③ *n.* 旗

① = signal ('sɪgnl̩)
= wave (wev)
② = weaken ('wikən)
= droop (drup)
= wilt (wɪlt)
= fade (fed)
③ = pennant ('pɛnənt)
= banner ('bænɚ)
= standard ('stændɚd)
= colors ('kʌlɚz)

flair (flɛr) *n.* 天賦

= talent ('tælənt)
= perception (pɚ'sɛpʃən)
= insight ('ɪn,saɪt)

flamboyant (flæm'bɔɪənt) *adj.*
如火的；燦爛的

= flaming ('flemɪŋ)
= brilliant ('brɪljənt)
= striking ('straɪkɪŋ)
= ornate (ɔr'net)
= vivid ('vɪvɪd)
= dazzling ('dæzlɪŋ , 'dæzl̩ɪŋ)
= fancy ('fænsɪ)

flame (flem) *v.* 燃燒

= blaze (blez)
= burn (bɜn)

flank (flæŋk) ① *n.* 一側
② *v.* 攻擊

① = side (saɪd)
= border ('bɔrdə)
② = attack (ə'tæk)
= strike (straɪk)

flare (flɛr) *v.* ①閃耀 ②展開

① = flame (flem)
= blaze (blez)
= glow (glo)
= burn (bɜn)
② = spread (sprɛd)
= expand (ɪk'spænd)
= unfold (ʌn'fold)
= *open up*

flash (flæʃ) *n.* ①閃光 ②電報

① = flame (flem)
= flare (flɛr)
= blaze (blez)
② = telegraph ('tɛlə,græf , -,grɑf)

= wire (waɪr)
= cable ('kebl̩)
= radio ('redɪ,o)

flat (flæt) ① *adj.* 平坦的
② *adj.* 平淡的　③ *adj.* 走調的
④ *n.* (英) 公寓

① = level ('lɛvl̩)
= even ('ivən)
= horizontal (,hɔrə'zɑntl̩)
= smooth (smuð)
② = dull (dʌl)
= lifeless ('laɪflɪs)
③ = off-key ('ɔf'ki , 'ɑf-)
= unmusical (ʌn'mjuzɪkl̩)
④ = apartment (ə'pɑrtmənt)
= suite (swit)

flatter ('flætə) *v.* 奉承

= praise (prez)
= compliment ('kɑmpləmənt)

flaunt (flɔnt) *v.* 炫耀

= display (dɪ'sple)
= exhibit (ɪg'zɪbɪt)
= parade (pə'red)

flavor ('flevə) *v.* 加味於

= season ('sizn̩)
= spice (spaɪs)
= *give taste to*

flaw (flɔ) *n.* 毛病

= damage ('dæmɪdʒ)
= defect (dɪ'fɛkt , 'difɛkt)
= crack (kræk)

F

= fault (fɔlt)

= weakness ('wiknɪs)

= blemish ('blɛmɪʃ)

flay (fle) v. ①剝⋯的皮 ②嚴責

① = peel (pil)

= skin (skɪn)

= strip (strɪp)

② = criticize ('krɪtə,saɪz)

= attack (ə'tæk)

= assail (ə'sel)

fleck (flɛk) n. 斑點

= spot (spɑt)

= mark (mɑrk)

= speckle ('spɛkḷ)

= dot (dɑt)

flee (fli) v. 逃走

= disappear (,dɪsə'pɪr)

= *run away*

fleece (flis) ① v. 騙取
② n. 羊毛

① = rob (rɑb)

= cheat (tʃit)

= swindle ('swɪndḷ)

② = wool (wʊl)

fleet (flit) ① adj. 快速的
② n. 艦隊 ③ n. 隊

① = rapid ('ræpɪd)

= swift (swɪft)

= fast (fæst)

= quick (kwɪk)

= nimble ('nɪmbḷ)

② = ships (ʃɪps)

③ = group (grup)

= band (bænd)

= company ('kʌmpənɪ)

flesh (flɛʃ) n. ①肉 ②皮
③骨肉

① = meat (mit)

= body ('bɑdɪ)

② = skin (skɪn)

③ = family ('fæməlɪ)

flex (flɛks) v. 彎曲

= bend (bɛnd)

= arch (ɑrtʃ)

= curve (kɜv)

flick (flɪk) v. 輕打

= strike (straɪk)

= snap (snæp)

= crack (kræk)

= jerk (dʒɜk)

= flip (flɪp)

flicker ('flɪkə) n. ①搖
②啄木鳥

① = flutter ('flʌtə)

= waver ('wevə)

② = woodpecker ('wʊd,pɛkə)

flimsy ('flɪmzɪ) adj. 脆弱的

= slight (slaɪt)

= frail (frel)

= weak (wik)

= delicate ('dɛləkət , -kɪt)

= dainty ('dentɪ)

= fragile ('frædʒəl , 'frædʒaɪl)

flinch ﹝ flɪntʃ ﹞ v. 退縮

  = shrink ﹝ ʃrɪŋk ﹞

  = cringe ﹝ krɪndʒ ﹞

  = recoil ﹝ rɪ'kɔɪl ﹞

  = *draw back*

fling ﹝ flɪŋ ﹞ v. ①投 ②慶祝

① = throw ﹝ θro ﹞

  = sling ﹝ slɪŋ ﹞

  = pitch ﹝ pɪtʃ ﹞

  = toss ﹝ tɔs ﹞

  = cast ﹝ kæst , kɑst ﹞

  = hurl ﹝ hɝl ﹞

② = celebration ﹝ ˌsɛlə'breʃən ﹞

  = spree ﹝ spri ﹞

  = escapade ﹝ 'ɛskəˌped , ˌɛskə'ped ﹞

  = lark ﹝ lɑrk ﹞

flip ﹝ flɪp ﹞ v. ①彈投 ②輕打

① = toss ﹝ tɔs ﹞

  = throw ﹝ θro ﹞

  = fling ﹝ flɪŋ ﹞

  = sling ﹝ slɪŋ ﹞

  = pitch ﹝ pɪtʃ ﹞

  = cast ﹝ kæst , kɑst ﹞

  = hurl ﹝ hɝl ﹞

② = jerk ﹝ dʒɝk ﹞

  = snap ﹝ snæp ﹞

  = flick ﹝ flɪk ﹞

flippant ﹝ 'flɪpənt ﹞ adj. 輕率的

  = rude ﹝ rud ﹞

  = disrespectful ﹝ ˌdɪsrɪ'spɛktfəl ﹞

  = saucy ﹝ 'sɔsɪ ﹞

  = pert ﹝ pɝt ﹞

  = impudent ﹝ 'ɪmpjədənt ﹞

  = cocky ﹝ 'kɑkɪ ﹞

  = flip ﹝ flɪp ﹞

  = cheeky ﹝ 'tʃikɪ ﹞

  = smart ﹝ smɑrt ﹞

  = smart-alecky ﹝ ˌsmɑrt'æləkɪ ﹞

flit ﹝ flɪt ﹞ v. 飛躍

  = fly ﹝ flaɪ ﹞

  = glide ﹝ glaɪd ﹞

  = flutter ﹝ 'flʌtə ﹞

float ﹝ flot ﹞ ① v. 支持 ② n. 筏
③ n. 遊行車

① = sustain ﹝ sə'sten ﹞

  = *buoy up*

  = *hold up*

② = raft ﹝ ræft ﹞

③ = *parade car*

flock ﹝ flɑk ﹞ n. 群

  = group ﹝ grup ﹞

  = crowd ﹝ kraʊd ﹞

  = throng ﹝ θrɔŋ ﹞

  = mob ﹝ mɑb ﹞

  = bunch ﹝ bʌntʃ ﹞

  = pack ﹝ pæk ﹞

  = multitude ﹝ 'mʌltəˌtjud ﹞

flog ﹝ flɑg ﹞ v. 重打

  = beat ﹝ bit ﹞

  = whip ﹝ hwɪp ﹞

  = lash ﹝ læʃ ﹞

  = spank ﹝ spæŋk ﹞

  = thrash ﹝ θræʃ ﹞

flood ﹝ flʌd ﹞ v. 氾濫

  = overfill ﹝ ˌovə'fɪl ﹞

F

= drench〔drɛntʃ〕
= overflow〔,ovəˈflo〕
= inundate〔ˈɪnʌn,det , ɪnˈʌndet〕
= oversupply〔,ovəsəˈplaɪ〕
= deluge〔ˈdɛljudʒ〕

floor〔flor , flɔr〕① v. 打倒
② n. 地板　③ n. 樓；層

① = defeat〔dɪˈfit〕
= overcome〔,ovəˈkʌm〕
= upset〔ʌpˈsɛt〕
= overthrow〔,ovəˈθro〕
② = ground〔graʊnd〕
= pavement〔ˈpevmənt〕
③ = level〔ˈlɛvḷ〕
= story〔ˈstorɪ〕

flop〔flɑp〕v. ①落　②失敗

① = drop〔drɑp〕
= fall〔fɔl〕
= sink〔sɪŋk〕
= droop〔drup〕
= slump〔slʌmp〕
= sag〔sæg〕
= *go down*
② = fail〔fel〕
= lose〔luz〕

flounder〔ˈflaʊndə〕① v. 掙扎
② n. 比目魚

① = struggle〔ˈstrʌgḷ〕
= stumble〔ˈstʌmbḷ〕
= *have trouble*
② = fish〔fɪʃ〕

flourish〔ˈflɝɪʃ〕v. ①茂盛
②揮舞

① = thrive〔θraɪv〕
= prosper〔ˈprɑspə〕
= grow〔gro〕
= develop〔dɪˈvɛləp〕
= sprout〔spraʊt〕
= bloom〔blum〕
= fade〔fed〕
② = wave〔wev〕
= flaunt〔flɔnt〕
= display〔dɪˈsple〕
= parade〔peˈred〕
= exhibit〔ɪgˈzɪbɪt〕
= show〔ʃo〕

flout〔flaʊt〕v. 嘲弄

= sneer〔snɪr〕
= insult〔ɪnˈsʌlt〕
= mock〔mɑk〕
= ridicule〔ˈrɪdɪ,kjul〕
= jeer〔dʒɪr〕
= taunt〔tɔnt〕

flow〔flo〕v. 流動

= glide〔glaɪd〕
= stream〔strim〕
= pour〔por , pɔr〕
= run〔rʌn〕
= gush〔gʌʃ〕

flower〔ˈflaʊə〕v. 開花；旺盛

= blossom〔ˈblɑsəm〕
= bloom〔blum〕
= develop〔dɪˈvɛləp〕
= flourish〔ˈflɝɪʃ〕
= thrive〔θraɪv〕

fluffy ('flʌfɪ) adj. 柔軟如毛的

= soft (sɔft)

= downy ('daʊnɪ)

= feathery ('fɛðərɪ)

= woolly ('wʊlɪ)

= furry ('fɜɪ)

fluid ('fluɪd) adj. 流動的

= liquid ('lɪkwɪd)

= flowing ('floɪŋ)

= watery ('wɔtərɪ)

flurry ('flɜɪ) ① v. 使慌亂
② n. 騷動　③ n. 一陣驟雪

① = fluster ('flʌstɚ)

= excite (ɪk'saɪt)

= agitate ('ædʒə,tet)

= confuse (kən'fjuz)

= ruffle ('rʌfḷ)

② = commotion (kə'moʃən)

= confusion (kən'fjuʒən)

= disturbance (dɪ'stɜbəns)

③ = *light snowstorm*

flush (flʌʃ) ① v. 面紅
② v. 猛衝　③ adj. 平的
④ adj. 豐足的

① = blush (blʌʃ)

= redden ('rɛdṇ)

= color ('kʌlɚ)

② = rush (rʌʃ)

= chase (tʃes)

③ = level ('lɛvḷ)

= flat (flæt)

= even ('ivən)

④ = full (fʊl)

= stuffed (stʌft)

= packed (pækt)

fluster ('flʌstɚ) v. 使驚慌

= excite (ɪk'saɪt)

= confuse (kən'fjuz)

flutter ('flʌtɚ) v. 擺動

= wave (wev)

= flap (flæp)

= flourish ('flɜɪʃ)

= tremble ('trɛmbḷ)

= move (muv)

fly (flaɪ) ① v. 飛行；航行
② v. 逃走　③ n. 昆蟲

① = glide (glaɪd)

= coast (kost)

= sail (sel)

= wing (wɪŋ)

② = flee (fli)

= *run away*

③ = insect ('ɪnsɛkt)

foam (fom) n. 泡沫

= bubble ('bʌbḷ)

= lather ('læðɚ)

= froth (frɔθ , frɑθ)

focus ('fokəs) v. 集中

= adjust (ə'dʒʌst)

= concentrate ('kɑnsṇ,tret)

foe (fo) n. 敵人

= enemy ('ɛnəmɪ)

F

= adversary ('ædvə‚sɛrɪ)
= opponent (ə'ponənt)

fog (fɑg , fɔg) v. 使模糊
= cloud (klaud)
= blur (blɝ)
= dim (dɪm)
= confuse (kən'fjuz)

foil (fɔɪl) ① v. 打敗 ② n. 箔
③ n. 劍
① = outwit (aut'wɪt)
= frustrate ('frʌstret)
= thwart (θwɔrt)
= spoil (spɔɪl)
= ruin ('ruɪn)
② = metal ('mɛtḷ)
③ = sword (sord , sɔrd)

fold (fold) ① v. 摺疊
② n. 圍欄 ③ n. 教會
① = bend (bɛnd)
= double *over*
② = pen (pɛn)
= enclosure (ɪn'kloʒə)
③ = church (tʃɝtʃ)

folk (fok) n. ①人民 ②種族
① = people ('pipḷ)
= persons ('pɝsṇz)
= society (sə'saɪətɪ)
= public ('pʌblɪk)
② = tribe (traɪb)
= nation ('neʃən)
= race (res)
= clan (klæn)
= breed (brid)

follow ('falo) v. ①跟隨
②沿…而行 ③遵循
① = succeed (sək'sid)
= ensue (ɪn'su, ɪn'sju)
= trail (trel)
= *come next*
② = pursue (pə'su, -'sju)
= trace (tres)
③ = use (juz)
= obey (ə'be, o'be)
= *act according to*

folly ('falɪ) n. 愚蠢；愚行
= foolishness ('fulɪʃnɪs)
= silliness ('sɪlɪnɪs)
= stupidity (stju'pɪdətɪ)

fond (fand) adj. 愛好的；愛憐的
= loving ('lʌvɪŋ)
= liking ('laɪkɪŋ)
= affectionate (ə'fɛkʃənɪt)
= adoring (ə'dorɪŋ, ə'dɔrɪŋ)
= romantic (ro'mæntɪk)
= tender ('tɛndə)
= sentimental (‚sɛntə'mɛntḷ)

fondle ('fandḷ) v. 撫愛
= pet (pɛt)
= caress (kɛ'rɛs)
= cuddle ('kʌdḷ)

font (fant) n. ①泉 ②聖水盆
① = fountain ('fauntṇ, -tɪn)
= spring (sprɪŋ)
② = basin ('besṇ)

food (fud) *n.* 食品；滋養品

= edibles ('ɛdəbl̩z)

= provisions (prə'vɪʒənz)

= nutriment ('njurəmənt , 'nu-)

= nourishment ('nɜɪʃmənt)

fool (ful) ① *v.* 開玩笑
② *v.* 欺騙   ③ *n.* 傻子

① = play (ple)

= joke (dʒok)

② = deceive (dɪ'siv)

= trick (trɪk)

= mislead (mɪs'lid)

③ = ninny ('nɪnɪ)

= ignoramus (ˌɪgnə'reməs)

= dunce (dʌns)

= blockhead ('blɑk,hɛd)

= scatterbrain ('skætə,bren)

= simpleton ('sɪmpl̩tən)

= know-nothing ('no,nʌθɪŋ)

foolhardy ('ful,hardɪ) *adj.*
愚勇的

= bold (bold)

= rash (ræʃ)

= daring ('dɛrɪŋ)

= audacious (ɔ'deʃəs)

= reckless ('rɛklɪs)

foolproof ('ful,pruf) *adj.*
安全的；不失敗的

= safe (sef)

= tight (taɪt)

= resistant (rɪ'zɪstənt)

foot (fʊt) ① *v.* 步行   ② *n.* 足部
③ *n.* 底部

① = walk (wɔk)

= march (martʃ)

= hike (haɪk)

= *hoof it*

② = sole (sol)

= kicker ('kɪkə)

= *part of body*

③ = base (bes)

= foundation (faʊn'deʃən)

= *lowest part*

forage ('fɔrɪdʒ , 'far-) ① *v.* 搜尋
② *n.* 牛馬的飼料

① = hunt (hʌnt)

= search (sɜtʃ)

= look (lʊk)

= explore (ɪk'splor , -'splɔr)

② = fodder ('fadə)

= feed (fid)

= grain (gren)

= *animal food*

foray ('fɔre , 'fare) *v.* 搶劫；
掠奪

= plunder ('plʌndə)

= pillage ('pɪlɪdʒ)

= raid (red)

= invade (ɪn'ved)

forbear (fɔr'bɛr , fə-) *v.* 戒絕；
抑制

= refrain (rɪ'fren)

= abstain (əb'sten , æb-)

= avoid (ə'vɔɪd)

= *control oneself*

= *hold back*

F

forbid (fə'bɪd) *v.* 禁止

= prohibit (pro'hɪbɪt)

= disallow (,dɪsə'lau)

= bar (bar)

= ban (bæn)

= taboo (tə'bu)

= prevent (prɪ'vɛnt)

= deter (dɪ'tɝ)

force (fors , fɔrs) ① *v.* 迫使
② *v.* 強行；突破　③ *n.* 力量
④ *n.* 組；群

① = compel (kəm'pɛl)

= make (mek)

= drive (draɪv)

= oblige (ə'blaɪdʒ)

= motivate ('motə,vet)

= pressure ('prɛʃɚ)

② = thrust (θrʌst)

= push (puʃ)

= shove (ʃʌv)

= ram (ræm)

= *break through*

③ = power ('pauɚ)

= strength (strɛnθ , strɛŋkθ)

= might (maɪt)

= vigor ('vɪgɚ)

= energy ('ɛnɚdʒɪ)

④ = group (grup)

= body ('badɪ)

= staff (stæf)

= personnel (,pɝsn̩'ɛl)

= crew (kru)

= gang (gæŋ)

fore (for , fɔr) *adj.* 在前的

= front (frʌnt)

= forward ('fɔrwəd)

= foremost ('for,most , 'fɔr-)

= first (fɝst)

= chief (tʃif)

= head (hɛd)

= primary ('praɪ,mɛrɪ , -mərɪ)

foreboding (fɔr'bodɪŋ , for-)
n. 預言；警告

= warning ('wɔrnɪŋ)

= prediction (prɪ'dɪkʃən)

= foretelling (for'tɛlɪŋ , fɔr-)

= forecast ('for,kæst)

= promise ('pramɪs)

= omen ('omɪn , 'omən)

= prophecy ('prafəsɪ)

= premonition (,primə'nɪʃən)

forecast ('for,kæst) *n.* 預言；
預兆

= prophecy ('prafəsɪ)

= prediction (prɪ'dɪkʃən)

= foretelling (for'tɛlɪŋ , fɔr-)

= promise ('pramɪs)

= omen ('omɪn , 'omən)

forefather ('for,faðɚ , 'fɔr-)
n. 祖先

= ancestor ('ænsɛstɚ)

= predecessor (,prɛdɪ'sɛsɚ)

= forebear ('for,bɛr , 'fɔr-)

foreign ('fɔrɪn , 'farɪn) *adj.*
外國的

= alien ('elɪən , 'eljən)

= external (ɪk'stɝnl̩)

foreman ('formən , 'fɔr-) *n.*
領班；監督者

= supervisor ('supəˌvaɪzə)
= superintendent
  (ˌsuprɪn'tɛndənt)
= overseer ('ovəˌsiə)
= boss (bɔs)

foremost ('fɔrˌmost , 'fɔr-) *adj.*
首要的

= first (fɝst)
= chief (tʃif)
= leading ('lidɪŋ)
= main (men)
= principal ('prɪnsəpḷ)
= dominant ('dɑmənənt)
= primary ('praɪˌmɛrɪ , -mərɪ)

foresee (for'si , fɔr-) *v.* 預知

= anticipate (æn'tɪsəˌpet)
= predict (prɪ'dɪkt)
= forecast ('forˌkæst)
= foretell (for'tɛl , fɔr-)
= prophesy ('prɑfəˌsaɪ)

forest ('fɔrɪst , 'fɑr-) *n.* 森林

= wood (wʊd)

foretell (fɔr'go) *v.* 放棄

= sacrifice ('sækrəˌfaɪs , -ˌfaɪz)
= surrender (sə'rɛndə)
= yield (jild)
= relinquish (rɪ'lɪŋkwɪʃ)
= *do without*
= *give up*

fork (fork) *n.* ①叉子
②分岔之物

① = silverware ('sɪlvəˌwɛr)
② = branch (bræntʃ)
  = offshoot ('ɔfˌʃut , 'ɑf-)

forlorn (fə'lɔrn) *adj.* 絕望的；
被遺棄的

= hopeless ('hoplɪs)
= miserable ('mɪzərəbḷ , 'mɪzrə-)
= desperate ('dɛspərɪt)
= despondent (dɪ'spandənt)
= forsaken (fə'sekən)
= abandoned (ə'bændənd)
= deserted (dɪ'zɝtɪd)
= defenseless (dɪ'fɛnslɪs)
= helpless ('hɛlplɪs)
= resistant (rɪ'zɪstənt)

form (fɔrm) ① *v.* 形成
② *n.* 形式；種類
③ *n.* 方式；方法

① = develop (dɪ'vɛləp)
  = compose (kəm'poz)
  = make (mek)
  = create (krɪ'et)
  = fashion ('fæʃən)
  = construct (kən'strʌkt)
  = shape (ʃep)
  = mold (mold)
② = kind (kaɪnd)
  = sort (sort)
  = class (klæs)
  = grade (gred)
  = type (taɪp)
  = variety (və'raɪətɪ)

= species（'spiʃɪz , -ʃiz ）
= make（ mek ）
③ = manner（'mænɚ ）
= method（'mεθəd ）
= fashion（'fæʃən ）
= style（ staɪl ）
= way（ we ）
= procedure（ prə'sidʒɚ ）

formal（'fɔrml̩ ）*adj.* 正式的；
合式的

= orderly（'ɔrdɚlɪ ）
= regular（'rεgjəlɚ ）
= systematic（,sɪstə'mætɪk ）
= businesslike（'bɪznɪs,laɪk ）
= stiff（ stɪf ）
= arranged（ ə'rendʒd ）
= structural（'strʌktʃərəl ）
= correct（ kə'rεkt ）
= proper（'prɑpɚ ）
= customary（'kʌstəm,εrɪ ）

former（'fɔrmɚ ）*adj.* 在前的

= earlier（'ɝlɪɚ ）
= past（ pæst ）
= previous（'privɪəs ）
= preceding（ prɪ'sidɪŋ ）
= prior（'praɪɚ ）
= first（ fɝst ）

formidable（'fɔrmɪdəbl̩ ）*adj.*
困難的

= difficult（'dɪfə,kʌlt ）
= hard（ hard ）
= rough（ rʌf ）
= rugged（'rʌgɪd ）
= tough（ tʌf ）

formulate（'fɔrmjə,let ）*v.*
陳述；說明

= define（ dɪ'faɪn ）
= describe（ dɪ'skraɪb ）
= express（ ɪk'sprεs ）
= voice（ vɔɪs ）
= put（ pʊt ）

forsake（ fɚ'sek ）*v.* 放棄

= leave（ liv ）
= abandon（ ə'bændən ）
= quit（ kwɪt ）
= *give up*

forth（ forθ , fɔrθ ）*adv.* 向前

= forward（'fɔrwəd ）
= onward（'ɑnwəd ）
= on（ ɑn ）
= ahead（ ə'hεd ）

forthcoming（'forθ'kʌmɪŋ ）
adj. 即將到來的

= approaching（ ə'protʃɪŋ ）
= imminent（'ɪmənənt ）
= coming（'kʌmɪŋ ）
= near（ nɪr ）
= close（ klos ）

forthwith（ forθ'wɪθ , fɔrθ- ,
-'wɪð ）*adv.* 立刻

= immediately（ ɪ'midɪɪtlɪ ）
= promptly（'prɑmptlɪ ）
= instantly（'ɪnstəntlɪ ）
= quickly（'kwɪklɪ ）
= swiftly（'swɪftlɪ ）
= *without delay*
= *at once*

fortify ('fɔrtə,faɪ) v. 加強

= strengthen ('strɛŋ(k)θən)

= brace (bres)

= invigorate (ɪn'vɪgə,ret)

= reinforce (,riɪn'fors)

fortitude ('fɔrtə,tjud) n. 堅毅

= courage ('kɝɪdʒ)

= strength (strɛŋθ , strɛŋkθ)

= vigor ('vɪgɚ)

= vitality (vaɪ'tælətɪ)

= stamina ('stæmənə)

= spunk (spʌŋk)

fortunate ('fɔrtʃənɪt) adj. 幸運的

= luck ('lʌkɪ)

= auspicious (ɔ'spɪʃəs)

fortune ('fɔrtʃən) n. ①財富 ②命運

① = riches ('rɪtʃɪz)

= wealth (wɛlθ)

= prosperity (pras'pɛrətɪ)

= treasure ('trɛʒɚ)

② = luck (lʌk)

= chance (tʃæns)

= fate (fet)

= lot (lɑt)

= destiny ('dɛstənɪ)

forum ('forəm , 'fɔrəm) n. ①廣場 ②討論 ③法庭

① = square (skwɛr)

= plaza ('plæzə , 'plɑzə)

② = discussion (dɪ'skʌʃən)

= debate (dɪ'bet)

= deliberation (dɪ,lɪbə'reʃən)

= consideration (kən,sɪdə'reʃən)

= study ('stʌdɪ)

③ = tribunal (trɪ'bjunḷ , traɪ-)

= *law court*

forward ('fɔrwəd) ① v. 轉遞 ② adj. , adv. 向前的（地） ③ adj. 大膽無禮的

① = send (sɛnd)

= dispatch (dɪ'spætʃ)

= deliver (dɪ'lɪvɚ)

= pass (pæs , pas)

② = onward ('ɑnwəd)

= ahead (ə'hɛd)

= frontward ('frʌntwəd)

= advanced (əd'vænst)

③ = pert (pɝt)

= bold (bold)

= aggressive (ə'grɛsɪv)

= insolent ('ɪnsələnt)

= presumptuous (prɪ'zʌmptʃuəs)

= brazen ('brezṇ)

= immodest (ɪ'mɑdɪst)

fossil ('fɑsḷ) n. 化石；遺跡

= remains (rɪ'menz)

= trace (tres)

= vestige ('vɛstɪdʒ)

= relic ('rɛlɪk)

foster ('fɔstɚ , 'fas-) v. 養育

= nourish ('nɝɪʃ)

= nurture ('nɝtʃɚ)

= feed (fid)

= cultivate ('kʌltə,vet)
= nurse (nɜs)
= support (sə'port , -'port)
= mind (maind)
= tend (tɛnd)
= rear (rɪr)
= *care for*

foul (faʊl) *adj.* ①污穢的
②邪惡的　③不公平的

① = dirty ('dɝtɪ)
= nasty ('næstɪ)
= smelly ('smɛlɪ)
= stinking ('stɪŋkɪŋ)
= offensive (ə'fɛnsɪv)
= disgusting (dɪs'gʌstɪŋ)
② = vile (vaɪl)
= wicked ('wɪkɪd)
= vicious ('vɪʃəs)
= evil ('ivl̩)
= bad (bæd)
= wrong (rɔŋ)
= sinful ('sɪnful , -fəl)
= base (bes)
= low (lo)
③ = unfair (ʌn'fɛr)

foundation (faʊn'deʃən) *n.*
①根基　②建設

① = base (bes)
= ground (graʊnd)
② = establishment (ə'stæblɪʃmənt)
= institution (,ɪnstə'tjuʃən)
= organization (,ɔrgənə'zeʃən)

founder ('faʊndɚ) ① *v.* 跌倒
② *v.* 失敗；崩潰　③ *n.* 建立者

① = fall (fɔl)
= stumble ('stʌmbl̩)
= tumble ('tʌmbl̩)
= topple ('tapl̩)
② = collapse (kə'læps)
= sink (sɪŋk)
= fail (fel)
= *break down*
③ = producer (prə'djusɚ)
= creator (krɪ'etɚ)
= maker ('mekɚ)
= author ('ɔθɚ)
= originator (ə'rɪdʒɪ,netɚ)
= inventor (ɪn'vɛntɚ)
= builder ('bɪldɚ)

foundling ('faʊndlɪŋ) *n.* 棄兒

= orphan ('ɔrfən)
= waif (wef)

foundry ('faʊndrɪ) *n.* 鑄造工廠

= forge (fordʒ , fɔrdʒ)
= smelter ('smɛltɚ)
= *blacksmith's shop*

fountain ('faʊntn̩ , -tɪn) *n.*
①噴水　② *n.* 泉源

① = spring (sprɪŋ)
= spout (spaʊt)
= spray (spre)
② = source (sors , sɔrs)

fowl (faʊl) *n.* 家禽

= bird (bɝd)
= poultry ('poltrɪ)

oxy ('faksı) *adj.* 狡猾的

= crafty ('kræftı , 'kraftı)

= shrewd (ʃrud)

= artful ('artfəl , -f!̩)

= cunning ('kʌnɪŋ)

= knowing ('noɪŋ)

= sly (slaɪ)

= clever ('klɛvɚ)

= canny ('kænɪ)

raction ('frækʃən) *n.* 部分

= part (part)

= portion ('porʃən , 'pɔr-)

= division (də'vɪʒən)

= segment ('sɛgmənt)

= section ('sɛkʃən)

racture ('fræktʃɚ) *v.* 碎裂

= break (brek)

= crack (kræk)

= burst (bɜst)

= rupture ('rʌptʃɚ)

= chip (tʃɪp)

ragile ('frækdʒəl , -aɪl) *adj.*
易碎的；脆弱的

= delicate ('dɛləkət , -kɪt)

= frail (frel)

= slight (slaɪt)

= dainty ('dentɪ)

= breakable ('brekəb!̩)

= flimsy ('flɪmzɪ)

= brittle ('brɪt!̩)

ragment ('frægmənt) *n.* 碎片

= part (part)

= portion ('porʃən , 'pɔr-)

= segment ('sɛgmənt)

= section ('sɛkʃən)

= fraction ('frækʃən)

= division (də'vɪʒən)

fragrant ('fregrənt) *adj.* 芳香的

= perfumed (pɚ'fjumd)

= odorous ('odərəs)

= aromatic (,ærə'mætɪk)

= sweet-smelling ('swit'smɛlɪŋ)

frail (frel) *adj.* 脆弱的

= weak (wik)

= slight (slaɪt)

= delicate ('dɛləkət , -kɪt)

= dainty ('dentɪ)

= fragile ('frædʒəl)

frame (frem) ① *v.* 構造；設計
② *n.* 邊緣 ③ *n.* 體形 ④ *n.* 支架

① = make (mek)

= plan (plæn)

= build (bɪld)

= construct (kən'strʌkt)

= form (fɔrm)

= design (dɪ'zaɪn)

= devise (dɪ'vaɪz)

= arrange (ə'rendʒ)

= *put together*

② = border ('bɔrdɚ)

= edge (edʒ)

= bound (baʊnd)

= time (trɪm)

③ = body ('badɪ)

= figure ('fɪgjɚ , 'fɪgɚ)

F

= form (fɔrm)

④ = support (sə'port , -'pɔrt)

= skeleton ('skɛlətn̩)

frank (fræŋk) *adj.* 坦白的

= open ('opən)

= candid ('kændɪd)

= sincere (sɪn'sɪr)

= straightforward (,stret'fɔrwəd)

= forthright (,forθ'raɪt)

= outspoken ('aut'spokən)

= blunt (blʌnt)

frantic ('fræntɪk) *adj.* 發狂的

= excited (ɪk'saɪtɪd)

= frenzied ('frɛnzɪd)

= wild (waɪld)

= violent ('vaɪələnt)

= delirious (dɪ'lɪrɪəs)

= hysterical (hɪs'tɛrɪkl̩)

fraternal (frə'tɜnl̩ , fre-) *adj.*
友愛的

= brotherly ('brʌðəlɪ)

= kind (kaɪnd)

= sympathetic (,sɪmpə'θɛtɪk)

= friendly ('frɛndlɪ)

= congenial (kən'dʒinjəl)

= sociable ('soʃəbl̩)

fraud (frɔd) *n.* 欺騙

= cheating ('tʃitɪŋ)

= trickery ('trɪkərɪ)

= dishonesty (dɪs'ɑnɪstɪ)

= swindle ('swɪndl̩)

fraught (frɔt) *adj.* 充滿…的

= loaded ('lodɪd)

= filled (fɪld)

fray (fre) ① *v.* 磨損   ② *n.* 衝突

① = rub (rʌb)

= tatter ('tætə)

= *wear away*

② = fight (faɪt)

= quarrel ('kwɔrəl , 'kwɑr-)

= battle ('bætl̩)

= conflict ('kɑnflɪkt)

= clash (klæʃ)

= brush (brʌʃ)

= tussle ('tʌsl̩)

= skirmish ('skɜmɪʃ)

= scuffle ('skʌfl̩)

= struggle ('strʌgl̩)

= melee (me'le , 'mele)

freak (frik) *adj.* 怪誕的

= unusual (ʌn'juʒuəl)

= queer (kwɪr)

= incredible (ɪn'krɛdəbl̩)

= grotesque (gro'tɛsk)

= bizarre (bɪ'zɑr)

free (fri) ① *v.* 釋放
② *adj.* 無束縛的   ③ *adj.* 自主的
④ *adj.* 免費的

① = clear (klɪr)

= acquit (ə'kwɪt)

= dismiss (dɪs'mɪs)

= release (rɪ'lis)

= discharge (dɪs'tʃɑrdʒ)

= relieve (rɪ'liv)

F

= reprieve (rɪ'priv)

= deliver (dɪ'lɪvə)

= liberate ('lɪbə,ret)

= emancipate (ɪ'mænsə,pet)

) = loose (lus)

= unfastened (ʌn'fæsn̩d)

= untied (ʌn'taɪd)

) = independent (,ɪndɪ'pɛndənt)

= open ('opən)

= unrestrained (,ʌnrɪ'strend)

= *at liberty*

= complimentary

   (,kɑmplə'mɛntərɪ)

= gratis ('gretɪs , 'grætɪs)

= untaxed (ʌn'tækst)

= without *charge*

reeze (friz) *v.* ①使冰冷
②變僵硬

) = chill (tʃɪl)

= refrigerate (rɪ'frɪdʒə,ret)

) = stiffen ('stɪfən)

= *remain motionless*

reight (fret) *n.* 貨物

= load (lod)

= cargo ('kɑrgo)

= burden ('bɝdn̩)

= shipment ('ʃɪpmənt)

= goods (gʊdz)

renzy ('frɛnzɪ) *n.* 狂亂；暴怒

= fury ('fjʊrɪ)

= madness ('mædnɪs)

= excitement (ɪk'saɪtmənt)

= passion ('pæʃən

= rage (redʒ)

= agitation (,ædʒə'teʃən)

= fit (fɪt)

= delirium (dɪ'lɪrɪəm)

frequent (*v.* frɪ'kwɛnt ,
adj. 'frikwənt) ① *v.* 常去
② *adj.* 時常的

① = haunt (hɔnt , hɑnt)

   = *visit often*

② = many ('mɛnɪ)

   = recurrent (rɪ'kɝənt)

   = common ('kɑmən)

   = prevalent ('prɛvələnt)

   = regular ('rɛgjələ)

   = habitual (hə'bɪtʃʊəl)

fresh (frɛʃ) *adj.* ①新鮮的
②淡的 ③有生氣的

① = new (nju)

   = unused (ʌn'juzd)

   = firsthand ('fɝst'hænd)

   = original (ə'rɪdʒənl̩)

② = unsalty (ʌn'sɔltɪ)

③ = bright (braɪt)

   = alert (ə'lɝt)

   = unfaded (ʌn'fedɪd)

   = brisk (brɪsk)

   = vigorous ('vɪgərəs)

   = energetic (,ɛnə'dʒɛtɪk)

   = refreshed (rɪ'frɛʃt)

fret (frɛt) *v.* 煩躁

= fuss (fʌs)

= worry ('wɝɪ)

F

friction ('frɪkʃən) *n.* 衝突

= resistance (rɪ'zɪstəns)
= clash (klæʃ)
= conflict ('kɑnflɪkt)
= grinding ('graɪndɪŋ)
= scraping ('skrepɪŋ)

friend (frɛnd) *n.* 朋友

= acquaintance (ə'kwentəns)
= intimate ('ɪntəmɪt)
= companion (kəm'pænjən)
= comrade ('kɑmræd , 'kɑmrɪd)
= mate (met)
= associate (ə'soʃɪɪt)
= colleague ('kɑlig)
= partner ('pɑrtnɚ)
= crony ('kronɪ)
= playmate ('ple,met)
= chum (tʃʌm)
= buddy ('bʌdɪ)

fright (fraɪt) *n.* ①驚嚇
②令人吃驚的人（物）

① = fear (fɪr)
= terror ('tɛrɚ)
= alarm (ə'lɑrm)
= dismay (dɪs'me)
= dread (drɛd)
= awe (ɔ)
= horror ('hɑrɚ)
= phobia ('fobɪə)
= panic ('pænɪk)
② = eyesore ('aɪ,sor , -,sɔr)
= mess (mɛs)

frigid ('frɪdʒɪd) *adj.* ①冷漠的
②嚴寒的

① = cold (kold)
= stiff (stɪf)
= chilling ('tʃɪlɪŋ)
= icy ('aɪsɪ)
= reserved (rɪ'zɜvd)
= unfeeling (ʌn'filɪŋ)
= aloof (ə'luf)
= distant ('dɪstənt)
= restrained (rɪ'strend)
② = freezing ('frizɪŋ)
= wintry ('wɪntrɪ)
= crisp (krɪsp)
= brisk (brɪsk)
= nippy ('nɪpɪ)
= raw (rɔ)
= sharp (ʃɑrp)
= frosty ('frɔstɪ , 'frɑstɪ)

frill (frɪl) *n.* （衣飾之）縐邊

= ornament ('ɔrnəmənt)
= ruffle ('rʌfl̩)
= flounce (flauns)
= embellishment (ɪm'bɛlɪʃmənt

fringe (frɪndʒ) *n.* 邊緣

= border ('bɔrdɚ)
= trimming ('trɪmɪŋ)
= edge (ɛdʒ)
= brim (brɪm)
= rim (rɪm)

frisk (frɪsk) *v.* 雀躍

= frolic ('frɑlɪk)
= play (ple)
= romp (rɑmp)
= caper ('kepɚ)

F

frivolous ('frɪvələs) *adj.* 愚蠢的；不重要的

= silly ('sɪlɪ)
= shallow ('ʃælo)
= unimportant (ˌʌnɪm'pɔrtn̩t)
= light (laɪt)
= trivial ('trɪvɪəl)
= foolish ('fulɪʃ)
= inane (ɪn'en)

frock (frɑk) *n.* 長袍

= gown (gaʊn)
= dress (drɛs)
= garment ('gɑrmənt)
= robe (rob)

frolic ('frɑlɪk) *v.* 雀躍

= play (ple)
= frisk (frɪsk)
= romp (rɑmp)
= caper ('kepɚ)

front (frʌnt) *n.* 前部

= fore (for , fɔr)
= face (fes)
= head (hɛd)
= *first part*

frontier (frʌn'tɪr , 'frʌntɪr) *n.* 邊界

= border ('bɔrdɚ)
= outskirts ('aʊtˌskɝts)
= *back country*

frost (frɔst , frɑst) *n.* 嚴寒

= freezing ('frizɪŋ)

= cold (kold)

frosting ('frɔstɪŋ , 'frɑstɪŋ) *n.* 覆於糕點上之糖霜

= icing ('aɪsɪŋ)
= topping ('tɑpɪŋ)

froth (frɔθ , frɑθ) *n.* ①泡沫 ②瑣事

① = foam (fom)
= lather ('læðɚ)
② = trivia ('trɪvɪə)
= rubbish ('rʌbɪʃ)
= *unimportant things*

frown (fraʊn) *v.* 蹙額；不悅

= scowl (skaʊl)
= pout (paʊt)
= *look sullen*
= *look displeased*

frugal ('frugl̩) *adj.* 節儉的

= economical (ˌikə'nɑmɪkl̩ , ˌɛk-)
= thrifty ('θrɪftɪ)
= saving ('sevɪŋ)
= prudent ('prudn̩t)

fruit (frut) *n.* ①果實 ②成果

① = *plant product*
② = yield (jild)
= result (rɪ'zʌlt)

frustrate ('frʌstret) *v.* 挫敗

= foil (fɔɪl)
= thwart (θwɔrt)
= defeat (dɪ'fit)

F

fry (fraɪ) v. 油煎；油炸

= cook (kʊk)
= saute (so'te)

fuel ('fjuəl) n. 燃料

= kindling ('kɪndlɪŋ)
= combustible (kəm'bʌstəbḷ)

F

fugitive ('fjudʒətɪv) adj.
①逃亡的 ②瞬時即逝的

① = runaway ('rʌnə,we)
= escaping (ə'skepɪŋ , ɪ- , ɛ-)
② = temporary ('tɛmpə,rɛrɪ)
= passing ('pæsɪŋ)
= transient ('trænʃənt , -zɪənt)

fulfill (fʊl'fɪl) v. 實踐；完成

= perform (pə'fɔrm)
= do (du)
= execute ('ɛksɪ,kjut)
= finish ('fɪnɪʃ)
= complete (kəm'plit)
= transact (træns'ækt , trænz-)
= discharge (dɪs'tʃɑrdʒ)
= satisfy ('sætɪs,faɪ)
= carry out

full (fʊl) adj. ①滿的；完全的
②肥胖豐滿的 ③寬廣的

① = complete (kəm'plit)
= entire (ɪn'taɪr)
= stuffed (stʌft)
= packed (pækt)

= crammed (kræmd)
② = plump (plʌmp)
= round (raʊnd)
= fat (fæt)
③ = broad (brɔd)
= wide (waɪd)
= expansive (ɪk'spænsɪv)
= roomy ('rumɪ)

fumble ('fʌmbḷ) v. 笨拙地處理

= bungle ('bʌŋgḷ)
= blunder ('blʌndə)
= muff (mʌf)
= grope awkwardly

fume (fjum) ① v. 忿怒
② n. 煙霧；蒸氣

① = burn (bɝn)
= seethe (sið)
= rage (redʒ)
= storm (stɔrm)
= rave (rev)
= be angry
② = smoke (smok)
= vapor ('vepə)

fumigate ('fjumə,get) v.
將…消毒

= disinfect (,dɪsɪn'fɛkt)
= sterilize ('stɛrə,laɪz)
= sanitize ('sænə,taɪz)

fun (fʌn) n. 樂趣

= amusement (ə'mjuzmənt)
= playfulness ('plefəlnɪs)
= joking ('dʒokɪŋ)

= sport (sport , sport)

= pleasure ('plɛʒɚ)

= entertainment (,ɛntɚ'tenmənt)

= enjoyment (ɪn'dʒɔɪmənt)

= *good time*

function ('fʌŋkʃən)

① *v.* 擔任工作 ② *n.* 典禮；集會

① = work (wɜk)

= act (ækt)

= operate ('ɑpə,ret)

= perform (pɚ'fɔrm)

= serve (sɜv)

= *be used*

② = ceremony ('sɛrə,monɪ)

= gathering ('gæðrɪŋ)

= service ('sɜvɪs)

= rite (raɪt)

= ritual ('rɪtʃuəl)

= exercise ('ɛksɚ,saɪz)

fund (fʌnd) *n.* 貯藏；資產

= stock (stɑk)

= supply (sə'plaɪ)

= resources (rɪ'sorsɪz , rɪ'sɔrsɪz)

= assets ('æsɛts)

fundamental (,fʌndə'mɛntḷ)

adj. 基本的

= essential (ə'sɛnʃəl)

= basic ('besɪk)

= underlying ('ʌndɚ,laɪɪŋ)

= primary ('praɪ,mɛrɪ , -mərɪ)

= elementary (,ɛlə'mɛntərɪ)

funeral ('fjunərəl) *n.* 葬禮

= burial ('bɛrɪəl)

= *last rites*

funnel ('fʌnḷ) *n.* 管狀物

= channel ('tʃænḷ)

= siphon ('saɪfən)

= pipe (paɪp)

fur (fɜ) *n.* 獸皮

= pelt (pɛlt)

= hide (haɪd)

= skin (skɪn)

furious ('fjurɪəs) *adj.* 生氣的

= raging ('redʒɪŋ)

= violent ('vaɪələnt)

= angry ('æŋgrɪ)

= mad (mæd)

= rabid ('ræbɪd)

= overwrought ('ovɚ'rɔt)

= upset ('ʌp'sɛt)

= enraged (ɪn'redʒd , ɛn-)

= infuriated (ɪn'fjurɪ,etɪd)

furl (fɜl) *v.* 捲起；疊起

= fold (fold)

= *roll up*

furlough ('fɜlo) *n.* 休假

= vacation (ve'keʃən , və-)

= sabbatical (sə'bætɪkḷ)

= *leave of absence*

furnace ('fɜnɪs) *n.* 火爐

= stove (stov)

= heater ('hitɚ)

F

= oven ('ʌvən)

= kiln (kɪl , kɪln)

= forge (fɔrdʒ , fordʒ)

furnish ('fɜnɪʃ) v. 供給；裝備

= supply (sə'plaɪ)

= provide (prə'vaɪd)

= give (gɪv)

= equip (ɪ'kwɪp)

= outfit ('aʊt,fɪt)

furrow ('fɜo) n. 皺紋；犁溝

= wrinkle ('rɪŋkḷ)

= crease (kris)

= groove (gruv)

further ('fɜðɚ) ① v. 促進
② adv. 更進一步地

① = aid (ed)

= advance (əd'væns)

= promote (prə'mot)

② = farther ('farðɚ)

= beyond (bɪ'jand)

= past (pæst , past)

= over ('ovɚ)

furthermore ('fɜðɚ,mor ,
-,mɔr) adv. 此外；同樣地

= then (ðɛn)

= again (ə'gɛn , ə'gen)

= also ('ɔlso)

= too (tu)

= besides (bɪ'saɪdz)

= similarly ('sɪmələlɪ)

= likewise ('laɪk,waɪz)

= *in addition*

= *by the same token*

furtive ('fɜtɪv) adj. 秘密的

= secret ('sikrɪt)

= sly (slaɪ)

= stealthy ('stɛlθɪ)

= sneaky ('snikɪ)

= underhanded ('ʌndɚ'hændɪd)

fuse (fjuz) ① v. 融合；結合
② n. 導火線

① = join (dʒɔɪn)

= blend (blɛnd)

= melt (mɛlt)

= unite (ju'naɪt)

= combine (kəm'baɪn)

= weld (wɛld)

= solder ('sadɚ)

= glue (glu)

= *stick together*

② = exploder (ɪk'splodɚ)

= blaster ('blæstɚ)

fuss (fʌs) v. 煩擾

= worry ('wɜɪ)

= bother ('baðɚ)

= fret (frɛt)

futile ('fjutḷ , -tɪl) adj. 徒勞的

= useless ('juslɪs)

= vain (ven)

= unsuccessful (,ʌnsək'sɛstfəl)

= ineffective (,ɪnə'fɛktɪv)

future ('fjutʃɚ) n. 將來

= coming ('kʌmɪŋ)

= hereafter (hɪr'æftɚ , -'af-)

= tomorrow (tə'moro)

fuzz (fʌz) *n.* 絨毛

  = fluff (flʌf)

  = fur (fɜ)

  = down (daʊn)

G

gadget ('gædʒɪt) *n.* 設計精巧的小機械

  = device (dɪ'vaɪs)

  = tool (tul)

  = instrument ('ɪnstrəmənt)

  = implement ('ɪmpləmənt)

  = utensil (ju'tɛnsḷ)

  = apparatus (ˌæpə'retəs , -'rætəs)

  = appliance (ə'plaɪəns)

  = contraption (kən'træpʃən)

gag (gæg) ① *v.* 強制緘默 ② *n.* 玩笑

① = silence ('saɪləns)

  = muzzle ('mʌzḷ)

  = muffle ('mʌfḷ)

  = restrain (rɪs'tren)

  = *stop one's mouth*

② = joke (dʒok)

  = jest (dʒɛst)

gain (gen) *v.* ①獲得 ②獲益 ③進步

① = get (gɛt)

  = obtain (əb'ten)

  = secure (sɪ'kjʊr)

  = acquire (ə'kwaɪr)

  = earn (ɜn)

  = receive (rɪ'siv)

② = benefit ('bɛnəfɪt)

③ = advance (əd'væns)

  = improve (ɪm'pruv)

  = *look up*

  = *pick up*

  = *make progress*

  = *come along*

gait (get) *n.* 步法;步行

  = pace (pes)

  = walk (wɔk)

  = step (stɛp)

  = stride (straɪd)

gala ('gelə , 'gɑlə) *adj.* 快樂的

  = festive ('fɛstɪv)

  = merry ('mɛrɪ)

  = gay (ge)

  = jolly ('dʒɑlɪ)

  = joyous ('dʒɔɪəs)

  = joyful ('dʒɔɪfəl)

gale (gel) *n.* ①大風 ②一陣鬧聲

① = wind (wɪnd)

  = windstorm ('wɪnd,stɔrm)

  = tempest ('tɛmpɪst)

  = squall (skwɔl)

② = shout (ʃaʊt)

  = *noisy outburst*

gall (gɔl) *n.* ①怨恨;卑鄙 ②膽汁

① = bitterness ('bɪtənɪs)

  = impudence ('ɪmpjədəns)

  = nerve (nɜv)

② = bile (baɪl)

G

gallant ('gælənt) *adj.* ①勇敢的
②壯麗的

① = brave (brev)
　 = courageous (kə'redʒəs)
　 = valiant ('væljənt)
　 = bold (bold)
　 = heroic (hɪ'ro·ɪk)
② = noble ('nobḷ)
　 = chivalrous ('ʃɪvḷrəs)
　 = splendid ('splɛndɪd)
　 = knightly ('naɪtlɪ)
　 = manly ('mænlɪ)
　 = fine (faɪn)
　 = grand (grænd)
　 = stately ('stetlɪ)

gallery ('gælərɪ , -lrɪ) *n.* ①走廊
②看臺

① = passage ('pæsɪdʒ)
　 = corridor ('kɔrədə· , -,dɔr ,
　　 'kɑr-)
　 = hallway ('hɔl,we)
　 = arcade (ɑr'ked)
② = balcony ('bælkənɪ)
　 = grandstand ('græn,stænd)

gallop ('gæləp) *v.* 飛馳

　 = run (rʌn)
　 = ride (raɪd)
　 = sprint (sprɪnt)
　 = bound (baʊnd)
　 = trot (trɑt)

gallows ('gæloz , -əz) *n.* 絞刑

　 = hanging ('hæŋɪŋ)
　 = execution (,ɛksɪ'kjuʃən)

　 = rope (rop)
　 = noose (nus)

galosh (gə'laʃ) *n.* 膠質套鞋

　 = rubber ('rʌbə·)
　 = overshoe ('ovə·,ʃu)
　 = boot (but)

gamble ('gæmbḷ) *v.* 打賭

　 = speculate ('spɛkjə,let)
　 = risk (rɪsk)
　 = bet (bɛt)
　 = wager ('wedʒə·)
　 = *try one's luck*

gambol ('gæmbḷ , -bəl) *v.* 雀躍

　 = frolic ('frɑlɪk)
　 = run (rʌn)
　 = play (ple)
　 = sport (sport , spɔrt)
　 = romp (rɑmp)
　 = caper ('kepə·)
　 = cavort (kə'vɔrt)
　 = *carry on*

game (gem) ① *adj.* 有膽量的
② *n.* 比賽　③ *n.* 策略
④ *n.* 獵物（集合稱）

① = brave (brev)
　 = plucky ('plʌkɪ)
　 = spirited ('spɪrɪtɪd)
　 = daring ('dɛrɪŋ)
② = contest ('kɑntɛst)
　 = match (mætʃ)
　 = play (ple)
　 = fun (fʌn)

G

③ = scheme〔skim〕
　= plan〔plæn〕
　= plot〔plɑt〕
④ = wildlife〔'waɪld͵laɪf〕
　= quarry〔'kwɑrɪ , 'kwɔrɪ〕
　= prey〔pre〕
　= *hunted animals*

gang〔gæŋ〕*n.* 一群

　= group〔grup〕
　= crew〔kru〕
　= ring〔rɪŋ〕
　= band〔bænd〕
　= party〔'pɑrtɪ〕
　= company〔'kʌmpənɪ〕
　= pack〔pæk〕
　= troop〔trup〕
　= bunch〔bʌntʃ〕
　= crowd〔kraʊd〕

gangway〔'gæŋ͵we〕*n.* 通道

　= passageway〔'pæsɪdʒ͵we〕
　= bridge〔brɪdʒ〕

gap〔gæp〕*n.* ①裂縫　②空白

① = break〔brek〕
　= opening〔'opənɪŋ〕
　= pass〔pæs〕
　= cleft〔klɛft〕
　= crevice〔'krɛvɪs〕
　= rift〔rɪft〕
　= gulf〔gʌlf〕
　= hole〔hol〕
② = blank〔blæŋk〕
　= *unfilled space*

gape〔gep〕① *v.* 張嘴；打呵欠
② *n.* 裂縫

① = yawn〔jɔn〕
　= *open mouth wide*
② = gap〔gæp〕
　= gulf〔gʌlf〕
　= hole〔hol〕
　= opening〔'opənɪŋ〕

garage〔gə'rɑʒ , gə'rɑdʒ〕*n.*
①車庫　②修車廠

① = carport〔'kɑr͵port〕
② = *auto repair shop*

garb〔gɑrb〕*n.* 衣服

　= clothing〔'kloðɪŋ〕
　= apparel〔ə'pærəl〕
　= dress〔drɛs〕
　= attire〔ə'taɪr〕
　= garments〔'gɑrmənts〕

garbage〔'gɑrbɪdʒ〕*n.* 垃圾

　= waste〔west〕
　= scraps〔skræps〕
　= refuse〔'rɛfjus〕
　= rubbish〔'rʌbɪʃ〕
　= trash〔træʃ〕
　= debris〔də'bri , (英)'debri〕
　= litter〔'lɪtə〕
　= junk〔dʒʌŋk〕

garden〔'gɑrdṇ〕*v.* 栽培花木

　= grow〔gro〕
　= raise〔rez〕
　= cultivate〔'kʌltə͵vet〕
　= plant〔plænt〕

G

gargle (ˈgɑrgl̩) *n.* 漱口劑

= mouthwash (ˈmauθ,waʃ , -,wɔʃ)

= antiseptic (,æntəˈsɛptɪk)

gargoyle (ˈgɑrgɔɪl) *n.* 筧嘴；
滴水嘴

= waterspout (ˈwɔtə,spaut)

garland (ˈgɑrlənd) *n.* 花圈

= wreath (riθ)

= spray (spre)

= bouquet (buˈke , boˈke)

= lei (ˈleɪ)

garment (ˈgɑrmənt) *n.* 衣著

= robe (rob)

= frock (frak)

= togs (tagz)

= *article of clothing*

garner (ˈgɑrnə) *v.* 收藏

= store (stor , stɔr)

= collect (kəˈlɛkt)

= accumulate (əˈkjumjə,let)

= amass (əˈmæs)

= stockpile (ˈstak,paɪl)

= *save up*

garnish (ˈgɑrnɪʃ) *v.* 裝飾

= decorate (ˈdɛkə,ret)

= trim (trɪm)

= adorn (əˈdɔrn)

= beautify (ˈbjutə,faɪ)

= embellish (ɪmˈbɛlɪʃ)

= *dress up*

= *spruce up*

= *fix up*

garret (ˈgærɪt) *n.* 閣樓

= attic (ˈætɪk)

= loft (lɔft , laft)

garrison (ˈgærəsn̩) *n.* ①要塞
②衛戌部隊

① = fort (fort , fɔrt)

= stronghold (ˈstrɔŋ,hold)

② = regiment (ˈrɛdʒəmənt)

= battalion (bəˈtæljən , bæˈtæl-)

= company (ˈkʌmpənɪ)

= troop (trup)

= *military unit*

gas (gæs) *n.* ①氣體 ②汽油

① = vapor (ˈvepə)

= fume (fjum)

② = gasoline (ˈgæsl̩,in)

= petroleum (pəˈtrolɪəm)

gash (gæʃ) *n.* 創傷

= cut (kʌt)

= wound (wund)

= laceration (,læsəˈreʃən)

gasoline (ˈgæsl̩,in) *n.* 汽油；
石油

= petroleum (peˈtrolɪəm)

gasp (gæsp , gɑsp) *v.* 喘氣

= pant (pænt)

= puff (pʌf)

= choke (tʃok)

G

gate 〔 get 〕 *n.* 籬笆門

  = fence 〔 fɛns 〕
  = barrier 〔 'bærɪə 〕
  = choke 〔 tʃok 〕

gateway 〔 'get,we 〕 *n.* 大門口

  = door 〔 dor , dɔr 〕
  = portal 〔 'portl , 'pɔr- 〕
  = choke 〔 tʃok 〕
  = entry 〔 'ɛntrɪ 〕
  = opening 〔 'opənɪŋ 〕

gather 〔 'gæðə 〕 *v.* ①聚集 ②摺皺

① = collect 〔 kə'lɛkt 〕
  = assemble 〔 ə'sɛmbl 〕
  = accumulate 〔 ə'kjumjə,let 〕
  = amass 〔 ə'mæs 〕
  = bunch 〔 bʌntʃ 〕
  = group 〔 grup 〕
  = cluster 〔 'klʌstə 〕
  = compile 〔 kəm'paɪl 〕
  = *bring together*
② = fold 〔 fold 〕
  = tuck 〔 tʌk 〕
  = pleat 〔 plit 〕

gaudy 〔 'gɔdɪ 〕 *adj.* 俗麗的

  = showy 〔 'ʃoɪ 〕
  = tasteless 〔 'testlɪs 〕
  = garish 〔 'gɛrɪʃ , 'gærɪʃ 〕
  = vulgar 〔 'vʌlgə 〕

gate 〔 get 〕 *v.* 評估

  = measure 〔 'mɛʒə 〕
  = estimate 〔 'ɛstə,met 〕

  = judge 〔 dʒʌdʒ 〕
  = rate 〔 ret 〕
  = appraise 〔 ə'prez 〕
  = assess 〔 ə'sɛs 〕
  = *size up*

gaunt 〔 gɔnt , gɑnt 〕 *adj.*
①憔悴的 ②荒涼的；空虛的

① = thin 〔 θɪn 〕
  = lean 〔 lin 〕
  = skinny 〔 'skɪnɪ 〕
  = scrawny 〔 'skrɔnɪ 〕
  = lanky 〔 'læŋkɪ 〕
  = bony 〔 'bonɪ 〕
② = desolate 〔 'dɛslɪt 〕
  = blank 〔 blæŋk 〕
  = bleak 〔 blik 〕
  = empty 〔 'ɛmptɪ 〕

gavel 〔 'gævl 〕 *n.* 小木槌

  = mallet 〔 'mælɪt 〕

gay 〔 ge 〕 *adj.* ①快樂的 ②五光十色的

① = happy 〔 'hæpɪ 〕
  = merry 〔 'mɛrɪ 〕
  = spirited 〔 'spɪrɪtɪd 〕
  = lively 〔 'laɪvlɪ 〕
  = animated 〔 'ænə,metɪd 〕
  = pleasant 〔 'plɛznt 〕
  = playful 〔 'plefəl 〕
  = joyful 〔 'dʒɔɪfəl 〕
  = joyous 〔 'dʒɔɪəs 〕
  = jolly 〔 'dʒɑlɪ 〕
  = jovial 〔 'dʒovɪəl 〕
  = cheerful 〔 'tʃɪrfəl 〕

G

= vivacious〔vaɪˈveʃəs, vɪ-〕

= blithe〔blaɪð〕

② = colorful〔ˈkʌləfəl〕

= bright〔braɪt〕

= vivid〔ˈvɪvɪd〕

= rich〔rɪtʃ〕

gaze〔gez〕v. 凝視

= stare〔stɛr〕

= gape〔gep〕

= gawk〔gɔk〕

gear〔gɪr〕① v. 裝備
② n. 齒輪

① = equip〔ɪˈkwɪp〕

= furnish〔ˈfɜnɪʃ〕

= outfit〔ˈaʊtˌfɪt〕

= rig〔rɪg〕

② = wheel〔hwil〕

gem〔dʒɛm〕n. ①寶石
②珍貴之物

① = jewel〔ˈdʒuəl〕

= *precious stone*

② = treasure〔ˈtrɛʒə〕

= joy〔dʒɔɪ〕

= first-rater〔ˈfɜstˈretə〕

= *good thing*

general〔ˈdʒɛnərəl〕
① adj. 普通的   ② n. 將軍

① = common〔ˈkamən〕

= widespread〔ˈwaɪdˈsprɛd〕

= indefinite〔ɪnˈdɛfənɪt〕

= vague〔veg〕

= broad〔brɔd〕

= universal〔ˌjunəˈvɜsḷ〕

= ordinary〔ˈɔrdṇˌɛrɪ〕

② = officer〔ˈɔfəsə, ˈɑf-〕

= commander〔kəˈmændə〕

generate〔ˈdʒɛnəˌret〕v. 產生

= produce〔prəˈdjus〕

= cause〔kɔz〕

= create〔krɪˈet〕

= originate〔əˈrɪdʒəˌnet〕

= *bring about*

generous〔ˈdʒɛnərəs〕adj.
①慷慨的   ②大量的

① = unselfish〔ʌnˈsɛlfɪʃ〕

= giving〔ˈgɪvɪŋ〕

= kind〔kaɪnd〕

= liberal〔ˈlɪbərəl〕

= openhanded〔ˈopənˈhændɪd〕

= bighearted〔ˈbɪgˌhɑrtɪd〕

② = large〔lɑrdʒ〕

= plentiful〔ˈplɛntɪfəl〕

= ample〔ˈæmpḷ〕

genial〔ˈdʒinjəl〕adj. 愉快的；
和藹的

= pleasant〔ˈplɛzṇt〕

= cheerful〔ˈtʃɪrfəl〕

= friendly〔ˈfrɛndlɪ〕

= kindly〔ˈkaɪndlɪ〕

= warm〔wɔrm〕

= cordial〔ˈkɔrdʒəl〕

= agreeable〔əˈgriəbḷ〕

= amiable〔ˈemɪəbḷ〕

= comforting〔ˈkʌmfətɪŋ〕

= good-natured〔ˈgʊdˈnetʃəd〕

G

genius (′dʒinjəs) *n.* ①天賦
②天才；神奇之人

① = intelligence (ɪn′tɛlədʒəns)
= inspiration (ˌɪnspə′reʃən)
= talent (′tælənt)
= gift (gɪft)
= *creative thought*
② = prodigy (′prɑdədʒɪ)
= master (′mæstɚ)
= wizard (′wɪzɚd)

genocide (′dʒɛnəˌsaɪd) *n.*
大屠殺

= slaughter (′slɔtɚ)
= massacre (′mæsəkɚ)
= killing (′kɪlɪŋ)
= butchery (′bʊtʃərɪ)
= carnage (′kɑrnɪdʒ)

gentle (′dʒɛtḷ) *adj.* ①溫和的
②友善的   ③文雅的

① = mild (maɪld)
= soft (sɔft)
= moderate (′mɑdərɪt)
= tender (′tɛndɚ)
② = kindly (′kaɪndlɪ)
= friendly (′frɛndlɪ)
= cordial (′kɔrdʒəl)
= genial (′dʒinjəl)
= amiable (′emɪəbḷ)
= humane (hju′men)
= good-natured (′gʊd′netʃɚd)
= sympathetic (ˌsɪmpə′θɛtɪk)
③ = refined (rɪ′faɪnd)
= cultured (′kʌltʃɚd)
= polished (′pɑlɪʃt)
= genteel (dʒɛn′til)

= noble (′nobḷ)
= well-bred (′wɛl′brɛd)

genuine (′dʒɛnjʊɪn) *adj.* 眞正的

= real (ril)
= true (tru)
= authentic (ɔ′θɛntɪk)
= pure (pjʊr)
= legitimate (lɪ′dʒɪtəmɪt)
= sincere (sɪn′sɪr)
= *bona fide*

germ (dʒɝm) *n.* ①根源   ②細菌

① = seed (sid)
= origin (′ɔrədʒɪn , ′ɑr-)
= beginning (bɪ′gɪnɪŋ)
② = microorganism
(ˌmaɪkro′ɔrgənˌɪzəm)

germinate (′dʒɝməˌnet) *v.*
發芽；發育

= grow (gro)
= develop (dɪ′vɛləp)
= sprout (spraʊt)
= flourish (′flɝɪʃ)
= thrive (θraɪv)

gesture (′dʒɛstʃɚ) *n.* 表情；姿勢

= signal (′sɪgnḷ)
= sign (saɪn)
= motion (′moʃən)
= movement (′muvmənt)

get (gɛt) *v.* ①獲得   ②變成
③促使   ④招致

① = obtain (əb′ten)

G

= receive (rɪ'siv)
= gain (gen)
= fetch (fɛtʃ)
= bring (brɪŋ)
= retrieve (rɪ'triv)
= acquire (ə'kwaɪr)
② = become (bɪ'kʌm)
= turn (tɜn)
= grow (gro)
③ = persuade (pɚ'swed)
= influence ('ɪnfluəns)
= induce (ɪn'djus)
④ = incur (ɪn'kɝ)
= *bring about*

geyser ('gaɪzɚ , 'gaɪsɚ) *n.*
間歇泉

= spring (sprɪŋ)
= steam (stim)
= jet (dʒɛt)
= gush (gʌʃ)
= fountain ('faʊntṇ , -tɪn)
= *volcanic water*

ghastly ('gæstlɪ , 'gɑst-) *adj.*
①可怕的 ②面色蒼白的

① = horrible ('hɑrəbḷ)
= terrible ('tɛrəbḷ)
= dreadful ('drɛdfəl)
= deplorable (dɪ'plorəbḷ ,
-'plɔr-)
= outrageous (aʊt'redʒəs)
= vile (vaɪl)
= wretched ('rɛtʃɪd)
= detestable (dɪ'tɛstəbḷ)

= contemptible (kən'tɛmptəbḷ)
= frightful ('fraɪtfəl)
= shocking ('ʃɑkɪŋ)
= appalling (ə'pɔlɪŋ)
= repulsive (rɪ'pʌlsɪv)
② = pale (pel)
= sallow ('sælo)
= deathlike ('dɛθ,laɪk)

ghost (gost) *n.* 幽靈

= spirit ('spɪrɪt)
= specter ('spɛktɚ)
= phantom ('fæntəm)
= spook (spuk , spʊk)

giant ('dʒaɪənt) *adj.* 巨大的

= huge (hjudʒ)
= immense (ɪ'mɛns)
= vast (væst)
= enormous (ɪ'nɔrməs)
= tremendous (trɪ'mɛndəs)
= colossal (kə'lɑsḷ)
= monumental (,mɑnjə'mɛntḷ)
= mammoth ('mæməθ)
= gigantic (dʒaɪ'gæntɪk)

gibe (dʒaɪb) *v.* 嘲弄

= jeer (dʒɪr)
= sneer (snɪr)
= scoff (skɔf , skɑf)
= mock (mɑk)
= taunt (tɔnt)
= boo (bu)
= hiss (hɪs)
= hoot (hut)

giddy ('gɪdɪ) *adj.* ①頭暈的
②輕浮的

① = dizzy ('dɪzɪ)
  = reeling ('rilɪŋ)
② = silly ('sɪlɪ)
  = flighty ('flaɪtɪ)
  = scatterbrained ('skætɚ,brend)

gift (gɪft) *n.* ①禮物　②天賦

① = present ('prɛznt)
  = offering ('ɔfərɪŋ , 'af-)
② = ability (ə'bɪlətɪ)
  = talent ('tælənt)
  = endowment (ɪn'daʊmənt)
  = power ('paʊɚ)
  = aptitude ('æptə , tjud , -tud)

gigantic (dʒaɪ'gæntɪk) *adj.*
巨大的

  = huge (hjudʒ)
  = immense (ɪ'mɛns)
  = vast (væst)
  = enormous (ɪ'nɔrməs)
  = tremendous (trɪ'mɛndəs)
  = colossal (kə'lɑsḷ)
  = monumental (,mɑnjə'mɛntḷ)
  = mammoth ('mæməθ)

giggle ('gɪgḷ) *v.* 格格地笑

  = laugh (læf)
  = chuckle ('tʃʌkḷ)
  = titter ('tɪtɚ)
  = snicker ('snɪkɚ)

gild (gɪld) *v.* ①鍍金　②修飾；
粉飾

① = coat (kot)
  = paint (pent)
  = cover ('kʌvɚ)
② = sweeten ('switṇ)
  = embellish (ɪm'bɛlɪʃ)

gird (gɝd) *v.* ①束；緊；纏
②圍繞　③準備從事

① = bind (baɪnd)
  = belt (bɛlt)
  = tie (taɪ)
  = wrap (ræp)
② = surround (sə'raʊnd)
  = encircle (ɪn'sɝkḷ)
③ = prepare (prɪ'pɛr)
  = ready ('rɛdɪ)
  = *get set*

girl (gɝl) *n.* 女孩

  = lass (læs)
  = female ('fimel)
  = maiden ('medṇ)
  = damsel ('dæmzḷ)
  = miss (mɪs)

girth (gɝθ) *n.* 周圍；大小

  = size (saɪz)
  = dimensions (də'mɛnʃənz)
  = measure ('mɛʒɚ)
  = proportions (prə'porʃənz ,
    -'pɔr-)
  = width (wɪdθ)
  = expanse (ɪk'spæns)

give (gɪv) *v.* ①給予　②讓步

① = present (prɪ'zɛnt)

G

= offer ('ɔfɚ , 'afɚ)

= bestow (bɪ'sto)

= donate ('donet)

= contribute (kən'trɪbjut)

= grant (grænt)

= award (ə'word)

= furnish ('fɜnɪʃ)

= provide (prə'vaɪd)

= supply (sə'plaɪ)

= allot (ə'lat)

= deliver (dɪ'lɪvɚ)

= *deal out*

= *hand over*

= *dole out*

= *mete out*

② = yield (jild)

= bend (bɛnd)

given ('gɪvən) *adj.* ①贈予的
②假設的 ③習慣…的

① = presented (prɪ'zɛntɪd)

= *handed over*

② = stated ('stetɪd)

= supposed (sə'pozd)

= assumed (ə'sumd , ə'sjumd)

③ = inclined (ɪn'klaɪnd)

= disposed (dɪ'spozd)

= addicted (ə'dɪktɪd)

= bent (bɛnt)

glacier ('gleʃɚ) *n.* 冰河

= iceberg ('aɪs,bɜg)

glad (glæd) *adj.* 高興的

= joyous ('dʒɔɪəs)

= happy ('hæpɪ)

= pleased ('plizd)

= bright (braɪt)

= gay (ge)

= delighted (dɪ'laɪtɪd)

= charmed (tʃɑrmd)

= thrilled (θrɪld)

= tickled ('tɪkl̩d)

= gratified ('grætə,faɪd)

= satisfied ('sætɪs,faɪd)

= joyful ('dʒɔɪfəl)

= cheerful ('tʃɪrfəl)

glade (gled) *n.* 森林中的空地

= clearing ('klɪrɪŋ)

= *open space*

gladiator ('glædɪ,etɚ) *n.*
格鬥者

= fighter ('faɪtɚ)

= battler ('bætl̩ɚ)

= combatant ('kɑmbətənt)

= contestant (kən'tɛstənt)

= contender (kən'tɛndɚ)

= competitor (kəm'pɛtətɚ)

glamorous ('glæmərəs ,
'glæmrəs) *adj.* 迷人的

= fascinating ('fæsn̩,etɪŋ)

= charming ('tʃɑrmɪŋ)

= entrancing (ɪn'trænsɪŋ , ɛn-)

= enchanting (ɪn'tʃæntɪŋ)

= bewitching (bɪ'wɪtʃɪŋ)

= spellbinding ('spɛl,baɪndɪŋ)

= alluring (ə'lʊrɪŋ)

= captivating ('kæptə,vetɪŋ)

= enthralling (ɪn'θrɔlɪŋ)

G

= attractive〔ə'træktɪv〕
= interesting〔'ɪnt(ə)rɪstɪŋ〕
= appealing〔ə'pilɪŋ〕
= enticing〔ɪn'taɪsɪŋ, ɛn-〕

glance〔glæns, glɑns〕v. 一瞥

= look〔lʊk〕
= glimpse〔glɪmps〕
= skim〔skɪm〕

glare〔glɛr〕v. ①怒目而視 ②發強光

① = stare〔stɛr〕
= scowl〔skaʊl〕
= glower〔'glaʊɚ〕
② = shine〔ʃaɪn〕
= glow〔glo〕
= burn〔bɝn〕
= glaze〔glez〕
= flash〔flæʃ〕
= flare〔flɛr〕
= dazzle〔'dæzl̩〕
= blind〔blaɪnd〕

glass〔glæs, glɑs〕n. ①玻璃杯 ②玻璃

① = goblet〔'gɑblɪt〕
= cup〔kʌp〕
= tumbler〔'tʌmblɚ〕
② = crystal〔'krɪstl̩〕
= pane〔pen〕

glaze〔glez〕v. 使光滑；塗以光滑劑

= gloss〔glɔs〕
= polish〔'pɑlɪʃ〕

= luster〔'lʌstɚ〕
= buff〔bʌf〕
= wax〔wæks〕
= coat〔kot〕
= cover〔'kʌvɚ〕

gleam〔glim〕v. 發光；閃爍

= shine〔ʃaɪn〕
= glow〔glo〕
= beam〔bim〕
= glare〔glɛr〕
= radiate〔'redɪ,et〕
= burn〔bɝn〕
= glimmer〔'glɪmɚ〕
= glisten〔'glɪsn̩〕
= twinkle〔'twɪŋkl̩〕
= sparkle〔'spɑrkl̩〕

glean〔glin〕v. 拾取（稻穗）；蒐集

= gather〔'gæðɚ〕
= harvest〔'hɑrvɪst〕
= reap〔rip〕
= pick〔pɪk〕
= separate〔'sɛpə,ret〕
= select〔sə'lɛkt〕

glee〔gli〕n. 歡樂

= joy〔dʒɔɪ〕
= delight〔dɪ'laɪt〕
= mirth〔mɝθ〕
= happiness〔'hæpɪnɪs〕
= gladness〔'glædnɪs〕
= cheer〔tʃɪr〕
= enchantment〔ɪn'tʃæntmənt〕
= elation〔ɪ'leʃən〕

G

= bliss (blɪs)

= merriment ('mɛrɪmənt)

glen (glɛn) *n.* 峽谷

= valley ('vælɪ)

= ravine (rə'vin)

glide (glaɪd) *v.* 滑動

= cruise (kruz)

= coast (kost)

= skim (skɪm)

= slide (slaɪd)

= sweep (swip)

= flow (flo)

= sail (sel)

= fly (flaɪ)

= *move easily*

glimmer ('glɪmɚ) *n.* ①閃爍
②暗示

① = shimmer ('ʃɪmɚ)

= blink (blɪŋk)

= flicker ('flɪkɚ)

② = hint (hɪnt)

= indication (ˌɪndə'keʃən)

= suggestion (sə(g)'dʒɛstʃən)

= inkling ('ɪŋklɪŋ)

= clue (klu)

glimpse (glɪmps) *v.* 一瞥

= glance (glæns , glɑns)

= see (si)

= notice ('notɪs)

= *catch sight of*

glint (glɪnt) *v.* 閃爍

= gleam (glim)

= flash (flæʃ)

= shine (ʃaɪn)

= sparkle ('spɑrkḷ)

= glitter ('glɪtɚ)

glisten ('glɪsṇ) *v.* 閃爍

= sparkle ('spɑrkḷ)

= glitter ('glɪtɚ)

= shine (ʃaɪn)

= glimmer ('glɪmɚ)

= twinkle ('twɪŋkḷ)

glitter ('glɪtɚ) *v.* 閃爍

= sparkle ('spɑrkḷ)

= glimmer ('glɪmɚ)

= twinkle ('twɪŋkḷ)

= shine (ʃaɪn)

= glisten ('glɪsṇ)

gloat (glot) *v.* 沾沾自喜

= exult (ɪg'zʌlt , ɛg-)

= triumph ('traɪəmf)

= glory ('glorɪ , 'glɔrɪ)

globe (glob) *n.* ①球體 ②世界
③地球儀

① = sphere (sfɪr)

= ball (bɔl)

② = earth (ɝθ)

= world (wɝld)

= universe ('junəˌvɝs)

③ = map (mæp)

gloomy ('glumɪ) *adj.* ①陰暗的；
令人沮喪的 ②悲傷的

① = dark〔dɑrk〕
= dim〔dɪm〕
= dismal〔'dɪzml̩〕
= dreary〔'drɪr〕
= somber〔'dɑmbɚ〕
= bleak〔blik〕
= depressing〔dɪ'prɛsɪŋ〕
= discouraging〔dɪs'kɝɪdʒɪŋ〕
② = sad〔sæd〕
= melancholy〔'mɛlən,kɑlɪ〕
= glum〔glʌm〕

glorify〔'glorə,faɪ , 'glɔr-〕v.
稱讚；崇拜
= worship〔'wɝʃəp〕
= praise〔prez〕
= laud〔lɔd〕
= exalt〔ɪg'zɔlt〕
= extol〔ɪk'stɑl , -'stol , ɛk-〕
= honor〔'ɑnɚ〕
= ennoble〔ɪ'nobl̩ , ɛn'no-〕

glorious〔'glorɪəs , 'glɔr-〕adj.
輝煌燦爛的
= magnificent〔mæg'nɪfəsn̩t〕
= splendid〔'splɛndɪd〕
= grand〔grænd〕
= superb〔sʊ'pɝb , sə-〕
= fine〔faɪn〕
= impressive〔ɪm'prɛsɪv〕
= proud〔praʊd〕
= stately〔'stetlɪ〕
= majestic〔mə'dʒɛstɪk〕
= elegant〔'ɛləgənt〕
= luxurious〔lʌg'ʒʊrɪəs , lʌk'ʃʊr-〕
= extravagant〔ɪk'strævəgənt〕

gloss〔glɔs〕v. 使有光澤
= shine〔ʃaɪn〕
= luster〔'lʌstɚ〕
= sheen〔ʃin〕
= glow〔glo〕
= gleam〔glim〕

glossary〔'glɑsərɪ , 'glɔs-〕n.
字典
= dictionary〔'dɪkʃən,ɛrɪ〕
= wordbook〔'wɝd,bʊk〕
= thesaurus〔θɪ'sɔrəs〕

glow〔glo〕v. ①發光 ②變紅
③顫抖

G

① = burn〔bɝn〕
= blaze〔blez〕
= flame〔flem〕
= flare〔flɛr〕
= flicker〔'flɪkɚ〕
= shine〔ʃaɪn〕
= radiate〔'redɪ,et〕
= glare〔glɛr〕
= dazzle〔'dæzl̩〕
② = redden〔'rɛdn̩〕
= blush〔blʌʃ〕
= flush〔flʌʃ〕
③ = tingle〔'tɪŋgl̩〕
= tremble〔'trɛmbl̩〕
= shiver〔'ʃɪvɚ〕
= quiver〔'kwɪvɚ〕
= quake〔kwek〕
= thrill〔θrɪl〕

glower〔'glaʊɚ〕v. 皺眉怒視
= stare〔stɛr〕

= scowl〔skaʊl〕

= glare〔glɛr〕

= frown〔fraʊn〕

glue〔glu〕*v.* 黏

= fasten〔'fæsn̩ , 'fɑsn̩〕

= bind〔baɪnd〕

= paste〔pest〕

= cement〔sə'mɛnt〕

= *stick together*

glum〔glʌm〕*adj.* 快快不樂的

= sad〔sæd〕

= gloomy〔'glumɪ〕

= dismal〔'dɪzml̩〕

= sullen〔'sʌlɪn , -ən〕

= moody〔'mudɪ〕

glutton〔'glʌtn̩〕*n.* 貪食者

= *greedy eater*

gnarled〔'nɑrld〕*adj.* 粗糙的；多節的

= knotted〔'nɑtɪd〕

= twisted〔'twɪstɪd〕

= rugged〔'rʌgɪd〕

gnash〔næʃ〕*v.* 咬

= crunch〔'krʌntʃ〕

= gnaw〔nɔ〕

= grind〔graɪnd〕

gnaw〔nɔ〕*v.* 咬

= grind〔graɪnd〕

= gnash〔næʃ〕

= chew〔tʃu〕

go〔go〕*v.* ①去 ②活動 ③變成 ④運行 ⑤通；達 ⑥歸於

① = move〔muv〕

= leave〔liv〕

= travel〔'trævl̩〕

= pass〔pæs〕

= proceed〔prə'sid〕

= advance〔əd'væns〕

② = act〔ækt〕

= work〔wɝk〕

③ = become〔bɪ'kʌm〕

= turn〔tɝn〕

= *get to be*

= *grow into*

④ = operate〔'ɑpə,ret〕

= function〔'fʌŋkʃən〕

⑤ = aim〔em〕

= lead〔lid〕

= reach〔ritʃ〕

= point〔pɔɪnt〕

= *head for*

⑥ = belong〔bə'lɔŋ〕

= *have place*

goad〔god〕*v.* 驅使

= urge〔ɝdʒ〕

= drive〔draɪv〕

= incite〔ɪn'saɪt〕

= push〔pʊʃ〕

= shove〔ʃʌv〕

= poke〔pok〕

= prick〔prɪk〕

= spur〔spɝ〕

goal〔gol〕*n.* ①目標 ②得分

① = end〔ɛnd〕

= finish ('fɪnɪʃ)
= destination (,dɛstə'neʃən)
= objective (əb'dʒɛktɪv)
= aim (em)
= object ('abdʒɪkt)
= target ('tɑrgɪt)
② = score (skor , skɔr)
= point (pɔɪnt)

gobble ('gabḷ) ① v. 狼吞虎嚥
② n. 火雞的叫聲

① = devour (dɪ'vaʊr)
= gulp (gʌlp)
= gorge (gɔrdʒ)
= stuff (stʌf)
= *eat fast*
② = *turkey talk*

goblet ('gablɪt) n. 高腳玻璃杯

= glass (glæs)
= cup (kʌp)

goblin ('gablɪn) n. 小妖精

= spirit ('spɪrɪt)
= elf (ɛlf)
= troll (trol)
= dwarf (dwɔrf)

God (gɑd) n. 上帝

= Lord (lɔrd)
= *the Maker*
= *the Creator*
= *the Supreme Being*
= *the Almighty*

godly ('gɑdlɪ) adj. 神聖的；
虔誠的

= religious (rɪ'lɪdʒəs)
= pious ('paɪəs)
= obeying (ə'beɪŋ , o'beɪŋ)
= loving ('lʌvɪŋ)
= holy ('holɪ)
= righteous ('raɪtʃəs)
= spiritual ('spɪrɪtʃʊəl)
= pure (pjʊr)
= saintly ('sentlɪ)
= divine (də'vaɪn)

golden ('goldn) adj. ①金製的
②金色的 ③極好的；寶貴的

① = metallic (mə'tælɪk)
② = shining ('ʃaɪnɪŋ)
= bright ('braɪt)
③ = superior (sə'pɪrɪɚ , su-)
= excellent ('ɛksḷənt)
= fine (faɪn)
= nice (naɪs)
= splendid ('splɛndɪd)
= valuable ('væljʊəbḷ)
= *very good*

gong (gɔŋ) n. 電鈴

= bell (bɛl)
= chimes (tʃaɪmz)

good (gʊd) ① adj. 美好的
② adj. 循規蹈矩的 ③ adj. 適當的
④ adj. 善良的 ⑤ adj. 真實的
⑥ n. 利益

① = excellent ('ɛksḷənt)
= fine (faɪn)
= nice (naɪs)
= splendid ('splɛndɪd)

G

② = proper ('prɑpɚ)
  = well-behaved ('wɛlbɪ'hevd)
③ = desirable (dɪ'zaɪrəbḷ)
  = right (raɪt)
  = appropriate (ə'proprɪɪt)
  = fitting ('fɪtɪŋ)
  = suitable ('sutəbḷ , 'sju-)
  = becoming (bɪ'kʌmɪŋ)
  = satisfying ('sætɪs,faɪɪŋ)
  = seemly ('simlɪ)
  = nice (naɪs)
  = decent ('disṇt)
④ = kind (kaɪnd)
  = friendly ('frɛndlɪ)
  = gracious ('greʃəs)
  = nice (naɪs)
  = warmhearted ('wɔrm'hɑrtɪd)
  = sympathetic (,sɪmpə'θɛtɪk)
  = brotherly ('brʌðəlɪ)
  = fraternal (frə't3nḷ)
⑤ = real (ril)
  = genuine ('dʒɛnjuɪn)
  = authentic (ɔ'θɛntɪk)
  = legitimate (lɪ'dʒɪtəmɪt)
  = *bona fide*
⑥ = benefit ('bɛnəfɪt)
  = profit ('prɑfɪt)
  = advantage (əd'væntɪdʒ)

good-by (gʊd'baɪ) *n.* 再見
  = farewell (,fɛr'wɛl)
  = adieu (ə'dju , ə'du)
  = *so long*

goods (gʊdz) *n. pl.* ①所有物
②貨物

① = belongings (bə'lɔŋɪŋz)
  = property ('prɑpətɪ)
  = holdings ('holdɪŋz)
  = possessions (pə'zɛʃənz)
② = wares (wɛrz)
  = merchandise ('m3tʃən,daɪz)

good will ('gʊd'wɪl) *n.* 善意;
親切
  = willingness ('wɪlɪŋnɪs)
  = agreeability (ə,grɪə'bɪlətɪ)
  = readiness ('rɛdɪnɪs)
  = harmony ('hɑrmənɪ)
  = *friendly relations*

gorge (gɔrdʒ) ① *v.* 狼吞虎嚥
② *n.* 峽谷
① = stuff (stʌf)
  = devour (dɪ'vaʊr)
  = gulp (gʌlp)
  = gobble ('gɑbḷ)
② = valley ('vælɪ)
  = ravine (rə'vin)
  = gully ('gʌlɪ)

gorgeous ('gɔrdʒəs) *adj.*
華麗燦爛的
  = splendid ('splɛndɪd)
  = beautiful ('bjutəfəl)
  = ravishing ('rævɪʃɪŋ)
  = stunning ('stʌnɪŋ)
  = glorious ('glorɪəs , 'glɔr-)
  = diving (də'vaɪn)
  = brilliant ('brɪljənt)
  = dazzling ('dæzlɪŋ , 'dæzḷɪŋ)

gory ('gorɪ , 'gɔrɪ) *adj.* 血腥的

= bloody ('dlʌdɪ)

gossamer ('gasəmə) *adj.*
①纖細的　②極輕而薄的

① = fine (faɪn)
= delicate ('dɛləkət , -kɪt)
= dainty ('dentɪ)
② = filmy ('fɪlmɪ)
= sheer (ʃɪr)
= transparent (træns'pɛrənt)

gossip ('gasəp) *v.* 說閒話

= chat (tʃæt)
= talk (tɔk)
= tattle ('tætḷ)
= prattle ('prætḷ)

gouge (gaʊdʒ) *v.* 挖鑿

= dig (dɪg)
= scoop (skup)
= excavate ('ɛkskə,vet)
= burrow ('bɝo)
= chisel ('tʃɪzḷ)
= carve (karv)

govern ('gʌvən) *v.* 治理；支配

= rule (rul)
= control (kən'trol)
= manage ('mænɪdʒ)
= regulate ('rɛgjə,let)
= influence ('ɪnfluəns)
= determine (dɪ'tɝmɪn)
= head (hɛd)
= lead (lid)
= command (kə'mænd)

= direct (də'rɛkt , daɪ-)
= supervise ('supə,vaɪz)
= minister ('mɪnɪstə)
= guide (gaɪd)
= conduct (kən'dʌkt)
= handle ('hændḷ)
= run (rʌn)
= boss (bɔs)
= *preside over*

gown (gaʊn) *n.* 長服

= dress (drɛs)
= robe (rob)
= garment ('garmənt)
= frock (frak)

grab (græb) *v.* 抓握

= snatch (snætʃ)
= seize (siz)
= grasp (græsp)
= grip (grɪp)
= clutch (klʌtʃ)

grace (gres) ① *v.* 使有光榮
② *n.* 優美　③ *n.* 文雅
④ *n.* 仁慈；寬赦　⑤ *n.* 善意
⑥ *n.* 感恩禱告

① = honor ('anə)
= dignify ('dɪgnə,faɪ)
= distinguish (dɪ'stɪŋgwɪʃ)
② = beauty ('bjutɪ)
= loveliness ('lʌvlɪnɪs)
= attractiveness (ə'træktɪvnɪs)
③ = charm (tʃarm)
= elegance ('ɛləgəns)
= taste (test)

G

= refinement (rɪ'faɪnmənt)

= polish ('palɪʃ)

= culture ('kʌltʃə)

④ = sympathy ('sɪmpəθɪ)

= clemency ('klɛmənsɪ)

= mercy ('mɝsɪ)

= pardon ('pardn̩)

= excuse (ɪk'skjus)

= reprieve (rɪ'priv)

⑤ = favor ('fevə)

⑥ = thanks (θæŋks)

= prayer (prɛr)

= thanksgiving (ˌθæŋks'gɪvɪŋ)

= blessing ('blɛsɪŋ)

gracious ('greʃəs) *adj.* 親切的；仁慈的

= pleasant ('plɛznt)

= kindly ('kaɪndlɪ)

= good (gʊd)

= nice (naɪs)

= merciful ('mɝsɪfəl)

= obliging (ə'blaɪdʒɪŋ)

= clement ('klɛmənt)

= sympathetic (ˌsɪmpə'θɛtɪk)

= polite (pə'laɪt)

= respectful (rɪ'spɛktfəl)

= cordial ('kɔrdʒəl)

= friendly ('frɛndlɪ)

= hospitable ('haspɪtəbl̩)

= generous ('dʒɛnərəs)

= warmhearted ('wɔrm'hartɪd)

grade (gred) ① *v.* 分級 ② *n.* 傾斜（面）；坡度

① = arrange (ə'rendʒ)

= sort (sort)

= classify ('klæsəˌfaɪ)

= group (grup)

= rank (ræŋk)

= rate (ret)

= mark (mark)

= place (ples)

② = slope (slop)

= incline (ɪn'klaɪn , 'ɪn-)

= hill (hɪl)

graft (græft , graft) ① *v.* 移植 ② *n.* 貪污

① = transplant (træns'plænt)

= join (dʒɔɪn)

② = bribery ('braɪbərɪ)

= corruption (kə'rʌpʃən)

grain (gren) *n.* ①顆粒；少許 ②穀物 ③紋 ④天性

① = particle ('partɪkl̩)

= speck (spɛk)

= bit (bɪt)

② = plant (plænt)

= seed (sid)

③ = texture ('tɛkstʃə)

= finish ('fɪnɪʃ)

= markings ('markɪŋz)

= fiber ('faɪbə)

④ = character ('kærɪktə , -ək-)

= temper ('tɛmpə)

= nature ('netʃə)

= disposition (ˌdɪspə'zɪʃən)

= tendency ('tɛndənsɪ)

grand (grænd) *adj.* ①雄偉的 ②顯要的；莊嚴堂皇的

G

① = large〔lɑrdʒ〕
  = great〔gret〕
  = considerable〔kən'sɪdərəbḷ〕
  = sizable〔'saɪzəbḷ〕
② = important〔ɪm'pɔrtṇt〕
  = main〔men〕
  = outstanding〔'aʊt'stændɪŋ〕
  = prominent〔'prɑmənənt〕
  = distinguished〔dɪ'stɪŋgwɪʃt〕
  = magnificent〔mæg'nɪfəsṇt〕
  = glorious〔'gloriəs , 'glɔr-〕
  = impressive〔ɪm'prɛsɪv〕
  = majestic〔mə'dʒɛstɪk〕
  = dignified〔'dɪgnə,faɪd〕
  = stately〔'stetlɪ〕

grandstand〔'græn,stænd ,
'grænd-〕*n.* 正面觀衆席

  = gallery〔'gælərɪ , -lrɪ〕
  = bleachers〔'blitʃəz〕

granite〔'grænɪt〕*n.* 花崗岩

  = rock〔rɑk〕
  = stone〔ston〕

grant〔grænt〕*v.* ①給予
②允許

① = give〔gɪv〕
  = donate〔'donet〕
  = present〔prɪ'zɛnt〕
  = bestow〔bɪ'sto〕
  = award〔ə'wɔrd〕
  = allot〔ə'lɑt〕
② = allow〔ə'laʊ〕
  = permit〔pə'mɪt〕
  = let〔lɛt〕

  = consent〔kən'sɛnt〕
  = admit〔əd'mɪt〕
  = *give out*
  = *deal out*
  = *mete out*
  = *dole out*

graph〔græf , grɑf〕*v.*
畫（曲線圖）

  = diagram〔'daɪə,græm〕
  = chart〔tʃɑrt〕
  = plot〔plɑt〕
  = outline〔'aʊt,laɪn〕
  = *draw up*

graphic〔'græfɪk〕*adj.* 生動的

  = lifelike〔'laɪf,laɪk〕
  = vivid〔'vɪvɪd〕
  = meaningful〔'minɪŋfḷ〕
  = significant〔sɪg'nɪfəkənt〕
  = representative〔,rɛprɪ'zɛntətɪv〕
  = descriptive〔dɪ'skrɪptɪv〕
  = pictorial〔pɪk'torɪəl , -'tɔr-〕

grapple〔'græpḷ〕*v.* ①抓住
②格鬥

① = seize〔siz〕
  = grip〔grɪp〕
  = grab〔græb〕
  = grasp〔græsp〕
  = clutch〔klʌtʃ〕
  = clasp〔klæsp〕
  = hold〔hold〕
② = struggle〔'strʌgḷ〕
  = fight〔faɪt〕

G

grasp ﹝ græsp ﹞① v. 抓住
② n. 控制 ③ n. 領會

① = seize ﹝ siz ﹞
= hold ﹝ hold ﹞
= grapple ﹝ 'græpl̩ ﹞
= clutch ﹝ klʌtʃ ﹞
= clasp ﹝ klæsp ﹞
= grip ﹝ grɪp ﹞

② = control ﹝ kən'trol ﹞
= possession ﹝ pə'zɛʃən ﹞
= hold ﹝ hold ﹞
= command ﹝ kən'mænd ﹞
= domination ﹝ dɑmə'neʃən ﹞

③ = understanding ﹝ ˌʌndɚ'stændɪŋ ﹞
= comprehension
﹝ˌkɑmprɪ'hɛnʃən ﹞

grate ﹝ gret ﹞① v. 磨碎
② v. 發磨擦聲 ③ v. 使難受
④ n. 鐵柵欄

① = grind ﹝ graɪnd ﹞
= file ﹝ faɪl ﹞
= scrape ﹝ skrep ﹞
= pulverize ﹝ 'pʌlvəˌraɪz ﹞

② = scrape ﹝ skrep ﹞
= scratch ﹝ skrætʃ ﹞
= rasp ﹝ ræsp ﹞

③ = annoy ﹝ ə'nɔɪ ﹞
= irritate ﹝ 'ɪrəˌtet ﹞
= *rub sb. the wrong way*
= *get on one's nerves*

④ = grillwork ﹝ 'grɪlˌwɝk ﹞
= *iron bars*

grateful ﹝ 'gretfəl ﹞ *adj.* 感謝的
= thankful ﹝ 'θæŋkfəl ﹞

= appreciative ﹝ ə'priʃɪˌetɪv ﹞
= obliged ﹝ ə'blaɪdʒd ﹞

gratify ﹝ 'grætəˌfaɪ ﹞ *v.* 使高興
= satisfy ﹝ 'sætɪsˌfaɪ ﹞
= please ﹝ pliz ﹞

gratitude ﹝ 'grætəˌtjud ﹞ *n.* 感謝
= thankfulness ﹝ 'θæŋkfəlnɪs ﹞
= gratefulness ﹝ 'gretfəlnɪs ﹞
= appreciation ﹝ əˌpriʃɪ'eʃən ﹞

grave ﹝ grev ﹞① *adj.* 嚴肅的；
沈思的 ② *adj.* 莊嚴的
③ *adj.* 重大的 ④ *n.* 墓地

① = serious ﹝ 'sɪrɪəs ﹞
= solemn ﹝ 'sɑləm ﹞
= grim ﹝ grɪm ﹞
= earnest ﹝ 'ɝnɪst , -əst ﹞
= thoughtful ﹝ 'θɔtfəl ﹞
= sober ﹝ 'sobɚ ﹞
= somber ﹝ 'sɑmbɚ ﹞

② = dignified ﹝ 'dɪgnəˌfaɪd ﹞
= stately ﹝ 'stetlɪ ﹞
= imposing ﹝ ɪm'pozɪŋ ﹞
= majestic ﹝ mə'dʒɛstɪk ﹞
= slow-moving ﹝ 'slo'muvɪŋ ﹞

③ = important ﹝ ɪm'pɔrtn̩t ﹞
= vital ﹝ 'vaɪtl̩ ﹞
= essential ﹝ ə'sɛnʃəl ﹞

④ = *burial place*

gravel ﹝ 'grævl̩ ﹞ *n.* 碎石
= pebbles ﹝ 'pɛbl̩z ﹞
= stones ﹝ stonz ﹞
= grain ﹝ gren ﹞

G

gravitate（'grævə,tet）v. 移向；被吸引（到⋯）

= incline（ɪn'klaɪn）
= lean（lin）
= tend（tɛnd）
= *move toward*

graze（grez）v. ①吃草 ②磨擦；輕觸

① = feed（fid）
② = scrape（skrep）
= rub（rʌb）
= contact（'kɑntækt , kɑn'tækt）
= brush（brʌʃ）
= skim（skɪm）
= *touch lightly*

grease（gris）n. 油；脂肪

= oil（ɔɪl）
= lubrication（,lubrɪ'keʃən）
= fat（fæt）

great（gret）adj. ①巨大的 ②偉大的

① = large（lɑrdʒ）
= grand（grænd）
= sizable（'saɪzəbl̩）
= considerable（kən'sɪdərəbl̩）
② = outstanding（'aʊt'stændɪŋ）
= prominent（'prɑmənənt）
= famous（'feməs）
= main（men）
= distinguished（dɪ'stɪŋgwɪʃt）
= remarkable（rɪ'mɑrkəbl̩）
= honorable（'ɑnərəbl̩）
= glorious（'glorɪəs , 'glɔr-）

= magnificent（mæg'nɪfəsn̩t）
= impressive（ɪm'prɛsɪv）
= majestic（mə'dʒɛstɪk）
= stately（'stetlɪ）

greed（grid）n. 貪慾

= avarice（'ævərɪs）
= piggishness（'pɪgɪʃnɪs）
= hoggishness（'hɑgɪʃnɪs）
= lust（lʌst）
= desire（dɪ'zaɪr）

green（grin）adj. ①未成熟的 ②無經驗的

① = undeveloped（,ʌndɪ'vɛləpt）
= unripe（ʌn'raɪp）
= immature（,ɪmə'tjʊr）
② = untrained（ʌn'trend）
= new（nju）
= inexperienced（,ɪnɪk'spɪrɪənst）
= ignorant（'ɪgnərənt）

greenhouse（'grin,haʊs）n. 溫室

= hothouse（'hɑt,haʊs）
= *plant nursery*

greet（grit）v. ①問候 ②映入眼簾

① = address（ə'drɛs）
= hail（hel）
= *talk to*
② = meet（mit）
= approach（ə'protʃ）

grieve（griv）v. 悲傷

= hurt（hɝt）

G

= mourn (morn , mɔrn)

= lament (lə'mɛnt)

= sorrow ('saro)

= *brood over*

grievance ('grivəns) *n.* 委屈

= wrong (rɔŋ)

= evil ('ivḷ)

= protest ('protɛst)

= objection (əb'dʒɛkʃən)

= injury ('ɪndʒərɪ)

= injustice (ɪn'dʒʌstɪs)

= complaint (kəm'plent)

grievous ('grivəs) *adj.*
①極惡的;重大的 ②悲慘的

① = severe (sə'vɪr)

= outrageous (aut'redʒəs)

= terrible ('tɛrəbḷ)

= deplorable (dɪ'plorəbḷ ,
-'plɔr-)

= awful ('ɔful , 'ɔfəl)

= wretched ('rɛtʃɪd)

= contemptible (kən'tɛmptəbḷ)

② = sorrowful ('sarofəl)

grill (grɪl) ① *v.* 烤 ② *v.* 烤問
③ *n.* 鐵柵欄

① = broil (brɔɪl)

= cook (kuk)

= barbecue ('barbɪ,kju)

② = question ('kwɛstʃən)

= cross-examine ('krɔsɪg'zæmɪn)

= interrogate (ɪn'tɛrə,get)

③ = gridiron ('grɪd,aɪən)

= grating ('gretɪŋ)

grim (grɪm) *adj.* ①嚴酷的
②可怕的

① = stern (stɜn)

= strict (strɪkt)

= harsh (harʃ)

= fierce (fɪrs)

= merciless ('mɜsɪlɪs)

= rough (rʌf)

= unyielding (ʌn'jildɪŋ)

= rigid ('rɪdʒɪd)

= inflexible (ɪn'flɛksəbḷ)

= adamant ('ædə,mænt , -mənt)

② = horrible ('hɑrəbḷ)

= frightful ('fraɪtfəl)

= ghastly ('gæstlɪ , 'gɑst-)

= dreadful ('drɛdfəl)

= terrible ('tɛrəbḷ)

grimace (grɪ'mes) *n.* 鬼臉

= *wry face*

grime (graɪm) *n.* 污穢

= dirt (dɜt)

= soot (sut , sut)

= smut (smʌt)

= mud (mʌd)

= slime (slaɪm)

= filth (fɪlθ)

grin (grɪn) *v.* 露齒而笑

= smile (smaɪl)

= smirk (smɜk)

= beam (bim)

grind (graɪnd) *v.* ①磨碎
②磨尖;磨光 ③刻苦用功

① = crush〔krʌʃ〕
  = pulverize〔'pʌlvə,raɪz〕
  = grate〔gret〕
  = crumble〔'krʌmbḷ〕
  = mash〔mæʃ〕
  = squash〔skwaʃ〕
② = sharpen〔'ʃarpən〕
  = smooth〔smuð〕
  = rub〔rʌb〕
  = edge〔ɛdʒ〕
  = whet〔hwɛt〕
  = file〔faɪl〕
③ = study〔'stʌdɪ〕
  = work〔wɜk〕
  = drudge〔drʌdʒ〕
  = plod〔plad〕

grip〔grɪp〕① v. 抓住
② n. 手提箱 ③ n. 控制
④ n. 領會

① = seize〔siz〕
  = hold〔hold〕
  = grasp〔græsp〕
  = clutch〔klʌtʃ〕
  = clasp〔klæsp〕
  = clench〔klɛntʃ〕
② = suitcase〔'sut,kes, 'sjut-〕
  = handbag〔'hænd,bæg, 'hæn-〕
  = valise〔və'lis〕
③ = control〔kən'trol〕
  = command〔kə'mænd〕
  = domination〔damə'neʃən〕
  = possession〔pə'zɛʃən〕
④ = understanding〔,ʌndə'stændɪŋ〕
  = comprehension
    〔,kamprɪ'hɛnʃən〕

grit〔grɪt〕① v. 磨擦 ② n. 砂礫
③ n. 勇氣

① = grind〔graɪnd〕
  = rub〔rʌb〕
  = grate〔gret〕
② = gravel〔'grævḷ〕
  = sand〔sænd〕
  = grain〔gren〕
③ = courage〔'kɜɪdʒ〕
  = pluck〔plʌk〕
  = stamina〔'stæmənə〕

groan〔gron〕n. 呻吟；歎息

  = moan〔mon〕
  = wail〔wel〕
  = howl〔haʊl〕
  = *harsh sound*

groom〔grum〕① v. 整飾
② n. 新郎

① = tidy〔'taɪdɪ〕
  = tend〔tɛnd〕
  = preen〔prin〕
  = *clean up*
② = newlywed〔'njulɪ,wɛd, 'nu-〕

groove〔gruv〕n. ①溝槽
②老套

① = channel〔'tʃænḷ〕
  = furrow〔'fɜo〕
  = track〔træk〕
② = routine〔ru'tin〕

grope〔grop〕v. 摸索

  = fumble〔'fʌmbḷ〕

G

= *feel around*
= *poke around*

gross〔 gros 〕*adj.* ①全部的
②嚴重的；遲鈍的 ③不雅的
④肥大的 ⑤濃密的

① = whole〔 hol 〕
= entire〔 ɪn'taɪr 〕
= total〔 'totl̩ 〕
② = bad〔 bæd 〕
= terrible〔 'tɛrəbl̩ 〕
= stupid〔 'stjupɪd 〕
③ = coarse〔 kors , kɔrs 〕
= vulgar〔 'vʌlgɚ 〕
= unrefined〔 ˌʌnrɪ'faɪnd 〕
= crude〔 krud 〕
④ = big〔 bɪg 〕
= fat〔 fæt 〕
= obese〔 o'bis 〕
= bulky〔 'bʌlkɪ 〕
= massive〔 'mæsɪv 〕
= clumsy〔 'klʌmzɪ 〕
⑤ = thick〔 θɪk 〕
= heavy〔 'hɛvɪ 〕
= dense〔 dɛns 〕

grotesque〔 gro'tɛsk 〕*adj.*
①古怪可笑的 ②醜怪的

① = fantastic〔 fæn'tæstɪk 〕
= incredible〔 ɪn'krɛdəbl̩ 〕
= bizarre〔 bɪ'zɑr 〕
= monstrous〔 'mɑnstrəs 〕
= ridiculous〔 rɪ'dɪkjələs 〕
= absurd〔 əb'sɝd 〕
② = deformed〔 dɪ'fɔrmd 〕
= unnatural〔 ʌn'nætʃərəl 〕

= queer〔 kwɪr 〕
= odd〔 od 〕
= disfigured〔 dɪs'fɪgɚd 〕
= ill-shaped〔 'ɪl'ʃept 〕
= ugly〔 'ʌglɪ 〕

grotto〔 'grato 〕*n.* 巖穴；小洞穴

= cave〔 kev 〕
= cavern〔 'kævən 〕
= tunnel〔 'tʌnl̩ 〕
= hole〔 hol 〕

grouch〔 grautʃ 〕*v.* 心懷不滿

= complain〔 kəm'plen 〕
= grumble〔 'grʌmbl̩ 〕
= mutter〔 'mʌtɚ 〕
= mope〔 mop 〕
= sulk〔 sʌlk 〕
= fret〔 frɛt 〕

ground〔 graund 〕① *v.* 建基礎
於～ ② *n.* 土地

① = fix〔 fɪks 〕
= establish〔 ə'stæblɪʃ 〕
= root〔 rut 〕
= set〔 sɛt 〕
② = surface〔 'sɝfɪs 〕
= soil〔 sɔɪl 〕
= sod〔 sad 〕
= dirt〔 dɝt 〕
= land〔 lænd 〕
= base〔 bes 〕
= floor〔 flor , flɔr 〕

grounds〔 graundz 〕*n.* ①院子
②渣滓 ③根據；理由

① = lawns〔lɔnz〕
= garden〔'gɑrdn̩〕
= *real estate*

② = dregs〔drɛgz〕
= leftovers〔'lɛft,ovəz〕
= sediment〔'sɛdəmənt〕

③ = foundation〔faʊn'deʃən〕
= basis〔'besɪs〕
= reason〔'rizn̩〕
= cause〔kɔz〕
= premise〔'prɛmɪs〕
= motive〔'motɪv〕

group〔grup〕*v.* 成群；分類

= arrange〔ə'rendʒ〕
= assemble〔ə'sɛmbl̩〕
= cluster〔'klʌstə〕
= organize〔'ɔrgən,aɪz〕
= grade〔gred〕
= sort〔sɔrt〕
= classify〔'klæsə,faɪ〕
= gather〔'gæðə〕
= collect〔kə'lɛkt〕
= bunch〔bʌntʃ〕

grovel〔'grɑvl̩, 'grʌvl̩〕*v.* 匍匐

= crawl〔krɔl〕
= creep〔krip〕
= cower〔'kaʊə〕

grow〔gro〕*v.* ①發展；變成
②栽種

① = increase〔ɪn'kris〕
= mature〔mə'tjʊr, -tʃʊr〕
= become〔bɪ'kʌm〕
= advance〔əd'væns〕

= gain〔gen〕
= rise〔raɪz〕
= develop〔dɪ'vɛləp〕
= age〔edʒ〕
= progress〔prə'grɛs〕

② = raise〔rez〕
= farm〔fɑrm〕
= cultivate〔'kʌltə,vet〕

growl〔graʊl〕*v.* 鳴不平；咆哮

= snarl〔snɑrl〕
= complain〔kəm'plen〕
= grumble〔'grʌmbl̩〕

grub〔grʌb〕① *v.* 挖掘
② *v.* 作苦工　③ *n.* 蛆　④ *n.* 食物

① = dig〔dɪg〕
= gouge〔gaʊdʒ〕
= excavate〔'ɛkskə,vet〕
= tunnel〔'tʌnl̩〕
= burrow〔'bʒo〕
= *scoop out*

② = toil〔tɔɪl〕
= drudge〔drʌdʒ〕
= plod〔plɑd〕

③ = larva〔'lɑrvə〕

④ = food〔fud〕

grudge〔grʌdʒ〕*n.* 惡意

= dislike〔dɪs'laɪk〕
= *ill will*

grudgingly〔'grʌdʒɪŋlɪ〕*adv.*
勉強地

= unwillingly〔ʌn'wɪlɪŋlɪ〕
= reluctantly〔rɪ'lʌktəntlɪ〕

G

= involuntarily (ɪn'vɑlən,tɛrɪlɪ)
= *under protest*
= *against one's will*

gruff (grʌf) *adj.* ①聲音沙啞的
②行為粗暴的；粗魯的

① = deep (dip)
= husky ('hʌskɪ)
= coarse (kors , kɔrs)
= harsh (hɑrʃ)
② = rough (rʌf)
= rude (rud)
= unfriendly (ʌn'frɛndlɪ)
= brusque (brʌsk , brʊsk)
= curt (kɝt)
= blunt (blʌnt)

grumble ('grʌmbḷ) *v.* 抱怨；
訴苦

= complain (kəm'plen)
= mutter ('mʌtɚ)

grunt (grʌnt) *v.* (豬等) 發低沈
之咕嚕聲

= snort (snɔrt)

guarantee (,gærən'ti) *v.* 保證

= promise ('prɑmɪs)
= secure (sɪ'kjʊr)
= pledge (plɛdʒ)
= swear (swɛr)
= warrant ('wɔrənt , 'wɑrənt)
= assure (ə'ʃʊr)
= certify ('sɝtə,faɪ)
= sponsor ('spɑnsɚ)
= back (bæk)

= endorse (ɪn'dɔrs , ɛn-)
= underwrite (,ʌndɚ'raɪt)
= *stand for*

guard (gɑrd) *v.* ①保護
②當心

① = watch (wɑtʃ)
= defend (dɪ'fɛnd)
= shield (ʃild)
= protect (prə'tɛkt)
= secure (sɪ'kjʊr)
② = check (tʃɛk)
= restrain (rɪ'stren)
= control (kən'trol)
= curb (kɝb)

guess (gɛs) *v.* 臆測；相信

= think (θɪŋk)
= believe (bɪ'liv)
= suppose (sə'poz)
= assume (ə'sjum)
= imagine (ɪ'mædʒɪn)
= consider (kən'sɪdɚ)
= conjecture (kən'dʒɛktʃɚ)

guest (gɛst) *n.* 來賓

= visitor ('vɪzɪtɚ)
= caller ('kɔlɚ)
= company ('kʌmpənɪ)

guide (gaɪd) *v.* ①引導 ②管理

① = lead (lid)
= direct (də'rɛkt , daɪ-)
= show (ʃo)
= steer (stɪr)
= escort (ɪ'skɔrt)

= conduct〔kən'dʌkt〕

= squire〔skwaɪr〕

= usher〔'ʌʃɚ〕

= manage〔'mænɪdʒ〕

= control〔kən'trol〕

= regulate〔'rɛgjə,let〕

= advise〔əd'vaɪz〕

= instruct〔ɪn'strʌkt〕

= govern〔'gʌvɚn〕

= rule〔rul〕

uild〔gɪld〕*n.* 協會

= society〔sə'saɪətɪ〕

= union〔'junjən〕

uile〔gaɪl〕*n.* 狡詐

= deceit〔dɪ'sit〕

= cunning〔'kʌnɪŋ〕

= craftiness〔'kræftɪnɪs〕

= sneakiness〔'snikɪnɪs〕

uilty〔'gɪltɪ〕*adj.* 有罪的

= criminal〔'krɪmənḷ〕

= blameworthy〔'blem,wɝðɪ〕

= culpable〔'kʌlpəbḷ〕

= *to blame*

= *at fault*

uise〔gaɪz〕*n.* ①服裝 ②外表

= garb〔gɑrb〕

= dress〔drɛs〕

= cover〔'kʌvɚ〕

= coat〔kot〕

= attire〔ə'taɪr〕

= clothes〔kloz , kloðz〕

= apparel〔ə'pærəl〕

② = appearance〔ə'pɪrəns〕

= look〔lʊk〕

= show〔ʃo〕

= form〔fɔrm〕

= manner〔'mænɚ〕

gulch〔gʌltʃ〕*n.* 峽谷

= valley〔'vælɪ〕

= gorge〔gɔrdʒ〕

= ravine〔rə'vin〕

= gully〔'gʌlɪ〕

= canyon〔'kænjən〕

gulf〔gʌlf〕*n.* ①隔閡；裂縫 ②海灣

① = separation〔,sɛpə'reʃən〕

= break〔brek〕

= cut〔kʌt〕

= cleft〔klɛft〕

= crack〔kræk〕

= crevice〔'krɛvɪs〕

= hole〔hol〕

= rift〔rɪft〕

= opening〔'opənɪŋ〕

= gap〔gæp〕

= chasm〔'kæzəm〕

= pit〔pɪt〕

② = bay〔be〕

gullible〔'gʌləbḷ〕*adj.* 易受騙的

= naive〔nɑ'iv〕

= deceivable〔dɪ'sivəbḷ〕

= *easily fooled*

gully〔'gʌlɪ〕*n.* 溪谷；溝渠

= gorge〔gɔrdʒ〕

G

= valley (ˈvælɪ)
= ditch (ˈdɪtʃ)
= ravine (rəˈvin)
= gulf (gʌlf)
= gulch (gʌltʃ)

gulp (gʌlp) v. ①吞　②壓抑

① = swallow (ˈswɑlo)
= devour (dɪˈvaʊr)
② = choke (tʃok)
= repress (rɪˈprɛs)
= gasp (gæsp , gɑsp)
= secure (sɪˈkjʊr)

gun (gʌn) ① v. 開槍射擊
② n. 槍

① = shoot (ʃut)
= fire (faɪr)
= discharge (dɪsˈtʃɑrdʒ)
② = weapon (ˈwɛpən)
= firearm (ˈfaɪrˌɑrm)
= pistol (ˈpɪstl̩)
= rifle (ˈraɪfl̩)
= revolver (rɪˈvɑlvɚ)

gurge (gɝdʒ) v. 迴旋

= whirlpool (ˈhwɝlˌpul)
= eddy (ˈɛdɪ)
= gyrate (ˈdʒaɪret)
= purl (pɝl)
= revolve (rɪˈvɑlv)
= swirl (swɝl)

gurgle (ˈgɝgl̩) n. 潺潺聲
= *bubbling sound*

gush (gʌʃ) v. ①傾流
②滔滔不絕地說

① = pour (por , pɔr)
= flow (flo)
= spout (spaʊt)
= surge (sɝdʒ)
= flush (flʌʃ)
= flood (flʌd)
= spurt (spɝt)
= *rush out*
② = chatter (ˈtʃætɚ)
= babble (ˈbæbl̩)
= prattle (ˈprætl̩)

gust (gʌst) n. ①陣風　②一陣

① = wind (wɪnd)
= blast (blæst)
② = outbreak (ˈaʊtˌbrek)
= outburst (ˈaʊtˌbɝst)
= eruption (ɪˈrʌpʃən)
= flare-up (ˈflɛrˌʌp)

gutta (ˈgʌtə) n. 小滴

= dribble (ˈdrɪbl̩)
= droplet (ˈdrɑplɪt)
= dropping (ˈdrɑpɪŋ)
= trickle (ˈtrɪkl̩)

gutter (ˈgʌtɚ) n. 溝槽

= channel (ˈtʃænl̩)
= groove (gruv)
= trench (trɛntʃ)
= ditch (dɪtʃ)

guy (gaɪ) n. 人；傢伙

= fellow (ˈfɛlo)

G

gyrate ('dʒaɪret) v. 迴旋

  = gurge (gɝdʒ)
  = whirlpool ('hwɝl,pul)
  = eddy ('ɛdɪ)
  = purl (pɝl)
  = revolve (rɪ'vɑlv)
  = swirl (swɝl)

gymnastics (dʒɪm'næstɪks) n.
體操

  = exercise ('ɛksɚ,saɪz)
  = drill (drɪl)
  = athletics (æθ'lɛtɪks)
  = calisthenics (,kæləs'θɛnɪks)
  = sports (sports , sprts)
  = acrobatics (,ækrə'bætɪks)

gyp (dʒɪp) n. 欺騙

  = cheat (tʃit)
  = swindle ('swɪndḷ)
  = defraud (dɪ'frɔd)

gypsy ('dʒɪpsɪ) n. 流浪者

  = nomad ('nomæd , 'nɑmæd)

H

habit ('bæbɪt) n. ①習性 ②法服

① = custom ('kʌstəm)
  = practice ('præktɪs)
  = nature ('netʃɚ)
  = pattern ('pætən)
  = trait (tret)
  = tendency ('tɛndənsɪ)
  = fashion ('fæʃən)
  = manner ('mænɚ)

  = routine (ru'tin)
  = addition (ə'dɪʃən)
② = costume ('kɑstjum)
  = clothes (kloz , kloðz)
  = *religious dress*

habitation (,hæbə'teʃən) n.
住所

  = abode (ə'bod)
  = residence ('rɛzədəns)
  = lodging ('lɑdʒɪŋ)
  = housing ('haʊzɪŋ)
  = occupancy ('ɑkjəpənsɪ)
  = domicile ('dɑməsḷ , -saɪl)
  = home (hom)
  = *abiding place*
  = *dwelling place*

habitual (hə'bɪtʃʊəl) adj.
習慣的；通常的

  = regular ('rɛgjələ)
  = ordinary ('ɔrdn̩,ɛrɪ , 'ɔrdnɛrɪ)
  = usual ('juʒʊəl)
  = customary ('kʌstəm,ɛrɪ)
  = familiar (fə'mɪljɚ)
  = accustomed (ə'kʌstəmd)
  = general ('dʒɛnərəl)
  = established (ə'stæblɪʃt)
  = normal ('nɔrml̩)

hack (hæk) v. ①斧劈 ②乾咳

① = cut (kʌt)
  = sever ('sɛvɚ)
  = split (splɪt)
  = cleave (kliv)
  = chop (tʃɑp)
② = cough (kɔf)

H

hades (ˈhediz) *n.* 地獄；冥府

= hell (hɛl)

= underworld (ˈʌndə-ˌwɜld)

= inferno (ɪnˈfɜno)

= abyss (əˈbɪs)

= Styx (stɪks)

hag (hæg) *n.* 女巫；巫婆

= witch (wɪtʃ)

= crone (kron)

haggard (ˈhægəd) *adj.* 憔悴的；形容枯槁的

= thin (θɪn)

= poor (pʊr)

= pale (pel)

= deathlike (ˈdɛθˌlaɪk)

= seedy (ˈsidɪ)

= wild-eyed (ˈwaɪldˌaɪd)

= tired-looking (ˈtaɪrdˌlʊkɪŋ)

= lean (lin)

= wornout (ˈwornˈaʊt, ˈwɔrn-)

= worried (ˈwɜɪd)

= wrinkled (ˈrɪŋkḷd)

= exhausted (ɪgˈzɔstɪd, ɛg-)

hail (hel) *v.* ①歡呼 ②下冰雹

① = greet (grit)

= cheer (tʃɪr)

= welcome (ˈwɛlkəm)

= call (kɔl)

= shout (ʃaʊt)

② = sleet (slit)

hale (hel) ① *v.* 拖曳

② *adj.* 強壯的

① = drag (dræg)

= haul (hɔl)

= pull (pʊl)

= tug (tʌg)

= tow (to)

② = strong (strɔŋ)

= mighty (ˈmaɪtɪ)

= powerful (ˈpaʊə-fəl)

= healthy (ˈhɛlθɪ)

= sturdy (ˈstɜdɪ)

= rugged (ˈrʌgɪd)

= strapping (ˈstræpɪŋ)

= hardy (ˈhɑrdɪ)

= robust (roˈbʌst)

= vigorous (ˈvɪgərəs)

hall (hɔl) *n.* ①走廊 ②會堂

① = passageway (ˈpæsɪdʒˌwe)

= corridor (ˈkɔrədə-, -ˌdɔr, ˈkɑr-)

= arcade (ɑrˈked)

= vestibule (ˈvɛstəˌbjul)

= lobby (ˈlɑbɪ)

= foyer (ˈfɔɪə-, ˈfɔɪ-e)

② = assembly (əˈsɛmblɪ)

= auditorium (ˌɔdəˈtorɪəm)

= building (ˈbɪldɪŋ)

= theater (ˈθiətə-, ˈθɪə-)

= *large meeting room*

= *community center*

halo (ˈhelo) *n.* ①光環 ②榮耀

① = circle (ˈsɜkḷ)

= ring (rɪŋ)

② = glory (ˈglorɪ, ˈglɔrɪ)

= glamour (ˈglæmə-)

halt (hɔlt) *v.* 停止

= stop (stɑp)

= check (tʃɛk)

= arrest (ə'rɛst)

= quit (kwɪt)

= cease (sis)

= end (ɛnd)

= *come to a standstill*

halve (hæv) *v.* 分開

= divide (də'vaɪd)

= dissect (dɪ'sɛkt)

= split (splɪt)

= share (ʃɛr)

hamlet ('hæmlɪt) *n.* 小村

= village ('vɪlɪdʒ)

hammer ('hæmɚ) ① *v.* 鎚打
② *v.* 重申 ③ *n.* 鎚

① = hit (hɪt)

= drive (draɪv)

= pound (paʊnd)

= beat (bit)

= knock (nɑk)

= bang (bæŋ)

② = repeat (rɪ'pit)

= drill (drɪl)

③ = mallet ('mælɪt)

hamper ('hæmpɚ) ① *v.* 妨礙
② *n.* 有蓋籃子

① = hinder ('hɪndɚ)

= impede (ɪm'pid)

= cramp (kræmp)

= obstruct (əb'strʌk)

= block (blɑk)

= restrain (rɪ'stren)

= limit ('lɪmɪt)

② = basket ('bæskɪt)

hand (hænd) ① *v.* 交給；傳遞
② *n.* 勞工　③ *n.* 控制　④ *n.* 筆跡

① = give (gɪv)

= deliver (dɪ'lɪvɚ)

= transfer (træns'fɝ)

= pass (pæs)

= *turn over*

② = worker ('wɝkɚ)

= person ('pɝsn̩)

= laborer ('lebərɚ)

③ = possession (pə'zɛʃən)

= command (kə'mænd)

= grasp (græsp)

= clutches ('klʌtʃɪz)

= *central power*

④ = handwriting ('hænd,raɪtɪŋ)

= penmanship ('pɛnmən,ʃɪp)

handbag ('hænd,bæg , 'hæn-)
n. 女用手提包

= pocketbook ('pɑkɪt,bʊk)

= purse (pɝs)

handicap ('hændɪ,kæp) *n.*
不利；障礙

= hindrance ('hɪndrəns)

= burden ('bɝdn̩)

= disadvantage (,dɪsəd'væntɪdʒ)

= load (lod)

H

handle〔'hændḷ〕v. ①以手觸動；操作 ②管理 ③買賣

① = touch〔tʌtʃ〕
= feel〔fil〕
= finger〔'fɪŋgɚ〕
= manipulate〔mə'nɪpjə‚let〕
= use〔juz〕
② = manage〔'mænɪdʒ〕
= direct〔də'rɛkt , daɪ-〕
= regulate〔'rɛgjə‚let〕
= govern〔'gʌvɚn〕
= run〔rʌn〕
= *carry on*
③ = *deal in*
= *trade in*

handsome〔'hænsəm〕adj. ①美貌的 ②巨大的

① = attractive〔ə'træktɪv〕
= good-looking〔'gʊd'lʊkɪŋ〕
② = large〔lɑrdʒ〕
= considerable〔kən'sɪdərəbḷ〕
= big〔bɪg〕
= generous〔'dʒɛnərəs〕
= liberal〔'lɪbərəl〕

handwriting〔'hænd‚raɪtɪŋ〕n. 筆跡；書法

= penmanship〔'pɛnmən‚ʃɪp〕

handy〔'hændɪ〕adj. ①方便的 ②熟練的

① = useful〔'jusfəl〕
= convenient〔kən'vinjənt〕
= nearby〔'nɪr‚baɪ〕
= available〔ə'veləbḷ〕

= ready〔'rɛdɪ〕
② = skillful〔'skɪlfəl〕
= adept〔ə'dɛpt〕
= apt〔æpt〕
= proficient〔prə'fɪʃənt〕

hang〔hæŋ〕v. ①懸掛 ②絞死 ③垂（首）

① = suspend〔sə'spɛnd〕
= *fasten up*
② = execute〔'ɛksɪ‚kjut〕
= *string up*
③ = droop〔drup〕
= sag〔sæg〕
= *bend down*

haphazard〔‚hæp'hæzɚd〕adj. 偶然的；隨便的

= chance〔tʃæns〕
= random〔'rændəm〕
= casual〔'kæʒuəl〕

happen〔'hæpən〕v. ①發生 ②恰逢

① = occur〔ə'kɝ〕
= pass〔pæs〕
= *take place*
= *come off*
② = chance〔tʃæns〕
= *turn up*

happy〔'hæpɪ〕adj. 快樂的；滿足的

= contented〔kən'tɛntɪd〕
= glad〔glæd〕
= joyful〔'dʒɔɪfəl〕

= cheerful ('tʃɪrfəl)
= bright (braɪt)
= blissful ('blɪsfəl)
= radiant ('redɪənt)

arass ('hærəs , hə'ræs) v.
①侵擾 ②使煩惱

① = trouble ('trʌbl)
= torment (tɔr'mɛnt)
= molest (mə'lɛst)
= bother ('bɑðɚ)
= badger ('bædʒɚ)
= plague (pleg)
= persecute ('pɜsɪ,kjut)
= haunt (hɔnt , hɑnt)
= bully ('bʊlɪ)
= threaten ('θrɛtn)
② = disturb (dɪ'stɜb)
= worry ('wɜɪ)
= vex (vɛks)
= beset (bɪ'sɛt)

arbor ('hɑrbɚ) ① v. 庇護
② v. 心懷 ③ n. 港

① = shelter ('ʃɛltɚ)
= protect (prə'tɛkt)
= shield (ʃild)
= defend (dɪ'fɛnd)
= guard (gɑrd)
= screen (skrin)
= cover ('kʌvɚ)
= house (haʊz)
② = consider (kən'sɪdɚ)
= think (θɪŋk)
= *keep in mind*
= *entertain the idea*

③ = port (port , pɔrt)
= dock (dɑk)
= wharf (hwɔrf)
= pier (pɪr)

hard (hɑrd) ① adj. 堅固的
② adj. 嚴厲的 ③ adj. 艱難的
④ adv. 努力地 ⑤ adj. 難堪的

① = firm (fɜm)
= solid ('sɑlɪd)
= stony ('stonɪ)
= rigid ('rɪdʒɪd)
② = stern (stɜn)
= unyielding (ʌn'jildɪŋ)
= strict (strɪkt)
= inflexible (ɪn'flɛksəbl)
③ = difficult ('dɪfə,kʌlt , 'dɪfəkəlt ,
   -kl̩t)
= rough (rʌf)
= rugged ('rʌgɪd)
= tough (tʌf)
④ = laboriously (lə'borɪəslɪ ,
   -'bɔr-)
= strenuously ('strɛnjʊəslɪ)
= *with effort*
= *with vigor*
⑤ = unpleasant (ʌn'plɛznt)
= harsh (hɑrʃ)
= ugly ('ʌglɪ)
= severe (sə'vɪr)
= callous ('kæləs)

hardly ('hɑrdlɪ) adv. 幾乎不;
恰好

= barely ('bɛrlɪ)
= just (dʒʌst)

H

= scarcely ('skɛrslɪ)
= narrowly ('nærolɪ)
= nearly ('nɪrlɪ)
= *not quite*

hardship ('hardʃɪp) *n.* 艱難

= trouble ('trʌbḷ)
= *ups and downs*

hardy ('hardɪ) *adj.* ①強壯的
②勇敢的

① = strong (strɔŋ)
= healthy ('hɛlθɪ)
= robust (ro'bʌst)
= mighty ('maɪtɪ)
= powerful ('pauɚfəl)
= sturdy ('stɝdɪ)
= rugged ('rʌgɪd)
= hale (hel)
② = bold (bold)
= daring ('dɛrɪŋ)
= courageous (kə'redʒəs)
= valiant ('væljənt)
= heroic (hɪ'ro·ɪk)

hark (hark) *v.* 聽

= listen ('lɪsṇ)
= heed (hid)

harm (harm) *v.* 傷害

= hurt (hɝt)
= damage ('dæmɪdʒ)
= wrong (rɔŋ)
= injure ('ɪndʒɚ)
= impair (ɪm'pɛr)

harmonious (har'monɪəs) *adj.*
①協調的　②音調和諧的

① = agreeing (ə'griɪŋ)
= congenial (kən'dʒinjəl)
= compatible (kəm'pætəbḷ)
= *in accord*
② = musical ('mjuzɪkḷ)
= blending ('blɛndɪŋ)
= *in tune*

harness ('harnɪs) *v.* ①控制
②束以馬具

① = control (kən'trol)
= use (juz)
② = saddle ('sædḷ)
= yoke (jok)
= *hitch up*
= *hook up*

harp (harp) *v.* 不停地說

= elaborate (ɪ'læbə,ret)
= *dwell on*

harrow ('hæro) *v.* ①使傷心；
使痛苦　②耙（掘）

① = hurt (hɝt)
= wound (wund)
= pain (pen)
= afflict (ə'flɪkt)
= distress (dɪ'strɛs)
= irritate ('ɪrə,tet)
= torment (tɔr'mɛnt)
= torture ('tɔrtʃɚ)
= agonize ('ægə,naɪz)
② = rake (rek)
= plow (plau)

H

harry ('hærɪ) v. ①掠奪
②使痛苦；苦惱

① = raid (red)
= rob (rɑb)
= storm (stɔrm)
= besiege (bɪ'sidʒ)
= invade (ɪn'ved)
② = trouble ('trʌbḷ)
= worry ('wɜɪ)
= torment (tɔr'mɛnt)
= vex (vɛks)
= harass ('hærəs , hə'ræs)

harsh (hɑrʃ) adj. ①粗糙的；
刺耳的　②嚴苛的

① = rough (rʌf)
= coarse (kors , kɔrs)
= husky ('hʌskɪ)
= grating ('gretɪŋ)
= raspy ('ræspɪ , 'rɑs-)
② = cruel ('kruəl)
= unfeeling (ʌn'filɪŋ)
= severe (sə'vɪr)
= bitter ('bɪtɚ)
= sharp (ʃɑrp)
= cutting ('kʌtɪŋ)
= piercing ('pɪrsɪŋ)
= gruff (grʌf)
= brusque (brʌsk , brusk)
= curt (kɜt)
= strict (strɪkt)
= stern (stɜn)
= tough (tʌf)

harvest ('hɑrvɪst) ① v. 收割
② n. 收穫　③ n. 成果

① = reap (rip)
= gather ('gæðɚ)
= pick (pɪk)
② = crop (krɑp)
= yield (jild)
= product ('prɑdəkt , -dʌkt)
= proceeds ('prosidz)
③ = result (rɪ'zʌlt)
= consequences ('kɑnsə,kwɛnsɪz)
= effect (ə'fɛkt , ɪ- , ɛ-)
= outcome ('aut,kʌm)

hash (hæʃ) n. ①混雜
②亂七八糟

① = mixture ('mɪkstʃɚ)
= assortment (ə'sɔrtmənt)
= mix (mɪks)
② = mess (mɛs)
= muddle ('mʌdḷ)
= jumble ('dʒʌmbḷ)
= scramble ('skræmbḷ)
= fiasco (fɪ'æsko)

hasty ('hestɪ) adj. ①急忙的
②草率的　③易怒的

① = quick (kwɪk)
= hurried ('hɜɪd)
= fast (fæst)
= swift (swɪft)
= speedy ('spidɪ)
= rapid ('ræpɪd)
= fleet (flit)
② = rash (ræʃ)
= reckless ('rɛklɪs)
= unprepared (,ʌnprɪ'pɛrd)
= sudden ('sʌdṇ)

= premature (ˌprɪmə'tjʊr ,
   'prɪmə,tʃʊr)

= impulsive (ɪm'pʌlsɪv)

= impetuous (ɪm'pɛtʃʊəs)

③ = hotheaded ('hɑt'hɛdɪd)

= quick-tempered
   ('kwɪk'tɛmpɚd)

hat (hæt) *n.* 帽子

= headdress ('hɛd,drɛs)

= chapeau (ʃæ'po)

= millinery ('mɪlə,nɛrɪ , -nərɪ)

= cap (kæp)

hatch (hætʃ) ① *v.* 計畫
② *v.* 孵（卵） ③ *n.* 艙口

① = arrange (ə'rendʒ)

= plan (plæn)

= plot (plɑt)

= scheme (skim)

= intrigue (ɪn'trig)

= invent (ɪn'vɛnt)

= concoct (kɑn'kɑkt , kən-)

= *make up*

② = produce (prə'djus)

= generate ('dʒɛnə,ret)

= incubate ('ɪnkjə,bet)

= breed (brid)

= brood (brud)

= *be born*

③ = opening ('opənɪŋ)

= door (dor , dɔr)

= trap (træp)

hatchet ('hætʃɪt) *n.* 斧頭

= ax (æks)

= tomahawk ('tɑmə,hɔk , 'tɑmɪ-)

hate (het) *v.* 憎恨

= dislike (dɪs'laɪk)

= loathe (loð)

= detest (dɪ'tɛst)

= abhor (əb'hɔr , æb-)

= abominate (ə'bɑmə,net)

haughty ('hɔtɪ) *adj.* 傲慢的

= arrogant ('ærəgənt)

= proud (praʊd)

= lofty ('lɔftɪ , 'lɑftɪ)

= scornful ('skɔrnfəl)

haul (hɔl) *v.* ①拖曳
②逮逋而押至法庭

① = pull (pʊl)

= drag (dræg)

= draw (drɔ)

= heave (hiv)

= tug (tʌg)

= tow (to)

② = take (tek)

= catch (kætʃ)

haunch (hɔntʃ , hɑntʃ) *n.* 腰

= hip (hɪp)

= side (saɪd)

= flank (flæŋk)

haunt (hɔnt , hɑnt) *v.* ①常至
②縈擾於心

① = frequent (frɪ'kwɛnt)

= *visit often*

= *hang around*

②= obsess (əb'sɛs)
　= torment (tɔr'mɛnt)

ᴴave (hæv) v. ①有　②必須
③令；使　④經歷　⑤ n. 忍耐

①= hold (hold)
　= possess (pə'zɛs)
　= own (on)

②= must (mʌst)
　= should (ʃud , ʃəd)
　= ought (ɔt)
　= need (nid)
　= *be forced*

③= cause (kɔz)
　= make (mek)
　= compel (kəm'pɛl)
　= require (rɪ'kwaɪr)

④= experience (ɪk'spɪrɪəns)
　= feel (fil)
　= meet (mit)
　= undergo (ˌʌndə'go)
　= endure (ɪn'djur)

⑤= permit (pə'mɪt)
　= tolerate ('tɑləˌret)
　= suffer ('sʌfə)
　= *stand for*
　= *put up with*

ᴴaven ('hevən) n. 避難所

　= shelter ('ʃɛltə)
　= safety ('seftɪ)
　= harbor ('hɑrbə)
　= refuge ('rɛfjudʒ)
　= sanctuary ('sæŋktʃuˌɛrɪ)

ᴴavoc ('hævək) n. 大破壞

= destruction (dɪ'strʌkʃən)
= ruin ('ruɪn)
= devastation (ˌdɛvəs'teʃən)
= ravage ('rævɪdʒ)
= damage ('dæmɪdʒ)
= harm (hɑrm)
= injury ('ɪndʒərɪ)

hawk (hɔk) v. ①狩獵
②沿街叫賣

①= hunt (hʌnt)
　= chase (tʃes)
②= peddle ('pɛdl̩)
　= sell (sɛl)
　= vend (vɛnd)

hay (he) n. 乾草

　= fodder ('fɑdə)
　= feed (fid)

hazard ('hæzəd) n. 賭

　= risk (rɪsk)
　= chance (tʃæns)
　= gamble ('gæmbl̩)
　= bet (bɛt)
　= wager ('wedʒə)

hazy ('hezɪ) adj. ①有薄霧的
②模糊的

①= misty ('mɪstɪ)
　= smoky ('smokɪ)
　= dim (dɪm)
　= cloudy ('klaudɪ)
　= overcast ('ovəˌkæst , ˌovə'kæst)
　= foggy ('fɑgɪ , 'fɔgɪ)
②= obscure (əb'skjur)

H

= indistinct (ˌɪndɪ'stɪŋkt)
= unclear (ʌn'klɪr)
= indefinite (ɪn'dɛfənɪt)
= vague (veg)
= faint (fent)
= blurred (blɝd)
= fuzzy ('fʌzɪ)
= uncertain (ʌn'sɝtn̩ , -'sɝtɪn)
= confused (kən'fjuzd)
= muddled ('mʌdl̩d)

head (hɛd) ① v. 領頭
② v. 領導   ③ v. 走向   ④ n. 頭部
⑤ n. 才智   ⑥ n. 危機；結論

① = lead (lid)
= precede (pri'sid , prɪ-)
= initiate (ɪ'nɪʃɪˌet)
= *come first*
② = govern ('gʌvən)
= command (kə'mænd)
= lead (lid)
= direct (də'rɛkt , daɪ-)
= manage ('mænɪdʒ)
= supervise ('supəˌvaɪz)
= administer (əd'mɪnəstə , æd-)
= control (kən'trol)
= rule (rul)
= dominate ('dɑməˌnet)
= conduct (kən'dʌkt)
= run (rʌn)
③ = proceed (prə'sid)
= go (go)
= gravitate ('grævəˌtet)
= *move toward*
④ = pate (pet)
= crown (kraʊn)

= top (tɑp)
⑤ = mind (maɪnd)
= intelligence (ɪn'tɛlədʒəns)
= understanding (ˌʌndə'stændɪŋ)
= mentality (mɛn'tælətɪ)
= brain (bren)
⑥ = crisis ('kraɪsɪs)
= conclusion (kən'kluʒən)

headfirst ('hɛd'fɝst) *adv.*
不顧前後地；急忙地

= hastily ('hestlɪ , -tɪlɪ)
= rashly ('ræʃlɪ)
= impetuously (ɪm'pɛtʃʊəslɪ)
= impulsively (ɪm'pʌlsɪvlɪ)
= recklessly ('rɛklɪslɪ)
= carelessly ('kɛrlɪslɪ)

heading ('hɛdɪŋ) *n.* 標題

= topic ('tɑpɪk)
= title ('taɪtl̩)
= subject ('sʌbdʒɪkt)
= issue ('ɪʃʊ , 'ɪʃju)
= question ('kwɛstʃən)
= theme (θim)
= headline ('hɛdˌlaɪn)

headquarters ('hɛd'kwɔrtəz ,
-ˌkwɔr-) *n.* 總部

= base (bes)
= *central station*
= *main office*

headstrong ('hɛdˌstrɔŋ) *adj.*
頑固的

= obstinate ('ɑbstənɪt)

= stubborn ('stʌbən)
= willful ('wɪlfəl)
= bullheaded ('bul'hɛdɪd)

headway ('hɛd,we) *n.* 進步

= progress ('prɑgrɛs)
= advance (əd'væns)
= improvement (ɪm'pruvmənt)

heal (hil) *v.* 治癒

= cure (kjur)
= remedy ('rɛmədɪ)
= correct (kə'rɛkt)
= mend (mɛnd)
= repair (rɪ'pɛr)

health (hɛlθ) *n.* 健康；身體狀況

= well-being ('wɛl'biɪŋ)
= *physical condition*

heap (hip) *v.* 堆積

= pile (paɪl)
= gather ('gæðə)
= fill (fɪl)
= stack (stæk)
= load (lod)

hear (hɪr) *v.* 聽

= listen ('lɪsn̩)
= heed (hid)

hearsay ('hɪr,se) *n.* 謠傳

= gossip ('gɑsəp)
= rumor ('rumə)
= *common talk*

heart (hɑrt) *n.* ①心臟 ②心情
③愛心 ④熱誠 ⑤中心 ⑥主旨
⑦任何表示想念之事物

① = *body pump*
② = feelings ('filɪŋz)
= soul (sol)
= spirit ('spɪrɪt)
= temperament ('tɛmprəmənt ,
-pərə-)
③ = kindness ('kaɪndnɪs)
= sympathy ('sɪmpəθɪ)
= warmth (wɔrmθ)
= love (lʌv)
= affection (ə'fɛkʃən)
④ = courage ('kɜɪdʒ)
= enthusiasm (ɪn'θjuzɪ,æzəm)
= stamina ('stæmənə)
⑤ = middle ('mɪdl̩)
= center ('sɛntə)
= core (kor)
= nucleus ('njuklɪəs)
= hub (hʌb)
⑥ = substance ('sʌbstəns)
= meat (mit)
= *main part*
⑦ = valentine ('væləntaɪn)

hearten ('hɑrtn̩) *v.* 鼓勵

= cheer (tʃɪr)
= encourage (ɪn'kɜɪdʒ)
= inspire (ɪn'spaɪr)
= gladden ('glædn̩)

heartfelt ('hɑrt,fɛlt) *adj.* 衷心的

= sincere (sɪn'sɪr)
= genuine ('dʒɛnjuɪn)

H

= profound (prə'faʊnd)

= deep (dip)

hearth (hɑrθ) *n.* 爐床;家庭

= fireplace ('faɪr,ples)

= fireside ('faɪr,saɪd)

= home (hom)

heartily ('hɑrtɪlɪ) *adv.* 熱忱地;完全地

= sincerely (sɪn'sɪrlɪ)

= warmly ('wɔrmlɪ)

= devotedly (dɪ'votɪdlɪ)

= completely (kəm'plitlɪ)

= fervently ('fɝvəntlɪ)

= ardently ('ɑrdn̩tlɪ)

heat (hit) *v.* ①使熱 ②烹飪 ③使激動

① = warm (wɔrm)

= *make hot*

② = cook (kʊk)

= prepare (prɪ'pɛr)

③ = excite (ɪk'saɪt)

= move (muv)

= affect (ə'fɛkt)

= stir (stɝ)

= provoke (prə'vok)

= arouse (ə'raʊz)

= kindle ('kɪndl̩)

= inflame (ɪn'flem)

heave (hiv) *v.* ①用力舉起 ②喘息 ③凸起

① = lift (lɪft)

= raise (rez)

= hoist (hɔɪst)

= pull (pʊl)

= haul (hɔl)

= lug (lʌg)

= tug (tʌg)

= tow (to)

= drag (dræg)

② = pant (pænt)

= *breathe hard*

③ = swell (swɛl)

= rise (raɪz)

= bulge (bʌldʒ)

= billow ('bɪlo)

= surge (sɝdʒ)

heaven ('hɛvən) *n.* ①天空 ②天堂;極樂

① = sky (skaɪ)

= space (spes)

② = paradise ('pærə,daɪs)

= bliss (blɪs)

= ecstasy ('ɛkstəsɪ)

heavy ('hɛvɪ) *adj.* 沈重的

= weighty ('wetɪ)

= laden ('ledn̩)

= bulky ('bʌlkɪ)

= fat (fæt)

= hefty ('hɛftɪ)

hectic ('hɛktɪk) *adj.* ①發熱的 ②緊張忙碌的

① = feverish ('fivərɪʃ)

= heated ('hitɪd)

= hot (hɑt)

= burning ('bɝnɪŋ)

H

② = exciting〔ɪk'saɪtɪŋ〕
  = stirring〔'stɝɪŋ〕
  = frantic〔'fræntɪk〕
  = moving〔'muvɪŋ〕
  = busy〔'bɪzɪ〕

hedge〔hɛdʒ〕① v. 閃避問題
② n. 限制

① = dodge〔dɑdʒ〕
  = sidestep〔'saɪd,stɛp〕
  = duck〔dʌk〕
  = *evade questions*
② = boundary〔'baʊndərɪ , 'baʊndrɪ〕
  = limit〔'lɪmɪt〕
  = border〔'bɔrdɚ〕
  = borderline〔'bɔrdɚ,laɪn〕

heed〔hid〕v. 注意到

  = notice〔'notɪs〕
  = observe〔əb'zɝv〕
  = follow〔'fɑlo〕
  = care〔kɛr〕
  = mind〔maɪnd〕
  = attend〔ə'tɛnd〕

height〔haɪt〕n. ①高度 ②頂點

① = altitude〔'æltə,tjud〕
  = elevation〔,ɛlə'veʃən〕
  = tallness〔'tɔlnɪs〕
  = stature〔'stætʃɚ〕
② = top〔tɑp〕
  = summit〔'sʌmɪt〕
  = peak〔pik〕
  = crown〔kraʊn〕
  = tip〔tɪp〕
  = apex〔'epɛks〕

  = acme〔'ækmɪ , 'ækmi〕
  = *highest point*

hello〔hə'lo〕int. 喂;哈囉

  = greetings〔'gritɪŋz〕
  = salutations〔,sæljə'teʃənz〕
  = *good day*

helm〔hɛlm〕n. 舵;駕駛盤

  = control〔kən'trol〕
  = reins〔renz〕
  = *driver's seat*

help〔hɛlp〕v. ①幫助 ②減輕
③避免

① = aid〔ed〕
  = assist〔ə'sɪst〕
  = avail〔ə'vel〕
  = benefit〔'bɛnə,fɪt〕
② = relieve〔rɪ'liv〕
  = *lend a hand*
③ = avoid〔ə'vɔɪd〕
  = prevent〔prɪ'vɛnt〕
  = deter〔dɪ'tɝ〕
  = *keep from*

hem〔hɛm〕n. 邊緣

  = border〔'bɔrdɚ〕
  = edge〔ɛdʒ〕
  = rim〔rɪm〕

hence〔hɛns〕adv. ①因此
②滾開【古】 ③從此

① = therefore〔'ðɛr,for , -,fɔr〕
  = consequently〔'kɑnsə,kwɛntlɪ〕
  = accordingly〔ə'kɔrdɪŋlɪ〕

H

= thus (ðʌs)
= *because of this*

② = away (ə'we)
= elsewhere ('ɛls,hwɛr)

③ = later ('letɚ)
= *from now on*
= *in future time*

herald ('hɛrəld) ① v. 宣布
② n. 報信者

① = announce (ə'nauns)
= proclaim (pro'klem)
= shout (ʃaut)
= *cry out*
= *bring news*

② = messenger ('mɛsn̩dʒɚ)

herd (hɝd) v. 使成群；放牧

= flock (flɑk)
= assemble (ə'sɛmbl̩)
= collect (kə'lɛkt)
= shepherd ('ʃɛpɚd)
= drive (draɪv)
= gather ('gæðɚ)
= *join together*

here (hɪr) ① adv. 在這裏
② adv. 現在 ③ int. (點名時回答)
到；有

① = *this place*
= *this spot*

② = now (nau)
= *at present*
= *at this time*

③ = present ('prɛzn̩t)
= *in attendance*

hereditary (hə'rɛdə,tɛrɪ) adj.
世襲的

= inborn (ɪn'bɔrn , 'ɪn,bɔrn)
= inherited (ɪn'hɛrɪtɪd)

heresy ('hɛrəsɪ) n. 異端邪說

= dissent (dɪ'sɛnt)
= misbelief (,mɪsbə'lif)

heritage ('hɛrətɪdʒ) n. 遺產；
與生俱來的權利

= heredity (hə'rɛdətɪ)
= birthright ('bɝθ,raɪt)

hermit ('hɝmɪt) n. 隱士

= recluse ('rɛklus , rɪ'klus)
= shut-in ('ʃʌt,ɪn)

heroic (hɪ'ro·ɪk) adj. 英勇的

= bold (bold)
= courageous (kə'redʒəs)
= stalwart ('stɔlwɚt)
= valiant ('væljənt)
= gallant ('gælənt)
= brave (brev)
= chivalrous ('ʃɪvl̩rəs)

hesitate ('hɛzə,tet) v. ①停頓
②猶豫

① = pause (pɔz)
= rest (rɛst)
= *let up*

② = flounder ('flaundɚ)
= waver ('wevɚ)
= falter ('fɔltɚ)

= *feel doubtful*

= *be undecided*

hew〔hju〕*v.* 砍；伐

= cut〔kʌt〕

= chop〔tʃɑp〕

= sever〔'sɛvɚ〕

= split〔splɪt〕

= cleave〔kliv〕

hibernate〔'haɪbɚˌnet〕*v.* 冬眠；蟄伏

= sleep〔slip〕

= slumber〔'slʌmbɚ〕

= *hole up*

hide〔haɪd〕① *v.* 遮蔽；隱瞞 ② *n.* 獸皮

① = conceal〔kən'sil〕

= screen〔skrin〕

= veil〔vel〕

= cloak〔klok〕

= mask〔mæsk , mɑsk〕

= *cover up*

② = skin〔skɪn〕

= pelt〔pɛlt〕

hideous〔'hɪdɪəs〕*adj.* 醜惡的；可怕的

= ugly〔'ʌglɪ〕

= frightful〔'fraɪtfəl〕

= horrible〔'hɑrəbḷ〕

= horrid〔'hɔrɪd , 'hɑr- 〕

= dreadful〔'drɛdfəl〕

= terrible〔'tɛrəbḷ〕

= repulsive〔rɪ'pʌlsɪv〕

= ghastly〔'gæstlɪ , 'gɑst- 〕

high〔haɪ〕*adj.* ①高的 ②主要的 ③尖銳的

① = tall〔tɔl〕

= long〔lɔŋ , lɑŋ〕

= lofty〔'lɔftɪ , 'lɑftɪ 〕

= elevated〔'ɛləˌvetɪd 〕

= steep〔stip〕

= towering〔'tauərɪŋ 〕

= soaring〔'sorɪŋ 〕

② = great〔gret〕

= chief〔tʃif〕

= main〔men〕

= important〔ɪm'pɔrtn̩t 〕

= eminent〔'ɛmənənt 〕

= exalted〔ɪg'zɔltɪd 〕

= grand〔grænd〕

③ = shrill〔ʃrɪl〕

= sharp〔ʃɑrp〕

= piercing〔'pɪrsɪŋ 〕

= screechy〔'skritʃɪ 〕

high-strung〔'haɪ'strʌŋ〕*adj.* 敏感的；緊張的

= sensitive〔'sɛnsətɪv 〕

= nervous〔'nɝvəs 〕

= excitable〔ɪk'saɪtəbḷ 〕

= edgy〔'ɛdʒɪ 〕

= jumpy〔'dʒʌmpɪ 〕

highway〔'haɪˌwe〕*n.* 公路

= road〔rod〕

= thoroughfare〔'θɝoˌfɛr 〕

= turnpike〔'tɝnˌpaɪk 〕

= expressway〔ɪk'sprɛsˌwe 〕

= thruway〔'θruˌwe 〕

= freeway〔'friˌwe 〕

H

hike (haɪk) *n.* 遠足;行軍

= walk (wɔk)
= march (mɑrtʃ)
= tramp (træmp)
= parade (pə'red)

hilarious (hə'lɛrɪəs , hɪ- , haɪ-)
adj. 高興的

= merry ('mɛrɪ)
= gay (ge)
= joyful ('dʒɔɪfəl)
= gleeful ('glifəl)

hill (hɪl) *n.* 小山;小土堆

= elevation (ˌɛlə'veʃən)
= mound (maʊnd)
= heap (hip)

hind (haɪnd) *adj.* 後部的

= back (bæk)
= rear (rɪr)

hinder ('hɪndɚ) *v.* 妨礙;阻止

= stop (stɑp)
= obstruct (əb'strʌkt)
= impede (ɪm'pid)
= curb (kɝb)
= check (tʃɛk)
= retard (rɪ'tɑrd)
= restrain (rɪ'stren)
= *hold back*

hinge (hɪndʒ) *v.* ①裝以鉸鏈
②依靠

① = fasten ('fæsn̩)
= clasp (klæsp)

= lock (lɑk)
= separate ('sɛpəˌret)
② = depend (dɪ'pɛnd)
= *rest on*
= *revolve on*

hint (hɪnt) *n.* 暗示

= suggest (səg'dʒɛst , sə'dʒɛst)
= imply (ɪm'plaɪ)
= intimate ('ɪntəmɪt)
= insinuate (ɪn'sɪnjuˌet)

hire (haɪr) *v.* ①僱 ②租

① = employ (ɪm'plɔɪ)
= engage (ɪn'gedʒ)
= use (juz)
② = lease (lis)
= let (lɛt)
= rent (rɛnt)
= charter ('tʃɑrtɚ)

hiss (hɪs) *v.* 發嘶嘶聲

= boo (bu)
= hoot (hut)

history ('hɪstrɪ , 'hɪstərɪ) *n.* 歷史

= record ('rɛkəd)
= chronicle ('krɑnɪkl̩)
= annals ('ænl̩z)

hit (hɪt) ① *v.* 打擊 ② *v.* 發現
③ *v.* 影響 ④ *n.* 成功

① = strike (straɪk)
= blow (blo)
= knock (nɑk)
= pouch (pautʃ)

= poke〔pok〕
= smack〔smæk〕
= whack〔hwæk〕
= slug〔slʌg〕
= bat〔bæt〕
= crack〔kræk〕
= swat〔swɑt〕
= sock〔sɑk〕
= clout〔klaʊt〕
② = meet〔mit〕
= find〔faɪnd〕
= discover〔dɪs'kʌvɚ〕
= reach〔ritʃ〕
= *arrive at*
= *come upon*
③ = affect〔ə'fɛkt〕
= impress〔ɪm'prɛs〕
= strike〔straɪk〕
④ = success〔sək'sɛs〕

hitch〔hɪtʃ〕① *v.* 繫住
② *v.* 猛拉 ③ *n.* 障礙

① = fasten〔'fæsn̩〕
= hook〔hʊk〕
= clasp〔klæsp〕
= bind〔baɪnd〕
= tie〔taɪ〕
② = jerk〔dʒɝk〕
= yank〔jæŋk〕
③ = obstacle〔'ɑbstəkl̩〕
= stopping〔'stɑpɪŋ〕
= block〔blɑk〕
= catch〔kætʃ〕
= snag〔snæg〕
= difficulty〔'dɪfə,kʌltɪ〕
= drawback〔'drɔ,bæk〕

hoard〔hord, hɔrd〕*v.*
貯藏金錢，貨物等

= save〔sev〕
= store〔stor, stɔr〕
= collect〔kə'lɛkt〕
= accumulate〔ə'kjumjə,let〕
= amass〔ə'mæs〕
= gather〔'gæðɚ〕

hoarse〔hors〕*adj.* 嘶啞的

= rough〔rʌf〕
= gruff〔grʌf〕
= harsh〔harʃ〕
= husky〔'hʌskɪ〕

hoary〔'horɪ〕*adj.* 灰白的；
鬢髮斑白的

= old〔old〕
= aged〔'edʒɪd〕
= elderly〔'ɛldɚlɪ〕
= white〔hwaɪt〕
= gray〔gre〕

hobble〔'hɑbl̩〕*v.* 蹣跚

= limp〔lɪmp〕
= totter〔'tɑtɚ〕
= stagger〔'stægɚ〕

hobby〔'hɑbɪ〕*n.* 嗜好

= avocation〔,ævə'keʃən〕
= pastime〔'pæs,taɪm, 'pɑs-〕

hobgoblin〔'hɑbgɑblɪn〕*n.*
妖鬼；惡鬼

= goblin〔'gɑblɪn〕
= imp〔ɪmp〕

H

= elf (ɛlf)

= ghost (gost)

hobo ('hobo) *n.* 流浪漢

= tramp (træmp)

= vagabond ('vægə,band)

= vagrant ('vegrənt)

hodgepodge ('hadʒ,padʒ) *n.*
混雜物

= mixture ('mɪkstʃə)

= mess (mɛs)

= jumble ('dʒʌmbļ)

= scramble ('skræmbļ)

hoe (ho) *v.* 鋤;掘

= plow (plau)

= dig (dɪg)

= loosen ('lusṇ)

= till (tɪl)

hog (hag) *n.* ①豬 ②貪婪者

① = pig (pɪg)

= swine (swaɪn)

② = glutton ('glʌtṇ)

= *greedy person*

hoist (hɔɪst) *v.* 升起

= raise (rez)

= lift (lɪft)

= elevate ('ɛlə,vet)

= boost (bust)

hold (hold) *v.* ①握住 ②容納
③佔有 ④有效 ⑤認爲

① = grasp (græsp)

= keep (kip)

= grip (grɪp)

= clutch (klʌtʃ)

= retain (rɪ'ten)

= *cling to*

② = contain (kən'ten)

= support (sə'port)

= bear (bɛr)

= carry ('kærɪ)

③ = have (hæv)

= maintain (men'ten , mən'ten)

= occupy ('akjə,paɪ)

④ = apply (ə'plaɪ)

= *stand up*

= *be true*

⑤ = think (θɪŋk)

= consider (kən'sɪdə)

= suppose (sə'poz)

= assume (ə'sjum)

= presume (prɪ'zum)

= regard (rɪ'gard)

= surmise (sə'maɪz)

holding ('holdɪŋ) *n.* 土地;財產

= land (lænd)

= property ('prapətɪ)

= possession (pə'zɛʃən)

= ownership ('onə,ʃɪp)

= title ('taɪtļ)

= claim (klem)

= stake (stek)

hole (hol) *n.* 洞

= opening ('openɪŋ)

= hollow ('halo)

= pit (pɪt)

= gap (gæp)

= chasm ('kæzəm)
= cavity ('kævətɪ)

holiday ('hɑlə‚de) *n.* 假日

= vacation (ve'keʃən , və-)
= leave (liv)
= furlough ('fɝlo)

hollow ('hɑlo) *adj.* ①空的
②凹陷的 ③虛偽的 ④飢餓的

① = empty ('ɛmptɪ)
= vacant ('vekənt)
= bare (bɛr)
= void (vɔɪd)
= blank (blæŋk)
= barren ('bærən)
② = deep (dip)
= sunken ('sʌŋkən)
= concave (kɑn'kev , 'kɑnkev)
③ = false (fɔls)
= unreal (ʌn'riəl , ʌn'ril)
= insincere (‚ɪnsɪn'sɪr)
④ = hungry ('hʌŋgrɪ)
= starved (stɑrvd)
= famished ('fæmɪʃt)
= ravenous ('rævənəs)
= empty ('ɛmptɪ)

holy ('holɪ) *adj.* 聖潔的

= sacred ('sekrɪd)
= spiritual ('spɪrɪtʃuəl)
= pure (pjur)
= religious (rɪ'lɪdʒəs)
= godly ('gɑdlɪ)

homage ('hɑmɪdʒ , 'am-) *n.* 尊重

= respect (rɪ'spɛkt)

= honor ('ɑnɚ)
= reverence ('rɛvərəns)
= regard (rɪ'gɑrd)
= esteem (ə'stim)
= deference ('dɛfərəns)
= acknowledgment
(ək'nɑlɪdʒmənt)

home (hom) *n.* ①住所
②庇護所

① = abode (ə'bod)
= dwelling ('dwɛlɪŋ)
= residence ('rɛzədəns)
= hearth (hɑrθ)
= habitat ('hæbə‚tæt)
② = institution (‚ɪnstə'tjuʃən)
= sanitarium (‚sænə'tɛrɪəm)
= hospital ('hɑspɪtl̩)
= asylum (ə'saɪləm)

homeland ('hom‚lænd) *n.* 故鄉

= *native land*
= *mother country*

homely ('homlɪ) *adj.* ①醜的
②普通的 ③似家的

① = ugly ('ʌglɪ)
= plain (plen)
= unattractive (‚ʌnə'træktɪv)
② = simple ('sɪmpl̩)
= ordinary ('ɔrdn̩‚ɛrɪ , 'ɔrdnɛrɪ)
= common ('kɑmən)
③ = homelike ('hom‚laɪk)
= comfortable ('kʌmfɚtəbl̩)
= cozy ('kozɪ)
= domestic (də'mɛstɪk)

H

homestead (ˈhomˌstɛd) *n.* 田園

= farm (fɑrm)
= plantation (plænˈteʃən)
= *house and grounds*

homework (ˈhomˌwɝk) *n.*
家庭作業

= lesson (ˈlɛsn̩)
= task (tæsk , tɑsk)
= assignment (əˈsaɪnmənt)
= duty (ˈdjutɪ)
= exercise (ˈɛksɚˌsaɪz)

honest (ˈɑnɪst) *adj.* 誠實的

= fair (fɛr)
= upright (ˈʌpˌraɪt , ʌpˈraɪt)
= truthful (ˈtruθfəl)
= frank (fræŋk)
= open (ˈopən)
= genuine (ˈdʒɛnjuɪn)
= pure (pjur)
= sincere (sɪnˈsɪr)

honk (hɔŋk , hɑŋk) *v.* 吹(響);
鳴(笛)

= toot (tut)
= blast (blæst)
= blare (blɛr , blær)

honor (ˈɑnɚ) *n.* 聲譽

= glory (ˈglorɪ , ˈglɔrɪ)
= fame (fem)
= renown (rɪˈnaun)
= respect (rɪˈspɛkt)
= regard (rɪˈgɑrd)
= esteem (əˈstim)
= homage (ˈhɑmɪdʒ , ˈɑm-)

= deference (ˈdɛfərəns)
= praise (prez)

hood (hud) *n.* 覆蓋之物

= cover (ˈkʌvɚ)
= lid (lɪd)
= veil (vel)
= cap (kæp)

hoodlum (ˈhudləm) *n.* 流氓

= rowdy (ˈraudɪ)
= ruffian (ˈrʌfɪən , ˈrʌfjən)
= thug (θʌg)
= tough (tʌf)

hoof (huf , huf) *n.* 足掌

= foot (fut)
= paw (pɔ)

hook (huk) ① *v.* 鉤
② *v.* 引(人)上鉤;欺騙
③ *n.* 掛物鉤

① = fasten (ˈfæsn̩ , ˈfɑsn̩)
= clasp (klæsp)
= bind (baɪnd)
= clip (klɪp)
= snap (snæp)
= latch (lætʃ)
② = catch (kætʃ)
= snare (snɛr)
= trap (træp)
③ = hanger (ˈhæŋɚ)
= wire (waɪr)
= crook (kruk)

hoop (hup) *n.* 圈狀物

= circle (ˈsɝkl̩)

= band（bænd）
= ring（rɪŋ）

hoot（hut）*n.* 喊叫聲

= yell（jɛl）
= call（kɔl）
= cry（kraɪ）

hop（hɑp）*n. v.* 跳躍

= spring（sprɪŋ）
= jump（dʒʌmp）
= vault（vɔlt）

hope（hop）*v.* 希望

= desire（dɪ'zaɪr）
= expect（ɪk'spɛkt）
= *wish for*
= *yearn for*

horde（hord , hɔrd）*n.* 群衆

= crowd（kraud）
= swarm（swɔrm）
= multitude（'mʌltə,tjud）
= throng（θrɔŋ）
= mob（mɑb）
= force（fors , fɔrs）
= pack（pæk）

horizontal（,hɔrə'zɑrntḷ）*adj.* 平的

= level（'lɛvḷ）
= flat（flæt）
= even（'ivən）
= plane（plen）

horrible（'hɑrəbḷ）*adj.* 可怕的

= frightful（'fraɪtfəl）

= shocking（'ʃɑkɪŋ）
= terrible（'tɛrəbḷ）
= dreadful（'drɛdfəl）
= outrageous（aut'redʒəs）
= horrid（'hɔrɪd）
= ghastly（'gæstlɪ , 'gɑst-）
= deplorable（dɪ'plorəbḷ , -'plɔr-）
= scandalous（'skændḷəs）

horse（hɔrs）*n.* 馬

= steed（stid）
= colt（kolt）
= mare（mɛr）
= stallion（'stæljən）
= stud（stʌd）

horseplay（'hɔrs,ple）*n.* 惡作劇

= rowdiness（'raudɪnəs）
= *boisterous fun*

hose（hoz）*n.* ①襪子　②管子

① = stockings（'stɑkɪŋz）
= socks（sɑks）
② = tube（tjub）
= pipe（paɪp）

hospitable（'hɑspɪtəbḷ）*adj.* 招待慇懃的；好客的

= friendly（'frɛndlɪ）
= receptive（rɪ'sɛptɪv）
= welcoming（'wɛlkəmɪŋ）
= cordial（'kɔrdʒəl）
= amiable（'emɪəbḷ）
= gracious（'greʃəs）
= neighborly（'nebəlɪ）
= generous（'dʒɛnərəs）

H

hospital ('hɑspɪtḷ) *n.* 醫院

  = sanitarium (ˌsænə'tɛrɪəm)
  = clinic ('klɪnɪk)

host (host) *n.* ①主人 ②極多

① = receptionist (rɪ'sɛpʃənɪst)
  = proprietor (prə'praɪətə)
② = quantity ('kwɑntətɪ)
  = multitude ('mʌltəˌtjud)
  = score (skor , skɔr)
  = flock (flɑk)
  = army ('ɑrmɪ)
  = swarm (swɔrm)
  = *large number*

hostel ('hɑstḷ) *n.* 旅社

  = inn (ɪn)
  = hotel (ho'tɛl)
  = tavern ('tævən)
  = roadhouse ('rodˌhaʊs)

hostile ('hɑstḷ , 'hɑstaɪl) *adj.*
敵對的

  = unfriendly (ʌn'frɛndlɪ)
  = unfavorable (ʌn'fevrəbḷ)
  = bitter ('bɪtə)
  = antagonistic (ænˌtægə'nɪstɪk)
  = aggressive (ə'grɛsɪv)
  = belligerent (bə'lɪdʒərənt)
  = militant ('mɪlətənt)

hot (hɑt) *adj.* ①極熱的 ②辣的
③新鮮的

① = torrid ('tɔrɪd , 'tɑr-)
  = burning ('bɜnɪŋ)
  = boiling ('bɔɪlɪŋ)

  = fiery ('faɪrɪ , 'faɪərɪ)
② = spicy ('spaɪsɪ)
  = sharp (ʃɑrp)
  = pepper ('pɛpə)
  = nippy ('nɪpɪ)
  = tangy ('tæŋɪ)
③ = fresh (frɛʃ)
  = new (nju , nu)

hotel (ho'tɛl) *n.* 旅館

  = inn (ɪn)
  = tavern ('tævən)
  = roadhouse ('rodˌhaʊs)
  = lodging ('lɑdʒɪŋ)
  = hostel ('hɑstḷ)
  = motel (mo'tɛl)

hothouse ('hɑtˌhaʊs) *n.* 溫室

  = nursery ('nɜsərɪ)
  = conservatory (kən'sɜvəˌtorɪ ,
    -ˌtɔrɪ)
  = greenhouse ('grinˌhaʊs)

hound (haʊnd) ① *v.* 追捕
② *v.* 激勵 ③ *n.* 獵犬

① = hunt (hʌnt)
  = chase (tʃes)
  = seek (sik)
  = search (sɜtʃ)
  = follow ('falo)
② = urge (ɜdʒ)
  = press (prɛs)
  = insist (ɪn'sɪst)
③ = dog (dɔg)

house (haʊs) *n.* ①住所 ②觀眾

① = shelter ('ʃɛltə)

= building ('bɪldɪŋ)
= dwelling ('dwɛlɪŋ)
= lodge (ladʒ)
= residence ('rɛzədəns)
= home (hom)
② = audience ('ɔdɪəns)
= congregation (,kaŋgrɪ'geʃən)

household ('haʊs,hold , -,old)
n. 家庭

= family ('fæməlɪ)
= brood (brud)
= folks (foks)

housekeeper ('haʊs,kipɚ) *n.*
主婦

= mistress ('mɪstrɪs)
= homemaker ('hom,mekɚ)
= housewife ('haʊs,waɪf)

hovel ('hʌvl̩ , 'havl̩) *n.*
簡陋的房屋

= shack (ʃæk)
= pigsty ('pɪg,staɪ)

hover ('hʌvɚ , 'havɚ) *v.* ①漂流
②躊躇

① = float (flot)
= sail (sel)
= drift (drɪft)
② = waver ('wevɚ)
= hesitate ('hɛzə,tet)
= pause (pɔz)
= falter ('fɔltɚ)

however (haʊ'ɛvɚ) *adv.* ①雖然
②不論如何

① = nevertheless (,nɛvɚðɚ'lɛs)
= although (ɔl'ðo)
= notwithstanding
(,natwɪθ'stændɪŋ)
= yet (jɛt)
= still (stɪl)
= but (bət)
② = whatever (hwat'ɛvɚ)
= whatsoever (,hwatso'ɛvɚ)

howl (haʊl) *n. v.* 咆哮

= cry (kraɪ)
= yell (jɛl)
= shout (ʃaʊt)
= bawl (bɔl)
= scream (skrim)
= screech (skritʃ)
= roar (ror , rɔr)
= bellow ('bɛlo)
= bark (bark)
= yelp (jɛlp)
= wail (wel)

hub (hʌb) *n.* 中心

= center ('sɛntɚ)
= middle ('mɪdl̩)
= nucleus ('njuklɪəs)
= core (kor)

hubbub ('hʌbʌb) *n.* 嘈雜聲

= noise (nɔɪz)
= uproar ('ʌp,ror , -,rɔr)
= racket ('rækɪt)
= din (dɪn)
= clamor ('klæmɚ)
= tumult ('tjumʌlt)

H

= fracas ('frekəs)

= ado (ə'du)

= fuss (fʌs)

= turmoil ('tɜmɔɪl)

= bustle ('bʌsḷ)

= row (raʊ)

= commotion (kə'moʃən)

= rumpus ('rʌmpəs)

huddle ('hʌdḷ) v. 聚集

= assemble (ə'sɛmbḷ)

= crowd (kraʊd)

= gather ('gæðə)

= cluster ('klʌstə)

= congregate ('kɑŋgrɪ,get)

= *flock together*

hue (hju) n. 色度

= color ('kʌlə)

= tint (tɪnt)

= shade (ʃed)

huff (hʌf) ① v. 噴氣；吹氣
② n. 發怒

① = puff (pʌf)

= blow (blo)

= exhale (ɛks'hel , ɪg'zel)

② = *fit of anger*

hug (hʌg) v. 緊抱

= hold (hold)

= clasp (klæsp)

= embrace (ɪm'bres)

= press (prɛs)

= enfold (ɪn'fold)

= squeeze (skwiz)

huge (hjudʒ) adj. 巨大的

= great (gret)

= vast (væst , vɑst)

= immense (ɪ'mɛns)

= enormous (ɪ'nɔrməs)

= gigantic (dʒaɪ'gæntɪk)

= tremendous (trɪ'mɛndəs)

= monumental (,mɑnjə'mɛntḷ)

= *very large*

hulk (hʌlk) n. ①廢船
②笨大的人或物

① = ship (ʃɪp)

= boat (bot)

② = clod (klɑd)

= oaf (of)

hum (hʌm) v. ①閉口低唱；
哼唱 ②忙碌

① = drone (dron)

= buzz (bʌz)

= murmur ('mɜmə)

② = activate ('æktɪ,vet)

= busy ('bɪzɪ)

human ('hjumən) n. 人

= man (mæn)

= person ('pɜsn̩)

= mortal ('mɔrtḷ)

= being ('biɪŋ)

humane (hju'men) adj.
仁愛的；有人情味的

= kind (kaɪnd)

= good (gʊd)

= gracious ('greʃəs)

= warmhearted ('wɔrm'hɑrtɪd)

= brotherly ('brʌðəlɪ)

= sympathetic (ˌsɪmpə'θɛtɪk)

humble ('hʌmbḷ) *adj.* 謙遜的

= modest ('mɑdɪst)

= meek (mik)

= plain (plen)

= simple ('sɪmpḷ)

= homely ('homlɪ)

= unpretentious (ˌʌnprɪ'tɛnʃəs)

humbug ('hʌmˌbʌg) *v.* 欺騙

= cheat (tʃit)

= deceive (dɪ'siv)

= trick (trɪk)

= hoax (hoks)

humid ('hjumɪd) *adj.* 潮濕的

= moist (mɔɪst)

= damp (dæmp)

= wet (wɛt)

= muggy ('mʌgɪ)

humiliate (hju'mɪlɪˌet) *v.* 屈辱

= embarrass (ɪm'bærəs)

= disgrace (dɪs'gres)

= shame (ʃem)

= mortify ('mɔrtəˌfaɪ)

= offend (ə'fɛnd)

= insult (ɪn'sʌlt)

= dishonor (dɪs'ɑnə)

humor ('hjumə , 'ju-) ① *v.* 縱容
② *n.* 幽默感 ③ *n.* 心情

① = pamper ('pæmpə)

= spoil (spɔɪl)

= coddle ('kɑdḷ)

= oblige (ə'blaɪdʒ)

= please (pliz)

= satisfy ('sætɪsˌfaɪ)

= *cater to*

= *give in to*

② = wit (wɪt)

= pleasantry ('plɛzn̩trɪ)

= comedy ('kɑmədɪ)

③ = mood (mud)

= temper ('tɛmpə)

= disposition (ˌdɪspə'zɪʃən)

= *frame of mind*

hump (hʌmp) *n.* 圓丘

= bump (bʌmp)

= bulge (bʌldʒ)

= ridge (rɪdʒ)

= hunch (hʌntʃ)

hunch (hʌntʃ) *n.* ①瘤　②預感

① = hump (hʌmp)

= bump (bʌmp)

= bulge (bʌldʒ)

② = feeling ('filɪŋ)

= suspicion (sə'spɪʃən)

= impression (ɪm'prɛʃən)

hunger ('hʌŋgə) *n.* 慾望

= desire (dɪ'zaɪr)

= eagerness ('igənɪs)

= appetite ('æpəˌtaɪt)

= craving ('krevɪŋ)

hunk (hʌŋk) *n.* 塊

= lump (lʌmp)

H

= piece (pis)

= mass (mæs)

= bulk (bʌlk)

= wad (wɑd)

= gob (gɑb)

= chunk (tʃʌŋk)

hunt (hʌnt) *v.* 捕捉

= search (sɝtʃ)

= seek (sik)

= look (lʊk)

= pursue (pɚˈsu , -sju)

= chase (tʃes)

hurdle (ˈhɝdḷ) ① *v.* 跳越
② *n.* 障礙

① = leap (lip)

= jump (dʒʌmp)

= vault (vɔlt)

= bound (baʊnd)

② = obstacle (ˈɑbstəkḷ)

= block (blɑk)

= difficulty (ˈdɪfəˌkʌltɪ)

= hitch (hɪtʃ)

= catch (kætʃ)

= snag (snæg)

= barrier (ˈbærɪɚ)

hurl (hɝl) *v.* 擲

= throw (θro)

= fling (flɪŋ)

= sling (slɪŋ)

= pitch (pɪtʃ)

= toss (tɔs)

= cast (kæst , kɑst)

= heave (hiv)

= chuck (tʃʌk)

= flip (flɪp)

hurrah (həˈrɔ , -ˈrɑ) *n.*
歡呼聲

= cheer (tʃɪr)

= cry (kraɪ)

= shout (ʃaʊt)

= yell (jɛl)

= applause (əˈplɔz)

hurricane (ˈhɝɪˌken) *n.* 颶風

= storm (stɔrm)

= cyclone (ˈsaɪklon)

= blizzard (ˈblɪzɚd)

= tornado (tɔrˈnedo)

= squall (skwɔl)

hurry (ˈhɝɪ) *v.* 趕快

= hasten (ˈhesn̩)

= speed (spid)

= urge (ɝdʒ)

= rush (rʌʃ)

= accelerate (ækˈsɛləˌret)

= hustle (ˈhʌsḷ)

hurt (hɝt) *v.* 傷害

= injure (ˈɪndʒɚ)

= bruise (bruz)

= harm (hɑrm)

= damage (ˈdæmɪdʒ)

= wrong (rɔŋ)

= impair (ɪmˈpɛr)

= pain (pen)

= wound (wund)

= distress (dɪˈstrɛs)

H

= grieve〔griv〕
= offend〔əˈfɛnd〕

hurtle〔ˈhɝtl̩〕*v.* 碰撞

= jostle〔ˈdʒɑsl̩〕
= collide〔kəˈlaɪd〕
= clash〔klæʃ〕
= strike〔straɪk〕
= bump〔bʌmp〕
= crash〔kræʃ〕

husband〔ˈhʌzbənd〕① *v.* 節儉
② *n.* 丈夫

① = save〔sev〕
= economize〔ɪˈkɑnəˌmaɪz, i-〕
= preserve〔prɪˈzɝv〕
= keep〔kip〕
= reserve〔rɪˈzɝv〕
= scrimp〔skrɪmp〕
= skimp〔skɪmp〕
② = spouse〔spaʊz〕
= mate〔met〕
= *married man*

hush〔hʌʃ〕*v.* 使安靜

= silence〔ˈsaɪləns〕
= quiet〔ˈkwaɪət〕
= mute〔mjut〕
= muffle〔ˈmʌfl̩〕
= calm〔kɑm〕

husky〔ˈhʌskɪ〕① *adj.* 壯碩的
② *adj.* 粗糙的　③ *n.* 愛斯基摩犬

① = strong〔strɔŋ〕
= sturdy〔ˈstɝdɪ〕
= mighty〔ˈmaɪtɪ〕

= powerful〔ˈpaʊəfəl〕
= rugged〔ˈrʌgɪd〕
= muscular〔ˈmʌskjələ〕
= athletic〔æθˈlɛtɪk〕
= hefty〔ˈhɛftɪ〕
= beefy〔ˈbifɪ〕
= strapping〔ˈstræpɪŋ〕
= well-built〔ˈwɛlˈbɪlt〕
② = hoarse〔hors〕
= harsh〔harʃ〕
= rough〔rʌf〕
= coarse〔kors, kɔrs〕
= raspy〔ˈræspɪ, ˈrɑs-〕
③ = *Eskimo dog*

hustle〔ˈhʌsl̩〕*v.* ①催促　②推擠

① = hasten〔ˈhesn̩〕
= speed〔spid〕
= urge〔ɝdʒ〕
= rush〔rʌf〕
② = push〔puʃ〕
= shove〔ʃʌv〕
= jostle〔ˈdʒɑsl̩〕
= prod〔prɑd〕
= bump〔bʌmp〕
= jolt〔dʒolt〕
= bounce〔baʊns〕

hut〔hʌt〕*n.* 簡陋的小屋

= cabin〔ˈkæbɪn〕
= shed〔ʃɛd〕
= shanty〔ˈʃæntɪ〕
= shack〔ʃæk〕

hybrid〔ˈhaɪbrɪd〕*n.* 混血兒

= mongrel〔ˈmʌŋgrəl, ˈmɑŋ-〕

H

= crossbreed ('krɔs,brid)

= half-breed ('hæf,brid)

hydrophobia (,haɪdrə'fobɪə)
n. 恐水症

= rabies ('rebiz)

hymn (hɪm) *n.* 讚美詩

= psalm (sɑm)

= spiritual ('spɪrɪtʃuəl)

= *song of praise*

hypnotize ('hɪpnə,taɪz) *v.* 對…
施催眠術

= entrance (ɪn'træns)

= spellbind ('spɛl,baɪnd)

= mesmerize ('mɛsmə,raɪz ,
'mɛz-)

hypocrite ('hɪpə,krɪt) *n.* 偽善者

= pretender (prɪ'tɛndə)

hysterical (hɪs'tɛrɪkḷ) *adj.*
過度興奮的

= uncontrollable (,ʌnkən'troləbḷ)

= frenzied ('frɛnzɪd)

= frantic ('fræntɪk)

= delirious (dɪ'lɪrɪəs)

= overexcited (,ovərɪk'saɪtɪd)

= upset ('ʌp'sɛt)

= *beside oneself*

I

ice (aɪs) *n.* 冰

= sleet (slit)

= *frozen water*

icebox ('aɪs,bɑks) *n.* 冰箱

= refrigerator (rɪ'frɪdʒə,retə)

ice cream ('aɪs'krim) *n.* 冰淇淋

= sherbet ('ʃɜbɪt)

= *frozen dessert*

icing ('aɪsɪŋ) *n.* 糖霜

= frosting ('frɔstɪŋ , 'frɑst-)

= topping ('tɑpɪŋ)

idea (aɪ'diə , -'dɪə) *n.* 意見

= thought (θɔt)

= plan (plæn)

= notion ('noʃən)

= fancy ('fænsɪ)

= opinion (ə'pɪnjən)

ideal (aɪ'diəl , aɪ'dil , aɪ'dɪəl)
adj. 理想的

= perfect ('pɜfɪkt)

= faultless ('fɔltlɪs)

= flawless ('flɔlɪs)

= model ('mɑdḷ)

identical (aɪ'dɛntɪkḷ) *adj.*
完全相同的

= same (sem)

= alike (ə'laɪk)

= duplicate ('djupləkɪt)

= *exactly like*

identify (aɪ'dɛntə,faɪ) *v.* 認出；
分辨

= recognize ('rɛkəg,naɪz)

= know〔no〕
= place〔ples〕
= distinguish〔dɪ'stɪŋgwɪʃ〕
= name〔nem〕
= spot〔spat〕
= nail〔nel〕
= tell〔tɛl〕
= label〔'lebḷ〕
= tag〔tæg〕
= designate〔'dɛzɪgˌnet〕
= *make out*

idiot〔'ɪdɪət〕*n.* 白癡

= simpleton〔'sɪmpḷtən〕
= imbecile〔'ɪmbəsḷ, -ˌsɪl〕
= moron〔'moran, 'mɔr-〕
= fool〔ful〕
= half-wit〔'hæfˌwɪt〕

idle〔'aɪdḷ〕*adj.* ①不忙的
②懶惰的 ③無用的 ④無由的

① = inactive〔ɪn'æktɪv〕
= unoccupied〔ʌn'akjəˌpaɪd〕
= *at leisure*
② = lazy〔'lezɪ〕
= loafing〔'lofɪŋ〕
③ = useless〔'juslɪs〕
= vain〔ven〕
= futile〔'fjutḷ, -tɪl〕
= worthless〔'wɜθlɪs〕
④ = unwarranted〔ʌn'wɔrəntɪd, -'war-〕
= groundless〔'graundlɪs〕
= unfounded〔ʌn'faundɪd〕

idol〔'aɪdḷ〕*n.* ①偶像 ②寵愛物

① = god〔gad〕
② = favorite〔'fevərɪt〕
= darling〔'darlɪŋ〕

igloo〔'ɪglu〕*n.* 用雪砌的小屋

= *ice hut*
= *Eskimo hut*

ignite〔ɪg'naɪt〕*v.* 燃燒

= burn〔bɜn〕
= light〔laɪt〕
= kindle〔'kɪndḷ〕
= stoke〔stok〕
= *set afire*

ignoble〔ɪg'nobḷ〕*adj.* 下流的

= mean〔min〕
= base〔bes〕
= low〔lo〕
= shameful〔'ʃemfʊl〕
= disgraceful〔dɪs'gresfəl〕
= *without honor*

ignorant〔'ɪgnərənt〕*adj.* 無知的

= unintelligent〔ˌʌnɪn'tɛlədʒənt〕
= foolish〔'fulɪʃ〕
= uninformed〔ˌʌnɪn'fɔrmd〕
= unaware〔ˌʌnə'wɛr〕
= uneducated〔ʌn'ɛdʒəˌketɪd〕

ignore〔ɪg'nor, -'nɔr〕*v.* 忽視

= disregard〔ˌdɪsrɪ'gard〕
= overlook〔ˌovə'luk〕
= snub〔snʌb〕
= slight〔slaɪt〕
= avoid〔ə'vɔɪd〕

I

ill ﹝ ɪl ﹞ *adj.* ①生病的　②邪惡的

① = sick ﹝ sɪk ﹞
　 = ailing ﹝ 'elɪŋ ﹞
　 = unwell ﹝ ʌn'wɛl ﹞
　 = indisposed ﹝ ˌɪndɪ'spozd ﹞
　 = rocky ﹝ 'rɑkɪ ﹞
　 = *out of sorts*
　 = *below par*
　 = *under the weather*
② = evil ﹝ 'ivḷ ﹞
　 = bad ﹝ bæd ﹞
　 = wrong ﹝ rɔŋ ﹞

illegal ﹝ ɪ'ligḷ ﹞ *adj.* 犯法的

　 = unlawful ﹝ ʌn'lɔfəl ﹞
　 = criminal ﹝ 'krɪmənḷ ﹞
　 = illegitimate ﹝ ˌɪlɪ'dʒɪtəmɪt ﹞

illegible ﹝ ɪ'lɛdʒəbḷ ﹞ *adj.* 難讀的

　 = unclear ﹝ ʌn'klɪr ﹞
　 = indistinct ﹝ ˌɪndɪ'stɪŋkt ﹞
　 = unreadable ﹝ ʌn'ridəbḷ ﹞

illiterate ﹝ ɪ'lɪtərɪt ﹞ *adj.*
目不識丁的

　 = uneducated ﹝ ʌn'ɛdʒəˌketɪd ﹞
　 = uncultured ﹝ ʌn'kʌltʃəd ﹞
　 = unlearned ﹝ ʌn'lɝnɪd ﹞
　 = ignorant ﹝ 'ɪgnərənt ﹞

ill-natured ﹝ 'ɪl'netʃəd ﹞ *adj.*
性情惡劣的

　 = cross ﹝ krɔs ﹞
　 = disagreeable ﹝ ˌdɪsə'griəbḷ ﹞
　 = bad-tempered ﹝ 'bæd'tɛmpəd ﹞

illogical ﹝ ɪ'lɑdʒɪkḷ ﹞ *adj.*
不合邏輯的

　 = unreasonable ﹝ ʌn'riznəbḷ ﹞
　 = senseless ﹝ 'sɛnslɪs ﹞
　 = unsound ﹝ ʌn'saund ﹞
　 = unscientific ﹝ ˌʌnsaɪən'tɪfɪk ﹞

illuminate ﹝ ɪ'luməˌnet , ɪ'lju- ﹞
v. ①照明　②說明

① = light ﹝ laɪt ﹞
　 = brighten ﹝ 'braɪtṇ ﹞
　 = spotlight ﹝ 'spɑtˌlaɪt ﹞
② = clarify ﹝ 'klærəˌfaɪ ﹞
　 = explain ﹝ ɪk'splen ﹞
　 = simplify ﹝ 'sɪmpləˌfaɪ ﹞
　 = show ﹝ ʃo ﹞
　 = illustrate ﹝ 'ɪləstret , ɪ'lʌstret ﹞

illusion ﹝ ɪ'ljuʒən ﹞ *n.* 幻影

　 = deception ﹝ dɪ'sɛpʃən ﹞
　 = delusion ﹝ dɪ'luʒən ﹞
　 = trick ﹝ trɪk ﹞
　 = misconception
　 　 ﹝ ˌmɪskən'sɛpʃən ﹞

illustrate ﹝ 'ɪləstret , ɪ'lʌstret ﹞
v. ①說明　②畫插圖

① = clarify ﹝ 'klærəˌfaɪ ﹞
　 = explain ﹝ ɪk'splen ﹞
　 = show ﹝ ʃo ﹞
　 = demonstrate ﹝ 'dɛmənˌstret ﹞
② = picture ﹝ 'pɪktʃə ﹞
　 = portray ﹝ por'tre , pɔr- ﹞
　 = represent ﹝ ˌrɛprɪ'zɛnt ﹞

I

illustrious (ɪˈlʌstrɪəs) *adj.*
著名的

= famous (ˈfeməs)
= great (gret)
= outstanding (ˈaʊtˈstændɪŋ)
= splendid (ˈsplɛndɪd)
= radiant (ˈredɪənt)
= bright (braɪt)
= shining (ˈʃaɪnɪŋ)
= glorious (ˈglorɪəs , ˈglɔr-)

image (ˈɪmɪdʒ) *n.* 肖像

= likeness (ˈlaɪknɪs)
= representation (ˌrɛprɪzɛnˈteʃən)
= picture (ˈpɪktʃə)
= reflection (rɪˈflɛkʃən)
= vision (ˈvɪʒən)
= appearance (əˈpɪrəns)
= resemblance (rɪˈzɛmbləns)

imagine (ɪˈmædʒɪn) *v.* ①幻想
②以爲

① = envision (ɛnˈvɪʒən , ɪn-)
= fancy (ˈfænsɪ)
= conceive (kənˈsiv)
= dream (drim)
② = suppose (səˈpoz)
= guess (gɛs)
= assume (əˈsjum)
= presume (prɪˈzum)
= gather (ˈgæðə)

imbecile (ˈɪmbəsḷ , -ˌsɪl) *n.* 白癡

= simpleton (ˈsɪmpḷtən)
= idiot (ˈɪdɪət)
= moron (ˈmoran , ˈmɔr-)

= fool (ful)
= half-wit (ˈhæfˌwɪt)

imbed (ɪmˈbɛd) *v.* 圍繞

= enclose (ɪnˈkloz)
= fix (fɪks)
= inset (ɪnˈsɛt)
= inlay (ɪnˈle)

imitate (ˈɪməˌtet) *v.* 仿效

= copy (ˈkapɪ)
= repeat (rɪˈpit)
= mirror (ˈmɪrə)
= reflect (rɪˈflɛkt)
= echo (ˈɛko)
= emulate (ˈɛmjəˌlet)
= *act like*

immaculate (ɪˈmækjəlɪt) *adj.*
純潔的

= pure (pjʊr)
= clean (klin)
= spotless (ˈspatlɪs)

immature (ˌɪməˈtjʊr) *adj.*
未成熟的

= undeveloped (ˌʌndɪˈvɛləpt)
= unripe (ʌnˈraɪp)
= inexperienced (ˌɪnɪkˈspɪrɪənst)
= green (grin)
= childish (ˈtʃaɪldɪʃ)

immeasurable (ɪˈmɛʒərəbḷ ,
ɪmˈmɛʒ-) *adj.* 無限的

= great (gret)
= boundless (ˈbaʊndlɪs)

I

= endless ('ɛndlɪs)
= unlimited (ʌn'lɪmɪtɪd)
= infinite ('ɪnfənɪt)

immediately (ɪ'midɪɪtlɪ) *adv.*
立刻地

= instantly ('ɪnstəntlɪ)
= now (naʊ)
= promptly ('prɑmptlɪ)
= straightway ('stret,we)
= forthwith (forθ'wɪθ , forθ- ,
  -'wɪð)
= quickly ('kwɪklɪ)
= swiftly ('swɪftlɪ)
= directly (də'rɛktlɪ , daɪ-)
= *at once*
= *without delay*

immense (ɪ'mɛns) *adj.*
極廣大的

= huge (hjudʒ)
= large (lɑrdʒ)
= vast (væst , vɑst)
= great (gret)
= stupendous (stju'pɛndəs)
= enormous (ɪ'nɔrməs)
= monumental (,mɑnjə'mɛntḷ)
= mammoth ('mæməθ)
= gigantic (dʒaɪ'gæntɪk)
= giant ('dʒaɪənt)

immerse (ɪ'mɝs) *v.* ①浸
②沈迷於

① = submerge (səb'mɝdʒ)
= plunge (plʌndʒ)
= sink (sɪŋk)

= dip (dɪp)
= inundate ('ɪnʌn,det , ɪn'ʌndet)
= drown (draʊn)
= dunk (dʌŋk)
② = absorb (əb'sɔrb)
= engross (ɪn'gros , ɛn-)
= occupy ('ɑkjə,paɪ)
= engage (ɪn'gedʒ)
= grip (grɪp)
= hold (hold)
= fascinate ('fæsn̩,et)
= enthrall (ɪn'θrɔl)

immigrate ('ɪmə,gret) *v.*
移居入境

= enter ('ɛntɚ)
= *come into*

imminent ('ɪmənənt) *adj.*
即將來臨的

= forthcoming ('forθ'kʌmɪŋ ,
  'forθ-)
= approaching (ə'protʃɪŋ)
= nearing ('nɪrɪŋ)
= impending (ɪm'pɛndɪŋ)

immoral (ɪ'mɔrəl) *adj.* 邪惡的

= wrong (rɔŋ)
= wicked ('wɪkɪd)
= evil ('ivḷ)
= bad (bæd)
= sinful ('sɪnful , -fəl)

immortal (ɪ'mɔrtḷ) *adj.* 不死的

= everlasting (,ɛvɚ'læstɪŋ)
= undying (ʌn'daɪɪŋ)
= eternal (ɪ'tɝnḷ)

immovable (ɪ'muvəbḷ , ɪm'muv-) *adj.* 固定的

= fixed (fɪkst)
= firm (fɜm)
= steadfast ('stɛd,fæst , -fəst)
= stable ('stebḷ)
= stationary ('steʃən,ɛrɪ)

immune (ɪ'mjun) *adj.* 免除的

= resistant (rɪ'zɪstənt)
= exempt (ɪg'zɛmpt , ɛg-)
= clear (klɪr)
= excused (ɪk'skjuzd)
= spared (spɛrd)
= free (fri)

imp (ɪmp) *n.* ①小鬼 ②頑童

① = pixie ('pɪksɪ)
= sprite (spraɪt)
= elf (ɛlf)
= gremlin ('grɛmlɪn)
= *little devil*
② = brat (bræt)
= whippersnapper
('hwɪpə,snæpə)
= mischief-maker
('mɪstʃɪf,mekə)

impact ('ɪmpækt) *n.* 撞擊

= collision (kə'lɪʒən)
= crash (kræʃ)
= bump (bʌmp)
= clash (klæʃ)
= shock (ʃɑk)
= brunt (brʌnt)

impair (ɪm'pɛr) *v.* 傷害

= damage ('dæmɪdʒ)
= harm (hɑrm)
= weaken ('wikən)
= hurt (hɜt)
= break (brek)
= *make worse*

impartial (ɪm'pɑrʃəl) *adj.* 公平的

= fair (fɛr)
= neutral ('njutrəl)
= unprejudiced (ʌn'prɛdʒədɪst)
= unbiased (ʌn'baɪəst)
= indifferent (ɪn'dɪfərənt)
= uninfluenced (ʌn'ɪnfluənst)

impassable (ɪm'pæsəbḷ , -pɑs) *adj.* 不能通行的

= unapproachable (,ʌnə'protʃəbḷ)
= inaccessible (,ɪnək'sɛsəbḷ , ,ɪnæk-)

impassioned (ɪm'pæʃənd) *adj.* 慷慨激昂的

= emotional (ɪ'moʃənḷ)
= ardent ('ɑrdṇt)
= passionate ('pæʃənɪt)
= fervent ('fɜvənt)
= sincere (sɪn'sɪr)
= serious ('sɪrɪəs)
= excited (ɪk'saɪtɪd)
= earnest ('ɜnɪst , -əst)

impassive (ɪm'pæsɪv) *adj.* 麻木的

= unmoved (ʌn'muvd)

I

= unfeeling (ʌn'filɪŋ)

= unemotional (ˌʌnɪ'moʃənḷ)

= unresponsive (ˌʌnrɪ'spɑnsɪv)

= unsympathetic

 (ˌʌnsɪmpə'θɛtɪk)

impatient (ɪm'peʃənt) *adj.*
不耐煩的

= restless ('rɛstlɪs)

= anxious ('æŋkʃəs , 'æŋʃəs)

= eager ('igə)

= intolerant (ɪn'tɑlərənt)

impeach (ɪm'pitʃ) *v.* 控告

= accuse (ə'kjuz)

= charge (tʃɑrdʒ)

= indict (ɪn'daɪt)

= arraign (ə'ren)

= denounce (dɪ'naʊns)

= reproach (rɪ'protʃ)

impede (ɪm'pid) *v.* 阻礙

= hinder ('hɪndə)

= obstruct (əb'strʌkt)

= curb (kɝb)

= inhibit (ɪn'hɪbɪt)

= arrest (ə'rɛst)

= check (tʃɛk)

= retard (rɪ'tard)

= delay (dɪ'le)

= limit ('lɪmɪt)

= confine (kən'faɪn)

= cramp (kræmp)

= hamper ('hæmpə)

= interrupt (ˌɪntə'rʌpt)

impel (ɪm'pɛl) *v.* 推進

= drive (draɪv)

= force (fors , fɔrs)

= cause (kɔz)

= push (pʊʃ)

= move (muv)

= propel (prə'pɛl)

= stimulate ('stɪmjəˌlet)

= compel (kəm'pɛl)

= make (mek)

impenetrable (ɪm'pɛnətrəbḷ)
adj. ①不能進入的　②無法了解的

① = unapproachable (ˌʌnə'protʃəbḷ)

= inaccessible (ˌɪnæk'sɛsəbḷ)

= impassable (ɪm'pæsəbḷ ,
 -'pas-)

= dense (dɛns)

② = obscure (əb'skjʊr)

= unclear (ʌn'klɪr)

= vague (veg)

= unintelligible (ˌʌnɪn'tɛlədʒəbḷ)

imperative (ɪm'pɛrətɪv) *adj.*
必要的

= urgent ('ɝdʒənt)

= necessary ('nɛsəˌsɛrɪ)

= compulsory (kəm'pʌlsərɪ)

= compelling (kəm'pɛlɪŋ)

= pressing ('prɛsɪŋ)

= crucial ('kruʃəl)

= critical ('krɪtɪkḷ)

= mandatory ('mændəˌtorɪ , -ˌtɔrɪ)

imperceptible (ˌɪmpə'sɛptəbḷ)
adj. 微小的

= slight (slaɪt)

= vague (veg)

= unclear (ʌn'klɪr)

imperfect (ɪm'pɝfɪkt) *adj.*
有缺點的

= defective (dɪ'fɛktɪv)

= faulty ('fɔltɪ)

= incomplete (ˌɪnkəm'plit)

= inadequate (ɪn'ædəkwɪt)

= impaired (ɪm'pɛrd)

= blemished ('blɛmɪʃt)

= marred (mɑrd)

= deficient (dɪ'fɪʃənt)

imperial (ɪm'pɪrɪəl) *adj.*
至尊的

= supreme (sə'prim , su-)

= majestic (mə'dʒɛstɪk)

= magnificent (mæg'nɪfəsn̩t)

= regal ('rigl̩)

= royal ('rɔɪəl)

imperious (ɪm'pɪrɪəs) *adj.*
①傲慢的　②急需的

① = haughty ('hɔtɪ)

= arrogant ('ærəgənt)

= domineering (ˌdɑmə'nɪrɪŋ)

= overbearing (ˌovə'bɛrɪŋ)

② = urgent ('ɝdʒənt)

= necessary ('nɛsəˌsɛrɪ)

= compelling (kəm'pɛlɪŋ)

= pressing ('prɛsɪŋ)

= crucial ('kruʃəl)

= critical ('krɪtɪkl̩)

= imperative (ɪm'pɛrətɪv)

impersonal (ɪm'pɝsn̩l̩) *adj.*
客觀的

= impartial (ɪm'pɑrʃəl)

= neutral ('njutrəl)

= unbiased (ʌn'baɪəst)

= detached (dɪ'tætʃt)

= unprejudiced (ʌn'prɛdʒədɪst)

impertinence (ɪm'pɝtn̩əns)
n. 無禮

= insolence ('ɪnsələns)

= impudence ('ɪmpjədəns)

= rudeness ('rudnɪs)

= brazenness ('brez(ə)nnɪs)

= cockiness ('kɑkɪnɪs)

impetuous (ɪm'pɛtʃuəs) *adj.*
猛烈的

= hasty ('hestɪ)

= rash (ræʃ)

= sudden ('sʌdn̩)

= abrupt (ə'brʌpt)

= impulsive (ɪm'pʌlsɪv)

= unexpected (ˌʌnɪk'spɛktɪd)

= reckless ('rɛklɪs)

impetus ('ɪmpətəs) *n.* 衝力；
衝勁

= momentum (mo'mɛntəm)

= thrust (θrʌst)

= push (puʃ)

= *driving force*

implement (*v.* 'ɪmpləˌmɛnt ,
n. 'ɪmpləmənt) ① *v.* 完成
② *n.* 工具

① = complete (kəm'plit)

= *carry out*

= *get done*

= *bring about*

② = tool (tul)

= utensil (ju'tɛnsḷ)

= instrument ('ɪnstrəmənt)

= apparatus (,æpə'retəs ,
,æpə'rætəs)

= device (dɪ'vaɪs)

= appliance (ə'plaɪəns)

= contraption (kən'træpʃən)

implore (ɪm'plor , -'plɔr) v.
懇求

= beg (bɛg)

= plead (plid)

= appeal (ə'pil)

= entreat (ɪn'trit)

= beseech (bɪ'sitʃ)

= pray (pre)

imply (ɪm'plaɪ) v. 暗示

= suggest (səg'dʒɛst , sə'dʒɛst)

= hint (hɪnt)

= intimate ('ɪntə,met)

= infer (ɪn'fɝ)

= insinuate (ɪn'sɪnju,et)

impolite (,ɪmpə'laɪt) adj.
不客氣的

= rude (rud)

= discourteous (dɪs'kɝtɪəs)

= disrespectful (,dɪsrɪ'spɛktfəl)

= insolent ('ɪnsələnt)

= ill-mannered ('ɪl'mænɚd)

import (v. ɪm'port , n. 'ɪmport)

① v. 輸入 ② n. 意義

① = receive (rɪ'siv)

= admit (əd'mɪt)

= introduce (,ɪntrə'djus)

= *bring in*

= *take in*

② = meaning ('minɪŋ)

= significance (sɪg'nɪfəkəns)

= implication (,ɪmplɪ'keʃən)

= substance ('sʌbstəns)

= effect (ə'fɛkt , ɪ- , ɛ-)

= importance (ɪm'pɔrtṇs)

important (ɪm'pɔrtṇt) adj.
重要的

= meaningful ('minɪŋfḷ)

= valuable ('væljʊəbḷ)

= influential (,ɪnflʊ'ɛnʃəl)

= significant (sɪg'nɪfəkənt)

= substantial (səb'stænʃəl)

= prominent ('prɑmənənt)

= outstanding ('aʊt'stændɪŋ)

impose (ɪm'poz) v. 加 (負擔) 於

= put (pʊt)

= place (ples)

= set (sɛt)

= charge (tʃɑrdʒ)

= levy ('lɛvɪ)

= tax (tæks)

= force (fors , fɔrs)

= *burden with*

imposing (ɪm'pozɪŋ) adj.
壯麗的

= impressive (ɪm'prɛsɪv)
= dramatic (drə'mætɪk)
= spectacular (spɛk'tækjələ)
= grand (grænd)
= magnificent (mæg'nɪfəsn̩t)
= splendid ('splɛndɪd)
= noble ('nobl̩)
= glorious ('glorɪəs , 'glɔr-)
= proud (praʊd)
= stately ('stetlɪ)
= elegant ('ɛləgənt)
= majestic (mə'dʒɛstɪk)

impossible (ɪm'pɑsəbl̩) *adj.*
不可能的

= inconceivable (,ɪnkən'sivəbl̩)
= unimaginable (,ʌnɪ'mædʒɪnəbl̩)
= absurd (əb'sɝd)
= unthinkable (ʌn'θɪŋkəbl̩)

impostor (ɪm'pɑstə) *n.* 騙子

= pretender (prɪ'tɛndə)
= deceiver (dɪ'sivə)
= cheat (tʃit)
= impersonator (ɪm'pɝsn̩,etə)
= fraud (frɔd)
= faker ('fekə)

impoverish (ɪm'pɑvərɪʃ) *v.*
耗盡

= ruin ('ruɪn)
= break (brek)
= bankrupt ('bæŋkrʌpt)
= exhaust (ɪg'zɔst , ɛg-)
= deplete (dɪ'plit)
= *make poor*

impractical (ɪm'præktɪkl̩) *adj.*
不切實際的

= unfeasible (ʌn'fizəbl̩)
= unworkable (ʌn'wɝkəbl̩)
= unrealistic (,ʌnrɪə'lɪstɪk)

impregnable (ɪm'prɛgnəbl̩)
adj. 攻不破的；堅定不移的

= resistant (rɪ'zɪstənt)
= strong (strɔŋ)
= unconquerable (ʌn'kɑŋkərəbl̩)
= unassailable (,ʌnə'seləbl̩)
= invincible (ɪn'vɪnsəbl̩)

impress (ɪm'prɛs) *v.* ①影響
②建立 ③銘記

① = affect (ə'fɛkt)
= strike (straɪk)
② = fix (fɪks)
= establish (ə'stæblɪʃ)
= root (rut)
= plant (plænt)
③ = stamp (stæmp)
= mark (mɑrk)
= imprint (ɪm'prɪnt)
= engrave (ɪn'grev)

imprint (ɪm'prɪnt) *v.* 銘記

= mark (mɑrk)
= engrave (ɪn'grev)
= impress (ɪm'prɛs)
= stamp (stæmp)

imprison (ɪm'prɪzn̩) *v.* 禁錮；
監禁

= jail (dʒel)

I

= confine〔kən'faɪn〕

= *lock up*

improbable〔ɪm'prɑbəbl̩〕*adj.*
未必然的；不太可能的

= unlikely〔ʌn'laɪklɪ〕

= doubtful〔'daʊtfəl〕

= questionable〔'kwɛstʃənəbl̩〕

improper〔ɪm'prɑpɚ〕*adj.*
①錯誤的 ②不合適的

① = wrong〔rɔŋ〕

= incorrect〔,ɪnkə'rɛkt〕

= unsuitable〔ʌn'sjutəbl̩, -'sut-〕

= inappropriate〔,ɪnə'proprɪɪt〕

= unfit〔ʌn'fɪt〕

= bad〔bæd〕

② = indecent〔ɪn'disn̩t〕

= unbecoming〔,ʌnbɪ'kʌmɪŋ〕

improve〔ɪm'pruv〕*v.* 改善

= better〔'bɛtɚ〕

= perfect〔pɚ'fɛkt〕

= progress〔prə'grɛs〕

= mend〔mɛnd〕

= develop〔dɪ'vɛləp〕

= advance〔əd'væns〕

improvise〔'ɪmprə,vaɪz,
,ɪmprə'vaɪz〕*v.* 即席而作

= invent〔ɪn'vɛnt〕

= devise〔dɪ'vaɪz〕

= originate〔ə'rɪdʒ,net〕

= ad-lib〔æd'lɪb〕

= *make up*

= *dream up*

= *dash off*

imprudent〔ɪm'prudn̩t〕*adj.*
不加思慮的；輕率的

= rash〔ræʃ〕

= indiscreet〔,ɪndɪ'skrit〕

= overconfident
〔'ovɚ'kɑnfədənt〕

= unwise〔ʌn'waɪz〕

= unsound〔ʌn'saʊnd〕

= unreasonable〔ʌn'riznəbl̩〕

= unintelligent〔,ʌnɪn'tɛlədʒənt〕

= ill-advised〔'ɪləd'vaɪzd〕

impudent〔'ɪmpjədənt〕*adj.*
鹵莽的

= forward〔'fɔrwəd〕

= bold〔bold〕

= immodest〔ɪ'mɑdɪst〕

= pert〔pɝt〕

= impertinent〔ɪm'pɝtn̩ənt〕

= rude〔rud〕

= disrespectful〔,dɪsrɪ'spɛktfəl,
-fʊl〕

= brash〔bræʃ〕

= saucy〔'sɔsɪ〕

impulse〔'ɪmpʌls〕*n.* ①刺激
②情感的衝動

① = thrust〔θrʌst〕

= push〔pʊʃ〕

= urge〔ɝdʒ〕

= pressure〔'prɛʃɚ〕

= compulsion〔kəm'pʌlʃən〕

② = notion〔'noʃən〕

= fancy〔'fænsɪ〕

= flash〔flæʃ〕

= inspiration〔,ɪnspə'reʃən〕

= *sudden thought*

impure (ɪm'pjʊr) *adj.* ①髒的
②猥褻的

① = dirty ('dɝtɪ)
  = unclean (ʌn'klin)
  = polluted (pə'lutɪd)
  = contaminated
    (kən'tæmə,netɪd)
  = infected (ɪn'fɛktɪd)
② = bad (bæd)
  = corrupt (kə'rʌpt)
  = indecent (ɪn'disn̩t)
  = obscene (əb'sin)
  = foul (faʊl)
  = filthy ('fɪlθɪ)
  = nasty ('næstɪ)

inability (,ɪnə'bɪlətɪ) *n.* 無能力

  = incapability (,ɪnkepə'bɪlətɪ ,
    ɪn,ke-)
  = ineptitude (ɪn'ɛptə,tjud)
  = incompetence (ɪn'kampətəns)

inaccessible (,ɪnək'sɛsəbl̩ ,
,ɪnæk-) *adj.* 不能到達的

  = unreachable (ʌn'ritʃəbl̩)
  = unapproachable (,ʌnə'protʃəbl̩)
  = out-of-the-way ('aʊtəvðə,we)
  = *out of reach*

inaccurate (ɪn'ækjərɪt) *adj.* 不正確的

  = incorrect (,ɪnkə'rɛkt)
  = inexact (,ɪnɪg'zækt)

inactive (ɪn'æktɪv) *adj.* 懶惰的

  = idle ('aɪdl̩)

  = sluggish ('slʌgɪʃ)
  = motionless ('moʃənlɪs)
  = still (stɪl)
  = calm (kɑm)

inadequate (ɪn'ædəkwɪt) *adj.* 不充分的

  = deficient (dɪ'fɪʃənt)
  = lacking ('lækɪŋ)
  = wanting ('wɑntɪŋ)
  = insufficient (,ɪnsə'fɪʃənt)
  = unsatisfactory (,ʌnsætɪs'fæktrɪ ,
    -tərɪ)
  = *short of*

inadvisable (,ɪnəd'vaɪzəbl̩) *adj.* 不智的

  = unwise (ʌn'waɪz)
  = imprudent (ɪm'prudn̩t)
  = ill-advised ('ɪləd'vaɪzd)
  = ill-considered ('ɪlkən'sɪdəd)

inappropriate (,ɪnə'proprɪɪt) *adj.* 不適合的

  = unfitting (ʌn'fɪtɪŋ)
  = unsuitable (ʌn'sjutəbl̩ , -'sut-)
  = improper (ɪm'prɑpɚ)

inattentive (,ɪnə'tɛntɪv) *adj.* 疏忽的

  = unmindful (ʌn'maɪndfəl)
  = heedless ('hidlɪs)
  = unobserving (,ʌnəb'zɝvɪŋ)
  = distracted (dɪ'stræktɪd)
  = negligent ('nɛglədʒənt)
  = wandering ('wɑndərɪŋ)

I

inaugurate (ɪn'ɔgjə,ret) v.
開創

= begin (bɪ'gɪn)
= install (ɪn'stɔl)
= introduce (,ɪntrə'djus)
= launch (lɔntʃ , lɑntʃ)
= admit (əd'mɪt)
= initiate (ɪ'nɪʃɪ,et)
= instate (ɪn'stet)

inborn (ɪn'bɔrn , 'ɪn,bɔrn) adj.
天生的

= natural ('nætʃərəl)
= innate (ɪ'net , ɪn'net)
= hereditary (hə'rɛdə,tɛrɪ)
= instinctive (ɪn'stɪŋktɪv)

incapable (ɪn'kepəbḷ) adj.
不能…的;無能的

= unable (ʌn'ebḷ)
= incompetent (ɪn'kɑmpətənt)
= unqualified (ʌn'kwɑlə,faɪd)
= unfit (ʌn'fɪt)

incense (v. ɪn'sɛns , n. 'ɪnsɛns)
① v. 激怒 ② n. 香氣

① = provoke (prə'vok)
= anger ('æŋgə)
= annoy (ə'nɔɪ)
= irritate ('ɪrə,tet)
= vex (vɛks)
= exasperate (ɛg'zæspə,ret , ɪg-)
= ruffle ('rʌfḷ)
= pique (pik)
② = fragrance ('fregrəns)
= perfume ('pɝfjum)
= aroma (ə'romə)

= scent (sɛnt)

incentive (ɪn'sɛntɪv) n. 刺激;
動機

= motive ('motɪv)
= stimulus ('stɪmjələs)
= encouragement (ɪn'kɝɪdʒmənt ,
  ɛn-)
= inducement (ɪn'djusmənt)

incessant (ɪn'sɛsṇt) adj. 不斷的

= continual (kən'tɪnjʊəl)
= uninterrupted (,ʌnɪntə'rʌptɪd)
= unbroken (ʌn'brokən)
= constant ('kɑnstənt)
= ceaseless ('sislɪs)
= endless ('ɛndlɪs)
= nonstop ('nɑn'stɑp)
= infinite ('ɪnfənɪt)
= perpetual (pə'pɛtʃʊəl)
= steady ('stɛdɪ)

incident ('ɪnsədənt) n. 事件

= happening ('hæpənɪŋ)
= event (ɪ'vɛnt)
= occurrence (ə'kɝəns)
= experience (ɪk'spɪrɪəns)
= adventure (əd'vɛntʃə)

incinerator (ɪn'sɪnə,retə) n.
焚化爐

= furnace ('fɝnɪs)
= burner ('bɝnə)

incipient (ɪn'sɪpɪənt) adj.
初期的

= beginning (bɪ'gɪnɪŋ)

= initial (ɪ'nɪʃəl)
= introductory (ˌɪntrə'dʌktərɪ)

incite (ɪn'saɪt) *v.* 鼓勵

= stir (stɜ)
= urge (ɜdʒ)
= rouse (raʊz)
= agitate ('ædʒə,tet)
= excite (ɪk'saɪt)
= inflame (ɪn'flem)
= provoke (prə'vok)
= instigate ('ɪnstə,get)

inclement (ɪn'klɛmənt) *adj.*
嚴酷的

= rough (rʌf)
= stormy ('stɔrmɪ)
= cold (kold)
= harsh (harʃ)
= severe (sə'vɪr)
= cruel ('kruəl)

incline (ɪn'klaɪn) *v.* ①傾向
②影響　③使彎曲　④傾斜（面）；
坡度

① = tend (tɛnd)
   = *be willing*
   = *be game*
② = influence ('ɪnfluəns)
   = affect (ə'fɛkt)
   = sway (swe)
   = move (muv)
   = induce (ɪn'djus)
   = persuade (pə'swed)
③ = lead (lid)
   = bend (bɛnd)
   = bow (baʊ)

= tilt (tɪlt)
= tip (tɪp)
④ = slope (slop)
   = hill (hɪl)
   = grade (gred)

include (ɪn'klud) *v.* 包括

= contain (kən'ten)
= comprise (kəm'praɪz)
= cover ('kʌvə)
= enclose (ɪn'kloz)

income ('ɪn,kʌm , 'ɪŋ,kʌm) *n.*
收入

= receipts (rɪ'sits)
= returns (rɪ'tɜnz)
= profits ('prafɪts)
= earnings ('ɜnɪŋz)
= proceeds ('prosidz)
= wages ('wedʒɪz)
= payment ('pemənt)

incomparable (ɪn'kampərəbl̩)
adj. 不能比較的

= matchless ('mætʃlɪs)
= unequaled (ʌn'ikwəld)

incompetent (ɪn'kampətənt)
adj. 無能力的

= unable (ʌn'ebl̩)
= incapable (ɪn'kepəbl̩)
= unqualified (ʌn'kwalə,faɪd)
= unfit (ʌn'fɪt)

incomplete (ˌɪnkəm'plit) *adj.*
不完全的

= unfinished (ʌn'fɪnɪʃt)

I

= deficient (dɪˈfɪʃənt)
= wanting (ˈwɑntɪŋ)
= lacking (ˈlækɪŋ)
= partial (ˈpɑrʃəl)
= imperfect (ɪmˈpɝfɪkt)

incomprehensible

(ˌɪnkɑmprɪˈhɛnsəb!̩) adj.
不能理解的

= unintelligible (ˌʌnɪnˈtɛlədʒəb!̩)
= vague (veg)
= obscure (əbˈskjʊr)
= difficult (ˈdɪfəˌkʌlt)

inconceivable (ˌɪnkənˈsivəb!̩)

adj. 不可想像的

= unbelievable (ˌʌnbɪˈlivəb!̩)
= unthinkable (ʌnˈθɪŋkəb!̩)
= unconvincing (ˌʌnkənˈvɪnsɪŋ)
= incredible (ɪnˈkrɛdəb!̩)

inconsiderate (ˌɪnkənˈsɪdərɪt)

adj. 不體貼的

= thoughtless (ˈθɔtlɪs)
= unmindful (ʌnˈmaɪndfəl)

inconsistent (ˌɪnkənˈsɪstənt)

adj. 矛盾的

= disagreeing (ˌdɪsəˈgriɪŋ)
= illogical (ɪˈlɑdʒɪk!̩)
= unreasonable (ʌnˈriznəb!̩)
= senseless (ˈsɛnslɪs)
= invalid (ɪnˈvælɪd)

inconspicuous

(ˌɪnkənˈspɪkjʊəs) adj. 不太顯眼的

= unseen (ʌnˈsin)
= unnoticed (ʌnˈnotɪst)
= unapparent (ˌʌnəˈpærənt)

inconvenient (ˌɪnkənˈvinjənt)

adj. 不便的

= untimely (ʌnˈtaɪmlɪ)
= inappropriate (ˌɪnəˈpropriɪt)
= unfavorable (ʌnˈfev(ə)rəb!̩)
= bothersome (ˈbɑðəˌsəm)
= awkward (ˈɔkwəd)
= troublesome (ˈtrʌb!̩səm)

incorporate (ɪnˈkɔrpəˌret) v.

合併

= join (dʒɔɪn)
= unite (juˈnaɪt)
= combine (kəmˈbaɪn)
= unify (ˈjunəˌfaɪ)
= merge (mɝdʒ)

incorrect (ˌɪnkəˈrɛkt) adj.

不正確的

= wrong (rɔŋ)
= faulty (ˈfɔltɪ)
= inaccurate (ɪnˈækjərɪt)
= improper (ɪmˈprɑpə)

increase (ɪnˈkris) v. 增加

= enlarge (ɪnˈlɑrdʒ)
= extend (ɪkˈstɛnd)
= expand (ɪkˈspænd)
= advance (ədˈvæns)
= raise (rez)
= add to

incredible〔 ɪnˈkrɛdəbḷ 〕 *adj.*
難以相信的

= unbelievable 〔ˌʌnbɪˈlivəbḷ 〕
= doubtful 〔ˈdautfəl 〕
= questionable 〔ˈkwɛstʃənəbḷ 〕
= staggering 〔ˈstægərɪŋ 〕
= preposterous 〔 prɪˈpastərəs 〕
= absurd 〔 əbˈsɜd 〕
= ridiculous 〔 rɪˈdɪkjələs 〕
= unconvincing 〔ˌʌnkənˈvɪnsɪŋ 〕

incur 〔 ɪnˈkɜ 〕 *v.* 招致

= contract 〔 kənˈtrækt 〕
= catch 〔 kætʃ 〕
= *bring on*

incurable 〔 ɪnˈkjurəbḷ 〕 *adj.*
無可救藥的

= hopeless 〔ˈhoplɪs 〕
= *beyond remedy*

indebted 〔 ɪnˈdɛtɪd 〕 *adj.* 負債的

= owing 〔ˈo·ɪŋ 〕
= obliged 〔 əˈblaɪdʒd 〕
= involved 〔 ɪnˈvalvd 〕

indeed 〔 ɪnˈdid 〕 *adv.* 的確

= really 〔ˈriəlɪ , ˈrɪlɪ 〕
= absolutely 〔ˈæbsəˌlutlɪ 〕
= positively 〔ˈpazətɪvlɪ 〕
= certainly 〔ˈsɜtṇlɪ 〕
= definitely 〔ˈdɛfənɪtlɪ 〕
= surely 〔ˈʃurlɪ 〕
= perfectly 〔ˈpɜfɪktlɪ 〕
= *in fact*
= *in truth*

= *of course*

indefinite 〔 ɪnˈdɛfənɪt 〕 *adj.*
不確定的

= unclear 〔 ʌnˈklɪr 〕
= vague 〔 veg 〕
= indistinct 〔ˌɪndɪˈstɪŋkt 〕
= obscure 〔 əbˈskjur 〕
= confused 〔 kənˈfjuzd 〕
= hazy 〔ˈhezɪ 〕
= general 〔ˈdʒɛnərəl 〕
= broad 〔 brɔd 〕

indelible 〔 ɪnˈdɛləbḷ 〕 *adj.* 難忘的

= permanent 〔ˈpɜmənənt 〕
= indestructible 〔ˌɪndɪˈstrʌktəbḷ 〕
= unforgettable 〔ˌʌnfəˈgɛtəbḷ 〕
= fixed 〔 fɪkst 〕

indent 〔 ɪnˈdɛnt 〕 *v.* 切割

= dent 〔 dɛnt 〕
= notch 〔 natʃ 〕
= cut 〔 kʌt 〕
= nick 〔 nɪk 〕

independent 〔ˌɪndɪˈpɛndənt 〕
adj. 獨立的

= unconnected 〔ˌʌnkəˈnɛktɪd 〕
= unassociated 〔ˌʌnəˈsoʃɪˌetɪd 〕
= self-reliant 〔ˌsɛlfrɪˈlaɪənt 〕
= *acting alone*

indescribable 〔ˌɪndɪˈskraɪbəbḷ 〕
adj. 難以形容的

= unexplainable 〔ˌʌnɪkˈsplenəbḷ 〕
= extraordinary 〔 ɪkˈstrɔrdṇˌɛrɪ 〕

I

= exceptional (ɪk'sɛpʃənḷ)

= remarkable (rɪ'mɑrkəbḷ)

index ('ɪndɛks) *n.* 索引

= list (lɪst)

= chart (tʃɑrt)

= file (faɪl)

= table ('tebḷ)

= sign (saɪn)

= symbol ('sɪmbḷ)

= guide (gaɪd)

indicate ('ɪndə,ket) *v.* 指出

= show (ʃo)

= exhibit (ɪg'zɪbɪt)

= demonstrate ('dɛmən,stret)

= disclose (dɪs'kloz)

= reveal (rɪ'vil)

= display (dɪ'sple)

= present (prɪ'zɛnt)

= express (ɪk'sprɛs)

= suggest (səg'dʒɛst , sə'dʒɛst)

= hint (hɪnt)

= imply (ɪm'plaɪ)

= signify ('sɪgnə,faɪ)

= *point out*

indifferent (ɪn'dɪfərənt) *adj.*
漠不關心的

= unbiased (ʌn'baɪəst)

= impartial (ɪm'pɑrʃəl)

= detached (dɪ'tætʃt)

= disinterested (dɪs'ɪnt(ə)rəstɪd)

= cool (kul)

= neutral ('njutrəl)

= impersonal (ɪm'pɝsṇḷ)

= unconcerned (,ʌnkən's3nd)

indigenous (ɪn'dɪdʒənəs) *adj.*
土產的

= native ('netɪv)

= original (ə'rɪdʒənḷ)

= *natural to*

indignant (ɪn'dɪgnənt) *adj.*
憤怒的

= angry ('æŋgrɪ)

= irate ('aɪret , aɪ'ret)

indignity (ɪn'dɪgnətɪ) *n.* 侮辱

= insult ('ɪnsʌlt)

= affront (ə'frʌnt)

= offense (ə'fɛns)

= injury ('ɪndʒərɪ)

indirect (,ɪndə'rɛkt) *adj.* 間接的

= devious ('divɪəs)

= roundabout ('raʊndə,baʊt)

= out-of-the-way ('aʊtəvðə'we)

indiscreet (,ɪndɪ'skrit) *adj.*
不智的

= unwise (ʌn'waɪz)

= imprudent (ɪm'prudṇt)

= unsound (ʌn'saʊnd)

= unreasonable (ʌn'riznəbḷ)

= ill-advised ('ɪləd'vaɪzd)

indispensable (,ɪndɪs'pɛnsəbḷ)
adj. 不可缺少的

= essential (ə'sɛnʃəl)

= necessary ('nɛsə,sɛrɪ)

= needed ('nidɪd)
= required (rɪ'kwaɪrd)
= vital ('vaɪtḷ)

indisposed (ˌɪndɪ'spozd) *adj.*
①微感不適的　②不願意的

① = ill (ɪl)
= sick (sɪk)
= ailing ('elɪŋ)
② = unwilling (ʌn'wɪlɪŋ)
= forced (forst , fɔrst)

indistinct (ˌɪndɪ'stɪŋkt) *adj.*
模糊的

= unclear (ʌn'klɪr)
= confused (kən'fjuzd)
= dim (dɪm)
= obscure (əb'skjur)
= vague (veg)
= cloudy ('klaʊdɪ)
= hazy ('hezɪ)
= blurred (blɝd)

individual (ˌɪndə'vɪdʒʊəl)
① *adj.* 個別的　② *n.* 人

① = single ('sɪŋgḷ)
= separate ('sɛpərɪt , -prɪt)
= one (wʌn)
= personal ('pɝsṇḷ)
= special ('spɛʃəl)
② = human ('hjumən)
= man (mæn)
= being ('biɪŋ)

indivisible (ˌɪndə'vɪzəbḷ) *adj.*
不能分割的

= inseparable (ɪn'sɛpərəbḷ)
= solid ('salɪd)

indolent ('ɪndələnt) *adj.* 怠惰的

= lazy ('lezɪ)
= shiftless ('ʃɪftlɪs)
= unenterprising
(ʌn'ɛntəˌpraɪzɪŋ)
= slothful ('sloθfəl , 'slɔθfəl)
= do-nothing ('duˌnʌθɪŋ)

indomitable (ɪn'damətəbḷ)
adj. 不屈不撓的；不氣餒的

= unconquerable (ʌn'kaŋkərəbḷ)
= unyielding (ʌn'jildɪŋ)
= invincible (ɪn'vɪnsəbḷ)
= uncontrollable (ʌnkən'troləbḷ)
= unruly (ʌn'rulɪ)
= unmanageable (ʌn'mænɪdʒəbḷ)
= unbeatable (ʌn'bitəbḷ)

induce (ɪn'djus) *v.* 引誘；招致

= influence ('ɪnfluəns)
= persuade (pə'swed)
= cause (kɔz)
= elicit (ɪ'lɪsɪt)
= evoke (ɪ'vok)
= prompt (prampt)
= move (muv)
= sway (swe)
= *lead on*

induct (ɪn'dʌkt) *v.* 使正式加入；
介紹

= introduce (ˌɪntrə'djus)
= install (ɪn'stɔl)

I

= place (ples)
= inaugurate (ɪn'ɔgjə,ret)
= enlist (ɪn'lɪst)
= enroll (ɪn'rol)
= draft (dræft)
= *bring in*

indulge (ɪn'dʌldʒ) *v.* 放縱；
遷就

= humor ('hjumɚ , 'ju-)
= favor ('fevɚ)
= oblige (ə'blaɪdʒ)
= please (pliz)
= gratify ('grætə,faɪ)
= satisfy ('sætɪs,faɪ)
= pamper ('pæmpɚ)
= coddle ('kɑdl̩)
= spoil (spɔɪl)
= *cater to*

industrious (ɪn'dʌstrɪəs) *adj.*
勤勉的

= diligent ('dɪlədʒənt)
= energetic (,ɛnɚ'dʒɛtɪk)
= tireless ('taɪrlɪs)
= hard-working ('hɑrd'wɝkɪŋ)

industry ('ɪndəstrɪ) *n.* 產業；
製造業

= trade (tred)
= business ('bɪznɪs)
= manufacture (,mænjə'fæktʃɚ)
= labor ('lebɚ)
= work (wɝk)
= concern (kən'sɝn)
= dealings ('dilɪŋz)

inedible (ɪn'ɛdəbl̩) *adj.*
不可吃的

= uneatable (ʌn'itəbl̩)

ineffectual (,ɪnə'fɛktʃʊəl) *adj.*
無用的；無益的

= useless ('juslɪs)
= futile ('fjutl̩)
= ineffective (,ɪnə'fɛktɪv)
= powerless ('paʊɚlɪs)
= unsuccessful (,ʌnsək'sɛsfəl)

inefficient (ɪnə'fɪʃənt) *adj.*
無效率的；無能的

= unable (ʌn'ebl̩)
= incapable (ɪn'kepəbl̩)
= incompetent (ɪn'kɑmpətənt)
= unfit (ʌn'fɪt)
= inept (ɪn'ɛpt)
= unskillful (ʌn'skɪlfəl)

inequality (,ɪnɪ'kwɑlətɪ) *n.*
不平等；不平均

= unevenness (ʌn'ivənnɪs)
= irregularity (,ɪrɛgjə'lærətɪ)
= imbalance (ɪm'bæləns)

inert (ɪn'ɝt) *adj.* 無生命的；
遲鈍的

= lifeless ('laɪflɪs)
= slow (slo)
= sluggish ('slʌgɪʃ)
= motionless ('moʃənlɪs)
= inactive (ɪn'æktɪv)
= stagnant ('stægnənt)
= listless ('lɪstlɪs)

inevitable (ɪn'ɛvətəbl̩) *adj.*
不可避免的

= destined ('dɛstɪnd)
= fated ('fetɪd)
= doomed (dumd)
= unavoidable (ˌʌnə'vɔɪdəbl̩)
= sure (ʃur)
= inescapable (ˌɪnə'skepəbl̩)
= certain ('sɝtn̩)

inexact (ˌɪnɪg'zækt) *adj.*
不精確的

= vague (veg)
= indefinite (ɪn'dɛfənɪt)
= broad (brɔd)
= general ('dʒɛnərəl)
= unclear (ʌn'klɪr)
= obscure (əb'skjur)
= inaccurate (ɪn'ækjərɪt)
= incorrect (ˌɪnkə'rɛkt)

inexcusable (ˌɪnɪk'skjuzəbl̩)
adj. 無可辯解的；不能原諒的

= unpardonable (ʌn'pardnəbl̩)
= unforgivable (ʌnfɚ'gɪvəbl̩)
= unjustifiable (ʌn'dʒʌstə,faɪəbl̩)

inexhaustible (ˌɪnɪg'zɔstəbl̩)
adj. ①不疲乏的　②無窮盡的

① = tireless ('taɪrlɪs)
② = endless ('ɛndlɪs)
= unlimited (ʌn'lɪmɪtɪd)
= infinite ('ɪnfənɪt)

inexpensive (ˌɪnɪk'spɛnsɪv) *adj.*
廉價的；不貴重的

= cheap (tʃip)
= reasonable ('riznəbl̩)
= low-priced ('lo'praɪst)

inexperienced (ˌɪnɪk'spɪrɪənst)
adj. 缺乏經驗的

= unpracticed (ʌn'præktɪst)
= untried (ʌn'traɪd)
= green (grin)
= unfamiliar (ˌʌnfə'mɪljɚ)
= immature (ˌɪmə'tjur)
= undeveloped (ˌʌndɪ'vɛləpt)
= ignorant ('ɪgnərənt)

inexplicable (ɪn'ɛksplɪkəbl̩)
adj. 不可解釋的；神秘的

= unexplainable (ˌʌnɪk'splenəbl̩)
= mysterious (mɪs'tɪrɪəs)

infallible (ɪn'fæləbl̩) *adj.*
絕對可靠的；必然的

= reliable (rɪ'laɪəbl̩)
= sure (ʃur)
= unerring (ʌn'ɝɪŋ , -'ɛrɪŋ)
= right (raɪt)

infamous ('ɪnfəməs) *adj.*
無恥的；惡名昭彰的

= wicked ('wɪkɪd)
= bad (bæd)
= disgraceful (dɪs'gresfəl)
= evil ('ivl̩)
= base (bes)
= low (lo)
= shameful ('ʃemfʊl)
= notorious (no'torɪəs)

= terrible ('tɛrəbḷ)

= scandalous ('skændləs , -dləs)

= outrageous (aʊt'redʒəs)

infancy ('ɪnfənsɪ) *n.* 初期；幼年

= beginning (bɪ'gɪnɪŋ)

= babyhood ('bebɪ,hʊd)

infantry ('ɪnfəntrɪ) *n.* 步兵(團)

= army ('ɑrmɪ)

= *foot soldiers*

infect (ɪn'fɛkt) *v.* ①傳染 ②影響

① = disease (dɪ'ziz)

= contaminate (kən'tæmə,net)

= communicate (kə'mjunə,ket)

= pollute (pə'lut)

= poison ('pɔɪzṇ)

= corrupt (kə'rʌpt)

② = influence ('ɪnfluəns)

infer (ɪn'fɝ) *v.* ①推論 ②暗指

① = conclude (kən'klud)

= reason ('rizṇ)

= deduce (dɪ'djus , -'dus)

= gather ('gæðɚ)

= derive (də'raɪv)

= assume (ə'sjum)

= presume (prɪ'zum)

= suppose (sə'poz)

= expect (ɪk'spɛkt)

= reckon ('rɛkən)

= calculate ('kælkjə,let)

= imagine (ɪ'mædʒɪn)

② = indicate ('ɪndə,ket)

= imply (ɪm'plaɪ)

= suggest (səg'dʒɛst , sə'dʒɛst)

= hint (hɪnt)

inferior (ɪn'fɪrɪɚ) *adj.* 較低的；較劣的

= lower ('loɚ)

= worse (wɝs)

= subordinate (sə'bɔrdṇɪt)

= secondary ('sɛkən,dɛrɪ)

= lesser ('lɛsɚ)

infernal (ɪn'fɝnḷ) *adj.* 地獄的

= hellish ('hɛlɪʃ)

infest (ɪn'fɛst) *v.* 騷亂；蹂躪

= overrun (,ovɚ'rʌn)

= plague (pleg)

= beset (bɪ'sɛt)

= *crawl with*

infidel ('ɪnfədḷ) *n.* 不信教的人

= unbeliever (,ʌnbɪ'livɚ)

= skeptic ('skɛptɪk)

infinite ('ɪnfənɪt) *adj.* 無限的

= limitless ('lɪmɪtlɪs)

= boundless ('baʊndlɪs)

= endless ('ɛndlɪs)

= immeasurable (ɪ'mɛʒərəbḷ)

= everlasting (,ɛvɚ'læstɪŋ)

= eternal (ɪ'tɝnḷ)

= ceaseless ('sislɪs)

= perpetual (pɚ'pɛtʃuəl)

infirm (ɪn'fɝm) *adj.* 虛弱的

= weak〔wik〕

= feeble〔'fibḷ〕

= unstable〔ʌn'stebḷ〕

= sickly〔'sɪklɪ〕

= unsound〔ʌn'saʊnd〕

= frail〔frel〕

nflame〔ɪn'flem〕*v.* ①激動
②使紅腫

① = excite〔ɪk'saɪt〕

= stir〔stɝ〕

= move〔muv〕

= affect〔ə'fɛkt〕

= provoke〔prə'vok〕

= arouse〔ə'raʊz〕

= incite〔ɪn'saɪt〕

= anger〔'æŋgɚ〕

= irritate〔'ɪrə,tet〕

② = redden〔'rɛdṇ〕

= swell〔swɛl〕

nflate〔ɪn'flet〕*v.* 膨脹

= swell〔swɛl〕

= expand〔ɪk'spænd〕

= broaden〔'brɔdṇ〕

= enlarge〔ɪn'lɑrdʒ〕

= stretch〔strɛtʃ〕

= increase〔ɪn'kris〕

= *puff out*

= *blow up*

nflexible〔ɪn'flɛksəbḷ〕*adj.*
坚強的；不屈的

= stiff〔stɪf〕

= rigid〔'rɪdʒɪd〕

= firm〔fɝm〕

= unbending〔ʌn'bɛndɪŋ〕

= unyielding〔ʌn'jildɪŋ〕

= stubborn〔'stʌbən〕

= inelastic〔,ɪnɪ'læstɪk〕

inflict〔ɪn'flɪkt〕*v.* 給予；使遭受

= give〔gɪv〕

= cause〔kɔz〕

= impose〔ɪm'poz〕

= effect〔ə'fɛkt , ɪ- , ɛ-〕

= produce〔prə'djus〕

= wreak〔rik〕

= *bring about*

influence〔'ɪnflʊəns〕*v.* 影響；
改變

= sway〔swe〕

= affect〔ə'fɛkt〕

= move〔muv〕

= induce〔ɪn'djus〕

= persuade〔pə'swed〕

= prejudice〔'prɛdʒədɪs〕

inform〔ɪn'fɔrm〕*v.* ①報告；
通知　②告發

① = tell〔tɛl〕

= communicate〔kə'mjunə,ket〕

= advise〔əd'vaɪz〕

= enlighten〔ɪn'laɪtṇ〕

= instruct〔ɪn'strʌkt〕

= notify〔'notə,faɪ〕

= report〔rɪ'port〕

② = accuse〔ə'kjuz〕

= tattle〔'tætḷ〕

= blab〔blæb〕

= snitch〔snɪtʃ〕

I

= squeal (skwil)

= betray (bɪ'tre)

infrequent (ɪn'frikwənt) adj.
罕見的

= rare (rɛr)

= scarce (skɛrs)

= sparse (spɑrs)

= scattered ('skætəd)

= occasional (ə'keʒṇḷ)

= uncommon (ʌn'kɑmən)

= irregular (ɪ'rɛgjələ)

infringe (ɪn'frɪndʒ) v. 侵犯；
違背

= violate ('vaɪə,let)

= break (brek)

= trespass ('trɛspəs)

= overstep (,ovə'stɛp)

infuriate (ɪn'fjʊrɪ,et) v. 激怒

= enrage (ɪn'redʒ , ɛn-)

= anger ('æŋgə)

= madden ('mædṇ)

= antagonize (æn'tægə,naɪz)

= provoke (prə'vok)

= irritate ('ɪrə,tet)

= incite (ɪn'saɪt)

= agitate ('ædʒə,tet)

infuse (ɪn'fjuz) v. ①注入
②鼓舞　③浸泡

① = instill (ɪn'stɪl)

= *put in*

② = inspire (ɪn'spaɪr)

= lift (lɪft)

= infect (ɪn'fɛkt)

= animate ('ænə,met)

③ = drench (drɛntʃ)

= saturate ('sætʃə,ret)

= bathe (beð)

ingenious (ɪn'dʒinjəs) adj.
智巧的；靈敏的

= clever ('klɛvə)

= skillful ('skɪlfəl)

= proficient (prə'fɪʃənt)

= masterful ('mæstəfəl , 'mɑs-)

= inventive (ɪn'vɛntɪv)

= original (ə'rɪdʒənḷ)

= creative (krɪ'etɪv)

= imaginative (ɪ'mædʒə,netɪv)

= productive (prə'dʌktɪv)

= inspired (ɪn'spaɪrd)

ingenuous (ɪn'dʒɛnjuəs) adj.
①坦白的　②純樸的

① = frank (fræŋk)

= open ('opən)

= sincere (sɪn'sɪr)

= candid ('kændɪd)

= straightforward (,stret'fɔrwəd)

② = simple ('sɪmpḷ)

= natural ('nætʃərəl)

= innocent ('ɪnəsṇt)

= plain (plen)

= unsophisticated
　(,ʌnsə'fɪstɪ,ketɪd)

ingredient (ɪn'gridɪənt) n.
成份

= part (pɑrt)

= element (ˈɛləmənt)

= factor (ˈfæktɚ)

= component (kəmˈponənt)

inhabit (ɪnˈhæbɪt) v. 居住

= live (lɪv)

= dwell (dwɛl)

= occupy (ˈɑkjəˌpaɪ)

= reside (rɪˈzaɪd)

= lodge (lɑdʒ)

= stay (ste)

= room (rum)

inhale (ɪnˈhel) v. 吸

= gasp (gæsp , gɑsp)

= sniff (snɪf)

= smell (smɛl)

= *breathe in*

inherent (ɪnˈhɪrənt) adj.
與生俱來的

= internal (ɪnˈtɜnḷ)

= natural (ˈnætʃərəl)

= implanted (ɪmˈplæntɪd)

= existing (ɪgˈzɪstɪŋ)

= belonging (bɪˈlɔŋɪŋ)

= instinctive (ɪnˈstɪŋktɪv)

inherit (ɪnˈhɛrɪt) v. 繼承；遺傳

= receive (rɪˈsiv)

= *come into*

inhospitable (ɪnˈhɑspɪtəbḷ)
adj. 冷淡的

= uncordial (ʌnˈkɔrdjəl)

= unfriendly (ʌnˈfrɛndlɪ)

= unreceptive (ʌnrɪˈsɛptɪv)

= ungracious (ʌnˈgreʃəs)

= unneighborly (ʌnˈnebɚlɪ)

inhuman (ɪnˈhjumən , -ˈjumən)
adj. 無人性的

= unfeeling (ʌnˈfilɪŋ)

= cruel (ˈkruəl)

= brutal (ˈbrutḷ)

= ruthless (ˈruθlɪs)

= uncivilized (ʌnˈsɪvḷˌaɪzd)

iniquity (ɪˈnɪkwətɪ) n. 不公平；
邪惡

= injustice (ɪnˈdʒʌstɪs)

= evil (ˈivḷ)

= sin (sɪn)

= wrong (rɔŋ)

= crime (kraɪm)

= outrage (ˈaʊtˌredʒ)

initial (ɪˈnɪʃəl) ① adj. 最初的
② n. 字母

① = first (fɜst)

= earliest (ˈɜlɪɪst)

= beginning (bɪˈgɪnɪŋ)

= primary (ˈpraɪˌmɛrɪ , -mərɪ)

= introductory (ˌɪntrəˈdʌktərɪ)

② = letter (ˈlɛtɚ)

initiate (ɪˈnɪʃɪˌet) v. ①創始
②引入 ③介紹

① = start (stɑrt)

= begin (bɪˈgɪn)

= originate (əˈrɪdʒəˌnet)

= pioneer (ˌpaɪəˈnɪr)

I

= lead〔lid〕
= head〔hɛd〕
= institute〔'ɪnstə,tjut〕
= introduce〔,ɪntrə'djus〕
= launch〔lɔntʃ, lantʃ〕
= *break the ice*
② = admit〔əd'mɪt〕
= receive〔rɪ'siv〕
= install〔ɪn'stɔl〕
= *let in*
= *take in*
③ = instruct〔ɪn'strʌkt〕
= introduce〔,ɪntrə'djus〕
= educate〔'ɛdʒə,ket, -dʒʊ-〕

inject〔ɪn'dʒɛkt〕*v.* 投入;注射
= fill〔fɪl〕
= insert〔ɪn'sɝt〕
= *force into*

injure〔'ɪndʒɚ〕*v.* 傷害;損害
= damage〔'dæmɪdʒ〕
= harm〔harm〕
= hurt〔hɝt〕
= wound〔wund〕
= wrong〔rɔŋ〕
= impair〔ɪm'pɛr〕

injustice〔ɪn'dʒʌstɪs〕*n.*
不公正
= inequity〔ɪn'ɛkwɪtɪ〕
= unfairness〔ʌn'fɛrnɪs〕
= unjustness〔ʌn'dʒʌstnɪs〕

inkling〔'ɪŋklɪŋ〕*n.* 略知;暗示
= hint〔hɪnt〕

= suggestion〔səg'dʒɛstʃən, sə'dʒ-〕
= notion〔'noʃən〕
= indication〔,ɪndə'keʃən〕
= glimmer〔'glɪmɚ〕
= clue〔klu〕
= suspicion〔sə'spɪʃən〕
= impression〔ɪm'prɛʃən〕
= idea〔aɪ'diə, -'dɪə〕

inlaid〔'ɪn,led〕*adj.* 鑲嵌的;
嵌入的
= embedded〔ɪm'bɛdɪd〕
= inset〔'ɪn,sɛt〕
= lined〔laɪnd〕

inlet〔'ɪn,lɛt〕*n.* 入口;通路
= entrance〔'ɛntrəns〕
= entry〔'ɛntrɪ〕
= opening〔'opənɪŋ〕
= passageway〔'pæsɪdʒ,we〕

inmate〔'ɪnmet〕*n.* 居住者
= occupant〔'akjəpənt〕
= resident〔'rɛzədənt〕
= tenant〔'tɛnənt〕
= inhabitant〔ɪn'hæbətənt〕

inmost〔'ɪn,most〕*adj.*
①最深處的 ②最奧秘的
① = deepest〔'dipɪst〕
= *farthest in*
② = private〔'praɪvɪt〕
= secret〔'sikrɪt〕

inn〔ɪn〕*n.* 客棧;酒店
= hotel〔ho'tɛl〕

= tavern ('tævən)
= roadhouse ('rod,haus)
= lodge (lɑdʒ)

nnocent ('ɪnəsn̩t) *adj.* ①無罪的
②無害的

① = guiltless ('gɪltlɪs)
= faultless ('fɔltlɪs)
= blameless ('blemlɪs)
= sinless ('sɪnlɪs)
② = harmless ('hɑrmlɪs)

innovate ('ɪnə,vet) *v.* 改革

= introduce (,ɪntrə'djus)
= change (tʃendʒ)
= modernize ('mɑdən,aɪz)

innumerable (ɪ'njumərəbl̩ ,
-'nu-) *adj.* 無數的

= countless ('kauntlɪs)
= unlimited (ʌn'lɪmɪtɪd)
= many ('mɛnɪ)
= infinite ('ɪnfənɪt)

inoculate (ɪn'ɑkjə,let) *v.* 接種

= immunize ('ɪmjə,naɪz)
= vaccinate ('væksn̩,et)

inoffensive (,ɪnə'fɛnsɪv) *adj.*
無害的

= harmless ('hɑrmlɪs)
= unobjectionable
  (,ʌnəb'dʒɛkʃ(ə)nəbl̩)

inquire (ɪn'kwaɪr) *v.* 詢問

= ask (æsk)

= question ('kwɛstʃən)

inquisitive (ɪn'kwɪzətɪv) *adj.*
好奇的

= curious ('kjʊrɪəs)
= prying ('praɪɪŋ)
= snooping ('snupɪŋ)
= meddlesome ('mɛdl̩səm)

inroad ('ɪn,rod) *n.* 攻擊；損害

= raid (red)
= attack (ə'tæk)
= invasion (ɪn'veʒən)
= foray ('fɔre , 'fɑre)

insane (ɪn'sen) *adj.* 瘋狂的；
極愚蠢的

= crazy ('krezɪ)
= foolish ('fulɪʃ)
= mad (mæd)
= unbalanced (ʌn'bælənst)
= deranged (dɪ'rendʒd)

insatiable (ɪn'seʃɪəbl̩) *adj.*
貪心的

= greedy ('gridɪ)
= unquenchable (ʌn'kwɛntʃəbl̩)
= covetous ('kʌvɪtəs)

inscribe (ɪn'skraɪb) *v.* 題記；
刻銘

= write (raɪt)
= engrave (ɪn'grev)
= mark (mɑrk)
= imprint (ɪm'prɪnt)
= impress (ɪm'prɛs)
= stamp (stæmp)

I

insensible ﹝ ɪnˈsɛnsəbḷ ﹞ *adj.*
無感覺的

= unfeeling ﹝ ʌnˈfilɪŋ ﹞

= unaware ﹝ ˌʌnəˈwɛr ﹞

= unconscious ﹝ ʌnˈkɑnʃəs ﹞

= numb ﹝ nʌm ﹞

= unknowing ﹝ ʌnˈnoɪŋ ﹞

inseparable ﹝ ɪnˈsɛpərəbḷ ﹞ *adj.*
不能分離的

= indivisible ﹝ ˌɪndəˈvɪzəbḷ ﹞

= solid ﹝ ˈsɑlɪd ﹞

= joined ﹝ dʒɔɪnd ﹞

insert ﹝ ɪnˈsɝt ﹞ *v.* 插入

= introduce ﹝ ˌɪntrəˈdjus ﹞

= inject ﹝ ɪnˈdʒɛkt ﹞

= enter ﹝ ˈɛntə ﹞

= *put in*

= *set in*

inside ﹝ *prep.* ɪnˈsaɪd ,
adj. ˈɪnˈsaɪd ﹞ ① *prep.* 在⋯裏面
② *adj.* 內部的

① = in ﹝ ɪn ﹞

= into ﹝ ˈɪntu , ˈɪntʊ ﹞

= within ﹝ wɪðˈɪn , wɪθˈɪn ﹞

② = interior ﹝ ɪnˈtɪrɪə ﹞

= innermost ﹝ ˈɪnəmost ﹞

insight ﹝ ˈɪnˌsaɪt ﹞ *n.* 洞察力;
見識

= wisdom ﹝ ˈwɪzdəm ﹞

= perception ﹝ pəˈsɛpʃən ﹞

= intuition ﹝ ˌɪntjuˈɪʃən ﹞

insignia ﹝ ɪnˈsɪgnɪə ﹞ *n.* 徽章;
標幟

= emblems ﹝ ˈɛmbləmz ﹞

= badges ﹝ ˈbædʒɪz ﹞

= symbols ﹝ ˈsɪmbḷz ﹞

insignificant ﹝ ˌɪnsɪgˈnɪfəkənt ﹞
adj. 無意義的;不重要的

= unimportant ﹝ ˌʌnɪmˈpɔrtṇt ﹞

= meaningless ﹝ ˈminɪŋlɪs ﹞

= negligible ﹝ ˈnɛglədʒəbḷ ﹞

= small ﹝ smɔl ﹞

= little ﹝ ˈlɪtḷ ﹞

= slight ﹝ slaɪt ﹞

insincere ﹝ ˌɪnsɪnˈsɪr ﹞ *adj.*
不誠懇的

= dishonest ﹝ dɪsˈɑnɪst ﹞

= false ﹝ fɔls ﹞

= superficial ﹝ supəˈfɪʃəl ﹞

= artificial ﹝ ˌɑrtəˈfɪʃəl ﹞

insinuate ﹝ ɪnˈsɪnjuˌet ﹞ *v.* 暗指;
暗示

= hint ﹝ hɪnt ﹞

= suggest ﹝ sə(g)ˈdʒɛst ﹞

= imply ﹝ ɪmˈplaɪ ﹞

= intimate ﹝ ˈɪntəˌmet ﹞

= indicate ﹝ ˈɪndəˌket ﹞

insist ﹝ ɪnˈsɪst ﹞ *v.* 堅持;強調

= urge ﹝ ɝdʒ ﹞

= press ﹝ prɛs ﹞

= maintain ﹝ menˈten , mənˈten ﹞

= stress ﹝ strɛs ﹞

= demand ﹝ dɪˈmænd ﹞

■nsolent (ˈɪnsələnt) *adj.* 無禮的

= rude (rud)
= insulting (ɪnˈsʌltɪŋ)
= impudent (ˈɪmpjədənt)
= arrogant (ˈærəgənt)
= haughty (ˈhɔtɪ)
= defiant (dɪˈfaɪənt)
= bold (bold)

■nsoluble (ɪnˈsaljəbļ) *adj.*
不能解決的

= unexplainable (ˌʌnɪkˈsplenəbļ)
= unsolvable (ʌnˈsalvəbļ)

■nspect (ɪnˈspɛkt) *v.* 檢查

= examine (ɪgˈzæmɪn)
= observe (əbˈzɝv)
= study (ˈstʌdɪ)
= contemplate (ˈkantəmˌplet)

■nspire (ɪnˈspaɪr) *v.* 激發；影響

= influence (ˈɪnfluəns)
= cause (kɔz)
= prompt (prampt)
= encourage (ɪnˈkɝɪdʒ)

■nstall (ɪnˈstɔl) *v.* ①使正式就職
②安置

① = admit (ədˈmɪt)
= establish (əˈstæblɪʃ)
= inaugurate (ɪnˈɔgjəˌret)
= instate (ɪnˈstet)
= receive (rɪˈsiv)
= *let in*
② = place (ples)
= fix (fɪks)

= plant (plænt)
= set (sɛt)
= *put in*

instance (ˈɪnstəns) *n.* 實例；
步驟

= example (ɪgˈzæmpļ)
= case (kes)
= occasion (əˈkeʒən)
= circumstance (ˈsɝkəmˌstæns)

instant (ˈɪnstənt) ① *adj.* 立刻的
② *n.* 片刻

① = immediate (ɪˈmidɪɪt)
= pressing (ˈprɛsɪŋ)
= urgent (ˈɝdʒənt)
= prompt (prampt)
= quick (kwɪk)
② = moment (ˈmomənt)
= second (ˈsɛkənd)

instead (of) (ɪnˈstɛd) *adv.* 代替

= *in place of*
= *rather than*
= *in lieu of*

instinct (ˈɪnstɪŋkt) *n.* 直覺；
本能

= *natural feeling*
= *natural tendency*

institute (ˈɪnstəˌtjut) ① *v.* 創設
② *n.* 學會；研究所

① = establish (əˈstæblɪʃ)
= begin (bɪˈgɪn)
= create (krɪˈet)

I

= organize (ˈɔrgənˌaɪz)

= form (fɔrm)

= launch (lɔntʃ , lɑntʃ)

= *set up*

② = society (səˈsaɪətɪ)

= organization (ˌɔrgənəˈzeʃən , -aɪˈze-)

= school (skul)

= establishment (əˈstæblɪʃmənt)

= foundation (faʊnˈdeʃən)

instruct (ɪnˈstrʌkt) *v.* ①教導 ②通知；命令

① = teach (titʃ)

= educate (ˈɛdʒəˌket)

= show (ʃo)

= guide (gaɪd)

② = inform (ɪnˈfɔrm)

= direct (dəˈrɛkt , daɪ-)

= tell (tɛl)

= command (kəˈmænd)

= order (ˈɔrdɚ)

= dictate (ˈdɪktet , dɪkˈtet)

= advise (ədˈvaɪz)

instrument (ˈɪnstrəmənt) *n.* 工具；方法

= tool (tul)

= device (dɪˈvaɪs)

= means (minz)

= implement (ˈɪmpləmənt)

= utensil (juˈtɛnsḷ)

= apparatus (ˌæpəˈretəs , ˌæpəˈræ-)

= gadget (ˈgædʒɪt)

= appliance (əˈplaɪəns)

= contraption (kənˈtræpʃən)

insufferable (ɪnˈsʌfrəbḷ , -fərə-) *adj.* 難受的

= unbearable (ʌnˈbɛrəbḷ)

= intolerable (ɪnˈtɑlərəbḷ)

insufficient (ˌɪnsəˈfɪʃənt) *adj.* 不夠的

= inadequate (ɪnˈædəkwɪt)

= unsatisfactory (ˌʌnsætɪsˈfæktrɪ -tərɪ)

= deficient (dɪˈfɪʃənt)

= *not enough*

insulate (ˈɪnsəˌlet , ˈɪnsju-) *v.* 隔離

= isolate (ˈaɪsḷˌet , ˈɪs-)

= separate (ˈsɛpəˌret)

insult (ɪnˈsʌlt) *v.* 侮辱

= offend (əˈfɛnd)

= affront (əˈfrʌnt)

= humiliate (hjuˈmɪlɪˌet)

insure (ɪnˈʃʊr) *v.* ①確保 ②保證 ③使確實

① = protect (prəˈtɛkt)

= safeguard (ˈsefˌgɑrd)

= defend (dɪˈfɛnd)

= shelter (ˈʃɛltɚ)

= cover (ˈkʌvɚ)

② = guarantee (ˌgærənˈti)

= warrant (ˈwɔrənt , ˈwɑrənt)

= assure (əˈʃʊr)

= endorse (ɪnˈdɔrs , ɛn-)

= certify (ˈsɝtəˌfaɪ)

= sponsor (ˈspɑnsɚ)

I

= back〔bæk〕
③ = affirm〔əˈfɝm〕
= vouch〔vautʃ〕
= determine〔dɪˈtɝmɪn〕
= *make sure*

insurgent〔ɪnˈsɝdʒənt〕*n.*
暴動者;叛徒

= rebel〔ˈrɛbḷ〕
= rioter〔ˈraɪətɚ〕
= revolter〔rɪˈvoltɚ〕
= agitator〔ˈædʒəˌtetɚ〕
= ringleader〔ˈrɪŋˌlidɚ〕
= troublemaker〔ˈtrʌbḷˌmekɚ〕
= instigator〔ˈɪnstəˌgetɚ〕
= rabble-rouser〔ˈræbḷˌrauzɚ〕

insurrection〔ɪnsəˈrɛkʃən〕*n.*
造反;起義

= revolt〔rɪˈvolt〕
= rebellion〔rɪˈbɛljən〕
= mutiny〔ˈmjutn̩ɪ〕
= riot〔ˈraɪət〕
= uprising〔ˈʌpraɪzɪŋ, ʌpˈraɪ-〕
= sedition〔sɪˈdɪʃən〕

intact〔ɪnˈtækt〕*adj.* 完整的

= untouched〔ʌnˈtʌtʃt〕
= whole〔hol〕
= uninjured〔ʌnˈɪndʒɚd〕
= undamaged〔ʌnˈdæmɪdʒd〕
= unchanged〔ʌnˈtʃendʒd〕
= complete〔kəmˈplit〕

intake〔ˈɪnˌtek〕*n.* ①引入之量
②收入

① = input〔ˈɪnˌput〕
= entry〔ˈɛntrɪ〕
② = income〔ˈɪnˌkʌm, ˈɪŋˌkʌm〕
= earnings〔ˈɝnɪŋz〕
= revenue〔ˈrɛvəˌnju〕
= receipts〔rɪˈsits〕
= proceeds〔ˈprosidz〕
= profits〔ˈprɑfɪts〕

intangible〔ɪnˈtændʒəbḷ〕*adj.*
無實體的

= untouchable〔ʌnˈtʌtʃəbḷ〕
= unsubstantial〔ˌʌnsəbˈstænʃəl〕

integrate〔ˈɪntəˌgret〕*v.*
①使平等　②使完全

① = equalize〔ˈikwəlˌaɪz〕
= balance〔ˈbæləns〕
= coordinate〔koˈɔrdn̩ˌet〕
= proportion〔prəˈporʃən, -ˈpor-〕
② = amass〔əˈmæs〕
= *form a whole*

integrity〔ɪnˈtɛgrətɪ〕*n.* ①正直
②完整

① = honesty〔ˈɑnɪstɪ〕
= sincerity〔sɪnˈsɛrətɪ〕
= uprightness〔ˈʌpˌraɪtnɪs, ʌpˈraɪ-〕
= honor〔ˈɑnɚ〕
= respectability〔rɪˌspɛktəˈbɪlətɪ〕
② = wholeness〔ˈholnɪs〕
= completeness〔kəmˈplitnɪs〕
= totality〔toˈtælətɪ〕
= entirety〔ɪnˈtaɪrtɪ〕

I

intelligent (ɪn'tɛlədʒənt) *adj.*
聰明的

= sensible ('sɛnsəbḷ)
= bright (braɪt)
= knowing ('noɪŋ)
= understanding (ˌʌndə'stændɪŋ)
= rational ('ræʃənḷ)
= aware (ə'wɛr)
= perceptive (pə'sɛptɪv)

intemperate (ɪn'tɛmpərɪt) *adj.*
無節制的

= excessive (ɪk'sɛsɪv)
= extreme (ɪk'strim)
= unreasonable (ʌn'riznəbḷ)
= unrestrained (ˌʌnrɪ'strend)

intend (ɪn'tɛnd) *v.* 意指；打算

= mean (min)
= plan (plæn)
= propose (prə'poz)
= aim (em)
= contemplate ('kɑntəmˌplet)
= *have in mind*

intense (ɪn'tɛns) *adj.* ①非常的
②強烈的

① = great (gret)
= considerable (kən'sɪdərəbḷ)
= extreme (ɪk'strim)
= drastic ('dræstɪk)
② = forceful ('forsfəl , 'fɔrs-)
= strong (strɔŋ)
= dynamic (daɪ'næmɪk)
= fierce (fɪrs)
= severe (sə'vɪr)
= rigorous ('rɪgərəs)

inter (ɪn'tɝ) *v.* 埋葬

= bury ('bɛrɪ)
= entomb (ɪn'tum , ɛn-)

intercede (ˌɪntə'sid) *v.* 說人情；
調停

= interfere (ˌɪntə'fɪr)
= intervene (ˌɪntə'vin)
= mediate ('midɪˌet)
= negotiate (nɪ'goʃɪˌet)
= arbitrate ('ɑrbəˌtret)
= umpire ('ʌmpaɪr)
= referee (ˌrɛfə'ri)
= *go between*

intercept (ˌɪntə'sɛpt) *v.*
中途攔截

= interrupt (ˌɪntə'rʌpt)
= check (tʃɛk)
= stop (stɑp)
= arrest (ə'rɛst)
= *hold up*

interchange (ˌɪntə'tʃendʒ) *v.*
交換

= exchange (ɪk'stʃendʒ)
= change (tʃendʒ)
= switch (swɪtʃ)
= trade (tred)
= substitute ('sʌbstəˌtjut)

intercourse ('ɪntəˌkors ,
-ˌkɔrs) *n.* ①交際　②交媾

① = communication
　　(kəˌmjunə'keʃən)

I

= dealings ('dilɪŋz)

② = copulation (,kɑpjə,leʃən)

= *sexual relations*

interest ('ɪntərɪst , 'ɪntrɪst) *n.*
①關心；趣味　②股份　③利益
④事物

① = concern (kən'sɝn)

= curiosity (,kjʊrɪ'ɑsətɪ)

= intrigue (ɪn'trig , 'ɪntrig)

② = share (ʃɛr)

= portion ('porʃən , 'por-)

= part (pɑrt)

= percentage (pə'sɛntɪdʒ)

③ = premium ('primɪəm)

= rate (ret)

= profit ('prɑfɪt)

④ = business ('bɪznɪs)

= affair (ə'fɛr)

= matters ('mætəz)

interesting ('ɪntərɪstɪŋ ,
'ɪntrɪstɪŋ) *adj.* 令人感興趣的

= arousing (ə'rauzɪŋ)

= provocative (prə'vɑkətɪv)

= fascinating ('fæsn̩,etɪŋ)

= enthralling (ɪn'θrɔlɪŋ)

= captivating ('kæptɪ,vetɪŋ)

= intriguing (ɪn'trigɪŋ)

= gripping ('grɪpɪŋ)

= absorbing (əb'sɔrbɪŋ)

= entertaining (,ɛntə'tenɪŋ)

= inviting (ɪn'vaɪtɪŋ)

= engrossing (ɛn'grosɪŋ)

= spellbinding ('spɛl,baɪndɪŋ)

= attractive (ə'træktɪv)

= appealing (ə'pilɪŋ)

= thought-provoking
('θɔtprə,vokɪŋ)

interfere (,ɪntə'fɪr) *v.* ①調停
②干涉

① = intervene (,ɪntə'vin)

= intercede (,ɪntə'sid)

= mediate ('midɪ,et)

= arbitrate ('ɑrbə,tret)

= umpire ('ʌmpaɪr)

= referee (,rɛfə'ri)

② = meddle ('mɛdl̩)

= intrude (ɪn'trud)

= encroach (ɪn'krotʃ)

= interrupt (,ɪntə'rʌpt)

interior (ɪn'tɪrɪə) *n.* 內部

= inside ('ɪn'saɪd)

= inner ('ɪnə)

= middle ('mɪdl̩)

= heart (hɑrt)

= core (kor)

= nucleus ('njuklɪəs)

interject (,ɪntə'dʒɛkt) *v.* 插入

= insert (ɪn'sɝt)

= implant (ɪm'plænt , -'plɑnt)

= interpose (,ɪntə'poz)

= *put between*

interlace (,ɪntə'les) *v.* 編織；
使交錯

= weave (wiv)

= intertwine (,ɪntə'twaɪn)

= braid (bred)

I

interlock (͵ɪntə'lɑk) v. 連結

= join (dʒɔɪn)
= link (lɪŋk)
= connect (kə'nɛkt)
= mesh (mɛʃ)
= engage (ɪn'gedʒ)

interlude ('ɪntə͵lud) n.
中間間隔之時間

= intermission (͵ɪntə'mɪʃən)
= interval ('ɪntəvl̩)
= interim ('ɪntərɪm)
= respite ('rɛspɪt)
= break (brek)
= pause (pɔz)
= recess (rɪ'sɛs , 'risɛs)
= interruption (͵ɪntə'rʌpʃən)

intermediate (͵ɪntə'midɪ͵et)
adj. 居間的；中間的

= middle ('mɪdl̩)
= intervening (͵ɪntə'vinɪŋ)
= in between

interminable (ɪn'tɜmɪnəbl̩)
adj. 冗長的

= endless ('ɛndlɪs)
= long (lɔŋ)
= lengthy ('lɛŋkθɪ , -ŋθɪ)
= infinite ('ɪnfənɪt)
= perpetual (pə'pɛtʃʊəl)

intermingle (͵ɪntə'mɪŋgl̩) v.
混合

= mix (mɪks)
= blend (blɛnd)

= merge (mɝdʒ)
= combine (kəm'baɪn)
= mingle ('mɪŋgl̩)

intermission (͵ɪntə'mɪʃən) n.
休息時間

= pause (pɔz)
= interruption (͵ɪntə'rʌpʃən)
= interlude ('ɪntə͵lud)
= interval ('ɪntəvl̩)
= interim ('ɪntərɪm)
= respite ('rɛspɪt)
= break (brek)
= recess (rɪ'sɛs , 'risɛs)

intermittent (͵ɪntə'mɪtn̩t) adj.
間歇的；斷續的

= periodic (͵pɪrɪ'ɑdɪk)
= recurrent (rɪ'kɝənt)
= sporadic (spo'rædɪk , spə-)
= broken ('brokən)
= irregular (ɪ'rɛgjələ)
= unsteady (ʌn'stɛdɪ)

internal (ɪn'tɝnl̩) adj. 內部的

= inner ('ɪnə)
= inside ('ɪn'saɪd)
= interior (ɪn'tɪrɪə)
= innermost ('ɪnəmost)

interpret (ɪn'tɝprɪt) v. 解釋；
說明

= explain (ɪk'splen)
= clarify ('klærə͵faɪ)
= translate ('trænslet , træn'slet)
= analyze ('ænl̩͵aɪz)

nterrogate (ɪn'tɛrəˌget) *v.*
質問；訊問

= question ('kwɛstʃən)
= examine (ɪg'zæmɪn)
= quiz (kwɪz)
= test (tɛst)
= grill (grɪl)
= cross-examine ('krɔsɪg'zæmɪn)
= *inquire of*

nterrupt (ˌɪntə'rʌpt) *v.* 打斷

= hinder ('hɪndə)
= stop (stɑp)
= intrude (ɪn'trud)
= interfere (ˌɪntə'fɪr)
= *break in*

ntertwine (ɪntə'twaɪn) *v.*
纏；編織

= interlace (ˌɪntə'les)
= weave (wiv)
= braid (bred)

terval ('ɪntəvḷ) *n.* 中間時間；
歇

= interruption (ˌɪntə'rʌpʃən)
= intermission (ˌɪntə'mɪʃən)
= interlude ('ɪntəˌlud)
= interim ('ɪntərɪm)
= respite ('rɛspɪt)
= break (brek)
= pause (pɔz)
= recess (rɪ'sɛs , 'rɪsɛs)

tervention (ˌɪntə'vɛnʃən) *v.*
裁；調停

= interference (ˌɪntə'fɪrəns)
= intrusion (ɪn'truʒən)
= infringement (ɪn'frɪndʒmənt)
= meddling ('mɛdḷɪŋ)

interview ('ɪntəˌvju) *v.* 訪問；
面談

= question ('kwɛstʃən)
= interrogate (ɪn'tɛrəˌget)
= quiz (kwɪz)
= test (tɛst)
= examine (ɪg'zæmɪn)

1. **intimate** ('ɪntəmɪt) *adj.*
①親密的 ②祕密的

① = close (klos)
= familiar (fə'mɪljə)
② = innermost ('ɪnəmost)
= private ('praɪvɪt)
= secret ('sikrɪt)

2. **intimate** ('ɪntəˌmet) *v.* 暗指；
暗示

= hint (hɪnt)
= suggest (sə(g)'dʒɛst)
= imply (ɪm'plaɪ)
= indicate ('ɪndəˌket)
= insinuate (ɪn'sɪnjʊˌet)

intimidate (ɪn'tɪməˌdet) *v.*
恐嚇

= frighten ('fraɪtṇ)
= threaten ('θrɛtṇ)
= menace ('mɛnɪs)
= cow (kaʊ)
= browbeat ('braʊˌbit)
= bully ('bʊlɪ)

I

= harass（'hærəs , hə'ræs）

= terrorize（'tɛrə,raɪz）

intolerable（ɪn'talərəbḷ）*adj.*
無法忍受的

= unbearable（ʌn'bɛrəbḷ）

= insufferable（ɪn'sʌfrəbḷ,
-fərə-）

intolerant（ɪn'talərənt）*adj.*
固執己見的

= impatient（ɪm'peʃənt）

= unsympathetic
（,ʌnsɪmpə'θɛtɪk）

= bigoted（'bɪgətɪd）

= prejudiced（'prɛdʒədɪst）

intoxicated（ɪn'taksə,ketɪd）
adj. ①醉酒的　②興奮的

① = drunk（drʌŋk）

= inebriated（ɪn'ibrɪ,etɪd）

② = excited（ɪk'saɪtɪd）

= impassioned（ɪm'pæʃənd）

= moved（muvd）

= touched（tʌtʃt）

= impressed（ɪm'prɛst）

= affected（ə'fɛktɪd）

intrepid（ɪn'trɛpɪd）*adj.* 勇敢的

= fearless（'fɪrlɪs）

= dauntless（'dɔntlɪs , 'dan-）

= brave（brev）

= courageous（kə'redʒəs）

= bold（bold）

= valiant（'væljənt）

= heroic（hɪ'ro·ɪk）

intricate（'ɪntrəkɪt）*adj.*
錯綜複雜的

= complicated（'kamplə,ketɪd）

= perplexing（pə'plɛksɪŋ）

= entangled（ɪn'tæŋgḷd , ɛn-）

= complex（kəm'plɛks）

= confused（kən'fjuzd）

= involved（ɪn'valvd）

intrigue（ɪn'trig , 'ɪntrig）*n.*
①陰謀　②風流韻事；私通

① = plot（plat）

= scheme（skim）

= conspiracy（kən'spɪrəsɪ）

② = romance（'romæns , ro'mæns）

= amour（ə'mʊr , æ-）

= *love affair*

intriguing（ɪn'trigɪŋ）*adj.*
吸引的

= fascinating（'fæsṇ,etɪŋ）

= alluring（ə'lʊrɪŋ）

= captivating（'kæptɪ,vetɪŋ）

= charming（'tʃarmɪŋ）

= enchanting（ɪn'tʃæntɪŋ）

= enthralling（ɪn'θrɔlɪŋ）

= attractive（ə'træktɪv）

= interesting（'ɪntərɪstɪŋ,
'ɪntrɪstɪŋ）

= appealing（ə'pilɪŋ）

= enticing（ɪn'taɪsɪŋ , ɛn-）

= inviting（ɪn'vaɪtɪŋ）

= tantalizing（'tæntə,laɪzɪŋ）

= bewitching（bɪ'wɪtʃɪŋ）

= winning（'wɪnɪŋ）

= thrilling（'θrɪlɪŋ）

= tempting ('tɛmptɪŋ)

= provocative (prə'vɑkətɪv)

ntroduce (ˌɪntrə'djus) v.
①提倡;引入 ②介紹

= inaugurate (ɪn'ɔgjəˌret)

= institute ('ɪnstəˌtjut)

= launch (lɔntʃ , lɑntʃ)

= innovate ('ɪnəˌvet)

= *bring in*

= present (prɪ'zɛnt)

= *acquaint with*

ntrude (ɪn'trud) v. 干擾

= interfere (ˌɪntə'fɪr)

= infringe (ɪn'frɪndʒ)

= encroach (ɪn'krotʃ)

= trespass ('trɛspəs)

= meddle ('mɛdl̩)

= overstep (ˌovə'stɛp)

undate ('ɪnʌnˌdet , ɪn'ʌndet)
氾濫

= flood (flʌd)

= overflow (ˌovə'flo)

= cascade (kæs'ked)

= deluge ('dɛljudʒ)

= drench (drɛntʃ)

= *run over*

vade (ɪn'ved) v. 侵犯;干擾

= intrude (ɪn'trud)

= overrun (ˌovə'rʌn)

= encroach (ɪn'krotʃ)

= trespass ('trɛspəs)

= infringe (ɪn'frɪndʒ)

= raid (red)

= attack (ə'tæk)

= *advance upon*

invalid (①'ɪnvəlɪd , ② ɪn'vælɪd)
adj. ①有病的 ②無效的

① = sickly ('sɪklɪ)

= weak (wik)

= unhealthy (ʌn'hɛlθɪ)

= infirm (ɪn'fɜm)

= frail (frel)

= debilitated (dɪ'bɪləˌtetɪd)

② = void (vɔɪd)

= ineffective (ˌɪnə'fɛktɪv)

= *without value*

invaluable (ɪn'væljəbl̩) *adj.*
無價的

= priceless ('praɪslɪs)

= precious ('prɛʃəs)

= dear (dɪr)

= worthwhile ('wɜθ'hwaɪl)

invariable (ɪn'vɛrɪəbl̩) *adj.*
不變的

= consistent (kən'sɪstənt)

= unchanging (ʌn'tʃendʒɪŋ)

= constant ('kɑnstənt)

= permanent ('pɜmənənt)

= uniform ('junəˌfɔrm)

= steady ('stɛdɪ)

invent (ɪn'vɛnt) v. 創作;虛構

= originate (ə'rɪdʒəˌnet)

= devise (dɪ'vaɪz)

= develop (dɪ'vɛləp)

I

= contrive (kən'traɪv)
= concoct (kɑn'kɑkt , kən-)
= *make up*

inventory ('ɪnvən,torɪ , -,tɔrɪ)
n. 詳細目錄

= stock (stɑk)
= collection (kə'lɛkʃən)
= list (lɪst)

invert (ɪn'vɝt) *v.* 倒轉

= reverse (rɪ'vɝs)
= *turn around*

invest (ɪn'vɛst) *v.* ①以…爲賭注
②授權予

① = venture ('vɛntʃə)
= stake (stek)
② = empower (ɪm'pauə)
= place (ples)
= provide (prə'vaɪd)
= endow (ɪn'dau)

investigate (ɪn'vɛstə,get) *v.*
調查；研究

= search (sɝtʃ)
= explore (ɪk'splor , -'splɔr)
= examine (ɪg'zæmɪn)
= inspect (ɪn'spɛkt)
= study ('stʌdɪ)
= review (rɪ'vju)
= probe (prob)
= scrutinize ('skrutn̩,aɪz)

invigorating (ɪn'vɪgə,retɪŋ)
adj. 鼓舞的

= stimulating ('stɪmjə,letɪŋ)
= exhilarating (ɪg'zɪlə,retɪŋ , ɛg-
= energizing ('ɛnə,dʒaɪzɪŋ)
= bracing ('bresɪŋ)
= refreshing (rɪ'frɛʃɪŋ)

invincible (ɪn'vɪnsəbl̩) *adj.*
難以克服的

= unbeatable (ʌn'bitəbl̩)
= unconquerable (ʌn'kɑŋkərəbl̩
= invulnerable (ɪn'vʌlnərəbl̩)
= impregnable (ɪm'prɛgnəbl̩)

invite (ɪn'vaɪt) *v.* ①請求
②引誘

① = ask (æsk)
= request (rɪ'kwɛst)
= call (kɔl)
= summon ('sʌmən)
② = attract (ə'trækt)
= tempt (tɛmpt)
= interest ('ɪntərɪst , 'ɪntrɪ-)
= appeal (ə'pil)

invoke (ɪn'vok) *v.* 求（神）
保護；祈求

= pray (pre)
= beseech (bɪ'sitʃ)
= entreat (ɪn'trit)
= beg (bɛg)
= implore (ɪm'plor , -'plɔr)
= appeal (ə'pil)
= plead (plid)

involuntary (ɪn'vɑlən,tɛrɪ)
adj. ①非本意的 ②本能的

= unwilling (ʌn'wɪlɪŋ)
= forced (fɔrst)

= instinctive (ɪn'stɪŋktɪv)
= automatic (ˌɔtə'mætɪk)
= mechanical (mə'kænɪkl̩)
= spontaneous (spɑn'tenɪəs)
= reflex (rɪ'flɛks)
= unconscious (ʌn'kɑnʃəs)
= compulsive (kəm'pʌlsɪv)
= unthinking (ʌn'θɪŋkɪŋ)
= unintentional (ˌʌnɪn'tɛnʃən̩l)

nvolve (ɪn'vɑlv) v. ①包括
)使複雜   ③專心於

= include (ɪn'klud)
= concern (kən'sɜn)
= affect (ə'fɛkt)
= entail (ɪn'tel , ɛn-)
= implicate ('ɪmplɪˌket)
= envelop (ɪn'vɛləp)
= encompass (ɪn'kʌmpəs , ɛn-)
= complicate ('kɑmpləˌket)
= tangle ('tæŋgl̩)
= confuse (kən'fjuz)
= confound (kɑn'faʊnd , kən-)
= occupy ('ɑkjəˌpaɪ)
= absorb (əb'sɔrb)
= engross (ɪn'gros , ɛn-)

ate ('aɪret , aɪ'ret) adj. 生氣的

= angry ('æŋgrɪ)
= mad (mæd)
= indignant (ɪn'dɪgnənt)
= infuriated (ɪn'fjʊrɪˌetɪd)

ksome ('ɜksəm) adj.
人厭煩的

= tiresome ('taɪrsəm)
= tedious ('tidɪəs , 'tidʒəs)
= wearisome ('wɪrɪsəm)
= troublesome ('trʌblsəm)
= trying ('traɪɪŋ)
= annoying (ə'nɔɪɪŋ)
= irritating ('ɪrəˌtetɪŋ)
= bothersome ('bɑðəsəm)

irregular (ɪ'rɛgjələ) adj.
①不合常規的   ②不整齊的

① = unnatural (ʌn'nætʃərəl)
   = abnormal (æb'nɔrml̩)
② = uneven (ʌn'ivən)
   = erratic (ə'rætɪk , ɪ-)
   = rough (rʌf)
   = distorted (dɪs'tɔrtɪd)

irrelevant (ɪ'rɛləvənt) adj.
離題的

   = unfitting (ʌn'fɪtɪŋ)
   = inappropriate (ˌɪnə'proprɪɪt)
   = unrelated (ˌʌnrɪ'letɪd)
   = far-fetched ('fɑr'fɛtʃt)

irresistible (ˌɪrɪ'zɪstəbl̩)
adj. 不可抵抗的

   = compelling (kəm'pɛlɪŋ)
   = moving ('muvɪŋ)

irresolute (ɪ'rɛzəˌlut ,
-'rɛzl̩ˌjut) adj. 猶豫不決的

   = hesitating ('hɛzəˌtetɪŋ)
   = uncertain (ʌn'sɜtn̩)
   = unsure (ʌn'ʃur)
   = indecisive (ˌɪndɪ'saɪsɪv)
   = fickle ('fɪkl̩)

I

irreverent (ɪ'rɛvərənt) *adj.*
不恭敬的

= disrespectful (ˌdɪsrɪ'spɛktfəl ,
    -fʊl)
= discourteous (dɪs'kɝtɪəs)
= insolent ('ɪnsələnt)
= impudent ('ɪmpjədənt)
= impious ('ɪmpɪəs , ɪm'paɪəs)

irritable ('ɪrətəbḷ) *adj.* 過敏的；
易怒的

= impatient (ɪm'peʃənt)
= cross (krɔs)
= cranky ('kræŋkɪ)
= irascible (aɪ'ræsəbḷ , ɪ'ræsə-)
= testy ('tɛstɪ)

irritate ('ɪrəˌtet) *v.* ①激怒
②使感不適

① = annoy (ə'nɔɪ)
= vex (vɛks)
= incite (ɪn'saɪt)
= agitate ('ædʒəˌtet)
= provoke (prə'vok)
= instigate ('ɪnstəˌget)
= foment (fo'mɛnt)
= infuriate (ɪn'fjʊrɪˌet)
= madden ('mædṇ)
= anger ('æŋgɚ)
= *stir up*
② = pain (pen)
= hurt (hɝt)
= wound (wund)
= chafe (tʃef)
= rub (rʌb)
= grate (gret)
= *make sore*

isolate ('aɪsḷˌet , 'ɪs-) *v.* 隔離

= separate ('sɛpəˌret)
= segregate ('sɛgrɪˌget)
= quarantine ('kwɔrənˌtin ,
    'kwar-)
= seclude (sɪ'klud)
= *set apart*

issue ('ɪʃʊ , 'ɪʃjʊ) *n.* ①結果；
問題 ②發行

① = cause (kɔz)
= principle ('prɪnsəpḷ)
= campaign (kæm'pen)
= problem ('prɑbləm)
= topic ('tɑpɪk)
= subject ('sʌbdʒɪkt)
= theme (θim)
= text (tɛkst)
= question ('kwɛstʃən)
= point (pɔɪnt)
② = publication (ˌpʌblɪ'keʃən)
= edition (ɪ'dɪʃən)
= copy ('kɑpɪ)

itch (ɪtʃ) *n.* ①發癢 ②渴望

① = *prickly feeling*
② = desire (dɪ'zaɪr)
= craving ('krevɪŋ)

item ('aɪtəm) *n.* 條款；項目

= part (pɑrt)
= segment ('sɛgmənt)
= portion ('porʃən , 'pɔr-)
= subdivision (ˌsʌbdə'vɪʒən)
= object ('ɑbdʒɪkt)
= unit ('junɪt)

= component (kəm'ponənt)

= piece (pis)

= article ('ɑrtɪkḷ)

= notation (no'teʃən)

= entry ('ɛntrɪ)

temize ('aɪtəm,aɪz) v. 詳列

= list (lɪst)

= total ('totḷ)

= summarize ('sʌmə,raɪz)

= *sum up*

J

ab (dʒæb) v. 刺戳

= poke (pok)

= push (puʃ)

= thrust (θrʌst)

= nudge (nʌdʒ)

= prod (prɑd)

agged ('dʒægɪd) adj. 有鋸齒形的

= pointy ('pɔɪntɪ)

= ragged ('rægɪd)

= notched (nɑtʃt)

= serrated ('sɛretɪd)

ail (dʒel) v. 監禁

= imprison (ɪm'prɪzṇ)

= incarcerate (ɪn'kɑrsə,ret)

= *lock up*

= *hold captive*

am (dʒæm) ① v. 塞滿
② n. 果醬

= crowd (kraʊd)

= stuff (stʌf)

= load (lod)

= cram (kræm)

= press (prɛs)

= squeeze (skwiz)

= push (puʃ)

= crush (krʌʃ)

= heap (hip)

② = jelly ('dʒɛlɪ)

= marmalade ('mɑrmḷ,ed , -'led)

= preserves (prɪ'zɝvz)

jar (dʒɑr) ① v. 刺激
② n. 大口瓶

① = shake (ʃek)

= rattle ('rætḷ)

= jolt (dʒolt)

= bounce (baʊns)

② = *glass container*

jaunt (dʒɔnt , dʒɑ-) n. 遠足；
遊覽

= trip (trɪp)

= journey ('dʒɝnɪ)

= excursion (ɪk'skɝʒən , -ʃən)

= tour (tʊr)

= voyage ('vɔɪ·ɪdʒ)

= outing ('aʊtɪŋ)

= expedition (,ɛkspɪ'dɪʃən)

jealous ('dʒɛləs) adj. 嫉妒的

= envious ('ɛnvɪəs)

= covetous ('kʌvɪtəs)

= *desirous of*

jeer (dʒɪr) v. 嘲弄

= taunt (tɔnt)

J

= scoff ﹙ skɔf , skɑf ﹚
= mock ﹙ mɑk ﹚
= *make fun of*

jeopardize ﹙ 'dʒɛpəd,aɪz ﹚ *v.*
冒…之險

= risk ﹙ rɪsk ﹚
= endanger ﹙ ɪn'dendʒə , ɛn- ﹚
= imperil ﹙ ɪm'pɛrəl , -ɪl ﹚
= hazard ﹙ 'hæzəd ﹚
= expose ﹙ ɪk'spoz ﹚

jerk ﹙ dʒɝk ﹚ *v.* 急拉；急動

= jolt ﹙ dʒolt ﹚
= *pull suddenly*
= *twist suddenly*

jest ﹙ dʒɛst ﹚ *n.* 笑話；嘲弄

= joke ﹙ dʒok ﹚
= fun ﹙ fʌn ﹚
= mock ﹙ mɑk ﹚
= tease ﹙ tiz ﹚

jetty ﹙ 'dʒɛtɪ ﹚ *n.* 防波堤；碼頭

= breakwater ﹙ 'brek,wɔtə ,
    -,wɑtə ﹚
= pier ﹙ pɪr ﹚
= buttress ﹙ 'bʌtrɪs ﹚
= bulwark ﹙ 'bulwək ﹚

jewel ﹙ 'dʒuəl ﹚ *n.* 珠寶

= stone ﹙ ston ﹚
= gem ﹙ dʒɛm ﹚
= ornament ﹙ 'ɔrnəmənt ﹚

jingle ﹙ 'dʒɪŋgl ﹚ *v.* 叮噹地響

= ring ﹙ rɪŋ ﹚

= chime ﹙ tʃaɪm ﹚
= tinkle ﹙ 'tɪŋkl ﹚

job ﹙ dʒɑb ﹚ *n.* 工作；職位

= work ﹙ wɝk ﹚
= business ﹙ 'bɪznɪs ﹚
= employment ﹙ ɪm'plɔɪmənt ﹚
= task ﹙ tæsk ﹚
= assignment ﹙ ə'saɪnmənt ﹚
= duty ﹙ 'djutɪ ﹚
= position ﹙ pə'zɪʃən ﹚
= labor ﹙ 'lebə ﹚
= toil ﹙ tɔɪl ﹚

jog ﹙ dʒɑg ﹚ *n.* 小步慢跑

= run ﹙ rʌn ﹚
= trot ﹙ trɑt ﹚
= gait ﹙ get ﹚
= sprint ﹙ sprɪnt ﹚
= lope ﹙ lop ﹚

join ﹙ dʒɔɪn ﹚ *v.* 連接；加入

= connect ﹙ kə'nɛkt ﹚
= fasten ﹙ 'fæsn , 'fɑ- ﹚
= clasp ﹙ klæsp ﹚
= unite ﹙ ju'naɪt ﹚
= combine ﹙ kəm'baɪn ﹚
= couple ﹙ 'kʌpl ﹚
= link ﹙ lɪŋk ﹚
= attach ﹙ ə'tætʃ ﹚
= annex ﹙ ə'nɛks ﹚
= *put together*

joke ﹙ dʒok ﹚ *n.* 笑話；笑柄

= jest ﹙ dʒɛst ﹚
= quip ﹙ kwɪp ﹚

J

= banter（'bæntə）

= tease（tiz）

lly（'dʒalı）*adj.* 歡樂的

= merry（'mɛrı）

= cheerful（'tʃɪrfəl）

= pleasant（'plɛznt）

= joyful（'dʒɔɪfəl）

= jovial（'dʒovɪəl）

= gleeful（'glifəl , -fḷ）

lt（dʒolt）*v.* 搖晃

= jerk（dʒɝk）

= jar（dʒar）

= shake（ʃek）

= startle（'startḷ）

= jounce（dʒaʊns）

stle（'dʒasḷ）*v.* 推；擠

= push（pʊʃ）

= shove（ʃʌv）

= thrust（θrʌst）

= bump（bʌmp）

t（dʒat）*v.* 匆匆而記

= write（raıt）

= note（not）

= record（rı'kɔrd）

= *mark down*

unce（dʒaʊns）*v.* 搖撼；震動

= jolt（dʒolt）

= bounce（baʊns）

= bump（bʌmp）

urnal（'dʒɝnḷ）*n.* ①日記
報紙；雜誌

① = account（ə'kaʊnt）

= log（lag , lɔg）

= diary（'daɪərı）

= chronicle（'kranıkḷ）

= *daily record*

② = newspaper（'njuz,pepə , 'njus- ,
'nu- ）

= magazine（,mægə'zin , 'mæ- ）

journey（'dʒɝnı）*n.* 旅行

= trip（trıp）

= voyage（'vɔı·ıdʒ）

= tour（tʊr）

= expedition（,ɛkspı'dıʃən）

= excursion（ık'skɝʒən , -ʃən）

= jaunt（dʒant , dʒɔnt）

= outing（'aʊtıŋ）

= junket（'dʒʌŋkıt）

jovial（'dʒovɪəl）*adj.* 快樂的

= kindly（'kaındlı）

= merry（'mɛrı）

= joyful（'dʒɔɪfəl）

= gleeful（'glifəl , -fḷ）

= jolly（'dʒalı）

= good-natured（'gʊd'netʃəd）

= good-hearted（'gʊd'hartıd）

= good-humored（'gʊd'hjuməd ,
-'ju- ）

joyful（'dʒɔɪfəl）*adj.* 歡喜的

= glad（glæd）

= happy（'hæpı）

= cheerful（'tʃɪrfəl）

= blissful（'blısfəl）

= merry（'mɛrı）

J

= jovial ('dʒovɪəl)
= gleeful ('glifəl , -fḷ)

jubilant ('dʒublənt) *adj.* 喜悅的

= rejoicing (rɪ'dʒɔɪsɪŋ)
= overjoyed (,ovɚ'dʒɔɪd)
= gay (ge)
= delighted (dɪ'laɪtɪd)
= elated (ɪ'letɪd)

judge (dʒʌdʒ) ① *v.* 審判
② *n.* 裁判人

① = decide (dɪ'saɪd)
= consider (kən'sɪdɚ)
= *form an opinion*
② = mediator ('midɪ,etɚ)
= referee (,rɛfə'ri)
= umpire ('ʌmpaɪr)

judicious (dʒu'dɪʃəs) *adj.*
明智的

= wise (waɪz)
= sensible ('sɛnsəbḷ)
= thoughtful ('θɔtfəl)
= well-advised ('wɛləd'vaɪzd)

jumble ('dʒʌmbḷ) *v.* 混雜

= mix (mɪks)
= confuse (kən'fjuz)
= scramble ('skræmbḷ)
= muddle ('mʌdḷ)

jumbo ('dʒʌmbo) *adj.* 巨大的

= big (bɪg)
= huge (hjudʒ)
= enormous (ɪ'nɔrməs)
= immense (ɪ'mɛns)

= colossal (kə'lɑsḷ)
= giant ('dʒaɪənt)
= gigantic (dʒaɪ'gæntɪk)
= mammoth ('mæməθ)
= monstrous ('mɑnstrəs)
= tremendous (trɪ'mɛndəs)

jump (dʒʌmp) *v.* 跳躍

= spring (sprɪŋ)
= leap (lip)
= bound (baund)
= vault (vɔlt)
= hurdle ('hɝdḷ)
= hop (hɑp)

junction ('dʒʌŋkʃən) *n.* 聯絡；
連接

= joining ('dʒɔɪnɪŋ)
= connection (kə'nɛkʃən)
= union ('junjən)
= linking ('lɪŋkɪŋ)
= coupling ('kʌplɪŋ)
= hookup ('huk,ʌp)
= meeting ('mitɪŋ)
= tie-up ('taɪ,ʌp)

junior ('dʒunjɚ) *adj.* ①年少的
②下級的

① = younger ('jʌŋgɚ)
② = lower ('loɚ)
= lesser ('lɛsɚ)
= secondary ('sɛkənd,ɛrɪ)
= subordinate (sə'bɔrdṇɪt)
= minor ('maɪnɚ)

junk (dʒʌŋk) *n.* ①破爛物
②中國大帆船

① = rubbish ('rʌbɪʃ)

= trash (træʃ)

= scrap (skræp)

= litter ('lɪtə)

= debris (də'bri , 'debri)

② = ship (ʃɪp)

= *Chinese sailing vessel*

ust (dʒʌst) ① *adj.* 確實的
② *adv.* 僅 ③ *adj.* 公正的

① = exact (ɪg'zækt)

= precise (prɪ'saɪs)

② = only ('onlɪ)

= merely ('mɪrlɪ)

③ = righteous ('raɪtʃəs)

= fair (fɛr)

= proper ('prɑpə)

= good (gʊd)

= moral ('mɔrəl)

= virtuous ('vɜtʃʊəs)

ut (dʒʌt) *v.* 突出

= project (prə'dʒɛkt)

= protrude (prə'trud)

= *stick out*

= *stand out*

uvenile ('dʒuvənḷ , -‚naɪl) *adj.*
力年的

= young (jʌŋ)

= youthful ('juθfəl)

K

een (kin) *adj.* ①銳利的
②聰明的；敏捷的

① = sharp (ʃɑrp)

= cutting ('kʌtɪŋ)

= fine (faɪn)

= acute (ə'kjut)

② = quick (kwɪk)

= exact (ɪg'zækt)

= smart (smɑrt)

= bright (braɪt)

= clever ('klɛvə)

= sharp-witted ('ʃɑrp'wɪtɪd)

keep (kip) *v.* 保持；保衛

= have (hæv)

= hold (hold)

= maintain (men'ten , mən'ten)

= preserve (prɪ'zɜv)

= conserve (kən'sɜv)

= save (sev)

= tend (tɛnd)

= protect (prə'tɛkt)

= guard (gɑrd)

kennel ('kɛnḷ) *n.* 狗舍

= doghouse ('dɔg‚haʊs)

= pound (paʊnd)

key (ki) *n.* ①鑰匙　②解答
③聲調

① = opener ('opənə)

② = clue (klu)

= answer ('ænsə)

= explanation (‚ɛksplə'neʃən)

= lead (lid)

③ = tone (ton)

= pitch (pɪtʃ)

= note (not)

K

kid〔kɪd〕① v. 嘲弄 ② n. 小孩
③ n. 小山羊

① = tease〔tiz〕
= joke〔dʒok〕
= fool〔ful〕
= jest〔dʒɛst〕
② = child〔tʃaɪld〕
= tot〔tat〕
③ = *young goat*

kidnap〔'kɪdnæp〕v. 綁架

= snatch〔snætʃ〕
= abduct〔æb'dʌkt, əb'-〕
= shanghai〔'ʃæŋhaɪ, 'ʃæŋ'haɪ〕
= *carry off*

kill〔kɪl〕v. 殺

= slay〔sle〕
= slaughter〔'slɔtɚ〕
= murder〔'mɝdɚ〕
= destroy〔dɪ'strɔɪ〕
= end〔ɛnd〕
= finish〔'fɪnɪʃ〕
= annihilate〔ə'naɪə,let〕
= execute〔'ɛksɪ,kjut〕

kin〔kɪn〕n. 親戚

= family〔'fæməlɪ〕
= relatives〔'rɛlətɪvz〕
= relations〔rɪ'leʃənz〕
= folks〔folks〕

kind〔kaɪnd〕① adj. 慈愛的
② n. 種；屬

① = friendly〔'frɛndlɪ〕
= gentle〔'dʒɛntl̩〕

= decent〔'disn̩t〕
= generous〔'dʒɛnərəs〕
= considerate〔kən'sɪdərɪt, -'sɪdrɪt〕
= tender〔'tɛndɚ〕
= sympathetic〔,sɪmpə'θɛtɪk〕
= thoughtful〔'θɔtfəl〕
= warmhearted〔'wɔrm'hɑrtɪd〕
② = sort〔sɔrt〕
= type〔taɪp〕
= variety〔və'raɪətɪ〕
= species〔'spiʃiz, -ʃɪs〕
= nature〔'netʃɚ〕
= make〔mek〕

kindle〔'kɪndl̩〕v. ①燃起
②激起

① = light〔laɪt〕
= ignite〔ɪg'naɪt〕
= *set afire*
② = arouse〔ə'rauz〕
= start〔stɑrt〕
= trigger〔'trɪgɚ〕
= move〔muv〕
= provoke〔prə'vok〕
= *stir up*

king〔kɪŋ〕n. 君主；最高者

= ruler〔'rulɚ〕
= sovereign〔'sɑvrɪn, 'sʌv-〕
= monarch〔'mɑnɚk〕
= chief〔tʃif〕
= potentate〔'potn̩,tet〕

kink〔kɪŋk〕① v. 使糾結
② n. 糾纏 ③ n. 奇想

① = curl〔kɝl〕

= twist (twist)

) = complication (ˌkɑmpləˈkeʃən)

) = quirk (kwɝk)

= *mental twist*

= *queer idea*

kiss (kɪs) *v.* 吻

= osculate (ˈɑskjəˌlet)

= buss (bʌs)

= *touch with lips*

kit (kɪt) *n.* 工具

= equipment (ɪˈkwɪpmənt)

= set (sɛt)

= outfit (ˈaʊtˌfɪt)

= furnishings (ˈfɝnɪʃɪŋz)

= gear (gɪr)

= rig (rɪg)

knack (næk) *n.* 技巧；竅門

= skill (skɪl)

= talent (ˈtælənt)

= art (ɑrt)

= know-how (ˈnoˈhaʊ)

knave (nev) *n.* 騙子

= rascal (ˈræskḷ)

= rogue (rog)

= scoundrel (ˈskaʊndrəl)

= villain (ˈvɪlən)

= *tricky man*

knead (nid) *v.* 揉；按摩

= mix (mɪks)

= blend (blɛnd)

= combine (kəmˈbaɪn)

= massage (məˈsɑʒ)

knife (naɪf) *n.* 小刀

= blade (bled)

= sword (sord , sɔrd)

knit (nɪt) *v.* 編結；黏合

= join (dʒɔɪn)

= fasten (ˈfæsṇ , ˈfɑ-)

= connect (kəˈnɛkt)

= unite (juˈnaɪt)

knock (nɑk) *v.* 敲擊

= hit (hɪt)

= strike (straɪk)

= punch (pʌntʃ)

= jab (dʒæb)

= pound (paʊnd)

= beat (bit)

= hammer (ˈhæmə)

= rap (ræp)

= bang (bæŋ)

know (no) *v.* 知道；了解

= understand (ˌʌndəˈstænd)

= comprehend (ˌkɑmprɪˈhɛnd)

= perceive (pəˈsiv)

= recognize (ˈrɛkəgˌnaɪz)

= indentify (aɪˈdɛntəˌfaɪ)

= *be sure of*

= *be aware of*

L

label (ˈlebḷ) *n.* 標籤

= name (nem)

= title (ˈtaɪtḷ)

= tag (tæg)

labor ('lebɚ) *n.* 勞動

  = work (wɜk)
  = industry ('ɪndəstrɪ)
  = toil (tɔɪl)
  = employment (ɪm'plɔɪmənt)
  = effort ('ɛfɚt)
  = task (tæsk)

labyrinth ('læbə,rɪnθ) *n.* 迷宮

  = maze (mez)
  = complex ('kɑmplɛks)
  = tangle ('tæŋgl̩)

lacerate ('læsə,ret) *v.* 撕裂；
傷害

  = mangle ('mæŋgl̩)
  = wound (wund)
  = *tear roughly*

lack (læk) *v.* 缺乏

  = want (wɑnt)
  = need (nid)
  = require (rɪ'kwaɪr)
  = *fall short*

lacquer ('lækɚ) *v.* 漆（器）

  = varnish ('vɑrnɪʃ)
  = polish ('pɑlɪʃ)
  = gild (gɪld)

lad (læd) *n.* 少年；青年

  = boy (bɔɪ)
  = youth (juθ)

laden ('ledn̩) *adj.* 充滿…的

  = loaded ('lodɪd)
  = burdened ('bɝdn̩d)
  = weighted ('wetɪd)

ladle ('ledl̩) *n.* 長柄杓

  = dipper ('dɪpɚ)
  = scoop (skup)

lady ('ledɪ) *n.* 淑女；主婦

  = woman ('wʊmən , 'wu-)
  = matron ('metrən)

lag (læg) *v.* 逗留；延遲

  = linger ('lɪŋgɚ)
  = loiter ('lɔɪtɚ)
  = dawdle ('dɔdl̩)
  = poke (pok)
  = dillydally ('dɪlɪ,dælɪ)
  = delay (dɪ'le)
  = tarry ('tærɪ)

lament (lə'mɛnt) *v.* 哀悼

  = mourn (morn , mɔrn)
  = sorrow ('sɑro)
  = grieve (griv)
  = bewail (bɪ'wel)
  = bemoan (bɪ'mon)

lance (læns , lɑns) *v.* 刺破；切開

  = pierce (pɪrs)
  = stab (stæb)
  = perforate ('pɝfə,ret)
  = knife (naɪf)
  = impale (ɪm'pel)
  = cut (kʌt)
  = puncture ('pʌŋktʃɚ)

and (lænd) ① *n.* 陸地
② *v.* 使著地

① = ground (graʊnd)
  = soil (sɔɪl)
  = sod (sɑd)
  = shore (ʃor , ʃɔr)
  = surface ('sɝfɪs)
  = earth (ɝθ)
② = descend (dɪ'sɛnd)
  = arrive (ə'raɪv)
  = alight (ə'laɪt)
  = *touch down*

andmark ('lænd,mɑrk , 'læn-)
. 顯著的目標

  = point (pɔɪnt)
  = milestone ('maɪl,ston)

ane (len) *n.* 小路

  = path (pæθ)
  = road (rod)
  = pass (pæs)
  = aisle (aɪl)
  = alley ('ælɪ)
  = avenue ('ævə,nju)
  = channel ('tʃænḷ)
  = artery ('ɑrtərɪ)
  = *narrow way*

anguage ('læŋgwɪdʒ) *n.* 語言

  = speech (spitʃ)
  = words (wɝdz)
  = tongue (tʌŋ)
  = talk (tɔk)

anguid ('læŋgwɪd) *adj.*
精神不振的

  = weak (wik)
  = drooping ('drupɪŋ)
  = feeble ('fibḷ)
  = debilitated (dɪ'bɪlə,tetɪd)
  = listless ('lɪstlɪs)
  = dull (dʌl)
  = sluggish ('slʌgɪʃ)
  = lethargic (lɪ'θɑrdʒɪk)

lank (læŋk) *adj.* 瘦長的

  = slender ('slɛndɚ)
  = thin (θɪn)
  = lean (lin)
  = skinny ('skɪnɪ)
  = gaunt (gɔnt , gɑnt)
  = scrawny ('skrɔnɪ)

lap (læp) *v.* ①舔 ②重疊

① = lick (lɪk)
  = drink (drɪŋk)
② = *wrap around*
  = *fold over*

lapse (læps) *v.* 消失

  = sink (sɪŋk)
  = decline (dɪ'klaɪn)
  = slump (slʌmp)
  = *go down*

larceny ('lɑrsṇɪ) *n.* 竊盜罪

  = theft (θɛft)
  = stealing ('stilɪŋ)
  = robbery ('rɑbərɪ)

lard (lɑrd) *n.* 豬油

  = fat (fæt)
  = grease (gris)

L

large ﹝ lardʒ ﹞ *adj.* 大的

= big ﹝ bɪg ﹞

= sizable ﹝ 'saɪzəbḷ ﹞

= great ﹝ gret ﹞

= grand ﹝ grænd ﹞

= huge ﹝ hjudʒ ﹞

= vast ﹝ væst ﹞

= immense ﹝ ɪ'mɛns ﹞

= colossal ﹝ kə'lɑsḷ ﹞

= giant ﹝ 'dʒaɪənt ﹞

= gigantic ﹝ dʒaɪ'gæntɪk ﹞

= mammoth ﹝ 'mæməθ ﹞

= massive ﹝ 'mæsɪv ﹞

= enormous ﹝ ɪ'nɔrməs ﹞

lariat ﹝ 'lærɪət ﹞ *n.* 繫繩

= rope ﹝ rop ﹞

= lasso ﹝ 'læso ﹞

lark ﹝ lark ﹞ *n.* 嬉樂

= fun ﹝ fʌn ﹞

= fling ﹝ flɪŋ ﹞

= joke ﹝ dʒok ﹞

= spree ﹝ spri ﹞

= celebration ﹝ ˌsɛlə'breʃən ﹞

= revel ﹝ 'rɛvḷ ﹞

lash ﹝ læʃ ﹞ *v.* 打擊；鞭策

= strike ﹝ straɪk ﹞

= blow ﹝ blo ﹞

= beat ﹝ bit ﹞

= hit ﹝ hɪt ﹞

= whip ﹝ hwɪp ﹞

= flog ﹝ flag ﹞

lass ﹝ læs ﹞ *n.* 少女；女孩

= girl ﹝ gɝl ﹞

= youth ﹝ juθ ﹞

lasso ﹝ 'læso ﹞ *n.* 套索

= rope ﹝ rop ﹞

= lariat ﹝ 'lærɪət ﹞

last ﹝ læst ﹞ *adj.* 最後的

= latest ﹝ 'letɪst ﹞

= end ﹝ ɛnd ﹞

= final ﹝ 'faɪnḷ ﹞

= conclusive ﹝ kən'klusɪv ﹞

= ultimate ﹝ 'ʌltəmɪt ﹞

= hindmost ﹝ 'haɪndˌmost ﹞

= *once and for all*

latch ﹝ lætʃ ﹞ *n.* 門拴

= hook ﹝ hʊk ﹞

= clasp ﹝ klæsp ﹞

= lock ﹝ lak ﹞

= fastener ﹝ 'fæsn̩ɚ , 'fa- ﹞

= catch ﹝ kætʃ ﹞

= closing ﹝ 'klozɪŋ ﹞

= seal ﹝ sil ﹞

late ﹝ let ﹞ *adj.* 遲的

= behind ﹝ bɪ'haɪnd ﹞

= slow ﹝ slo ﹞

= tardy ﹝ 'tardɪ ﹞

latent ﹝ 'letn̩t ﹞ *adj.* 潛在的

= hidden ﹝ 'hɪdn̩ ﹞

= concealed ﹝ kən'sild ﹞

= covered ﹝ 'kʌvɚd ﹞

= obscured ﹝ əb'skjurd ﹞

= underlying ﹝ 'ʌndɚ'laɪɪŋ ﹞

L

ather ('læðə) *n.* 肥皂泡沫

= soap (sop)
= foam (fom)
= suds (sʌdz)
= froth (frɔθ , frɑθ)

latter ('lætə) *adj.* 較後的

= later ('letə)
= *more recent*

laud (lɔd) *v.* 讚美

= praise (prez)
= commend (kə'mɛnd)
= glorify ('glorə,faɪ , 'glɔr-)
= compliment ('kɑmpləmənt)
= extol (ɪk'stɑl , -'stol , ɛk-)

laugh (læf , lɑf) *v.* 笑

= giggle ('gɪgḷ)
= chuckle ('tʃʌkḷ)
= smile (smaɪl)
= grin (grɪn)
= titter ('tɪtə)
= snicker ('snɪkə)
= guffaw (gʌ'fɔ , gə'fɔ)
= howl (haʊl)
= roar (ror , rɔr)

launch (lɔntʃ , lɑntʃ) *v.* 創辦；發動

= start (stɑrt)
= introduce (,ɪntrə'djus)
= fire (faɪr)
= spring (sprɪŋ)
= *set afloat*
= *set going*

launder ('lɔndə , 'lɑn-) *v.* 洗（衣）；洗熨（衣）

= wash (wɑʃ)
= bathe (beð)
= scour (skaʊr)
= scrub (skrʌb)

lavatory ('lævə,torɪ) *n.* 盥洗室

= bathroom ('bæθ,rum , -,rʊm)
= toilet ('tɔɪlɪt)
= latrine (lə'trin)
= washroom ('wɑʃ,rum , -,rʊm)

lavish ('lævɪʃ) *adj.* 過多的

= free (fri)
= abundant (ə'bʌndənt)
= liberal ('lɪbərəl)
= plentiful ('plɛntɪfəl)
= ample ('æmpḷ)
= extravagant (ɪk'strævəgənt)
= generous ('dʒɛnərəs)
= prodigal ('prɑdɪgḷ)

law (lɔ) *n.* 法律

= rule (rul)
= principle ('prɪnsəpḷ)
= standard ('stændəd)
= formula ('fɔrmjələ)
= ordinance ('ɔrdṇəns)
= act (ækt)
= decree (dɪ'kri)
= proclamation (,prɑklə'meʃən)
= edict ('idɪkt)
= regulation (,rɛgjə'leʃən)

lax (læks) *adj.* 鬆弛的

= loose (lus)

L

= slack (slæk)

= careless ('kɛrlɪs)

= lenient ('linɪənt , 'linjənt)

= vague (veg)

= lazy ('lezɪ)

lay (le) *v.* 放置

= put (pʊt)

= place (ples)

= set (sɛt)

= rest (rɛst)

= deposit (dɪ'pɑzɪt)

= arrange (ə'rendʒ)

lazy ('lezɪ) *adj.* 怠惰的

= lax (læks)

= inactive (ɪn'æktɪv)

= indolent ('ɪndələnt)

lea (li) *n.* 牧場

= meadow ('mɛdo)

= pasture ('pæstʃɚ , 'pɑs-)

= *grassy field*

lead (lid) *v.* 引導

= head (hɛd)

= escort (ɪ'skɔrt)

= guide (gaɪd)

= conduct (kən'dʌkt)

= direct (də'rɛkt , daɪ-)

= run (rʌn)

= *come first*

league (lig) *n.* 聯盟

= union ('junjən)

= alliance (ə'laɪəns)

= association (ə,sosɪ'eʃən , -soʃɪ)

= society (sə'saɪətɪ)

= federation (,fɛdə'reʃən)

= group (grup)

= band (bænd)

leak (lik) *v.* 漏

= drip (drɪp)

= dribble ('drɪbl̩)

= *run out*

lean (lin) ① *adj.* 瘦的
② *v.* 傾斜；倚靠

① = thin (θɪn)

= scant (skænt)

= spare (spɛr)

= lanky ('læŋkɪ)

= meager ('migɚ)

= slight (slaɪt)

= slim (slɪm)

= slender ('slɛndɚ)

= narrow ('næro)

= skinny ('skɪnɪ)

= scrawny ('skrɔnɪ)

② = bend (bɛnd)

= rest (rɛst)

= slope (slop)

= slant (slænt)

= incline (ɪn'klaɪn)

= tip (tɪp)

leap (lip) *v.* 跳躍

= jump (dʒʌmp)

= spring (sprɪŋ)

= vault (vɔlt)

= hop (hɑp)

= bound (baʊnd)

= hurdle ('hɜdḷ)

= dive (daɪv)

= plunge (plʌndʒ)

= pounce (paʊns)

learn (lɜn) *v.* 學習;得知

= memorize ('mɛmə,raɪz)

= discover (dɪs'kʌvə)

= *gain knowledge*

= *find out*

lease (lis) *v.* 租得;租出

= rent (rɛnt)

= hire (haɪr)

= let (lɛt)

= charter ('tʃɑrtə)

leash (liʃ) *n.* (牽狗用的) 皮帶

= strap (stræp)

= chain (tʃen)

= rein (ren)

= collar ('kɑlə)

= shackle ('ʃækḷ)

least (list) *adj.* 最少 (小) 的

= fewest ('fjuɪst)

= smallest ('smɔlɪst)

= minimum ('mɪnəməm)

leave (liv) *v.* 離開;遺棄

= go (go)

= depart (dɪ'pɑrt)

= quit (kwɪt)

= abandon (ə'bændən)

= withdraw (wɪð'drɔ , wɪθ-)

= vacate ('veket)

= exit ('ɛgzɪt , 'ɛgsɪt)

lecture ('lɛktʃə) *n.* 演講

= speech (spitʃ)

= talk (tɔk)

= sermon ('sɜmən)

= address (ə'drɛs , 'ædrɛs)

= recitation (,rɛsə'teʃən)

= discourse ('dɪskors , dɪ'skors)

= oration (o'reʃən , ɔ-)

ledge (lɛdʒ) *n.* 架

= shelf (ʃɛlf)

= ridge (rɪdʒ)

= edge (ɛdʒ)

= rim (rɪm)

legal ('ligḷ) *adj.* 法律的;合法的

= lawful ('lɔfəl)

= legitimate (lɪ'dʒɪtə,mɪt)

= authorized ('ɔθə,raɪzd)

= permitted (pə'mɪtɪd)

= allowed (ə'laʊd)

= admissible (əd'mɪsəbḷ)

= valid ('vælɪd)

= sound (saʊnd)

= just (dʒʌst)

legend ('lɛdʒənd) *n.* 傳奇

= story ('storɪ)

= fiction ('fɪkʃən)

= myth (mɪθ)

= fable ('febḷ)

= folklore ('fok,lor , -,lɔr)

= *fairy tale*

L

legible ('lɛdʒəbḷ) *adj.* 易讀的

= readable ('ridəbḷ)

= plain (plen)

= clear (klɪr)

legion ('lidʒən) *n.* 軍團；一群人或物

= unit ('junɪt)

= outfit ('aut,fɪt)

= regiment ('rɛdʒəmənt)

= troop (trup)

= battalion (bə'tæljən , bæ-)

= company ('kʌmpənɪ)

= squad (skwɑd)

= team (tim)

= division (də'vɪʒən)

= army ('ɑrmɪ)

= force (fors , fɔrs)

legislation (,lɛdʒɪs'leʃən) *n.* 立法

= lawmaking ('lɔ,mekɪŋ)

= resolution (,rɛzə'ljuʃən , -zḷ'-)

= regulation (,rɛgjə'leʃən)

= ruling ('rulɪŋ)

= decree (dɪ'kri)

= ordinance ('ɔrdn̩əns)

= statute ('stætʃut)

= enactment (ɪn'æktmənt , ɛn-)

legitimate (lɪ'dʒɪtəmɪt) *adj.* 合法的

= lawful ('lɔfəl)

= rightful ('raɪtfəl)

= allowed (ə'laud)

= legal ('ligḷ)

= authorized ('ɔθə,raɪzd)

= permitted (pɚ'mɪtɪd)

= admissible (əd'mɪsəbḷ)

= valid ('vælɪd)

= sound (saund)

= just (dʒʌst)

leisure ('liʒɚ , 'lɛʒɚ) *n.* 空閒

= freedom ('fridəm)

= *spare time*

lend (lɛnd) *v.* 借出

= give (gɪv)

= loan (lon)

= advance (əd'væns)

length (lɛŋkθ , lɛŋθ) *n.* 長度

= extent (ɪk'stɛnt)

= measure ('mɛʒɚ)

= span (spæn)

= reach (ritʃ)

= stretch (strɛtʃ)

= distance ('dɪstəns)

lenient ('linɪənt , 'linjənt) *adj.* 寬大的

= mild (maɪld)

= gentle ('dʒɛntḷ)

= merciful ('mɜsɪfəl)

= lax (læks)

= loose (lus)

= relaxed (rɪ'lækst)

= soft (sɔft)

= easy ('izɪ)

= unrestrained (,ʌnrɪ'strend)

L

less (lɛs) *adj.* 較小的

= smaller ('smɔlɚ)

= fewer ('fjuɚ)

= reduced (rɪ'djust)

lesson ('lɛsn̩) *n.* 課業

= teaching ('titʃɪŋ)

= instruction (ɪn'strʌkʃən)

= assignment (ə'saɪmmənt)

= exercise ('ɛksɚˌsaɪz)

= course (kors , kɔrs)

= study ('stʌdɪ)

let (lɛt) *v.* ①允許　②出租

① = allow (ə'lau)

= permit (pɚ'mɪt)

= leave (liv)

= consent (kən'sɛnt)

= grant (grænt)

= admit (əd'mɪt)

② = rent (rɛnt)

= lease (lis)

= charter ('tʃɑrtɚ)

= contract ('kɑntrækt)

= *hire out*

letter ('lɛtɚ) *n.* ①字母　②書信

① = character ('kærɪktɚ , -rək-)

= symbol ('sɪmbl̩)

= *alphabet sign*

② = message ('mɛsɪdʒ)

= note (not)

= communication

　(kəˌmjunə'keʃən)

= dispatch (dɪ'spætʃ)

level ('lɛvl̩) *adj.* 平的

= flat (flæt)

= even ('ivən)

= equal ('ikwəl)

= uniform ('junəˌform)

= constant ('kɑnstənt)

= steady ('stɛdɪ)

= smooth (smuð)

liable ('laɪəbl̩) *adj.* ①易於

②有責任的

① = likely ('laɪklɪ)

= probable ('prɑbəbl̩)

= apt (æpt)

② = responsible (rɪ'spɑnsəbl̩)

= accountable (ə'kauntəbl̩)

= answerable ('ænsərəbl̩ , -srə-)

liar ('laɪɚ) *n.* 說謊者

= fibber ('fɪbɚ)

= falsifier ('fɔlsəˌfaɪɚ)

= fabricator ('fæbrɪˌketɚ)

= perjurer ('pɝdʒərɚ)

= storyteller ('storɪˌtɛlɚ)

liberal ('lɪbərəl) *adj.* ①大方的

②寬厚的

① = generous ('dʒɛnərəs)

= plentiful ('plɛntɪfəl)

= abundant (ə'bʌndənt)

= ample ('æmpl̩)

= extravagant (ɪk'strævəgənt)

= lavish ('lævɪʃ)

= extensive (ɪk'stɛnsɪv)

= unselfish (ʌn'sɛlfɪʃ)

② = tolerant ('tɑlərənt)

L

= freethinking ('friθɪŋkɪŋ)
= progressive (prə'grɛsɪv)
= broad-minded ('brɔd'maɪndɪd)

liberty ('lɪbɚtɪ) *n.* 自由

= freedom ('fridəm)
= independence (ˌɪndɪ'pɛndəns)
= autonomy (ɔ'tɑnəmɪ)
= emancipation (ɪˌmænsə'peʃən)

license ('laɪsn̩s) *n.* 許可

= permit ('pɝmɪt , pə'mɪt)
= warrant ('wɔrənt , 'wɑrənt)
= consent (kən'sɛnt)
= authorization (ˌɔθərə'zeʃən)
= sanction ('sæŋkʃən)
= approval (ə'pruvl̩)

lick (lɪk) *v.* 舔

= lap (læp)
= taste (test)

lid (lɪd) *n.* 蓋

= cover ('kʌvɚ)
= top (tɑp)
= cap (kæp)
= stopper ('stɑpɚ)

lie (laɪ) *v.* ①撒謊　②躺

①= fib (fɪb)
= falsify ('fɔlsəˌfaɪ)
= fabricate ('fæbrɪˌket)
= exaggerate (ɪg'zædʒəˌret)
②= recline (rɪ'klaɪn)
= repose (rɪ'poz)

life (laɪf) *n.* 生命

= existence (ɪg'zɪstəns)
= being ('biɪŋ)

lift (lɪft) *v.* 抬起

= raise (rez)
= elevate ('ɛləˌvet)
= hoist (hɔɪst)
= *pick up*

light (laɪt) *adj.* ①明亮的
②輕的

①= bright (braɪt)
= clear (klɪr)
= open ('opən , 'opm̩)
= lucid ('lusɪd , 'lɪu-)
②= weightless ('wetlɪs)
= airy ('ɛrɪ)
= delicate ('dɛləkət , -kɪt)

like (laɪk) *v.* 喜好

= prefer (prɪ'fɝ)
= fancy ('fænsɪ)
= enjoy (ɪn'dʒɔɪ)
= appreciate (ə'priʃɪˌet)
= *go for*
= *care for*
= *be fond of*

likeness ('laɪknɪs) *n.* 相似

= similarity (ˌsɪmə'lærətɪ)
= resemblance (rɪ'zɛmbləns)

likewise ('laɪkˌwaɪz) *adv.* 相同地

= similarly ('sɪmələ˺lɪ)

= also ('ɔlso)

= moreover (mor'ovɚ , mɔr-)

= too (tu)

= *as well*

limber ('lɪmbɚ) *adj.* 易彎曲的

= flexible ('flɛksəbḷ)

= bending ('bɛndɪŋ)

= pliable ('plaɪəbḷ)

= elastic (ɪ'læstɪk)

limit ('lɪmɪt) *n.* 界限

= end (ɛnd)

= boundary ('baʊndərɪ , 'baʊndrɪ)

= restriction (rɪ'strɪkʃən)

= extreme (ɪk'strim)

= tip (tɪp)

= confine ('kɑnfaɪn)

limp (lɪmp) *adj.* 軟弱的

= weak (wik)

= drooping ('drupɪŋ)

= sagging ('sægɪŋ)

= flimsy ('flɪmzɪ)

= loose (lus)

= soft (sɔft)

= floppy ('flɑpɪ)

limpid ('lɪmpɪd) *adj.* 清澈的；透明的

= clear (klɪr)

= transparent (træns'pɛrənt)

= lucid ('lusɪd , 'lɪu-)

= translucent (træns'lusn̩t , -'lɪu-)

line (laɪn) *n.* ①繩 ②線條 ③邊界 ④排；列 ⑤種類

① = rope (rop)

= cord (kɔrd)

= wire (waɪr)

= string (strɪŋ)

② = mark (mɑrk)

= stroke (strok)

= stripe (straɪp)

= streak (strik)

= dash (dæʃ)

③ = edge (ɛdʒ)

= boundary ('baʊndərɪ , 'baʊndrɪ)

= limit ('lɪmɪt)

= confine ('kɑnfaɪn)

④ = row (ro)

= arrangement (ə'rendʒmənt)

= series ('sɪrɪz , 'sɪrɪz)

= sequence ('sikwəns)

⑤ = type (taɪp)

= kind (kaɪnd)

= brand (brænd)

= sort (sɔrt)

= make (mek)

L

lineage ('lɪnɪɪdʒ) *n.* 血統；家世

= race (res)

= family ('fæməlɪ)

= ancestry ('ænsɛstrɪ)

linger ('lɪŋgɚ) *v.* 逗留

= stay (ste)

= wait (wet)

= delay (dɪ'le)

= remain (rɪ'men)

= tarry ('tærɪ)

= loiter (ˈlɔɪtɚ)

= dawdle (ˈdɔdḷ)

= dillydally (ˈdɪlɪˌdælɪ)

= lag (læg)

link (lɪŋk) v. 連結

= unite (juˈnaɪt)

= connect (kəˈnɛkt)

= join (ˈdʒɔɪn)

= combine (kəmˈbaɪn)

= couple (ˈkʌpḷ)

= bridge (brɪdʒ)

= *put together*

liquid (ˈlɪkwɪd) n. 液體

= fluid (ˈfluɪd)

liquor (ˈlɪkɚ) n. 酒

= whiskey (ˈhwɪskɪ)

= drink (drɪŋk)

= alcohol (ˈælkəˌhɔl)

= spirits (ˈspɪrɪts)

list (lɪst) ① n. 目錄   ② v. 傾斜

① = enumeration (ɪˌnjuməˈreʃən , ɪˌnu-)

= schedule (ˈskɛdʒul)

= record (ˈrɛkɚd)

= register (ˈrɛdʒɪstɚ)

= inventory (ˈɪnvənˌtorɪ , -ˌtɔrɪ)

= line-up (ˈlaɪnˌʌp)

② = tilt (tɪlt)

= tip (tɪp)

= slant (slænt)

= slope (slop)

= lean (lin)

listen (ˈlɪsn̩) v. 聽

= hear (hɪr)

= eavesdrop (ˈivzˌdrɑp)

listless (ˈlɪstlɪs) adj. 倦怠的

= tired (taɪrd)

= uninterested (ʌnˈɪntərɪstɪd)

= unconcerned (ˌʌnkənˈsɝnd)

= lethargic (lɪˈθɑrdʒɪk)

= apathetic (ˌæpəˈθɛtɪk)

literally (ˈlɪtərəlɪ) adv. 逐字地

= exactly (ɪgˈzæktlɪ)

= actually (ˈæktʃuəlɪ)

= really (ˈriəlɪ , ˈrɪlɪ)

= word-for-word (ˈwɝdfɚˈwɝd)

literate (ˈlɪtərɪt) adj. 受教育的

= learned (ˈlɝnɪd)

= scholarly (ˈskɑlɚlɪ)

= cultured (ˈkʌltʃɚd)

= educated (ˈɛdʒəˌketɪd)

literature (ˈlɪtərətʃɚ) n. 文獻

= writings (ˈraɪtɪŋz)

= books (buks)

= publications (ˌpʌblɪˈkeʃənz)

lithe (laɪð) adj. 易彎的

= bending (ˈbɛndɪŋ)

= supple (ˈsʌpḷ)

= elastic (ɪˈlæstɪk)

= flexible (ˈflɛksəbḷ)

= pliable (ˈplaɪəbḷ)

= plastic (ˈplæstɪk)

= limber (ˈlɪmbɚ)

L

litter ('lɪtə) *n.* 垃圾

= clutter ('klʌtə)
= rubbish ('rʌbɪʃ)
= trash (træʃ)
= scrap (skræp)
= rubble ('rʌbl̩)
= debris (də'bri , 'debri)
= junk (dʒʌŋk)

little ('lɪtl̩) *adj.* 小的

= small (smɔl)
= short (ʃɔrt)
= tiny ('taɪnɪ)
= bit (bɪt)
= minimum ('mɪnəməm)
= slight (slaɪt)
= miniature ('mɪnɪətʃə)
= mini ('mɪnɪ)
= puny ('pjunɪ)
= teeny ('tinɪ)
= wee (wi)

live (lɪv) *v.* ①生存　②居住

① = exist (ɪg'zɪst)
= *be alive*
② = reside (rɪ'zaɪd)
= occupy ('ɑkjə,paɪ)
= dwell (dwɛl)
= stay (ste)
= house (haʊz)
= room (rum)
= inhabit (ɪn'hæbɪt)

livelihood ('laɪvlɪ,hʊd) *n.* 生計

= support (sə'port , -'pɔrt)
= keep (kip)

= maintenance ('mentənəns , -tɪn-)
= sustenance ('sʌstənəns)
= subsistence (səb'sɪstəns)

lively ('laɪvlɪ) *adj.* 活潑的

= exciting (ɪk'saɪtɪŋ , ɛk-)
= bright ('braɪt)
= cheerful ('tʃɪrfəl)
= vivid ('vɪvɪd)
= vigorous ('vɪgərəs)
= gay (ge)
= active ('æktɪv)
= energetic (,ɛnə'dʒɛtɪk)
= interesting ('ɪntərɪstɪŋ , 'ɪntrɪstɪŋ)
= spirited ('spɪrɪtɪd)
= animated ('ænə,metɪd)
= vivacious (vaɪ'veʃəs , vɪ-)
= spry (spraɪ)

livestock ('laɪv,stɑk) *n.* 家畜

= cattle ('kætl̩)
= animals ('ænəml̩z)

livid ('lɪvɪd) *adj.* ①土色的 ②生氣的

① = pale (pel)
= grayish ('greɪʃ)
② = furious ('fjʊrɪəs)
= enraged (ɪn'redʒd , ɛn-)
= *very angry*

load (lod) ① *n.* 負擔　② *v.* 裝載

① = burden ('bɝdn̩)
= pack (pæk)

L

= cargo ('kargo)

= freight (fret)

= shipment ('ʃɪpmənt)

② = fill (fɪl)

= stuff (stʌf)

= charge (tʃardʒ)

loaf (lof) *v.* 游手好閒

= idle ('aɪdl̩)

= lounge (laʊndʒ)

= loiter ('lɔɪtɚ)

= *lie around*

loan (lon) *v.* 借 (出)

= lend (lɛnd)

= advance (əd'væns)

= give (gɪv)

loath (loθ) *adj.* 勉強的

= unwilling (ʌn'wɪlɪŋ)

= reluctant (rɪ'lʌktənt)

loathe (loð) *v.* 厭惡

= hate (het)

= dislike (dɪs'laɪk)

= abhor (əb'hɔr , æb-)

= detest (dɪ'tɛst)

= abominate (ə'bamə,net)

= despise (dɪ'spaɪz)

lobby ('labɪ) *n.* 門廊

= entrance ('ɛntrəns)

= passageway ('pæsɪdʒ,we)

= vestibule ('vɛstə,bjul)

= foyer ('fɔɪ·e , 'fɔɪɚ)

local ('lokl̩) *adj.* 局部的

= regional ('ridʒn̩əl)

= limited ('lɪmɪtɪd)

= particular (pɚ'tɪkjələ , pə- , par-)

= restricted (rɪ'strɪktɪd)

location (lo'keʃən) *n.* 位置

= position (pə'zɪʃən)

= place (ples)

= region ('ridʒən)

= area ('ɛrɪə , 'erɪə)

= zone (zon)

= territory ('tɛrə,torɪ , -,tɔrɪ)

= district ('dɪstrɪkt)

= section ('sɛkʃən)

= neighborhood ('nebɚ,hʊd)

= spot (spat)

= site (saɪt)

= situation (,sɪtʃʊ'eʃən)

lock (lak) *v.* 鎖

= fasten ('fæsn̩ , 'fasn̩)

= close (kloz)

= hook (hʊk)

= clasp (klæsp)

= latch (lætʃ)

= shut (ʃʌt)

= seal (sil)

locomotion (,lokə'moʃən) *n.*
運動;移動

= travel ('trævl̩)

= movement ('muvmənt)

= motion ('moʃən)

= transit ('trænsɪt , -zɪt)

L

odge ﹝lɑdʒ﹞ *v.* 住宿

= live ﹝lɪv﹞
= reside ﹝rɪ'zaɪd﹞
= inhabit ﹝ɪn'hæbɪt﹞
= occupy ﹝'ɑkjə,paɪ﹞
= dwell ﹝dwɛl﹞
= room ﹝rum﹞
= stay ﹝ste﹞

ofty ﹝'lɔftɪ , 'lɑftɪ﹞ *adj.* 高的

= high ﹝haɪ﹞
= grand ﹝grænd﹞
= dignified ﹝'dɪgnə,faɪd﹞
= proud ﹝praʊd﹞
= haughty ﹝'hɔtɪ﹞
= eminent ﹝'ɛmənənt﹞
= prominent ﹝'prɑmənənt﹞

og ﹝lɔg , lɑg﹞ *n.* ①木頭 ②記錄

① = wood ﹝wʊd﹞
= lumber ﹝'lʌmbɚ﹞
= timber ﹝'tɪmbɚ﹞
= board ﹝bord , bɔrd﹞
② = record ﹝'rɛkɚd﹞
= register ﹝'rɛdʒɪstɚ﹞
= account ﹝ə'kaʊnt﹞
= scrapbook ﹝'skræp,bʊk﹞
= album ﹝'ælbəm﹞
= catalog ﹝'kætḷ,ɔg﹞
= journal ﹝'dʒɝnḷ﹞

logical ﹝'lɑdʒɪkḷ﹞ *adj.* 合理的

= reasonable ﹝'riznəbḷ﹞
= sensible ﹝'sɛnsəbḷ﹞
= sound ﹝saʊnd﹞
= sane ﹝sen﹞
= rational ﹝'ræʃənḷ﹞

loiter ﹝'lɔɪtɚ﹞ *v.* 徘徊

= linger ﹝'lɪŋgɚ﹞
= idle ﹝'aɪdḷ﹞
= stop ﹝stɑp﹞
= dillydally ﹝'dɪlɪ,dælɪ﹞
= wait ﹝wet﹞
= delay ﹝dɪ'le﹞
= stay ﹝ste﹞
= tarry ﹝'tærɪ﹞

loll ﹝lɑl﹞ *v.* 懶洋洋地倚靠

= droop ﹝drup﹞
= hang ﹝hæŋ﹞
= sprawl ﹝sprɔl﹞
= repose ﹝rɪ'poz﹞
= recline ﹝rɪ'klaɪn﹞
= relax ﹝rɪ'læks﹞

lonely ﹝'lonlɪ﹞ *adj.* 孤單的

= alone ﹝ə'lon﹞
= solitary ﹝'sɑlə,tɛrɪ﹞
= isolated ﹝'aɪsḷ,etɪd﹞
= unaccompanied
﹝,ʌnə'kʌmpənɪd﹞
= friendless ﹝'frɛndlɪs﹞
= desolate ﹝'dɛsḷɪt﹞

long ﹝lɔŋ , lɑŋ﹞ *adj.* 長的

= lengthy ﹝'lɛŋkθɪ , -ŋθ-﹞
= extensive ﹝ɪk'stɛnsɪv﹞
= far-reaching ﹝'fɑr'ritʃɪŋ﹞

look ﹝lʊk﹞ *v.* ①看 ②似乎

① = see ﹝si﹞

L

= search (sɝtʃ)

= hunt (hʌnt)

= explore (ɪk'splor , -'splɔr)

= stare (stɛr)

= glance (glæns , glɑns)

= peek (pik)

= peer (pɪr)

= gaze (gez)

= gape (gep)

= gawk (gɔk)

② = seem (sim)

= appear (ə'pɪr)

loom (lum) *v.* 隱現;隱約可見

= appear (ə'pɪr)

= emerge (ɪ'mɝdʒ)

= *show up*

= *come in sight*

loose (lus) *adj.* ①鬆的
②自由的;含糊的

① = limp (lɪmp)

= drooping ('drupɪŋ)

= slack (slæk)

= unfastened (ʌn'fæsn̩d)

= untied (ʌn'taɪd)

② = vague (veg)

= free (fri)

= unclear (ʌn'klɪr)

= confused (kən'fjuzd)

= hazy ('hezɪ)

= inexact (,ɪnɪg'zækt)

loot (lut) *v.* 掠奪

= rob (rɑb)

= plunder ('plʌndɚ)

= burglarize ('bɝglə,raɪz)

lope (lop) *v.* 跳躍而行

= run (rʌn)

= sprint (sprɪnt)

= bound (baʊnd)

= race (res)

= gallop ('gæləp)

lord (lɔrd) *n.* 領主

= owner ('onɚ)

= ruler ('rulɚ)

= master('mæstɚ , 'mɑs-)

= boss (bɔs)

= proprietor (prə'praɪətɚ)

lose (luz) *v.* ①輸　②遺失

① = fail (fel)

= flop (flɑp)

= forfeit ('fɔrfɪt)

= sacrifice ('sækrə,faɪs , -,faɪz)

= *be unsuccessful*

② = misplace (mɪs'ples)

= mislay (mɪs'le)

lot (lɑt) *n.* ①一批　②總量
③運氣　④土地

① = many ('mɛnɪ)

= bunch (bʌntʃ)

= group (grup)

= cluster ('klʌstɚ)

= clump (klʌmp)

② = quantity ('kwɑntətɪ)

= amount (ə'maʊnt)

= sum (sʌm)

= number ('nʌmbɚ)

L

= portion ('porʃən , 'pɔr-)

③ = fate (fet)

= fortune ('fɔrtʃən)

= chance (tʃæns)

= luck (lʌk)

= destiny ('dɛstənɪ)

= end (ɛnd)

① = field (fild)

= plot (plɑt)

= tract (trækt)

lotion ('loʃən) *n.* 洗劑

= ointment ('ɔɪntmənt)

= salve (sæv)

= cream (krim)

= balm (bɑm)

lottery ('lɑtərɪ) *n.* 抽籤

= raffle ('ræfḷ)

= drawing ('drɔ·ɪŋ)

loud (laʊd) *adj.* 大聲的

= thunderous ('θʌndrəs , -dərəs)

= roaring ('rorɪŋ , 'rɔr-)

= resounding (rɪ'zaʊndɪŋ)

= noisy ('nɔɪzɪ)

lounge (laʊndʒ) *v.* 懶洋洋地橫靠

= relax (rɪ'læks)

= loaf (lof)

= rest (rɛst)

= repose (rɪ'poz)

= laze (lez)

= *sit around*

= *lie down*

= *take it easy*

love (lʌv) *v.* 喜好

= adore (ə'dor , ə'dɔr)

= like (laɪk)

= fancy ('fænsɪ)

= idolize ('aɪdḷ,aɪz)

= cherish ('tʃɛrɪʃ)

= *care for*

= *be fond of*

lovely ('lʌvlɪ) *adj.* 可愛的

= delightful (dɪ'laɪtfəl)

= exquisite ('ɛkskwɪzɪt , ɪk's-)

= charming ('tʃɑrmɪŋ)

= appealing (ə'pilɪŋ)

= enchanting (ɪn'tʃæntɪŋ)

= beautiful ('bjutəfəl)

= pretty ('prɪtɪ)

= attractive (ə'træktɪv)

= fetching ('fɛtʃɪŋ)

low (lo) *adj.* ①較差的
②低級的

① = inferior (ɪn'fɪrɪɚ)

= lesser ('lɛsɚ)

= short (ʃɔrt)

② = mean (min)

= coarse (kors , kɔrs)

= vulgar ('vʌlgɚ)

= base (bes)

= wicked ('wɪkɪd)

= evil ('ivḷ)

= bad (bæd)

= sinful ('sɪnfəl , -fʊl)

= vile (vaɪl)

L

loyal ('lɔɪəl , 'lɔjəl) *adj.* 忠貞的

= true (tru)

= faithful ('feθfəl)

= obedient (ə'bidɪənt)

= dutiful ('djutɪfəl)

= devoted (dɪ'votɪd)

= trustworthy ('trʌst,wɜðɪ)

lubricate ('lubrɪ,ket) *v.* 使潤滑

= grease (griz , gris)

= oil (ɔɪl)

= anoint (ə'nɔɪnt)

lucid ('lusɪd , 'lɪu-) *adj.* ①清澈的 ②明白的

① = clear (klɪr)

= shining ('ʃaɪnɪŋ)

= light (laɪt)

= transparent ('træns'pɛrənt)

= translucent (træns'lusn̩t , -'lju-)

② = understandable (,ʌndə'stændəbl̩)

= plain (plen)

= distinct (dɪ'stɪŋkt)

= explicit (ɪk'splɪsɪt)

= clear-cut ('klɪr'kʌt)

luck (lʌk) *n.* 運氣

= chance (tʃæns)

= fortune ('fɔrtʃən)

= fate (fet)

= lot (lat)

= fortuity (fɔr'tjuətɪ , -'tu-)

ludicrous ('ludɪkrəs , 'lɪu-) *adj.* 可笑的

= ridiculous (rɪ'dɪkjələs)

= absurd (əb's3d)

lug (lʌg) *v.* 拉

= drag (dræg)

= pull (pul)

= haul (hɔl)

= tug (tʌg)

luggage ('lʌgɪdʒ) *n.* 行李

= baggage ('bægɪdʒ)

= valises (və'lisɪz)

= bags (bægz)

lull (lʌl) *n.* 平息

= quiet ('kwaɪət)

= calm (kɑm)

= hush (hʌʃ)

= silence ('saɪləns)

= stillness ('stɪlnɪs)

= pause (pɔz)

= rest (rɛst)

= break (brek)

= recess (rɪ'sɛs , 'risɛs)

= intermission (,ɪntə'mɪʃən)

= respite ('rɛspɪt)

= lapse (læps)

= letup ('lɛt,ʌp)

lumber ('lʌmbə) *n.* 木材

= timber ('tɪmbə)

= logs (lɔgz , lɑgz)

= wood (wud)

luminous ('lumənəs) *adj.* 光亮的

= light (laɪt)

= shining ('ʃaɪnɪŋ)
= radiant ('redɪənt)
= beaming ('bimɪŋ)
= gleaming ('glimɪŋ)
= glowing ('gloɪŋ)
= bright (braɪt)
= clear (klɪr)

lump (lʌmp) *n.* 堆；團

= swelling ('swɛlɪŋ)
= bump (bʌmp)
= mass (mæs , mɑs)
= hunk (hʌŋk)
= chunk (tʃʌŋk)

lunge (lʌndʒ) *v.* 擊

= thrust (θrʌst)
= attack (ə'tæk)
= push (puʃ)

lurch (lɝtʃ) *v.* 傾斜

= sway (swe)
= topple ('tɑpḷ)
= tip (tɪp)
= rock (rɑk)
= roll (rol)
= toss (tɔs)
= tumble ('tʌmbḷ)
= pitch (pɪtʃ)

lure (lʊr) *v.* 引誘

= pull (pʊl)
= attract (ə'trækt)
= entice (ɪn'taɪs , ɛn-)
= seduce (sɪ'djus)
= tempt (tɛmpt)
= *draw on*

lurid ('lʊrɪd) *adj.* 可怖的

= terrible ('tɛrəbḷ)
= sensational (sɛn'seʃənḷ)
= startling ('stɑrtlɪŋ)
= melodramatic
  (,mɛlədrə'mætɪk)

lurk (lɝk) *v.* 藏躲

= hide (haɪd)
= sneak (snik)
= slink (slɪŋk)
= prowl (praʊl)
= creep (krip)

luscious ('lʌʃəs) *adj.* 美味的

= delicious (dɪ'lɪʃəs)
= savory ('sevərɪ , 'sevrɪ)
= pleasing ('plizɪŋ)
= tasty ('testɪ)
= appetizing ('æpə,taɪzɪŋ)

luster ('lʌstɚ) *n.* 光彩；光輝

= shine (ʃaɪn)
= brightness ('braɪtnɪs)
= brilliance ('brɪljəns)
= sheen (ʃin)
= glow (glo)
= gleam (glim)
= gloss (glɔs)

lusty ('lʌstɪ) *adj.* 壯健的

= strong (strɔŋ)
= healthy ('hɛlθɪ)
= vigorous ('vɪgərəs)
= powerful ('paʊɚfəl)
= mighty ('maɪtɪ)

L

= sturdy ('stɜdɪ)
= rugged ('rʌgɪd)
= strapping ('stræpɪŋ)
= robust (ro'bʌst)
= hardy ('hɑrdɪ)
= hale (hel)
= husky ('hʌskɪ)
= hefty ('hɛftɪ)

luxury ('lʌkʃərɪ) *n.* 奢華

= extravagance (ɪk'strævəgəns)
= frills (frɪlz)
= prosperity (prɑs'pɛrətɪ)
= elegance ('ɛləgəns)
= comfort ('kʌmfət)
= magnificence (mæg'nɪfəsns)
= grandeur ('grændʒə)
= splendor ('splɛndə)
= swankiness ('swæŋkənəs)
= well-being ('wɛl'biɪŋ)

lyrical ('lɪrɪkl̩) *adj.* 詩的

= musical ('mjuzɪkl̩)
= poetic (po'ɛtɪk)

M

mad (mæd) *adj.* ①瘋狂的
②生氣的

① = crazy ('krezɪ)
= insane (ɪn'sen)
= wild (waɪld)
= foolish ('fulɪʃ)
= lunatic ('lunə,tɪk)
= daft (dæft , dɑft)
= demented (dɪ'mɛntɪd)

= deranged (dɪ'rendʒd)
= unbalanced (ʌn'bælənst)
② = angry ('æŋgrɪ)
= annoyed (ə'nɔɪd)
= irritated ('ɪrə,tetɪd)
= exasperated (ɛg'zæspə,retɪd ,
ɪg-)
= enraged (ɪn'redʒd)
= furious ('fjʊrɪəs)
= cross (krɔs)
= irritable ('ɪrətəbl̩)
= ornery ('ɔrnərɪ)
= disagreeable (,dɪsə'griəbl̩)
= raging ('redʒɪŋ)

magazine (,mægə'zin ,
'mægə,zin) *n.* 雜誌

= periodical (,pɪrɪ'ɑdɪkl̩)
= publication (,pʌblɪ'keʃən)
= journal ('dʒɜnl̩)

magic ('mædʒɪk) *n.* 巫術

= wizardry ('wɪzədrɪ)
= sorcery ('sɔrsərɪ)
= voodoo ('vudu , vu'du)
= witchcraft ('wɪtʃ,kræft ,
-,krɑft)

magistrate ('mædʒɪs,tret , -trɪt)
n. 法官

= judge (dʒʌdʒ)

magnetic (mæg'nɛtɪk) *adj.*
吸引人的

= attractive (ə'træktɪv)
= pulling ('pʊlɪŋ)

= drawing ('drɔ·ɪŋ)
= alluring (ə'lurɪŋ)

magnificent (mæg'nɪfəsn̩t)
adj. 華麗的

= splendid ('splɛndɪd)
= grand (grænd)
= stately ('stetlɪ)
= majestic (mə'dʒɛstɪk)
= superb (su'pɝb , sə-)
= exquisite (ɪk'skwɪzɪt , 'ɛks-)
= marvelous ('mɑrvl̩əs)
= wonderful ('wʌndəfəl)
= grandiose ('grændɪˌos)
= glorious ('glorɪəs , 'glɔr-)
= imposing (ɪm'pozɪŋ)
= elaborate (ɪ'læbərɪt)
= impressive (ɪm'prɛsɪv)
= brilliant ('brɪljənt)

magnify ('mægnəˌfaɪ) *v.* 放大

= exaggerate (ɪg'zædʒəˌret)
= increase (ɪn'kris)
= intensify (ɪn'tɛnsəˌfaɪ)
= expand (ɪk'spænd)
= enhance (ɪn'hæns)
= enlarge (ɪn'lɑrdʒ)
= extend (ɪk'stɛnd)
= broaden ('brɔdn̩)
= stretch (strɛtʃ)
= inflate (ɪn'flet)

maid (med) *n.* 僕人

= servant ('sɝvənt)
= helper ('hɛlpə)
= domestic (də'mɛstɪk)

= housekeeper ('haʊsˌkipə)

mail (mel) ① *v.* 郵寄
② *n.* 郵件

① = send (sɛnd)
= dispatch (dɪ'spætʃ)
= post (post)
② = letters ('lɛtəz)
= correspondence
(ˌkɔrə'spɑndəns)

maim (mem) *v.* 使殘廢

= cripple ('krɪpl̩)
= disable (dɪs'ebl̩)
= injure ('ɪndʒə)
= hurt (hɝt)
= wound (wund)

main (men) *adj.* 最主要的

= chief (tʃif)
= principal ('prɪnsəpl̩)
= foremost ('forˌmost , 'fɔr- ,
-məst)
= leading ('lidɪŋ)
= primary ('praɪˌmɛrɪ , -mərɪ)
= dominant ('dɑmənənt)
= first (fɝst)
= *most important*

maintain (men'ten , mən'ten)
v. 保持

= keep (kip)
= uphold (ʌp'hold)
= possess (pə'zɛs)
= support (sə'port , -'pɔrt)
= bear (bɛr)

M

⊜stain（sə'sten）

⊜reserve（prɪ'zɜv）

⊜ve（sev）

⊜uard（gard）

⊜rotect（prə'tɛkt）

⊜tain（rɪ'ten）

ma⊜stic（mə'dʒɛstɪk）*adj.*
高貴的

= grand（grænd）

= stately（'stetlɪ）

= noble（'nobl）

= great（gret）

= kingly（'kɪŋlɪ）

= dignified（'dɪgnə,faɪd）

= high（haɪ）

= prominent（'pramənənt）

= eminent（'ɛmənənt）

= regal（'rigl）

= royal（'rɔɪəl）

= imperial（ɪm'pɪrɪəl）

= sovereign（'savrɪn , 'sʌv-）

= grandiose（'grændɪ,os）

= magnificent（mæg'nɪfəsn̩t）

= impressive（ɪm'prɛsɪv）

= elegant（'ɛləgənt）

= imposing（ɪm'pozɪŋ）

= proud（praud）

major（'medʒɚ）*adj.* 主要的

= larger（'lardʒɚ）

= greater（'gretɚ）

= superior（sə'pɪrɪɚ , su-）

= higher（'haɪɚ）

= senior（'sinjɚ）

make（mek）① *v.* 製造
② *v.* 致使   ③ *n.* 牌子

① = build（bɪld）

 = form（fɔrm）

 = shape（ʃep）

 = compose（kəm'poz）

 = create（krɪ'et）

 = assemble（ə'sɛmbl̩）

 = manufacture（,mænjə'fæktʃɚ）

 = fashion（'fæʃən）

 = fabricate（'fæbrɪ,ket）

 = construct（kən'strʌkt）

 = produce（prə'djus）

 = do（du）

 = execute（'ɛksɪ,kjut）

② = cause（kɔz）

 = force（fors , fɔrs）

 = compel（kəm'pɛl）

③ = kind（kaɪnd）

 = brand（brænd）

 = type（taɪp）

 = line（laɪn）

 = sort（sɔrt）

malady（'mælədɪ）*n.* 疾病

 = sickness（'sɪknɪs）

 = illness（'ɪlnɪs）

 = disease（dɪ'ziz）

 = ailment（'elmənt）

 = disorder（dɪs'ɔrdɚ）

 = infirmity（ɪn'fɝmətɪ）

male（mel）*adj.* 男性的

 = manly（'mænlɪ）

 = masculine（'mæskjəlɪn）

malice ('mælɪs) *n.* 惡意

= spite (spaɪt)
= meanness ('minnɪs)
= *ill will*

malign (mə'laɪn) *v.* 詆毀

= slur (slɜ)
= slander ('slændɚ)
= defame (dɪ'fem)
= smear (smɪr)
= *speak evil of*

malignant (mə'lɪgnənt) *adj.*
有害的

= deadly ('dɛdlɪ)
= harmful ('hɑrmfəl)
= destructive (dɪ'strʌktɪv)
= killing ('kɪlɪŋ)
= fatal ('fetḷ)
= mortal ('mɔrtḷ)
= lethal ('liθəl)

malleable ('mælɪəbḷ) *adj.*
易適應的

= adaptable (ə'dæptəbḷ)
= changeable ('tʃendʒəbḷ)
= flexible ('flɛksəbḷ)
= pliant ('plaɪənt)
= yielding ('jildɪŋ)
= plastic ('plæstɪk)
= elastic (ɪ'læstɪk)
= bendable ('bɛndəbḷ)
= supple ('sʌpḷ)

maltreat (mæl'trit) *v.* 虐待

= abuse (ə'bjuz)

= mistreat (mɪs'trit)

mammoth ('mæməθ) *adj.*
龐大的

= huge (hjudʒ)
= gigantic (dʒaɪ'gæntɪk)
= immense (ɪ'mɛns)
= vast (væst , vɑst)
= enormous (ɪ'nɔrməs)
= giant ('dʒaɪənt)
= colossal (kə'lɑsḷ)
= titanic (taɪ'tænɪk)
= monumental (,mɑnjə'mɛntḷ)

man (mæn) *n.* ①人類　②男子

① = person ('pɜsṇ)
= folk (fok)
= society (sə'saɪətɪ)
= mortal ('mɔrtḷ)
= individual (,ɪndə'vɪdʒuəl)
= soul (sol)
= *Homo sapiens*
= *human being*
② = male (mel)
= fellow ('fɛlo)
= gentleman ('dʒɛntḷmənt)

manage ('mænɪdʒ) *v.* 支配；
處理

= control (kən'trol)
= conduct (kən'dʌkt)
= handle ('hændḷ)
= direct (də'rɛkt , daɪ-)
= operate ('ɑpə,ret)
= work (wɜk)
= regulate ('rɛgjə,let)

M

= govern ('gʌvən)
= lead (lid)
= supervise ('supə‚vaız)
= administer (əd'mınəstə‚ æd-)
= run (rʌn)

mandate ('mændet , -dɪt) *n.*
命令；授權

= command (kə'mænd)
= order ('ɔrdə)
= dictate ('dıktet)
= referendum (‚rɛfə'rɛndəm)
= injunction (ın'dʒʌŋkʃən)

maneuver (mə'nuvə) *v.* 操縱

= operate ('ɑpə‚ret)
= work (wɝk)
= run (rʌn)
= conduct (kən'dʌkt)
= handle ('hændḷ)
= drive (draıv)
= manipulate (mə'nıpjə‚let)
= engineer (‚ɛndʒə'nır)
= plot (plɑt)
= scheme (skim)
= intrigue (ın'trig)
= conspire (kən'spaır)
= plan (plæn)

mangle ('mæŋgḷ) *v.* 傷害；撕裂

= cut (kʌt)
= lacerate ('læsə‚ret)
= mutilate ('mjutḷ‚et)
= maim (mem)
= injure ('ındʒə)
= wound (wund)

= hurt (hɝt)
= *tear apart*

manhood ('mænhud) *n.* 成年

= manliness ('mænlınəs)
= maturity (mə'tjurətı , -'tʃu-)
= adulthood (ə'dʌlthud)

mania ('menıə) *n.* 狂亂

= craze (krez)
= insanity (ın'sænətı)
= madness ('mædnıs)
= infatuation (ın‚fætʃu'eʃən)
= enthusiasm (ın'θjuzı‚æzəm)
= desire (dı'zaır)

manifest ('mænə‚fɛst) *adj.*
明顯的

= apparent (ə'pærənt , ə'pɛrənt)
= clear (klır)
= plain (plen)
= visible ('vızəbḷ)
= open ('opən , 'opm)
= exposed (ık'spozd)
= perceptible (pə'sɛptəbḷ)
= discernible (dı'zɝnəbḷ , -'sɝn-)
= evident ('ɛvədənt)
= obvious ('ɑbvıəs)
= open-and-shut ('opənən'ʃʌt)

manifold ('mænə‚fold) *adj.*
多種的

= many ('mɛnı)
= various ('vɛrıəs)
= multiple ('mʌltəpḷ)

manipulate (mə'nɪpjə‚let) *v.*
操作

  = handle ('hændḷ)
  = manage ('mænɪdʒ)
  = touch (tʌtʃ)
  = feel (fil)
  = operate ('ɑpə‚ret)
  = work (wɜk)
  = conduct (kən'dʌkt)
  = maneuver (mə'nuvɚ)

man-made ('mæn‚med) *adj.*
人造的

  = artificial (‚ɑrtə'fɪʃəl)
  = *not natural*

manner ('mænɚ) *n.* 方法

  = way (we)
  = kind (kaɪnd)
  = mode (mod)
  = style (staɪl)
  = fashion ('fæʃən)
  = form (fɔrm)
  = nature ('netʃɚ)
  = character ('kærɪktɚ , -ək-)
  = means (minz)
  = method ('mɛθəd)

manor ('mænɚ) *n.* 領地；莊園

  = estate (ə'stet)
  = land (lænd)
  = property ('prɑpɚtɪ)
  = domain (do'men)
  = mansion ('mænʃən)
  = palace ('pælɪs , -əs)
  = castle ('kæsḷ , 'kɑsḷ)

  = chateau (ʃæ'to)
  = villa ('vɪlə)
  = *large house*

manslaughter ('mæn‚slɔtɚ)
n. 殺人

  = killing ('kɪlɪŋ)
  = homicide ('hɑmə‚saɪd)
  = murder ('mɜdɚ)
  = assassination (ə‚sæsn̩'eʃən)
  = elimination (ɪ‚lɪmə'neʃən)

mantle ('mæntḷ) *n.* 外套

  = cloak (klok)
  = cover ('kʌvɚ)
  = coat (kot)
  = robe (rob)
  = wrap (ræp)

manual ('mænjuəl) ① *n.* 手冊
② *adj.* 手工的

  ① = guidebook ('gaɪd‚bʊk)
    = directory (də'rɛktərɪ , daɪ-)
    = handbook ('hænd‚bʊk)
  ② = *by hand*

manufacture (‚mænjə'fæktʃɚ)
v. 製造

  = make (mek)
  = invent (ɪn'vɛnt)
  = create (krɪ'et)
  = fashion ('fæʃən)
  = construct (kən'strʌkt)
  = build (bɪld)
  = erect (ɪ'rɛkt)
  = compose (kəm'poz)

M

= prepare (prɪ'pɛr)

= devise (dɪ'vaɪz)

= fabricate ('fæbrɪˌket)

manuscript ('mænjəˌskrɪpt) *n.* 草稿

= writing ('raɪtɪŋ)

= copy ('kɑpɪ)

= composition (ˌkɑmpə'zɪʃən)

= work (wɜk)

= paper ('pepɚ)

= document ('dɑkjəmənt)

many ('mɛnɪ) *adj.* 許多的

= numerous ('njumərəs)

= various ('vɛrɪəs)

= multitudinous (ˌmʌltə'tjudn̩əs , -'tud-)

= myriad ('mɪrɪəd)

= several ('sɛvərəl)

= considerable (kən'sɪdərəbl̩)

map (mæp) *n.* 地圖

= chart (tʃɑrt)

mar (mɑr) *v.* 損毀

= damage ('dæmɪdʒ)

= injure ('ɪndʒɚ)

= blemish ('blɛmɪʃ)

= disfigure (dɪs'fɪgjɚ)

= scar (skɑr)

= deform (dɪ'fɔrm)

= spoil (spɔɪl)

= ruin ('ruɪn , 'rɪʊɪn)

marathon ('mærəˌθɑn , -θən) *n.* 馬拉松賽跑

= race (res)

= relay (rɪ'le , 'rile)

= contest ('kɑntɛst)

march (mɑrtʃ) *v.* 前進

= walk (wɔk)

= hike (haɪk)

= parade (pə'red)

= tramp (træmp)

margin ('mɑrdʒɪn) *n.* 邊緣；餘地

= border ('bɔrdɚ)

= edge (ɛdʒ)

= rim (rɪm)

= leeway ('liˌwe)

= room (rum)

mariner ('mærənɚ) *n.* 水手

= sailor ('selɚ)

= seaman ('simən)

= navigator ('nævəˌgetɚ)

= tar (tɑr)

= salt (sɔlt)

marionette (ˌmærɪə'nɛt) *n.* 木偶

= puppet ('pʌpɪt)

= doll (dɑl)

mark (mɑrk) *n.* ①符號 ②等級

① = line (laɪn)

= sign (saɪn)

= evidence ('ɛvədəns)

= indication (ˌɪndə'keʃən)

= manifestation (ˌmænəfɛs'teʃən

M

② = grade (gred)
   = rating ('retɪŋ)

marked (mɑrkt) *adj.* 明顯的

   = noticeable ('notɪsəbḷ)
   = plain (plen)
   = evident ('ɛvədənt)
   = noted ('notɪd)
   = apparent (ə'pærənt , ə'pɛrənt)
   = decided (dɪ'saɪdɪd)

market ('mɑrkɪt) *n.* 市場

   = store (stor , stɔr)
   = shop (ʃɑp)
   = mart (mɑrt)

marriage ('mærɪdʒ) *n.* 婚禮

   = union ('junjən)
   = joining ('dʒɔɪnɪŋ)
   = coupling ('kʌplɪŋ)
   = linking ('lɪŋkɪŋ)
   = wedding ('wɛdɪŋ)
   = matrimony ('mætrə,monɪ)
   = nuptials ('nʌpʃəlz)

marshal ('mɑrʃəl) *v.* 排列；
引導

   = arrange (ə'rendʒ)
   = lead (lid)
   = conduct (kən'dʌkt)
   = escort (ɪ'skɔrt)
   = guide (gaɪd)
   = usher ('ʌʃə)
   = squire (skwaɪr)

mart (mɑrt) *n.* 市場

   = market ('mɑrkɪt)
   = shop (ʃɑp)
   = store (stor , stɔr)

martial ('mɑrʃəl) *adj.* 好戰的

   = militant ('mɪlətənt)
   = warlike ('wɔr,laɪk)
   = military ('mɪlə,tɛrɪ)
   = combative (kəm'bætɪv ,
      'kɑmbətɪv , 'kʌm-)
   = belligerent (bə'lɪdʒərənt)
   = aggressive (ə'grɛsɪv)
   = hostile ('hɑstɪl)

martyr ('mɑrtə) *n.* 烈士

   = sufferer ('sʌfərə)
   = victim ('vɪktɪm)
   = protomartyr (,protə'mɑrtə)

marvelous ('mɑrvḷəs) *adj.*
不可思議的

   = wonderful ('wʌndəfəl)
   = extraordinary (ɪk'strɔrdṇ,ɛrɪ ,
      ,ɛkstrə'ɔr-)
   = miraculous (mə'rækjələs)
   = astounding (ə'staʊndɪŋ)
   = superb (su'pɜb , sə-)
   = magnificent (mæg'nɪfəsṇt)
   = glorious ('glorɪəs , 'glɔr-)
   = divine (də'vaɪn)
   = exceptional (ɪk'sɛpʃənḷ)
   = remarkable (rɪ'mɑrkəbḷ)

masculine ('mæskjəlɪn) *adj.*
雄壯的

   = manly ('mænlɪ)

M

= strong (strɔŋ)

= vigorous ('vɪgərəs)

= virile ('vɪrəl , 'vaɪrəl)

mash (mæʃ) v. 搗碎

= crush (krʌʃ)

= mix (mɪks)

= soften ('sɔfən)

= crumble ('krʌmbḷ)

= grind (graɪnd)

= grate (gret)

= granulate ('grænjə,let)

= pulverize ('pʌlvə,raɪz)

mask (mæsk , mɑsk) v. 掩飾

= disguise (dɪs'gaɪz)

= cover ('kʌvɚ)

= camouflage ('kæmə,flɑʒ)

masquerade (,mæskə'red) v.
偽裝

= disguise (dɪs'gaɪz)

= pretend (prɪ'tɛnd)

= impersonate (ɪm'pɝsn̩,et)

= pose (poz)

mass (mæs) n. 團;塊

= bulk (bʌlk)

= lump (lʌmp)

= quantity ('kwɑntətɪ)

= load (lod)

= amount (ə'maʊnt)

= measure ('mɛʒɚ)

= volume ('valjəm)

= accumulation (ə,kjumjə'leʃən)

= hunk (hʌŋk)

= chunk (tʃʌŋk)

= lots (lɑts)

= pile (paɪl)

= stack (stæk)

= heap (hip)

= slew (slu)

= batch (bætʃ)

massacre ('mæsəkɚ) n. 大屠殺

= slaughter ('slɔtɚ)

= killing ('kɪlɪŋ)

= butchery ('bʊtʃərɪ)

= carnage ('kɑrnɪdʒ)

= pogrom ('pogrəm , 'pɑg- ,
po'grɑm)

massage (mə'sɑʒ) v. 按摩

= rub (rʌb)

= knead (nid)

= stroke (strok)

massive ('mæsɪv) adj. 大的;
有力的

= big (bɪg)

= large (lɑrdʒ)

= heavy ('hɛvɪ)

= solid ('salɪd)

= sturdy ('stɝdɪ)

= strong (strɔŋ)

= clumsy ('klʌmzɪ)

= ponderous ('pɑndərəs)

= thick (θɪk)

= coarse (kors , kɔrs)

master ('mæstɚ , 'mɑs-) n.
指揮者

= director (də'rɛktɚ , daɪ-)
= commander (kə'mændɚ)
= ruler ('rulɚ)
= head (hɛd)
= controller (kən'trolɚ)
= chief (tʃif)

masterly ('mæstɚlɪ , 'mɑs-) *adj.* 巧妙的

= expert (ɪk'spɝt , 'ɛkspɝt)
= skillful ('skɪlfəl)
= proficient (prə'fɪʃənt)
= adept (ə'dɛpt)
= handy ('hændɪ)
= clever ('klɛvɚ)

mat (mæt) *n.* 蓆

= rug (rʌg)
= cover ('kʌvɚ)

match (mætʃ) *n.* ①火柴 ②競賽 ③配偶；相似之人或物

① = lighter ('laɪtɚ)
② = contest ('kɑntɛst)
= battle ('bætḷ)
= engagement (ɪn'gedʒmənt)
= encounter (ɪn'kaʊntɚ)
= game (gem)
= sport (sport , spɔrt)
= play (ple)
③ = duplicate ('djupləkɪt)
= twin (twɪn)
= double ('dʌbḷ)
= companion (kəm'pænjən)
= mate (met)
= fellow ('fɛlo)
= counterpart ('kaʊntɚ,pɑrt)

= complement ('kɑmpləmənt)
= equivalent (ɪ'kwɪvələnt)
= equal ('ikwəl)

mate (met) *n.* 配偶

= pair (pɛr , pær)
= couple ('kʌpḷ)
= team (tim)

material (mə'tɪrɪəl) *n.* 物質

= substance ('sʌbstəns)
= fabric ('fæbrɪk)
= stuff (stʌf)
= matter ('mætɚ)
= composition (,kɑmpə'zɪʃən)
= goods (gʊdz)

maternal (mə'tɝnḷ) *adj.* 母親的

= motherly ('mʌðɚlɪ)

mathematics (,mæθə'mætɪks) *n.* 數學

= numbers ('nʌmbɚz)
= measurements ('mɛʒɚmənts)
= figures ('fɪgjɚz , 'fɪgɚz)
= calculation (,kælkjə'leʃən)
= computation (,kɑmpjə'teʃən)

matrimony ('mætrə,monɪ) *n.* 婚禮

= marriage ('mærɪdʒ)
= wedding ('wɛdɪŋ)
= nuptials ('nʌpʃəlz)

matron ('metrən) *n.* 主婦

= woman ('wʊmən , 'wu-)
= lady ('ledɪ)

M

matter ('mætɚ) *n.* ①物質
②事件

① = material (mə'tɪrɪəl)
= substance ('sʌbstəns)
= composition (,kɑmpə'zɪʃən)
= content ('kɑntɛnt , kən'tɛnt)

② = affair (ə'fɛr)
= business ('bɪznɪs)
= concern (kən'sɝn)
= transaction (træns'ækʃən ,
trænz-)
= activity (æk'tɪvətɪ)

mature (mə'tjur , -'tʃur) *adj.*
成熟的

= ripe (raɪp)
= developed (dɪ'vɛləpt)
= mellow ('mɛlo)
= adult (ə'dʌlt , 'ædʌlt)
= ready ('rɛdɪ)
= prime (praɪm)
= full-blown ('ful'blon)
= full-grown ('ful'gron)

maul (mɔl) *v.* 毆打

= bruise (bruz)
= batter ('bætɚ)
= abuse (ə'bjuz)

mausoleum (,mɔsə'liəm) *n.* 墓

= tomb (tum)
= vault (vɔlt)
= crypt (krɪpt)
= shrine (ʃraɪn)

maxim ('mæksɪm) *n.* 格言

= proverb ('prɑvɝb)
= saying ('seɪŋ)
= rule (rul)
= law (lɔ)
= code (kod)
= principle ('prɪnsəpl̩)
= adage ('ædɪdʒ)
= regulation (,rɛgjə'leʃən)

maximum ('mæksəməm) *adj.*
最大量的

= largest ('lɑrdʒɪst)
= highest ('haɪɪst)
= greatest ('gretɪst)
= uppermost ('ʌpɚ,most)
= head (hɛd)
= chief (tʃif)

may (me) *aux.* 可能

= can (kæn , kən)
= *be able to*
= *be allowed to*

maybe ('mebi , 'mebɪ) *adv.* 大概

= possibly ('pɑsəblɪ)
= perhaps (pɚ'hæps)
= conceivably (kən'sivəblɪ)
= perchance (pɚ'tʃæns)

maze (mez) *n.* 迷惘；混亂

= network ('nɛt,wɝk)
= complex ('kɑmplɛks)
= tangle ('tæŋgl̩)
= labyrinth ('læbə,rɪnθ)
= confusion (kən'fjuʒən)
= muddle ('mʌdl̩)

meadow ('mɛdo) *n.* 草地

= grassland ('græs,lænd)
= pasture ('pæstʃə , 'pɑs-)
= range (rendʒ)
= field (fild)

meager ('migə) *adj.* 貧乏的

= poor (pur)
= scanty ('skæntɪ)
= thin (θɪn)
= lean (lin)
= sparse (spɑrs)
= skimpy ('skɪmpɪ)

meal (mil) *n.* 一餐

= repast (rɪ'pæst)
= spread (sprɛd)

mean (min) ① *v.* 意謂
② *adj.* 卑鄙的　③ *adj.* 中庸的

① = signify ('sɪgnə,faɪ)
= intend (ɪn'tɛnd)
= denote (dɪ'not)
= imply (ɪm'plaɪ)
= indicate ('ɪndə,ket)
= suggest (səg'dʒɛst , sə'dʒɛst)
= connote (kə'not)
② = petty ('pɛtɪ)
= unkind (ʌn'kaɪnd)
= malicious (mə'lɪʃəs)
= ill-humored ('ɪl'hjuməd , 'ɪl'ju-)
= cross (krɔs)
= irritable ('ɪrətəbl̩)
= testy ('tɛstɪ)
③ = average ('ævərɪdʒ)
= medium ('midɪəm)

= normal ('nɔrml̩)
= middle ('mɪdl̩)

meander (mɪ'ændə) *v.* 漫遊

= wander ('wɑndə)
= wind (waɪnd)
= twist (twɪst)
= stray (stre)

measure ('mɛʒə) *v.* 測量；估量

= size (saɪz)
= grade (gred)
= rank (ræŋk)
= compare (kəm'pɛr)
= assess (ə'sɛs)
= appraise (ə'prez)
= rate (ret)
= estimate ('ɛstə,met)

mechanic (mə'kænɪk) *n.* 技師

= machinist (mə'ʃinɪst)
= repairman (rɪ'pɛr,mæn , -mən)
= craftsman ('kræftsmən ,
　'krɑfts-)
= technician (tɛk'nɪʃən)

medal ('mɛdl̩) *n.* 獎章

= award (ə'wɔrd)
= honor ('ɑnə)
= reward (rɪ'wɔrd)
= medallion (mɪ'dæljən , mə-)
= prize (praɪz)

meddle ('mɛdl̩) *v.* 擾亂

= interfere (,ɪntə'fɪr)
= interpose (,ɪntə'poz)

M

= intrude (ɪn'trud)
= interrupt (ˌɪntə'rʌpt)
= intervene (ˌɪntə'vin)
= trespass ('trɛspəs)

media ('midɪə) *n. pl.* 媒體

= instruments ('ɪnstrəmənts)
= tools (tulz)
= agents ('edʒənts)
= implements ('ɪmpləmənts)

mediate ('midɪˌet) *v.* 調停

= settle ('sɛtḷ)
= negotiate (nɪ'goʃɪˌet)
= intercede (ˌɪntə'sid)
= intervene (ˌɪntə'vin)
= referee (ˌrɛfə'ri)
= umpire ('ʌmpaɪr)
= arbitrate ('ɑrbəˌtret)
= *make peace*

medicinal (mə'dɪsn̩l) *adj.*
治療的

= healing ('hilɪŋ)
= helping ('hɛlpɪŋ)
= relieving (rɪ'livɪŋ)
= remedial (rɪ'midɪəl)
= corrective (kə'rɛktɪv)
= therapeutic (ˌθɛrə'pjutɪk)

mediocre ('midɪˌokə ,
ˌmidɪ'okə) *adj.* 平常的

= average ('ævərɪdʒ)
= ordinary ('ɔrdn̩ˌɛrɪ , 'ɔrdnɛrɪ)
= fair (fɛr)
= moderate ('mɑdərɪt)

= adequate ('ædəkwɪt)
= medium ('midɪəm)
= acceptable (ək'sɛptəbḷ , æk-)
= passable ('pæsəbḷ)
= so-so ('soˌso)

meditate ('mɛdəˌtet) *v.* 考慮

= think (θɪŋk)
= reflect (rɪ'flɛkt)
= consider (kən'sɪdə)
= contemplate ('kɑntəmˌplet ,
  kən'tɛmplet)
= study ('stʌdɪ)
= ponder ('pɑndə)
= weigh (we)
= brood (brud)
= deliberate (dɪ'lɪbəˌret)

medium ('midɪəm)
① *adj.* 中等的 ② *n.* 媒體

① = middle ('mɪdḷ)
= average ('ævərɪdʒ)
= mean (min)
= halfway ('hæf'we)
= mediocre (ˌmidɪ'okə ,
  'midɪˌokə)
= fair (fɛr)
② = instrument ('ɪnstrəmənt)
= tool (tul)
= agent ('edʒənt)
= implement ('ɪmpləmənt)

medley ('mɛdlɪ) *n.* 混合

= mixture ('mɪkstʃə)
= hodgepodge ('hɑdʒˌpɑdʒ)
= assortment (ə'sɔrtmənt)

= conglomeration
  (kən,glɑmə'reʃən)
= combination (,kɑmbə'neʃən)

meek (mik) *adj.* 溫順的

= mild (maɪld)
= patient ('peʃənt)
= submissive (səb'mɪsɪv)
= gentle ('dʒɛntḷ)
= tame (tem)
= subdued (səb'djud)
= uncomplaining
  (,ʌnkəm'plenɪŋ)
= passive ('pæsɪv)
= modest ('mɑdɪst)
= unassuming (,ʌnə'sumɪŋ,
  -'sjum-)
= unpretentious (,ʌnprɪ'tɛnʃəs)

meet (mit) *v.* 會合

= join (dʒɔɪn)
= unite (ju'naɪt)
= connect (kə'nɛkt)
= assemble (ə'sɛmbḷ)
= gather ('gæðɚ)
= encounter (ɪn'kaʊntɚ)
= converge (kən'vɝdʒ)
= *come together*

melancholy ('mɛlən,kɑlɪ) *adj.*
憂鬱的

= sad (sæd)
= gloomy ('glumɪ)
= blue (blu)
= pensive ('pɛnsɪv)
= wistful ('wɪstfəl)

= depressing (dɪ'prɛsɪŋ)
= dismal ('dɪzmḷ)

mellow ('mɛlo) *adj.* 成熟的

= mature (mə'tjʊr , -'tʃʊr)
= ripe (raɪp)
= developed (dɪ'vɛləpt)
= soft (sɔft)
= full-grown ('fʊl'gron)

melody ('mɛlədɪ) *n.* 曲調

= tune (tjun)
= song (sɔŋ , sɑŋ)

melt (mɛlt) *v.* 融化

= dissolve (dɪ'zɑlv)
= change (tʃendʒ)
= soften ('sɔfən)
= liquefy ('lɪkwə,faɪ)

member ('mɛmbɚ) *n.* 組成分子

= part (pɑrt)
= offshoot ('ɔf,ʃut , 'ɑf-)
= branch (bræntʃ)
= organ ('ɔrgən)

membrane ('mɛmbren) *n.* 膜

= covering ('kʌvərɪŋ)
= tissue ('tɪʃu)
= layer ('leɚ)

M

memorable ('mɛmərəbḷ) *adj.*
值得紀念的

= notable ('notəbḷ)
= rememberable (rɪ'mɛmbərəbḷ)

memorandum

(ˌmɛməˈrændəm) *n.* 便箋；備忘錄

= note (not)

= letter (ˈlɛtɚ)

= report (rɪˈport)

= reminder (rɪˈmaɪndɚ)

= memo (ˈmɛmo)

memorize (ˈmɛməˌraɪz) *v.* 記住

= remember (rɪˈmɛmbɚ)

= *learn by heart*

menace (ˈmɛnɪs) *n.* 威脅

= threat (θrɛt)

menagerie (məˈnædʒərɪ , -ˈnæʒ-) *n.* 動物展覽；動物園

= zoo (zu)

= collection (kəˈlɛkʃən)

= kennel (ˈkɛnḷ)

mention (ˈmɛnʃən) *v.* 提及

= remark (rɪˈmark)

= comment (ˈkamɛnt)

= observe (əbˈzɝv)

= say (se)

= note (not)

= state (stet)

= name (nem)

= specify (ˈspɛsəˌfaɪ)

= stipulate (ˈstɪpjəˌlet)

= designate (ˈdɛzɪgˌnet)

menu (ˈmɛnju , ˈmenju) *n.* 菜單

= list (lɪst)

= account (əˈkaʊnt)

= line-up (ˈlaɪnˌʌp)

= *bill of fare*

merchandise (ˈmɝtʃənˌdaɪz) *n.* 商品

= goods (gʊds)

= wares (wɛrz)

= commodities (kəˈmadətɪz)

= products (ˈpradəkts , -dʌkts)

mercy (ˈmɝsɪ) *n.* 慈悲

= kindness (ˈkaɪndnɪs)

= compassion (kəmˈpæʃən)

= pity (ˈpɪtɪ)

= sympathy (ˈsɪmpəθɪ)

= charity (ˈtʃærətɪ)

merely (ˈmɪrlɪ) *adv.* 僅

= simply (ˈsɪmplɪ)

= only (ˈonlɪ)

= purely (ˈpjʊrlɪ)

= barely (ˈbɛrlɪ)

merge (mɝdʒ) *v.* 吞沒；合併

= absorb (əbˈsɔrb)

= swallow (ˈswalo)

= combine (kəmˈbaɪn)

= unite (juˈnaɪt)

= mix (mɪks)

= blend (blɛnd)

= fuse (fjuz)

= join (dʒɔɪn)

= mingle (ˈmɪŋgḷ)

= scramble (ˈskræmbḷ)

merit ('mɛrɪt) *n.* 價值；優點

= quality ('kwalətɪ)
= value ('vælju)
= worth (wɜθ)
= goodness ('gʊdnɪs)
= excellence ('ɛksḷəns)
= fineness ('faɪnnɪs)

merry ('mɛrɪ) *adj.* 快樂的

= gay (ge)
= joyful ('dʒɔɪfəl)
= jolly ('dʒalɪ)
= jovial ('dʒovɪəl)
= gleeful ('glifəl)
= mirthful ('mɜθfəl)
= festive ('fɛstɪv)

mesh (mɛʃ) *n.* 網

= net (nɛt)
= screen (skrin)
= web (wɛb)
= complex ('kamplɛks)

mess (mɛs) *v.* 使混亂

= dirty ('dɜtɪ)
= disfigure (dɪs'fɪgjə)
= contaminate (kən'tæmə,net)
= pollute (pə'lut)
= corrupt (kə'rʌpt)

message ('mɛsɪdʒ) *n.* 訊息；音信

= word (wɜd)
= communication
  (kə,mjunə'keʃən)
= dispatch (dɪ'spætʃ)
= letter ('lɛtə)

= epistle (ɪ'pɪsḷ)
= note (not)

mete (mit) *v.* 分配

= distribute (dɪ'strɪbjut)
= share (ʃɛr)
= give (gɪv)
= allot (ə'lat)
= grant (grænt)
= present (prɪ'zɛnt)
= dispense (dɪ'spɛns)
= measure ('mɛʒə)
= *deal out*
= *dole out*
= *hand out*

meteoric (,mitɪ'ɔrɪk , -'ar-) *adj.* 疾速的

= swift (swɪft)
= flashing ('flæʃɪŋ)
= brief (brif)
= blazing ('blezɪŋ)

meter ('mitə) *n.* 計量器

= measure ('mɛʒə)
= record ('rɛkəd)
= gauge (gedʒ)

M

method ('mɛθəd) *n.* 方法

= system ('sɪstəm)
= way (we)
= manner ('mænə)
= means (minz)
= mode (mod)
= fashion ('fæʃən)
= style (staɪl)

= procedure (prə'sidʒə)
= process ('prasɛs , 'prosɛs)
= form (fɔrm)
= course (kors , kɔrs)
= plan (plæn)
= scheme (skim)
= design (dɪ'zaɪn)
= arrangement (ə'rendʒmənt)

metropolitan (,mɛtrə'palətṇ)
adj. 大都市的

= city ('sɪtɪ)
= civic ('sɪvɪk)
= urban ('ɜbən)
= municipal (mju'nɪsəpḷ)

mettle ('mɛtḷ) *n.* 勇氣

= spirit ('spɪrɪt)
= courage ('kɜɪdʒ)
= nerve (nɜv)
= stamina ('stæmənə)
= pluck (plʌk)
= spunk (spʌŋk)

microscopic (,maɪkrə'skapɪk)
adj. 微小的

= infinitesimal (,ɪnfɪnə'tɛsəmḷ)
= tiny ('taɪnɪ)
= minute (mə'njut , maɪ)

middle ('mɪdḷ) *n.* 中心

= center ('sɛntə)
= heart (hart)
= core (kor)
= nucleus ('njuklɪəs)
= hub (hʌb)

midget ('mɪdʒɪt) *n.* 侏儒

= dwarf (dwɔrf)
= pygmy ('pɪgmɪ)
= runt (rʌnt)

mien (min) *n.* 態度

= manner ('mænə)
= way (we)
= conduct ('kandʌkt)
= behavior (bɪ'hevjə)
= semblance ('sɛmbləns)

might (maɪt) *aux.* 可能

= can (kæn , kən)
= *be able to*
= *be allowed to*

mighty ('maɪtɪ) *adj.* 有力的

= strong (strɔŋ)
= powerful ('pauəfəl)
= great (gret)
= grand (grænd)
= potent ('potṇt)
= muscular ('mʌskjələ)
= forceful ('forsfəl , 'fɔrs-)
= vigorous ('vɪgərəs)
= stout (staut)
= sturdy ('stɜdɪ)
= rugged ('rʌgɪd)
= robust (ro'bʌst)
= hearty ('hartɪ)

migrant ('maɪgrənt) *adj.* 移居的

= roving ('rovɪŋ)
= traveling ('trævḷɪŋ , 'trævlɪŋ)
= wandering ('wandərɪŋ)

M

= roaming ('romɪŋ)
= rambling ('ræmblɪŋ)
= meandering (mɪ'ændrɪŋ)
= drifting ('drɪftɪŋ)
= straying ('streɪŋ)
= transient ('trænʃənt)

mild (maɪld) *adj.* 溫柔的

= gentle ('dʒɛntl̩)
= kind (kaɪnd)
= calm (kɑm)
= warm (wɔrm)
= temperate ('tɛmprɪt)
= moderate ('mɑdərɪt)
= lenient ('linɪənt , 'linjənt)
= good-natured ('gʊd'netʃəd)
= good-humored ('gʊd'jumæd ,
  -'hju-)

militant ('mɪlətənt) *adj.* 好戰的

= fighting ('faɪtɪŋ)
= warlike ('wɔr,laɪk)
= combative (kəm'bætɪv ,
  'kɑmbətɪv , 'kʌm-)
= belligerent (bə'lɪdʒərənt)
= hostile ('hɑstɪl)
= antagonistic (æn,tægə'nɪstɪk ,
  ,æntægə-)
= contentious (kən'tɛnʃəs)
= pugnacious (pʌg'neʃəs)
= aggressive (ə'grɛsɪv)
= bellicose ('bɛlə,kos)

military ('mɪlə,tɛrɪ) *n.* 軍隊

= army ('ɑrmɪ)
= troops (trups)

= soldiers ('soldʒəz)
= service ('sɝvɪs)
= *armed forces*

mimic ('mɪmɪk) *v.* 模仿

= imitate ('ɪmə,tet)
= copy ('kɑpɪ)
= ape (ep)
= mock (mɑk)
= mime (maɪm)
= parrot ('pærət)
= copycat ('kɑpɪ,kæt)

mince (mɪns) *v.* 粉碎

= chop (tʃɑp)
= shatter ('ʃætæ)
= crush (krʌʃ)
= smash (smæʃ)
= fragment ('frægmənt)

mind (maɪnd) ① *n.* 智力
② *v.* 服從 ③ *v.* 注意

① = brain (bren)
= intelligence (ɪn'tɛlədʒəns)
= intellect ('ɪntl̩,ɛkt)
= *mental ability*
② = obey (ə'be , o'be)
= heed (hid)
= regard (rɪ'gɑrd)
= comply (kəm'plaɪ)
= *listen to*
③ = attend (ə'tɛnd)
= watch (wɑtʃ)
= observe (əb'zɝv)
= notice ('notɪs)

M

mine (maɪn) *v.* ①挖 ②炸毀

① = excavate ('ɛkskə,vet)

= dig (dɪg)

= *scoop out*

② = blast (blæst)

= *blow up*

mingle ('mɪŋgl̩) *v.* 混合

= mix (mɪks)

= associate (ə'soʃɪ,et)

= blend (blɛnd)

= combine (kəm'baɪn)

miniature ('mɪnɪətʃə) *adj.* 微小的

= small (smɔl)

= tiny ('taɪnɪ)

= minute (mə'njut , maɪ-)

minimum ('mɪnəməm) *adj.* 最小的

= least (list)

= lowest ('loɪst)

= smallest ('smɔlɪst)

minister ('mɪnɪstə) *n.* 牧師

= clergyman ('klɝdʒɪmən)

= pastor ('pæstə , 'pɑs-)

= chaplain ('tʃæplɪn)

= *spiritual guide*

minor ('maɪnə) *adj.* ①較小的 ②未成年的

① = smaller ('smɔlə)

= lesser ('lɛsə)

= inferior (ɪn'fɪrɪə)

= secondary ('sɛkən,dɛrɪ)

= lower ('loə)

② = underage ('ʌndə,edʒ)

= immature (,ɪmə'tjʊr)

minstrel ('mɪnstrəl) *n.* 吟遊詩人;音樂家

= musician (mju'zɪʃən)

= bard (bɑrd)

= troubadour ('trubə,dʊr , -,dor , -,dɔr)

minus ('maɪnəs) *prep.* 缺少;無

= less (lɛs)

= lacking ('lækɪŋ)

= without (wɪð'aʊt , wɪθ-)

= excepting (ɪk'sɛptɪŋ , ɛk-)

1. **minute** ('mɪnɪt) *n.* 瞬間;片刻

= instant ('ɪnstənt)

= moment ('momənt)

= twinkling ('twɪŋklɪŋ)

2. **minute** (mə'njut , maɪ-) *adj.* 微小的

= small (smɔl)

= tiny ('taɪnɪ)

= miniature ('mɪnɪətʃə)

= slight (slaɪt)

= negligible ('nɛglədʒəbl̩)

= insignificant (,ɪnsɪg'nɪfəkənt)

miraculous (mə'rækjələs) *adj.* 神奇的;特異的

= wonderful ('wʌndəfəl)

M

= marvelous（'mɑrvḷəs）
= remarkable（rɪ'mɑrkəbḷ）
= incredible（ɪn'krɛdəbḷ）
= phenomenal（fə'nɑmənḷ）
= extraordinary（ɪk'strɔrdn̩,ɛrɪ, ,ɛkstrə'ɔr-）

nire（maɪr）*n.* 泥濘；泥沼

= mud（mʌd）
= slush（slʌʃ）
= muck（mʌk）
= slime（slaɪm）

mirror（'mɪrə）*v.* 反映

= reflect（rɪ'flɛkt）
= echo（'ɛko）
= copy（'kɑpɪ）
= imitate（'ɪmə,tet）

nirth（mɝθ）*n.* 歡樂

= fun（fʌn）
= laughter（'læftə, 'lɑf-）
= joy（dʒɔɪ）
= glee（gli）
= levity（'lɛvətɪ）
= amusement（ə'mjuzmənt）

nisbehave（,mɪsbɪ'hev）*v.*
行為不檢

= *behave badly*
= *act up*

niscellaneous（,mɪsḷ'enɪəs）
adj. 混雜的

= mixed（mɪkst）
= combined（kəm'baɪnd）

= blended（'blɛndɪd）
= conglomerate（kən'glɑmərɪt, -'glɑmrɪt）
= scrambled（'skræmbḷd）
= jumbled（'dʒʌmbḷd）

mischievous（'mɪstʃɪvəs）*adj.*
淘氣的

= naughty（'nɔtɪ）
= harmful（'hɑrmfəl）
= devilish（'dɛvlɪʃ）
= impish（'ɪmpɪʃ）
= playful（'plefəl）
= prankish（'præŋkɪʃ）
= elfish（'ɛlfɪʃ, 'ɛlvɪʃ）

miser（'maɪzə）*n.* 守財奴

= moneygrubber（'mʌnɪ,grʌbə）

miserable（'mɪzərəbḷ, 'mɪzrə-）
adj. 可憐的

= poor（pur）
= mean（min）
= wretched（'rɛtʃɪd）
= unhappy（ʌn'hæpɪ）
= pitiful（'pɪtɪfəl）
= shabby（'ʃæbɪ）
= woeful（'wofəl）
= sorry（'sɔrɪ, 'sɑrɪ）

misfortune（mɪs'fɔrtʃən）*n.*
不幸；災禍

= difficulty（'dɪfə,kʌltɪ）
= trouble（'trʌbḷ）
= distress（dɪ'strɛs）
= hardship（'hɑrdʃɪp）

M

= ruin ('ruɪn)

= disaster (dɪz'æstɚ)

= catastrophe (kə'tæstrəfɪ)

= calamity (kə'læmətɪ)

= tragedy ('trædʒədɪ)

= accident ('æksədənt)

= mishap ('mɪs,hæp , mɪs'hæp)

misgiving (mɪs'gɪvɪŋ) *n.*
疑惑；擔憂

= doubt (daʊt)

= suspicion (sə'spɪʃən)

= anxiety (æŋ'zaɪətɪ)

= question ('kwɛstʃən)

= skepticism ('skɛptə,sɪzəm)

= qualm (kwɑm , kwɔm)

= concern (kən'sɝn)

= uneasiness (ʌn'izɪnɪs)

mishap (mɪs'hæp , 'mɪs,hæp)
n. 不幸；災禍

= misfortune (mɪs'fɔrtʃən)

= difficulty ('dɪfə,kʌltɪ)

= trouble ('trʌbl̩)

= distress (dɪ'strɛs)

= hardship ('hɑrdʃɪp)

= ruin ('ruɪn)

= disaster (dɪz'æstɚ)

= catastrophe (kə'tæstrəfɪ)

= calamity (kə'læmətɪ)

= tragedy ('trædʒədɪ)

= accident ('æksədənt)

misjudge (mɪs'dʒʌdʒ) *v.*
判斷錯誤

= mistake (mə'stek)

= err (ɝ)

= miscalculate (mɪs'kælkjə,let)

= *slip up*

mislay (mɪs'le) *v.* 誤放

= lose (luz)

= miss (mɪs)

= misplace (mɪs'ples)

mislead (mɪs'lid) *v.* 使入歧途

= deceive (dɪ'siv)

= misdirect (,mɪsdə'rɛkt)

= misinform (,mɪsɪn'fɔrm ,
  ,mɪsn̩-)

misplace (mɪs'ples) *v.* 誤放

= mislay (mɪs'le)

= lose (luz)

= miss (mɪs)

miss (mɪs) *v.* 喪失

= fail (fel)

= lose (luz)

= forfeit ('fɔrfɪt)

= sacrifice ('sækrə,faɪs , -,faɪz)

misshapen (mɪs'ʃepən) *adj.*
畸形的

= deformed (dɪ'fɔrmd)

= disfigured (dɪs'fɪgjɚd)

= grotesque (gro'tɛsk)

missile ('mɪsl̩) *n.* 火箭

= rocket ('rɑkɪt)

= projectile (prə'dʒɛktl̩)

missing (ˈmɪsɪŋ) *adj.* 缺少的

= lacking (ˈlækɪŋ)
= wanting (ˈwɑntɪŋ)
= lost (lɔst)
= absent (ˈæbsn̩t)
= nonexistent (ˌnɑnɪgˈzɪstənt)
= gone (gɔn)
= vanished (ˈvænɪʃt)

mission (ˈmɪʃən) *n.* 使命；任務

= errand (ˈɛrənd)
= business (ˈbɪznɪs)
= purpose (ˈpɜpəs)
= task (tæsk, tɑsk)
= work (wɜk)
= stint (stɪnt)
= job (dʒɑb)
= assignment (əˈsaɪnmənt)
= chore (tʃor, tʃɔr)
= charge (tʃɑrdʒ)
= duty (ˈdjutɪ)

mist (mɪst) *n.* 霧

= cloud (klaʊd)
= fog (fɑg, fɔg)
= vapor (ˈvepɚ)
= haze (hez)
= film (fɪlm)
= dimness (ˈdɪmnɪs)
= blur (blɜ)

mistake (məˈstek) *n.* 錯誤；
誤會

= error (ˈɛrɚ)
= blunder (ˈblʌndɚ)
= fault (fɔlt)

= miss (mɪs)
= slip (slɪp)
= oversight (ˈovɚˌsaɪt)
= *faux pas*

mistreat (mɪsˈtrit) *v.* 虐待；
苛待

= abuse (əˈbjuz)
= molest (məˈlɛst)
= bruise (bruz)
= ill-treat (ˌɪlˈtrit)

mistress (ˈmɪstrɪs) *n.* 主婦

= woman (ˈwʊmən)
= matron (ˈmetrən)
= housekeeper (ˈhaʊsˌkipɚ)

mistrust (mɪsˈtrʌst) *v.* 懷疑

= doubt (daʊt)
= suspect (səˈspɛkt)
= distrust (dɪsˈtrʌst)
= question (ˈkwɛstʃən)
= challenge (ˈtʃælɪndʒ)
= dispute (dɪˈspjut)
= *be skeptical*

misunderstanding
(ˌmɪsʌndɚˈstændɪŋ) *n.* 誤會

= disagreement (ˌdɪsəˈgrimənt)
= difficulty (ˈdɪfəˌkʌltɪ)
= difference (ˈdɪfərəns)
= misinterpretation
 (ˌmɪsɪnˌtɜprɪˈteʃən)
= mistake (məˈstek)
= error (ˈɛrɚ)

M

misuse (mɪsˈjuz) *v.* 誤用

= mishandle (mɪsˈhændl̩)

= *treat badly*

mitt (mɪt) *n.* 手套

= glove (glʌv)

mix (mɪks) *v.* 混合

= stir (stɝ)

= join (dʒɔɪn)

= blend (blɛnd)

= combine (kəmˈbaɪn)

= fuse (fjuz)

= mingle (ˈmɪŋgl̩)

= merge (mɝdʒ)

moan (mon) *v.* 呻吟

= wail (wel)

= groan (gron)

= howl (haʊl)

= cry (kraɪ)

= bawl (bɔl)

= suffer (ˈsʌfɚ)

= agonize (ˈægəˌnaɪz)

= complain (kəmˈplen)

moat (mot) *n.* 壕溝

= trench (trɛntʃ)

= fortification (ˌfɔrtəfəˈkeʃən)

= channel (ˈtʃænl̩)

= ditch (dɪtʃ)

= entrenchment (ɪnˈtrɛntʃmənt)

mob (mab) *n.* 民眾

= crowd (kraʊd)

= mass (mæs)

= throng (θrɔŋ)

= multitude (ˈmʌltəˌtjud)

= horde (hord , hɔrd)

= pack (pæk)

= bunch (bʌntʃ)

mobile (ˈmobl̩ , ˈmobɪl) *adj.* 動的

= movable (ˈmuvəbl̩)

= changeable (ˈtʃendʒəbl̩)

= fluid (ˈfluɪd)

mock (mak) *v.* 模仿；嘲弄

= mimic (ˈmɪmɪk)

= imitate (ˈɪməˌtet)

= ape (ep)

= ridicule (ˈrɪdɪkjul)

= scoff (skaf , skɔf)

= jeer (dʒɪr)

= taunt (tɔnt)

= deride (dɪˈraɪd)

= *laugh at*

mode (mod) *n.* 作法；方式

= manner (ˈmænɚ)

= way (we)

= style (staɪl)

= fashion (ˈfæʃən)

= form (fɔrm)

= vogue (vog)

= custom (ˈkʌstəm)

= method (ˈmɛθəd)

model (ˈmadl̩) *n.* 模型

= copy (ˈkapɪ)

= shape (ʃep)

= design (dɪˈzaɪn)

M

= reproduction (ˌriprə'dʌkʃən)

= duplicate ('djupləkɪt)

= replica ('rɛplɪkə)

= standard ('stændəd)

= prototype ('protəˌtaɪp)

= image ('ɪmɪdʒ)

= likeness ('laɪknɪs)

moderate ('madərɪt) *adj.*
適度的；溫和的

= calm (kɑm)

= fair (fɛr)

= medium ('midɪəm)

= mild (maɪld)

= conservative (kən's3vətɪv)

= gentle ('dʒɛntḷ)

= restrained (rɪ'strend)

= lenient ('liniənt, 'linjənt)

= temperate ('tɛmprɪt)

modern ('madən) *adj.* 現代的

= contemporary (kən'tɛmpəˌrɛrɪ)

= progressive (prə'grɛsɪv)

= up-to-date ('ʌptə'det)

= forward-looking
('fɔrwəd,lukɪŋ)

modest ('madɪst) *adj.* 謙遜的；
質樸的

= humble ('hʌmbḷ)

= bashful ('bæʃfəl)

= shy (ʃaɪ)

= quiet ('kwaɪət)

= unpretentious (ˌʌnprɪ'tɛnʃəs)

= plain (plen)

= simple ('sɪmpḷ)

modify ('madəˌfaɪ) *v.* 變更；
修改

= change (tʃendʒ)

= alter ('ɔltə)

= vary ('vɛrɪ)

= diversify (də'v3səˌfaɪ)

= qualify ('kwaləˌfaɪ)

= adjust (ə'dʒʌst)

= fix (fɪks)

moist (mɔɪst) *adj.* 潮濕的

= wet (wɛt)

= damp (dæmp)

= humid ('hjumɪd)

= dank (dæŋk)

= watery ('wɔtərɪ)

mold (mold) *v.* ①塑造 ②發黴

① = shape (ʃep)

= form (fɔrm)

= sculpture ('skʌlptʃə)

= carve (kɑrv)

= model ('madḷ)

② = decay (dɪ'ke)

= rot (rat)

= spoil (spɔɪl)

= deteriorate (dɪ'tɪrɪəˌret)

= disintegrate (dɪs'ɪntəˌgret)

= crumble ('krʌmbḷ)

= *go bad*

molest (mə'lɛst) *v.* 妨害；干擾

= trouble ('trʌbḷ)

= injure ('ɪndʒə)

= harm (hɑrm)

= hurt (h3t)

M

= damage ('dæmɪdʒ)
= wrong (rɔŋ)
= disturb (dɪ'stɝb)
= mistreat (mɪs'trit)
= annoy (ə'nɔɪ)
= abuse (ə'bjuz)
= torment (tɔr'mɛnt)
= harass (hə'ræs , 'hærəs)
= badger ('bædʒɚ)
= pester ('pɛstɚ)
= plague (pleg)

moment ('momənt) *n.* 瞬間；片刻

= instant ('ɪnstənt)
= minute ('mɪnɪt)
= twinkling ('twɪŋklɪŋ)

momentous (mo'mɛntəs) *adj.* 極重要的

= important (ɪm'pɔrtn̩t)
= great (gret)
= outstanding (aut'stændɪŋ)
= considerable (kən'sɪdərəbl̩)
= eventful (ɪ'vɛntfəl)
= stirring ('stɝɪŋ)
= influential (,ɪnflu'ɛnʃəl)
= powerful ('pauɚfəl)
= effective (ə'fɛktɪv)

momentum (mo'mɛntəm) *n.* 動力

= force (fors , fɔrs)
= impetus ('ɪmpətəs)
= thrust (θrʌst)
= push (puʃ)

monarch ('manɚk) *n.* 統治者

= ruler ('rulɚ)
= sovereign ('savrɪn , 'sʌv-)
= head (hɛd)
= emperor ('ɛmpərɚ)
= king (kɪŋ)
= queen (kwin)
= chief (tʃif)

money ('mʌnɪ) *n.* 貨幣；金錢

= currency ('kɝənsɪ)
= cash (kæʃ)
= dollars ('dalɚz)
= *legal tender*

mongrel ('mʌŋgrəl) *n.* 混血兒

= crossbreed ('krɔs,brid)
= hybrid ('haɪbrɪd)

monitor ('manətɚ) *n.* ①級長 ②書記 ③勸誡者

① = helper ('hɛlpɚ)
= assistant (ə'sɪstənt)
② = recorder (rɪ'kɔrdɚ)
= clerk (klɝk)
③ = adviser (əd'vaɪzɚ)
= informant (ɪn'fɔrmənt)
= counselor ('kaunslɚ)
= reporter (rɪ'portɚ)
= announcer (ə'naunsɚ)

monogram ('manə,græm) *n.* 印章；簽字

= signature ('sɪgnətʃɚ)
= mark (mark)
= seal (sil)
= stamp (stæmp)

M

monopoly (mə'nɑpḷɪ) *n.* 壟斷

= control (kən'trol)
= corner ('kɔrnə)
= possession (pə'zɛʃən)

nonotonous (mə'nɑtṇəs) *adj.* 單調的

= boring ('borɪŋ)
= humdrum ('hʌm,drʌm)
= repetitious (,rɛpɪ'tɪʃəs)
= tedious ('tidɪəs , 'tidʒəs)
= dreary ('drɪrɪ , 'drirɪ)
= dull (dʌl)

nonsoon (mɑn'sun) *n.* 季風

= rains (renz)
= storm (stɔrm)
= winds (wɪndz)

nonstrous ('mɑnstrəs) *adj.* 恐怖的；怪異的

= horrible ('hɑrəbḷ)
= dreadful ('drɛdfəl)
= shocking ('ʃɑkɪŋ)
= grotesque (gro'tɛsk)
= deformed (dɪ'fɔrmd)
= disfigured (dɪs'fɪgjəd)

monument ('mɑnjəmənt) *n.* 紀念碑

= tower ('tauə)
= memorial (mə'morɪəl)
= shrine (ʃraɪn)
= pillar ('pɪlə)

monumental (mɑnjə'mɛntḷ) *adj.* 巨大的；不朽的

= important (ɪm'pɔrtṇt)
= weighty ('wetɪ)
= great (gret)
= vast (væst)
= immense (ɪ'mɛns)
= stupendous (stju'pɛndəs)
= enormous (ɪ'nɔrməs)
= huge (hjudʒ)
= notable ('notəbḷ)
= remarkable (rɪ'mɑrkəbḷ)
= extraordinary (ɪk'strɔrdṇ,ɛrɪ)
= exceptional (ɪk'sɛpʃənḷ)
= special ('spɛʃəl)
= memorable ('mɛmərəbḷ)

mood (mud) *n.* 心境；心情

= feeling ('filɪŋ)
= temperament ('tɛmprəmənt)
= humor ('hjumə , 'ju-)
= disposition (,dɪspə'zɪʃən)
= nature ('netʃə)
= phase (fez)
= *frame of mind*

moody ('mudɪ) *adj.* 憂鬱的

= gloomy ('glumɪ)
= sullen ('sʌlɪn , -ən)
= glum (glʌm)
= mopish ('mopɪʃ)
= morose (mo'ros , mə-)
= sulky ('sʌlkɪ)

moor (mur) *v.* 使停泊

= anchor ('æŋkə)
= fasten ('fæsṇ , 'fɑsṇ)
= secure (sɪ'kjur)

M

= dock〔dɑk〕
= tie〔taɪ〕

mop〔mɑp〕*v.* 洗擦

= wipe〔waɪp〕
= wash〔wɑʃ〕
= scrub〔skrʌb〕
= scour〔skaʊr〕
= swab〔swɑb〕

mope〔mop〕*v.* 抑鬱不樂

= sulk〔sʌlk〕
= grieve〔griv〕
= sorrow〔'saro〕
= fret〔frɛt〕
= *brood over*

moral〔'mɔrəl〕*adj.* 公正的；道德的

= right〔raɪt〕
= just〔dʒʌst〕
= ethical〔'ɛθɪkḷ〕
= honorable〔'ɑnərəbḷ〕
= reputable〔'rɛpjətəbḷ〕
= upstanding〔ʌp'stændɪŋ〕
= respectable〔rɪ'spɛktəbḷ〕
= virtuous〔'vɝtʃʊəs〕
= good〔gʊd〕
= righteous〔'raɪtʃəs〕
= law-abiding〔'lɔə,baɪdɪŋ〕

morale〔mo'ræl , mo'ral〕*n.* 士氣；民心

= spirit〔'spɪrɪt〕
= enthusiasm〔ɪn'θjuzɪ,æzəm〕

morass〔mo'ræs , mə-〕*n.* 沼地

= swamp〔swɑmp〕
= marsh〔mɑrʃ〕
= bog〔bɑg , bɔg〕
= mire〔maɪr〕

morbid〔'mɔrbɪd〕*adj.* ①病態的 ②可怕的

① = unhealthy〔ʌn'hɛlθɪ〕
= sickly〔'sɪklɪ〕
= diseased〔dɪ'zizd〕
= unwholesome〔ʌn'holsəm〕
② = ghastly〔'gæstlɪ , 'gɑst-〕
= horrible〔'hɑrəbḷ〕
= dreadful〔'drɛdfəl〕
= awful〔'ɔfl〕
= shocking〔'ʃɑkɪŋ〕
= appalling〔ə'pɔlɪŋ〕

more〔mor〕*adj.* 另外的；更多的

= greater〔'gretɚ〕
= further〔'fɝðɚ〕
= farther〔'fɑrðɚ〕
= extra〔'ɛkstrə〕
= another〔ə'nʌðɚ〕

moreover〔mor'ovɚ , mɔr-〕*adv.* 而且；此外

= besides〔bɪ'saɪdz〕
= also〔'ɔlso〕
= furthermore〔'fɝðɚ,mor , -,mɔr〕
= too〔tu〕
= *as well*

morose〔mo'ros , mə-〕*adj.* 憂鬱的

= gloomy〔'glumɪ〕

= sullen ('sʌlən , -ɪn)
= sulky ('sʌlkɪ)
= moody ('mudɪ)
= glum (glʌm)

morsel ('mɔrsəl) *n.* 少量

= piece (pis)
= fragment ('frægmənt)
= particle ('pɑrtɪkḷ)
= bit (bɪt)
= crumb (krʌm)
= scrap (skræp)
= shred (ʃrɛd)

mortal ('mɔrtḷ) ① *n.* 人
② *adj.* 致命的

①= man (mæn)
= person ('pɝsṇ)
= soul (sol)
= individual (ˌɪndə'vɪdʒʊəl)
= body ('bɑdɪ)
= *human being*
②= deadly ('dɛdlɪ)
= fatal ('fetḷ)
= lethal ('liθəl)
= killing ('kɪlɪŋ)
= destructive (dɪ'strʌktɪv)
= malignant (mə'lɪgnənt)

mortify ('mɔrtə,faɪ) *v.* 使羞辱

= wound (wund)
= humiliate (hju'mɪlɪ,et)
= shame (ʃem)
= embarrass (ɪm'bærəs)
= disgrace (dɪs'gres)

most (most) *adj.* 最多的；最大的

= greatest ('gretɪst)
= extreme (ɪk'strim)
= maximum ('mæksəməm)
= supreme (sə'prim , su-)
= highest ('haɪɪst)

mostly ('mostlɪ) *adv.* 主要地

= mainly ('menlɪ)
= chiefly ('tʃiflɪ)
= nearly ('nɪrlɪ)
= *almost all*

mother ('mʌðɚ) ① *v.* 產生
② *n.* 母親 ③ *v.* 照顧

①= originate (ə'rɪdʒə,net)
= produce (prə'djus)
= cause (kɔz)
= breed (brid)
= *bring about*
②= mommy ('mamɪ)
= mama ('mamə , mə'ma)
= mom (mam)
= *female parent*
③= watch (watʃ)
= mind (maɪnd)
= foster ('fɔstɚ , 'fa-)
= nurse (nɝs)
= nurture ('nɝtʃɚ)
= *care for*
= *attend to*
= *look after*

motion ('moʃən) *n.* ①動作
②提議

①= movement ('muvmənt)
= activity (æk'tɪvətɪ)

M

= proceedings (prə'sidɪŋz)

= doings ('duɪŋz)

② = suggestion (səg'dʒɛstʃən)

= proposal (prə'pozl̩)

= legislation (,lɛdʒɪs'leʃən)

= resolution (,rɛzə'ljuʃən)

= proposition (,prɑpə'zɪʃən)

motive ('motɪv) *n.* 動機

= reason ('rizn̩)

= cause (kɔz)

= ground (graund)

= basis ('besɪs)

= motivation (,motə'veʃən)

= prompting ('prɑmptɪŋ)

motley ('mɑtlɪ) *adj.* 混雜的

= mixed (mɪkst)

= varied ('vɛrɪd)

= assorted (ə'sɔrtɪd)

= diversified (daɪ'vɜsə,faɪd , də-)

= various ('vɛrɪəs)

= many ('mɛnɪ)

= several ('sɛvərəl)

motor ('motɚ) *n.* 引擎；發動機

= engine ('ɛndʒən)

= machine (mə'ʃin)

mottled ('mɑtl̩d) *adj.* 有斑點的

= spotted ('spɑtɪd)

= streaked (strikt)

= dappled ('dæpl̩d)

= speckled ('spɛkl̩d)

= flecked (flɛkt)

= piebald ('paɪ,bɔld)

motto ('mato) *n.* 箴言

= saying ('seɪŋ)

= maxim ('mæksɪm)

= proverb ('prɑvɜb)

= adage ('ædɪdʒ)

mound (maund) *n.* 土堆；丘陵

= heap (hip)

= hill (hɪl)

= swell (swɛl)

= pile (paɪl)

= stack (stæk)

mount (maunt) *v.* ①上升
②增加　③放置

① = rise (raɪz)

= ascend (ə'sɛnd)

= climb (klaɪm)

= board (bord , bɔrd)

= *get on*

= *go up*

② = increase (ɪn'kris)

= gain (gen)

= grow (gro)

= advance (əd'væns)

③ = position (pə'zɪʃən)

= place (ples)

= fix (fɪks)

= set (sɛt)

mountain ('mauntn̩ , -tɪn) *n.*
①山　②大量之物

① = hill (hɪl)

= elevation (,ɛlə've ʃən)

② = quantity ('kwɑntətɪ)

= volume ('valjəm)

M

= mass〔mæs〕

= abundance〔ə'bʌndəns〕

= much〔mʌtʃ〕

= *large amount*

nourn〔morn , mɔrn〕*v.* 憂傷

= grieve〔griv〕

= sorrow〔'saro〕

= lament〔lə'mɛnt〕

= bewail〔bɪ'wel〕

= bemoan〔bɪ'mon〕

nove〔muv〕*v.* ①移動 ②煽動；影響

① = change〔tʃendʒ〕

= budge〔bʌdʒ〕

= stir〔stɝ〕

= stimulate〔'stɪmjə,let〕

= impel〔ɪm'pɛl〕

= motivate〔'motə,vet〕

= animate〔'ænəmet〕

② = influence〔'ɪnfluəns〕

= sway〔swe〕

= affect〔ə'fɛkt〕

= persuade〔pə'swed〕

= induce〔ɪn'djus〕

= arouse〔ə'rauz〕

= prompt〔prɑmpt〕

= convince〔kən'vɪns〕

now〔mo〕*v.* 割

= cut〔kʌt〕

= clip〔klɪp〕

= crop〔krɑp〕

= prune〔prun〕

= shear〔ʃɪr〕

= shave〔ʃev〕

much〔mʌtʃ〕*n.* 許多

= quantity〔'kwɑntətɪ〕

= abundance〔ə'bʌndəns〕

= volune〔'vɑljəm〕

= mass〔mæs〕

mucilage〔'mjuslɪdʒ〕*n.* 膠水

= glue〔glu〕

= adhesive〔əd'hisɪv〕

= cement〔sə'mɛnt〕

= paste〔pest〕

muck〔mʌk〕*n.* 髒物；污物

= dirt〔dɝt〕

= filth〔fɪlθ〕

= rot〔rɑt〕

= slime〔slaɪm〕

= mire〔maɪr〕

mud〔mʌd〕*n.* 泥

= mire〔maɪr〕

= muck〔mʌk〕

= slush〔slʌʃ〕

= slime〔slaɪm〕

= dirt〔dɝt〕

muddle〔'mʌdl̩〕*n.* 混亂

= mess〔mɛs〕

= disorder〔dɪs'ɔrdə〕

= confusion〔kən'fjuʒən〕

= chaos〔'keas〕

muff〔mʌf〕*v.* 拙劣地做

= bungle〔'bʌŋgl̩〕

= blunder〔'blʌndə〕

M

= fumble ('fʌmbḷ)

= botch (batʃ)

= spoil (spɔɪl)

= mess (mɛs)

muffle ('mʌfḷ) v. 消音

= silence ('saɪləns)

= mute (mjut)

= dull (dʌl)

= soften ('sɔfən)

= deaden ('dɛdn̩)

= cushion ('kuʃən , 'kuʃɪn)

= smother ('smʌðɚ)

= stifle ('staɪfḷ)

= suppress (sə'prɛs)

muggy ('mʌgɪ) adj. 潮濕的；
悶熱的

= warm (wɔrm)

= damp (dæmp)

= close (klos)

= stuffy ('stʌfɪ)

= humid ('hjumɪd)

= dank (dæŋk)

= sticky ('stɪkɪ)

mulish ('mjulɪʃ) adj. 倔強的

= stubborn ('stʌbən)

= obstinate ('abstənɪt)

= willful ('wɪlfəl)

= headstrong ('hɛd,strɔŋ)

= tenacious (tɪ'neʃəs)

= unyielding (ʌn'jildɪŋ)

= inflexible (ɪn'flɛksəbḷ)

= rigid ('rɪdʒɪd)

= adamant ('ædə,mænt , -mənt)

multiply ('mʌltə,plaɪ) v. 增加

= increase (ɪn'kris)

= advance (əd'væns)

= gain (gen)

= grow (gro)

= rise (raɪz)

= procreate ('prokrɪ,et)

mum (mʌm) adj. 沈默的

= silent ('saɪlənt)

= mute (mjut)

= speechless ('spitʃlɪs)

= quiet ('kwaɪət)

mumble ('mʌmbḷ) v. 喃喃自語

= mutter ('mʌtɚ)

= *speak indistinctly*

municipal (mju'nɪsəpḷ) adj.
市政的

= civic ('sɪvɪk)

= urban ('ɚbən)

= metropolitan (,mɛtrə'palətn̩)

murder ('mɝdɚ) v. ①謀殺
②破壞

① = kill (kɪl)

= assassinate (ə'sæsn̩,et)

= eliminate (ɪ'lɪmə,net)

= purge (pɝdʒ)

= liquidate ('lɪkwɪ,det)

= slaughter ('slɔtɚ)

= massacre ('mæsəkɚ)

② = spoil (spɔɪl)

= ruin ('ruɪn)

= botch (batʃ)

= muff〔mʌf〕
= mar〔mɑr〕
= butcher〔'butʃɚ〕
= *make a mess*

murky〔'mɝkɪ〕*adj.* 黑暗的

= dark〔dɑrk〕
= gloomy〔'glumɪ〕

murmur〔'mɝmɚ〕*v. n.* 低語

= mutter〔'mʌtɚ〕
= whisper〔'hwɪspɚ〕

muscle〔'mʌsḷ〕*n.* 力量;肌肉

= strength〔strɛŋθ, strɛŋkθ〕
= brawn〔brɔn〕

muse〔mjuz〕*v.* 沈思;冥想

= dream〔drim〕
= think〔θɪŋk〕
= envision〔ɛn'vɪʒən〕
= ponder〔'pɑndɚ〕
= contemplate〔'kɑntəm,plet〕
= reflect〔rɪ'flɛkt〕
= deliberate〔dɪ'lɪbə,ret〕
= consider〔kən'sɪdɚ〕

musical〔'mjuzɪkḷ〕*adj.* 音樂的

= melodious〔mə'lodɪəs〕
= tuneful〔'tjunfəl, -fḷ〕
= lyrical〔'lɪrɪkḷ〕
= dulcet〔'dʌlsɪt, -sɛt〕
= harmonious〔hɑr'monɪəs〕
= symphonic〔sɪm'fɑnɪk〕

muss〔mʌs〕*v.* 使混亂

= rumple〔'rʌmpḷ〕
= mess〔mɛs〕
= disarrange〔,dɪsə'rendʒ〕
= disorganize〔dɪs'ɔrgə,naɪz〕
= disarray〔,dɪsə're〕
= litter〔'lɪtɚ〕
= clutter〔'klʌtɚ〕

must〔mʌst〕*aux.* 必須

= should〔ʃud, ʃəd〕
= *ought to*
= *be obliged to*
= *have to*
= *need to*
= *be forced to*

muster〔'mʌstɚ〕*v.* 召集;集中

= assemble〔ə'sɛmbḷ〕
= gather〔'gæðɚ〕
= collect〔kə'lɛkt〕
= summon〔'sʌmən〕
= cluster〔'klʌstɚ〕
= amass〔ə'mæs〕
= group〔grup〕
= compile〔kəm'paɪl〕
= recruit〔rɪ'krut〕
= accumulate〔ə'kjumjə,let〕

musty〔'mʌstɪ〕*adj.* 發霉的

= moldy〔'moldɪ〕
= mildewed〔'mɪl,djud, -,dud〕

mute〔mjut〕*adj.* 沈默的

= silent〔'saɪlənt〕
= dumb〔dʌm〕
= voiceless〔'vɔɪslɪs〕
= speechless〔'spitʃlɪs〕

M

mutilate ('mjutḷ,et) v. 切斷

= cut (kʌt)

= tear (tɛr)

= amputate ('æmpjə,tet)

= clip (klɪp)

= lacerate ('læsə,ret)

= *break off*

mutiny ('mjutṇɪ) n. 叛變

= rebellion (rɪ'bɛljən)

= revolt (rɪ'volt)

= riot ('raɪət)

= insurrection (,ɪnsə'rɛkʃən)

= uprising ('ʌp,raɪzɪŋ)

= insurgence (ɪn's ɝdʒəns)

mutter ('mʌtɚ) v. 喃喃地說

= mumble ('mʌmbḷ)

= complain (kəm'plen)

= grumble ('grʌmbḷ)

= murmur ('mɝmɚ)

= whisper ('hwɪspɚ)

mutual ('mjutʃʊəl) adj. 相互的；
共同的

= reciprocal (rɪ'sɪprəkḷ)

= joint (dʒɔɪnt)

= common ('kɑmən)

muzzle ('mʌzḷ) v. 使緘默；克制

= silence ('saɪləns)

= restrain (rɪ'stren)

= gag (gæg)

= bind (baɪnd)

= bridle ('braɪdḷ)

myriad ('mɪrɪəd) adj. 無數的

= many ('mɛnɪ)

= numerous ('njumərəs)

= multitudinous (,mʌltə'tjudṇəs)

= considerable (kən,sɪdərəbḷ)

mysterious (mɪs'tɪrɪəs) adj.
神祕的

= secret ('sikrɪt)

= hidden ('hɪdṇ)

= profound (prə'faʊnd)

= mystical ('mɪstɪkḷ)

= recondite ('rɛkən,daɪt ,
rɪ'kɑndaɪt)

= occult (ə'kʌlt , 'ɑkʌlt)

mystify ('mɪstə,faɪ) v. 使困惑

= bewilder (bɪ'wɪldɚ)

= puzzle ('pʌzḷ)

= perplex (pɚ'plɛks)

= baffle ('bæfḷ)

= confound (kɑn'faʊnd , kən-)

myth (mɪθ) n. 神話

= legend ('lɛdʒənd)

= story ('storɪ)

= fiction ('fɪkʃən)

= fantasy ('fæntəzɪ , -sɪ)

= fable ('febḷ)

= fabrication (,fæbrɪ'keʃən)

= falsehood ('fɔlshʊd)

= *fairy tale*

N

nag (næg) ① v. 抱怨；嘮叨；
煩擾 ② n. 小馬

① = pester ('pɛstɚ)

M

= annoy〔ə'nɔɪ〕
= bother〔'baðɚ〕
② = horse〔hɔrs〕
= pony〔'ponɪ〕

nail〔nel〕v. ①固定 ②抓住

① = fasten〔'fæsn̩ , 'fasn̩〕
= hold〔hold〕
= fix〔fɪks〕
= secure〔sɪ'kjʊr〕
② = catch〔kætʃ〕
= seize〔siz〕
= hook〔hʊk〕
= snare〔snɛr〕
= trap〔træp〕
= capture〔'kæptʃɚ〕
= apprehend〔,æprɪ'hɛnd〕

naked〔'nekɪd〕adj. 未遮蓋的

= uncovered〔ʌn'kʌvɚd〕
= exposed〔ɪk'spozd〕
= nude〔njud〕
= bare〔bɛr〕
= undressed〔ʌn'drɛst〕

name〔nem〕n. 名稱

= title〔'taɪtl̩〕
= label〔'lebl̩〕
= tag〔tæg〕
= appellation〔,æpə'leʃən〕

nap〔næp〕n. 小睡；微睡

= sleep〔slip〕
= doze〔doz〕
= drowse〔draʊz〕
= siesta〔sɪ'ɛstə〕

narcotics〔nɑr'kɑtɪks〕n.
鎮靜劑

= drugs〔drʌgz〕
= opiates〔'opɪ,ets〕
= tranquilizers〔'træŋkwɪ,laɪzɚz〕
= sedatives〔'sɛdətɪvz〕
= barbiturates〔,bɑrbɪ'tjurets〕

narrate〔næ'ret , 'næret〕v.
敘述

= tell〔tɛl〕
= relate〔rɪ'let〕
= recount〔rɪ'kaʊnt〕
= report〔rɪ'port〕
= recite〔rɪ'saɪt〕
= review〔rɪ'vju〕
= describe〔dɪ'skraɪb〕

narrow〔'næro〕adj. 窄的

= slender〔'slɛndɚ〕
= close〔klos〕
= tight〔taɪt〕
= restricted〔rɪ'strɪktɪd〕
= cramped〔kræmpt〕
= confined〔kən'faɪnd〕
= meager〔'migɚ〕
= limited〔'lɪmɪtɪd〕

nasty〔'næstɪ〕adj. 不愉快的；
討厭的；骯髒的

= unpleasant〔ʌn'plɛznt〕
= revolting〔rɪ'voltɪŋ〕
= disgusting〔dɪs'gʌstɪŋ〕
= repulsive〔rɪ'pʌlsɪv〕
= offensive〔ə'fɛnsɪv〕
= foul〔faʊl〕

N

= vile (vaɪl)
= sickening ('sɪkənɪŋ)
= nauseating ('nɔʒɪ,etɪŋ , -zɪ-)
= filthy ('fɪlθɪ)
= odious ('odɪəs)
= obnoxious (əb'nɑkʃəs , ɑb-)
= dirty ('dɜtɪ)

nation ('neʃən) *n.* 國家

= country ('kʌntrɪ)
= land (lænd)
= society (sə'saɪətɪ)
= commuunity (kə'mjunətɪ)

native ('netɪv) *adj.* 自然的；
生來的

= natural ('nætʃərəl)
= original (ə'rɪdʒənḷ)
= indigenous (ɪn'dɪdʒənəs)

natural ('nætʃərəl) *adj.*
自然的；正常的

= genuine ('dʒɛnjuɪn)
= typical ('tɪpɪkḷ)
= real ('riəl , 'rɪəl)
= authentic (ɔ'θɛntɪk)
= legitimate (lɪ'dʒɪtəmɪt)
= honest ('ɑnɪst)
= pure (pjʊr)
= original (ə'rɪdʒənḷ)
= true (tru)
= characteristic (,kærɪktə'rɪstɪk)
= normal ('nɔrmḷ)

naturally ('nætʃərəlɪ) *adv.*
自然地；必然地

= plainly ('plenlɪ)
= certainly ('sɜtṇlɪ , -ənlɪ)
= surely ('ʃʊrlɪ)
= indeed (ɪn'did)
= *of course*

naught (nɔt) *n.* 無

= nothing ('nʌθɪŋ)
= zero ('zɪro)
= nil (nɪl)

naughty ('nɔtɪ) *adj.* 頑皮的；
不妥的

= bad (bæd)
= disobedient (,dɪsə'bidɪənt)
= misbehaving (,mɪsbɪ'hevɪŋ)
= disorderly (dɪs'ɔrdəlɪ , dɪz-)
= evil ('ivḷ)
= wrong (rɔŋ)

navigate ('nævə,get) *v.* 航行；
領航

= sail (sel)
= steer (stɪr)
= cruise (kruz)
= guide (gaɪd)

near (nɪr) *adj.* 近的

= close (klos)
= imminent ('ɪmənənt)
= *at hand*

nearly ('nɪrlɪ) *adv.* 幾乎；近乎

= almost ('ɔl,most , ɔl'most)
= approximately (ə'prɑksə,mɪtlɪ)
= *close to*
= *just about*

neat (nit) *adj.* ①整潔的
②靈巧的

① = clean (klin)
= orderly ('ɔrdəlɪ)
= trim (trɪm)
= tidy ('taɪdɪ)
= shipshape ('ʃɪp,ʃep)
= well-kept ('wɛl'kɛpt)
② = skillful ('skɪlfəl)
= clever ('klɛvə)
= apt (æpt)
= adept (ə'dɛpt , 'ædɛpt)
= proficient (prə'fɪʃənt)
= handy ('hændɪ)
= expert ('ɛkspɜt)
= masterful ('mæstəfəl , 'mɑs-)
= well-done ('wɛl'dʌn)

necessary ('nɛsə,sɛrɪ) *adj.*
必要的

= required (rɪ'kwaɪrd)
= compulsory (kəm'pʌlsərɪ)
= urgent ('ɜdʒənt)
= important (ɪm'pɔrtṇt)
= obligatory (ə'blɪgə,torɪ)
= compelling (kəm'pɛlɪŋ)
= needed ('nidɪd)
= essential (ə'sɛnʃəl)
= exigent ('ɛksədʒənt)
= imperative (ɪm'pɛrətɪv)

need ('nid) *v.* 缺乏；需要

= want (wɑnt , wɔnt)
= lack (læk)
= require (rɪ'kwaɪr)

neglect (nɪ'glɛkt) *v.* 疏忽

= overlook (,ovə'lʊk)
= disregard (,dɪsrɪ'gɑrd)
= ignore (ɪg'nor , -'nɔr)
= slight (slaɪt)
= omit (o'mɪt , ə-)
= *be inattentive*
= *pass over*
= *be careless*
= *be thoughtless*
= *be inconsiderate*

negligent ('nɛglədʒənt) *adj.*
不留心的

= careless ('kɛrlɪs)
= indifferent (ɪn'dɪfərənt)
= neglectful (nɪ'glɛktfəl)
= inattentive (ɪnə'tɛntɪv)
= remiss (rɪ'mɪs)

negotiate (nɪ'goʃɪ,et) *v.* 商議

= arrange (ə'rendʒ)
= settle ('sɛtḷ)
= mediate ('midɪ,et)
= intervene (,ɪntə'vin)
= umpire ('ʌmpaɪr)
= arbitrate ('ɑrbə,tret)
= referee (,rɛrə'ri)
= *talk over*

neighboring ('nebərɪŋ) *adj.*
附近的；鄰界的

= near (nɪr)
= bordering ('bɔrdərɪŋ)
= adjoining (ə'dʒɔɪnɪŋ)
= adjacent (ə'dʒesṇt)
= surrounding (sə'raʊndɪŋ)

N

neighborly (ˈnebəlɪ) *adj.*
友善的

= friendly (ˈfrɛndlɪ)
= kind (kaɪnd)
= amiable (ˈemɪəbḷ)
= congenial (kənˈdʒinjəl)
= cordial (ˈkɔrdʒəl)
= warm (wɔrm)
= amicable (ˈæmɪkəbḷ)

nerve (nɜv) *n.* 勇氣

= strength (strɛŋθ, strɛŋkθ)
= courage (ˈkɜɪdʒ)
= stamina (ˈstæmənə)
= daring (ˈdɛrɪŋ)
= bravado (brəˈvado, -ˈvedo)
= mettle (ˈmɛtḷ)

nervous (ˈnɜvəs) *adj.* 不安的；
緊張的

= upset (ˈʌpˈsɛt)
= restless (ˈrɛstlɪs)
= excited (ɪkˈsaɪtɪd)
= disturbed (dɪˈstɜbd)
= ruffled (ˈrʌfḷd)
= shaken (ˈʃekən)
= flustered (ˈflʌstəd)
= agitated (ˈædʒɪˌtetɪd)
= perturbed (pəˈtɜbd)
= tense (tɛns)
= strained (strend)
= edgy (ˈɛdʒɪ)
= jittery (ˈdʒɪtərɪ)
= high-strung (ˈhaɪˈstrʌŋ)

nestle (ˈnɛsḷ) *v.* 擁抱

= snuggle (ˈsnʌgḷ)

= cuddle (ˈkʌdḷ)
= *hold closely*

net (nɛt) ① *n.* 陷阱 ② *n.* 網
③ *v.* 淨得

① = trap (træp)
= snare (snɛr)
② = mesh (mɛʃ)
= web (wɛb)
= *lacelike cloth*
③ = gain (gen)
= earn (ɜn)
= acquire (əˈkwaɪr)
= get (gɛt)
= obtain (əbˈten)
= secure (sɪˈkjur)

nettle (ˈnɛtḷ) *v.* 激怒

= irritate (ˈɪrəˌtet)
= provoke (prəˈvok)
= annoy (əˈnɔɪ)
= vex (vɛks)
= anger (ˈæŋgə)
= disturb (dɪˈstɜb)

neutral (ˈnjutrəl) *adj.* 中立的

= impartial (ɪmˈpɑrʃəl)
= detached (dɪˈtætʃt)
= unprejudiced (ʌnˈprɛdʒədɪst)
= cool (kul)
= indifferent (ɪnˈdɪfərənt)
= independent (ˌɪndɪˈpɛndənt)

nevertheless (ˌnɛvəðəˈlɛs) *adv.*
雖然如此

= however (hauˈɛvə)

N

= notwithstanding
(,nɑtwɪθ'stændɪŋ)
= although (ɔl'ðo)
= but (bʌt)
= regardless (rɪ'gɑrdlɪs)
= anyway ('ɛnɪ,we)

ew (nju , nu) *adj.* 新的

= fresh (frɛʃ)
= modern ('mɑdən)
= recent ('risn̩t)
= original (ə'rɪdʒən̩l)
= young (jʌŋ)
= unused (ʌn'juzd)
= firsthand ('fɜst'hænd)

ews (njuz , nuz) *n.* 新聞；消息

= tidings ('taɪdɪŋz)
= information (,ɪnfə'meʃən)
= word (wɜd)
= story ('storɪ)

ext (nɛkst) *adj.* 其次的

= following ('fɑləwɪŋ)
= nearest ('nɪrɪst)
= closest ('klozɪst)
= succeeding (sək'sidɪŋ)
= successive (sək'sɛsɪv)
= subsequent ('sʌbsɪ,kwɛnt)

bble ('nɪbl̩) *v.* 輕咬

= chew (tʃu)
= munch (mʌntʃ)

ce (naɪs) *adj.* 愉快的；好的

= pleasing ('plizɪŋ)

= agreeable (ə'griəbl̩)
= satisfactory (,sætɪs'fæktərɪ)
= enjoyable (ɪn'dʒɔɪəbl̩)
= desirable (dɪ'zaɪrəbl̩)
= gratifying ('grætə,faɪɪŋ)
= good (gud)
= fine (faɪn)

niche (nɪtʃ) *n.* 壁龕；適當位置

= nook (nuk)
= corner ('kɔrnə)
= cranny ('krænɪ)
= recess (rɪ'sɛs , 'risɛs)
= alcove ('ælkov)

nick (nɪk) *n.* 刻痕

= notch (nɑtʃ)
= cut (kʌt)
= dash (dæʃ)
= indentation (,ɪndɛn'teʃən)

niggardly ('nɪgədlɪ) *adj.*
吝嗇的

= stingy ('stɪndʒɪ)
= cheap (tʃip)
= miserly ('maɪzə-lɪ)

nimble ('nɪmbl̩) *adj.* 迅速的

= light (laɪt)
= quick (kwɪk)
= active ('æktɪv)
= fast (fæst , fɑst)
= swift (swɪft)
= speedy ('spidɪ)
= agile ('ædʒəl , -aɪl)

N

nip〔nɪp〕① v. 箝；夾　② n. 刺寒
③ n. 小飲

① = pinch〔pɪntʃ〕
　 = bite〔baɪt〕
　 = squeeze〔skwiz〕
② = cold〔kold〕
　 = chill〔tʃɪl〕
　 = crispness〔'krɪspnɪs〕
③ = sip〔sɪp〕
　 = *small drink*

noble〔'nobḷ〕*adj.* 高貴的；
偉大的

　 = great〔gret〕
　 = grand〔grænd〕
　 = majestic〔mə'dʒɛstɪk〕
　 = distinguished〔dɪ'stɪŋgwɪʃt〕
　 = lofty〔'lɔftɪ , 'lɑftɪ〕
　 = eminent〔'ɛmənənt〕
　 = prominent〔'prɑmənənt〕
　 = important〔ɪm'pɔrtṇt〕
　 = grandiose〔'grændɪ,os〕
　 = magnificent〔mæg'nɪfəsṇt〕
　 = stately〔'stetlɪ〕
　 = aristocratic〔ə,rɪstə'krætɪk ,
　　,ærɪstə-〕
　 = dignified〔'dɪgnə,faɪd〕

nocturnal〔nɑk't3nḷ〕*adj.*
夜間的

　 = nightly〔'naɪtlɪ〕

nod〔nɑd〕*v.* 點頭

　 = bow〔baʊ〕
　 = bob〔bɑb〕
　 = tip〔tɪp〕

　 = bend〔bɛnd〕
　 = signal〔'sɪgnḷ〕

noise〔nɔɪz〕*n.* 喧聲

　 = sounds〔saʊndz〕
　 = clamor〔'klæmɚ〕
　 = din〔dɪn〕
　 = racket〔'rækɪt〕
　 = clatter〔'klætɚ〕
　 = uproar〔'ʌp,ror , -,rɔr〕
　 = tumult〔'tjumʌlt〕
　 = bedlam〔'bɛdləm〕
　 = hubbub〔'hʌbʌb〕
　 = commotion〔kə'moʃən〕
　 = ballyhoo〔'bælɪ,hu , bælɪ'hu〕
　 = rumpus〔'rʌmpəs〕

nomad〔'nomæd , 'nɑmæd〕*n.*
流浪者

　 = wanderer〔'wɑndərɚ〕
　 = traveler〔'trævlɚ〕
　 = rover〔'rovɚ〕
　 = roamer〔'romɚ〕
　 = vagrant〔'vegrənt〕
　 = migrant〔'maɪgrənt〕

nomination〔,nɑmə'neʃən〕*n.*
提名

　 = naming〔'nemɪŋ〕
　 = appointment〔ə'pɔɪntmənt〕
　 = selection〔sə'lɛkʃən〕
　 = choice〔tʃɔɪs〕
　 = designation〔,dɛzɪg'neʃən〕

nonchalant〔'nɑnʃələnt〕*adj.*
不在乎的

= indifferent (ɪn'dɪfərənt)
= unconcerned (ˌʌnkən'sɜnd)
= cool (kul)
= blasé (blɑ'ze , 'blɑze)
= easygoing ('izɪ'goɪŋ)
= casual ('kæʒuəl)
= lackadaisical (ˌlækə'dezɪkl̩)
= devil-may-care ('dɛvl̩me'kɛr)

nsense ('nɑnsɛns) *n.* 無意義

= foolishness ('fulɪʃnɪs)
= ridiculousness (rɪ'dɪkjələsnɪs)
= folly ('fɑlɪ)
= absurdity (əb'sɜdətɪ)
= stupidity (stju'pɪdətɪ)
= rubbish ('rʌbɪʃ)
= poppycock ('pɑpɪˌkɑk)

ok (nʊk) *n.* 角落;屋隅

= corner ('kɔrnɚ)
= niche (nɪtʃ)
= cranny ('krænɪ)
= recess (rɪ'sɛs , 'risɛs)
= alcove ('ælkov)

ose (nus) *n.* 繩索

= rope (rop)
= snare (snɛr)
= lasso ('læso)

rmal ('nɔrml̩) *adj.* 正常的

= usual ('juʒuəl)
= regular ('rɛgjəlɚ)
= average ('ævərɪdʒ)
= standard ('stændɚd)
= ordinary ('ɔrdn̩ˌɛrɪ , 'ɔrdnɛrɪ)

= typical ('tɪpɪkl̩)
= characteristic (ˌkærɪktə'rɪstɪk)
= *true to form*

notable ('notəbl̩) *adj.* 著名的;
重要的

= striking ('straɪkɪŋ)
= important (ɪm'pɔrtn̩t)
= remarkable (rɪ'mɑrkəbl̩)
= noteworthy ('notˌwɜðɪ)
= special ('spɛʃəl)
= casual ('kæʒuəl)
= extraordinary (ˌɛkstrə'ɔrdn̩ˌɛrɪ)
= exceptional (ɪk'sɛpʃənl̩)
= rare (rɛr)
= famous ('feməs)
= distinguished (dɪ'stɪŋgwɪʃt)
= renowned (rɪ'naund)
= celebrated ('sɛləbretɪd)
= popular ('pɑpjələ)
= notorious (no'torɪəs)
= memorable ('mɛmərəbl̩)
= well-known ('wɛl'non)
= prominent ('prɑmənənt)

notch (nɑtʃ) *n.* 刻痕

= nick (nɪk)
= cut (kʌt)
= gash (gæʃ)
= indentation (ˌɪndɛn'teʃən)

N

note (not) *v.* ①記錄　②留心

① = write (raɪt)
= record (rɪ'kɔrd)
= inscribe (ɪn'skraɪb)
= list (lɪst)

= indicate ('ɪndə,ket)
= mark (mark)
= comment ('kamɛnt)
= *mark down*
= *jot down*
② = observe (əb'zɝv)
= heed (hid)
= regard (rɪ'gard)
= notice ('notɪs)

notice ('notɪs) *v.* 注意

= note (not)
= observe (əb'zɝv)
= heed (hid)
= regard (rɪ'gard)
= see (si)

notify ('notə,faɪ) *v.* 通知；警告

= inform (ɪn'fɔrm)
= advise (əd'vaɪz)
= report (rɪ'port)
= tell (tɛl)
= instruct (ɪn'strʌkt)
= remind (rɪ'maɪnd)
= warn (wɔrn)
= *announce to*

notion ('noʃən) *n.* 觀念；意見

= idea (aɪ'diə , -'dɪə)
= understanding (,ʌndə'stændɪŋ)
= opinion (ə'pɪnjən)
= view (vju)
= belief (bɪ'lif)
= thought (θɔt)
= impression (ɪm'prɛʃən)
= sentiment ('sɛntəmənt)

notorious (no'torɪəs) *adj.* 著名的；聲名狼藉的

= famous ('feməs)
= renowned (rɪ'naund)
= celebrated ('sɛləbretɪd)
= popular ('papjələ)
= infamous ('ɪnfəməs)
= well-known ('wɛl'non)

nourish ('nɝʃ) *v.* 養育；支持

= feed (fid)
= nurture ('nɝtʃə)
= nurse (nɝs)
= strengthen ('strɛŋθən)
= sustain (sə'sten)
= maintain (men'ten , mən'ten)

novel ('navl̩) *adj.* 新奇的

= new (nju , nu)
= original (ə'rɪdʒənl̩)
= fresh (frɛʃ)
= unique (ju'nik)
= firsthand ('fɝst'hænd)
= different ('dɪfərənt)
= unusual (ʌn'juʒʊəl)

novice ('navɪs) *n.* 新手

= beginner (bɪ'gɪnə)
= newcomer ('nju,kʌmə)
= tyro ('taɪro)
= greenhorn ('grin,hɔrn)
= freshman ('frɛʃmən)

now (nau) *adv.* ①馬上 ②此時

① = immediately (ɪ'midɪɪtlɪ)
= *at once*

= *right away*
= presently ('prɛzn̩tlɪ)
= today (tə'de)
= *at this time*

oxious ('nɑkʃəs) *adj.* 有害的
= harmful ('hɑrmfəl)
= poisonous ('pɔɪznəs)
= damaging ('dæmɪdʒɪŋ)
= detrimental (,dɛtrə'mɛntl̩)
= toxic ('tɑksɪk)

ucleus ('njuklɪəs) *n.* 中心
= middle ('mɪdl̩)
= core (kor)
= heart (hɑrt)
= kernel ('kɜnl̩)
= hub (hʌb)
= focus ('fokəs)

ıdge (nʌdʒ) *v.* 輕推
= push (puʃ)
= prod (prɑd)
= shove (ʃʌv)
= poke (pok)
= jab (dʒæb)
= prompt (prɑmpt)

ıgget ('nʌgɪt) *n.* 堆；塊
= lump (lʌmp)
= clump (klʌmp)
= mass (mæs)
= wad (wɑd)
= hunk (hʌŋk)
= chunk (tʃʌŋk)

nuisance ('njusn̩s) *n.* 討厭的人
或物
= annoyance (ə'nɔɪəns)
= pest (pɛst)
= bother ('bɑðɚ)
= trouble ('trʌbl̩)
= irritation (,ɪrə'teʃən)

numb (nʌm) *adj.* 麻木的
= dull (dʌl)
= unfeeling (ʌn'filɪŋ)
= deadened ('dɛdn̩d)
= insensitive (ɪn'sɛnsətɪv)

number ('nʌmbɚ) *n.* ①數目；
量 ②數字
① = quantity ('kwɑntətɪ)
= sum (sʌm)
= count (kaʊnt)
= collection (kə'lɛkʃən)
= amount (ə'maʊnt)
= bulk (bʌlk)
= portion ('porʃən , 'pɔr-)
= multitude ('mʌltə,tjud)
= measure ('mɛʒɚ)
② = numeral ('njumərəl)
= figure ('fɪgjɚ , 'fɪgɚ)
= digit ('dɪdʒɪt)
= symbol ('sɪmbl̩)

numeral ('njumərəl) *n.* 數字
= number ('nʌmbɚ)
= figure ('fɪgjɚ , 'fɪgɚ)
= digit ('dɪdʒɪt)
= symbol ('sɪmbl̩)

N

numerous （'njumərəs ）*adj.*
極多的

= many （'mɛnɪ ）

= multitudinous （,mʌltə'tjudn̩əs ）

= several （'sɛvərəl ）

= abundant （ ə'bʌndənt ）

= myriad （'mɪrɪəd ）

= considerable （ kən'sɪdərəb̩l ）

= various （'vɛrɪəs ）

nurse （ nɜs ） *v.* 養育；看護

= nurture （'nɜtʃɚ ）

= nourish （'nɜɪʃ ）

= foster （'fɔstɚ , 'fas- ）

= feed （ fid ）

= sustain （ sə'sten ）

= mind （ maɪnd ）

= *tend to*

= *care for*

nurture （'nɜtʃɚ ） *v.* 養育

= rear （ rɪr ）

= foster （'fɔstɚ , 'fas- ）

= train （ tren ）

= raise （ rez ）

= feed （ fid ）

= tend （ tɛnd ）

= mind （ maɪnd ）

= nurse （ nɜs ）

= nourish （'nɜɪʃ ）

= *bring up*

= *care for*

nutrition （ nju'trɪʃən ） *n.* 食物；
營養

= food （ fud ）

= nourishment （'nɜɪʃmənt ）

O

oaf （ of ） *n.* 笨人；傻瓜

= lummox （'lʌməks ）

= clown （ klaʊn ）

= clod （ klad ）

= lout （ laʊt ）

= fool （ ful ）

= dunce （ dʌns ）

= blockhead （'blak,hɛd ）

oath （ oθ ） *n.* 誓約；承諾

= promise （'pramɪs ）

= pledge （'plɛdʒ ）

= vow （ vaʊ ）

= agreement （ ə'grimənt ）

= commitment （ kə'mɪtmənt ）

= bond （ band ）

obey （ ə'be , o'be ） *v.* 服從

= yield （ jild ）

= submit （ səb'mɪt ）

= comply （ kəm'plaɪ ）

= mind （ maɪnd ）

= heed （ hid ）

= *listen to*

object （'abdʒɪkt ） *n.* ①物件
②目的

① = thing （ θɪŋ ）

= article （'artɪk̩l ）

② = purpose （'pɜpəs ）

= end （ ɛnd ）

= goal （ gol ）

= target （'targɪt ）

= intent （ ɪn'tɛnt ）

= aim （ em ）

bjection (əb'dʒɛkʃən) *n.* 反對

= protest ('protɛst)
= challenge ('tʃælɪndʒ)
= dissent (dɪ'sɛnt)
= disapproval (,dɪsə'pruvl̩)
= complaint (kəm'plent)
= criticism ('krɪtə,sɪzəm)

bligate ('ablə,get) *v.* 使負義務

= require (rɪ'kwaɪr)
= oblige (ə'blaɪdʒ)
= bind (baɪnd)
= pledge (plɛdʒ)
= compel (kəm'pɛl)
= force (fors , fɔrs)

bliging (ə'blaɪdʒɪŋ) *adj.*
切的；體貼的

= helpful ('hɛlpfəl)
= considerate (kən'sɪdərɪt)
= thoughtful ('θɔtfəl)
= accommodating
  (ə'kamə,detɪŋ)
= well-meaning ('wɛl'minɪŋ)

bliterate (ə'blɪtə,ret) *v.* 擦掉

= destroy (dɪ'strɔɪ)
= erase (ɪ'res)
= demolish (dɪ'malɪʃ)
= delete (dɪ'lit)
= *wipe out*
= *blot out*

blivious (ə'blɪvɪəs) *adj.*
掉的

= forgetful (fə'gɛtfəl)

= unconscious (ʌn'kanʃəs)
= senseless ('sɛnslɪs)
= preoccupied (pri'akjə,paɪd)

obnoxious (əb'nakʃəs) *adj.*
可憎的

= offensive (ə'fɛnsɪv)
= disagreeable (,dɪsə'griəbl̩)
= hateful ('hetfəl)
= nasty ('næstɪ)
= repulsive (rɪ'pʌlsɪv)
= dreadful ('drɛdfəl)
= deplorable (dɪ'plorəbl̩)
= disgusting (dɪs'gʌstɪŋ)
= loathsome ('loðsəm)
= vile (vaɪl)
= terrible ('tɛrəbl̩)
= wretched ('rɛtʃɪd)
= abominable (ə'bamnəbl̩)
= detestable (dɪ'tɛstəbl̩)
= despicable ('dɛspɪkəbl̩)
= contemptible (kən'tɛmptəbl̩)

obscene (əb'sin) *adj.* 淫穢的

= dirty ('dɜtɪ)
= smutty ('smʌtɪ)
= filthy ('fɪlθɪ)
= lewd (lud)
= bawdy ('bɔdɪ)
= pornographic (,pɔrnə'græfɪk)
= unclean (ʌn'klin)
= indecent (ɪn'disn̩t)

O

obscure (əb'skjʊr) *adj.*
不清楚的

= indistinct (,ɪndɪ'stɪŋkt)

= unclear (ʌn'klɪr)

= indefinite (ɪn'dɛfənɪt)

= faint (fent)

= dim (dɪm)

= vague (veg)

= dark (dɑrk)

= shadowy ('ʃædəwɪ)

= hazy ('hezɪ)

= blurred (blɜd)

= fuzzy ('fʌzɪ)

observe (əb'zɝv) v. ①觀察
②慶祝　③遵守

① = see (si)

= note (not)

= examine (ɪg'zæmɪn)

= study ('stʌdɪ)

= perceive (pɚ'siv)

= behold (bɪ'hold)

= inspect (ɪn'spɛkt)

= scrutinize ('skrutn̩‚aɪz)

= contemplate ('kɑntəm‚plet)

= review (rɪ'vju)

② = celebrate ('sɛlə‚bret)

= commemorate (kə'mɛmə‚ret)

③ = keep (kip)

= practice ('præktɪs)

= obey (ə'be)

= heed (hid)

= follow ('falo)

= *comply with*

obsolete ('ɑbsə‚lit) adj. 過時

= extinct (ɪk'stɪŋkt)

= passé (pæ'se , 'pæse)

= dated ('detɪd)

= outmoded (aʊt'modɪd)

= discontinued (‚dɪskən'tɪnjud)

= antiquated ('æntə‚kwetɪd)

= old-fashioned ('old'fæʃənd)

obstacle ('ɑbstəkl̩) n. 障礙

= barrier ('bærɪɚ)

= obstruction (əb'strʌkʃən)

= block (blɑk)

= stoppage ('stɑpɪdʒ)

= hindrance ('hɪndrəns)

= deterrent (dɪ'tɝrənt)

= impediment (ɪm'pɛdəmənt)

= hitch (hɪtʃ)

= snag (snæg)

= catch (kætʃ)

obstinate ('ɑbstənɪt) adj.
頑固的

= stubborn ('stʌbən)

= willful ('wɪlfəl)

= headstrong ('hɛd‚strɔŋ)

= bullheaded ('bʊl'hɛdɪd)

= pigheaded ('pɪg'hɛdɪd)

= unyielding (ʌn'jildɪŋ)

= unbending (ʌn'bɛndɪŋ)

= inflexible (ɪn'flɛksəbl̩)

= adamant ('ædə‚mænt)

= firm (fɝm)

= stiff (stɪf)

= rigid ('rɪdʒɪd)

obstruct (əb'strʌkt) v. 阻礙

= block (blɑk)

= hinder ('hɪndɚ)

= clog (klɑg , klɔg)

= delay (dɪ'le)

= bar (bɑr)

= impede (ɪm'pid)

= retard (rɪ'tɑrd)

= hamper ('hæmpɚ)

obtain (əb'ten) v. 獲得

= get (gɛt)

= acquire (ə'kwaɪr)

= gain (gen)

= secure (sɪ'kjʊr)

= procure (pro'kjʊr)

= earn (ɜn)

= receive (rɪ'siv)

obtuse (əb'tjus) adj. ①遲鈍的
②不銳利的

① = slow (slo)

= stupid ('stjupɪd)

= dense (dɛns)

= slow-witted ('slo'wɪtɪd)

② = blunt (blʌnt)

= dull (dʌl)

= unsharpened (ʌn'ʃɑrpənd)

obvious ('ɑbvɪəs) adj. 顯然的

= understandable
  (ˌʌndɚ'stændəbḷ)

= apparent (ə'pærənt)

= clear (klɪr)

= plain (plen)

= evident ('ɛvədənt)

= manifest ('mænəˌfɛst)

= explicit (ɪk'splɪsɪt)

= distinct (dɪ'stɪŋkt)

occasionally (ə'keʒənḷɪ) adv.
有時

= sometimes ('sʌmˌtaɪmz)

= now and then

= once in a while

= from time to time

occupant ('ɑkjəpənt) n. 居住者

= tenant ('tɛnənt)

= resident ('rɛzədənt)

= lodger ('lɑdʒɚ)

= inhabitant (ɪn'hæbətənt)

= dweller ('dwɛlɚ)

= boarder ('bordɚ , 'bɔrdɚ)

occupation (ˌɑkjə'peʃən) n.
①職業 ②占有

① = business ('bɪznɪs)

= employment (ɪm'plɔɪmənt)

= trade (tred)

= work (wɜk)

= activity (æk'tɪvətɪ)

= affair (ə'fɛr)

= matter ('mætɚ)

= concern (kən'sɜn)

= interest ('ɪntərɪst , 'ɪntrɪst)

= capacity (kə'pæsətɪ)

= role (rol)

= function ('fʌŋkʃən)

= duty ('djutɪ)

= task (tæsk)

= stint (stɪnt)

= job (dʒɑb)

② = possession (pə'zɛʃən)

= holding ('holdɪŋ)

= ownership ('onɚˌʃɪp)

O

occur (ə'kɝ) v. 發生

= happen ('hæpən)
= transpire (træn'spaɪr)
= *come about*
= *take place*

odd (ɑd) adj. ①古怪的
②剩餘的

① = strange (strendʒ)
= peculiar (pɪ'kjuljə)
= queer (kwɪr)
= unusual (ʌn'juʒʊəl)
= curious ('kjʊrɪəs)
= unique (ju'nik)
= eccentric (ɪk'sɛntrɪk)
= weird (wɪrd)
= bizarre (bɪ'zɑr)
② = extra ('ɛkstrə)
= remaining (rɪ'menɪŋ)
= spare (spɛr)
= *left over*

odious ('odɪəs) adj. 可憎的

= hateful ('hetfəl)
= offensive (ə'fɛnsɪv)
= displeasing (dɪs'plizɪŋ)
= revolting (rɪ'voltɪŋ)
= repulsive (rɪ'pʌlsɪv)
= disgusting (dɪs'gʌstɪŋ)
= vile (vaɪl)
= foul (faʊl)
= obnoxious (əb'nɑkʃəs)
= horrible ('harəbḷ)
= terrible ('tɛrəbḷ)
= wretched ('rɛtʃɪd)

odor ('odə) n. 氣味

= smell (smɛl)
= fragrance ('fregrəns)
= scent (sɛnt)
= essence ('ɛsn̩s)
= aroma (ə'romə)

offend (ə'fɛnd) v. 觸怒

= displease (dɪs'pliz)
= hurt (hɝt)
= pain (pen)
= grieve (griv)
= wound (wund)
= disgust (dɪs'gʌst)
= sicken ('sɪkən)
= horrify ('hɔrə,faɪ , 'har-)
= affront (ə'frʌnt)
= insult (ɪn'sʌlt)

offer ('ɔfə , 'afə) v. 提供

= present (prɪ'zɛnt)
= propose (prə'poz)
= try (traɪ)
= submit (səb'mɪt)
= attempt (ə'tɛmpt)
= suggest (səg'dʒɛst , sə'dʒɛst)

office ('ɔfɪs , 'afɪs) n. ①任務
②辦公處

① = position (pə'zɪʃən)
= duty ('djutɪ)
= task (tæsk)
= job (dʒab)
= work (wɝk)
= function ('fʌŋkʃən)
= capacity (kə'pæsətɪ)

O

= role (rol)

= post (post)

② = room (rum)

= workplace ('wɜk,ples)

= headquarters ('hɛd'kwɔrtəz)

= studio ('stjudɪ,o)

= department (dɪ'pɑrtmənt)

ffset (ɔf'sɛt) *v.* 彌補

= neutralize ('njutrəl,aɪz)

= balance ('bæləns)

= cushion ('kuʃən)

= compensate ('kɑmpən,set)

= counteract (,kaʊntə'ækt)

= soften ('sɔfən)

ffshoot ('ɔf,ʃut) *n.* 分枝；
行生物

= branch (bræntʃ)

= byproduct ('baɪ,prɑdəkt)

= outgrowth ('aʊt,groθ)

= appendage (ə'pɛndɪdʒ)

= supplement ('sʌpləmənt)

= accessory (æk'sɛsərɪ)

= addition (ə'dɪʃən)

ffspring ('ɔf,sprɪŋ) *n.* 子孫

= child (tʃaɪld)

= descendant (dɪ'sɛndənt)

= young (jʌŋ)

ften ('ɔfən , 'ɔftən) *adv.* 時常地

= repeatedly (rɪ'pitɪdlɪ)

= frequently ('frikwəntlɪ)

= *many times*

gre ('ogə) *n.* 醜怪殘暴之人

= monster ('mɑnstə)

= fiend (find)

= demon ('dimən)

= devil ('dɛvl̩)

old (old) *adj.* ①古老的
②過時的

① = aged ('edʒɪd)

= ancient ('enʃənt)

= elderly ('ɛldəlɪ)

= antique (æn'tik)

= mature (mə'tjʊr , mə'tʃʊr)

② = former ('fɔrmə)

= obsolete ('ɑbsə,lit)

= abandoned (ə'bændənd)

= discontinued (,dɪskən'tɪnjud)

= stale (stel)

= outworn ('aʊt'wɔrn)

= discarded (dɪs'kɑrdɪd)

omen ('omɪn , 'omən) *n.* 徵兆

= sign (saɪn)

= indication (,ɪndə'keʃən)

= warning ('wɔrnɪŋ)

= warning ('wɔrnɪŋ)

= portent ('pɔrtɛnt , 'por-)

ominous ('ɑmənəs) *adj.* 不吉的

= unfavorable (ʌn'fevrəbl̩)

= sinister ('sɪnɪstə)

= menacing ('mɛnɪsɪŋ)

= threatening ('θrɛtn̩ɪŋ)

omit (o'mɪt , ə'mɪt) *v.* 遺漏

= neglect (nɪ'glɛkt)

= exclude (ɪk'sklud)

O

= bar〔bɑr〕
= miss〔mɪs〕
= skip〔skɪp〕
= *leave out*

omnipotent〔ɑm'nɪpətənt〕*adj.*
全能的

= almighty〔ɔl'maɪtɪ〕
= divine〔də'vaɪn〕
= all-powerful〔'ɔl'paʊəfəl〕

one-sided〔'wʌn'saɪdɪd〕*adj.*
不公平的

= partial〔'pɑrʃəl〕
= unfair〔ʌn'fɛr〕
= prejudiced〔'prɛdʒədɪst〕
= biased〔'baɪəst〕

onlooker〔'ɑn,lʊkə〕*n.* 旁觀者

= spectator〔'spɛktetə, spɛk'tetə〕
= observer〔əb'zɝvə〕
= watcher〔'wɑtʃə〕
= bystander〔'baɪ,stændə〕
= witness〔'wɪtnɪs〕

only〔'onlɪ〕*adv.* 僅僅

= just〔dʒʌst〕
= merely〔'mɪrlɪ〕
= simply〔'sɪmplɪ〕

onset〔'ɑn,sɛt〕*n.* ①開始
②進攻

① = beginning〔bɪ'gɪnɪŋ〕
= commencement
〔kə'mɛnsmənt〕
= start〔stɑrt〕

= opening〔'opənɪŋ〕
② = attack〔ə'tæk〕
= assault〔ə'sɔlt〕
= offense〔ə'fɛns〕
= charge〔tʃɑrdʒ〕
= drive〔draɪv〕
= onslaught〔'ɑn,slɔt〕

onslaught〔'ɑn,slɔt〕*n.* 猛攻

= attack〔ə'tæk〕
= assault〔ə'sɔlt〕
= onset〔'ɑn,sɛt〕
= offense〔ə'fɛns〕
= charge〔tʃɑrdʒ〕
= drive〔draɪv〕
= push〔pʊʃ〕

onward〔'ɑnwəd〕*adj.* 向前的

= further〔'fɝðə〕
= forward〔'fɔrwəd〕
= ahead〔ə'hɛd〕

ooze〔uz〕*v.* 慢慢地流；滲

= leak〔lik〕
= seep〔sip〕
= filter〔'fɪltə〕
= drip〔drɪp〕
= flow〔flo〕

opaque〔ə'pek〕*adj.* 不透明的

= dark〔dɑrk〕
= dull〔dʌl〕
= filmy〔'fɪlmɪ〕
= cloudy〔'klaʊdɪ〕
= obtuse〔əb'tjus〕
= murky〔'mɝkɪ〕

= obscure (əb'skjur)

= vague (veg)

= unclear (ʌn'klɪr)

= indistinct (ˌɪndɪ'stɪŋkt)

pen ('opən) v. ①創立
打開；展示

= begin (bɪ'gɪn)

= start (stɑrt)

= launch (lɔntʃ)

= initiate (ɪ'nɪʃɪˌet)

= unfold (ʌn'fold)

= establish (ə'stæblɪʃ)

= originate (ə'rɪdʒəˌnet)

= expose (ɪk'spoz)

= uncover (ʌn'kʌvɚ)

= disclose (dɪs'kloz)

= reveal (rɪ'vil)

= show (ʃo)

= bare (bɛr)

penly ('opənlɪ) adv. 直率地

= sincerely (sɪn'sɪrlɪ)

= freely ('frilɪ)

= frankly ('fræŋklɪ)

perate ('ɑpəˌret) v. 轉動；操作

= work (wɜk)

= run (rʌn)

= manage ('mænɪdʒ)

= conduct (kən'dʌkt)

= handle ('hændḷ)

= act (ækt)

= perform (pɚ'fɔrm)

= function ('fʌŋkʃən)

= *carry on*

opinion (ə'pɪnjən) n. 評論

= belief (bɪ'lif)

= judgment ('dʒʌdʒmənt)

= estimate ('ɛstəmɪt)

= impression (ɪm'prɛʃən)

= feeling ('filɪŋ)

= sentiment ('sɛntəmənt)

= attitude ('ætəˌtjud)

= view (vju)

= theory ('θɪərɪ)

= conception (kən'sɛpʃən)

= thought (θɔt)

= idea (aɪ'diə)

= outlook ('aʊtˌlʊk)

= conviction (kən'vɪkʃən)

opponent (ə'ponənt) n. 對手

= enemy ('ɛnəmɪ)

= foe (fo)

= adversary ('ædvɚˌsɛrɪ)

= competitor (kəm'pɛtətɚ)

= rival ('raɪvḷ)

= combatant ('kɑmbətənt)

= contender (kən'tɛndɚ)

opportunity (ˌɑpɚ'tjunətɪ) n.
機會

= chance (tʃæns)

= occasion (ə'keʒən)

= time (taɪm)

= opening ('opənɪŋ)

= turn (tɜn)

= spell (spɛl)

oppose (ə'poz) v. 對抗

= counteract (ˌkaʊntɚ'ækt)

O

= refute (rɪ'fjut)

= fight (faɪt)

= struggle ('strʌgl̩)

= resist (rɪ'zɪst)

= dispute (dɪ'spjut)

= hinder ('hɪndɚ)

= contradict (,kantrə'dɪkt)

= cross (krɔs)

= *conflict with*

oppressive (ə'prɛsɪv) *adj.*
嚴苛的

= harsh (harʃ)

= severe (sə'vɪr)

= unjust (ʌn'dʒʌst)

= burdensome ('bɝdn̩səm)

= overbearing (,ovɚ'bɛrɪŋ)

= domineering (,damə'nɪrɪŋ)

= dictatorial (,dɪktə'torɪəl)

= tyrannical (tɪ'rænɪkl̩ , taɪ-)

optical ('aptɪkl̩) *adj.* 視覺的

= visual ('vɪʒʊəl)

= seeing ('siɪŋ)

optimistic (,aptə'mɪstɪk) *adj.*
樂觀的

= cheerful ('tʃɪrfəl)

= happy ('hæpɪ)

= bright (braɪt)

= pleasant ('plɛznt)

= radiant ('redɪənt)

= glad (glæd)

= lighthearted ('laɪt'hartɪd)

= jaunty ('dʒɔntɪ)

= carefree ('kɛr,fri)

optional ('apʃənl̩) *adj.* 可選擇的

= voluntary ('valən,tɛrɪ)

= elective (ɪ'lɛktɪv)

oral ('ɔrəl) *adj.* 口頭的

= spoken ('spokən)

= voiced (vɔɪst)

= vocalized ('vokl̩,aɪzd)

= sounded ('saʊndɪd)

= articulated (ar'tɪkjə,letɪd)

= verbal ('vɝbl̩)

= uttered ('ʌtɚd)

= said (sɛd)

orb (ɔrb) *n.* 球

= sphere (sfɪr)

= globe (glob)

= ball (bɔl)

orbit ('ɔrbɪt) *n.* 軌道

= path (pæθ)

= circuit ('sɝkɪt)

= circle ('sɝkl̩)

= revolution (,rɛvə'luʃən)

= route (rut , raʊt)

orchestra ('ɔrkɪstrə) *n.* 樂隊

= band (bænd)

= ensemble (an'sambl̩)

ordain (ɔr'den) *v.* 任命

= order ('ɔrdɚ)

= decide (dɪ'saɪd)

= decree (dɪ'kri)

= command (kə'mænd)

= dictate ('dɪktet)

= direct (də'rɛkt)
= instruct (ɪn'strʌkt)
= bid (bɪd)
= rule (rul)
= authorize ('ɔθə,raɪz)
= sanction ('sæŋkʃən)

rdeal ('ɔrdil , ɔr'dil) *n.*
嚴酷之考驗

= experience (ɪk'spɪrɪəns)
= test (tɛst)
= trial ('traɪəl)
= tribulation (,trɪbjə'leʃən)

rder ('ɔrdə) *n.* ①秩序 ②命令

① = arrangement (ə'rendʒmənt)
= condition (kən'dɪʃən)
= state (stet)
= manner ('mænə)
= mode (mod)
= way (we)
= disposition (,dɪspə'zɪʃən)
= formation (fɔr'meʃən)
= system ('sɪstəm)
② = command (kə'mænd)
= bid (bɪd)
= direction (də'rɛkʃən)
= instruction (ɪn'strʌkʃən)

rdinary ('ɔrdn̩,ɛrɪ) *adj.*
①普通的 ②中下等的

① = usual ('juʒuəl)
= common ('kɑmən)
= normal ('nɔrml̩)
= average ('ævərɪdʒ)
= regular ('rɛgjələ)

= everyday ('ɛvrɪ,de)
= standard ('stændəd)
② = mediocre ('midɪ,okə , ,midɪ'okə)
= inferior (ɪn'fɪrɪə)
= poor (pʊr)
= so-so ('so,so)

organize ('ɔrgən,aɪz) *v.* 組織;
建立

= arrange (ə'rendʒ)
= classify ('klæsə,faɪ)
= systematize ('sɪstəmə,taɪz)
= categorize ('kætəgə,raɪz)
= sort (sɔrt)
= orient ('orɪ,ɛnt)
= group (grup)
= establish (ə'stæblɪʃ)
= *set up*

origin ('ɔrədʒɪn) *n.* ①開端
②起源

① = beginning (bɪ'gɪnɪŋ)
= start (start)
= infancy ('ɪnfənsɪ)
= birth (bɜθ)
= inception (ɪn'sɛpʃən)
② = source (sors , sɔrs)
= parentage ('pɛrəntɪdʒ)
= derivation (,dɛrə'veʃən)
= root (rut)

ornament ('ɔrnəmənt) *n.*
裝飾品

= decoration (,dɛkə'reʃən)
= adornment (ə'dɔrnmənt)

O

= embellishment (ɪm'bɛlɪʃmənt)
= garnish ('garnɪʃ)
= trimming ('trɪmɪŋ)

ornery ('ɔrnərɪ) *adj.* 頑固的

= unruly (ʌn'rulɪ)
= disobedient (,dɪsə'bidɪənt)
= rebellious (rɪ'bɛljəs)
= contrary ('kantrɛrɪ)
= obstinate ('abstənɪt)
= stubborn ('stʌbən)
= willful ('wɪlfəl)
= headstrong ('hɛd,strɔŋ)
= firm (fɝm)
= stiff (stɪf)
= rigid ('rɪdʒɪd)
= adamant ('ædəmənt ,
    'ædə,mænt)
= difficult ('dɪfə,kʌlt , 'dɪfəkəlt)
= mean (min)
= malicious (mə'lɪʃəs)
= disagreeable (,dɪsə'griəbḷ)
= cross (krɔs)
= irritable ('ɪrətəbḷ)
= cranky ('kræŋkɪ)

orthodox ('ɔrθə,daks) *adj.*
慣常的

= usual ('juʒʊəl)
= customary ('kʌstəm,ɛrɪ)
= conventional (kən'vɛnʃənḷ)
= traditional (trə'dɪʃənḷ)
= accepted (ək'sɛptɪd)
= proper ('prapɚ)
= correct (kə'rɛkt)

ostentatious (,astən'teʃəs) *adj.*
虛飾的

= showy ('ʃoɪ)
= flashy ('flæʃɪ)
= pretentious (prɪ'tɛnʃəs)
= overdone ('ovɚ'dʌn)
= garish ('gɛrɪʃ , 'gærɪʃ)
= fancy ('fænsɪ)
= swanky ('swæŋkɪ)

other ('ʌðɚ) *adj.* 不同的

= different ('dɪfərənt)
= distinct (dɪ'stɪŋkt)
= additional (ə'dɪʃənḷ)
= extra ('ɛkstrə)
= supplementary (,sʌplə'mɛntərɪ)
= further ('fɝðɚ)
= fresh (frɛʃ)
= new (nju)

ought (ɔt) *aux.* 應當

= should ('ʃud)
= must (mʌst)
= *need to*
= *be obliged to*
= *have to*

outbreak ('aut,brek) *n.* 爆發

= revolt (rɪ'volt)
= riot ('raɪət)
= disturbance (dɪ'stɝbəns)
= uprising ('ʌp,raɪzɪŋ , ʌp'raɪzɪŋ)
= rebellion (rɪ'bɛljən)
= eruption (ɪ'rʌpʃən)
= outburst ('aut,bɝst)
= torrent ('tɔrənt , 'tarənt)

O

outburst ('aʊt,bɜst) *n.* 爆發

= eruption (ɪ'rʌpʃən)
= outbreak ('aʊt,brek)
= torrent ('tɔrənt , 'tɑrənt)
= discharge (dɪs'tʃɑrdʒ)
= ejection (ɪ'dʒɛkʃən)

outcast ('aʊt,kæst) *adj.* 被遺棄的

= homeless ('homlɪs)
= friendless ('frɛndlɪs)
= abandoned (ə'bændənd)
= deserted (dɪ'zɜtɪd)
= forlorn (fɚ'lɔrn)
= forsaken (fɚ'sekən)
= derelict ('dɛrə,lɪkt)
= rejected (rɪ'dʒɛktɪd)
= disowned (dɪs'ond)

outcome ('aʊt,kʌm) *n.* 結果

= result (rɪ'zʌlt)
= consequence ('kansə,kwɛns)
= effect (ə'fɛkt , ɪ- , ɛ-)
= upshot ('ʌp,ʃat)
= fruit (frut)
= conclusion (kən'kluʒən)

outcry ('aʊt,kraɪ) *n.* 叫喊

= noise (nɔɪz)
= clamor ('klæmɚ)
= uproar ('ʌp,ror)

outdated (aʊt'detɪd) *adj.* 過時的

= old (old)
= outmoded (aʊt'modɪd)
= unfashionable (ʌn'fæʃənəbḷ)
= old-fashioned ('old'fæʃənd)

outdo (aʊt'du) *v.* 超越

= surpass (sɚ'pæs)
= excel (ɪk'sɛl)
= outshine (aʊt'ʃaɪn)
= defeat (dɪ'fit)
= beat (bit)

outfit ('aʊt,fɪt) *v.* 裝備

= equip (ɪ'kwɪp)
= furnish ('fɜnɪʃ)
= prepare (prɪ'pɛr)
= rig (rɪg)
= fit (fɪt)

outgrowth ('aʊt,groθ) *n.*
自然的結果

= product ('pradəkt)
= result (rɪ'zʌlt)
= effect (ə'fɛkt , ɪ- , ɛ-)
= consequence ('kansə,kwɛns)
= outcome ('aʊt,kʌm)
= fruit (frut)
= upshot ('ʌp,ʃat)
= byproduct ('baɪ,pradəkt)

outing ('aʊtɪŋ) *n.* 遠足

= trip (trɪp)
= journey ('dʒɜnɪ)
= jaunt (dʒɔnt , dʒant)
= excursion (ɪk'skɜʒən)

outlandish (aʊt'lændɪʃ) *adj.*
奇異的

= odd (ad)
= queer (kwɪr)
= peculiar (pɪ'kjuljɚ)

O

= curious ('kjʊrɪəs)

= strange (strendʒ)

= weird (wɪrd)

outlaw ('aʊt,lɔ) *n.* 罪犯

= outcast ('aʊt,kæst)

= exile ('ɛksaɪl , 'ɛgzaɪl)

= criminal ('krɪmənḷ)

= convict ('kɑnvɪkt)

outlay ('aʊt,le) *n.* 花費

= spending ('spɛndɪŋ)

= expense (ɪk'spɛns)

= costs (kɔsts)

outline ('aʊt,laɪn) *n.* ①草稿
②輪廓

① = plan (plæn)

= sketch (skɛtʃ)

= diagram ('daɪə,græm)

= chart (tʃɑrt)

= draft (dræft)

= pattern ('pætən)

= drawing ('drɔɪŋ)

② = profile ('profaɪl)

= contour ('kɑntʊr)

= skeleton ('skɛlətṇ)

outlook ('aʊt,lʊk) *n.* 看法；見解

= view (vju)

= attitude ('ætə,tjud)

= position (pə'zɪʃən)

outlying ('aʊt,laɪɪŋ) *adj.* 邊遠的

= external (ɪk'stɜnḷ)

= outer ('aʊtə)

= remote (rɪ'mot)

outnumber (aʊt'nʌmbə) *v.*
比…多

= exceed (ɪk'sid)

output ('aʊt,pʊt) *n.* 生產量

= yield (jild)

= production (prə'dʌkʃən)

= proceeds ('pro,sidz)

= crop (krɑp)

= harvest ('hɑrvɪst)

outrageous (aʊt'redʒəs) *adj.*
暴亂的

= shocking ('ʃɑkɪŋ)

= insulting (ɪn'sʌltɪŋ)

= absurd (əb'sɜd)

= nonsensical (nɑn'sɛnsɪkḷ)

= ridiculous (rɪ'dɪkjələs)

= foolish ('fulɪʃ)

= crazy ('krezɪ)

= preposterous (prɪ'pɑstərəs)

= bizarre (bɪ'zɑr)

= excessive (ɪk'sɛsɪv)

= extreme (ɪk'strim)

= exorbitant (ɪg'zɔrbətənt)

= disgraceful (dɪs'gresfəl)

= shameful ('ʃemfəl)

= scandalous ('skændləs)

= unwarranted (ʌn'wɔrəntɪd)

outright ('aʊt'raɪt) *adv.* 完全地

= altogether (,ɔltə'gɛðə)

= entirely (ɪn'taɪrlɪ)

= completely (kəm'plitlɪ)

= thoroughly ('θɝolɪ)
= wholly ('holɪ)
= fully ('fʊlɪ)
= totally ('totl̩ɪ)
= quite (kwaɪt)
= freely ('frilɪ)
= openly ('opənlɪ)
= downright ('daʊn,raɪt)

outset ('aʊt,sɛt) *n.* 開始

= start (stɑrt)
= beginning (bɪ'gɪnɪŋ)
= commencement
  (kə'mɛnsmənt)
= opening ('opənɪŋ)

outspoken ('aʊt'spokən) *adj.*
坦白的

= frank (fræŋk)
= unreserved (,ʌnrɪ'zɝvd)
= unrestrained (,ʌnrɪ'strend)
= open ('opən)
= vocal ('vokl̩)
= candid ('kændɪd)
= straightforward (,stret'fɔrwɚd)
= direct (də'rɛkt)
= forthright (,forθ'raɪt , 'forθ,raɪt)
= reserved (rɪ'zɝvd)

outstanding ('aʊt'stændɪŋ) *adj.*
顯著的

= important (ɪm'pɔrtn̩t)
= great (gret)
= eminent ('ɛmənənt)
= famous ('feməs)
= prominent ('prɑmənənt)

= distinguished (dɪ'stɪŋgwɪʃt)
= conspicuous (kən'spɪkjʊəs)
= significant (sɪg'nɪfəkənt)
= noticeable ('notɪsəbl̩)
= striking ('straɪkɪŋ)
= bold (bold)
= well-known ('wɛl'non)

outwit (aʊt'wɪt) *v.* 以機智勝過

= outmaneuver (,aʊtmə'nuvɚ)
= outdo (aʊt'du)
= outsmart (aʊt'smɑrt)

overbearing (,ovɚ'bɛrɪŋ) *adj.*
自大的

= masterful ('mæstɚfəl)
= domineering (,dɑmə'nɪrɪŋ)
= dictatorial (,dɪktə'torɪəl)
= autocratic (,ɔtə'krætɪk)
= arbitrary ('ɑrbə,trɛrɪ)
= arrogant ('ærəgənt)
= bossy ('bɔsɪ)

overcast ('ovɚ,kæst) *adj.* 陰暗的

= cloudy ('klaʊdɪ)
= dark (dɑrk)
= gloomy ('glumɪ)
= dismal ('dɪzml̩)
= somber ('sɑmbɚ)
= bleak (blik)
= hazy ('hezɪ)
= misty ('mɪstɪ)

overcome (,ovɚ'kʌm) *v.* 擊敗

= conquer ('kɑŋkɚ)
= defeat (dɪ'fit)

O

= upset (ʌp'sɛt)
= overpower (,ovə'pauə)
= surmount (sə'maunt)
= frustrate ('frʌstret)
= *drive off*

overdo ('ovə'du) v. 過分

= exaggerate (ɪg'zædʒə,ret)
= stretch (strɛtʃ)
= magnify ('mægnə,faɪ)
= enlarge (ɪn'lardʒ)
= *carry too far*
= *go to extremes*

overflow (,ovə'flo) v. 氾濫

= flood (flʌd)
= cascade (kæs'ked)
= spill (spɪl)
= inundate ('ɪnʌn,det)
= *run over*

overhaul (,ovə'hɔl) v. 修理

= repair (rɪ'pɛr)
= service ('sɝvɪs)
= mend (mɛnd)
= fix (fɪks)
= condition (kən'dɪʃən)

overhead (adv. 'ovə'hɛd ; n. adj. 'ovə,hɛd) ① adj. adv. 在上 (地) ② n. 開支

① = above (ə'bʌv)
= high (haɪ)
= aloft (ə'lɔft)
② = costs (kɔsts)
= expenses (ɪk'spɛnsɪz)

overjoyed ('ovə'dʒɔɪd) adj. 極高興的

= delighted (dɪ'laɪtɪd)
= enchanted (ɪn'tʃæntɪd)
= ecstatic (ɪk'stætɪk)
= elated (ɪ'letɪd)
= enraptured (ɪn'ræptʃəd)
= jubilant ('dʒublənt)

overlook (,ovə'luk) v. ①忽略 ②俯瞰

① = neglect (nɪ'glɛkt)
= ignore (ɪg'nor , -'nɔr)
= disregard (,dɪsrɪ'gard)
= skip (skɪp)
= miss (mɪs)
= *pass over*
= *let slip*
② = face (fes)
= view (vju)
= watch (watʃ)

overpass ('ovə,pæs) n. 橋

= bridge (brɪdʒ)
= span (spæn)
= viaduct ('vaɪə,dʌkt)

overpower (,ovə'pauə) v. 擊敗

= master ('mæstə)
= overwhelm (,ovə'hwɛlm)
= surmount (sə'maunt)
= defeat (dɪ'fit)
= conquer ('kɔŋkə)
= crush (krʌʃ)
= vanquish ('væŋkwɪʃ)

overrun (,ovə'rʌn) v. 超過

= exceed (ɪk'sid)

= spread (sprɛd)

= infest (ɪn'fɛst)

= beset (bɪ'sɛt)

= abound (ə'baʊnd)

= flood (flʌd)

oversee (,ovə'si) v. 督導

= supervise (,supə'vaɪz)

= mange ('mænɪdʒ)

= direct (də'rɛkt)

= superintend (,suprɪn'tɛnd)

= administer (əd'mɪnəstə)

= preside (prɪ'zaɪd)

= boss (bɔs)

oversight ('ovə,saɪt) n. 疏忽

= slip (slɪp)

= negligence ('nɛglədʒəns)

= omission (o'mɪʃən)

= error ('ɛrə)

overstep (,ovə'stɛp) v. 超越

= exceed (ɪk'sid)

= surpass (sə'pæs)

= transcend (træn'sɛnd)

= trespass ('trɛspəs)

= *go beyond*

overthrow (,ovə'θro) v. 推翻；
使毀滅

= defeat (dɪ'fit)

= destroy (dɪ'strɔɪ)

= overcome (,ovə'kʌm)

= overpower (,ovə'paʊə)

= overturn (,ovə't₃n)

= dethrone (dɪ'θron)

= upset (ʌp'sɛt)

= unseat (ʌn'sit)

overture ('ovətʃə) n. ①提議
②序曲

① = proposal (prə'pozḷ)

= offer ('ɔfə , 'ɑfə)

= bid (bɪd)

② = prelude ('prɛljud)

= introduction (,ɪntrə'dʌkʃən)

overwhelm (,ovə'hwɛlm) v.
①壓倒 ②使困窘；使驚訝

① = crush (krʌʃ)

= overcome (,ovə'kʌm)

= defeat (dɪ'fit)

= surmount (sə'maʊnt)

= conquer ('kɔŋkə)

= vanquish ('væŋkwɪʃ)

② = astonish (ə'stɑnɪʃ)

= surprise (sə'praɪz)

= flabbergast ('flæbə,gæst)

= amaze (ə'mez)

= astound (ə'staʊnd)

= bewilder (bɪ'wɪldə)

= startle ('stɑrtḷ)

= dumbfound (,dʌm'faʊnd)

owe (o) v. 感激

= *be indebted*

= *be obliged*

= *be liable*

own (on) v. 擁有

= have (hæv)

O

= possess (pə'zɛs)

= hold (hold)

= maintain (men'ten)

= monopolize (mə'nɑpḷ,aɪz)

P

pace (pes) *n.* ①速度　②步

① = rate (ret)

= speed (spid)

② = stride (straɪd)

= walk (wɔk)

= tread (trɛd)

pacify ('pæsə,faɪ) *v.* 使平靜；
鎮壓

= quiet ('kwaɪət)

= calm (kɑm)

= tranquilize ('træŋkwɪ,laɪz)

= soothe (suð)

= appease (ə'piz)

= placate ('pleket)

= mollify ('mɑlə,faɪ)

pack (pæk) *n.* 包裹

= fill (fɪl)

= load (lod)

= stuff (stʌf)

= cram (kræm)

= stow (sto)

= box (bɑks)

pact (pækt) *n.* 協定

= agreement (ə'grimənt)

= contract ('kɑntrækt)

= understanding (,ʌndɚ'stændɪŋ)

= bargain ('bɑrgɪn)

= treaty ('tritɪ)

= alliance (ə'laɪəns)

pad (pæd) *n.* ①墊子
②便條紙簿

① = cushion ('kʊʃɪn)

= pillow ('pɪlo)

= wadding ('wɑdɪŋ)

② = notebook ('not,bʊk)

= tablet ('tæblɪt)

= ledger ('lɛdʒɚ)

= album ('ælbəm)

paddle ('pædḷ) ① *v.* 責打
② *n.* 槳

① = spank (spæŋk)

= whip (hwɪp)

= beat (bit)

= lick (lɪk)

= wallop ('wɑləp)

② = oar (or)

padlock ('pæd,lɑk) *n.* 扣鎖

= bolt (bolt)

= bar (bɑr)

= lock (lɑk)

page (pedʒ) *n.* ①頁　②僮僕

① = paper ('pepɚ)

= sheet (ʃit)

= leaf (lif)

② = attendant (ə'tɛndənt)

= usher ('ʌʃɚ)

= servant ('sɝvənt)

= *errand boy*

pageant ('pædʒənt) *n.* 壯觀

= show (ʃo)
= spectacle ('spɛktəkl̩)
= pomp (pamp)
= display (dɪ'sple)
= entertainment (,ɛntə'tenmənt)
= exhibition (,ɛksə'bɪʃən)
= presentation (,prɛzn̩'teʃən)
= parade (pə'red)
= review (rɪ'vju)

pail (pel) *n.* 桶

= bucket ('bʌkɪt)

pain (pen) *n.* 苦痛

= suffering ('sʌfrɪŋ)
= hurt (hɜt)
= discomfort (dɪs'kʌmfət)
= distress (dɪ'strɛs)
= ache (ek)
= pang (pæŋ)
= irritation (,ɪrə'teʃən)
= soreness ('sornɪs , 'sɔr-)

painstaking ('penz,tekɪŋ) *adj.* 極小心的

= careful ('kɛrfəl)
= particular (pə'tɪkjələ)
= thorough ('θɜo)
= elaborate (ɪ'læbərɪt)
= diligent ('dɪlədʒənt)
= exacting (ɪg'zaktɪŋ)
= meticulous (mə'tɪkjələs)
= scrupulous ('skrupjələs)
= precise (prɪ'saɪs)
= accurate ('ækjərɪt)

paint (pent) *v.* ①油漆；粉飾 ②描繪

① = coat (kot)
= color ('kʌlə)
= cover ('kʌvə)
= decorate ('dɛkə,ret)
= trim (trɪm)
= garnish ('garnɪʃ)
② = draw (drɔ)
= sketch (skɛtʃ)
= picture ('pɪktʃə)
= depict (dɪ'pɪkt)
= draft (dræft)
= portray (por'tre)
= represent (,rɛprɪ'zɛnt)

pair (pɛr) *n.* 一雙

= set (sɛt)
= two (tu)
= couple ('kʌpl̩)
= both (boθ)
= twins (twɪnz)
= mates (mets)
= team (tim)
= duo ('du:o)

pal (pæl) *n.* 同伴

= friend (frɛnd)
= playmate ('ple,met)
= companion (kəm'pænjən)
= fellow ('fɛlo)
= comrade ('kamræd)
= associate (ə'soʃɪɪt)
= crony ('kronɪ)
= colleague ('kalig)
= partner ('partnə)

P

palace ('pælɪs) *n.* 大廈

= castle ('kæsl̩ , 'kɑsl̩)

= mansion ('mænʃən)

= villa ('vɪlə)

= chateau (ʃæ'to)

palatable ('pælətəbl̩) *adj.* 味美的

= delicious (dɪ'lɪʃəs)

= luscious ('lʌʃəs)

= delectable (dɪ'lɛktəbl̩)

= savory ('sevrɪ , 'sevərɪ)

= tasty ('testɪ)

pale (pel) *adj.* 蒼白的；無力的

= dim (dɪm)

= colorless ('kʌlələɪs)

= whitish ('hwaɪtɪʃ)

= faint (fent)

= weak (wik)

= vague (veg)

= indistinct (,ɪndɪ'stɪŋkt)

= lifeless ('laɪflɪs)

= pallid ('pælɪd)

= wan (wɑn)

= sallow ('sælo)

palpitate ('pælpə,tet) *v.* 顫動

= tremble ('trɛmbl̩)

= quiver ('kwɪvə)

= beat (bit)

= throb (θrɑb)

= pulsate ('pʌlset)

= flutter ('flʌtə)

paltry ('pɔltrɪ) *adj.* 無價值的

= trifling ('traɪflɪŋ)

= petty ('pɛtɪ)

= worthless ('wɜθlɪs)

= poor (pur)

= miserable ('mɪzərəbl̩)

= cheap (tʃip)

pamper ('pæmpə) *v.* 縱容

= humor ('hjumə)

= favor ('fevə)

= indulge (ɪn'dʌldʒ)

= oblige (ə'blaɪdʒ)

= coddle ('kɑdl̩)

= spoil (spɔɪl)

= *cater to*

pamphlet ('pæmflɪt) *n.* 小冊子

= booklet ('buklɪt)

= brochure (bro'ʃur)

= leaflet ('liflɪt)

= folder ('foldə)

panel ('pænl̩) *n.* ①小組 ②鑲板

① = group (grup)

= forum ('forəm)

= board (bord)

② = partition (pɑr'tɪʃən)

= wall (wɔl)

= division (də'vɪʒən)

= separation (,sɛpə'reʃən)

= barrier ('bærɪə)

pang (pæŋ) *n.* 悲痛

= pain (pen)

= hurt (hɜt)

= discomfort (dɪs'kʌmfət)

P

= distress（dɪ'strɛs）

= ache（ek）

= soreness（'sornɪs , 'sɔr- ）

= irritation（,ɪrə'teʃən）

anic（'pænɪk）*n.* 恐慌

= fear（fɪr）

= fright（fraɪt）

= scare（skɛr）

= alarm（ə'lɑrm）

= dread（drɛd）

= awe（ɔ）

= terror（'tɛrɚ）

= phobia（'fobɪə）

anorama（,pænə'ræmə）*n.*
景

= scene（sin）

= vista（'vɪstə）

= lookout（'lʊk,aʊt）

= sight（saɪt）

ant（pænt）*v.* 喘息

= breathe（brið）

= puff（pʌf）

= gasp（gæsp）

= wheeze（hwiz）

ants（pænts）*n. pl.* 褲子

= trousers（'traʊzɚz）

= breeches（'brɪtʃɪz）

ar（pɑr）*adj.* 標準的

= average（'ævərɪdʒ）

= normal（'nɔrml̩）

parade（pə'red）*n.* 誇示；閱兵

= show（ʃo）

= display（dɪ'sple）

= review（rɪ'vju）

= promenade（,prɑmə'ned）

= march（mɑrtʃ）

= exhibition（,ɛksə'bɪʃən）

= pageant（'pædʒənt）

paradise（'pærə,daɪs）*n.* 樂園；
極樂

= heaven（'hɛvən）

= bliss（blɪs）

= glory（'glɔrɪ）

= ecstasy（'ɛkstəsɪ）

= elation（ɪ'leʃən）

= enchantment（ɪn'tʃæntmənt）

paralyze（'pærə,laɪz）*v.* 使麻痺

= deaden（'dɛdn̩）

= numb（nʌm）

= desensitize（di'sɛnsə,taɪz）

= disable（dɪs'ebl̩）

= cripple（'krɪpl̩）

paramount（'pærə,maʊnt）*adj.*
至上的

= chief（tʃif）

= foremost（'for,most）

= principal（'prɪnsəpl̩）

= leading（'lidɪŋ）

= uppermost（'ʌpɚ,most）

= dominant（'dɑmənənt）

= primary（'praɪ,mɛrɪ）

= main（men）

= maximum（'mæksəməm）

P

= top (tap)
= *most important*

parcel ('parsḷ) *n.* 包裹

= package ('pækɪdʒ)
= bundle ('bʌndḷ)
= pack (pæk)
= lot (lat)

parched (partʃt) *adj.* 枯乾的

= thirsty ('θɜstɪ)
= dry (draɪ)
= dehydrated (di'haɪdretɪd)

pardon ('pardṇ) *v.* 原諒

= absolve (æb'salv)
= acquit (ə'kwɪt)
= excuse (ɪk'skjuz)
= exculpate ('ɛkskʌl,pet)
= exonerate (ɪg'zanə,ret)
= forgive (fə'gɪv)
= vindicate ('vɪndə,ket)

pare (pɛr , pær) *v.* 剝；削

= peel (pil)
= trim (trɪm)
= skin (skɪn)
= strip (strɪp)
= scrape (skrep)

park (park) ① *n.* 公園
② *v.* 置放

① = garden ('gardṇ)
= *recreation ground*
② = settle ('sɛtḷ)

= place (ples)
= put (put)
= set (sɛt)
= station ('steʃən)
= fix (fɪks)

parry ('pærɪ) *v.* 躲避

= avoid (ə'vɔɪd)
= evade (ɪ'ved)
= dodge (dadʒ)
= hedge (hɛdʒ)
= sidestep ('saɪd,stɛp)
= *ward off*

part (part) *n.* ①部分 ②角色

① = portion ('porʃən)
= segment ('sɛgmənt)
= fraction ('frækʃən)
= share (ʃɛr)
= division (də'vɪʒən)
= section ('sɛkʃən)
= component (kəm'ponənt)
= cut (kʌt)
② = role (rol)

partake (pə'tek) *v.* 分享

= share (ʃɛr)
= participate (pə'tɪsə,pet , par-)
= contribute (kən'trɪbjut)
= *join in*

partial ('parʃəl) *adj.* 部分的

= partly ('partlɪ)
= fractional ('frækʃənḷ)
= fragmentary ('frægmən,tɛrɪ)
= limited ('lɪmɪtɪd)

P

articipate (pə'tɪsə,pet) v.
參與

= partake (pə'tek)
= contribute (kən'trɪbjut)
= *take part in*
= *have a hand in*
= *enter into*
= *join in*

articular (pə'tɪkjələ) adj.
①特殊的　②難以取悅的

① = special ('spɛʃəl)
= unusual (ʌn'juʒuəl)
= different ('dɪfərənt)
② = meticulous (mə'tɪkjələs)
= critical ('krɪtɪkḷ)
= discriminating
　(dɪ'skrɪmə,netɪŋ)
= fastidious (fæs'tɪdɪəs)
= finicky ('fɪnɪkɪ)
= exacting (ɪg'zæktɪŋ)
= fussy ('fʌsɪ)

arting ('partɪŋ) n. 離別

= departure (dɪ'partʃə)
= leaving ('livɪŋ)
= exit ('ɛgzɪt , 'ɛksɪt)
= withdrawal (wɪð'drɔəl)
= *going away*

artition (par'tɪʃən) n. 分隔

= separation (,sɛpə'reʃən)
= division (də'vɪʒən)
= wall (wɔl)

artner ('partnə) n. 夥伴

= companion (kəm'pænjən)
= mate (met)
= collaborator (kə'læbə,retə)
= assistant (ə'sɪstənt)
= participant (pə'tɪsəpənt)
= comrade ('kamræd)
= colleague ('kalig)

party ('partɪ) n. ①團體
②參與者　③集會

① = group (grup)
= company ('kampənɪ)
= gang (gæŋ)
= crew (kru)
= body ('badɪ)
= band (bænd)
= faction ('fækʃən)
② = person ('pɝsṇ)
= fellow ('fɛlo)
= individual (,ɪndə'vɪdʒuəl)
③ = festival ('fɛstəvḷ)
= fete (fet)
= affair (ə'fɛr)
= ball (bɔl)
= celebration (,sɛlə'breʃən)

pass (pæs) v. ①通過　②消耗
③傳送　④經過

① = succeed (sək'sid)
= *do well*
② = spend (spɛnd)
= use (juz)
= employ (ɪm'plɔɪ)
③ = deliver (dɪ'lɪvə)
= transfer (træns'fɝ)
= *hand over*

P

④ = go (go)
= travel ('trævḷ)
= move (muv)
= progress (prə'grɛs)

passage ('pæsɪdʒ) *n.* ①通道
②一段 ③航行

① = corridor ('kɔrədɚ)
= hallway ('hɔl,we)
= arcade (ɑr'ked)
= entranceway ('ɛntrəns,we)
= opening ('opənɪŋ)
= lane (len)
= channel ('tʃænḷ)
= artery ('ɑrtərɪ)
= passageway ('pæsɪdʒ,we)
② = section ('sɛkʃən)
= paragraph ('pærə,græf)
= chapter ('tʃæptɚ)
= excerpt ('ɛksɜpt)
= selection (sə'lɛkʃən)
= extract ('ɛkstrækt)
③ = voyage ('vɔɪ·ɪdʒ)
= cruise (kruz)
= crossing ('krɔsɪŋ)
= trip (trɪp)
= trek (trɛk)

passageway ('pæsɪdʒ,we) *n.*
通路

= passage ('pæsɪdʒ)
= corridor ('kɔrədɚ)
= hallway ('hɔl,we)
= arcade (ɑr'ked)
= entranceway ('ɛntrəns,we)
= opening ('opənɪŋ)
= lane (len)

= channel ('tʃænḷ)
= artery ('ɑrtərɪ)

passion ('pæʃən) *n.* ①熱情
②憤怒　③愛情

① = emotion (ɪ'moʃən)
= enthusiasm (ɪn'θjuzɪ,æzəm)
= craze (krez)
= fervor ('fɜvɚ)
= *strong feeling*
② = rage (redʒ)
= anger ('æŋgɚ)
= fury ('fjʊrɪ)
= violence ('vaɪələns)
③ = love (lʌv)
= affection (ə'fɛkʃən)
= fondness ('fɑndnɪs)
= ardor ('ɑrdɚ)
= lust (lʌst)
= desire (dɪ'zaɪr)

passive ('pæsɪv) *adj.* 消極的；
溫順的

= inactive (ɪn'æktɪv)
= dormant ('dɔrmənt)
= submissive (səb'mɪsɪv)
= unresisting (,ʌnrɪ'zɪstɪŋ)
= compliant (kəm'plaɪənt)
= yielding ('jildɪŋ)
= docile ('dɑsḷ)
= mild (maɪld)
= gentle ('dʒɛntḷ)

past (pæst , pɑst) *adj.* 過去的

= ended ('ɛndɪd)
= former ('fɔrmɚ)

P

= over ('ovɚ)
= previous ('privɪəs)
= preceding (prɪ'sidɪŋ)
= *gone by*

aste (pest) *n.* 漿糊；膠水

= glue (glu)
= adhesive (əd'hisɪv)
= cement (sə'mɛnt)
= mucilage ('mjuslɪdʒ)

astel (pæs'tɛl , 'pæs,tɛl) *adj.*
淺淡的

= pale (pel)
= soft (sɔft)
= light (laɪt)
= fair (fɛr)

astime ('pæs,taɪm) *n.* 消遣

= recreation (,rɛkrɪ'eʃən)
= amusement (ə'mjuzmənt)
= enjoyment (ɪn'dʒɔɪmənt)
= diversion (də'vɝʒən)
= relaxation (,rilæks'eʃən)

asture ('pæstʃɚ) *n.* 草地

= grassland ('græs,lænd)
= meadow ('mɛdo)
= range (rendʒ)

at (pæt) *n. v.* 輕拍

= tap (tæp)
= stroke (strok)
= rap (ræp)

atch (pætʃ) *v.* 補綴；修補

= mend (mɛnd)
= repair (rɪ'pɛr)
= fix (fɪks)
= service ('sɝvɪs)

paternal (pə'tɝnl) *adj.* 父親的

= fatherly ('fɑðɚlɪ)

path (pæθ , pɑθ) *n.* 小徑

= route (rut)
= track (træk)
= way (we)
= trail (trel)
= road (rod)
= line (laɪn)

pathetic (pə'θɛtɪk) *adj.* 可憐的

= pitiful ('pɪtɪfəl)
= deplorable (dɪ'plɔrəbl)
= miserable ('mɪzərəbl)
= touching ('tʌtʃɪŋ)
= moving ('muvɪŋ)
= sad (sæd)
= distressing (dɪ'strɛsɪŋ)

patience ('peʃəns) *n.* 容忍

= tolerance ('tɑlərəns)
= endurance (ɪn'djurəns)
= indulgence (ɪn'dʌldʒəns)
= perseverance (,pɝsə'vɪrəns)
= persistence (pə'sɪstəns)

patriotic (,petrɪ'ɑtɪk) *adj.*
愛國的

= loyal ('lɔɪəl)
= nationalistic (,næʃənl'ɪstɪk)
= chauvinistic (,ʃovɪ'nɪstɪk)

P

patrol (pəˈtrol) *v.* 巡查

= watch (wɑtʃ)
= guard (gɑrd)
= protect (prəˈtɛkt)
= police (pəˈlis)
= *keep vigil*

patronize (ˈpetrənˌaɪz) *v.*
①光顧 ②支援

① = *deal with*
= *trade with*
② = back (bæk)
= sponsor (ˈspɑnsə)
= finance (ˈfaɪnæns)
= promote (prəˈmot)
= support (səˈport)

patter (ˈpætə) *v.* ①輕拍
②閒談

① = drum (drʌm)
= beat (bit)
= pound (paʊnd)
= throb (θrɑb)
② = chatter (ˈtʃætə)
= chat (tʃæt)
= prattle (ˈprætḷ)
= babble (ˈbæbḷ)
= jabber (ˈdʒæbə)
= blab (blæb)

pattern (ˈpætən) *n.* ①圖案
②模型

① = arrangement (əˈrendʒmənt)
= design (dɪˈzaɪn)
= illustration (ˌɪləsˈtreʃən)

= picture (ˈpɪktʃə)
= print (prɪnt)
② = model (ˈmɑdḷ)
= example (ɪgˈzæmpḷ)
= standard (ˈstændəd)
= prototype (ˈprotəˌtaɪp)
= paragon (ˈpærəˌgɑn)

pauper (ˈpɔpə) *n.* 貧民

= *poor man*

pause (pɔz) *v.* 中止

= wait (wet)
= stop (stɑp)
= rest (rɛst)
= recess (rɪˈsɛs)
= cease (sis)

pave (pev) *v.* 舖（道路）

= cover (ˈkʌvə)
= floor (flor , flɔr)

pavilion (pəˈvɪljən) *n.* 建築

= building (ˈbɪldɪŋ)
= structure (ˈstrʌktʃə)
= edifice (ˈɛdəfɪs)

paw (pɔ) *v.* 用足觸或摸

= handle (ˈhændḷ)
= touch (tʌtʃ)
= feel (fil)

pawn (pɔn) *v.* 典當

= pledge (plɛdʒ)
= deposit (dɪˈpɑzɪt)

P

ay (pe) v. 報酬

= give (gɪv)
= remunerate (rɪ'mjunə,ret)
= compensate ('kɑmpən,set)

eaceful ('pisfəl) adj. 安靜的

= quiet ('kwaɪət)
= untroubled (ʌn'trʌbl̩d)
= placid ('plæsɪd)
= tranquil ('træŋkwɪl)
= still (stɪl)
= calm (kɑm)
= pacific (pə'sɪfɪk)
= serene (sə'rin)
= cool (kul)

eak (pik) n. 頂點

= top (tɑp)
= crest (krɛst)
= hilltop ('hɪl,tɑp)
= summit ('sʌmɪt)
= pinnacle ('pɪnək l̩)
= crown (kraʊn)
= tip (tɪp)
= apex ('epɛks)

eal (pil) n. 鈴聲

= ring (rɪŋ)
= chime (tʃaɪm)
= toll (tol)

eculiar (pɪ'kjuljə) adj.
奇異的 ②特殊的

= strange (strendʒ)
= odd (ɑd)
= unusual (ʌn'juʒʊəl)

= queer (kwɪr)
= curious ('kjʊrɪəs)
= weird (wɪrd)
= bizarre (bɪ'zɑr)
= eccentric (ɪk'sɛntrɪk)
② = special ('spɛʃəl)
= distinctive (dɪ'stɪŋktɪv)
= characteristic (,kærɪktə'rɪstɪk)
= typical ('tɪpɪk l̩)
= representative (,rɛprɪ'zɛntətɪv)

pedal ('pɛdl̩) v. 踩踏板

= drive (draɪv)
= push (pʊʃ)
= roll (rol)

peddle ('pɛdl̩) v. 叫賣

= vend (vɛnd)
= sell (sɛl)
= hawk (hɔk)

pedestrian (,pə'dɛstrɪən) n.
步行者

= walker (wɔkə)
= hiker ('haɪkə)

peek (pik) v. 偷看；瞥見

= glance (glæns)
= glimpse (glɪmps)
= peep (pip)
= *look slyly*

peel (pil) v. 剝皮

= strip (strɪp)
= pare (pɛr)
= skin (skɪn)

P

peep (pip) *v.* 窺看;瞥見

= peek (pik)

= glance (glæns)

= glimpse (glɪmps)

= *look slyly*

peer (pɪr) ① *n.* 同輩　② *v.* 細看

① = equal ('ikwəl)

= match (mætʃ)

= equivalent (ɪ'kwɪvələnt)

= like (laɪk)

② = look (luk)

= peek (pik)

= peep (pip)

peevish ('pivɪʃ) *adj.* 易怒的

= cross (krɔs)

= complaining (kəm'plenɪŋ)

= fretful ('frɛtfəl)

= petulant ('pɛtʃələnt)

pell-mell ('pɛl'mɛl) *adv.* 紛亂地

= headlong ('hɛd,lɔŋ)

= tumultuous (tju'mʌltʃuəs)

= hastily ('hestlɪ , -tɪlɪ)

= hurriedly ('hɜɪdlɪ)

= quickly ('kwɪklɪ)

= swiftly ('swɪftlɪ)

= speedily ('spidlɪ)

pelt (pɛlt) ① *v.* 投擊　② *n.* 毛皮

① = attack (ə'tæk)

= strike (straɪk)

= pound (paund)

= beat (bit)

= knock (nak)

= hammer ('hæmə)

= rap (ræp)

= bang (bæŋ)

= whip (hwɪp)

= thrash (θræʃ)

= wallop ('waləp)

② = skin (skɪn)

= hide (haɪd)

= fur (fɜ)

pen (pɛn) *v.* ①寫　②關入欄中

① = write (raɪt)

= inscribe (ɪn'skraɪb)

= record (rɪ'kɔrd)

② = enclose (ɪn'kloz)

= confine (kən'faɪn)

= *shut in*

penalize ('pinḷ,aɪz , 'pɛnḷ-) *v.* 科罰

= punish ('pʌnɪʃ)

= chastise (tʃæs'taɪz)

= discipline ('dɪsəplɪn)

= castigate ('kæstə,get)

pending ('pɛndɪŋ) ① *adj.* 未定　② *prep.* 直到;在~中

① = waiting ('wetɪŋ)

② = until (ən'tɪl)

= during (djurɪŋ)

penetrate ('pɛnə,tret) *v.* ①透　②了解

① = pierce (pɪrs)

= enter ('ɛntə)

= puncture ('pʌŋktʃə)

P

= bore (bor)

= perforate ('pɜfə,ret)

= understand (ˌʌndə'stænd)

= perceive (pə'siv)

= *see through*

enitence ('pɛnətəns) *n.* 悔悟

= sorrow ('saro)

= repentance (rɪ'pɛntəns)

= penance ('pɛnəns)

enmanship ('pɛnmən,ʃɪp) *n.*
法

= handwriting ('hænd,raitɪŋ)

= script (skrɪpt)

= calligraphy (kə'lɪgrəfɪ)

ennant ('pɛnənt) *n.* 旗

= flag (flæg)

= banner ('bænə)

= streamer ('strimə)

= ensign ('ɛnsain , 'ɛnsṇ)

= standard ('stændəd)

= colors ('kaləz)

enniless ('pɛnɪlɪs) *adj.* 貧困的

= poor (pur)

= destitute ('dɛstə,tjut , -,tut)

= down-and-out ('daunən'aut)

= bankrupt ('bæŋkrʌpt)

nsion ('pɛnʃən) *n.* 津貼

= allowance (ə'lauəns)

= aid (ed)

= assistance (ə'sɪstəns)

= help (hɛlp)

= subsidy ('sʌbsədɪ)

= grant (grænt)

= stipend ('staɪpɛnd)

pensive ('pɛnsɪv) *adj.* 沈思的；
苦心焦慮的

= thoughtful ('θɔtfəl)

= contemplative ('kantəm,pletɪv)

= reflective (rɪ'flɛktɪv)

= meditative ('mɛdə,tetɪv)

= deliberating (dɪ'lɪbə,retɪŋ)

= absorbed (əb'sɔrbd)

= engrossed (ɪn'grost)

= melancholy ('mɛlən,kalɪ)

= serious ('sɪrɪəs)

= wistful ('wɪstfəl)

people ('pipḷ) *n.* 人們

= persons ('pɜsṇz)

= folks (foks)

= community (kə'mjunətɪ)

= society (sə'saɪətɪ)

= public ('pʌblɪk)

= men (mɛn)

= *human beings*

pep (pɛp) *n.* 活力

= spirit ('spɪrɪt)

= energy ('ɛnə,dʒɪ)

= vim (vɪm)

= vigor ('vɪgə)

= verve (vɜv)

= punch (pʌntʃ)

= vivacity (vaɪ'væsətɪ)

= dash (dæʃ)

= drive (draɪv)

P

= animation (ˌænə'meʃən)

= life (laɪf)

perceive (pɚ'siv) v. 察覺

= sense (sɛns)

= observe (əb'zɝv)

= feel (fil)

= experience (ɪk'spɪrɪəns)

= detect (dɪ'tɛkt)

= recognize ('rɛkəg,naɪz)

= distinguish (dɪ'stɪŋgwɪʃ)

= *make out*

percentage (pɚ'sɛntɪdʒ) n.
百分率

= proportion (prə'porʃən)

= part (part)

= ratio ('reʃo)

= rate (ret)

= quota ('kwotə)

perch (pɝtʃ) v. 棲息

= rest (rɛst)

= sit (sɪt)

= settle ('sɛtl̩)

= straddle ('strædl̩)

perchance (pɚ'tʃæns) adv. 或許

= perhaps (pɚ'hæps)

= possibly ('pasəblɪ)

= maybe ('mebɪ)

= conceivably (kən'sivəblɪ)

perennial (pə'rɛnɪəl) adj.
不斷的

= continuous (kən'tɪnjuəs)

= constant ('kanstənt)

= perpetual (pɚ'pɛtʃuəl)

= steady ('stɛdɪ)

= regular ('rɛgjələ)

perfect ('pɝfɪkt) adj. 無瑕的

= faultless ('fɔltlɪs)

= flawless ('flɔlɪs)

= ideal (aɪ'diəl)

= correct (kə'rɛkt)

= accurate ('ækjərɪt)

= right (raɪt)

perforate ('pɝfə,ret) v. 貫穿

= pierce (pɪrs)

= penetrate ('pɛnə,tret)

= puncture ('pʌŋktʃɚ)

= enter ('ɛntɚ)

= bore (bor , bɔr)

perform (pɚ'fɔrm) v. 執行

= do (du)

= act (ækt)

= execute ('ɛksɪ,kjut)

= transact (træns'ækt)

= accomplish (ə'kamplɪʃ)

= achieve (ə'tʃiv)

= *carry out*

perhaps (pɚ'hæps) adv. 或許

= possibly ('pasəblɪ)

= maybe ('mebɪ , 'mebi)

= conceivably (kən'sivəblɪ)

peril ('pɛrəl) n. 危險

= danger ('dendʒɚ)

P

= harm〔hɑrm〕
= jeopardy〔'dʒɛpədɪ〕
= hazard〔'hæzəd〕
= risk〔rɪsk〕
= endangerment
　〔ɪn'dendʒəmənt〕

eriod〔'pɪrɪəd〕*n.* 時期

= interval〔'ɪntəvl̩〕
= span〔spæn〕
= time〔taɪm〕

eriodical〔pɪrɪ'ɑdɪkl̩〕*n.*
期刊物

= magazine〔,mægə'zin〕
= journal〔'dʒɜnl̩〕
= gazette〔gə'zɛt〕

erish〔'pɛrɪʃ〕*v.* 毀滅

= die〔daɪ〕
= decease〔dɪ'sis〕
= succumb〔sə'kʌm〕
= disappear〔,dɪsə'pɪr〕
= vanish〔'vænɪʃ〕
= decay〔dɪ'ke〕

rmanent〔'pɜmənənt〕*adj.*
久的

= lasting〔'læstɪŋ〕
= durable〔'djʊrəbl̩〕
= enduring〔ɪn'djʊrɪŋ〕
= long-lasting〔'lɔŋ 'læstɪŋ〕
= unchanging〔ʌn'tʃendʒɪŋ〕
= constant〔'kɑnstənt〕
= stable〔'stebl̩〕
= steady〔'stɛdɪ〕

permeate〔'pɜmɪ,et〕*v.* 彌漫

= penetrate〔'pɛnə,tret〕
= saturate〔'satʃə,ret〕
= pervade〔pə'ved〕
= soak〔sok〕
= *spread through*

permit〔pə'mɪt〕*v.* 允許

= allow〔ə'laʊ〕
= consent〔kən'sɛnt〕
= let〔lɛt〕
= grant〔grænt〕
= admit〔əd'mɪt〕

pernicious〔pə'nɪʃəs〕*adj.*
有害的

= harmful〔'hɑrmfəl〕
= hurtful〔'hɜtfəl〕
= damaging〔'damɪdʒɪŋ〕
= injurious〔ɪn'dʒʊrɪəs〕
= detrimental〔,dɛtrə'mɛntl̩〕
= malignant〔mə'lɪgnənt〕
= deadly〔'dɛdlɪ〕
= destructive〔dɪ'strʌktɪv〕
= fatal〔'fetl̩〕
= mortal〔'mɔrtl̩〕

perpendicular
〔,pɜpən'dɪkjələ〕*adj.* 垂直的

= upright〔'ʌp,raɪt〕
= vertical〔'vɜtɪkl̩〕

perpetrate〔'pɜpə,tret〕*v.* 做
（壞事）；犯（過失）

= commit〔kə'mɪt〕
= effect〔ə'fɛkt〕
= achieve〔ə'tʃiv〕

P

perpetual (pə'pɛtʃʊəl) *adj.*
永久的

= eternal (ɪ'tɜnḷ)
= lasting ('læstɪŋ)
= continuous (kən'tɪnjuəs)
= unceasing (ʌn'sisɪŋ)
= permanent ('pɜmənənt)
= infinite ('ɪnfənɪt)
= endless ('ɛndlɪs)
= incessant (ɪn'sɛsn̩t)
= constant ('kɑnstənt)

perplex (pə'plɛks) *v.* 使困惑

= puzzle ('pʌzḷ)
= bewilder (bɪ'wɪldə)
= baffle ('bæfḷ)
= confound (kɑn'faʊnd , kən-)
= mystify ('mɪstə,faɪ)

persecute ('pɜsɪ,kjut) *v.* 迫害

= harm (hɑrm)
= oppress (ə'prɛs)
= torment (tɔr'mɛnt)
= harass (hə'ræs)
= molest (mə'lɛst)
= torture ('tɔrtʃə)
= antagonize (æn'tægə,naɪz)
= badger ('bædʒə)

persevere (,pɜsə'vɪr) *v.* 堅持

= persist (pə'zɪst , -'sɪst)
= endure (ɪn'djʊr)
= continue (kən'tɪnju)
= *carry on*
= *keep on*

persist (pə'zɪst , -'sɪst) *v.* 持久

= last (læst)
= stay (ste)
= continue (kən'tɪnju)
= endure (ɪn'djʊr)
= prevail (prɪ'vel)
= persevere (,pɜsə'vɪr)
= *go on*

person ('pɜsṇ) *n.* 人

= individual (,ɪndə'vɪdʒʊəl)
= soul (sol)
= somebody ('sʌm,bɑdɪ)
= someone ('sʌm,wʌn)

personal ('pɜsṇḷ) *adj.* 個人的

= private ('praɪvɪt)
= special ('spɛʃəl)
= individual (,ɪndə'vɪdʒʊəl)
= specific (spɪ'sɪfɪk)
= particular (pə'tɪkjələ)

personality (,pɜsṇ'ælətɪ) *n.*
個性

= identity (aɪ'dɛntətɪ)
= individuality
  (,ɪndə,vɪdʒʊ'ælətɪ)

perspire (pə'spaɪr) *v.* 流汗

= sweat (swɛt)

persuade (pə'swed) *v.* 說服

= convince (kən'vɪns)
= convict (kən'vɪkt)
= convert (kən'vɜt)
= induce (ɪn'djus)
= *win over*

P

419

ert (pɜt) *adj.* 魯莽的

= bold (bold)
= saucy ('sɔsɪ)
= flippant ('flɪpənt)
= forward ('fɔrwəd)
= impudent ('ɪmpjədənt)
= impertinent (ɪm'pɜtn̩ənt)

ertain (pə'ten) *v.* 屬於

= belong (bə'lɔŋ)
= relate (rɪ'let)
= refer (rɪ'fɜ)
= concern (kən'sɜn)
= apply (ə'plaɪ)
= *be appropriate*
= *be connected*

erturb (pə'tɜb) *v.* 使心煩

= disturb (dɪ'stɜb)
= trouble ('trʌbl̩)
= distress (dɪ'strɛs)
= bother ('baðə)
= agitate ('ædʒə,tet)
= upset (ʌp'sɛt)

eruse (pə'ruz) *v.* 細察；細讀

= examine (ɪg'zæmɪn)
= study ('stʌdɪ)
= inspect (ɪn'spɛkt)
= review (rɪ'vju)
= *read carefully*

ervade (pə'ved) *v.* 遍布

= fill (fɪl)
= permeate ('pɜmɪ,et)
= penetrate ('pɛnə,tret)

= overrun (,ovə'rʌn)

perverse (pə'vɜs) *adj.*
①固執的　②錯誤的　③邪惡的

① = stubborn ('stʌbən)
= contrary ('kɑntrɛrɪ)
= willful ('wɪlfəl)
= difficult ('dɪfəkəlt)
= obstinate ('ɑbstənɪt)
② = wrong (rɔŋ)
= incorrect (,ɪnkə'rɛkt)
= untrue (ʌn'tru)
= false (fɔls)
= erroneous (ə'ronɪəs)
③ = wicked ('wɪkɪd)
= corrupt (kə'rʌpt)

perverted (pə'vɜtɪd) *adj.*
歪曲的

= distorted (dɪs'tɔrtɪd)
= twisted ('twɪstɪd)
= warped (wɔrpt)
= contorted (kən'tɔrtɪd)

pessimistic (,pɛsə'mɪstɪk) *adj.*
悲觀的

= unhappy (ʌn'hæpɪ)
= cheerless ('tʃɪrlɪs)
= joyless ('dʒɔɪlɪs)
= gloomy ('glumɪ)
= cynical ('sɪnɪkəl)

pester ('pɛstə) *v.* 使困擾

= annoy (ə'nɔɪ)
= vex (vɛks)
= trouble ('trʌbl̩)

P

= torment (tɔr'mɛnt)

= molest (mə'lɛst)

= bother ('baðə·)

= harass ('hærəs)

= badger ('bædʒə·)

= tease (tiz)

= nag (næg)

pestilence ('pɛstḷəns) *n.* 疾病

= plague (pleg)

= epidemic (ˌɛpə'dɛmɪk)

= disease (dɪ'ziz)

pet (pɛt) *v.* 愛撫

= stroke (strok)

= pat (pæt)

= caress (kə'rɛs)

= fondle ('fandḷ)

petite (pə'tit) *adj.* 小的

= little ('lɪtḷ)

= small (smɔl)

= slight (slaɪt)

= tiny ('taɪnɪ)

petition (pə'tɪʃən) *v.* 請願

= request (rɪ'kwɛst)

= demand (dɪ'mænd)

= requisition (ˌrɛkwə'zɪʃən)

= appeal (ə'pil)

= plea (pli)

petrify ('pɛtrəˌfaɪ) *v.* ①嚇呆
②使僵硬

① = terrify ('tɛrəˌfaɪ)

= horrify ('hɔrəˌfaɪ , 'har-)

= shock (ʃak)

= appall (ə'pɔl)

= frighten ('fraɪtṇ)

= stun (stʌn)

② = harden ('hardṇ)

= solidify (sə'lɪdəˌfaɪ)

= *become stone*

petty ('pɛtɪ) *adj.* ①次要的
②卑賤的

① = unimportant (ˌʌnɪm'pɔrtṇt)

= small (smɔl)

= trivial ('trɪvɪəl)

= puny ('pjunɪ)

= minor ('maɪnə·)

= inferior (ɪn'fɪrɪə·)

② = mean (min)

= base (bes)

= low (lo)

= wretched ('rɛtʃɪd)

= miserable ('mɪzərəbḷ)

= despicable ('dɛspɪkəbḷ)

= contemptible (kən'tɛmptəbḷ)

petulant ('pɛtʃələnt) *adj.* 暴躁
的

= irritable ('ɪrətəbḷ)

= peevish ('pivɪʃ)

= fretful ('frɛtfəl)

= grouchy ('graʊtʃɪ)

phantom ('fæntəm) *n.* 幻像；
幽靈

= illusion (ɪ'ljuʒən)

= fantasy ('fæntəsɪ)

= apparition (ˌæpə'rɪʃən)

= specter ('spɛktə·)

P

= ghost (gost)
= spirit ('spɪrɪt)
= vision ('vɪʒən)
= spook (spuk)

harmacist ('farməsɪst) *n.*
劑師

= druggist ('drʌgɪst)
= chemist ('kɛmɪst)

hase (fez) *n.* 階段

= stage (stedʒ)
= state (stet)
= aspect ('æspɛkt)

henomenal (fə'namənḷ) *adj.*
凡的

= extraordinary (ɪk'strɔrdṇ͵ɛrɪ)
= exceptional (ɪk'sɛpʃənḷ)
= remarkable (rɪ'markəbḷ)
= wonderful ('wʌndəfəl)
= marvelous ('marvḷəs)
= miraculous (mə'rækjələs)

hilanthropic (͵fɪlən'θrapɪk)
j. 慈善的

= charitable ('tʃærətəbḷ)
= kindly ('kaɪndlɪ)
= benevolent (bə'nɛvələnt)
= bighearted ('bɪg͵hartɪd)
= generous ('dʒɛnərəs)
= giving ('gɪvɪŋ)
= merciful ('mɜsɪfəl)
= humanitarian
   (hju͵mænə'tɛrɪən)

philosophical (͵fɪlə'safɪkəl)
adj. 賢明的;冷靜的

= wise (waɪz)
= reasonable ('riznəbḷ)
= calm (kɑm)

photograph ('fotə͵græf) *n.*
拍照

= snap (snæp)
= film (fɪlm)
= *take a picture*

phrase (frez) *n.* 片語

= clause (klɔz)
= part (part)
= section ('sɛkʃən)
= passage ('pæsɪdʒ)

physician (fə'zɪʃən) *n.* 醫生

= doctor ('daktə)
= medic ('mɛdɪk)

physique (fɪ'zik) *n.* 體格

= figure ('fɪgjə)
= form (fɔrm)
= shape (ʃep)
= build (bɪld)
= body ('badɪ)
= frame (frem)

pick (pɪk) *v.* 挑選

= choose (tʃuz)
= select (sə'lɛkt)
= harvest ('harvɪst)
= gather ('gæðə)
= cull (kʌl)

P

picket ('pɪkɪt) ① *n.* 示威者
② *v.* 以柵圍護

① = strike (straɪk)
= boycott ('bɔɪ,kat)
= revolt (rɪ'volt)
② = bar (bar)
= fence (fɛns)
= wall (wɔl)
= enclose (ɪn'kloz)

pickle ('pɪkḷ) *v.* 醃

= preserve (prɪ'zɝv)
= marinate ('mærə,net)

pickpocket ('pɪk,pakɪt) *n.* 扒手

= robber ('rabɚ)

picnic ('pɪknɪk) *n.* 野餐

= feast (fist)
= outing ('autɪŋ)
= festivity (fɛs'tɪvətɪ)

picture ('pɪktʃɚ) *v.* 描繪

= represent (,rɛprɪ'zɛnt)
= illustrate ('ɪləstret , ɪ'lʌstret)
= portray (por'tre)
= depict (dɪ'pɪkt)
= describe (dɪ'skraɪb)
= characterize ('kærɪktə,raɪz)

piece (pis) *n.* 片;部分

= part (part)
= bit (bɪt)
= portion ('porʃən)
= division (də'vɪʒən)

= segment ('sɛgmənt)
= section ('sɛkʃən)
= share (ʃɛr)

pier (pɪr) *n.* 碼頭

= dock (dak)
= wharf (hwɔrf)
= breakwater ('brek,watɚ)

pierce (pɪrs) *v.* 刺透;穿

= penetrate ('pɛnə,tret)
= puncture ('pʌŋktʃɚ)
= perforate ('pɝfə,ret)
= stab (stæb)
= bore (bor)

pigment ('pɪgmənt) *n.* 顏料

= coloring ('kʌlərɪŋ)
= shade (ʃed)
= stain (sten)
= dye (daɪ)

pile (paɪl) *n.* 一堆

= heap (hip)
= stack (stæk)
= mound (maund)
= collection (kə'lɛkʃən)
= slew (slu)
= batch (bætʃ)

pilfer ('pɪlfɚ) *v.* 偷

= steal (stil)
= thieve (θiv)
= take (tek)
= filch (fɪltʃ)
= rob (rab)

P

pilgrimage ('pɪlgrəmɪdʒ) *n.* 漫遊

= journey ('dʒɝnɪ)
= trip (trɪp)
= trek (trɛk)
= expedition (ˏɛkspɪ'dɪʃən)
= crusade (kru'sed)

pillage ('pɪlɪdʒ) *v.* 搶奪

= plunder ('plʌndɚ)
= rob (rɑb)
= loot (lut)
= burglarize ('bɝglə,raɪz)

pillar ('pɪlɚ) *n.* 柱子;柱石

= column ('kɑləm)
= support (sə'port)
= shaft (ʃæft)
= monument ('mɑnjəmənt)
= post (post)

pillow ('pɪlo) *n.* 枕頭;墊子

= cushion ('kuʃən)
= headrest ('hɛd,rɛst)
= bolster ('bolstɚ)

pilot ('paɪlət) *n.* 駕駛者

= operator ('ɑpə,retɚ)
= driver ('draɪvɚ)
= engineer (ˏɛndʒə'nɪr)
= conductor (kən'dʌktɚ)

pimple ('pɪmpḷ) *n.* 腫塊

= swelling ('swɛlɪŋ)
= bump (bʌmp)
= boil (bɔɪl)

pin (pɪn) *v.* 釘住;緊握

= clasp (klæsp)
= fasten ('fæsṇ)
= hook (huk)
= clip (klɪp)

pinch (pɪntʃ) *v.* 挾;捏

= squeeze (skwiz)
= press (prɛs)
= tweak (twik)
= nip (nɪp)

pinnacle ('pɪnəkḷ) *n.* 尖峰

= peak (pik)
= crown (kraʊn)
= summit ('sʌmɪt)
= crest (krɛst)
= top (tɑp)
= spire (spaɪr)
= apex ('epɛks)
= vertex ('vɝtɛks)
= acme ('ækmi , 'ækmɪ)
= zenith ('zinɪθ)

pioneer (ˏpaɪə'nɪr) *n.* 開墾者;先鋒

= settler ('sɛtlɚ)
= leader ('lidɚ)
= colonist ('kɑlənɪst)
= forerunner ('for,rʌnɚ)

pious ('paɪəs) *adj.* 虔誠的

= religious (rɪ'lɪdʒəs)
= devout (dɪ'vaʊt)
= reverent ('rɛvərənt)
= faithful ('feθfəl)
= believing (bɪ'livɪŋ)

P

pipe (paɪp) *n.* 管筒

= tube (tjub)

= reed (rid)

= hose (hoz)

pique (pik) *v.* 激怒

= arouse (ə'raʊz)

= stir (stɜ)

= incite (ɪn'saɪt)

= instigate ('ɪnstə,get)

= agitate ('ædʒə,tet)

= inflame (ɪn'flem)

= invoke (ɪn'vok)

= excite (ɪk'saɪt)

= foment (fo'mɛnt)

= infuriate (ɪn'fjʊrɪ,et)

= exasperate (ɛg'zæspə,ret)

= annoy (ə'nɔɪ)

= anger ('æŋgɚ)

= disturb (dɪ'stɜb)

piracy ('paɪrəsɪ) *n.* 偷竊

= stealing ('stilɪŋ)

= pillaging ('pɪlɪdʒɪŋ)

= plundering ('plʌndɚɪŋ)

= looting ('lutɪŋ)

= thievery ('θivərɪ)

pistol ('pɪstl̩) *n.* 手鎗

= gun (gʌn)

= firearm ('faɪr,ɑrm)

= revolver (rɪ'valvɚ)

pit (pɪt) *n.* 坑

= hole (hol)

= cavity ('kævətɪ)

= crater ('kretɚ)

= hollow ('halo)

pitch (pɪtʃ) *v.* ①擲 ②搖擺

① = throw (θro)

= fling (flɪŋ)

= hurl (hɜl)

= toss (tɔs)

= sling (slɪŋ)

= cast (kæst)

= heave (hiv)

② = sway (swe)

= fall (fɔl)

= topple ('tapl̩)

= flounder ('flaʊndɚ)

= stagger ('stægɚ)

= rock (rak)

= roll (rol)

= reel (ril)

= lurch (lɜtʃ)

pity ('pɪtɪ) *n.* 同情

= sympathy ('sɪmpəθɪ)

= sorrow ('saro)

= compassion (kəm'pæʃən)

= mercy ('mɜsɪ)

pivot ('pɪvət) *v.* 旋轉

= turn (tɜn)

= swivel ('swɪvl̩)

= swing (swɪŋ)

= rotate ('rotet)

= wheel (hwil)

= gyrate ('dʒaɪret)

P

lacard ('plækɑrd) *n.* 公告；
告示

= poster ('postɚ)

= notice ('notɪs)

= sign (saɪn)

= billboard ('bɪl,bord)

lace (ples) *v.* 放置

= arrange (ə'rendʒ)

= fix (fɪks)

= compose (kəm'poz)

= put (pʊt)

= locate (lo'ket)

= situate ('sɪtʃʊ,et)

= set (sɛt)

= station ('steʃən)

lacid ('plæsɪd) *adj.* 安靜的；
平靜的

= calm (kɑm)

= peaceful ('pisfəl)

= quiet ('kwaɪət)

= still (stɪl)

= tranquil ('træŋkwɪl)

= smooth (smuð)

= pacific (pə'sɪfɪk)

= untroubled (ʌn'trʌbḷd)

itfall ('pɪt,fɔl) *n.* 陷阱

= trap (træp)

= snare (snɛr)

lague (pleg) ① *n.* 疾病；瘟疫
② *v.* 苦惱

= disease (dɪ'ziz)

= epidemic (,ɛpə'dɛmɪk)

= pestilence ('pɛstḷəns)

② = annoy (ə'nɔɪ)

= vex (vɛks)

= bother ('bɑðɚ)

= torment ('tɔrmɛnt)

= molest (mə'lɛst)

= trouble ('trʌbḷ)

= harass ('hærəs , hə'ræs)

= badger ('bædʒɚ)

= worry ('wɝɪ)

= pester ('pɛstɚ)

= haunt (hɑnt , hɔnt)

plain (plen) *adj.* ①明白的
②樸素的

① = clear (klɪr)

= understandable
  ('ʌndɚ'stændəbḷ)

= simple ('sɪmpḷ)

= distinct (dɪ'stɪŋkt)

= obvious ('ɑbvɪəs)

= evident ('ɛvədənt)

② = homely ('homlɪ)

= unattractive (,ʌnə'træktɪv)

= ordinary ('ɔrdṇɛrɪ)

plan (plæn) *n.* 計畫；設計

= propose (prə'poz)

= intend (ɪn'tɛnd)

= design (dɪ'zaɪn)

= mean (min)

= aim (em)

= think (θɪŋk)

= devise (dɪ'vaɪz)

= arrange (ə'rendʒ)

= plot (plɑt)

P

= scheme (skim)
= maneuver (mə'nuvɚ)
= project (prə'dʒɛkt)

plane (plen) ① *adj.* 平坦的
② *n.* 飛機

① = flat (flæt)
= level ('lɛvḷ)
= horizontal (ˌhɑrə'zɑntḷ)
= even ('ivən)
= smooth (smuð)
② = airplane ('ɛrˌplen)
= aircraft ('ɛrˌkræft)

plank (plæŋk) *n.* 厚板

= board (bɔrd , bord)
= wood (wud)

plant (plænt) *v.* 種植

= establish (ə'stæblɪʃ)
= fix (fɪks)
= root (rut)
= settle ('sɛtḷ)
= sow (so)

plastic ('plæstɪk) *adj.* 易變的；
易塑造的

= changeable ('tʃendʒəbḷ)
= variable('vɛrɪəbḷ)
= mobile ('mobɪl)
= fluid ('fluɪd)
= flexible ('flɛksəbḷ)
= pliant ('plaɪənt)
= supple ('sʌpḷ)

platform ('plætˌfɔrm) *n.*
①月臺；講台 ②黨綱

① = stage (stedʒ)
= rostrum ('rɑstrəm)
= balcony ('bælkənɪ)
② = policy ('pɑləsɪ)
= program ('progræm)
= plan (plæn)
= course (kɔrs)

plausible ('plɔzəbḷ) *adj.*
似合理的

= reasonable ('riznəbḷ)
= logical ('lɑdʒɪkḷ)
= sound (saund)
= sensible ('sɛnsəbḷ)
= believable (bɪ'livəbḷ)

playful ('plefəl) *adj.* 嬉戲的

= frisky ('frɪskɪ)
= sportive ('sportɪv)
= gay (ge)
= spirited ('spɪrɪtɪd)
= lively ('laɪvlɪ)
= animated ('ænəˌmetɪd)
= vivacious (vaɪ'veʃəs)
= frolicsome ('frɑlɪksəm)
= impish ('ɪmpɪʃ)
= mischievous ('mɪstʃɪvəs)
= devilish ('dɛvḷɪʃ , 'dɛvəlɪʃ)

plaza ('plɑzə) *n.* 大廣場

= square (skwɛr)

plea (pli) *n.* ①請求 ②辯解

① = request (rɪ'kwɛst)
= appeal (ə'pil)
= petition (pə'tɪʃən)

P

= asking ('æskɪŋ)

= excuse (ɪk'skjus)

= defense (dɪ'fɛns)

leasant ('plɛzn̩t) *adj.* 愉悅的

= pleasing ('plizɪŋ)

= enjoyable (ɪn'dʒɔɪəbl̩)

= likable ('laɪkəbl̩)

= desirable (dɪ'zaɪrəbl̩)

= agreeable (ə'griəbl̩)

= gratifying ('grætə,faɪɪŋ)

= delightful (dɪ'laɪtfəl)

= charming ('tʃɑrmɪŋ)

= appealing (ə'pilɪŋ)

= enchanting (ɪn'tʃæntɪŋ)

= cheerful ('tʃɪrfəl)

= genial ('dʒinjəl)

= happy ('hæpɪ)

= satisfying ('sætɪs,faɪɪŋ)

leat (plit) *v.* 打摺

= fold (fold)

= crease (kris)

= tuck (tʌk)

ledge (plɛdʒ) *n.* 誓言；諾言

= promise ('prɑmɪs)

= vow (vaʊ)

= oath (oθ)

= assurance (ə'ʃʊrəns)

= guarantee (,gærən'ti)

= word (wɜd)

lentiful ('plɛntɪfəl) *adj.* 豐盛的

= ample ('æmpl̩)

= enough (ə'nʌf , ɪ'nʌf)

= abundant (ə'bʌndənt)

= generous ('dʒɛnərəs)

= sufficient (sə'fɪʃənt)

= lavish ('lævɪʃ)

pliable ('plaɪəbl̩) *adj.* 易曲的

= flexible ('flɛksəbl̩)

= supple ('sʌpl̩)

= plastic ('plæstɪk)

= elastic (ɪ'læstɪk)

= yielding ('jildɪŋ)

= limber ('lɪmbɚ)

= suggestible (səg'dʒɛstəbl̩)

= compliant (kəm'plaɪənt)

plight (plaɪt) *n.* 困境

= predicament (prɪ'dɪkəmənt)

= pinch (pɪntʃ)

= complication (,kɑmplə'keʃən)

= muddle ('mʌdl̩)

= difficulty ('dɪfə,kʌltɪ)

= dilemma (də'lɛmə , daɪ'lɛmə)

plod (plɑd) *v.* 吃力地走

= trudge (trʌdʒ)

= lumber ('lʌmbɚ)

plot (plɑt) *n.* ①陰謀 ②輪廓

① = plan (plæn)

= scheme (skim)

= intrigue (ɪn'trig)

= conspire (kən'spaɪr)

= contrive (kən'traɪv)

= maneuver (mə'nuvɚ)

= concoct (kən'kɑkt)

② = outline ('aʊt,laɪn)

P

= sketch (skɛtʃ)
= graph (grɑf , græf)
= map (mæp)
= chart (tʃɑrt)
= blueprint ('blu,prɪnt)
= diagram ('daɪə,græm)

plow (plaʊ) *v.* 耕種

= cultivate ('kʌltə,vet)
= work (wɜk)
= till (tɪl)
= furrow ('fɜo)

pluck (plʌk) *v.* 急拉

= pull (pʊl)
= pick (pɪk)
= jerk (dʒɜk)
= tug (tʌg)
= yank (jæŋk)

plucky ('plʌkɪ) *adj.* 有勇氣的

= courageous (kə'redʒəs)
= spirited ('spɪrɪtɪd)
= brave (brev)
= bold (bold)
= valiant ('væljənt)
= gallant ('gælənt)
= heroic (hɪ'ro·ɪk)
= resolute ('rɛzḷ,jut)
= game (gem)
= mettlesome ('mɛtḷsəm)
= spunky ('spʌŋkɪ)
= nervy ('nɜvɪ)

plug (plʌg) *v.* 填塞

= block (blɑk)
= clog (klɔg)
= stop (stɑp)
= obstruct (əb'strʌkt)
= stuff (stʌf)
= jam (dʒæm)
= congest (kən'dʒɛst)

plump (plʌmp) *adj.* 肥胖的

= fat (fæt)
= round (raʊnd)
= stuffed (stʌft)
= stout (staʊt)
= obese (o'bis)
= fleshy ('flɛʃɪ)
= corpulent ('kɔrpjələnt)
= pudgy ('pʌdʒɪ)
= chubby ('tʃʌbɪ)
= stocky ('stɑkɪ)
= chunky ('tʃʌŋkɪ)
= tubby ('tʌbɪ)

plunder ('plʌndə) *v.* 搶奪

= rob (rɑb)
= steal (stil)
= loot (lut)
= pillage ('pɪlɪdʒ)
= fleece (flis)

plunge (plʌndʒ) *v.* 使投入；
跳入

= dive (daɪv)
= plummet ('plʌmɪt)
= drop (drɑp)
= fall (fɔl)
= *swoop down*

lush (plʌʃ) *adj.* 豪華的

= luxurious (lʌgˈʒʊrɪəs , lʌkˈʃʊr-)
= sumptuous (ˈsʌmptʃuəs)
= elegant (ˈɛləgənt)
= elaborate (ɪˈlæbəˌret)
= grand (grænd)
= magnificent (mægˈnɪfəsn̩t)
= glorious (ˈglorɪəs)
= impressive (ɪmˈprɛsɪv)
= majestic (məˈdʒɛstɪk)

ocket (ˈpakɪt) *v.* 放入袋中；
吞；佔為己有

= load (lod)
= pack (pæk)
= stow (sto)
= accept (əkˈsɛpt)
= receive (rɪˈsiv)
= take (tek)
= get (gɛt)
= acquire (əˈkwaɪr)
= *take in*

oetry (ˈpo·ətrɪ) *n.* 詩；韻文

= verse (vɝs)
= rhyme (raɪm)
= lyric (ˈlɪrɪk)
= ode (od)

oint (pɔɪnt) *v.* 指示

= direct (dəˈrɛkt)
= aim (em)
= show (ʃo)
= indicate (ˈɪndəˌket)

oised (pɔɪzd) *adj.* 鎮定的

= composed (kəmˈpozd)
= collected (kəˈlɛktɪd)
= balanced (ˈbælənst)
= confident (ˈkɑnfədənt)
= assured (əˈʃʊrd)

poisonous (ˈpɔɪznəs) *adj.*
有毒的

= toxic (ˈtɑksɪk)
= deadly (ˈdɛdlɪ)
= destructive (dɪˈstrʌktɪv)
= noxious (ˈnɑkʃəs)
= harmful (ˈhɑrmfəl)
= malignant (məˈlɪgnənt)
= venomous (ˈvɛnəməs)

poke (pok) *v.* 驅迫；衝；刺

= thrust (θrʌst)
= push (pʊʃ)
= shove (ʃʌv)
= ram (ræm)
= jab (dʒæb)
= goad (god)
= spur (spɝ)

pole (pol) *n.* 竿；柱

= bar (bar)
= rod (rad)
= shaft (ʃaft)
= post (post)
= beam (bim)
= stick (stɪk)

police (pəˈlis) *v.* 整頓；管理

= guard (gard)
= watch (watʃ)

P

= patrol (pə'trol)

= shield (ʃild)

policy ('pɑləsɪ) *n.* 政策;方針

= plan (plæn)

= program ('progræm)

= procedure (prə'sidʒə)

= course (kɔrs)

= principles ('prɪnsəplz)

= line (laɪn)

= platform ('plæt,fɔrm)

polish ('pɑlɪʃ) *v.* 磨亮;擦光

= shine (ʃaɪn)

= burnish ('bɜnɪʃ)

= gloss (glɔs)

= rub (rʌb)

= buff (bʌf)

= glaze (glez)

= wax (wæks)

= furbish ('fɜbɪʃ)

polite (pə'laɪt) *adj.* 有禮的

= refined (rɪ'faɪnd)

= courteous ('kɜtɪəs)

= civil ('sɪvḷ)

= gracious ('greʃəs)

= respectful (rɪ'spɛktfəl)

= well-mannered ('wɛl'mænəd)

= tactful ('tæktfəl)

poll (pol) *n.* 投票;民意調查

= canvass ('kænvəs)

= survey (sə've)

= vote (vot)

= questionnaire (,kwɛstʃən'ɛr)

pollute (pə'lut) *n.* 污染

= contaminate (kəm'tæmənet)

= infect (ɪn'fɛkt)

= taint (tent)

= tarnish ('tɑrnɪʃ)

= defile (dɪ'faɪl)

= foul (faʊl)

= poison ('pɔɪzṇ)

pomp (pɑmp) *n.* 壯麗

= spectacle ('spɛktəkḷ)

= display (dɪ'sple)

= sight (saɪt)

= exhibition (,ɛksə'bɪʃən)

= show (ʃo)

= pageant ('pædʒənt)

= ostentation (,ɑstən'teʃən)

= magnificence (mæg'nɪfəsṇs)

ponder ('pɑndə) *v.* 考慮

= consider (kən'sɪdə)

= contemplate ('kɑntəm,plet)

= reflect (rɪ'flɛkt)

= deliberate (dɪ'lɪbə,ret)

= meditate ('mɛdə,tet)

= muse (mjuz)

= brood (brud)

= *think over*

ponderous ('pɑndərəs) *adj.*
沈重的

= heavy ('hɛvɪ)

= clumsy ('klʌmzɪ)

= bulky ('bʌlkɪ)

= massive ('mæsɪv)

= weighty ('wetɪ)

P

= cumbersome (ˈkʌmbɚsəm)
= unwieldy (ʌnˈwildɪ)

pool (pul) ① *n.* 水塘
② *v.* 聯合

① = lake (lek)
= pond (pɑnd)
= puddle (ˈpʌdl̩)
= reservoir (ˈrɛzɚˌvɔr)
② = contribute (kənˈtrɪbjut)
= combine (kəmˈbaɪn)

poor (pʊr) *adj.* ①貧困的
②可憐的

① = needy (ˈnidɪ)
= penniless (ˈpɛnɪlɪs)
= impoverished (ɪmˈpɑvərɪʃt)
= destitute (ˈdɛstəˌtjut)
② = pitiful (ˈpɪtɪfəl)
= unfortunate (ʌnˈfɔrtʃənɪt)
= wretched (ˈrɛtʃɪd)
= miserable (ˈmɪzərəbl̩)

pop (pɑp) *v.* 發出爆裂聲

= shoot (ʃut)
= burst (bɝst)
= bang (bæŋ)
= fire (faɪr)
= crack (kræk)
= explode (ɪkˈsplod)
= detonate (ˈdɛtəˌnet)

popular (ˈpɑpjələ) *adj.*
①普遍的 ②受喜愛的

① = common (ˈkɑmən)
= usual (ˈjuʒʊəl)

= regular (ˈrɛgjələ)
= customary (ˈkʌstəmˌɛrɪ)
= ordinary (ˈɔrdnɛrɪ , ˈɔrdn̩ˌɛrɪ)
= everyday (ˈɛvrɪˈde)
= conventional (kənˈvɛnʃənl̩)
= prevalent (ˈprɛvələnt)
= traditional (trəˈdɪʃənl̩)
② = well-liked (ˈwɛlˈlaɪkt)
= dear (dɪr)
= beloved (bɪˈlʌvd)
= adored (əˈdɔrd)
= admired (ədˈmaɪrd)
= cherished (ˈtʃɛrɪʃt)
= favorite (ˈfevərɪt)
= pet (pɛt)

population (ˌpɑpjəˈleʃən) *n.*
人口;居民

= inhabitants (ɪnˈhæbətənts)
= people (ˈpipl̩)

port (pɔrt) *n.* 港口

= harbor (ˈhɑrbə)
= dock (dɑk)
= wharf (hwɔrf)
= pier (pɪr)

portable (ˈpɔrtəbl̩) *adj.*
可攜帶的

= movable (ˈmuvəbl̩)
= transferable (trænsˈfɝəbl̩)
= conveyable (kənˈveəbl̩)

portal (ˈpɔrtl̩) *n.* 大門;正門

= door (dɔr)
= gate (get)

P

= entrance ('ɛntrəns)

= threshold ('θrɛʃold , 'θrɛʃhold)

portent ('pɔrtɛnt , 'pɔr-) *n.*
徵兆

= forewarning (for'wɔrnɪŋ)

= omen ('omən , 'omɪn)

= sign (saɪn)

= premonition (,primə'nɪʃən)

portion ('pɔrʃən) *n.* 部分

= part (part)

= share (ʃɛr)

= division (də'vɪʒən)

= segment ('sɛgmənt)

= section ('sɛkʃən)

= fraction ('frækʃən)

= fragment ('frægmənt)

= piece (pis)

portly ('pɔrtlɪ) *adj.* ①肥胖的
②莊嚴的

① = stout (staʊt)

= fat (fæt)

= obese (o'bis)

= plump (plʌmp)

= pudgy ('pʌdʒɪ)

= stocky ('stakɪ)

= chubby ('tʃʌbɪ)

= heavyset ('hɛvɪ'sɛt)

② = dignified ('dɪgnə,faɪd)

= stately ('stetlɪ)

= imposing (ɪm'pozɪŋ)

= grand (grænd)

= noble ('nobḷ)

= majestic (mə'dʒɛstɪk)

portray (pɔr'tre) *v.* 描繪

= represent (,rɛprɪ'zɛnt)

= picture ('pɪktʃɚ)

= depict (dɪ'pɪkt)

= illustrate (ɪ'lʌstret , 'ɪləstret)

= characterize ('kærɪktə,raɪz)

= impersonate (ɪm'pɜsn̩,et)

= describe (dɪ'skraɪb)

pose (poz) *n.* ①姿勢　②偽裝

① = posture ('pastʃɚ)

= position (pə'zɪʃən)

= bearing ('bɛrɪŋ)

= carriage ('kærɪdʒ)

② = pretense (prɪ'tɛns)

position (pə'zɪʃən) *n.* ①位置
②職位

① = place (ples)

= location (lo'keʃən)

= situation (,sɪtʃʊ'eʃən)

= spot (spat)

② = job (dʒab)

= duty ('djutɪ)

= function ('fʌŋkʃən)

= role (rol)

= office ('ɔfɪs , 'afɪs)

= capacity (kə'pæsətɪ)

= situation (,sɪtʃʊ'eʃən)

= post (post)

positive ('pazətɪv) *adj.* 確實的

= sure (ʃʊr)

= definite ('dɛfənɪt)

= certain ('sɜtn̩)

= absolute ('æbsə,lut)

= convinced (kən'vɪnst)

= assured (ə'ʃʊrd)

possess (pə'zɛs) v. 擁有;具有

= own (on)

= have (hæv)

= hold (hold)

= control (kən'trol)

= maintain (mən'ten , men'ten)

= occupy ('akjə,paɪ)

possible ('pasəbḷ) adj. 可能的

= likely ('laɪklɪ)

= conceivable (kən'sivəbḷ)

= imaginable (ɪ'mædʒɪnəbḷ)

= feasible ('fizəbḷ)

= probable ('prabəbḷ)

= credible ('krɛdəbḷ)

= achievable (ə'tʃivəbḷ)

= attainable (ə'tenəbḷ)

= plausible ('plɔzəbḷ)

post (post) ① v. 公布
② n. 職位

① = list (lɪst)

= schedule ('skɛdʒʊl)

= notify ('notəfaɪ)

= inform (ɪn'fɔrm)

② = position (pə'zɪʃən)

= situation (sɪtʃʊ'eʃən)

= office ('ɔfɪs)

= duty ('djutɪ)

= job (dʒab)

postpone (post'pon) v. 拖延

= delay (dɪ'le)

= defer (dɪ'fɜ)

= suspend (sə'spɛnd)

= shelve (ʃɛlv)

= stall (stɔl)

= procrastinate (pro'kræstə,net)

= table ('tebḷ)

= *put off*

= *hold over*

posture ('pastʃɚ) n. 姿勢

= position (pə'zɪʃən)

= carriage ('kærɪdʒ)

= bearing ('bɛrɪŋ)

potent ('potṇt) adj. 有力的

= powerful ('pauɚfəl)

= strong (strɔŋ)

= forceful ('fɔrsfəl)

= mighty ('maɪtɪ)

potential (pə'tɛnʃəl) adj.
可能的;有潛力的

= possible ('pasəbḷ)

= promising ('pramɪsɪŋ)

= hidden ('hɪdṇ)

= likely ('laɪklɪ)

= conceivable (kən'sivəbḷ)

potion ('poʃən) n. (藥之)
一服;飲料

= drink (drɪŋk)

= dose (dos)

pouch (pautʃ) n. 小包

= sack (sæk)

= bag (bæg)

P

pounce (pauns) v. 跳躍

= jump (dʒʌmp)

= swoop (swup)

= leap (lip)

= spring (sprɪŋ)

= hop (hɑp)

= bound (baund)

= hurdle ('hɜdl̩)

= vault (vɔlt)

= plunge (plʌndʒ)

= dive (daɪv)

pound (paund) v. 打擊

= beat (bit)

= strike (straɪk)

= knock (knɑk)

= hit (hɪt)

= hammer ('hæmə)

= rap (ræp)

= bang (bæŋ)

= batter ('bætə)

= drum (drʌm)

pour (pɔr) v. 灌;澆

= drain (dren)

= stream (strim)

= spill (spɪl)

= spew (spju)

= *flow out*

pout (paut) v. 不悅;憂慮

= sulk (sʌlk)

= mope (mop)

= fret (frɛt)

= frown (fraun)

= scowl (skaul)

powder ('paudə) v. 撒;灑

= sprinkle ('sprɪŋkl̩)

= dust (dʌst)

= spatter ('spætə)

power ('pauə) n. 力量

= strength (strɛŋθ)

= might (maɪt)

= force (fɔrs)

= vigor ('vɪgə)

= energy ('ɛnədʒɪ)

= potency ('potn̩sɪ)

= authority (ə'θɔrətɪ)

= right (raɪt)

= control (kən'trol)

= influence ('ɪnfluəns)

= command (kə'mænd)

= dominion (də'mɪnjən)

= mastery ('mæstərɪ , 'mɑs-)

practically ('præktɪkl̩ɪ) adv.
①有益地 ②幾乎

① = usefully ('jusfəlɪ)

= profitably ('prɑfɪtəblɪ)

= advantageously
(ˌædvən'tedʒəslɪ)

② = almost (ɔl'most)

= about (ə'baut)

= nearly ('nɪrlɪ)

= really ('riəlɪ , 'rɪəlɪ , 'rɪlɪ)

= essentially (ə'sɛnʃəlɪ)

= fundamentally (ˌfʌndə'mɛntl̩ɪ)

= basically ('besɪkəlɪ)

practice ('præktɪs) v. 練習

= repeat (rɪ'pit)

P

= train (tren)

= drill (drɪl)

= exercise ('ɛksə,saɪz)

= prepare (prɪ'pɛr)

= condition (kən'dɪʃən)

= rehearse (rɪ'hɜs)

praise (prez) v. 讚美

= compliment ('kɑmpləmənt)

= extol (ɪk'stɑl , -'stol , ɛk-)

= commend (kə'mɛnd)

= laud (lɔd)

= glorify ('glorə,faɪ)

= flatter ('flætə)

= *approve of*

prance (præns , prɑns) v. 漫步

= romp (rɑmp)

= stroll (strol)

= saunter ('sɔntə , 'sɑn-)

= strut (strʌt)

= promenade (,prɑmə'ned , -'nɑd)

= bounce (bauns)

= swagger ('swægə)

prank (præŋk) n. 惡作劇

= mischief ('mɪstʃɪf)

= caper ('kepə)

= antic ('æntɪk)

= whim (hwɪm)

= caprice (kə'pris)

= trick (trɪk)

prattle ('prætl̩) v. 閒談

= babble ('bæbl̩)

= blab (blæb)

= chatter ('tʃætə)

= jabber ('dʒæbə)

pray (pre) v. 祈求

= appeal (ə'pil)

= beseech (bɪ'sitʃ)

= beg (bɛg)

= entreat (ɪn'trit)

= implore (ɪm'plor)

= petition (pə'tɪʃən)

= plead (plid)

preach (pritʃ) v. 說教

= advise (əd'vaɪz)

= expound (ɪk'spaund)

= lecture ('lɛktʃə)

= sermonize ('sɜmən,aɪz)

= urge (ɜdʒ)

precarious (prɪ'kɛrɪəs) adj. 危險的

= dangerous ('dendʒərəs)

= unsafe (ʌn'sef)

= uncertain (ʌn'sɜtn̩)

= hazardous ('hæzədəs)

= critical ('krɪtɪkl̩)

= ticklish ('tɪklɪʃ)

= touchy ('tʌtʃɪ)

= delicate ('dɛləkət , -kɪt)

= unsure (ʌn'ʃur)

= unsound (ʌn'saund)

= shaky ('ʃekɪ)

precaution (prɪ'kɔʃən) n. 預防

= forewarning (for'wɔrnɪŋ)

= notification (,notəfə'keʃən)

P

precede (pri'sid , prɪ-) *v.*
在前；在先

= lead (lid)
= head (hɛd)
= forerun (for'rʌn)
= *come first*

precept ('prisɛpt) *n.* 箴言

= rule (rul)
= saying ('seɪŋ)
= belief (bɪ'lif)
= axiom ('æksɪəm)
= principle ('prɪnsəpl)
= proposition (,prɑpə'zɪʃən)

precinct ('prisɪŋkt) *n.* 區域

= district ('dɪstrɪkt)
= boundary ('baʊndrɪ , -dərɪ)
= limit ('lɪmɪt)
= community (kə'mjunətɪ)
= vicinity (və'sɪnətɪ)
= neighborhood ('nebɚ,hʊd)

precious ('prɛʃəs) *adj.* 珍貴的

= adored (ə'dɔrd)
= valuable ('væljuəbl)
= cherished ('tʃɛrɪʃt)
= expensive (ɪk'spɛnsɪv)
= admired (əd'maɪrd)
= prized ('praɪzd)
= special ('spɛʃəl)
= costly ('kɔstlɪ)
= dear (dɪr)
= loved (lʌvd)
= priceless (,pælə'sed)

precipice ('prɛsəpɪs) *n.* 懸崖

= bluff (blʌf)
= cliff (klɪf)
= slope (slop)
= palisade (,pælə'sed)

precipitation (prɪ,sɪpə'teʃən)
n. ①雨；雪 ②慌忙

① = rain (ren)
= snow (sno)
= moisture ('mɔɪstʃɚ)
② = haste (hest)
= speed (spid)
= impetuousness (ɪm'pɛtʃuəsnɪs)
= impulsiveness (ɪm'pʌlsɪvnɪs)
= rashness ('ræʃnɪs)

precise (prɪ'saɪs) *adj.* 正確的

= exact (ɪg'zækt)
= accurate ('ækjərɪt)
= definite ('dɛfənɪt)
= positive ('pɑzətɪv)
= strict (strɪkt)
= careful ('kɛrfəl)
= absolute ('æbsə,lut)
= meticulous (mə'tɪkjələs)
= detailed (dɪ'teld)
= explicit (ɪk'splɪsɪt)
= clear-cut ('klɪr'kʌt)

preclude (prɪ'klud) *v.* 妨礙

= forbid (fɚ'bɪd)
= bar (bɑr)
= prohibit (pro'hɪbɪt)
= deter (dɪ'tɝ)
= prevent (prɪ'vɛnt)

P

= exclude (ɪk'sklud)
= *shut out*

recocious (prɪ'koʃəs) *adj.*
早熟的

= advanced (əd'vænst)
= forward ('fɔrwəd)
= premature ('primə,tʃʊr ,
,primə'tjʊr)

redecessor ('prɛdɪ,sɛsə) *n.*
前輩；祖先

= leader ('lidə)
= forerunner ('fɔr,rʌnə)

redicament (prɪ'dɪkəmənt)
n. 困窘；困境

= mess (mɛs)
= complication (,kamplə'keʃən)
= plight (plaɪt)
= embarrassment
  (ɪm'bærəsmənt)
= pinch (pɪntʃ)
= dilemma (də'lɛmə)

redict (prɪ'dɪkt) *v.* 預測；預言

= foresee (fɔr'si)
= foretell (fɔr'tɛl)
= prophesy ('prafə,saɪ)
= divine (də'vaɪn)
= forecast (fɔr'kæst)
= portend (pɔr'tɛnd)

redominant (prɪ'damənənt)
adj. 主要的

= chief (tʃif)

= superior (sə'pɪrɪə)
= main (men)
= principal ('prɪnsəpl)
= leading ('lidɪŋ)
= foremost ('fɔr,most)

preface ('prɛfɪs) *n.* 序文；開端

= introduction (,ɪntrə'dʌkʃən)
= preamble (prɪ'æmbl)
= foreward ('fɔrwɜd)
= preliminary (prɪ'lɪmə,nɛrɪ)

prefer (prɪ'fɝ) *v.* 較喜愛

= choose (tʃuz)
= favor ('fevə)
= desire (dɪ'zaɪr)
= fancy ('fænsɪ)
= pick (pɪk)
= select (sə'lɛkt)

pregnant ('prɛgnənt) *adj.*
懷孕的；豐富的

= productive (prə'dʌktɪv)
= fertile ('fɝtl)
= full (fʊl)

prejudiced ('prɛdʒədɪst) *adj.*
有偏見的

= biased ('baɪəst)
= opinionated (ə'pɪnjən,etɪd)
= partial ('parʃəl)
= influenced ('ɪnfluənst)

preliminary (prɪ'lɪmə,nɛrɪ)
adj. 初步的

= prior ('praɪə)
= preceding (prɪ'sidɪŋ)

P

premature (ˌprimə'tjʊr) *adj.*
太早的

= early ('ɜlɪ)
= advanced (əd'vænst)
= forward ('fɔrwəd)
= hasty ('hestɪ)
= *too soon*

premeditated (prɪ'mɛdə,tetɪd)
adj. 事先計畫的

= calculated ('kælkjə,letɪd)
= planned (plænd)
= forethought ('for,θɔt , 'fɔr-)
= intended (ɪn'tɛndɪd)
= plotted ('platɪd)
= meant (mɛnt)
= deliberate (dɪ'lɪbərɪt)

prepare (prɪ'pɛr) *v.* 準備

= equip (ɪ'kwɪp)
= compose (kəm'poz)
= concoct (kan'kakt)
= provide (prə'vaɪd)
= arrange (ə'rendʒ)
= plan (plæn)
= fix (fɪks)
= rig (rɪg)
= ready ('rɛdɪ)

preposterous (prɪ'pastərəs)
adj. 荒謬的

= absurd (əb'sɜd)
= senseless ('sɛnslɪs)
= foolish ('fulɪʃ)
= ridiculous (rɪ'dɪkjələs)
= nonsensical (nan'sɛnsɪkḷ)

= crazy ('krezɪ)
= outrageous (aʊt'redʒəs)
= unreasonable (ʌn'riznəbḷ ,
  ʌn'riznəbḷ)
= silly ('sɪlɪ)

prescribe (prɪ'skraɪb) *v.* 指定

= advocate ('ædvə,ket)
= order ('ɔrdə)
= direct (də'rɛkt , daɪ-)
= assign (ə'saɪn)
= advise (əd'vaɪz)
= recommend (ˌrɛkə'mɛnd)
= suggest (sə'dʒɛst)

presence ('prɛzṇs) *n.* 出席;
在場

= attendance (ə'tɛndəns)
= being ('biɪŋ)
= existence (ɪg'zɪstəns)
= occurrence (ə'kɜəns)
= appearance (ə'pɪrəns)

present (prɪ'zɛnt) *v.* 給;提出

= give (gɪv)
= offer ('ɔfə , 'afə)
= tender ('tɛndə)
= submit (səb'mɪt)
= extend (ɪk'stɛnd)
= donate ('donet)
= bestow (bɪ'sto)
= grant (grænt)
= deliver (dɪ'lɪvə)
= award (ə'wɔrd)
= *hand over*

P

resently ('prɛzn̩tlɪ) *adv.*
I刻地

= shortly ('ʃɔrtlɪ)
= soon (sun)
= directly (də'rɛktlɪ)
= *before long*

reserve (prɪ'zɜv) *v.* 保護；
保存

= protect (prə'tɛkt)
= keep (kip)
= maintain (mən'ten)
= guard (gɑrd)
= defend (dɪ'fɛnd)
= save (sev)
= shelter ('ʃɛltə)
= shield (ʃild)
= screen (skrin)
= harbor ('hɑrbə)
= uphold (ʌp'hold)
= support (sə'port)
= reserve (rɪ'zɜv)
= conserve (kən'sɜv)
= sustain (sə'sten)
= retain (rɪ'ten)

reside (prɪ'zaɪd) *v.* 管理

= direct (də'rɛkt)
= administer (əd'mɪnəstə)
= officiate (ə'fɪʃɪˌet)
= govern ('gʌvən)

ress (prɛs) *v.* ①按；壓
②力勸 ③壓平

① = push (puʃ)
= force (fɔrs)

= squeeze (skwiz)
= clasp (klæsp)
= tighten ('taɪtn̩)
② = urge (ɜdʒ)
= insist (ɪn'sɪst)
= coax (koks)
= goad (god)
= prod (prɑd)
= stress (strɛs)
③ = iron ('aɪən)
= smooth (smuð)

pressing ('prɛsɪŋ) *adj.* 迫急的

= urgent ('ɜdʒənt)
= compelling (kəm'pɛlɪŋ)
= crucial ('kruʃəl)
= neccessary ('nɛsəˌsɛrɪ)
= driving ('draɪvɪŋ)

pressure ('prɛʃə) *n.* ①壓力
②壓迫；強制

① = weight (wet)
= force (fɔrs , fors)
= load (lod)
= burden ('bɜdn̩)
② = influence ('ɪnfluəns)
= power ('pauə)
= effect (ɪ'fɛkt)
= domination (dɑmə'neʃən)

prestige ('prɛstɪdʒ , prɛs'tiʒ) *n.*
威望

= importance (ɪm'pɔrtn̩s)
= greatness ('gretnɪs)
= distinction (dɪ'stɪŋkʃən)
= prominence ('prɑmənəns)

P

= significance (sɪg'nɪfəkəns)

= superiority (sə,pɪrɪ'ɔrətɪ)

= mastery ('mæstərɪ , 'mas-)

= power ('pauɚ)

= influence ('ɪnfluəns)

= authority (ə'θɔrətɪ)

presume (prɪ'zum) v. 假定

= suppose (sə'poz)

= assume (ə'sjum)

= surmise (sɝ'maɪz)

= guess (gɛs)

= think (θɪŋk)

= imagine (ɪ'mædʒɪn)

= fancy ('fænsɪ)

= imply (ɪm'plaɪ)

= infer (ɪn'fɝ)

presumptuous
(prɪ'zʌmptʃuəs) adj. 大膽的

= daring ('dɛrɪŋ)

= bold (bold)

= arrogant ('ærəgənt)

= insolent ('ɪnsələnt)

= brazen ('brezn̩)

pretend (prɪ'tɛnd) v. 佯裝

= act (ækt)

= feign (fen)

= bluff (blʌf)

= sham (ʃæm)

= fake (fek)

= *make believe*

pretentious (prɪ'tɛnʃəs) adj.
矯飾的

= showy ('ʃoɪ)

= ostentatious (,ɑstən'teʃəs ,
-tɛn-)

= flashy ('flæʃɪ)

= fancy ('fænsɪ)

= affected (ə'fɛktɪd)

pretext ('pritɛkst) n. 藉口

= pretense (prɪ'tɛns)

= excuse (ɪk'skjus)

= cover ('kʌvɚ)

= sham (ʃæm)

pretty ('prɪtɪ) adj. 漂亮的

= attractive (ə'træktɪv)

= lovely ('lʌvlɪ)

= beautiful ('bjutəfəl)

= handsome ('hænsəm)

= good-looking ('gud'lukɪŋ)

prevalent ('prɛvələnt) adj.
普遍的

= widespread ('waɪd'sprɛd)

= common ('kɑmən)

= fashionable ('fæʃənəbl̩)

= popular ('pɑpjəlɚ)

= customary ('kʌstəm,ɛrɪ)

= current ('kɝənt)

= standard ('stædɚd)

= usual ('juʒuəl)

= general ('dʒɛnərəl)

= universal (,junə'vɝsl̩)

= well-known ('wɛl'non)

prevent (prɪ'vɛnt) v. 阻礙

= prohibit (pro'hɪbɪt)

P

= forbid〔fə'bɪd〕
= deter〔dɪ'tɜ〕
= preclude〔prɪ'klud〕
= stop〔stɑp〕
= block〔blɑk〕
= thwart〔θwɔrt〕
= inhibit〔ɪn'hɪbɪt〕
= hinder〔'hɪndɚ〕
= *keep from*

revious〔'prɪvɪəs〕*adj.* 在前的
= prior〔'praɪɚ〕
= earlier〔'ɜlɪɚ〕
= former〔'fɔrmɚ〕
= preceding〔prɪ'sidɪŋ〕
= one-time〔'wʌn,taɪm〕

rice〔praɪs〕*n.* 價格
= cost〔kɔst〕
= value〔'væljʊ〕
= amount〔ə'maʊnt〕
= rate〔ret〕
= charge〔tʃɑrdʒ〕
= worth〔wɜθ〕
= expense〔ɪk'spɛns〕

riceless〔'praɪslɪs〕*adj.* 無價的
= valuable〔'væljəbḷ〕
= invaluable〔ɪn'væljəbḷ〕
= precious〔'prɛʃəs〕
= dear〔dɪr〕
= expensive〔ɪk'spɛnsɪv〕
= costly〔'kɔstlɪ〕

rickly〔'prɪklɪ〕*adj.* 刺痛的
= sharp〔ʃɑrp〕

= stinging〔'stɪŋɪŋ〕
= tingly〔'tɪŋglɪ〕

pride〔praɪd〕*n.* 自負；自尊
= self-respect〔,sɛlfrɪ'spɛkt〕
= self-esteem〔,sɛlfə'stim〕
= dignity〔'dɪgnətɪ〕
= vanity〔'vænətɪ〕
= egotism〔'igə,tɪzəm , 'ɛg-〕

prim〔prɪm〕*adj.* 一本正經的；
呆板的
= neat〔nit〕
= proper〔'prɑpɚ〕
= precise〔prɪ'saɪs〕
= prudish〔'prudɪʃ〕
= overmodest〔'ovɚ'mɑdɪst〕
= strait-laced〔'stret'lest〕
= puritanical〔,pjʊrə'tænɪkḷ〕
= formal〔'fɔrmḷ〕
= stiff〔stɪf〕
= stuffy〔'stʌfɪ〕

primary〔'praɪ,mɛrɪ , -mərɪ〕
adj. 首要的；初步的
= first〔fɜst〕
= important〔ɪm'pɔrtṇt〕
= chief〔tʃif〕
= main〔men〕
= principal〔'prɪnsəpḷ〕
= leading〔'lidɪŋ〕
= dominant〔'dɑmənənt〕
= essential〔ə'sɛnʃəl〕
= basic〔'besɪk〕
= fundamental〔,fʌndə'mɛntḷ〕
= foremost〔'for,most , 'fɔr-〕
= paramount〔'pærə,maʊnt〕

P

primitive ('prɪmətɪv) *adj.*
①原始的 ②簡單的

① = ancient ('enʃənt)
= original (ə'rɪdʒənl̩)
= prehistoric (,priɪs'tɔrɪk ,
,prihɪs-)
= uncivilized (ʌn'sɪvl̩,aɪzd)
= barbarous ('barbərəs)
= native ('netɪv)
② = simple ('sɪmpl̩)
= basic ('besɪk)
= fundamental (,fʌndə'mɛntl̩)
= elementary (,ɛlə'mɛntərɪ)
= beginning (bɪ'gɪnɪŋ)

principal ('prɪnsəpl̩) *adj.*
首要的

= chief (tʃif)
= main (men)
= important (ɪm'pɔrtn̩t)
= leading ('lidɪŋ)
= dominant ('damənənt)
= foremost ('for,most , 'fɔr-)
= primary ('praɪ,mɛrɪ , -mərɪ)
= head (hɛd)
= prominent ('pramənənt)
= essential (ə'sɛnʃəl)

principle ('prɪnsəpl̩) *n.* 原理；
眞諦

= rule (rul)
= law (lɔ)
= standard ('stændəd)
= belief (bɪ'lif)
= dogma ('dɔgmə)
= doctrine ('daktrɪn)
= truth (truθ)

print (prɪnt) *v.* ①印於 ②出版

① = stamp (stæmp)
= impress (ɪm'prɛs)
= mark (mark)
= etch (ɛtʃ)
= engrave (ɪn'grev)
② = publish ('pʌblɪʃ)
= issue ('ɪʃu , 'ɪʃju)
= publicize ('pʌblɪ,saɪz)
= *put out*

prior ('praɪə) *adj.* 較早的

= earlier ('ɝlɪə)
= before (bɪ'for , bɪ'fɔr)
= previous ('privɪəs)
= former ('fɔrmə)

prison ('prɪzn̩) *n.* 監牢

= jail (dʒel)
= penitentiary (,pɛnə'tɛnʃərɪ ,
-'tɛntʃərɪ)
= reformatory (rɪ'fɔrmə,torɪ ,
-,tɔrɪ)
= *penal institution*

privacy ('praɪvəsɪ) *n.* 秘密；
隱居

= secrecy ('sikrəsɪ)
= seclusion (sɪ'kluʒən)
= intimacy ('ɪntəməsɪ)
= retreat (rɪ'trit)
= hideaway ('haɪdə,we)
= sanctum ('sæŋktəm)
= cloister ('klɔɪstə)
= withdrawal (wɪð'drɔəl , wɪθ-)
= isolation (,aɪsl̩'eʃən , ,ɪsə-)
= solitude ('salə,tjud)

privilege ('prɪvḷɪdʒ) *n.* 特權

= advantage (əd'væntɪdʒ)
= license ('laɪsn̩s)
= favor ('fevɚ)
= liberty ('lɪbɚtɪ)
= freedom ('fridəm)
= grant (grænt)

prize (praɪz) ① *n.* 獎品
② *v.* 重視

= reward (rɪ'wɔrd)
= award (ə'wɔrd)
= treasure ('trɛʒɚ)
= value ('vælju)
= appreciate (ə'priʃɪˌet)
= hold (hold)
= dear (dɪr)
= cherish ('tʃɛrɪʃ)
= adore (ə'dor , ə'dɔr)
= idolize ('aɪdḷˌaɪz)
= worship ('wɜʃəp)
= respect (rɪ'spɛkt)
= revere (rɪ'vɪr)

probable ('prɑbəbḷ) *adj.* 可能的

= likely ('laɪklɪ)
= liable ('laɪəbḷ)
= apt (æpt)
= presumable (prɪ'zuməbḷ)
= promising ('prɑmɪsɪŋ)
= hopeful ('hopfəl)

probation (pro'beʃən) *n.* 試驗

= test (tɛst)
= trial ('traɪəl)
= try (traɪ)

= check (tʃɛk)

probe (prob) *v.* 探求

= examine (ɪg'zæmɪn)
= investigate (ɪn'vɛstəˌget)
= search (sɝtʃ)
= explore (ɪk'splor , -'splɔr)

problem ('prɑbləm , -lɛm) *n.* 問題

= issue ('ɪʃu , 'ɪʃju)
= question ('kwɛstʃən)
= mystery ('mɪstrɪ , 'mɪstərɪ)
= enigma (ɪ'nɪgmə)
= puzzle ('pʌzḷ)
= perplexity (pɚ'plɛksətɪ)
= conundrum (kə'nʌndrəm)

procedure (prə'sidʒɚ) *n.* 程序

= process ('prɑsɛs , 'prosɛs)
= course (kors , kɔrs)
= measure ('mɛʒɚ)
= custom ('kʌstəm)
= practice ('præktɪs)
= rule (rul)
= policy ('pɑləsɪ)
= plan (plæn)
= method ('mɛθəd)
= way (we)
= manner ('mænɚ)
= means (minz)

proceed (prə'sid) *v.* 進行

= progress (prə'grɛs)
= advance (əd'væns)
= *go forward*
= *go ahead*

P

proceeds ('prosidz) *n.* 收入

= receipts (rɪ'sits)

= income ('ɪn,kʌm , 'ɪŋ,kʌm)

= profits ('prɑfɪts)

= earnings ('ɜnɪŋz)

= returns (rɪ'tɜnz)

process ('prɑsɛs , 'prosɛs) *n.* 手續;方法

= operation (,ɑpə'reʃən)

= procedure (prə'sidʒɚ)

= course (kors , kɔrs)

= step (stɛp)

= act (ækt)

= way (we)

= manner ('mænɚ)

= means (minz)

= mode (mod)

proclaim (pro'klem) *v.* 宣布

= declare (dɪ'klɛr)

= announce (ə'naʊns)

= herald ('hɛrəld)

= publicize ('pʌblɪ,saɪz)

= voice (vɔɪs)

= advertise ('ædvɚ,taɪz)

procure (pro'kjʊr) *v.* 取得;採購

= obtain (əb'ten)

= get (gɛt)

= acquire (ə'kwaɪr)

= secure (sɪ'kjʊr)

= purchase ('pɜtʃəs , -ɪs)

= buy (baɪ)

prod (prɑd) *v.* 刺;刺激;驅使

= poke (pok)

= jab (dʒæb)

= goad (god)

= stir (stɜ)

= thrust (θrʌst)

= ram (ræm)

= drive (draɪv)

= butt (bʌt)

prodigal ('prɑdɪgḷ) *adj.* 浪費的

= wasteful ('westfəl)

= lavish ('lævɪʃ)

= extravagant (ɪk'strævəgənt)

= spendthrift ('spɛnd,θrɪft , 'spɛn,θrɪft)

= squandering ('skwɑndərɪŋ)

prodigious (prə'dɪdʒəs) *adj.* ①很大的 ②奇異的

① = great (gret)

= huge (hjudʒ)

= vast (væst , vɑst)

= immense (ɪ'mɛns)

= stupendous (stju'pɛndəs)

= enormous (ɪ'nɔrməs)

= colossal (kə'lɑsḷ)

= mammoth ('mæməθ)

= gigantic (dʒaɪ'gæntɪk)

② = wonderful ('wʌndɚfəl)

= marvelous ('marvḷəs)

= miraculous (mə'rækjələs)

= extraordinary (ɪk'strɔrdṇ,ɛrɪ)

= remarkable (rɪ'markəbḷ)

= exceptional (ɪk'sɛpʃənḷ)

P

rodigy (ˈprodədʒɪ) *n.*
丁驚的事物；天才

= marvel (ˈmɑrvḷ)
= wonder (ˈwʌndə)
= miracle (ˈmɪrəkḷ)
= phenomenon (fəˈnɑməˌnɑn)
= rarity (ˈrɛrətɪ)
= curiosity (ˌkjurɪˈɑsətɪ)
= genius (ˈdʒinjəs)
= first-rater (ˌfɜstˈretə)

roductive (prəˈdʌktɪv) *adj.*
沃的；多產的

= fruitful (ˈfrutfəl)
= fertile (ˈfɜtḷ)
= yielding (ˈjildɪŋ)
= prolific (prəˈlɪfɪk)
= creative (krɪˈetɪv)
= inventive (ɪnˈvɛntɪv)
= gainful (ˈgenfəl)
= profitable (ˈprɑfɪtəbḷ)

rofanity (prəˈfænətɪ) *n.* 不敬

= swearing (ˈswɛrɪŋ)
= cursing (ˈkɜsɪŋ)

rofess (prəˈfɛs) *v.* 聲稱

= claim (klem)
= allege (əˈlɛdʒ)
= maintain (menˈten , mənˈten)
= contend (kənˈtɛnd)

rofessional (prəˈfɛʃənḷ) *adj.*
業的

= occupational (ˌɑkjəˈpeʃənḷ)
= vocational (voˈkeʃənḷ)

proficient (prəˈfɪʃənt) *adj.*
精通的

= skilled (skɪld)
= expert (ɪkˈspɜt , ˈɛkspɜt)
= adept (əˈdɛpt , ˈædɛpt)
= apt (æpt)
= clever (ˈklɛvə)
= masterful (ˈmæstəfəl , ˈmɑs-)
= ingenious (ɪnˈdʒinjəs)
= deft (dɛft)
= effective (əˈfɛktɪv , ɪ-)
= competent (ˈkɑmpətənt)
= crack (kræk)

profit (ˈprɑfɪt) *n.* 利益

= gain (gen)
= benefit (ˈbɛnəfɪt)
= advantage (ədˈvæntɪdʒ)
= earnings (ˈɜnɪŋz)
= proceeds (ˈprosidz)
= returns (rɪˈtɜnz)
= receipts (rɪˈsits)

profound (prəˈfaʊnd) *adj.*
極深的

= deep (dip)
= great (gret)
= extreme (ɪkˈstrim)
= intense (ɪnˈtɛns)
= serious (ˈsɪrɪəs)

profuse (prəˈfjus) *adj.* 浪費的；
很多的

= lavish (ˈlævɪʃ)
= extravagant (ɪkˈstrævəgənt)
= abundant (əˈbʌndənt)

P

= generous ('dʒɛnərəs)

= liberal ('lıbərəl)

= free (fri)

= unsparing (ʌn'spɛrıŋ)

= bountiful ('bauntəfəl)

= bighearted ('bıg,hartıd)

= magnanimous (mæg'nænəməs)

= prodigal ('pradıgḷ)

program ('progræm) *n.* 節目;
計畫;節目表

= schedule ('skɛdʒul)

= plan (plæn)

= list (lıst)

= prospectus (prə'spɛktəs , pra-)

= bill (bıl)

= calendar ('kæləndə , 'kælın-)

progress (prə'grɛs) *v.* 進行

= advance (əd'væns)

= proceed (prə'sid)

= move (muv)

= *go ahead*

prohibit (pro'hıbıt) *v.* 禁止

= forbid (fə'bıd)

= bar (bar)

= ban (bæn)

= disallow (,dısə'lau)

= veto ('vito)

= deny (dı'naı)

= prevent (prı'vɛnt)

= deter (dı'tɝ)

= thwart (θwɔrt)

= restrict (rı'strıkt)

= foil (fɔıl)

1. **project** ('pradʒɛkt) *n.* 計畫

= plan (plæn)

= scheme (skim)

= proposal (prə'pozḷ)

= plot (plat)

= design (dı'zaın)

= intention (ın'tɛnʃən)

= undertaking (,ʌndə'tekıŋ)

= enterprise ('ɛntə,praız)

= venture ('vɛntʃə)

2. **project** (prə'dʒɛkt) *v.* ①突出
②投影

①= protrude (pro'trud)

= bulge (bʌldʒ)

= *stick out*

②= show (ʃo)

= screen (skrin)

prolific (prə'lıfık) *adj.* 多產的

= productive (prə'dʌktıv)

= rich (rıtʃ)

= plentiful ('plɛntıfəl)

= fruitful ('frutfəl)

= creative (krı'etıv)

prolong (prə'lɔŋ , -'laŋ) *v.* 延

= extend (ık'stɛnd)

= stretch (strɛtʃ)

= lengthen ('lɛŋkθən , 'lɛŋθ-)

= elongate (ı'lɔŋget)

= *drag out*

prominent ('pramənənt) *adj.*
顯著的

= important (ım'pɔrtṇt)

= outstanding (aʊt'stændɪŋ)
= distinguished (dɪ'stɪŋgwɪʃt)
= great (gret)
= eminent ('ɛmənənt)
= famous ('feməs)
= popular ('pɑpjələ)
= well-known ('wɛl'non)
= celebrated ('sɛlə,bretɪd)

romiscuous (prə'mɪskjʊəs)
i. 雜亂的

= indiscriminate
  (,ɪndɪ'skrɪmənɪt)
= uncritical (ʌn'krɪtɪkḷ)
= loose (lus)
= mixed (mɪkst)
= combined (kəm'baɪnd)
= scrambled ('skræmbḷd)
= unorganized (ʌn'ɔrgən,aɪzd)
= haphazard ('hæp'hæzəd)
= random ('rændəm)

omising ('prɑmɪsɪŋ) *adj.*
希望的

= hopeful ('hopfəl)
= encouraging (ɪn'kɝɪdʒɪŋ , ɛn-)
= favorable ('fevərəbḷ)
= probable ('prɑbəbḷ)
= likely ('laɪklɪ)

omotion (prə'moʃən) *n.*
豎

= advancement (əd'vænsmənt)
= forwarding ('fɔrwədɪŋ)
= improvement (ɪm'pruvmənt)
= lift (lɪft)

= rise (raɪz)
= betterment ('bɛtəmənt)
= progress ('prɑgrɛs , 'pro-)

prompt (prɑmpt)
① *adj.* 立刻的 ② *v.* 提示

① = punctual ('pʌŋktʃʊəl)
  = quick (kwɪk)
  = instant ('ɪnstənt)
  = immediate (ɪ'midɪɪt)
  = ready ('rɛdɪ)
② = remind (rɪ'maɪnd)
  = hint (hɪnt)
  = suggest (səg'dʒɛst , sə'dʒɛst)
  = coach (kotʃ)

prone (pron) *adj.* ①易於…的
②水平的

① = inclined (ɪn'klaɪnd)
  = liable ('laɪəbḷ)
  = willing ('wɪlɪŋ)
  = ready ('rɛdɪ)
② = flat (flæt)
  = level ('lɛvḷ)
  = horizontal (,hɑrə'zɑntḷ)
  = prostrate ('prɑstret)
  = reclining (rɪ'klaɪnɪŋ)
  = reposing (rɪ'pozɪŋ)

pronounce (prə'naʊns) *v.* 發音

= sound (saʊnd)
= utter ('ʌtə)
= articulate (ɑr'tɪkjə,let)
= voice (vɔɪs)
= enunciate (ɪ'nʌnsɪ,et , -ʃɪ-)
= express (ɪk'sprɛs)

P

pronounced (prə'naʊnst) *adj.*
顯著的

= distinct (dɪ'stɪŋkt)
= marked (mɑrkt)
= decided (dɪ'saɪdɪd)
= plain (plen)
= clear (klɪr)
= obvious ('ɑbvɪəs)
= evident ('ɛvədənt)
= definite ('dɛfənɪt)
= visible ('vɪzəbl̩)
= downright ('daʊn,raɪt)
= absolute ('æbsə,lut)
= conspicuous (kən'spɪkjʊəs)
= noticeable ('notɪsəbl̩)
= prominent ('prɑmənənt)
= bold (bold)
= striking ('straɪkɪŋ)
= outstanding (aʊt'stændɪŋ)
= flagrant ('flegrənt)
= glaring ('glɛrɪŋ)
= clear-cut ('klɪr'kʌt)

prop (prɑp) *v.* 支持

= support (sə'port , -'pɔrt)
= bolster ('bolstɚ)
= brace (bres)
= *hold up*

propagate ('prɑpə,get) *v.* 繁殖

= produce (prə'djus)
= increase (ɪn'kris)
= breed (brid)
= multiply ('mʌltə,plaɪ)
= generate ('dʒɛnə,ret)
= procreate ('prokrɪ,et)

propel (prə'pɛl) *v.* 驅策

= drive (draɪv)
= push (pʊʃ)
= shove (ʃʌv)
= move (muv)
= impel (ɪm'pɛl)
= motivate ('motə,vet)
= stimulate ('stɪmjə,let)

proper ('prɑpɚ) *adj.* 正確的 ;
高尚的

= correct (kə'rɛkt)
= right (raɪt)
= fitting ('fɪtɪŋ)
= decent ('disn̩t)
= respectful (rɪ'spɛktfəl)
= accurate ('ækjərɪt)
= perfect ('pɜfɪkt)
= faultless ('fɔltlɪs)
= tasteful ('testfəl)

property ('prɑpɚtɪ) *n.* 財產

= possession (pə'zɛʃən)
= holdings ('holdɪŋz)
= belongings (bə'lɔŋɪŋz)

prophesy ('prɑfə,saɪ) *v.* 預言

= predict (prɪ'dɪkt)
= foretell (for'tɛl , fɔr-)
= forecast (for'kæst)
= divine (də'vaɪn)
= foresee (for'si , fɔr-)
= soothsay ('suθ,se)

proportion (prə'porʃən ,
-'pɔr-) *n.* 比率

= ratio ('reʃo)

= measure ('mɛʒɚ)

= amount (ə'maʊnt)

= balance ('bæləns)

= portion ('porʃən , 'por-)

= share (ʃɛr)

= interest ('ɪntərɪst , 'ɪntrɪst)

= part (part)

= percentage (pɚ'sɛntɪdʒ)

roposal (prə'pozḷ) *n.* 提議

= plan (plæn)

= scheme (skim)

= suggestion (səg'dʒɛstʃən)

= offer ('ɔfɚ , 'afɚ)

= intent (ɪn'tɛnt)

= project ('pradʒɛkt)

= design (dɪ'zaɪn)

= motion ('moʃən)

rosecute ('prasɪ,kjut) *v.*
實行 ②告發

= complete (kəm'plit)

= fulfill (fʊl'fɪl)

= discharge (dɪs'tʃardʒ)

= execute ('ɛksɪ,kjut)

= transact (træns'ækt , trænz-)

= practice ('præktɪs)

= exercise ('ɛksɚ,saɪz)

= pursue (pɚ'su , -'sɪu)

= follow ('falo)

= *carry out*

= *bring suit*

= *take action against*

rospective (prə'spɛktɪv) *adj.*
期的

= expected (ɪk'spɛktɪd)

= anticipated (æn'tɪsə,petɪd)

= awaited (ə'wetɪd)

= coming ('kʌmɪŋ)

= promised ('pramɪst)

= due (dju)

= future ('fjutʃ)

= eventual (ɪ'vɛntʃʊəl)

prosperous ('praspərəs) *adj.*
成功的；繁盛的

= successful (sək'sɛsfəl)

= thriving ('θraɪvɪŋ)

= fortunate ('fɔrtʃənɪt)

= triumphant (traɪ'ʌmfənt)

= comfortable ('kʌmfətəbḷ)

= flourishing ('flɝɪʃɪŋ)

= wealthy ('wɛlθɪ)

= rich (rɪtʃ)

= opulent ('apjələnt)

= affluent ('æflʊənt)

= well-off ('wɛl'ɔf)

prostrate ('prastret) *adj.*
①無力的 ②平臥的

① = helpless ('hɛlplɪs)

= overcome (,ovɚ'kʌm)

= defenseless (dɪ'fɛnslɪs)

= powerless ('paʊɚlɪs)

② = prone (pron)

= horizontal (,harə'zantḷ)

= flat (flæt)

= lying ('laɪɪŋ)

= reclining (rɪ'klaɪnɪŋ)

protect (prə'tɛkt) *v.* 保護

= defend (dɪ'fɛnd)

P

= guard (gɑrd)

= shield (ʃild)

= safeguard ('sef,gɑrd)

= shelter ('ʃɛltə)

= screen (skrin)

= cover ('kʌvə)

= ensure (ɪn'ʃur)

= harbor ('hɑrbə)

protest (prə'tɛst) *v.* 反對

= object (əb'dʒɛkt)

= squawk (skwɔk)

= dispute (dɪ'spjut)

= challenge ('tʃælɪndʒ)

= dissent (dɪ'sɛnt)

= disapprove (,dɪsə'pruv)

protrude (pro'trud) *v.* 伸出

= project (prə'dʒɛkt)

= bulge (bʌldʒ)

= *stick out*

proud (praʊd) *adj.* ①極愉快的
②驕傲的

① = dignified ('dɪgnə,faɪd)

= elated (ɪ'letɪd)

= pleased (plizd)

= satisfied ('sætɪs,faɪd)

= gratified ('grætə,faɪd)

= delighted (dɪ'laɪtɪd)

② = arrogant ('ærəgənt)

= boastful ('bost,fəl)

= haughty ('hɔtɪ)

= vain (ven)

= lofty ('lɔftɪ , 'lɑftɪ)

= conceited (kən'sitɪd)

= bragging ('brægɪŋ)

prove (pruv) *v.* 證明

= show (ʃo)

= verify ('vɛrə,faɪ)

= check (tʃɛk)

= confirm (kən'fɝm)

= justify ('dʒʌstə,faɪ)

= certify ('sɝtə,faɪ)

= establish (ə'stæblɪʃ)

= substantiate (səb'stænʃɪ,et)

= demonstrate ('dɛmən,stret)

= document ('dɑkjəmənt)

proverb ('prɑvɝb) *n.* 格言

= maxim ('mæksɪm)

= adage ('ædɪdʒ)

= saying ('seɪŋ)

= dictum ('dɪktəm)

provide (prə'vaɪd) *v.* 供給

= supply (sə'plaɪ)

= give (gɪv)

= furnish ('fɝnɪʃ)

province ('prɑvɪns) *n.* ①部門
②範圍

① = division (də'vɪʒən)

= department (dɪ'pɑrtmənt)

= part (pɑrt)

= field (fild)

= sphere (sfɪr)

= domain (do'men)

② = region ('ridʒən)

= area ('ɛrɪə , 'erɪə)

= zone (zon)

= territory ('tɛrə,torɪ , -,tɔrɪ)

= district ('dɪstrɪkt)

P

= quarter（'kwɔrtɚ）

= place（ples）

= neighborhood（'nebɚ,hud）

= kingdom（'kɪŋdəm）

= empire（'ɛmpaɪr）

= principality（,prɪnsə'pælətɪ）

rovoke（prə'vok）v. 激怒

= anger（'æŋgɚ）

= vex（vɛks）

= excite（ɪk'saɪt）

= stir（stɝ）

= irritate（'ɪrə,tet）

= annoy（ə'nɔɪ）

= incense（ɪn'sɛns）

= exasperate（ɛg'zæspə,ret , ɪg-）

= pique（pik）

= ruffle（'rʌfḷ）

= enrage（ɪn'redʒ , ɛn-）

= infuriate（ɪn'fjʊrɪ,et）

= antagonize（æn'tægə,naɪz）

= irk（ɝk）

= nettle（'nɛtḷ）

= disturb（dɪ'stɝb）

= arouse（ə'raʊz）

= taunt（tɔnt）

= aggravate（'ægrə,vet）

= peeve（piv）

= rile（raɪl）

owess（'praʊɪs）n. 勇敢；
凡的技術

= daring（'dɛrɪŋ）

= courage（'kɝɪdʒ）

= valor（'vælɚ）

= gallantry（'gæləntrɪ）

= heroism（'hɛro,ɪzəm）

= boldness（'boldnəs）

= skill（skɪl）

prowl（praʊl）v. 潛行；徘徊

= sneak（snik）

= slink（slɪŋk）

= lurk（lɝk）

= steal（stil）

= creep（krip）

= rove（rov）

proxy（'prɑksɪ）n. 代理人

= agent（'edʒənt）

= substitute（'sʌbstə,tjut）

= deputy（'dɛpjətɪ）

= alternate（'æltɚnɪt , 'ɔltɚnɪt）

= replacement（rɪ'plesmənt）

= representative（,rɛprɪ'zɛntətɪv）

= surrogate（'sɝəgɪt）

prudent（'prudn̩t）adj. 謹慎的

= careful（'kɛrfəl）

= sensible（'sɛnsəbḷ）

= discreet（dɪ'skrit）

= cautious（'kɔʃəs）

= guarded（'gɑrdɪd）

= judicious（dʒu'dɪʃəs）

pry（praɪ）v. ①偵查　②撬開

① = meddle（'mɛdḷ）

= mix（mɪks）

= busybody（'bɪzɪ,bɑdɪ）

= peek（pik）

= peep（pip）

= search（sɝtʃ）

P

= grope〔grop〕

= snoop〔snup〕

② = loosen〔'lusn̩〕

= jimmy〔'dʒɪmɪ〕

= wrench〔rɛntʃ〕

public〔'pʌblɪk〕*n.* 大衆

= people〔'pipl̩〕

= populace〔'papjəlɪs , -ləs〕

= society〔sə'saɪətɪ〕

= persons〔'pɝsn̩z〕

= population〔,papjə'leʃən〕

= inhabitants〔ɪn'hæbətənts〕

publish〔'pʌblɪʃ〕*v.* 出版；公開

= divulge〔də'vʌldʒ〕

= reveal〔rɪ'vil〕

= circulate〔'sɝkjə,let〕

= broadcast〔'brɔd,kæst〕

= spread〔sprɛd〕

= advertise〔'ædvɚ,taɪz〕

= print〔prɪnt〕

= issue〔'ɪʃu , 'ɪʃju〕

= *make known*

pucker〔'pʌkɚ〕*v.* 皺起；摺疊

= wrinkle〔'rɪŋkl̩〕

= fold〔fold〕

= crumple〔'krʌmpl̩〕

puffy〔'pʌfɪ〕*adj.* 膨脹的

= swollen〔'swolən〕

= inflated〔ɪn'fletɪd〕

= bloated〔'blotɪd〕

= distended〔dɪ'stɛndɪd〕

= dilated〔daɪ'letɪd , də-〕

pull〔pʊl〕*v.* ①拉　②吸引

① = tug〔tʌg〕

= draw〔drɔ〕

= heave〔hiv〕

= haul〔hɔl〕

= tow〔to〕

= drag〔dræg〕

= yank〔jæŋk〕

= jerk〔dʒɝk〕

= strain〔stren〕

= stretch〔strɛtʃ〕

② = attract〔ə'trækt〕

= lure〔lʊr〕

= influence〔'ɪnfluəns〕

pulsate〔'pʌlset〕*v.* 震動

= beat〔bit〕

= throb〔θrab〕

= palpitate〔'pælpə,tet〕

= drum〔drʌm〕

= pound〔paʊnd〕

pulverize〔'pʌlvə,raɪz〕*v.* 研碎

= crumble〔'krʌmbl̩〕

= granulate〔'grænjə,let〕

= powder〔'paʊdɚ〕

= crush〔krʌʃ〕

= mash〔mæʃ〕

= smash〔smæʃ〕

= grind〔graɪnd〕

= grate〔gret〕

pummel〔'pʌml̩〕*v.* 打

= beat〔bit〕

= punch〔pʌntʃ〕

= thrash〔θræʃ〕

P

= flog (flɑg)
= strike (straɪk)
= pound (paʊnd)
= hammer ('hæmɚ)
= rap (ræp)
= bang (bæŋ)
= batter ('bætɚ)
= wallop ('wɑləp)

unch (pʌntʃ) v. 擊

= pummel ('pʌml̩)
= beat (bit)
= thrash (θræʃ)
= flog (flɑg)
= strike (straɪk)
= pound (paʊnd)
= hammer ('hæmɚ)
= rap (ræp)
= bang (bæŋ)
= batter ('bætɚ)
= wallop ('wɑləp)

unctual ('pʌŋktʃʊəl) adj.
ˈ時的

= prompt (prɑmpt)
= quick (kwɪk)
= immediate (ɪ'midɪɪt)
= exact (ɪg'zækt)
= precise (prɪ'saɪs)

uncture ('pʌŋktʃɚ) v. 穿孔

= pierce (pɪrs)
= perforate ('pɝfə,ret)
= penetrate ('pɛnə,tret)
= stab (stæb)
= bore (bor , bɔr)

= impale (ɪm'pel)

pungent ('pʌndʒənt) adj. 尖刻的

= sharp (ʃɑrp)
= biting ('baɪtɪŋ)
= bitter ('bɪtɚ)
= acid ('æsɪd)
= stinging ('stɪŋɪŋ)
= tangy ('tæŋɪ)
= spicy ('spaɪsɪ)

punish ('pʌnɪʃ) v. 處罰

= discipline ('dɪsəplɪn)
= chastise (tʃæs'taɪz)
= correct (kə'rɛkt)
= castigate ('kæstə,get)
= penalize ('pinl̩,aɪz , 'pɛnl-)

puny ('pjunɪ) adj. ①軟弱的
②細微的

① = weak (wik)
= meager ('migɚ)
= slight (slaɪt)
= little ('lɪtl̩)
= small (smɔl)
= frail (frel)
= delicate ('dɛləkət , -kɪt)
= fragile ('frædʒəl)
② = petty ('pɛtɪ)
= unimportant (,ʌnɪm'pɔrtn̩t)
= trivial ('trɪvɪəl)

pupil ('pjupl̩) n. 學生

= student ('stjudn̩t)
= scholar ('skɑlɚ)
= schoolchild ('skul,tʃaɪld)

P

puchase ('pɜtʃəs , -ɪs) *v.* 購買

= buy (baɪ)

= shop (ʃɑp)

purify ('pjʊrə,faɪ) *v.* 淨化

= cleanse (klɛnz)

= clarify ('klærə,faɪ)

= clean (klin)

= clear (klɪr)

= refine (rɪ'faɪn)

= filter ('fɪltɚ)

purpose ('pɜpəs) *n.* 目的；決心

= plan (plæn)

= aim (em)

= intention (ɪn'tɛnʃən)

= design (dɪ'zaɪn)

= object ('ɑbdʒɪkt)

= goal (gol)

= target ('tɑrgɪt)

= resolution (,rɛzə'ljuʃən , -zl̩'juʃən)

= determination (dɪ,tɜmə'neʃən)

= will (wɪl)

pursue (pɚ'su , -'sju) *v.* 追隨；追蹤

= chase (tʃes)

= follow ('falo)

= seek (sik)

= shadow ('ʃædo)

= trail (trel)

= heel (hil)

= quest (kwɛst)

= hunt (hʌnt)

= *go after*

push (pʊʃ) *v.* ①推 ②驅策

① = press (prɛs)

= thrust (θrʌst)

= shove (ʃʌv)

= force (fors , fɔrs)

= drive (draɪv)

= propel (prə'pɛl)

= nudge (nʌdʒ)

② = urge (ɜdʒ)

= encourage (ɪn'kɜɪdʒ)

= prod (prɑd)

= coax (koks)

= spur (spɜ)

= goad (god)

put (pʊt) *v.* 放；安置

= place (ples)

= lay (le)

= set (sɛt)

= arrange (ə'rendʒ)

= deposit (dɪ'pɑzɪt)

putrid ('pjutrɪd) *adj.* 腐朽的；極壞的

= rotten ('rɑtn̩)

= foul (faʊl)

= bad (bæd)

= decayed (dɪ'ked)

= spoiled (spɔɪld)

= stinking ('stɪŋkɪŋ)

= smelly ('smɛlɪ)

= rancid ('rænsɪd)

= reeking ('rikɪŋ)

= awful ('ɔful , 'ɔfl̩)

= atrocious (ə'troʃəs)

P

uzzle (ˈpʌzḷ) *n.* 難解之事；謎

= perplexity (pəˈplɛksətɪ)

= quandary (ˈkwɑndrɪ , -dərɪ)

= dilemma (dəˈlɛmə , daɪ-)

= confusion (kənˈfjuʒən)

= mystery (ˈmɪstrɪ , ˈmɪstərɪ)

= enigma (ɪˈnɪgmə)

= problem (ˈprɑbləm , -lɛm)

ygmy (ˈpɪgmɪ) *n.* 侏儒

= dwarf (dwɔrf)

= midget (ˈmɪdʒɪt)

Q

uack (kwæk) *n.* 冒充內行之人

= imposter (ɪmˈpɑstɚ)

= pretender (prɪˈtɛndɚ)

= charlatan (ˈʃɑrlətṇ)

= fake (fek)

uaff (kwæf , kwɑf) *v.* 飲

= drink (drɪŋk)

= sip (sɪp)

= imbibe (ɪmˈbaɪb)

= guzzle (ˈgʌzḷ)

uaint (kwent) *adj.* 古怪有趣的

= odd (ɑd)

= curious (ˈkjʊrɪəs , ˈkɪʊrɪ-)

= old-fashioned (ˈoldˈfæʃənd)

uake (kwek) *v.* 震動；戰慄

= shake (ʃek)

= tremble (ˈtrɛmbḷ)

= vibrate (ˈvaɪbret)

= quiver (ˈkwɪvɚ)

= shudder (ˈʃʌdɚ)

= shiver (ˈʃɪvɚ)

qualified (ˈkwɑləˌfaɪd) *adj.*
有資格的

= competent (ˈkɑmpətənt)

= fit (fɪt)

= capable (ˈkepəbḷ)

= efficient (əˈfɪʃənt , ɪ-)

= able (ˈebḷ)

= suited (ˈsutɪd , ˈsɪu-)

= eligible (ˈɛlɪdʒəbḷ)

quality (ˈkwɑlətɪ) *n.* 特性；
性質

= nature (ˈnetʃɚ)

= kind (kaɪnd)

= characteristic (ˌkærɪktəˈrɪstɪk)

= constitution (ˌkɑnstəˈtjuʃən)

= trait (tret)

= feature (ˈfitʃɚ)

= mark (mɑrk)

= type (taɪp)

= property (ˈprɑpɚtɪ)

qualm (kwɑm , kwɔm) *n.*
不安；疑懼

= uneasiness (ʌnˈizɪnɪs)

= doubt (daʊt)

= skepticism (ˈskɛptəˌsɪzəm)

= misgiving (mɪsˈgɪvɪŋ)

= question (ˈkwɛstʃən)

= suspicion (səˈspɪʃən)

= apprehension (ˌæprɪˈhɛnʃən)

= anxiety (æŋˈzaɪətɪ)

quandary ('kwɑndrɪ , 'kwɑndərɪ) *n.* 困惑

= dilemma (də'lɛmə , daɪ-)
= perplexity (pə'plɛksətɪ)
= predicament (prɪ'dɪkəmənt)
= confusion (kən'fjuʒən)
= puzzle ('pʌzḷ)
= uncertainty (ʌn'sɝtn̩tɪ)

quantity ('kwɑntətɪ) *n.* 數量

= amount (ə'maunt)
= number ('nʌmbə)
= sum (sʌm)
= measure ('mɛʒə)
= portion ('porʃən , 'por-)
= volume ('vɑljəm)
= mass (mæs)
= multitude ('mʌltə,tjud)

quarantine ('kwɔrən,tin , 'kwɑr-) *v.* 使孤立；隔離

= separate ('sɛpə,ret)
= segregate ('sɛgrɪ,get)
= isolate ('aɪsḷ,et , 'ɪs-)
= confine (kən'faɪn)
= seclude (sɪ'klud)

quarrelsome ('kwɔrəlsəm , 'kwɑr-) *adj.* 愛爭吵的

= argumentative (,ɑrgjə'mɛntətɪv)
= cranky ('kræŋkɪ)
= cross (krɔs)
= irritable ('ɪrətəbḷ)
= peevish ('pivɪʃ)
= belligerent (bə'lɪdʒərənt)

= grouchy ('grautʃɪ)

quaver ('kwevə) *v.* 震顫

= shake (ʃek)
= tremble ('trɛmbḷ)
= vibrate ('vaɪbret)
= quiver ('kwɪvə)
= shiver ('ʃɪvə)
= quake (kwek)

queer (kwɪr) *adj.* ①古怪的 ②同性戀的

① = odd (ɑd)
= strange (strendʒ)
= peculiar (pɪ'kjuljə)
= curious ('kjurɪəs , 'kɪurɪ-)
= eccentric (ɪk'sɛntrɪk , ɛk-)
= weird (wɪrd)
② = homosexual (,homə'sɛkʃuəl)
= deviant ('divɪənt)

quell (kwɛl) *v.* 使鎮靜；壓服

= calm (kɑm)
= subdue (səb'dju)
= quiet ('kwaɪət)
= pacify ('pæsə,faɪ)
= appease (ə'piz)
= cool (kul)
= hush (hʌʃ)
= mollify ('mɑlə,faɪ)
= lull (lʌl)
= smother ('smʌðə)
= crush (krʌʃ)
= reduce (rɪ'djus)
= suppress (sə'prɛs)
= extinguish (ɪk'stɪŋgwɪʃ)
= stifle ('staɪfḷ)

quench (kwɛntʃ) *v.* 結束；熄滅

= stop (stap)

= extinguish (ɪk'stɪŋgwɪʃ)

= stifle ('staɪfl̩)

= suppress (sə'prɛs)

= quell (kwɛl)

= squelch (skwɛltʃ)

= *put out*

query ('kwɪrɪ) *v.* 詢問

= question ('kwɛstʃən)

= ask (æsk)

= inquire (ɪn'kwaɪr)

= demand (dɪ'mænd)

= interrogate (ɪn'tɛrə,get)

= quiz (kwɪz)

quest (kwɛst) *v.* 搜尋

= search ('sɜtʃ)

= hunt (hʌnt)

= pursue (pə'su , -sɪu)

= seek (sik)

= explore (ɪk'splor , -'splɔr)

question ('kwɛstʃən) *v.* 詢問

= inquire (ɪn'kwaɪr)

= ask (æsk)

= query ('kwɪrɪ)

= demand (dɪ'mænd)

= interrogate (ɪn'tɛrə,get)

= quiz (kwɪz)

questionable ('kwɛstʃənəbl̩)
dj. 可疑的

= doubtful ('dautfəl)

= uncertain (ʌn'sɜtn̩ , -'sɜtɪn)

= dubious ('djubɪəs , 'du-)

= improbable (ɪm'prabəbl̩)

= unlikely (ʌn'laɪklɪ)

= implausible (ɪm'plɔzəbl̩)

quick (kwɪk) *adj.* ①迅速的
②機伶的

① = fast (fæst)

= swift (swɪft)

= hasty ('hestɪ)

= brisk (brɪsk)

= lively ('laɪvlɪ)

= speedy ('spidɪ)

= rapid ('ræpɪd)

= fleet (flit)

= expeditious (,ɛkspɪ'dɪʃəs)

② = alert (ə'lɜt)

= attentive (ə'tɛntɪv)

= smart (smart)

= bright (braɪt)

= keen (kin)

= sharp (ʃɑrp)

quiet ('kwaɪət) *adj.* 平靜的

= still (stɪl)

= silent ('saɪlənt)

= hushed (hʌʃt)

= peaceful ('pisfəl)

= serene (sə'rin)

= tranquil ('træŋkwɪl , 'træn-)

= calm (kɑm)

quip (kwɪp) *n.* 譏諷語；妙語

= joke (dʒok)

= witticism ('wɪtə,sɪzəm)

= pleasantry ('plɛzn̩trɪ)

= jibe (dʒaɪb)

Q

Q

quit ﹝ kwɪt ﹞ v. 停止;放棄

= stop ﹝ stɑp ﹞
= leave ﹝ liv ﹞
= cease ﹝ sis ﹞
= discontinue ﹝ ˌdɪskən'tɪnju ﹞
= end ﹝ ɛnd ﹞
= halt ﹝ hɔlt ﹞
= desist ﹝ dɪ'zɪst ﹞
= refrain ﹝ rɪ'fren ﹞
= depart ﹝ dɪ'pɑrt ﹞
= withdraw ﹝ wɪð'drɔ , wɪθ- ﹞
= retreat ﹝ rɪ'trit ﹞
= abandon ﹝ ə'bændən ﹞
= resign ﹝ rɪ'zaɪn ﹞
= vacate ﹝ 'veket ﹞

quite ﹝ kwaɪt ﹞ adv. 完全地;
相當;頗

= completely ﹝ kəm'plitlɪ ﹞
= absolutely ﹝ 'æbsəˌlutlɪ ﹞
= entirely ﹝ ɪn'taɪrlɪ ﹞
= really ﹝ 'riəlɪ , 'rɪəlɪ ﹞
= rather ﹝ 'ræðɚ , 'rɑðɚ ﹞
= truly ﹝ 'trulɪ ﹞
= very ﹝ 'vɛrɪ ﹞
= exceedingly ﹝ ɪk'sidɪŋlɪ ﹞

quiver ﹝ 'kwɪvɚ ﹞ v. 震顫;發抖

= shake ﹝ ʃek ﹞
= shiver ﹝ 'ʃɪvɚ ﹞
= tremble ﹝ 'trɛmbl̩ ﹞
= vibrate ﹝ 'vaɪbret ﹞
= quake ﹝ kwek ﹞
= quaver ﹝ 'kwevɚ ﹞
= shudder ﹝ 'ʃʌdɚ ﹞

quiz ﹝ kwɪz ﹞ v. 測驗;質問

= test ﹝ tɛst ﹞
= examine ﹝ ɪg'zæmɪn ﹞
= interrogate ﹝ ɪn'tɛrəˌget ﹞
= question ﹝ 'kwɛstʃən ﹞
= query ﹝ 'kwɪrɪ ﹞

quota ﹝ 'kwotə ﹞ n. 配額

= ratio ﹝ 'reʃo ﹞
= share ﹝ ʃɛr ﹞
= proportion ﹝ prə'porʃən , -'por-
= percentage ﹝ pɚ'sɛntɪdʒ ﹞
= allotment ﹝ ə'lɑtmənt ﹞

quote ﹝ kwot ﹞ v. 引證;引用

= cite ﹝ saɪt ﹞
= illustrate ﹝ 'ɪləstret , ɪ'lʌstret ﹞
= repeat ﹝ rɪ'pit ﹞
= echo ﹝ 'ɛko ﹞
= *refer to*

R

race ﹝ res ﹞ ① v. 跑;加速
② n. 種族

① = run ﹝ rʌn ﹞
= speed ﹝ spid ﹞
= rush ﹝ rʌʃ ﹞
= dash ﹝ dæʃ ﹞
= hurry ﹝ 'hɝɪ ﹞
= hasten ﹝ 'hesn̩ ﹞
= scoot ﹝ skut ﹞
= scamper ﹝ 'skæmpɚ ﹞
= scurry ﹝ 'skɝɪ ﹞
= sprint ﹝ sprɪnt ﹞
= bound ﹝ baʊnd ﹞

= bolt (bolt)

= accelerate (æk'sɛlə,ret)

= chase (tʃes)

= people ('pipl̩)

= folk (fok)

= clan (klæn)

= tribe (traɪb)

= nation ('neʃən)

= breed (brid)

= culture ('kʌltʃɚ)

= lineage ('lɪnɪɪdʒ)

ack (ræk) ① v. 使痛苦
) n. 架子

) = hurt (hɜt)

= torture ('tɔrtʃɚ)

= pain (pen)

= torment (tɔr'mɛnt)

= agonize ('æɡə,naɪz)

= punish ('pʌnɪʃ)

= harass ('hærəs , hə'ræs)

= distress (dɪ'strɛs)

= strain (stren)

) = framework ('frem,wɜk)

= shelf (ʃɛlf)

acket ('rækɪt) n. ①喧嚷
② (以威脅手段騙錢的) 計策

) = noise (nɔɪz)

= din (dɪn)

= commotion (kə'moʃən)

= tumult ('tjumʌlt)

= uproar ('ʌp,ror , -,rɔr)

= disturbance (dɪ'stɜbəns)

= hubbub ('hʌbʌb)

= fracas ('frekəs)

= ado (ə'du)

= fuss (fʌs)

= rumpus ('rʌmpəs)

= stir (stɜ)

= row (raʊ)

② = fraud (frɔd)

= swindle ('swɪndl̩)

= dishonesty (dɪs'ɑnɪstɪ)

radiant ('redɪənt) adj. 閃爍
明亮的

= shining ('ʃaɪnɪŋ)

= bright (braɪt)

= beaming ('bimɪŋ)

= luminous ('lumənəs)

= gleaming ('ɡlimɪŋ)

= glowing ('gloɪŋ)

= lustrous ('lʌstrəs)

radical ('rædɪkl̩) adj. 極端的

= extreme (ɪk'strim)

= greatest ('gretɪst)

= utmost ('ʌt,most)

radio ('redɪ,o) v. 以無線電廣播

= broadcast ('brɔd,kæst)

= transmit (træns'mɪt)

rage (redʒ) n. ①盛怒；瘋狂
②流行之物

① = anger ('æŋɡɚ)

= passion ('pæʃən)

= violence ('vaɪələns)

= storm (stɔrm)

= frenzy ('frɛnzɪ)

= furor ('fjʊror)

= fit (fɪt)

R

= delirium (dɪ'lɪrɪəm)

= mania ('menɪə)

= craze (krez)

= excitement (ɪk'saɪtmənt)

② = fad (fæd)

= fashion ('fæʃən)

= style (staɪl)

ragged ('rægɪd) *adj.* 衣衫襤褸的

= torn (torn , tɔrn)

= worn (worn , wɔrn)

= shabby ('ʃæbɪ)

= shoddy ('ʃɑdɪ)

= tattered ('tætəd)

= frayed (fred)

= frazzled ('fræzl̩d)

= seedy ('sidɪ)

raid (red) *v.* 襲擊；搶劫

= attack (ə'tæk)

= invade (ɪn'ved)

= assault (ə'sɔlt)

= plunder ('plʌndə)

= pillage ('pɪlɪdʒ)

= loot (lut)

= seize (siz)

rain (ren) *v.* 使傾注；下雨

= precipitate (prɪ'sɪpə,tet)

= shower ('ʃauə)

= pour (por , pɔr)

= sprinkle ('sprɪŋkl̩)

= drizzle ('drɪzl̩)

raise (rez) *v.* ①提高；增加
②產生

① = lift (lɪft)

= increase (ɪn'kris)

= elevate ('ɛlə,vet)

= hoist (hɔɪst)

= boost (bust)

② = produce (prə'djus)

= rear (rɪr)

= build (bɪld)

= create (krɪ'et)

= construct (kən'strʌkt)

rally ('rælɪ) *v.* ①收集　②復原

① = assemble (ə'sɛmbl̩)

= meet (mit)

= gather ('gæðə)

= congregate ('kɑŋgrɪ,get)

= collect (kə'lɛkt)

= throng (θrɔŋ)

= crowd (kraud)

= cluster ('klʌstə)

= convene (kən'vin)

② = improve (ɪm'pruv)

= recover (rɪ'kʌvə)

= recuperate (rɪ'kjupə,ret)

= mend (mɛnd)

= revive (rɪ'vaɪv)

ram (ræm) *v.* 撞；擠入

= strike (straɪk)

= push (puʃ)

= thrust (θrʌst)

= shove (ʃʌv)

= press (prɛs)

= bear (bɛr)

= drive (draɪv)

= prod (prɑd)

= goad (god)

amble ('ræmbl) v. 漫遊

= wander ('wɑndɚ)
= roam (rom)
= rove (rov)
= gad (gæd)
= drift (drɪft)
= stroll (strol)
= stray (stre)
= meander (mɪ'ændɚ)

ampage ('ræmpedʒ) n. 喧擾

= racket ('rækɪt)
= commotion (kə'moʃən)
= hubbub ('hʌbʌb)
= tumult ('tjumʌlt)
= uproar ('ʌp,ror , -,rɔr)
= disturbance (dɪ'stɝbəns)
= fracas ('frekəs)
= ado (ə'du)
= fuss (fʌs)
= rumpus ('rʌmpəs)
= stir (stɝ)
= row (rau)

anch (ræntʃ) n. 大農場

= farm (farm)
= range (rendʒ)
= plantation (plæn'teʃən)
= homestead ('hom,stɛd)

andom ('rændəm) adj. 隨便的

= haphazard (,hæp'hæzɚd)
= aimless ('emlɪs)
= irregular (ɪ'rɛgjəlɚ)
= unorganized (ʌn'ɔrgən,aɪzd)

ange (rendʒ) n. 範圍

= limit ('lɪmɪt)
= extent (ɪk'stɛnt)
= distance ('dɪstəns)
= reach (ritʃ)
= length (lɛŋkθ , lɛŋθ)
= scope (skop)

rank (ræŋk) ① v. 分類;評價
② adj. 使人厭惡的

① = grade (gred)
= class (klæs)
= position (pə'zɪʃən)
= rate (ret)
= value ('vælju)
= evaluate (ɪ'vælju,et)
= gauge (gedʒ)
= appraise (ə'prez)
= classify ('klæsə,faɪ)
= arrange (ə'rendʒ)
= group (grup)
= categorize ('kætəgə,raɪz)
② = offensive (ə'fɛnsɪv)
= repulsive (rɪ'pʌlsɪv)
= disgusting (dɪs'gʌstɪŋ)
= revolting (rɪ'voltɪŋ)
= foul (faul)
= vile (vaɪl)
= odious ('odɪəs)
= repugnant (rɪ'pʌgnənt)
= obnoxious (əb'nakʃəs , ab-)
= sickening ('sɪkənɪŋ)
= nasty ('næstɪ)
= putrid ('pjutrɪd)
= rotten ('ratn̩)

rankle ('ræŋkl̩) v. 使痛

= pain (pen)

= distress (dɪ'strɛs)
= inflame (ɪn'flem)
= irritate ('ɪrə,tet)
= fester ('fɛstə)
= ache (ek)
= hurt (hɜt)

ransack ('rænsæk) v. 搜索；
洗劫

= search (sɜtʃ)
= rummage ('rʌmɪdʒ)
= forage ('fɔrɪdʒ , 'far-)
= pillage ('pɪlɪdʒ)
= plunder ('plʌndə)
= loot (lut)
= raid (red)
= rifle ('raɪfḷ)

ransom ('rænsəm) v. 贖回；
補償

= redeem (rɪ'dim)
= reclaim (rɪ'klem)
= recover (rɪ'kʌvə)
= retrieve (rɪ'triv)
= regain (rɪ'gen)

rap (ræp) v. 敲

= knock (nak)
= tap (tæp)
= hammer ('hæmə)
= bang (bæŋ)

rapid ('ræpɪd) adj. 迅速的

= quick (kwɪk)
= swift (swɪft)
= fast (fæst)

= speedy ('spidɪ)
= fleet (flit)
= hasty ('hestɪ)
= expeditious (,ɛkspɪ'dɪʃəs)

rapture ('ræptʃə) n. 狂喜

= joy (dʒɔɪ)
= delight (dɪ'laɪt)
= ecstasy ('ɛkstəsɪ)
= bliss (blɪs)
= elation (ɪ'leʃən , i-)
= enchantment (ɪn'tʃæntmənt)
= glee (gli)
= happiness ('hæpɪnɪs)

rare (rɛr) adj. 罕有的

= scarce (skɛrs)
= sparse (spɑrs)
= uncommon (ʌn'kɑmən)
= infrequent (ɪn'frikwənt)
= peculiar (pɪ'kjuljə)
= unusual (ʌn'juʒʊəl)

rascal ('ræskḷ) n. 流氓

= rogue (rog)
= scoundrel ('skaundrəl)
= devil ('dɛvḷ)
= scamp (skæmp)
= trickster ('trɪkstə)

rash (ræʃ) ① adj. 輕率的
② n. 發疹

① = hasty ('hestɪ)
= careless ('kɛrlɪs)
= reckless ('rɛklɪs)
= impetuous (ɪm'pɛtʃʊəs)

= impulsive (ɪm'pʌlsɪv)
= sudden ('sʌdn̩)
= imprudent (ɪm'prudn̩t)
= brash (bræʃ)
) = breaking-out ('brekɪŋ'aʊt)

ate (ret) *v.* 評估

= grade (gred)
= classify ('klæsə,faɪ)
= position (pə'zɪʃən)
= rank (ræŋk)
= value ('vælju)
= evaluate (ɪ'vælju,et)
= appraise (ə'prez)
= group (grup)
= categorize ('kætəgə,raɪz)
= estimate ('ɛstə,met)
= measure ('mɛʒɚ)

atify ('rætə,faɪ) *v.* 批准

= confirm (kən'fɝm)
= approve (ə'pruv)
= validate ('vælə,det)
= certify ('sɝtə,faɪ)
= support (sə'port , -'pɔrt)
= uphold (ʌp'hold)
= authenticate (ɔ'θɛntɪ,ket)
= substantiate (səb'stænʃɪ,et)
= endorse (ɪn'dɔrs , ɛn-)
= accept (ək'sɛpt)
= pass (pæs)
= O. K. ('o'ke)

atio ('reʃo) *n.* 比例

= proportion (prə'pɔrʃən)
= comparison (kəm'pærəsn̩)
= percentage (pɚ'sɛntɪdʒ)

ration ('ræʃən , 'reʃən) *n.* 配給量

= allowance (ə'laʊəns)
= portion ('porʃən , 'pɔr-)
= share (ʃɛr)
= quota ('kwotə)
= allotment (ə'lɑtmənt)
= budget ('bʌdʒɪt)
= measure ('mɛʒɚ)
= supply (sə'plaɪ)
= amount (ə'maʊnt)

rational ('ræʃən̩l) *adj.* 合理的

= sensible ('sɛnsəbl̩)
= reasonable ('riznəbl̩)
= thinking ('θɪŋkɪŋ)
= logical ('lɑdʒɪkl̩)
= sound (saʊnd)
= level-headed ('lɛvl̩'hɛdɪd)

rattle (rætl̩) *v.* ①發嘎嘎聲
②使驚慌

① = clatter ('klætɚ)
= patter ('pætɚ)
② = confuse (kən'fjuz)
= disturb (dɪs'tɝb)
= upset (ʌp'sɛt)
= fluster ('flʌstɚ)
= ruffle ('rʌfl̩)
= unsettle (ʌn'sɛtl̩)

raucous ('rɔkəs) *adj.* 粗啞的

= harsh (hɑrʃ)
= hoarse (hors)
= husky ('hʌskɪ)
= gruff (grʌf)
= coarse (kors , kɔrs)

R

ravage（'rævɪdʒ）*v.* 破壞

= damage（'dæmɪdʒ）
= destroy（dɪ'strɔɪ）
= devastate（'dɛvəs,tet）
= ruin（'ruɪn）
= wreck（rɛk）

ravenous（'rævənəs）*adj.* ①餓的 ②貪婪的

① = hungry（'hʌŋgrɪ）
= starved（starvd）
= famished（'fæmɪʃt）
= empty（'ɛmptɪ）
② = greedy（'gridɪ）
= grasping（'græspɪŋ）
= piggish（'pɪgɪʃ）
= hoggish（'hagɪʃ）
= vulturous（'vʌltʃurəs）
= gluttonous（'glʌtṇəs）

ravishing（'rævɪʃɪŋ）*adj.* 迷人的

= enchanting（ɪn'tʃæntɪŋ）
= delightful（dɪ'laɪtfəl）
= lovely（'lʌvlɪ）
= appealing（ə'pilɪŋ）
= beautiful（'bjutəfəl）
= stunning（'stʌnɪŋ）
= dazzling（'dæzlɪŋ, 'dæzlɪŋ）
= gorgeous（'gɔrdʒəs）
= alluring（ə'ljurɪŋ）
= enticing（ɪn'taɪsɪŋ, ɛn-）
= fascinating（'fæsṇ,etɪŋ）
= charming（'tʃarmɪŋ）

raw（rɔ）*adj.* ①無經驗的 ②陰冷的 ③生的

① = immature（,ɪmə'tjur）
= inexperienced（,ɪnɪk'spɪrɪənst
= green（grin）
= undeveloped（,ʌndɪ'vɛləpt）
= callow（'kælo, 'kælə）
= crude（krud）
② = cold（kold）
= nippy（'nɪpɪ）
= wintry（'wɪntrɪ）
= freezing（'frizɪŋ）
= piercing（'pɪrsɪŋ）
= bitter（'bɪtɚ）
= wind-swept（'wɪnd'swɛpt）
③ = uncooked（ʌn'kukt）

ray（re）*n.* 光線

= light（laɪt）
= gleam（glim）
= beam（bim）
= stream（strim）

raze（rez）*v.* 摧毀

= destroy（dɪ'strɔɪ）
= level（'lɛvḷ）
= flatten（'flætṇ）
= demolish（dɪ'malɪʃ）
= *tear down*

reach（ritʃ）*v.* ①達到 ②伸展

① = approach（ə'protʃ）
= land（lænd）
= *come to*
= *arrive at*
② = extend（ɪk'stɛnd）
= stretch（strɛtʃ）

react (rɪ'ækt) v. 反應

= respond (rɪ'spɑnd)
= answer ('ænsə)

ready ('rɛdɪ) adj. 預備好的

= prepared (prɪ'pɛrd)
= set (sɛt)
= fit (fɪt)

real ('riəl , ril) adj. 真實的

= actual ('æktʃuəl)
= true (tru)
= genuine ('dʒɛnjuɪn)
= authentic (ɔ'θɛntɪk)
= substantial (səb'stænʃəl)
= certain ('sɜtṇ)
= legitimate (lɪ'dʒɪtəmɪt)
= sincere (sɪn'sɪr)
= honest ('ɑnɪst)
= pure (pjur)
= *bona fide*

realize ('riə,laɪz) v. 認知；了解

= understand (,ʌndə'stænd)
= grasp (græsp)
= conceive (kən'siv)
= comprehend (,kɑmprɪ'hɛnd)
= follow ('falo)
= appreciate (ə'priʃɪ,et)

realm (rɛlm) n. 地區

= region ('ridʒən)
= range (rendʒ)
= extent (ɪk'stɛnt)
= sphere (sfɪr)
= field (fild)

= province ('prɑvɪns)
= domain (do'men)

reap (rip) v. 收穫；獲得

= gather ('gæðə)
= acquire (ə'kwaɪr)
= gain (gen)
= obtain (əb'ten)
= get (gɛt)
= earn (ɜn)
= glean (glin)

rear (rɪr) ① adj. 後部的
② v. 養育

① = back (bæk)
= hind (haɪnd)
= posterior (pɑs'tɪrɪə)
② = raise (rez)
= produce (prə'djus)
= create (krɪ'et)
= nurse (nɜs)
= foster ('fɔstə , 'fastə)
= train (tren)

reason ('rizṇ) n. 原因；理由

= cause (kɔz)
= motive ('motɪv)
= explanation (,ɛksplə'neʃən)
= logic ('lɑdʒɪk)
= sense (sɛns)
= ground (graund)
= justification (,dʒʌstəfə'keʃən)
= basis ('besɪs)

reasonable ('riznəbḷ) adj.
合理的

= sensible ('sɛnsəbḷ)

R

= fair (fɛr)

= logical ('lɑdʒɪkl̩)

= just (dʒʌst)

= sound (saʊnd)

= sane (sen)

= rational ('ræʃənl̩)

= practical ('præktɪkl̩)

= realistic (,riə'lɪstɪk)

= justifiable ('dʒʌstə,faɪəbl̩)

rebel (rɪ'bɛl) v. 反叛

= revolt (rɪ'volt)

= defy (dɪ'faɪ)

= riot ('raɪət)

= mutiny ('mjutn̩ɪ)

= disobey (,dɪsə'be)

= disregard (,dɪsrɪ'gɑrd)

= *rise up*

rebuff (rɪ'bʌf) v. 拒絕；否認；
輕蔑

= reject (rɪ'dʒɛkt)

= renounce (rɪ'naʊns)

= deny (dɪ'naɪ)

= repudiate (rɪ'pjʊdɪ,et)

= disown (dɪs'on , dɪz-)

= disclaim (dɪs'klem)

= spurn (spɜn)

= scorn (skɔrn)

= disdain (dɪs'den)

= snub (snʌb)

rebuke (rɪ'bjuk) v. 責罵

= scold (skold)

= disapprove (,dɪsə'pruv)

= reprove (rɪ'pruv)

= reprimand ('rɛprə,mænd)

= lecture ('lɛktʃə)

= correct (kə'rɛkt)

= chide (tʃaɪd)

= berate (bɪ'ret)

recall (rɪ'kɔl) v. ①記起 ②召喚

① = remember (rɪ'mɛmbə)

= recollect (,rɛkə'lɛkt)

= review (rɪ'vju)

= reminisce (,rɛmə'nɪs)

② = summon ('sʌmən)

= *call back*

recede (rɪ'sid) v. 撤回

= retreat (rɪ'trit)

= withdraw (wɪð'drɔ , wɪθ-)

= regress (rɪ'grɛs)

receive (rɪ'siv) v. 收到

= secure (sɪ'kjʊr)

= obtain (əb'ten)

= accept (ək'sɛpt)

= admit (əd'mɪt)

= gain (gen)

= get (gɛt)

= *take in*

recent ('risn̩t) adj. 最近的

= new (nju)

= late (let)

= modern ('mɑdən)

= up-to-date ('ʌptə'det)

reception (rɪ'sɛpʃən) n. 歡迎會

= party ('pɑrtɪ)

= entertainment (ˌɛntəˈtenmənt)

= social (ˈsoʃəl)

= festivity (fɛsˈtɪvətɪ)

R

recess (rɪˈsɛs) *v.* ①休會 ②使凹入

① = pause (pɔz)

= hesitate (ˈhɛzəˌtet)

= rest (rɛst)

= adjourn (əˈdʒɝn)

② = indent (ɪnˈdɛnt)

= notch (nɑtʃ)

= *set back*

recipe (ˈrɛsəpɪ) *n.* 秘訣；處方

= formula (ˈfɔrmjələ)

= instructions (ɪnˈstrʌkʃənz)

= directions (dəˈrɛkʃənz, daɪ-)

= prescription (prɪˈskrɪpʃən)

recite (rɪˈsaɪt) *v.* 背誦

= narrate (næˈret, ˈnæret)

= tell (tɛl)

= relate (rɪˈlet)

= recount (rɪˈkaʊnt)

= rehearse (rɪˈhɝs)

= review (rɪˈvju)

= repeat (rɪˈpit)

reckless (ˈrɛklɪs) *adj.* 魯莽的

= rash (ræʃ)

= careless (ˈkɛrlɪs)

= heedless (ˈhidlɪs)

= thoughtless (ˈθɔtlɪs)

= inconsiderate (ˌɪnkənˈsɪdərɪt)

= hasty (ˈhestɪ)

= unmindful (ʌnˈmaɪndfəl)

= impetuous (ɪmˈpɛtʃʊəs)

reckon (ˈrɛkən) *v.* ①斷定；認為 ②計算；評估

① = think (θɪŋk)

= consider (kənˈsɪdɚ)

= judge (dʒʌdʒ)

= suppose (səˈpoz)

= hold (hold)

= regard (rɪˈgɑrd)

= deem (dim)

= imagine (ɪˈmædʒɪn)

= fancy (ˈfænsɪ)

= believe (bɪˈliv)

② = count (kaʊnt)

= calculate (ˈkælkjəˌlet)

= compute (kəmˈpjut)

= estimate (ˈɛstəˌmet)

= figure (ˈfɪgjɚ, ˈfɪgɚ)

= evaluate (ɪˈvæljʊˌet)

= appraise (əˈprez)

recline (rɪˈklaɪn) *v.* 斜倚

= repose (rɪˈpoz)

= lounge (laʊndʒ)

= rest (rɛst)

= *lie down*

recluse (rɪˈklus) *n.* 隱士

= hermit (ˈhɝmɪt)

= shut-in (ˈʃʌtˌɪn)

= isolationist (ˌaɪslˈeʃənɪst)

recognize (ˈrɛkəgˌnaɪz) *v.* ①認得 ②承認；准許

① = acknowledge (əkˈnɑlɪdʒ)

R

= see (si)
= behold (bɪ'hold)
= know (no)
② = realize ('rɪə,laɪz)
= appreciate (ə'priʃɪ,et)
= understand (,ʌndə'stænd)
= admit (əd'mɪt)
= allow (ə'laʊ)
= accept (ək'sɛpt)

recollect (,rɛkə'lɛkt) v. 憶起
= remember (rɪ'mɛmbə)
= recall (rɪ'kɔl)
= reminisce (,rɛmə'nɪs)
= review (rɪ'vju)
= reflect (rɪ'flɛkt)

recommend (,rɛkə'mɛnd) v. 勸告
= advise (əd'vaɪz)
= suggest (səg'dʒɛst , sə'dʒɛst)
= advocate ('ædvə,ket)
= instruct (ɪn'strʌkt)
= guide (gaɪd)
= direct (də'rɛkt , daɪ-)
= urge (ɝdʒ)

recompense ('rɛkəm,pɛns) v. 償還
= pay (pe)
= reward (rɪ'wɔrd)
= compensate ('kampən,set)

reconcile ('rɛkən,saɪl) v. 和解
= settle ('sɛtl̩)
= harmonize ('harmə,naɪz)

= mend (mɛnd)
= *fix up*
= *bring together*

record (rɪ'kɔrd) v. 記錄
= write (raɪt)
= inscribe (ɪn'skraɪb)
= register ('rɛdʒɪstə)
= enroll (ɪn'rol)
= list (lɪst)
= note (not)
= post (post)
= enter ('ɛntə)
= log (lɔg , lag)
= tabulate ('tæbjə,let)
= chronicle ('kranɪkl̩)
= *mark down*

recount (rɪ'kaʊnt) v. 詳述
= recite (rɪ'saɪt)
= narrate (næ'ret)
= tell (tɛl)
= relate (rɪ'let)
= review (rɪ'vju)

recover (rɪ'kʌvə) v. ①尋回 ②復原
① = regain (rɪ'gen)
= retrieve (rɪ'triv)
= rescue ('rɛskju)
= reclaim (rɪ'klem)
= *get back*
② = recuperate (rɪ'kjupə,ret)
= rally ('rælɪ)
= revive (rɪ'vaɪv)
= heal (hil)

= improve (ɪm'pruv)

= *come around*

= *get back in shape*

= *make a comeback*

= *get better*

ecreation (ˌrɛkrɪ'eʃən) *n.* 娛樂

= play (ple)

= amusement (ə'mjuzmənt)

= entertainment (ˌɛntə'tenmənt)

= pleasure ('plɛʒə)

= enjoyment (ɪn'dʒɔɪmənt)

= diversion (də'vɝʒən , daɪ-)

= relaxation (ˌrilæks'eʃən)

= pastime ('pæsˌtaɪm , 'pɑs-)

= fun (fʌn)

= sport (sport , spɔrt)

ecruit (rɪ'krut) *v.* 招募

= enlist (ɪn'lɪst)

= draft (dræft)

= muster ('mʌstə)

= enroll (ɪn'rol)

= *sign up*

rectify ('rɛktəˌfaɪ) *v.* 修正

= adjust (ə'dʒʌst)

= remedy ('rɛmədɪ)

= fix (fɪks)

= regulate ('rɛgjəˌlet)

= amend (ə'mɛnd)

= correct (kə'rɛkt)

= *set right*

recur (rɪ'kɝ) *v.* 重現；再發生

= repeat (rɪ'pit)

= return (rɪ'tɝn)

= *come again*

redeem (rɪ'dim) *v.* 收回；
實踐；賠償

= fulfill (fʊl'fɪl)

= rescue ('rɛskju)

= recover (rɪ'kʌvə)

= deliver (dɪ'lɪvə)

= *make good*

= *pay off*

redress (rɪ'drɛs) *v.* 修正

= repair (rɪ'pɛr)

= remedy ('rɛmədɪ)

= rectify ('rɛktəˌfaɪ)

= correct (kə'rɛkt)

= right (raɪt)

= fix (fɪks)

= mend (mɛnd)

= relieve (rɪ'liv)

reduce (rɪ'djus) *v.* 減少；降低

= lessen ('lɛsn̩)

= lower ('loə)

= decrease (dɪ'kris)

= diminish (də'mɪnɪʃ)

= cut (kʌt)

= moderate ('mɑdəˌret)

reek (rik) *n.* 氣味；臭味

= smell (smɛl)

= stink (stɪŋk)

reel (ril) ① *v.* 搖晃 ② *n.* 捲軸

① = sway (swe)

R

= rock〔rɑk〕
= swing〔swɪŋ〕
= lurch〔lɜtʃ〕
= roll〔rol〕
= wobble〔'wɑbl〕
= stagger〔'stægə〕
= pitch〔pɪtʃ〕
= flounder〔'flaʊndə〕
② = spool〔spul〕
= roller〔'rolə〕

refer〔rɪ'fɜ〕v. 提示；提交
= direct〔də'rɛkt , daɪ-〕
= point〔pɔɪnt〕
= recommend〔,rɛkə'mɛnd〕
= allude〔ə'lud , ə'lɪud〕
= send〔sɛnd〕

referee〔,rɛfə'ri〕n. 裁判員；
調解人
= judge〔dʒʌdʒ〕
= moderator〔'mɑdə,retə〕
= umpire〔'ʌmpaɪr〕
= arbitrator〔'ɑrbə,tretə〕
= mediator〔'midɪ,etə〕

refine〔rɪ'faɪn〕v. 精製；精錬
= perfect〔pə'fɛkt , 'pɜfɪkt〕
= develop〔dɪ'vɛləp〕
= improve〔ɪm'pruv〕
= purify〔'pjʊrə,faɪ〕
= cultivate〔'kʌltə,vet〕
= polish〔'pɑlɪʃ〕

reflect〔rɪ'flɛkt〕v. ①反映
②思考

① = mirror〔'mɪrə〕
= *send back*
② = think〔θɪŋk〕
= ponder〔'pɑndə〕
= study〔'stʌdɪ〕
= deliberate〔dɪ'lɪbə,ret〕
= consider〔kən'sɪdə〕
= contemplate〔'kɑntəm,plet〕
= meditate〔'mɛdə,tet〕
= muse〔mjuz〕
= *mull over*

reform〔rɪ'fɔrm〕v. 改進
= change〔tʃendʒ〕
= improve〔ɪm'pruv〕
= convert〔kən'vɜt〕
= revise〔rɪ'vaɪz〕

refrain〔rɪ'fren〕v. 抑制；戒
= avoid〔ə'vɔɪd〕
= abstain〔əb'sten , æb-〕
= forego〔fɔr'go〕
= shun〔ʃʌn〕

refrigerate〔rɪ'frɪdʒə,ret〕v.
冷凍
= cool〔kul〕
= chill〔tʃɪl〕

refuge〔'rɛfjudʒ〕n. 避難所
= shelter〔'ʃɛltə〕
= protection〔prə'tɛkʃən〕
= asylum〔ə'saɪləm〕
= retreat〔rɪ'trit〕
= haven〔'hevən〕
= port〔port , pɔrt〕

= harbor ('hɑrbɚ)

= sanctuary ('sæŋktʃu,ɛrɪ)

refund (rɪ'fʌnd) v. 償還

= repay (rɪ'pe)

= reimburse (,riɪm'bɝs)

= *pay back*

refuse (rɪ'fjuz) v. 拒絕

= decline (dɪ'klaɪn)

= reject (rɪ'dʒɛkt)

= rebuff (rɪ'bʌf)

= *say no*

refuse ('rɛfjus) n. 廢物

= waste (west)

= garbage ('gɑrbɪdʒ)

= rubbish ('rʌbɪʃ)

= rubble ('rʌbl̩)

= trash (træʃ)

= litter ('lɪtɚ)

= junk (dʒʌŋk)

refute (rɪ'fjut) v. 反駁

= argue ('ɑrgju)

= dispute (dɪ'spjut)

= contradict (,kɑntrə'dɪkt)

regal ('rigl̩) adj. ①王室的
②華麗的

= royal ('rɔɪəl)

= majestic (mə'dʒɛstɪk)

= sovereign ('sɑvrɪn , 'sʌ-)

= imperial (ɪm'pɪrɪəl)

= dignified ('dɪgnə,faɪd)

= stately ('stetlɪ)

= splendid ('splɛndɪd)

= magnificent (mæg'nɪfəsn̩t)

= imposing (ɪm'pozɪŋ)

regard (rɪ'gɑrd) v. 視為

= consider (kən'sɪdɚ)

= judge (dʒʌdʒ)

= *think of*

regardless (rɪ'gɑrdlɪs) adv.
不顧

= notwithstanding
('nɑtwɪθ'stændɪŋ)

region ('ridʒən) n. 地方；區域

= place (ples)

= space (spes)

= area ('ɛrɪə , 'erɪə)

= location (lo'keʃən)

= district ('dɪstrɪkt)

= zone (zon)

= territory ('tɛrə,torɪ , -,tɔrɪ)

= section ('sɛkʃən)

= vicinity (və'sɪnətɪ)

register ('rɛdʒɪstɚ) v. 登記

= record (rɪ'kɔrd)

= inscribe (ɪn'skraɪb)

= write (raɪt)

= enroll (ɪn'rol)

= list (lɪst)

= post (post)

= enter ('ɛntɚ)

= log (lɔg , lɑg)

= indicate ('ɪndə,ket)

regret 〔 rɪ'grɛt 〕 v. 後悔

= bemoan 〔 bɪ'mon 〕

= bewail 〔 bɪ'wel 〕

= rue 〔 ru 〕

= *be sorry for*

regular 〔'rɛgjələ 〕 adj. ①通常的 ②不變的

① = usual 〔'juʒʊəl 〕

= customary 〔'kʌstəm,ɛrɪ 〕

= steady 〔'stɛdɪ 〕

= habitual 〔 hə'bɪtʃʊəl 〕

= everyday 〔'ɛvrɪ'de 〕

= common 〔'kɑmən 〕

= typical 〔'tɪpɪkļ 〕

= normal 〔'nɔrmļ 〕

= routine 〔 ru'tin 〕

② = uniform 〔'junə,fɔrm 〕

= even 〔'ivən 〕

= orderly 〔'ɔrdəlɪ 〕

regulate 〔'rɛgjə,let 〕 v. ①管理 ②調節

① = manage 〔'mænɪdʒ 〕

= govern 〔'gʌvən 〕

= handle 〔'hændļ 〕

= direct 〔 də'rɛkt 〕

= rule 〔 rul 〕

= control 〔 kən'trol 〕

= organize 〔'ɔrgə,aɪz 〕

= run 〔 rʌn 〕

= command 〔 kə'mænd 〕

② = adjust 〔 ə'dʒʌst 〕

= remedy 〔'rɛmədɪ 〕

= rectify 〔'rɛktə,faɪ 〕

= correct 〔 kə'rɛkt 〕

rehearse 〔 rɪ'hɜs 〕 v. 預演

= practice 〔'præktɪs 〕

= repeat 〔 rɪ'pit 〕

= train 〔 tren 〕

= drill 〔 drɪl 〕

= exercise 〔'ɛksə,saɪz 〕

= prepare 〔 prɪ'pɛr 〕

reign 〔 ren 〕 v. 統治

= rule 〔 rul 〕

= prevail 〔 prɪ'vel 〕

reinforce 〔,riɪn'fors 〕 v. 增強

= fortify 〔'fɔrtə,faɪ 〕

= brace 〔 bres 〕

= intensify 〔 ɪn'tɛnsə,faɪ 〕

= strengthen 〔'strɛŋθən 〕

reiterate 〔 ri'ɪtə,ret 〕 v. 重述

= repeat 〔 rɪ'pit 〕

= recount 〔 rɪ'kaunt 〕

= retell 〔 rɪ'tɛl 〕

= review 〔 rɪ'vju 〕

reject 〔 rɪ'dʒɛkt 〕 v. 拒絕；抛棄

= exclude 〔 ɪk'sklud 〕

= bar 〔 bar 〕

= eliminate 〔 ɪ'lɪmə,net 〕

= expel 〔 ɪk'spɛl 〕

= discard 〔 dɪs'kard 〕

= decline 〔 dɪ'klaɪn 〕

= refuse 〔 rɪ'fjuz 〕

= *throw away*

= *dispose of*

= *cast off*

ejoice (rɪ'dʒɔɪs) v. 使高興

= cheer (tʃɪr)

= gladden ('glædṇ)

= celebrate ('sɛlə,bret)

= inspire (ɪn'spaɪr)

= hearten ('hartṇ)

= encourage (ɪn'kɜɪdʒ)

= glory ('glorɪ , 'glɔrɪ)

= delight (dɪ'laɪt)

elapse (rɪ'læps) v. 回復

= return (rɪ'tɜn)

= revert (rɪ'vɜt)

= regress (rɪ'grɛs)

= reverse (rɪ'vɜs)

= *slip back*

elate (rɪ'let) v. 敘述

= tell (tɛl)

= report (rɪ'port)

= recount (rɪ'kaʊnt)

= narrate (næ'ret , 'næret)

= recite (rɪ'saɪt)

= state (stet)

= declare (dɪ'klɛr)

elated (rɪ'letɪd) adj. 有關連的

= associated (ə'soʃɪ,etɪd)

= connected (kə'nɛktɪd)

= affiliated (ə'fɪlɪ,etɪd)

= allied (ə'laɪd , 'ælaɪd)

= akin (ə'kɪn)

elax (rɪ'læks) v. 放鬆

= rest (rɛst)

= loosen ('lusṇ)

= *ease up*

relay (rɪ'le , 'rile) v. 轉送；傳遞

= carry ('kærɪ)

= deliver (dɪ'lɪvə)

= pass (pæs)

= transfer (træns'fɜ)

= impart (ɪm'part)

= *hand on*

release (rɪ'lis) v. 釋放；免除

= free (fri)

= fire (faɪr)

= relieve (rɪ'liv)

= dismiss (dɪs'mɪs)

= discharge (dɪs'tʃardʒ)

= expel (ɪk'spɛl)

= sack (sæk)

= can (kæn , kən)

= bump (bʌmp)

= retire (rɪ'taɪr)

= relinquish (rɪ'lɪŋkwɪʃ)

= liberate ('lɪbə,ret)

= *let go*

relent (rɪ'lɛnt) v. 變溫和；變寬容

= yield (jild)

= bend (bɛnd)

= soften ('sɔfən)

= relax (rɪ'læks)

= submit (səb'mɪt)

= *give in*

relentless (rɪ'lɛntlɪs) adj. 殘忍的；不留情的

= harsh (harʃ)

= unsympathetic
(ˌʌnsɪmpə'θɛtɪk)
= merciless ('mɝsɪlɪs)
= ruthless ('ruθlɪs)
= heartless ('hɑrtlɪs)
= cruel (krul)
= strict (strɪkt)
= firm (fɝm)
= rigid ('rɪdʒɪd)
= inflexible (ɪn'flɛksəbl̩)
= unyielding (ʌn'jildɪŋ)
= uncompromising
(ʌn'kɑmprə,maɪzɪŋ)
= persevering (ˌpɝsə'vɪrɪŋ)
= persistent (pə'zɪstənt , -'sɪst-)
= steadfast ('stɛd,fæst , -fəst)
= hard (hɑrd)

relevant ('rɛləvənt) *adj.*
中肯的；有關的

= pertinent ('pɝtn̩ənt)
= applicable ('æplɪkəbl̩)
= apropos (ˌæprə'po)
= suitable ('sutəbl̩ , 'sɪu-)
= connected (kə'nɛktɪd)
= fitting ('fɪtɪŋ)

reliable (rɪ'laɪəbl̩) *adj.*
可信賴的

= trustworthy ('trʌst,wɝðɪ)
= dependable (dɪ'pɛndəbl̩)
= faithful ('feθfəl)
= steadfast ('stɛd,fæst)
= loyal ('lɔɪəl)
= true (tru)
= devoted (dɪ'votɪd)
= safe (sef)

= sure (ʃur)
= stable ('stebl̩)

relic ('rɛlɪk) *n.* 紀念物

= memento (mɪ'mɛnto)
= remembrance (rɪ'mɛmbrəns)
= token ('tokən)
= souvenir ('suvə,nɪr , ,suvə'nɪr)
= trophy ('trofɪ)
= keepsake ('kip,sek)

relief (rɪ'lif) *n.* ①解救 ②接着

① = freedom ('fridəm)
= ease (iz)
= alleviation (ə,livɪ'eʃən)
= release (rɪ'lis)
= help (hɛlp)
= assistance (ə'sɪstəns)
= aid (ed)
② = change (tʃendʒ)
= substitution (ˌsʌbstə'tjuʃən)
= replacement (rɪ'plesmənt)
= alternate ('ɔltə,net , 'æl-)
= proxy ('prɑksɪ)

religious (rɪ'lɪdʒəs) *adj.* 虔誠

= pious ('paɪəs)
= devout (dɪ'vaut)
= reverent ('rɛvərənt)
= faithful ('feθfəl)
= adoring (ə'dɔrɪŋ)

relinquish (rɪ'lɪŋkwɪʃ) *v.* 放棄

= surrender (sə'rɛndə)
= yield (jild)
= abandon (ə'bændən)

= waive (wev)
= release (rɪ'lis)
= sacrifice ('sækrə,faɪs , -,faɪz)
= forego (for'go , fɔr-)
= *give up*

elish ('rɛlɪʃ) v. 喜好；享受

= enjoy (ɪn'dʒɔɪ)
= like (laɪk)
= appreciate (ə'priʃɪ,et)
= savor ('sevə)

eluctant (rɪ'lʌktənt) adj.
情願的

= unwilling (ʌn'wɪlɪŋ)
= grudging ('grʌdʒɪŋ)
= disinclined (,dɪsɪn'klaɪnd)
= loath (loθ)

ely (rɪ'laɪ) v. 依賴

= trust (trʌst)
= confide (kən'faɪd)
= *depend on*
= *count on*

emain (rɪ'men) v. 依然

= continue (kən'tɪnju)
= endure (ɪn'djur)
= persist (pə'zɪst , -'sɪst)
= stay (ste)
= last (læst)
= *keep on*

emark (rɪ'mark) v. 評論

= comment ('kamɛnt)
= mention ('mɛnʃən)
= note (not)

= observe (əb'zɝv)
= say (se)
= state (stet)
= speak (spik)

remarkable (rɪ'markəbl̩) adj.
不平常的

= unusual (ʌn'juʒʊəl)
= noteworthy ('not,wɝðɪ)
= extraordinary (ɪk'strɔrdn̩,ɛrɪ)
= exceptional (ɪk'sɛpʃənl̩)
= wonderful ('wʌndə-fəl)
= marvelous ('marvl̩əs)
= great (gret)
= striking ('straɪkɪŋ)
= notable ('notəbl̩)
= special ('spɛʃəl)
= rare (rɛr)

remember (rɪ'mɛmbə) v. 想起

= remind (rɪ'maɪnd)
= recall (rɪ'kɔl)
= recollect (,rɛkə'lɛkt)
= recognize ('rɛkəg,naɪz)

remedy ('rɛmədɪ) v. 治療

= cure (kjur)
= correct (kə'rɛkt)
= fix (fɪks)
= rectify ('rɛktə,faɪ)
= heal (hil)
= treat (trit)
= doctor ('daktə)

remind (rɪ'maɪnd) v. 提醒

= prompt (prampt)
= *suggest to*

R

remnant ('rɛmnənt) *n.* 殘餘

= leftover ('lɛft,ovɚ)

= remains (rɪ'menz)

= residue ('rɛzə,dju , -,du)

= balance ('bæləns)

remorse (rɪ'mɔrs) *n.* 悔恨

= regret (rɪ'grɛt)

= sorrow ('saro)

= grief (grif)

remote (rɪ'mot) *adj.* 遙遠的

= far (far)

= distant ('dɪstənt)

= removed (rɪ'muvd)

= secluded (sɪ'kludɪd)

= isolated ('aɪsḷ,etɪd)

= hidden ('hɪdṇ)

remove (rɪ'muv) *v.* 除去

= withdraw (wɪð'drɔ , wɪθ-)

= extract (ɪk'strækt)

= eject (ɪ'dʒɛkt)

= expel (ɪk'spɛl)

= oust (aʊst)

= deduct (dɪ'dʌkt)

= subtract (səb'trækt)

= eliminate (ɪ'lɪmə,net)

= discard (dɪs'kard)

= doff (daf , dɔf)

= *take away*

= *dispose of*

render ('rɛndɚ) *v.* ①使變成 ②給與

① = cause (kɔz)

= make (mek)

= do (du)

= effect (ə'fɛkt , ɪ-)

② = give (gɪv)

= present (prɪ'zɛnt)

= grant (grænt)

= allow (ə'laʊ)

= allot (ə'lat)

rendezvous ('randə,vu , 'rɛn-) *n.* 集會

= meeting ('mitɪŋ)

= appointment (ə'pɔɪntmənt)

= session ('sɛʃən)

= get-together ('gɛttʊ,gɛðɚ)

renounce (rɪ'naʊns) *v.* 放棄

= yield (jild)

= waive (wev)

= relinquish (rɪ'lɪŋkwɪʃ)

= surrender (sə'rɛndɚ)

= abandon (ə'bændən)

= scorn (skɔrn)

= release (rɪ'lis)

= reject (rɪ'dʒɛkt)

= deny (dɪ'naɪ)

= disclaim (dɪs'klem)

= discard (dɪs'kard)

= spurn (spɜn)

= *give up*

renovate ('rɛnə,vet) *v.* 革新

= recondition (,rikən'dɪʃən)

= redo (ri'du)

= remake (rɪ'mek)

enowned (rɪ'naʊnd) *adj.*
著名的

= famous ('feməs)
= celebrated ('sɛlə,bretɪd)
= popular ('pɑpjələ)
= distinguished (dɪ'stɪŋgwɪʃt)
= notable ('notəbḷ)
= notorious (no'torɪəs)
= well-known ('wɛl'non)

ent (rɛnt) *v.* 出租

= hire (haɪr)
= lease (lis)
= charter ('tʃɑrtə)
= let (lɛt)

epair (rɪ'pɛr) *v.* 修理；修復

= mend (mɛnd)
= fix (fɪks)
= service ('sɜvɪs)
= overhaul (,ovə'hɔl)
= restore (rɪ'stor , rɪ'stɔr)
= *patch up*

epast (rɪ'pæst) *n.* 食物

= meal (mil)
= food (fud)
= refreshment (rɪ'frɛʃmənt)

epeal (rɪ'pil) *v.* 撤消

= withdraw (wɪð'drɔ , wɪθ'drɔ)
= abolish (ə'bɑlɪʃ)
= revoke (rɪ'vok)
= recall (rɪ'kɔl)
= cancel ('kænsḷ)
= annul (ə'nʌl)

= invalidate (ɪn'vælə,det)
= rescind (rɪ'sɪnd)
= overrule (,ovə'rul)
= *take back*

repeat (rɪ'pit) *v.* 重複說

= recite (rɪ'saɪt)
= reiterate (ri'ɪtə,ret)
= duplicate ('djuplə,ket)
= echo ('ɛko)
= *say again*

repel (rɪ'pɛl) *v.* ①驅逐 ②厭惡

① = rebuff (rɪ'bʌf)
= *drive back*
= *hold off*
② = repulse (rɪ'pʌls)
= offend (ə'fɛnd)
= revolt (rɪ'volt)
= disgust (dɪs'gʌst)
= nauseate ('nɔʒɪ,et , 'nɔzɪ,et)
= sicken ('sɪkən)

repent (rɪ'pɛnt) *v.* 懊悔

= regret (rɪ'grɛt)
= *be sorry*

replenish (rɪ'plɛnɪʃ) *v.* 補充

= provide (prə'vaɪd)
= supply (sə'plaɪ)
= furnish ('fɜnɪʃ)
= *fill again*

replica ('rɛplɪkə) *n.* 複製品

= copy ('kɑpɪ)
= reproduction (,riprə'dʌkʃən)

= duplicate ('djupləkɪt)
= double ('dʌbḷ)

reply (rɪ'plaɪ) v. 回答

= answer ('ænsə)
= respond (rɪ'spɑnd)
= retort (rɪ'tɔrt)
= acknowledge (ək'nɑlɪdʒ)
= react (rɪ'ækt)

report (rɪ'port) v. 報導

= describe (dɪ'skraɪb)
= tell (tɛl)
= repeat (rɪ'pit)
= relate (rɪ'let)
= narrate (næ'ret , 'næret)

repose (rɪ'poz) v. 休息;睡眠

= rest (rɛst)
= sleep (slip)
= recline (rɪ'klaɪn)
= lounge (laʊndʒ)

represent (,rɛprɪ'zɛnt) v.
①象徵;描寫 ②說明

① = portray (por'tre , pɔr-)
= depict (dɪ'pɪkt) =
illustrate ('ɪləstret , ɪ'lʌs-)
= symbolize ('sɪmbḷ,aɪz)
= characterize ('kærɪktə,raɪz)
= express (ɪk'sprɛs)
= describe (dɪ'skraɪb)
= *stand for*
② = exhibit (ɪg'zɪbɪt)
= show (ʃo)
= demonstrate ('dɛmən,stret)

= display (dɪ'sple)
= manifest ('mænə,fɛst)
= present (prɪ'zɛnt)
= reveal (rɪ'vil)
= disclose (dɪs'kloz)

repress (rɪ'prɛs) v. 壓抑

= restrain (rɪ'stren)
= suppress (sə'prɛs)
= quell (kwɛl)
= crush (krʌʃ)
= squash (skwɑʃ)
= smother ('smʌðə)
= stifle ('staɪfḷ)
= censor ('sɛnsə)
= muffle ('mʌfḷ)
= squelch (skwɛltʃ)
= *keep down*
= *hush up*

reproach (rɪ'protʃ) v. 責備

= blame (blem)
= accuse (ə'kjuz)
= denounce (dɪ'naʊns)
= condemn (kən'dɛm)

reprove (rɪ'pruv) v. 責備

= scold (skold)
= blame (blem)
= lecture ('lɛktʃə)
= reprimand (,rɛprə'mænd)
= chide (tʃaɪd)
= rebuke (rɪ'bjuk)

repudiate (rɪ'pjudɪ,et) v. 拒絕

= reject (rɪ'dʒɛkt)

= renounce (rɪ'naʊns)

= deny (dɪ'naɪ)

= disclaim (dɪs'klem)

= disown (dɪs'on , dɪz'on)

= discard (dɪs'kɑrd)

= spurn (spɝn)

= scorn (skɔrn)

= disdain (dɪs'den)

= exclude (ɪk'sklud)

pulsive (rɪ'pʌlsɪv) *adj.*
惡的

= disgusting (dɪs'gʌstɪŋ)

= frightful ('fraɪtfəl)

= ghastly ('gæstlɪ , 'gɑstlɪ)

= offensive (ə'fɛnsɪv)

= repugnant (rɪ'pʌgnənt)

= horrid ('hɔrɪd , 'hɑrɪd)

= hideous ('hɪdɪəs)

= dreadful ('drɛdfəl)

= terrible ('tɛrəbl̩)

= ugly ('ʌglɪ)

= repelling (rɪ'pɛlɪŋ)

= horrible ('hɑrəbl̩)

= revolting (rɪ'voltɪŋ)

= gruesome ('grusəm)

putable ('rɛpjətəbl̩) *adj.*
聲好的

= honorable ('ɑnərəbl̩)

= upstanding (ʌp'stændɪŋ)

= respectable (rɪ'spɛktəbl̩)

= well-thought-of ('wɛl'θɔt,ɑv)

= upright ('ʌpraɪt , ʌp'raɪt)

= principled ('prɪnsəpl̩d)

= moral ('mɔrəl)

= honest ('ɑnɪst)

request (rɪ'kwɛst) *v.* 請求

= ask (æsk)

= requisition (,rɛkwə'zɪʃən)

= *apply for*

require (rɪ'kwaɪr) *v.* ①需要
②命令

① = need (nid)

= necessitate (nə'sɛsə,tet)

= lack (læk)

= want (wɑnt , wɔnt)

② = demand (dɪ'mænd)

= order ('ɔrdɚ)

= command (kə'mænd)

= oblige (ə'blaɪdʒ)

rescue ('rɛskju) *v.* 解救

= release (rɪ'lis)

= retrieve (rɪ'triv)

= salvage ('sælvɪdʒ)

= redeem (rɪ'dim)

= extricate ('ɛkstrɪ,ket)

= recover (rɪ'kʌvɚ)

= liberate ('lɪbə,ret)

= save (sev)

= free (fri)

research (rɪ'sɝtʃ) *v.* 研究

= delve (dɛlv)

= dig (dɪg)

= search (sɝtʃ)

= investigate (ɪn'vɛstə,get)

= inquire (ɪn'kwaɪr)

= hunt (hʌnt)

= explore (ɪk'splor , -'splɔr)

= *look into*

R

resemblance (rɪ'zɛmbləns) *n.*
相似

= likeness ('laɪknɪs)
= similarity (,sɪmə'lærətɪ)
= sameness ('semnɪs)

resentment (rɪ'zɛntmənt) *n.*
憤恨

= displeasure (dɪs'plɛʒə)
= irritation (,ɪrə'teʃən)
= annoyance (ə'nɔɪəns)
= vexation (vɛks'eʃən)
= bitterness ('bɪtənɪs)
= wrath (ræθ , rɑθ)
= anger ('æŋgə)
= indignation (,ɪndɪg'neʃən)

reserve (rɪ'zɝv) *v.* 保留

= keep (kip)
= hold (hold)
= save (sev)
= store (stor , stɔr)
= preserve (prɪ'zɝv)
= *put aside*

reside (rɪ'zaɪd) *v.* 居住

= live (lɪv)
= dwell (dwɛl)
= inhabit (ɪn'hæbɪt)
= occupy ('akjə,paɪ)

residue ('rɛzə,dju , 'rɛzə,du) *n.*
殘餘

= remains (rɪ'menz)
= leftovers ('lɛft,ovəz)
= rest (rɛst)
= dregs (drɛgz)

= sediment ('sɛdəmənt)
= balance ('bæləns)

resign (rɪ'zaɪn) *v.* 放棄

= relinquish (rɪ'lɪŋkwɪʃ)
= surrender (sə'rɛndə)
= yield (jild)
= waive (wev)
= forego (for'go , fɔr-)
= abdicate ('æbdə,ket)
= vacate ('veket)
= quit (kwɪt)
= retire (rɪ'taɪr)
= renounce (rɪ'naʊns)
= abandon (ə'bændən)
= *give up*

resist (rɪ'zɪst) *v.* 抵抗

= oppose (ə'poz)
= withstand (wɪθ'stænd , wɪð-)
= counteract (,kaʊntə'ækt)

resolute ('rɛzə,lut , 'rɛzḷ,jut)
adj. 堅決的

= firm (fɝm)
= bold (bold)
= resolved (rɪ'zalvd)
= decided (dɪ'saɪdɪd)
= persevering (,pɝsə'vɪrɪŋ)
= obstinate ('abstənɪt)
= spirited ('spɪrɪtɪd)
= game (gem)
= willful ('wɪlfəl)
= unyielding (ʌn'jildɪŋ)
= unbending (ʌn'bɛndɪŋ)
= adamant ('ædə,mænt ,
  'ædəmənt)

esolve (rɪ'zɑlv) v. 決定

= determine (dɪ'tɜmɪn)

= decide (dɪ'saɪd)

= settle ('sɛtḷ)

esourceful (rɪ'sorsfəl , sor-) adj. 敏捷多智的

= smart (smɑrt)

= ingenious (ɪn'dʒinjəs)

= cunning ('kʌnɪŋ)

= skillful ('skɪlfḷ)

= clever ('klɛvɚ)

= adept (ə'dɛpt , 'ædɛpt)

= deft (dɛft)

espect (rɪs'pɛkt) v. 尊敬

= adore (ə'dor , ə'dɔr)

= revere (rɪ'vɪr)

= value ('væljʊ)

= appreciate (ə'priʃɪ,et)

= idolize ('aɪdḷ,aɪz)

= honor ('ɑnɚ)

= admire (əd'maɪr)

= regard (rɪ'gɑrd)

= esteem (ə'stim)

spective (rɪs'pɛktɪv) adj. 別的

= particular (pɚ'tɪkjələ , pə-)

= individual (,ɪndə'vɪdʒʊəl)

= special ('spɛʃəl)

= specific (spɪ'sɪfɪk)

= personal ('pɝsṇḷ)

spiration (,rɛspə'reʃən) n. 吸

= breathing ('briðɪŋ)

= inhalation (,ɪnhə'leʃən)

= exhalation (,ɛksə'leʃən)

respite ('rɛspɪt) n. 休息

= rest (rɛst)

= relief (rɪ'lif)

= lull (lʌl)

= pause (pɔz)

= recess (rɪ'sɛs , 'risɛs)

= break (brek)

= interruption (,ɪntə'rʌpʃən)

= intermission (,ɪntə'mɪʃən)

= breather ('briðɚ)

= reprieve (rɪ'priv)

resplendent (rɪ'splɛndənt) adj. 燦爛的

= flamboyant (flæm'bɔɪənt)

= bright (braɪt)

= shining ('ʃaɪnɪŋ)

= splendid ('splɛndɪd)

= brilliant ('brɪljənt)

= vivid ('vɪvɪd)

= dazzling ('dæzlɪŋ , 'dæzḷɪŋ)

= glorious ('glorɪəs , 'glɔr-)

= gorgeous ('gɔrdʒəs)

respond (rɪ'spɑnd) v. 回答

= answer ('ænsɚ)

= reply (rɪ'plaɪ)

= retort (rɪ'tɔrt)

= acknowledge (ək'nɑlɪdʒ)

= react (rɪ'ækt)

responsible (rɪ'spɑnsəbḷ) adj. ①有責任的 ②可靠的

① = accountable (ə'kaʊntəbḷ)

R

R

= answerable ('ænsərəbḷ , -srə-)
= liable ('laɪəbḷ)
② = trustworthy ('trʌst,wɜðɪ)
= reliable (rɪ'laɪəbḷ)
= dependable (dɪ'pɛndəbḷ)
= faithful ('feθfəl)
= loyal ('lɔɪəl , 'lɔjəl)

rest (rɛst) *n.* ①休息
②剩餘之物

① = repose (rɪ'poz)
= pause (pɔz)
= ease (iz)
= relaxation (,rilæks'eʃən)
= recess (rɪ'sɛs , 'risɛs)
= recline (rɪ'klaɪn)
= lounge (laʊndʒ)
② = remains (rɪ'menz)
= residue ('rɛzə,dju , 'rɛzə,du)
= leftovers ('lɛft,ovəz)
= balance ('bæləns)

restless ('rɛstlɪs) *adj.* 不安的

= uneasy (ʌn'izɪ)
= disturbed (dɪ'stɜbd)
= agitated ('ædʒɪ,tetɪd)
= excited (ɪk'saɪtɪd)
= disquieted (dɪs'kwaɪətɪd)
= anxious ('æŋkʃəs , 'æŋʃəs)
= nervous ('nɜvəs)
= impatient (ɪm'peʃənt)
= fidgety ('fɪdʒɪtɪ)
= troubled ('trʌbḷd)

restore (rɪ'stor , -'stɔr) *v.* 修復

= renovate ('rɛnə,vet)

= fix (fɪks)
= mend (mɛnd)
= repair (rɪ'pɛr)
= reinstate (,riɪn'stet)
= replace (rɪ'ples)
= renew (rɪ'nju)
= overhaul (,ovə'hɔl)
= *put back*

restrain (rɪ'stren) *v.* 抑制

= arrest (ə'rɛst)
= check (tʃɛk)
= control (kən'trol)
= inhibit (ɪn'hɪbɪt)
= curb (kɜb)
= suppress (sə'prɛs)
= limit ('lɪmɪt)
= impede (ɪm'pid)
= retard (rɪ'tɑrd)
= smother ('smʌðə)
= stifle ('staɪfḷ)
= restrict (rɪ'strɪkt)
= confine (kən'faɪn)
= *hold back*
= *keep down*

restrict (rɪ'strɪkt) *v.* 限制

= confine (kən'faɪn)
= limit ('lɪmɪt)
= bound (baʊnd)
= hamper ('hæmpə)
= cramp (kræmp)
= restrain (rɪ'stren)
= impede (ɪm'pid)

result (rɪ'zʌlt) *n.* 結果

= consequence ('kɑnsə,kwɛns)

R

= end (εnd)

= effect (ə'fεkt , ι- , ε-)

= outcome ('aυt,kʌm)

= upshot ('ʌp,ʃat)

= fruit (frut)

= product ('pradəkt , -dʌkt)

= conclusion (kən'kluʒən)

sume (rɪ'zum , -'zjum) *v.*
續

= continue (kən'tɪnju)

= *return to*

= *go on with*

tain (rɪ'ten) *v.* 保持

= keep (kip)

= hold (hold)

= maintain (men'ten , mən'ten)

= preserve (prɪ'zɜv)

= save (sev)

taliate (rɪ'tælɪ,et) *v.* 報復

= reciprocate (rɪ'sɪprə,ket)

= retort (rɪ'tɔrt)

= revenge (rɪ'vεndʒ)

= avenge (ə'vεndʒ)

= *strike back*

tard (rɪ'tard) *v.* 妨礙

= delay (dɪ'le)

= hinder ('hɪndə)

= inhibit (ɪn'hɪbɪt)

= impede (ɪm'pid)

= curb (kɜb)

= check (tʃεk)

= arrest (ə'rεst)

= detain (dɪ'ten)

= *keep back*

retire (rɪ'taɪr) *v.* ①放棄
②解職   ③撤退   ④就寢

① = resign (rɪ'zaɪn)

= quit (kwɪt)

= vacate ('veket)

= relinquish (rɪ'lɪŋkwɪʃ)

= abdicate ('æbdə,ket)

② = withdraw (wɪθ'drɔ , wɪð-)

= discharge (dɪs'tʃardʒ)

= dismiss (dɪs'mɪs)

= suspend (sə'spεnd)

= expel (ɪk'spεl)

= remove (rɪ'muv)

③ = retreat (rɪ'trit)

= recede (rɪ'sid)

④ = *go to bed*

retiring (rɪ'taɪrɪŋ) *adj.* 羞怯的

= shy (ʃaɪ)

= modest ('madɪst)

= reserved (rɪ'zɜvd)

= timid ('tɪmɪd)

= bashful ('bæʃfəl)

= restrained (rɪ'strend)

= distant ('dɪstənt)

retort (rɪ'tɔrt) *v.* 反駁

= reply (rɪ'plaɪ)

= answer ('ænsə)

= respond (rɪ'spand)

= retaliate (rɪ'tælɪ,et)

retract (rɪ'trækt) *v.* 收回；取消

= withdraw (wɪθ'drɔ , wɪð-)

R

= repeal (rɪ'pil)
= revoke (rɪ'vok)
= rescind (rɪ'sɪnd)
= cancel ('kænsḷ)
= recall (rɪ'kɔl)
= annul (ə'nʌl)
= invalidate (ɪn'vælə,det)

retreat (rɪ'trit) *v.* 撤退

= withdraw (wɪθ'drɔ , wɪð-)
= retire (rɪ'taɪr)
= reverse (rɪ'vɝs)
= *fall back*

retrieve (rɪ'triv) *v.* 恢復

= recover (rɪ'kʌvə)
= regain (rɪ'gen)
= recoup (rɪ'kup)
= reclaim (rɪ'klem)
= repossess (,ripə'zɛs)
= retake (rɪ'tek)
= salvage ('sælvɪdʒ)
= rescue ('rɛskju)
= redeem (rɪ'dim)
= save (sev)
= *get back*

return (rɪ'tɝn) *v.* ①回；歸
②歸還

① = revert (rɪ'vɝt)
= revisit (ri'vɪzɪt)
= *go back*
= *come back*
② = repay (rɪ'pe)
= reimburse (,riɪm'bɝs)
= *give back*

reunion (ri'junjən) *n.* 重聚

= gathering ('gæðrɪŋ)
= assembly (ə'sɛmblɪ)
= get-together ('gɛttʊ,gɛðə)
= social ('soʃəl)
= reception (rɪ'sɛpʃən)
= meeting ('mitɪŋ)

reveal (rɪ'vil) *v.* 透露

= exhibit (ɪg'zɪbɪt)
= show (ʃo)
= display (dɪ'sple)
= open ('opən , 'opm̩)
= disclose (dɪs'kloz)
= manifest ('mænə,fɛst)
= expose (ɪk'spoz)
= demonstrate ('dɛmən,stret)
= present (prɪ'zɛnt)
= bare (bɛr)
= divulge (dɪ'vʌldʒ)

revenge (rɪ'vɛndʒ) *v.* 報仇

= retaliate (rɪ'tælɪ,et)
= *get even with*

revenue ('rɛvə,nju) *n.* 收入總

= income ('ɪn,kʌm , 'ɪŋ-)
= earnings ('ɝnɪŋz)
= receipts (rɪ'sits)
= profits ('prafɪts)
= returns (rɪ'tɝnz)
= proceeds ('prosidz)

reverberate (rɪ'vɝbə,ret) *v.*
回響

= echo ('ɛko)

= resound (rɪ'zaʊnd)

= reflect (rɪ'flɛkt)

evere (rɪ'vɪr) v. 尊敬

= love (lʌv)

= respect (rɪ'spɛkt)

= honor ('ɑnɚ)

= admire (əd'maɪr)

= value ('vælju)

= idolize ('aɪdḷ,aɪz)

= adore (ə'dor , ə'dɔr)

= esteem (ə'stim)

= cherish ('tʃɛrɪʃ)

= worship ('wɝʃəp)

= prize (praɪz)

everse (rɪ'vɝs) v. 反轉

= revert (rɪ'vɝt)

= regress (rɪ'grɛs)

= return (rɪ'tɝn)

= *back up*

evert (rɪ'vɝt) v. 恢復

= regress (rɪ'grɛs)

= reverse (rɪ'vɝs)

= return (rɪ'tɝn)

= *change back*

eview (rɪ'vju) v. ①溫習
評論；視察

= study ('stʌdɪ)

= remember (rɪ'mɛmbɚ)

= recall (rɪ'kɔl)

= learn (lɝn)

= examine (ɪg'zæmɪn)

= inspect (ɪn'spɛkt)

= survey (sɚ've)

= observe (əb'zɝv)

= consider (kən'sɪdɚ)

= criticize ('krɪtə,saɪz)

= *look at*

= *size up*

revise (rɪ'vaɪz) v. 校訂

= correct (kə'rɛkt)

= change (tʃendʒ)

= improve (ɪm'pruv)

= alter ('ɔltɚ)

= rewrite (rɪ'raɪt)

= amend (ə'mɛnd)

revive (rɪ'vaɪv) v. 復原

= restore (rɪ'stor , rɪ'stɔr)

= refresh (rɪ'frɛʃ)

= renew (rɪ'nju)

= regenerate (rɪ'dʒɛnə,ret)

= resurrect (,rɛzə'rɛkt)

= resuscitate (rɪ'sʌsə,tet)

= revivify (rɪ'vɪvə,faɪ)

= *bring back*

revoke (rɪ'vok) v. 取消

= repeal (rɪ'pil)

= cancel ('kænsḷ)

= withdraw (wɪð'drɔ , wɪθ-)

= rescind (rɪ'sɪnd)

= retract (rɪ'trækt)

= recall (rɪ'kɔl)

= abolish (ə'bɑlɪʃ)

= annul (ə'nʌl)

= invalidate (ɪn'vælə,det)

= overrule (,ovɚ'rul)

R

revolt (rɪ'volt) v. ①反叛
②厭惡

① = rebel (rɪ'bɛl)
= mutiny ('mjutn̩ɪ)
= riot ('raɪət)
= revolutionize (ˌrɛvə'luʃənˌaɪz)
= *rise up*
② = offend (ə'fɛnd)
= repel (rɪ'pɛl)
= sicken ('sɪkən)
= nauseate ('nɔʒɪˌet , 'nɔzɪˌet)
= disgust (dɪs'gʌst)
= horrify ('hɔrəˌfaɪ , 'hɑrəˌfaɪ)
= appall (ə'pɔl)

revolution (ˌrɛvə'luʃən) n.
①改革 ②旋轉

① = change (tʃendʒ)
= revolt (rɪ'volt)
= overthrow (ˌovə'θro)
= rebellion (rɪ'bɛljən)
= riot ('raɪət)
= uprising ('ʌpˌraɪzɪŋ , ʌp'raɪzɪŋ)
② = circle ('sɝkl̩)
= circuit ('sɝkɪt)
= cycle ('saɪkl̩)
= orbit ('ɔrbɪt)
= turning ('tɝnɪŋ)

revolve (rɪ'vɑlv) v. 旋轉

= turn (tɝn)
= circle ('sɝkl̩)
= *go around*

reward (rɪ'wɔrd) v. 報答

= compensate ('kɑmpənˌset)

= pay (pe)
= remunerate (rɪ'mjunəˌret)
= award (ə'wɔrd)

rhythm ('rɪðəm) n. 節奏

= beat (bit)
= swing (swɪŋ)
= tempo ('tɛmpo)
= meter ('mitɚ)

rich (rɪtʃ) adj. ①富饒的
②有錢的 ③昂貴的 ④味濃的

① = abounding (ə'baʊndɪŋ)
= fertile ('fɝtl̩)
= productive (prə'dʌktɪv)
= prolific (prə'lɪfɪk)
② = wealthy ('wɛlθɪ)
= affluent ('æfluənt)
= prosperous ('prɑspərəs)
= opulent ('ɑpjələnt)
= comfortable ('kʌmfətəbl̩)
= well-to-do ('wɛltə'du)
③ = valuable ('væljuəbl̩)
= costly ('kɔstlɪ)
= elegant ('ɛləgənt)
= priceless ('praɪslɪs)
= expensive (ɪk'spɛnsɪv)
④ = flavorful ('flevɚfəl)

rickety ('rɪkətɪ , 'rɪkɪtɪ) adj.
柔弱的;搖晃的

= weak (wik)
= shaky ('ʃekɪ)
= unsteady (ʌn'stɛdɪ)

rid (rɪd) v. 解除

R

= clear (klɪr)
= free (fri)
= *do away with*

iddle ('rɪdḷ) *n.* 謎

= puzzle ('pʌzḷ)
= enigma (ɪ'nɪgmə)
= conundrum (kə'nʌndrəm)

idicule ('rɪdɪkjul) *v.* 嘲笑

= mock (mak)
= deride (dɪ'raɪd)
= scoff (skɔf , skaf)
= jeer (dʒɪr)
= taunt (tɔnt)
= *laugh at*
= *sneer at*

idiculous (rɪ'dɪkjələs) *adj.*
可笑的

= nonsensical (nan'sɛnsɪkḷ)
= foolish ('fulɪʃ)
= crazy ('krezɪ)
= preposterous (prɪ'pastərəs)
= outrageous (aut'redʒəs)
= bizarre (bɪ'zar)
= unbelievable (ˌʌnbɪ'livəbḷ)
= ludicrous ('ludɪkrəs)

ifle ('raɪfḷ) *v.* 搶劫

= rob (rab)
= ransack ('rænsæk)
= steal (stil)
= plunder ('plʌndə)
= loot (lut)
= pillage ('pɪlɪdʒ)

= despoil (dɪ'spɔɪl)

rift (rɪft) *n.* ①裂縫　②不和睦

① = split (splɪt)
= break (brek)
= crack (kræk)
= cleft (klɛft)
= fracture ('fræktʃə)
= fissure ('fɪʃə)
= gap (gæp)
= crevice ('krɛvɪs)
② = falling-out ('fɔlɪŋ'aut)
= estrangement (ə'strendʒmənt)
= difference ('dɪfərəns)
= parting ('partɪŋ)
= breach (britʃ)
= alienation (ˌeljən'eʃən , ˌelɪən-)
= separation (ˌsɛpə'reʃən)

rig (rɪg) *n.* 裝置

= fit (fɪt)
= equip (ɪ'kwɪp)
= outfit ('aut,fɪt)
= furnish ('fɜnɪʃ)
= prepare (prɪ'pɛr)

right (raɪt) *adj.* ①好的；合法的
②正確的

① = good (gud)
= just (dʒʌst)
= lawful ('lɔfəl)
= fitting ('fɪtɪŋ)
= suitable ('sutəbḷ , 'sju-)
= proper ('prapə)
= valid ('vælɪd)
= sound (saund)

② = correct (kə'rɛkt)

= true (tru)

= exact (ɪg'zækt)

= accurate ('ækjərɪt)

= perfect ('pɜfɪkt)

= faultless ('fɔltlɪs)

righteous ('raɪtʃəs) *adj.* 正當的

= virtuous ('vɜtʃuəs)

= just (dʒʌst)

= proper ('prɑpə)

= good (gud)

= moral ('mɔrəl)

= pure (pjur)

= worthy ('wɜðɪ)

rigid ('rɪdʒɪd) *adj.* ①堅固的
②嚴格的

① = stiff (stɪf)

= firm (fɜm)

= unbending (ʌn'bɛndɪŋ)

= unchanging (ʌn'tʃendʒɪŋ)

= hard (hɑrd)

② = stubborn ('stʌbən)

= unyielding (ʌn'jildɪŋ)

= adamant ('ædə,mænt)

= strict (strɪkt)

= taut (tɔt)

= tense (tɛns)

rigorous ('rɪgərəs) *adj.* 嚴厲的

= harsh (hɑrʃ)

= strict (strɪkt)

= severe (sə'vɪr)

= rigid ('rɪdʒɪd)

= relentless (rɪ'lɛntlɪs)

= hard (hɑrd)

rim (rɪm) *n.* 邊緣

= edge (ɛdʒ)

= border ('bɔrdə)

= margin ('mɑrdʒɪn)

= fringe (frɪndʒ)

ring (rɪŋ) *n.* ①鈴聲 ②環

① = sound (saund)

= peal (pil)

= toll (tol)

= chime (tʃaɪm)

= tinkle ('tɪŋkl̩)

= jingle ('dʒɪŋgl̩)

= clamor ('klæmə)

② = circle ('sɜkl̩)

= band (bænd)

riot ('raɪət) *v.* 騷動；暴動

= revolt (rɪ'volt)

= rebel (rɪ'bɛl)

= mutiny ('mjutn̩ɪ)

= brawl (brɔl)

= *rise up*

rip (rɪp) *v.* 撕；扯

= tear (tɛr)

= break (brek)

= cut (kʌt)

ripe (raɪp) *adj.* 成熟的

= developed (dɪ'vɛləpt)

= ready ('rɛdɪ)

= mature (mə'tjur , mə'tʃur)

= full-grown ('ful'gron)

R

ise (raɪz) v. ①起立 ②上升
③增加 ④起源 ⑤叛變

① = stand (stænd)
= *get up*

② = advance (əd'væns)
= ascend (ə'sɛnd)
= mount (maʊnt)
= *go up*

③ = increase (ɪn'kris)
= grow (gro)
= gain (gen)

④ = originate (ə'rɪdʒə,net)
= begin (bɪ'gɪn)
= start (stɑrt)
= appear (ə'pɪr)

⑤ = revolt (rɪ'volt)
= rebel (rɪ'bɛl)
= riot ('raɪət)
= mutiny ('mjutn̩ɪ)

isk (rɪsk) v. 冒險

= chance (tʃæns)
= hazard ('hæzəd)
= gamble ('gæmbl̩)
= venture ('vɛntʃə)
= endanger (ɪn'dendʒə, ɛn-)
= imperil (ɪm'pɛrəl, -rɪl)
= jeopardize ('dʒɛpəd,aɪz)
= expose (ɪk'spoz)

itual ('rɪtʃʊəl) n. 儀式

= ceremony ('sɛrə,monɪ)
= formality (fɔr'mælətɪ)
= service ('sɜvɪs)
= exercise ('ɛksə,saɪz)

rival ('raɪvl̩) v. 競爭

= match (mætʃ)
= *compete with*
= *vie with*

road (rod) n. 道路

= path (pæθ, pɑθ)
= track (træk)
= trail (trel)
= thoroughfare ('θɜo,fɛr)
= lane (len)

roam (rom) v. 閒逛

= wander ('wɑndə)
= rove (rov)
= gad (gæd)
= drift (drɪft)
= stray (stre)
= meander (mɪ'ændə)
= ramble ('ræmbl̩)

roar (ror, rɔr) v. 吼叫

= thunder ('θʌndə)
= boom (bum)
= clamor ('klæmə)

rob (rɑb) v. 搶劫；盜取

= steal (stil)
= burglarize ('bɜglə,raɪz)
= loot (lut)
= sack (sæk)
= pillage ('pɪlɪdʒ)
= plunder ('plʌndə)
= thieve (θiv)
= pilfer ('pɪlfə)
= filch (fɪltʃ)

R

robust (ro'bʌst) *adj.* 強壯的

= sturdy ('stɜdɪ)
= healthy ('hɛlθɪ)
= mighty ('maɪtɪ)
= powerful ('pauəfəl)
= potent ('potṇt)
= stalwart ('stɔlwət)
= vigorous ('vɪgərəs)
= heavy ('hɛvɪ)

rock (rɑk) ① *v.* 搖擺 ② *n.* 岩石

① = sway (swe)
= swing (swɪŋ)
= roll (rol)
= bob (bɑb)
= flounder ('flaundə)
= tumble ('tʌmbḷ)
= toss (tɔs)
② = stone (ston)

rogue (rog) *n.* 歹徒

= rascal ('ræskḷ)
= scamp (skæmp)
= scoundrel ('skaundrəl)
= villain ('vɪlən)

role (rol) *n.* 角色；職分

= capacity (kə'pæsətɪ)
= character ('kærɪktə)
= part (pɑrt)
= position (pə'zɪʃən)
= function ('fʌŋkʃən)

roll (rol) *v.* 轉

= turn (tɜn)
= move (muv)

= rotate ('rotet)
= pivot ('pɪvət , -vɪt)
= swivel ('swɪvḷ)
= gyrate ('dʒaɪret)
= wheel (hwil)

romp (rɑmp) *v.* 嬉戲

= play (ple)
= frolic ('frɑlɪk)
= caper ('kepə)
= *carry on*

room (rum) *n.* ①空間 ②房間

① = space (spes)
= scope (skop)
= margin ('mɑrdʒɪn)
= latitude ('lætə,tjud)
= leeway ('li,we)
② = chamber ('tʃembə)

root (rut) *n.* 原因

= cause (kɔz)
= source (sors , sɔrs)
= origin ('ɔrədʒɪn , 'ɑ-)
= derivation (,dɛrə've ʃən)

rosy ('rozɪ) *adj.* 光明的

= bright (braɪt)
= cheerful ('tʃɪrfəl)
= sunny ('sʌnɪ)
= optimistic (,ɑptə'mɪstɪk)
= favorable ('fevərəbḷ)
= encouraging (ɪn'kɜɪdʒɪŋ)

rot (rɑt) *v.* 腐爛；枯萎

= decay (dɪ'ke)

= spoil (spɔɪl)

= disintegrate (dɪs'ɪntə,gret)

= crumble ('krʌmbḷ)

= *go bad*

otate ('rotet) v. 旋轉

= spin (spɪn)

= turn (tɝn)

= gyrate ('dʒaɪret)

= swivel ('swɪvḷ)

= pivot ('pɪvət , -vɪt)

ough (rʌf) *adj.* ①粗糙的
②粗暴的

= coarse (kors , kɔrs)

= unsmooth (ʌn'smuð)

= bumpy ('bʌmpɪ)

= choppy ('tʃɑpɪ)

= shaggy ('ʃægɪ)

= broken ('brokən)

= uneven (ʌn'ivən)

= irregular (ɪ'rɛgjələ)

= harsh (harʃ)

= rowdy ('raʊdɪ)

= severe (sə'vɪr)

= fierce (fɪrs)

= difficult ('dɪfəkʌlt)

= gruff (grʌf)

= brusque (brʌsk , brusk)

= rude (rud)

= crude (krud)

= curt (kɝt)

= surly ('sɝlɪ)

= blunt (blʌnt)

= tough (tʌf)

= snippy ('snɪpɪ)

round (raʊnd) *adj.* 圓的

= circular ('sɝkjələ)

= globular ('glɑbjələ)

= rotund (ro'tʌnd)

= spherical ('sfɛrəkḷ)

rouse (raʊz) v. 驚動;激動

= stir (stɝ)

= excite (ɪk'saɪt)

= arouse (ə'raʊz)

= awaken (ə'wekən)

= move (muv)

= provoke (prə'vok)

= pique (pik)

= kindle ('kɪndḷ)

= inflame (ɪn'flem)

= foment (fo'mɛnt)

= stimulate ('stɪmjə,let)

= agitate ('ædʒə,tet)

= disturb (dɪs'tɝb)

= shake (ʃek)

rout (raʊt) v. 打敗

= defeat (dɪ'fit)

= conquer ('kɑŋkə)

= crush (krʌʃ)

= overcome (,ovə'kʌm)

= beat (bit)

= scatter ('skætə)

route (rut , raʊt) *n.* 路線

= course (kors , kɔrs)

= circuit ('sɝkɪt)

= path (pɑθ , pæθ)

= rounds (raʊndz)

= itinerary (aɪ'tɪnə,rɛrɪ , ɪ-)

R

routine (ru'tin) *n.* 慣例

= habit ('hæbɪt)

= method ('mɛθəd)

= system ('sɪstəm)

= arrangement (ə'rendʒmənt)

= order ('ɔrdə)

rove (rov) *v.* 漫遊

= wander ('wɑndə)

= roam (rom)

= gad (gæd)

= drift (drɪft)

= stray (stre)

= meander (mɪ'ændə)

= ramble ('ræmbḷ)

= tramp (træmp)

1. row (ro) ① *n.* 行列
② *v.* 划槳

① = line (laɪn)

= file (faɪl)

= string (strɪŋ)

= train (tren)

= series ('sɪrɪz , 'sirɪz)

= sequence ('sikwəns)

= succession (sək'sɛʃən)

= column ('kɑləm)

② = paddle ('pædḷ)

2. row (raʊ) *n.* 爭吵

= quarrel ('kwɔrəl , 'kwɑ-)

= noise (nɔɪz)

= fracas ('frekəs)

= brawl (brɔl)

= dispute (dɪs'pjut)

= squabble ('skwɑbḷ)

= rumpus ('rʌmpəs)

rowdy ('raʊdɪ) *adj.* 粗暴的

= rough (rʌf)

= naughty ('nɔtɪ)

= disorderly (dɪs'ɔrdəlɪ , dɪz-)

= misbehaving (,mɪsbɪ'hevɪŋ)

= bad (bæd)

= rambunctious (ræm'bʌŋkʃəs)

= boisterous ('bɔɪstərəs)

royal ('rɔɪəl) *adj.* 高貴的；
威嚴的

= majestic (mə'dʒɛstɪk)

= noble ('nobḷ)

= dignified ('dɪgnə,faɪd)

= stately ('stetlɪ)

= grand (grænd)

= regal ('rigḷ)

= imperial (ɪm'pɪrɪəl)

= aristocratic (ə,rɪstə'krætɪk)

rub (rʌb) *v.* 磨擦；按摩

= massage (mə'sɑʒ)

= scrub (skrʌb)

= scour (skaʊr)

= buff (bʌf)

= stroke (strok)

rubbish ('rʌbɪʃ) *n.* ①垃圾
②無意義的話

① = waste (west)

= trash (træʃ)

= garbage ('gɑrbɪdʒ)

= refuse ('rɛfjus)

= scrap (skræp)

= debris (də'bri , 'debri)

= litter ('lɪtə)

= junk (dʒʌŋk)

= nonsense ('nɑnsɛns)

= silliness ('sɪlɪnɪs)

= absurdity (əb's3dətɪ)

= poppycock ('pɑpɪ,kɑk)

ude (rud) *adj.* 無禮貌的

= impolite (,ɪmpə'laɪt)

= rough (rʌf)

= coarse (kors , kɔrs)

= discourteous (dɪ'sk3tɪəs)

= uncivil (ʌn'sɪvl̩)

= disrespectful (,dɪsrɪ'spɛktfəl)

= insolent ('ɪnsələnt)

= ill-behaved ('ɪl'bɪhevd)

= ill-mannered ('ɪl'mænəd)

= vulgar ('vʌlgə)

= boorish ('burɪʃ)

= gruff (grʌf)

= brusque (brusk , brʌsk)

= curt (k3t)

= blunt (blʌnt)

= harsh (harʃ)

= surly ('s3lɪ)

= impudent ('ɪmpjədənt)

= impertinent (ɪm'p3tn̩ənt)

= saucy ('sɔsɪ)

= crude (krud)

= crass (kræs)

= flip (flɪp)

= cocky ('kɑkɪ)

= cheeky ('tʃikɪ)

udiment ('rudəmənt) *n.* 基礎

= foundation (faʊn'deʃən)

= basis ('besɪs)

= groundwork ('graʊnd,w3k)

= beginning (bɪ'gɪnɪŋ)

= origin ('ɔrədʒɪn , 'ɑ-)

= seed (sid)

rue (ru) *v.* 悔恨

= regret (rɪ'grɛt)

= repent (rɪ'pɛnt)

= deplore (dɪ'plor)

= bemoan (bɪ'mon)

= bewail (bɪ'wel)

= *be sorry for*

ruffian ('rʌfɪən , 'rʌfjən) *n.*
惡棍

= rowdy ('raʊdɪ)

= rogue (rog)

= cad (kæd)

= tough (tʌf)

= bully ('bulɪ)

= brute (brut)

= hoodlum ('hudləm)

ruffle ('rʌfl̩) *v.* ①擾亂   ②使皺

① = disturb (dɪs't3b)

= annoy (ə'nɔɪ)

= provoke (prə'vok)

= irk (3k)

= vex (vɛks)

= excite (ɪk'saɪt)

= fluster ('flʌstə)

= upset (ʌp'sɛt)

= shake (ʃek)

= trouble ('trʌbl̩)

= perturb (pə'tɜb)

= agitate ('ædʒə,tet)

= rattle ('rætḷ)

= rile (raɪl)

② = fold (fold)

= crease (kris)

= wrinkle ('rɪŋkḷ)

= furrow ('fɜo)

rug (rʌg) *n.* 地毯

= carpet ('karpɪt)

= mat (mæt)

= covering ('kʌvərɪŋ)

rugged ('rʌgɪd) *adj.* ①多皺的
②強壯的

① = rough (rʌf)

= uneven (ʌn'ivṇ)

= jagged ('dʒægɪd)

= ragged ('rægɪd)

= rocky ('rakɪ)

= snaggy ('snægɪ)

② = sturdy ('stɜdɪ)

= vigorous ('vɪgərəs)

= strong (strɔŋ)

= powerful ('pauəfəl)

= potent ('potṇt)

= stalwart ('stɔlwət)

= hardy ('hardɪ)

= robust (ro'bʌst)

= muscular ('mʌskjələ)

= athletic (æθ'lɛtɪk)

= brawny ('brɔnɪ)

= well-built ('wɛl'bɪlt)

= healthy ('hɛlθɪ)

= hale (hel)

= husky ('hʌskɪ)

= hefty ('hɛftɪ)

= beefy ('bifɪ)

ruin ('ruɪn) *v.* 毀壞

= destroy (dɪ'strɔɪ)

= spoil (spɔɪl)

= mar (mar)

= upset (ʌp'sɛt)

= wreck (rɛk)

= devastate ('dɛvəs,tet)

= ravage ('rævɪdʒ)

= demolish (dɪ'malɪʃ)

rule (rul) *v.* ①管理 ②畫界

① = govern ('gʌvən)

= control (kən'trol)

= reign (ren)

= dominate ('damə,net)

= regulate ('rɛgjə,let)

= command (kə'mænd)

= head (hɛd)

= lead (lid)

= direct (də'rɛkt , daɪ'rɛkt)

= manage ('mænɪdʒ)

= supervise (,supə'vaɪz)

= administer (əd'mɪnəstə , æd-)

= decree (dɪ'kri)

= dictate ('dɪktet , dɪk'tet)

= order ('ɔrdə)

= instruct (ɪn'strʌkt)

= prevail (prɪ'vel)

= guide (gaɪd)

= influence ('ɪnfluəns)

② = measure ('mɛʒə)

= *mark off*

umble ('rʌmbḷ) *v.* 發隆隆聲

= roar (ror)

= thunder ('θʌndɚ)

= boom (bum)

= roll (rol)

ummage ('rʌmɪdʒ) *v.* 翻尋

= search (sɝtʃ)

= ransack ('rænsæk)

= scour (skaʊr)

= comb (kom)

umor ('rumɚ) *v.* 謠傳

= gossip ('gɑsəp)

= broadcast ('brɔd,kæst)

= circulate ('sɝkjə,let)

= *spread word*

umple ('rʌmpḷ) *v.* 起皺

= crumple ('krʌmpḷ)

= crush (krʌʃ)

= wrinkle ('rɪŋkḷ)

= crease (kris)

= dishevel (dɪ'ʃɛvḷ)

= *muss up*

umpus ('rʌmpəs) *n.* 騷擾；
喧鬧

= noise (nɔɪz)

= uproar ('ʌp,ror , 'ʌp,rɔr)

= disturbance (dɪs'tɝbəns)

= commotion (kə'moʃən)

= hubbub ('hʌbʌb)

= tumult ('tjumʌlt)

= racket ('rækɪt)

= fracas ('frekəs)

= ado (ə'du)

= fuss (fʌs)

= pandemonium
(,pændɪ'monɪəm , -'monjəm)

= row (raʊ)

= din (dɪn)

= clamor ('klæmɚ)

run (rʌn) *v.* ①跑 ②轉動
③延伸 ④流 ⑤繼續 ⑥競選
⑦管理 ⑧拆解 ⑨ *n.* 一段時間

① = hasten ('hesṇ)

= hurry ('hɝɪ)

= speed (spid)

= sprint (sprɪnt)

= bound (baʊnd)

= flee (fli)

= bolt (bolt)

= race (res)

② = go (go)

= move (muv)

= operate ('ɑpə,ret)

= work (wɝk)

③ = stretch (strɛtʃ)

= extend (ɪk'stɛnd)

= reach (ritʃ)

= range (rendʒ)

= lie (laɪ)

= spread (sprɛd)

④ = flow (flo)

= stream (strim)

= pour (por , pɔr)

= gush (gʌʃ)

= discharge (dɪs'tʃɑrdʒ)

⑤ = continue (kən'tɪnjʊ)

= last (læst , lɑst)

= endure (ɪn'djʊr)

= persist (pɚ'zɪst , pɚ'sɪst)

⑥ = campaign (kæm'pen)

= electioneer (ɪ,lɛkʃən'ɪr , ə-)

= stump (stʌmp)

⑦ = conduct (kən'dʌkt)

= manage ('mænɪdʒ)

= direct (də'rɛkt , daɪ-)

= regulate ('rɛgjə,let)

= handle ('hændl̩)

= govern ('gʌvɚn)

= administer (əd'mɪnəstɚ , æd-)

= lead (lid)

= head (hɛd)

= guide (gaɪd)

= steer (stɪr)

= pilot ('paɪlət)

= supervise (,supɚ'vaɪz)

= oversee (,ovɚ'si)

= boss (bɔs)

⑧ = tear (tɛr)

= ravel ('rævl̩)

⑨ = span (spæn)

= period ('pɪrɪəd , 'pi-)

= time (taɪm)

= spell (spɛl)

runway ('rʌn,we) *n.* 跑道

= path (pæθ , pɑθ)

= track (træk)

= road (rod)

rupture ('rʌptʃɚ) *v. n.* 破裂

= break (brek)

= burst (bɝst)

= fracture ('fræktʃɚ)

= crack (kræk)

rural ('rʊrəl) *adj.* 鄉村的

= countrified ('kʌntrɪ,faɪd)

= rustic ('rʌstɪk)

= provincial (prə'vɪnʃəl)

= bucolic (bju'kɑlɪk)

ruse (ruz) *n.* 計謀

= trick (trɪk)

= device (dɪ'vaɪs)

= hoax (hoks)

= deception (dɪ'sɛpʃən)

= fraud (frɔd)

= subterfuge ('sʌbtɚ,fjudʒ)

rush (rʌʃ) *v.* ①衝　②攻擊

① = speed (spid)

= hasten ('hesn̩)

= hurry ('hɝɪ)

= dash (dæʃ)

= dart (dɑrt)

= scurry ('skɝɪ)

= race (res)

= run (rʌn)

= expedite ('ɛkspɪ,daɪt)

= accelerate (æk'sɛlə,ret)

② = pressure ('prɛʃɚ)

= push (pʊʃ)

= attack (ə'tæk)

= charge (tʃɑrdʒ)

= besiege (bɪ'sidʒ)

= drive (draɪv)

= assault (ə'sɔlt)

= storm (stɔrm)

rustic ('rʌstɪk) *adj.* ①鄉村的
②單純的

) = rural (rurəl)

= countrified ('kʌntrɪˌfaɪd)

= provincial (prə'vɪnʃəl)

= bucolic (bju'kɑlɪk)

) = simple ('sɪmp!̣)

= plain (plen)

rusty ('rʌstɪ) *adj.* ①陳腐的
②不熟練的

) = corroded (kə'rodɪd)

= eroded (ɪ'rodɪd)

= worn (worn , worn)

= old (old)

② = unpracticed (ʌn'præktɪst)

rut (rʌt) *n.* 常規

= habit ('hæbɪt)

= routine (ru'tin)

ruthless ('ruθlɪs) *adj.* 殘忍的

= cruel ('kruəl)

= merciless ('mɝsɪlɪs)

= heartless ('hɑrtlɪs)

= cold (kold)

= unfeeling (ʌn'filɪŋ)

= brutal ('brut!̣)

= savage ('sævɪdʒ)

= inhumane (ˌɪnhju'men)

S

sack (sæk) ① *v.* 搶奪
② *n.* 袋；包

① = plunder ('plʌndɚ)

= steal (stil)

= pillage ('pɪlɪdʒ)

= loot (lut)

= rob (rɑb)

= fleece (flis)

② = bag (bæg)

= pack (pæk)

sacred ('sekrɪd) *adj.* 神聖的

= religious (rɪ'lɪdʒəs)

= holy ('holɪ)

= spiritual ('spɪrɪtʃuəl)

sacrifice ('sækrəˌfaɪs , -ˌfaɪz)
v. 犧牲

= relinquish (rɪ'lɪŋkwɪʃ)

= release (rɪ'lis)

= surrender (sə'rɛndɚ)

= yield (jild)

= waive (wev)

= forego (for'go , fɔr'go)

= lose (luz)

= forfeit ('fɔrfɪt)

= *give up*

sad (sæd) *adj.* 悲傷的

= sorrowful ('sɑrofəl)

= unhappy (ʌn'hæpɪ)

= dejected (dɪ'dʒɛktɪd)

= depressed (dɪ'prɛst)

= blue (blu)

= melancholy ('mɛlənˌkɑlɪ)

= downcast ('daʊnˌkæst)

= discouraged (dɪs'kɝɪdʒd)

= gloomy ('glumɪ)

= somber ('sɑmbɚ)

= glum (glʌm)

= morose (mo'ros , mə-)

= sullen ('sʌlɪn , -lən)
= grievous ('grivəs)
= miserable ('mɪzərəbḷ , 'mɪzrəbḷ)
= pathetic (pə'θɛtɪk)
= unfortunate (ʌn'fɔrtʃənɪt)
= forlorn (fə'lɔrn)

saddle ('sædḷ) v. ①配以馬鞍 ②使負擔

① = harness ('harnɪs)
= yoke (jok)
= *hitch up*
② = burden ('bɝdn)
= load (lod)
= encumber (ɪn'kʌmbə , ɛn-)
= oppress (ə'prɛs)
= *weigh down*

safe (sef) adj. 安全的

= secure (sɪ'kjur)
= unharmed (ʌn'harmd)
= protected (prə'tɛktɪd)
= guarded ('gardɪd)
= sheltered ('ʃɛltəd)
= shielded ('ʃildɪd)

safeguard ('sef,gard) v. 保護

= shield (ʃild)
= screen (skrin)
= bulwark ('bulwək)
= precaution (prɪ'kɔʃən)

sag (sæg) v. 下跌

= droop (drup)
= sink (sɪŋk)

= hang (hæŋ)
= dangle ('dæŋgḷ)
= slump (slʌmp)

saga ('sagə) n. 英雄故事

= story ('storɪ)
= tale (tel)
= yarn (jarn)
= epic ('ɛpɪk)
= account (ə'kaunt)
= anecdote ('ænɪk,dot)
= narrative ('nærətɪv)

sage (sedʒ) adj. 明智的

= wise (waɪz)
= knowing ('noɪŋ)
= learned ('lɝnɪd)
= profound (prə'faund)

sail (sel) n. 航行

= glide (glaɪd)
= coast (kost)
= skim (skɪm)
= navigate ('nævə,get)
= cruise (kruz)
= float (flot)

salary ('sælərɪ) n. 薪水

= pay (pe)
= wages ('wedʒɪz)
= remuneration (rɪ,mjunə're∫ən)
= compensation (,kampən'se∫ən)

salutary ('sæljə,tɛrɪ) adj. 有益健康的

= beneficial (,bɛnə'fɪʃəl)

= healthful（'hɛlθfəl）
= advantageous（,ædvən'tedʒəs）
= wholesome（'holsm̩）

salutation（,sæljə'teʃən）*n.*
寒喧；招呼

= greeting（'gritɪŋ）
= hail（hel）
= hello（hə'lo）

salvage（'sælvɪdʒ）*v.* 援救

= save（sev）
= rescue（'rɛskju）
= recover（rɪ'kʌvɚ）
= redeem（rɪ'dim）
= retrieve（rɪ'triv）

salve（sæv）*n.* 藥膏；軟膏

= ointment（'ɔɪntmənt）
= lotion（'loʃən）
= cream（krim）
= balm（bɑm）
= pomade（po'med，po'mɑd）

same（sem）*adj.* 同一的

= identical（aɪ'dɛntɪkl̩）
= alike（ə'laɪk）
= equivalent（ɪ'kwɪvələnt）

sample（'sæmpl̩）*v.* 試驗

= test（tɛst）
= experiment（ɪk'spɛrəmənt）
= try（traɪ）

sanction（'sæŋkʃən）*v.* 准許

= permit（pɚ'mɪt）

= approve（ə'pruv）
= allow（ə'lau）
= authorize（'ɔθə,raɪz）
= support（sə'port，-'pɔrt）
= license（'laɪsəns）
= accept（ək'sɛpt）
= O. K.（'o'ke）

sanctuary（'sæŋktʃu,ɛrɪ）*n.*
避難所

= refuge（'rɛfjudʒ）
= asylum（ə'saɪləm）
= haven（'hevən）

sand（sænd）*v.* 用砂紙磨光

= scrape（skrep）
= smooth（smuð）
= file（faɪl）
= grind（graɪnd）

sane（sen）*adj.* 頭腦清楚的

= sensible（'sɛnsəbl̩）
= sound（saund）
= rational（'ræʃənl̩）
= logical（'lɑdʒɪkl̩）

sanguine（'sæŋgwɪn）*adj.*
樂天的

= hopeful（'hopfəl）
= expectant（ɪk'spɛktənt，ɛk-）
= confident（'kɑnfədənt）
=·cheerful（'tʃɪrfəl）
= optimistic（,ɑptə'mɪstɪk）

sanitarium（,sænə'tɛrɪəm）*n.*
療養院

= infirmary（ɪn'fɝmərɪ）

= hospital ('hɑspɪtḷ)

= clinic ('klɪnɪk)

sanitary ('sænə,tɛrɪ) *adj.*
衛生的

= clean (klin)

= hygienic (,haɪdʒɪ'ɛnɪk)

= sterile ('stɛrəl)

= pure (pjʊr)

= prophylactic (,profə'læktɪk)

= spotless ('spɑtlɪs)

= healthful ('hɛlθfəl)

sap (sæp) *v.* 使衰弱

= weaken ('wikən)

= debilitate (dɪ'bɪlə,tet)

sarcastic (sɑr'kæstɪk) *adj.*
諷刺的

= sneering ('snɪrɪŋ)

= cutting ('kʌtɪŋ)

= stinging ('stɪŋɪŋ)

= bitter ('bɪtə)

= sharp (ʃɑrp)

= caustic ('kɔstɪk)

satisfy ('sætɪs,faɪ) *v.* ①使滿足
②使確信

① = please (pliz)

= gratify ('grætə,faɪ)

= content (kən'tɛnt)

= benefit ('bɛnəfɪt)

= suit (sut , sjut)

= appease (ə'piz)

② = convince (kən'vɪns)

= persuade (pə'swed)

= assure (ə'ʃʊr)

= comfort ('kʌmfət)

= relieve (rɪ'liv)

saturate ('sætʃə,ret) *v.* 使充斥

= fill (fɪl)

= load (lod)

= stuff (stʌf)

= pack (pæk)

= cram (kræm)

= gorge (gɔrdʒ)

= soak (sok)

= drench (drɛntʃ)

saucy ('sɔsɪ) *adj.* 無禮的

= rude (rud)

= impudent ('ɪmpjədənt)

= impertinent (ɪm'pɜtnənt)

= pert (pɜt)

= disrespectful (,dɪsrɪ'spɛktfəl)

= flippant ('flɪpənt)

= cocky ('kɑkɪ)

= flip (flɪp)

= cheeky ('tʃikɪ)

saunter ('sɔntə , 'sɑntə) *v.*
漫步

= stroll (strol)

= ramble ('ræmbḷ)

= wander ('wɑndə)

= meander (mɪ'ændə)

savage ('sævɪdʒ) *adj.* 蠻荒的

= uncivilized (ʌn'sɪvḷaɪzd)

= barbarous ('bɑrbərəs)

= fierce (fɪrs)

= cruel ('kruəl)

= wild (waɪld)

= untamed (ʌn'temd)

= ruthless ('ruθlɪs)

= inhumane (ˌɪnhju'men)

ave (sev) *v.* ①儲存　②援救

① = store (stor , stɔr)

= economize (ɪ'kɑnəˌmaɪz , i-)

= scrimp (skrɪmp)

= preserve (prɪ'zɜv)

= conserve (kən'sɜv)

= keep (kip)

= maintain (men'ten , mən-)

= reserve (rɪ'zɜv)

= accumulate (ə'kjumjəˌlet)

= gather ('gæðə)

② = rescue ('rɛskju)

= protect (prə'tɛkt)

= salvage ('sælvɪdʒ)

= recover (rɪ'kʌvə)

= redeem (rɪ'dim)

= retrieve (rɪ'triv)

avor ('sevə) *v.* 欣賞

= relish ('rɛlɪʃ)

= enjoy (ɪn'dʒɔɪ)

= like (laɪk)

ay (se) ① *v.* 說話
② *n.* 過問的權利

① = speak (spik)

= declare (dɪ'klɛr)

= recite (rɪ'saɪt)

= utter ('ʌtə)

= voice (vɔɪs)

= express (ɪk'sprɛs)

= tell (tɛl)

= communicate (kə'mjunɪˌket)

= remark (rɪ'mɑrk)

= comment ('kɑmɛnt)

= mention ('mɛnʃən)

= assert (ə'sɜt)

= relate (rɪ'let)

② = power ('pauə)

= authority (ə'θɔrətɪ)

= right (raɪt)

= prerogative (prɪ'rɑgətɪv)

scald (skɔld) *v. n.* 燙傷

= burn (bɜn)

= scorch (skɔrtʃ)

scamp (skæmp) *n.* 流氓

= rascal ('ræskl̩)

= rogue (rog)

= scoundrel ('skaundrəl)

= devil ('dɛvl̩)

= mischief-maker
　('mɪstʃɪfˌmekə)

scamper ('skæmpə) *v.* 疾馳

= scurry ('skɜɪ)

= rush (rʌʃ)

= tear (tɛr)

= dash (dæʃ)

= dart (dɑrt)

= run (rʌn)

= scoot (skut)

= race (res)

= hasten ('hesn̩)

= hurry ('hɜɪ)

S

= scuttle ('skʌtḷ)
= hustle ('hʌsḷ)

scan (skæn) v. 細察

= examine (ɪg'zæmɪn)
= inspect (ɪn'spɛkt)
= scrutinize ('skrutṇaɪz)
= study ('stʌdɪ)
= review (rɪ'vju)
= *look at*

scandal ('skændḷ) n. 恥辱

= disgrace (dɪs'gres)
= humiliation (hju,mɪlɪ'eʃən)
= shame (ʃem)
= slander ('slændɚ)

scanty ('skæntɪ) adj. 缺乏的

= meager ('migɚ)
= scarce (skɛrs)
= sparse (spɑrs)
= inconsiderable
　(,ɪnkən'sɪdərəbḷ)
= small (smɔl)
= slight (slaɪt)
= negligible ('nɛglədʒəbḷ)
= skimpy ('skɪmpɪ)

scar (skɑr) v. 使有疤痕

= blemish ('blɛmɪʃ)
= mar (mɑr)
= mark (mɑrk)
= wound (wund)
= deface (dɪ'fes)

scarce (skɛrs) adj. 缺乏的

= scanty ('skæntɪ)
= sparse (spɑrs)
= rare (rɛr)

scare (skɛr) v. 驚嚇

= frighten ('fraɪtən)
= alarm (ə'lɑrm)
= startle ('stɑrtḷ)
= unnerve (ʌn'nɝv)
= terrify ('tɛrə,faɪ)
= horrify ('hɔrə,faɪ , 'hɑr-)
= appall (ə'pɔl)

scatter ('skætɚ) v. 撒播；揮霍

= disperse (dɪ'spɝs)
= distribute (dɪ'strɪbjut)
= spread (sprɛd)
= separate ('sɛpə,ret , -prɪt)
= part (pɑrt)
= squander ('skwɑndɚ)
= strew (stru)
= *split up*

scene (sin) n. ①景色　②場景
③發脾氣

① = view (vju)
= picture ('pɪktʃɚ)
= sight (saɪt)
= vista ('vɪstə)
= lookout ('lʊk,aʊt)
= landscape ('lænskep , 'lænd-)
= setting ('sɛtɪŋ)
② = act (ækt)
③ = storm (stɔrm)
= outburst ('aʊt,bɝst)
= explosion (ɪk'sploʒən)
= flare-up ('flɛr,ʌp)

cent (sɛnt) *n.* 氣味

= smell (smɛl)

= odor ('odə)

= essence ('ɛsn̩s)

= fragrance ('fregrəns)

chedule ('skɛdʒʊl) *v.* 編製目錄

= list (lɪst)

= index ('ɪndɛks)

= post (post)

= enumerate (ɪ'njumə‚ret)

= slate (slet)

= program ('progræm)

= *line up*

cheme (skim) *v.* 計畫；圖謀

= plan (plæn)

= plot (plɑt)

= intrigue ('ɪntrig , ɪn'trig)

= conspire (kən'spaɪr)

= connive (kə'naɪv)

= contrive (kən'traɪv)

cholar ('skɑlə) *n.* 學者

= savant ('sævənt)

= student ('stjudn̩t)

= learned man

chool (skul) *v.* 教育

= educate ('ɛdʒə‚ket , -dʒʊ-)

= teach (titʃ)

= instruct (ɪn'strʌkt)

= enlighten (ɪn'laɪtn̩)

= direct (də'rɛkt , daɪ-)

= guide (gaɪd)

coff (skɔf , skɑf) *v.* 嘲笑

= mock (mɑk)

= jeer (dʒɪr)

= taunt (tɔnt)

= deride (dɪ'raɪd)

scold (skold) *v.* 責備

= blame (blem)

= reprove (rɪ'pruv)

= reprimand ('rɛprə‚mænd)

= chide (tʃaɪd)

= lecture ('lɛktʃə)

= admonish (əd'mɑnɪʃ)

= *talk to*

scoop (skup) *v.* 挖掘；舀

= dig (dɪg)

= excavate ('ɛkskə‚vet)

= gouge (gaʊdʒ)

= ladle ('ledl̩)

scoot (skut) *v.* 疾走

= dart (dɑrt)

= speed (spid)

= dash (dæʃ)

= rush (rʌʃ)

= tear (tɛr)

= scamper ('skæmpə)

= scurry ('skɜɪ)

= race (res)

= hasten ('hesn̩)

= hurry ('hɜɪ)

= run (rʌn)

= sprint (sprɪnt)

scope (skop) *n.* 範圍

= extent (ɪk'stɛnt)

S

= degree (dɪ'gri)

= measure ('mɛʒɚ)

= range (rendʒ)

= sphere (sfɪr)

= space (spes)

= reach (ritʃ)

scorch (skɔrtʃ) *v.* 燒焦

= burn (bɝn)

= sear (sɪr)

= singe (sɪndʒ)

= blister ('blɪstɚ)

= parch (partʃ)

= char (tʃar)

score (skor , skɔr) *v.* ①計算 ②得分 ③做記號

① = calculate ('kælkjə,let)

= compute (kəm'pjut)

= figure ('fɪgjɚ , 'fɪgɚ)

= tally ('tælɪ)

② = gain (gen)

= earn (ɝn)

= get (gɛt)

= acquire (ə'kwaɪr)

= attain (ə'ten)

= win (wɪn)

③ = cut (kʌt)

= mark (mark)

= line (laɪn)

= scratch (skrætʃ)

= stroke (strok)

scornful ('skɔrnfəl) *adj.* 輕視的

= mocking ('makɪŋ)

= disdainful (dɪs'denfəl , dɪz-)

= contemptuous (kən'tɛmptʃuəs)

scoundrel ('skaundrəl) *n.* 無賴

= villain ('vɪlən)

= rascal ('ræskl)

= rogue (rog)

= devil ('dɛvl)

scour (skaur) *v.* 磨亮;擦淨

= clean (klin)

= scrub (skrʌb)

= polish ('palɪʃ)

= wash (waʃ)

= rub (rʌb)

= buff (bʌf)

= massage (mə'saʒ)

= shine (ʃaɪn)

scourge (skɝdʒ) *v.* 鞭打

= whip (hwɪp)

= beat (bit)

= thrash (θræʃ)

= spank (spæŋk)

= flog (flag)

= lash (læʃ)

scout (skaut) *v.* 偵察

= hunt (hʌnt)

= *search out*

scowl (skaul) *n.* 不悅之色

= frown (fraun)

= pout (paut)

= glower ('glauɚ)

= *black look*

cramble ('skræmbḷ) v. ①湊合
①匆忙

= mix (mɪks)
= mingle ('mɪŋgḷ)
= blend (blɛnd)
= combine (kəm'baɪn)
= jumble ('dʒʌmbḷ)
= merge (mɝdʒ)
= fuse (fjuz)
= hurry ('hɝɪ)
= scurry ('skɝɪ)
= scamper ('skæmpɚ)
= hasten ('hesn̩)
= scoot (skut)
= rush (rʌʃ)
= tear (tɛr)
= dart (dart)
= hustle ('hʌsḷ)
= scuttle ('skʌtḷ)
= bustle ('bʌsḷ)

crap (skræp) ① v. 吵架
① n. 碎屑   ③ n. 殘物

① = fight (faɪt)
= quarrel ('kwɔrəl , 'kwa-)
= struggle ('strʌgḷ)
= squabble ('skwabḷ)
= tiff (tɪf)
= spat (spæt)
= bicker ('bɪkɚ)
= row (raʊ)
② = shred (ʃrɛd)
= snatch (snætʃ)
= speck (spɛk)
= particle ('partɪkḷ)
= *small amount*
③ = waste (west)

= litter ('lɪtɚ)
= debris (də'bri , 'debri)
= trash (træʃ)
= rubbish ('rʌbɪʃ)
= junk (dʒʌŋk)
= garbage ('garbɪdʒ)

scrape (skrep) ① v. 磨；擦
② n. 困境

① = rub (rʌb)
= brush (brʌʃ)
= skim (skɪm)
= graze (grez)
= grate (gret)
② = trouble ('trʌbḷ)
= predicament (prɪ'dɪkəmənt)
= plight (plaɪt)
= pinch (pɪntʃ)
= strait (stret)
= mess (mɛs)
= complication (,kamplə'keʃən)
= muddle ('mʌdḷ)
= embarrassment
   (ɪm'bærəsmənt)

scratch (skrætʃ) v. 抓

= scrape (skrep)
= mark (mark)
= cut (kʌt)
= graze (grez)
= score (skor , skɔr)
= scar (skar)
= engrave (ɪn'grev)

scrawl (skrɔl) v. 亂塗

= scribble ('skrɪbḷ)
= scratch (skrætʃ)

scrawny ('skrɔnɪ) *adj.* 細瘦的

= lean (lin)

= thin (θɪn)

= skinny ('skɪnɪ)

= spare (spɛr)

= gaunt (gɔnt , gɑnt)

= lanky ('læŋkɪ)

= bony ('bonɪ)

scream (skrim) *v.* 高聲尖叫

= yell (jɛl)

= cry (kraɪ)

= shout (ʃaʊt)

= howl (haʊl)

= shriek (ʃrik)

= screech (skritʃ)

= wail (wel)

= squall (skwɔl)

= bawl (bɔl)

screech (skritʃ) *v.* 尖叫

= shriek (ʃrik)

= scream (skrim)

= squeal (skwil)

= yell (jɛl)

= cry (kraɪ)

= shout (ʃaʊt)

= howl (haʊl)

screen (skrin) *v.* ①掩護
②篩選 ③調查

① = shelter ('ʃɛltɚ)

= protect (prə'tɛkt)

= hide (haɪd)

= cover ('kʌvɚ)

= cloak (klok)

= veil (vel)

= shade (ʃed)

= safeguard ('sef,gɑrd)

② = sift (sɪft)

= strain (stren)

= filter ('fɪltɚ)

= refine (rɪ'faɪn)

= sort (sɔrt)

= separate ('sɛpə,ret , -pret)

③ = inspect (ɪn'spɛkt)

= analyze ('ænḷ,aɪz)

= check (tʃɛk)

screw (skru) *v.* ①用螺絲釘釘住
②旋轉

① = fasten ('fæsṇ , 'fɑsṇ)

= tighten ('taɪtṇ)

② = twist (twɪst)

= rotate ('rotet)

= turn (tɜn)

scribble ('skrɪbḷ) *v.* 亂塗

= scrawl (skrɔl)

= scratch (skrætʃ)

scrimmage ('skrɪmɪdʒ) *n.* 混戰

= struggle ('strʌgḷ)

= fight (faɪt)

= encounter (ɪn'kaʊntɚ)

= battle ('bætḷ)

= fray (fre)

= clash (klæʃ)

= tussle ('tʌsḷ)

= scuffle ('skʌfḷ)

= melee (me'le , 'mele)

= hassle ('hæsḷ)

cript (skrɪpt) *n.* 手稿；筆跡

= writing ('raɪtɪŋ)

= penmanship ('pɛnmən‚ʃɪp)

crub (skrʌb) *v.* 擦洗

= scour (skaʊr)

= clean (klin)

= polish ('palɪʃ)

= wash (waʃ)

= rub (rʌb)

= buff (bʌf)

= massage (mə'saʒ)

= shine (ʃaɪn)

crupulous ('skrupjələs) *adj.* 謹慎的

= careful ('kɛrfəl)

= meticulous (mə'tɪkjələs)

= exacting (ɪg'zæktɪŋ , ɛg-)

= particular(pə'tɪkjələ , pa-)

= precise (prɪ'saɪs)

= fussy ('fʌsɪ)

= fastidious (fæs'tɪdɪəs)

crutinize ('skrutn‚aɪz) *v.* 細察

= inspect (ɪn'spɛkt)

= examine (ɪg'zæmɪn)

= observe (əb'zɝv)

= study ('stʌdɪ)

= contemplate ('kantəm‚plet)

= review (rɪ'vju)

= *look at*

cuffle ('skʌfl) *n.* 混戰

= struggle ('strʌgl)

= fight (faɪt)

= tussle ('tʌsl)

= melee (me'le , 'mele)

sculpture ('skʌlptʃə) *v.* 雕刻

= carve (karv)

= form (fɔrm)

= shape (ʃep)

= mold (mold)

= model ('madl)

= chisel ('tʃɪzl)

scurry ('skɝɪ) *v.* 疾走

= scamper ('skæmpə)

= rush (rʌʃ)

= tear (tɛr)

= dash (dæʃ)

= dart (dart)

= run (rʌn)

= scoot (skut)

= race (res)

= scuttle ('skʌtl)

= hasten ('hesn)

= hurry ('hɝɪ)

= hustle ('hʌsl)

scuttle ('skʌtl) *v.* 疾走

= scurry ('skɝɪ)

= scamper ('skæmpə)

= rush (rʌʃ)

= tear (tɛr)

= dash (dæʃ)

= dart (dart)

= run (rʌn)

= scoot (skut)

= race (res)

= hasten ('hesn)

S

S

= hurry ('hɝɪ)

= hustle ('hʌsḷ)

seal (sil) ① v. 封緘；密封

② v. 蓋章　③ n. 海豹

① = fasten ('fæsn̩ , 'fɑsn̩)

= close (kloz)

= shut (ʃʌt)

= lock (lɑk)

② = endorse (ɪn'dɔrs , ɛn-)

= sign (saɪn)

= mark (mɑrk)

= stamp (stæmp)

③ = sea lion

sear (sɪr) v. 燒焦

= burn (bɝn)

= scorch (skɔrtʃ)

= singe (sɪndʒ)

= char (tʃɑr)

search (sɝtʃ) v. 尋找

= seek (sik)

= hunt (hʌnt)

= explore (ɪk'splor , -'splɔr)

= look for

season ('sizn̩) v. 調味

= flavor ('flevɚ)

= spice (spaɪs)

secluded (sɪ'kludɪd) adj.
隔離的；退隱的

= concealed (kən'sild)

= hidden ('hɪdn̩)

= covered ('kʌvɚd)

= obscured (əb'skjʊrd)

= secret ('sikrɪt)

= private ('praɪvɪt)

= intimate ('ɪntəmɪt)

= undisturbed (ˌʌndɪ'stɝbd)

= withdrawn (wɪð'drɔn , wɪθ-)

= isolated ('aɪsḷˌetɪd)

= remote (rɪ'mot)

secret ('sikrɪt) adj. 隱秘的

= hidden ('hɪdn̩)

= mysterious (mɪs'tɪrɪəs)

= private ('praɪvɪt)

= concealed (kən'sild)

= secluded (sɪ'kludɪd)

secrete (sɪ'krit) v. 分泌

= discharge (dɪs'tʃɑrdʒ)

= excrete (ɛk'skrit , ɪk-)

= eliminate (ɪ'lɪməˌnet)

= exude (ɪg'zjud , ɪk'sjud)

section ('sɛkʃən) v. 切開

= divide (də'vaɪd)

= slice (slaɪs)

= split (splɪt)

= partition (par'tɪʃən , pɚ-)

= parcel ('pɑrsḷ)

= portion ('porʃən , 'pɔr-)

secure (sɪ'kjʊr) ① adj. 安全的
② v. 得到　③ v. 緊閉

① = safe (sef)

= protected (prə'tɛktɪd)

= sure (ʃʊr)

= sound (saʊnd)

= firm (fɜm)
= stable ('stebḷ)
= get (gɛt)
= obtain (əb'ten)
= acquire (ə'kwaɪr)
= close (kloz)
= fasten ('fæsn̩ , 'fasn̩)
= shut (ʃʌt)
= lock (lak)
= seal (sil)
= fix (fɪks)
= attach (ə'tætʃ)

educe (sɪ'djus) *v.* 引誘

= tempt (tɛmpt)
= persuade (pə'swed)
= lure (lʊr)
= entice (ɪn'taɪs , ɛn-)
= *lead on*

ek (sik) *v.* 尋求

= hunt (hʌnt)
= search (sɜtʃ)
= pursue (pə'su , -sɪʊ)
= quest (kwɛst)
= explore (ɪk'splor , -'splɔr)
= *look for*

em (sim) *v.* 看似

= appear (ə'pɪr)
= look (lʊk)

ep (sip) *v.* 滲入

= ooze (uz)
= trickle ('trɪkḷ)
= emit (ɪ'mɪt)

= excrete (ɪk'skrit)

seethe (sið) *v.* 沸騰；激昂

= burn (bɜn)
= fume (fjum)
= simmer ('sɪmə)
= boil (bɔɪl)
= stew (stju)
= *be angry*

segment ('sɛgmənt) *n.* 部分

= division (də'vɪʒən)
= section ('sɛkʃən)
= part (part)
= portion ('porʃən , 'pɔr-)
= fraction ('frækʃən)
= subdivision (ˌsʌbdə'vɪʒən , 'sʌbdəˌvɪʒən)

seize (siz) *v.* 抓住

= clutch (klʌtʃ)
= grasp (græsp)
= grab (græb)
= grip (grɪp)
= clasp (klæsp)
= snatch (snætʃ)

seldom ('sɛldəm) *adv.* 很少地

= rarely ('rɛrlɪ)
= infrequently (ɪn'frikwəntlɪ)
= hardly ('hardlɪ)
= *not often*

select (sə'lɛkt) *v.* 選擇

= pick (pɪk)
= choose (tʃuz)

S

self-conscious ('sɛlf'kɑnʃəs)
adj. 羞怯的

= shy (ʃaɪ)
= timid ('tɪmɪd)
= bashful ('bæʃfəl)
= coy (kɔɪ)
= demure (dɪ'mjʊr)

selfish ('sɛlfɪʃ) *adj.* 自私的

= egotistical (,ɪgə'tɪstɪkḷ , ,ɛg-)
= self-centered ('sɛlf'sɛntəd)
= possessive (pə'zɛsɪv)

sell (sɛl) *v.* 販賣

= market ('mɑrkɪt)
= vend (vɛnd)
= peddle ('pɛdḷ)

send (sɛnd) *v.* 派遣

= dispatch (dɪ'spætʃ)
= transmit (træns'mɪt)
= forward ('fɔrwəd)

senior ('sinjə) *adj.* 年長的

= elder ('ɛldə)
= older ('oldə)

sensational (sɛn'seʃənḷ) *adj.*
令人激動的

= exciting (ɪk'saɪtɪŋ , ɛk)
= startling ('stɑrtlɪŋ)
= superb (su'pɜb , sə-)
= exquisite ('ɛkskwɪzɪt , ɪk's-)
= magnificent (mæg'nɪfəsṇt)
= marvelous ('mɑrvḷəs)
= wonderful ('wʌndəfəl)

= glorious ('glorɪəs , 'glɔr-)

sense (sɛns) ① *v.* 理解
② *n.* 判斷力

① = feel (fil)
= perceive (pə'siv)
= understand (,ʌndə'stænd)
= realize ('rɪə,laɪz , 'rɪə-)
= comprehend (,kɑmprɪ'hɛnd)
= fathom ('fæðəm)
= follow ('fɑlo)
= grasp (græsp)
= discern (dɪ'zɜn , -'sɜn)
② = intelligence (ɪn'tɛlədʒəns)
= mentality (mɛn'tælətɪ)
= judgment ('dʒʌdʒmənt)

senseless ('sɛnslɪs) *adj.*
①無知覺的 ②愚蠢的

① = unconscious (ʌn'kɑnʃəs)
= lifeless ('laɪflɪs)
= inanimate (ɪn'ænəmɪt)
= oblivious (ə'blɪvɪəs)
② = foolish ('fulɪʃ)
= stupid ('stjupɪd)
= asinine ('æsṇ,aɪn)
= silly ('sɪlɪ)
= inane (ɪn'en)
= idiotic (,ɪdɪ'ɑtɪk)

sensible ('sɛnsəbḷ) *adj.* 明理的
合理的

= wise (waɪz)
= intelligent (ɪn'tɛlədʒənt)
= understanding (,ʌndə'stændɪŋ

= rational ('ræʃən!)

= bright (braɪt)

= sound (saʊnd)

= sane (sen)

= logical ('lɑdʒɪk!)

= practical ('præktɪk!)

= realistic (,rɪə'lɪstɪk , ,rɪə-)

ntimental (,sɛntə'mɛnt!) *adj.*
情的

= emotional (ɪ'moʃən!)

= tender ('tɛndɚ)

= affectionate (ə'fɛkʃənɪt)

parate ('sɛpə,ret , -prɪt) *v.*
開

= divide (də'vaɪd)

= part (pɑrt)

= segregate ('sɛgrɪ,get)

= sort (sɔrt)

= isolate ('aɪsḷ,et , 'ɪs-)

= partition (pɑr'tɪʃən , pə-)

quel ('sikwəl) *n.* 後續；結果

= continuation (kən,tɪnju'eʃən)

= supplement ('sʌpləmənt)

= outcome ('aʊt,kʌm)

= follow-up ('fɑlo,ʌp , 'fɑlə,wʌp)

quence ('sikwəns) *n.* 繼續

= succession (sək'sɛʃən)

= continuation (kən,tɪnju'eʃən)

= series ('sɪrɪz , 'sɪrɪz)

= progression (prə'grɛʃən)

ene (sə'rin) *adj.* 寧靜的

= peaceful ('pisfəl)

= calm (kɑm)

= tranquil ('trɑnkwɪl , 'træŋ-)

= quiet ('kwaɪət)

= untroubled (ʌn'trʌbḷd)

= pacific (pə'sɪfɪk)

serial ('sɪrɪəl) *adj.* 連續的

= consecutive (kən'sɛkjətɪv)

= sequential (sɪ'kwɛnʃəl)

= periodic (,pɪrɪ'ɑdɪk)

serious ('sɪrɪəs) *adj.* ①認真的
②重要的

① = thoughtful ('θɔtfəl)

= grave (grev)

= reflective (rɪ'flɛktɪv)

= pensive ('pɛnsɪv)

= solemn ('sɑləm)

= engrossed (ɪn'grost , ɛn-)

= sincere (sɪn'sɪr)

= earnest ('ɝnɪst , -əst)

= zealous ('zɛləs)

② = important (ɪm'pɔrtṇt)

= weighty ('wetɪ)

= momentous (mo'mɛntəs)

= profound (prə'faʊnd)

sermon ('sɝmən) *n.* 講道

= lecture ('lɛktʃɚ)

= talk (tɔk)

= discourse (dɪ'skors , 'dɪskors)

= recitation (,rɛsə'teʃən)

serpent ('sɝpənt) *n.* 蛇

= snake (snek)

= viper ('vaɪpɚ)

S

serve ﹝ sɜv ﹞ *v.* ①供應 ②服務

① = supply ﹝ sə'plaɪ ﹞
　 = furnish ﹝ 'fɜnɪʃ ﹞
　 = deliver ﹝ dɪ'lɪvə ﹞
　 = present ﹝ prɪ'zɛnt ﹞
② = help ﹝ hɛlp ﹞
　 = assist ﹝ ə'sɪst ﹞
　 = *work for*

set ﹝ sɛt ﹞ *v.* 安置

　 = place ﹝ ples ﹞
　 = position ﹝ pə'zɪʃən ﹞
　 = arrange ﹝ ə'rendʒ ﹞
　 = fix ﹝ fɪks ﹞
　 = adjust ﹝ ə'dʒʌst ﹞
　 = regulate ﹝ 'rɛgjə,let ﹞

setting ﹝ 'sɛtɪŋ ﹞ *n.* 環境；背景

　 = scenery ﹝ 'sinərɪ ﹞
　 = surroundings ﹝ sə'raʊndɪŋs ﹞
　 = background ﹝ 'bæk,graʊnd ﹞

settle ﹝ 'sɛtl̩ ﹞ *v.* ①決定；解決
②定居

① = determine ﹝ dɪ'tɜmɪn ﹞
　 = decide ﹝ dɪ'saɪd ﹞
　 = resolve ﹝ rɪ'zalv ﹞
　 = fix ﹝ fɪks ﹞
　 = reconcile ﹝ 'rɛkən,saɪl ﹞
　 = mend ﹝ mɛnd ﹞
　 = *patch up*
② = occupy ﹝ 'akjə,paɪ ﹞
　 = inhabit ﹝ ɪn'hæbɪt ﹞
　 = colonize ﹝ 'kalə,naɪz ﹞
　 = locate ﹝ lo'ket , 'loket ﹞

sever ﹝ 'sɛvə ﹞ *v.* 斷絕；切斷

　 = separate ﹝ 'sɛpə,ret ﹞
　 = part ﹝ part ﹞
　 = detach ﹝ dɪ'tætʃ ﹞
　 = chop ﹝ tʃap ﹞
　 = cleave ﹝ kliv ﹞
　 = split ﹝ splɪt ﹞
　 = *cut off*

several ﹝ 'sɛvərəl ﹞ *adj.* 數個的

　 = some ﹝ 'sʌm ﹞
　 = various ﹝ 'vɛrɪəs ﹞
　 = assorted ﹝ ə'sɔrtɪd ﹞
　 = diversified ﹝ də'vɜsə,faɪd ﹞
　 = many ﹝ 'mɛnɪ ﹞
　 = numerous ﹝ 'njumərəs ﹞

severe ﹝ sə'vɪr ﹞ *adj.* 嚴厲的

　 = strict ﹝ strɪkt ﹞
　 = stern ﹝ stɜn ﹞
　 = harsh ﹝ harʃ ﹞
　 = rough ﹝ rʌf ﹞
　 = stringent ﹝ 'strɪndʒənt ﹞
　 = austere ﹝ ɔ'stɪr ﹞

shabby ﹝ 'ʃæbɪ ﹞ *adj.* 衣衫襤褸

　 = worn ﹝ wɔrn ﹞
　 = ragged ﹝ 'rægɪd ﹞
　 = shoddy ﹝ 'ʃadɪ ﹞
　 = tattered ﹝ 'tætəd ﹞
　 = frayed ﹝ 'fred ﹞
　 = seedy ﹝ 'sidɪ ﹞

shack ﹝ ʃæk ﹞ *n.* 小木屋

　 = hut ﹝ hʌt ﹞
　 = shanty ﹝ 'ʃæntɪ ﹞

= shed (ʃɛd)

= cabin ('kæbɪn)

ackle ('ʃækl) v. 束縛

= tie (taɪ)

= bind (baɪnd)

= chain (tʃen)

= manacle ('mænəkl)

= handcuff ('hænd,kʌf , 'hæn-)

aggy ('ʃægɪ) adj. 蓬鬆的；
亂的

= rumpled ('rʌmpld)

= tousled ('tauzld)

= disheveled (dɪ'ʃɛvld , -əld)

= mussed up

ake (ʃek) v. ①顫抖 ②搖動

= vibrate ('vaɪbret)

= tremble ('trɛmbl)

= shiver ('ʃɪvə)

= quiver ('kwɪvə)

= quaver ('kwevə)

= jerk (dʒɝk)

= twitch (twɪtʃ)

= jar (dʒɑr)

= bump (bʌmp)

= bounce (bauns)

= pump (pʌmp)

= jolt (dʒolt)

= rock (rɑk)

= sway (swe)

allow ('ʃælo) adj. ①膚淺的
淺的

= featherbrained ('fɛðə,brend)

= simple ('sɪmpl)

= slow (slo)

= empty ('ɛmptɪ)

② = not deep

sham (ʃæm) n. 偽物；贋品

= fraud (frɔd)

= pretense (prɪ'tɛns)

= fake (fek)

= mock (mɑk)

= imitation (,ɪmə'teʃən)

= hoax ('hoks)

shambles ('ʃæmblz) n. 凌亂

= mess (mɛs)

= disorder (dɪs'ɔrdə)

= chaos ('keɑs)

shameful ('ʃemfʊl) adj. 可恥的

= disgraceful (dɪs'gresfəl)

= humiliating (hju'mɪlɪ,etɪŋ)

= scandalous ('skændləs)

= pitiful ('pɪtɪfəl)

= deplorable (dɪ'plorəbl)

shampoo (ʃæm'pu) v. 洗髮

= soap (sop)

= lather ('læðə)

= wash (wɑʃ)

shanty ('ʃæntɪ) n. 簡陋小屋

= shack (ʃæk)

= hut (hʌt)

= shed (ʃɛd)

= cabin ('kæbɪn)

S

shape (∫ep) *n.* 形狀

= form (fɔrm)

= fashion ('fæ∫ən)

= mold (mold)

= design (dı'zaın)

= develop (dı'vɛləp)

= adapt (ə'dæpt)

share (∫ɛr) *v.* 分配

= divide (də'vaıd)

= proportion (prə'por∫ən)

= apportion (ə'por∫ən)

= distribute (dı'strıbjut)

= allot (ə'lɑt)

sharp (∫ɑrp) *adj.* ①尖的
②刺骨的 ③聰明的

① = pointy ('pɔıntı)

= angular ('æŋgjələ)

② = severe (sə'vır)

= biting ('baıtıŋ)

= caustic ('kɔstık)

= bitter ('bıtə)

= harsh ('hɑr∫)

= curt (kɜt)

= gruff (grʌf)

= brusque (brʌsk)

= blunt (blʌnt)

= snippy ('snıpı)

③ = keen (kin)

= bright (braıt)

= smart (smɑrt)

= clever ('klɛvə)

= shrewd (∫rud)

= alert (ə'lɜt)

= brainy ('brenı)

shatter ('∫ætə) *v.* 損毀

= destroy (dı'strɔı)

= smash (smæ∫)

= fragment ('frægmənt)

= break (brek)

shear (∫ır) *v.* 修剪

= clip (klıp)

= crop (krɑp)

= *cut off*

shed (∫ɛd) ① *v.* 脫落；發散
② *n.* 小屋

① = cast (kæst)

= slough (slʌf)

= spread (sprɛd)

= radiate ('redı,et)

= *throw off*

② = hut (hʌt)

= shanty ('∫æntı)

= shack (∫æk)

sheen (∫in) *n.* 光輝

= luster ('lʌstə)

= shine (∫aın)

= brightness ('braıtnıs)

= gloss (glɔs)

= glow (glo)

= gleam (glim)

sheepish ('∫ipı∫) *adj.* 羞怯的

= bashful ('bæ∫fəl)

= embarrassed (ım'bærəst)

= flushed (flʌ∫t)

= blushing ('blʌ∫ıŋ)

= shamefaced ('∫em,fest)

= shy〔ʃaɪ〕
= timid〔'tɪmɪd〕

sheer〔ʃɪr〕*adj.* ①極薄的；
透明的 ②純粹的

① = transparent〔træns'pɛrənt〕
= translucent〔træns'lusn̩t〕
= clear〔klɪr〕
= thin〔θɪn〕
= diaphanous〔daɪ'æfənəs〕
② = simple〔'sɪmpl̩〕
= plain〔plen〕
= pure〔pjʊr〕

shelter〔'ʃɛltɚ〕*v.* 保護

= protect〔prə'tɛkt〕
= shield〔ʃild〕
= hide〔haɪd〕
= guard〔gard〕
= defend〔dɪ'fɛnd〕
= screen〔skrin〕
= cover〔'kʌvɚ〕
= harbor〔'harbɚ〕

shield〔ʃild〕*v.* 防禦

= defend〔dɪ'fɛnd〕
= protect〔prə'tɛkt〕
= guard〔gard〕
= shelter〔'ʃɛltɚ〕
= hide〔haɪd〕
= screen〔skrin〕
= cover〔'kʌvɚ〕
= cloak〔klok〕
= harbor〔'harbɚ〕

shift〔ʃɪft〕*v.* 變換

= change〔tʃendʒ〕

= substitute〔'sʌbstə,tjut〕
= alter〔'ɔltɚ〕
= vary〔'vɛrɪ〕

shiftless〔'ʃɪftlɪs〕*adj.* 懶惰的；
無能的

= lazy〔'lezɪ〕
= inefficient〔ɪnə'fɪʃənt〕
= indolent〔'ɪndələnt〕
= laggard〔'lægɚd〕
= do-nothing〔'du,nʌθɪŋ〕

shifty〔'ʃɪftɪ〕*adj.* 詭詐的

= tricky〔'trɪkɪ〕
= sneaky〔'snikɪ〕
= sly〔slaɪ〕
= furtive〔'fɝtɪv〕
= deceitful〔dɪ'sitfəl〕
= evasive〔ɪ'vesɪv〕
= crafty〔'kraftɪ〕
= foxy〔'faksɪ〕
= cunning〔'kʌnɪŋ〕
= artful〔'artfəl〕
= shrewd〔ʃrud〕
= canny〔'kænɪ〕

shimmer〔'ʃɪmɚ〕*v.* 發閃光

= gleam〔glim〕
= shine〔ʃaɪn〕
= glimmer〔'glɪmɚ〕
= twinkle〔'twɪŋkl̩〕
= sparkle〔'sparkl̩〕
= glisten〔'glɪsn̩〕

shine〔ʃaɪn〕*v.* ①發光
②出類拔萃

① = glow〔glo〕

S

S

= gleam (glim)

= glimmer ('glɪmə)

= twinkle ('twɪŋkḷ)

= sparkle ('sparkḷ)

= glisten ('glɪsn̩)

= glare (glɛr)

② = *be smart*

= *be bright*

ship (ʃɪp) *v.* 運送

= transport (træns'port)

= send (sɛnd)

= dispatch (dɪ'spætʃ)

= haul (hɔl)

shirk (ʃɝk) *v.* 躲避

= slack (slæk)

= avoid (ə'vɔɪd)

= malinger (mə'lɪŋgə)

shiver ('ʃɪvə) *v. n.* 顫抖

= shake (ʃek)

= quiver ('kwɪvə)

= quaver ('kwevə)

= quake (kwek)

= tremble ('trɛmbḷ)

shock (ʃak) *v.* 使震驚

= startle ('startḷ)

= frighten ('fraɪtn̩)

= terrify ('tɛrə,faɪ)

= horrify ('hɔrə,faɪ , 'har-)

= appall (ə'pɔl)

= awe (ɔ)

shoot (ʃut) *v.* 射擊

= fire (faɪr)

= discharge (dɪs'tʃardʒ)

shop (ʃap) *v.* 購物

= market ('markɪt)

= buy (baɪ)

= purchase ('pɝtʃəs , -ɪs)

shore (ʃor) *n.* 海岸

= coast (kost)

= beach (bitʃ)

= waterfront ('watə'frʌnt)

= bank (bæŋk)

short (ʃort) *adj.* ①短小的
②簡潔的

① = little ('lɪtḷ)

= small (smɔl)

= slight (slaɪt)

= puny ('pʌnɪ)

② = brief (brif)

= concise (kən'saɪs)

= succinct (sək'sɪŋkt)

= curt (kɝt)

shortage ('ʃortɪdʒ) *n.* 缺乏

= lack (læk)

= deficiency (dɪ'fɪʃənsɪ)

= want (want , wɔnt)

= need (nid)

= deficit ('dɛfəsɪt)

= absence ('æbsn̩s)

shortcoming ('ʃort,kʌmɪŋ) *n.*
缺點

= fault (fɔlt)

S

= defect (dɪ'fɛkt)

= flaw (flɔ)

= weakness ('wiknɪs)

= failing ('felɪŋ)

= imperfection (ˌɪmpə'fɛkʃən)

= inadequacy (ɪn'ædəkwəsɪ)

= deficiency (dɪ'fɪʃənsɪ)

shout (ʃaʊt) *v.* 喊叫

= yell (jɛl)

= call (kɔl)

= cry (kraɪ)

= scream (skrim)

= shriek (ʃrik)

= howl (haʊl)

= clamor ('klæmɚ)

shove (ʃʌv) *v.* 推擠

= push (puʃ)

= jostle ('dʒɑsl̩)

= thrust (θrʌst)

= ram (ræm)

= bump (bʌmp)

= prod (prɑd)

= goad (god)

= nudge (nʌdʒ)

show (ʃo) *v.* ①說明 ②顯示

= direct (də'rɛkt)

= point (pɔɪnt)

= aim (em)

= explain (ɪk'splen)

= clarify ('klærə,faɪ)

= demonstrate ('dɛmən,stret)

= illustrate (ɪ'lʌstret)

= indicate ('ɪndə,ket)

= denote (dɪ'not)

= manifest ('mænə,fɛst)

= guide (gaɪd)

② = display (dɪ'sple)

= exhibit (ɪg'zɪbɪt)

= reveal (rɪ'vil)

showy ('ʃoɪ) *adj.* 炫耀的

= flashy ('flæʃɪ)

= flaunting ('flɔntɪŋ)

= ostentatious (ˌɑstən'teʃəs)

shred (ʃrɛd) *n.* 微量

= fragment ('frægmənt)

= particle ('pɑrtɪkl̩)

= piece (pis)

= crumb (krʌm)

= scrap (skræp)

shrewd (ʃrud) *adj.* 精明的

= keen (kin)

= clever ('klɛvɚ)

= sharp (ʃɑrp)

= smart (smɑrt)

= artful ('ɑrtfəl)

= cunning ('kʌnɪŋ)

= knowing ('noɪŋ)

= crafty ('kræftɪ)

= foxy ('fɑksɪ)

= smooth (smuð)

= canny ('kænɪ)

shriek (ʃrik) *v.* 尖叫

= yell (jɛl)

= cry (kraɪ)

= call (kɔl)

= shout (ʃaʊt)
= howl (haʊl)
= scream (skrim)
= screech (skritʃ)

shrill (ʃrɪl) *adj.* 尖銳的

= piercing ('pɪrsɪŋ)
= sharp (ʃɑrp)
= screechy ('skritʃɪ)
= squeaky ('skwikɪ)
= harsh (hɑrʃ)
= grating ('gretɪŋ)

shrink (ʃrɪŋk) *v.* ①收縮
②退縮

① = shrivel ('ʃrɪvl)
= wither ('wɪðɚ)
= dwindle ('dwɪndl)
= *become smaller*
② = withdraw (wɪð'drɔ)
= recoil (rɪ'kɔɪl)
= retreat (rɪ'trit)
= flinch (flɪntʃ)
= cringe (krɪndʒ)
= *pull back*

shrivel ('ʃrɪvl) *v.* 使萎縮

= wither ('wɪðɚ)
= shrink (ʃrɪŋk)
= wrinkle ('rɪŋkl)

shroud (ʃraʊd) *v.* 遮蓋

= cover ('kʌvɚ)
= conceal (kən'sil)
= veil (vel)
= cloak (klok)
= screen (skrin)

shudder ('ʃʌdɚ) *v. n.* 戰慄

= tremble ('trɛmbl)
= quiver ('kwɪvɚ)
= shake (ʃek)
= quake (kwek)

shuffle ('ʃʌfl) *v.* ①拖著腳步走
②弄亂

① = scrape (skrep)
= drag (dræg)
= scuff (skʌf)
= trudge (trʌdʒ)
② = mix (mɪks)
= combine (kəm'baɪn)
= scramble ('skræmbl)
= jumble ('dʒʌmbl)

shun (ʃʌn) *v.* 避免

= avoid (ə'vɔɪd)
= evade (ɪ'ved)
= dodge (dɑdʒ)
= snub (snʌb)
= slight (slaɪt)
= ignore (ɪg'nor)

shut (ʃʌt) *v.* 關閉

= close (kloz)
= fasten ('fæsn)
= seal (sil)
= lock (lɑk)

shy (ʃaɪ) *adj.* 害羞的

= bashful ('bæʃfəl)
= timid ('tɪmɪd)
= coy (kɔɪ)
= demure (dɪ'mjʊr)

sick (sɪk) *adj.* 生病的

= ill (ɪl)
= ailing ('elɪŋ)
= indisposed (ˌɪndɪ'spozd)

sift (sɪft) *v.* 篩選

= sort (sɔrt)
= separate ('sɛpəˌret , -prɪt)
= divide (də'vaɪd)
= screen (skrin)
= filter ('fɪltə)
= refine (rɪ'faɪn)
= strain (stren)

sight (saɪt) *n.* 觀覽；景象

= vision ('vɪʒən)
= view (vju)
= look (lʊk)
= vista ('vɪstə)
= scene (sin)
= spectacle ('spɛktəkḷ)
= display (dɪ'sple)
= show (ʃo)

sign (saɪn) *v.* ①簽字　②做手勢

① = mark (mɑrk)
= endorse (ɪn'dɔrs)
= seal (sil)
= initial (ɪ'nɪʃəl)
② = signal ('sɪgnḷ)
= gesture ('dʒɛstʃə)
= motion ('moʃən)
= wave (wev)
= indicate ('ɪndəˌket)

signet ('sɪgnɪt) *n.* 印章

= seal (sil)
= insignia (ɪn'sɪgnɪə)
= label ('lebḷ)
= tag (tæg)
= stamp (stæmp)
= sticker ('stɪkə)
= brand (brænd)
= hallmark ('hɔlˌmɑrk)

significance (sɪg'nɪfəkəns) *n.*
意義；重要

= meaning ('minɪŋ)
= connotation (ˌkɑnə'teʃən)
= implication (ˌɪmplɪ'keʃən)
= drift (drɪft)
= substance ('sʌbstəns)
= gist (dʒɪst)
= effect (ə'fɛkt)
= importance (ɪm'pɔrtṇs)
= consequence ('kɑnsəˌkwɛns)

silent ('saɪlənt) *adj.* 安靜的

= quiet ('kwaɪət)
= still (stɪl)
= noiseless ('nɔɪzlɪs)
= soundless ('saʊndlɪs)
= hushed (hʌʃt)

silhouette (ˌsɪlʊ'ɛt) *n.* 輪廓

= outline ('aʊtˌlaɪn)
= contour ('kɑntʊr)
= profile ('profaɪl)
= configuration
　(kənˌfɪgjə'reʃən)
= shadow ('ʃædo)

S

silly ('sɪlɪ) *adj.* 愚蠢的

= foolish ('fulɪʃ)

= ridiculous (rɪ'dɪkjələs)

= inane (ɪn'en)

= senseless ('sɛnslɪs)

= asinine ('æsn̩,aɪn)

similar ('sɪmələ) *adj.* 相似的

= alike (ə'laɪk)

= like (laɪk)

= resembling (rɪ'zɛmblɪŋ)

= same (sem)

simmer ('sɪmə) *v.* ①煮 ②幾近爆發

① = boil (bɔɪl)

= stew (stju)

= cook (kʊk)

② = seethe (sið)

= fume (fjum)

= rage (redʒ)

= storm (stɔrm)

= rant (rænt)

= rave (rev)

simple ('sɪmpl̩) *adj.* ①簡易的 ②樸實的 ③無知的

① = easy ('izɪ)

= effortless ('ɛfətlɪs)

② = bare (bɛr)

= mere (mɪr)

= commom ('kamən)

= ordinary ('ɔrdn̩,ɛrɪ)

= sheer (ʃɪr)

= plain (plen)

③ = dull (dʌl)

= stupid ('stjupɪd)

= idiotic (,ɪdɪ'atɪk)

= half-witted ('hæf'wɪtɪd)

= moronic (mo'ranɪk)

= ignorant ('ɪgnərənt)

sin (sɪn) *n.* 罪惡

= wrongdoing ('rɔŋ'duɪŋ)

= misconduct (mɪs'kandʌkt)

= crime (kraɪm)

= vice (vaɪs)

= offense (ə'fɛns)

= evil ('ivl̩)

= error ('ɛrə)

= indiscretion (,ɪndɪ'skrɛʃən)

sincere (sɪn'sɪr) *adj.* 真實的

= genuine ('dʒɛnjuɪn)

= real (ril)

= honest ('anɪst)

= authentic (ɔ'θɛntɪk)

= legitimate (lɪ'dʒɪtəmɪt)

= unaffected (,ʌnə'fɛktɪd)

= *bona fide*

sinewy ('sɪnjəwɪ) *adj.* 強壯的

= strong (strɔŋ)

= powerful ('paʊəfəl)

= tough (tʌf)

= athletic (æθ'lɛtɪk)

= brawny ('brɔnɪ)

= muscular ('mʌskjələ)

= beefy ('bifɪ)

sing (sɪŋ) *v.* 歌唱

= vocalize ('vokl̩,aɪz)

= chant (tʃænt)

singe (sɪndʒ) v. 燒燙

= burn (bɜn)

= scorch (skɔrtʃ)

= sear (sɪr)

= char (tʃɑr)

sinister ('sɪnɪstɚ) adj. 邪惡的

= bad (bæd)

= evil ('ivḷ)

= dishonest (dɪs'ɑnɪst)

= wrong (rɔŋ)

= corrupt (kə'rʌpt)

= fraudulent ('frɔdʒələnt)

= crooked ('krʊkɪd)

sink (sɪŋk) v. ①沈降 ②使衰弱

① = fall (fɔl)

= decline (dɪ'klaɪn)

= slump (slʌmp)

= settle ('sɛtḷ)

= lower ('loɚ)

= submerge (səb'mɜdʒ)

= go down

② = weaken ('wikən)

= droop (drup)

= pine (paɪn)

= fade (fed)

sip (sɪp) v. 啜飲

= drink (drɪŋk)

= taste (test)

sire (saɪr) v. 爲…之父；出生

= father ('fɑðɚ)

= breed (brid)

= beget (bɪ'gɛt)

= propagate ('prɑpə,get)

= procreat ('prokrɪ,et)

= reproduce (,riprə,djus)

= produce (prə'djus)

siren ('saɪrən) n. 號笛

= alarm (ə'lɑrm)

= whistle ('hwɪsḷ)

= signal ('sɪgnḷ)

= noisemaker ('nɔɪz,mekɚ)

sit (sɪt) v. 坐

= perch (pɜtʃ)

= be seated

site (saɪt) n. 位置

= place (ples)

= location (lo'keʃən)

= position (pə'zɪʃən)

= situation (,sɪtʃu'eʃən)

= whereabouts ('hwɛrə,baʊts)

situation (,sɪtʃu'eʃən) n. ①位置
②情形

① = place (ples)

= location (lo'keʃən)

= position (pə'zɪʃən)

= whereabouts ('hwɛrə,baʊts)

② = circumstances
('sɜkəm,stænsɪz)

= case (kes)

= condition (kən'dɪʃən)

= terms (tɜms)

size (saɪz) *n.* 尺寸

= proportion (prə'porʃən)

= measure ('mɛʒɚ)

= extent (ɪk'stɛnt)

= scope (skop)

= dimensions (də'mɛnʃənz)

skillful ('skɪlfəl) *adj.* 熟練的

= expert (ɪk'spɝt)

= adept (ə'dɛpt)

= proficient (prə'fɪʃənt)

= apt (æpt)

= handy ('hændɪ)

= clever ('klɛvɚ)

= masterful ('mæstɚfəl)

= able ('ebḷ)

= capable ('kepəbḷ)

skim (skɪm) *v.* 掠過

= glide (glaɪd)

= coast (kost)

= sail (sel)

= slide (slaɪd)

= graze (grez)

= brush (brʌʃ)

skimpy ('skɪmpɪ) *adj.* 不足的

= scanty ('skæntɪ)

= scarce (skɛrs)

= sparse (spɑrs)

= meager ('migɚ)

skinny ('skɪnɪ) *adj.* 細瘦的

= lean (lin)

= spare (spɛr)

= scrawny ('skrɔnɪ)

= lanky ('læŋkɪ)

= gaunt (gɑnt , gɔnt)

= bony ('bonɪ)

skip (skɪp) *v.* ①跳躍　②遺漏

① = spring (sprɪŋ)

= jump (dʒʌmp)

= leap (lip)

② = omit (o'mɪt , ə-)

= bypass ('baɪ,pæs)

= *pass over*

skirmish ('skɝmɪʃ) *n.* 小衝突

= argument ('ɑrgjəmənt)

= conflict ('kɑnflɪkt)

= clash (klæʃ)

= scuffle ('skʌfḷ)

= brush (brʌʃ)

= struggle ('strʌgḷ)

= encounter (ɪn'kauntɚ)

= engagement (ɪn'gedʒmənt)

= melee (me'le , 'mele)

skirt (skɝt) *n.* 邊緣

= border ('bɔrdɚ)

= edge (ɛdʒ)

= rim (rɪm)

= margin ('mɑrdʒɪn)

= fringe (frɪndʒ)

skulk (skʌlk) *v.* 藏匿；潛行

= sneak (snik)

= hide (haɪd)

= lurk (lɝk)

= slink (slɪŋk)

= prowl (praʊl)

= steal〔stil〕

= creep〔krip〕

ack〔slæk〕*adj.* ①鬆弛的

懈怠的

= loose〔lus〕

= lax〔læks〕

= baggy〔'bægɪ〕

= hanging〔'hæŋɪŋ〕

= droopy〔'drupɪ〕

= slow〔slo〕

= dull〔dʌl〕

= lazy〔'lezɪ〕

= inactive〔ɪn'æktɪv〕

am〔slæm〕*v.* 關閉

= close〔kloz〕

= bang〔bæŋ〕

= shut〔ʃʌt〕

lander〔'slændɚ〕*v. n.* 誹謗

= libel〔'laɪbḷ〕

= slur〔slɝ〕

= discredit〔dɪs'krɛdɪt〕

= smear〔smɪr〕

lant〔slænt〕*v.* 使傾斜

= slope〔slop〕

= incline〔ɪn'klaɪn〕

= lean〔lin〕

= tip〔tɪp〕

= tilt〔tɪlt〕

lap〔slæp〕*v.* 拍擊

= hit〔hɪt〕

= crack〔kræk〕

= smack〔smæk〕

slash〔slæʃ〕*v.* 割砍

= cut〔kʌt〕

= gash〔gæʃ〕

= wound〔wund〕

= sever〔'sɛvɚ〕

slaughter〔'slɔtɚ〕*n.* 屠殺

= butchery〔'butʃərɪ〕

= massacre〔'mæsəkɚ〕

= killing〔'kɪlɪŋ〕

= carnage〔'kɑrnɪdʒ〕

= genocide〔'dʒɛnə,saɪd〕

slavery〔'slevərɪ〕*n.* 奴役

= bondage〔'bɑndɪdʒ〕

= servitude〔'sɝvə,tjud〕

= serfdom〔'sɝfdəm〕

slay〔sle〕*v.* 殺

= kill〔kɪl〕

= destroy〔dɪ'strɔɪ〕

= exterminate〔ɪk'stɝmə,net〕

= *put to death*

sleek〔slik〕*adj.* 光滑的

= smooth〔smuð〕

= glossy〔'glɔsɪ〕

= slick〔slɪk〕

= polished〔'pɑlɪʃt〕

sleep〔slip〕*n. v.* 睡眠

= slumber〔'slʌmbɚ〕

= doze〔doz〕

= drowse〔drauz〕

= nap〔næp〕

= rest〔rɛst〕

= snooze〔snuz〕

slender ('slɛndɚ) *adj.* 纖細的

= thin (θɪn)

= narrow ('næro)

= svelte (svɛlt)

= frail (frel)

= slight (slaɪt)

slice (slaɪs) *v.* 切割

= cut (kʌt)

= sever ('sɛvɚ)

= split (splɪt)

= carve (karv)

= slash (slæʃ)

= slit (slɪt)

slick (slɪk) *adj.* ①光滑的
②狡猾的

① = sleek (slik)

= smooth (smuð)

= glossy ('glɔsɪ)

= polished ('palɪʃt)

② = sly (slaɪ)

= tricky ('trɪkɪ)

= cunning ('kʌnɪŋ)

= shrewd (ʃrud)

= shifty ('ʃɪftɪ)

= crafty ('kræftɪ)

= foxy ('faksɪ)

slide (slaɪd) *v.* 滑行

= glide (glaɪd)

= coast (kost)

= skim (skɪm)

= skid (skɪd)

= slip (slɪp)

slight (slaɪt) ① *adj.* 輕小的
② *adj.* 苗條的 ③ *v.* 忽略

① = small (smɔl)

= petite (pə'tit)

= puny ('pjunɪ)

= tiny ('taɪnɪ)

② = slender ('slɛndɚ)

= frail (frel)

= delicate ('dɛləkət , -kɪt)

= dainty ('dentɪ)

= flimsy ('flɪmzɪ)

= thin (θɪn)

= svelte ('svɛlt)

③ = neglect (nɪ'glɛkt)

= disregard (,dɪsrɪ'gard)

= ignore (ɪg'nor)

= overlook (,ovɚ'luk)

slim (slɪm) *adj.* 細長的

= slender ('slɛndɚ)

= thin (θɪn)

= svelte (svɛlt)

= lean (lin)

= slight (slaɪt)

slime (slaɪm) *n.* 黏泥

= mud (mʌd)

= muck (mʌk)

= mire (maɪr)

= slush (slʌʃ)

sling (slɪŋ) ① *v.* 投擲
② *v.* 吊懸 ③ *n.* 吊腕帶

① = throw (θro)

= cast (kæst)

= hurl (hɝl)

= fling (flɪŋ)

= pitch (pɪtʃ)

= toss (tɔs)

= heave (hiv)

= flip (flɪp)

= suspend (sə'spɛnd)

= hang (hæŋ)

= bandage ('bændɪdʒ)

= support (sə'port)

= splint (splɪnt)

ink (slɪŋk) v. 潛行

= sneak (snik)

= lurk (lɜk)

= prowl (praʊl)

= creep (krip)

= steal (stil)

ip (slɪp) n. ①滑行 ②失誤

= slide (slaɪd)

= glide (glaɪd)

= skid (skɪd)

= mistake (mə'stek)

= error ('ɛrə)

= oversight ('ovə,saɪt)

= blunder ('blʌndə)

it (slɪt) v. 割裂

= cut (kʌt)

= sever ('sɛvə)

= split (splɪt)

= cleave (kliv)

= tear (tɛr)

logan ('slogən) n. 口號

= phrase (frez)

= expression (ɪk'sprɛʃən)

= cry (kraɪ)

= motto ('mato)

slope (slop) v. 使傾斜

= slant (slænt)

= incline (ɪn'klaɪn)

= tip (tɪp)

= lean (lin)

= tilt (tɪlt)

slug 這 S

sloppy ('slɑpɪ) adj. ①不小心的 ②濕的

① = careless ('kɛrlɪs)

= slovenly ('slʌvənlɪ)

= slipshod ('slɪp,ʃɑd)

= negligent ('nɛglədʒənt)

= haphazard ('hæp'hæzəd)

= messy ('mɛsɪ)

② = wet (wɛt)

= slushy ('slʌʃɪ)

slothful ('sloθfəl) adj. 懶惰的

= lazy ('lezɪ)

= sluggish ('slʌgɪʃ)

= do-nothing ('du,nʌθɪŋ)

= shiftless ('ʃɪftlɪs)

= indolent ('ɪndələnt)

= laggard ('lægəd)

slovenly ('slʌvənlɪ) adj. 潦草的

= untidy (ʌn'taɪdɪ)

= slipshod ('slɪp,ʃɑd)

= unkempt (ʌn'kɛmpt)

= shabby ('ʃæbɪ)

= seedy ('sidɪ)

= messy ('mɛsɪ)
= sloppy ('slɑpɪ)

slow (slo) *adj.* ①遲緩的
②愚鈍的

① = lingering ('lɪŋgərɪŋ)
= delaying (dɪ'leɪŋ)
= lackadaisical (ˌlækə'dezɪkḷ)
= leisurely ('lɛʒəlɪ)
= poking ('pokɪŋ)
= tarrying ('tærɪŋ)
= dillydallying ('dɪlɪˌdælɪŋ)
② = dull (dʌl)
= stupid ('stjupɪd)

slug (slʌg) *n.* ①重擊 ②金屬塊

① = strike (straɪk)
= hit (hɪt)
= knock (nɑk)
= poke (pok)
= punch (pʌntʃ)
= jab (dʒæb)
= smack (smæk)
= whack (hwæk)
= bat (bæt)
= crack (kræk)
= clout (klaʊt)
② = token ('tokən)
= coin (kɔɪn)

sluggish ('slʌgɪʃ) *adj.* 行動
遲緩的

= lethargic (lɪ'θɑrdʒɪk)
= slow-moving ('slo'muvɪŋ)
= inactive (ɪn'æktɪv)
= lackadaisical (ˌlækə'dezɪkḷ)

= poky ('pokɪ)
= listless ('lɪstlɪs)

slumber ('slʌmbə) *n. v.* 睡眠

= sleep (slip)
= doze (doz)
= drowse (draʊz)
= nap (næp)
= rest (rɛst)
= snooze (snuz)

slur (slɝ) *v.* ①忽視 ②蔑視

① = scan (skæn)
= *skim over*
= *glance at*
② = insult (ɪn'sʌlt)
= smear (smɪr)
= soil (sɔɪl)
= slander ('slændə)
= libel ('laɪbḷ)
= defame (dɪ'fem)
= slight (slaɪt)

sly (slaɪ) *adj.* 狡詐的

= shrewd (ʃrud)
= underhanded ('ʌndə'hændɪd)
= artful ('ɑrtfəl)
= cunning ('kʌnɪŋ)
= shifty ('ʃɪftɪ)
= smooth (smuð)
= crafty ('kræftɪ)
= canny ('kænɪ)
= sneaky ('snikɪ)
= clever ('klɛvə)
= tricky ('trɪkɪ)

mack (smæk) *n.* ①拍擊
②響吻

① = hit (hɪt)
= slap (slæp)
= crack (kræk)
= strike (straɪk)
= whack (hwæk)
② = kiss (kɪs)

mall (smɔl) *adj.* ①小的
②不重要的

① = little ('lɪtl̩)
= slight (slaɪt)
= puny ('pjunɪ)
② = insignificant (ˌɪnsɪg'nɪfəkənt)
= unimportant (ˌʌnɪm'pɔrtn̩t)
= trivial ('trɪvɪəl)

mart (smɑrt) ① *adj.* 聰明的
② *adj.* 時髦的 ③ *v.* 感到痛苦

① = bright (braɪt)
= clever ('klɛvɚ)
= keen (kin)
= intelligent (ɪn'tɛlədʒənt)
= quick (kwɪk)
= shrewd (ʃrud)
= alert (ə'lɜt)
= brainy ('brenɪ)
② = stylish ('staɪlɪʃ)
= well-dressed ('wɛl'drɛst)
= chic (ʃik , ʃɪk)
= natty ('nætɪ)
= dapper ('dæpɚ)
= fashionable ('fæʃənəbl̩)
③ = pain (pen)
= ache (ek)

= hurt (hɜt)

smash (smæʃ) *v.* ①破壞
②重擊

① = destroy (dɪ'strɔɪ)
= shatter ('ʃætɚ)
= ruin ('ruɪn)
= break (brek)
= crash (kræʃ)
= fragment ('frægmənt)
② = collide (kə'laɪd)
= clash (klæʃ)
= bump (bʌmp)
= strike (straɪk)
= knock (nɑk)
= bang (bæŋ)

smear (smɪr) *v.* ①弄髒
②毀謗

① = stain (sten)
= mark (mɑrk)
= soil (sɔɪl)
= tarnish ('tɑrnɪʃ)
= smudge (smʌdʒ)
= spot (spɑt)
② = spoil (spɔɪl)
= harm (hɑrm)
= blacken ('blækən)
= defile (dɪ'faɪl)
= slander ('slændɚ)

smell (smɛl) *n.* 味道

= scent (sɛnt)
= odor ('odɚ)
= essence ('ɛsn̩s)
= fragrance ('fregrəns)

S

smile (smaɪl) v. 微笑

= grin (grɪn)
= beam (bim)
= laugh (læf , lɑf)
= smirk (smɝk)
= chuckle ('tʃʌkl̩)

smog (smɑg) n. 煙霧

= fog (fɑg , fɔg)
= smoke (smok)
= haziness ('hezɪnɪs)
= cloudiness ('klaʊdɪnɪs)

smooth (smuð) adj. ①平滑的 ②有禮的；溫和的

① = sleek (slik)
= slick (slɪk)
= glossy ('glɔsɪ)
= polished ('pɑlɪʃt)
= even ('ivən)
= level ('lɛvl̩)
② = polite (pə'laɪt)
= pleasant ('plɛznt)
= suave (swɑv)
= chivalrous ('ʃɪvlrəs)
= cunning ('kʌnɪŋ)

smother ('smʌðɚ) v. 使窒息

= suffocate ('sʌfə,ket)
= stifle ('staɪfl̩)
= choke (tʃok)
= asphyxiate (æs'fɪksɪ,et)
= muffle ('mʌfl̩)
= suppress (sə'prɛs)

smudge (smʌdʒ) v. 弄髒

= smear (smɪr)
= mark (mɑrk)
= soil (sɔɪl)
= blacken ('blækən)
= spot (spɑt)
= stain (sten)

smug (smʌg) adj. 自滿的

= self-satisfied ('sɛlf'sætɪs,faɪd)
= confident ('kɑnfədənt)
= vain (ven)
= conceited (kən'sitɪd)
= arrogant ('ærəgənt)
= boastful ('bost,fəl)
= egotistical (,igə'tɪstɪkl̩)

snag (snæg) v. 奪取

= trap (træp)
= hook (hʊk)
= catch (kætʃ)
= snatch (snætʃ)
= snare (snɛr)

snake (snek) n. 蛇

= serpent ('sɝpənt)
= viper ('vaɪpɚ)

snap (snæp) v. ①爆裂 ②攫取

① = break (brek)
= burst (bɝst)
= split (splɪt)
= crack (kræk)
② = snatch (snætʃ)
= seize (siz)

snare (snɛr) v. 捕捉

= trap (træp)

= catch (kætʃ)

= hook (huk)

snarl (snɑrl) v. ①咆哮 ②糾結

① = growl (graul)

= grumble ('grʌmbḷ)

② = tangle ('tæŋgḷ)

= knot (nɑt)

= *mix up*

snatch (snætʃ) ① v. 奪取

② n. 小量

① = seize (siz)

= grasp (græsp)

= grab (græb)

= clutch (klʌtʃ)

= hook (huk)

= snag (snæg)

= snare (snɛr)

= trap (træp)

② = shred (ʃrɛd)

= scrap (skræp)

= bit (bɪt)

= *small amount*

sneak (snik) v. 潛行

= lurk (lɜk)

= prowl (praul)

= slink (slɪŋk)

= steal (stil)

= creep (krip)

sneer (snɪr) v. n. 譏誚

= mock (mɑk)

= scoff (skɔf)

= jeer (dʒɪr)

= taunt (tɔnt)

sniff (snɪf) v. 聞；吸氣

= smell (smɛl)

= scent (sɛnt)

= inhale (ɪn'hel)

snipe (snaɪp) v. 伏擊

= *shoot at*

= *fire at*

snobbish ('snɑbɪʃ) adj. 勢利的

= haughty ('hɔtɪ)

= arrogant ('ærəgənt)

= priggish ('prɪgɪʃ)

snoop (snup) v. 管閒事

= pry (praɪ)

= meddle ('mɛdḷ)

= intrude (ɪn'trud)

= interfere (ˌɪntə'fɪr)

snooze (snuz) v. 小睡

= sleep (slip)

= doze (doz)

= nap (næp)

snub (snʌb) v. 輕忽

= slight (slaɪt)

= ignore (ɪg'nor)

= avoid (ə'vɔɪd)

= shun (ʃʌn)

= spurn (spɜn)

= rebuff (rɪ'bʌf)

S

snug ﹝ snʌg ﹞ *adj.* ①舒適的 ②緊貼的

① = comfortable ﹝'kʌmfətəbḷ﹞
= warm ﹝ wɔrm ﹞
= sheltered ﹝'ʃɛltəd﹞
= cozy ﹝'kozɪ﹞
= homelike ﹝'hom،laɪk﹞
② = compact ﹝ kəm'pækt ﹞
= close ﹝ klos ﹞
= tight ﹝ taɪt ﹞

snuggle ﹝'snʌgḷ﹞ *v.* 挨近；依偎
= nestle ﹝'nɛsḷ﹞
= cuddle ﹝'kʌdḷ﹞

soak ﹝ sok ﹞ *v.* 浸濕
= wet ﹝ wɛt ﹞
= drench ﹝ drɛntʃ ﹞
= saturate ﹝'sætʃə،ret﹞
= steep ﹝ stip ﹞
= sop ﹝ sɑp ﹞

soap ﹝ sop ﹞ *n.* 肥皂
= lather ﹝'læðə﹞
= shampoo ﹝ ʃæm'pu ﹞

soar ﹝ sor ﹞ *v.* 高飛；升高
= fly ﹝ flaɪ ﹞
= glide ﹝ glaɪd ﹞
= aspire ﹝ ə'spaɪr ﹞
= tower ﹝'taʊə﹞
= hover ﹝'hʌvə﹞
= ascend ﹝ ə'sɛnd ﹞

sob ﹝ sɑb ﹞ *v. n.* 啜泣
= cry ﹝ kraɪ ﹞

= weep ﹝ wip ﹞
= bawl ﹝ bɔl ﹞
= blubber ﹝'blʌbə﹞
= snivel ﹝'snɪvḷ﹞
= wail ﹝ wel ﹞
= howl ﹝ haʊl ﹞

sober ﹝'sobə﹞ *adj.* ①冷靜的； 適度的 ②未醉的

① = sensible ﹝'sɛnsəbḷ﹞
= calm ﹝ kɑm ﹞
= moderate ﹝'mɑdərɪt﹞
= temperate ﹝'tɛmprɪt﹞
= mild ﹝ maɪld ﹞
= sound ﹝ saʊnd ﹞
= reasonable ﹝'riznəbḷ﹞
② = unintoxicated ﹝،ʌnɪn'tɑkəs،ketɪd﹞
= uninebriated﹝،ʌnɪn'ibrɪ،etɪd﹞

sociable ﹝'soʃəbḷ﹞ *adj.* 友善的
= friendly ﹝'frɛndlɪ﹞
= amiable ﹝'emɪəbḷ﹞
= congenial ﹝ kən'dʒinjəl ﹞
= cordial ﹝'kɔrdʒəl﹞
= gregarious ﹝ grɪ'gɛrɪəs ﹞

society ﹝ sə'saɪətɪ ﹞ *n.* ①社會 ②組織

① = people ﹝'pipḷ﹞
= folks ﹝ foks ﹞
= public ﹝'pʌblɪk﹞
= populace ﹝'pɑpjəlɪs﹞
= community ﹝ kə'mjunətɪ ﹞
= world ﹝ wɜld ﹞
② = company ﹝'kʌmpənɪ﹞

= organization (ˏɔrgənəˈzeʃən)
= association (əˏsoʃɪˈeʃən)
= alliance (əˈlaɪəns)
= league (lig)
= union (ˈjunjən)
= federation (ˏfɛdəˈreʃən)
= sect (sɛkt)

ock (sak) ① v. 重擊
② n. 短襪

① = strike (straɪk)
= hit (hɪt)
= knock (nak)
= jab (dʒæb)
= whack (hwæk)
= bat (bæt)
= crack (kræk)
② = stocking (ˈstakɪŋ)

od (sad) n. 草地

= soil (sɔɪl)
= earth (ɝθ)
= dirt (dɝt)
= ground (graʊnd)

oft (sɔft) adj. ①柔軟的
②溫和的

① = delicate (ˈdɛləkət)
= supple (ˈsʌpl̩)
= tender (ˈtɛndɚ)
= flexible (ˈflɛksəbl̩)
= pliable (ˈplaɪəbl̩)
= elastic (ɪˈlæstɪk)
② = mild (maɪld)
= kind (kaɪnd)
= gentle (ˈdʒɛntl̩)

= tender (ˈtɛndɚ)
= pleasant (ˈplɛznt)
= lenient (ˈlinɪənt)
= easygoing (ˈiziˈgoɪŋ)

soggy (ˈsagɪ) adj. 濕濕的

= damp (dæmp)
= soaked (sokt)
= saturated (ˈsætʃəˏretɪd)
= sopping (ˈsapɪŋ)
= waterlogged (ˈwɔtɚˏlagd)

soil (sɔɪl) ① v. 污損 ② v. 誹謗
③ n. 土地

① = dirty (ˈdɝtɪ)
= spot (spat)
= stain (sten)
= smudge (smʌdʒ)
= smear (smɪr)
② = slander (ˈslændɚ)
= libel (ˈlaɪbl̩)
= defile (dɪˈfaɪl)
③ = ground (graʊnd)
= earth (ɝθ)
= dirt (dɝt)
= land (lænd)

sojourn (ˈsodʒɝn , soˈdʒɝn) n.
逗留

= stay (ste)
= stopover (ˈstapˏovɚ)

solace (ˈsalɪs) v. 安慰

= comfort (ˈkʌmfɚt)
= relieve (rɪˈliv)
= cheer (tʃɪr)
= console (kənˈsol)

S

= encourage〔ɪn'kɜ·ɪdʒ〕

= reassure〔,riə'ʃʊr〕

= hearten〔'hɑrtn̩〕

solder〔'sɑdə·〕 v. 接合

= cement〔sə'mɛnt〕

= bind〔baɪnd〕

= weld〔wɛld〕

= fuse〔fjuz〕

= join〔dʒɔɪn〕

= mend〔mɛnd〕

= fasten〔'fæsn̩, 'fɑsn̩〕

sole〔sol〕 adj. 唯一的

= only〔'onlɪ〕

= single〔'sɪŋgl̩〕

= one〔wʌn〕

= individual〔,ɪndə'vɪdʒʊəl〕

= unique〔ju'nik〕

solem〔'saləm〕 adj. 憂鬱的

= serious〔'sɪrɪəs〕

= grave〔grev〕

= gloomy〔'glumɪ〕

= dismal〔'dɪzml̩〕

= somber〔'sambə·〕

= dreary〔'drirɪ, 'drɪrɪ〕

= glum〔glʌm〕

solicit〔sə'lɪsɪt〕 v. 懇求

= request〔rɪ'kwɛst〕

= appeal〔ə'pil〕

= ask〔æsk〕

= canvass〔'kænvəs〕

= beg〔bɛg〕

solid〔'salɪd〕 adj. ①牢固的 ②完全的

① = hard〔hard〕

= firm〔fɜm〕

= rigid〔'rɪdʒɪd〕

= substantial〔səb'stænʃəl〕

= sturdy〔'stɜ·dɪ〕

= strong〔strɔŋ〕

= durable〔'djʊrəbl̩〕

② = whole〔hol〕

= entire〔ɪn'taɪr〕

= continuous〔kən'tɪnjʊəs〕

= complete〔kəm'plit〕

solitary〔'salə,tɛrɪ〕 adj. 單一的

= single〔'sɪŋgl̩〕

= individual〔,ɪndə'vɪdʒʊəl〕

= lone〔lon〕

= isolated〔'aɪsl̩,etɪd〕

= unaccompanied
〔,ʌnə'kʌmpənɪd〕

solution〔sə'luʃən〕 n. ①解答 ②溶液

① = explanation〔,ɛksplə'neʃən〕

= answer〔'ænsə·〕

= resolution〔,rɛzə'ljuʃen〕

= finding〔'faɪndɪŋ〕

= outcome〔'aʊt,kʌm〕

= result〔rɪ'zʌlt〕

② = mixture〔'mɪkstʃə·〕

solve〔salv〕 v. 解釋

= answer〔'ænsə·〕

= explain〔ɪk'splen〕

= unriddle〔ʌn'rɪdl̩〕

= decipher (dɪ'saɪfɚ)

= decode (di'kod)

= *clear up*

= *work out*

= *figure out*

omber ('sɑmbɚ) *adj.* 憂鬱的

= dark (dɑrk)

= gloomy ('glumɪ)

= dismal ('dɪzml̩)

= dreary ('drɪrɪ , 'drirɪ)

= melancholy ('mɛlən,kɑlɪ)

= bleak (blik)

= uncheerful (ʌn'tʃɪrfəl)

= grave (grev)

= solemn ('sɑləm)

= grim (grɪm)

oon (sun) *adv.* 即刻

= promptly ('prɑmptlɪ)

= quickly ('kwɪklɪ)

= shortly ('ʃɔrtlɪ)

= presently ('prɛzn̩tlɪ)

= directly (də'rɛktlɪ)

= *before long*

oothe (suð) *v.* 安撫

= calm (kɑm)

= comfort ('kʌmfɚt)

= quiet ('kwaɪət)

= ease (iz)

= pacify ('pæsə,faɪ)

= relieve (rɪ'liv)

orcery ('sɔrsərɪ) *n.* 魔法

= witchcraft ('wɪtʃ,kræft)

= bewitchment (bɪ'wɪtʃmənt)

= entrancement (ɪn'trænsmənt)

= spell (spɛl)

= magic ('mædʒɪk)

= wizardry ('wɪzɚdrɪ)

= voodoo ('vudu , vu'du)

sordid ('sɔrdɪd) *adj.* 污穢的

= dirty ('dɝtɪ)

= filthy ('fɪlθɪ)

= slovenly ('slʌvənlɪ)

= squalid ('skwɑlɪd)

sore (sɔr , sor) *adj.* ①疼痛的 ②憤怒的

① = painful ('penfəl)

= aching ('ekɪŋ)

= tender ('tɛndɚ)

= smarting ('smɑrtɪŋ)

= raw (rɔ)

= irritated ('ɪrə,tetɪd)

= inflamed (ɪn'flemd)

= festering ('fɛstɚɪŋ)

= rankling ('ræŋkl̩ɪŋ)

= throbbing ('θrɑbɪŋ)

= distressing (dɪ'strɛsɪŋ)

② = angry ('æŋgrɪ)

= offended (ə'fɛndɪd)

= irate ('aɪret , aɪ'ret)

= indignant (ɪn'dɪgnənt)

sorrow ('sɑro) *n.* 憂愁

= grief (grif)

= sadness ('sædnɪs)

= regret (rɪ'grɛt)

= trouble ('trʌbl̩)

= misfortune (mɪs'fɔrtʃən)

= suffering ('sʌfərɪŋ , 'sʌfrɪŋ)

= woe (wo)

= anguish ('æŋgwɪʃ)

= misery ('mɪzərɪ)

= agony ('ægənɪ)

= remorse (rɪ'mɔrs)

sorry ('sɑrɪ) *adj.* ①抱歉的
②可惜的　③可憐的

① = regretful (rɪ'grɛtfḷ)

= remorseful (rɪ'mɔrsfəl)

= repentant (rɪ'pɛntənt)

= apologetic (ə,pɑlə'dʒɛtɪk)

② = sad (sæd)

= sympathetic (,sɪmpə'θɛtɪk)

= unhappy (ʌn'hæpɪ)

= miserable ('mɪzərəbḷ)

= displeased (dɪs'plizd)

③ = wretched ('rɛtʃɪd)

= poor (pur)

= pitiful ('pɪtɪfəl)

sort (sɔrt) *v.* 分類

= arrange (ə'rendʒ)

= separate ('sɛpə,ret)

= classify ('klæsə,faɪ)

= categorize ('kætəgə,raɪz)

= group (grup)

= divide (də'vaɪd)

= catalog ('kætḷ,ɔg)

sound (saund) ① *v.* 發聲
② *adj.* 健全的　③ *adj.* 穩固的
④ *adj.* 正確的

① = utter ('ʌtə)

= pronounce (prə'nauns)

= voice (vɔɪs)

= *make noise*

② = healthy ('hɛlθɪ)

= wholesome ('holsəm)

= hearty ('hɑrtɪ)

③ = strong (strɔŋ)

= safe (sef)

= secure (sɪ'kjur)

= stable ('stebḷ)

= substantial (səb'stænʃəl)

= firm (fɝm)

= solid ('sɑlɪd)

= solvent ('sɑlvənt)

④ = correct (kə'rɛkt)

= right (raɪt)

= reasonable ('riznəbḷ)

= sensible ('sɛnsəbḷ)

= sane (sen)

= logical ('lɑdʒɪkḷ)

= rational ('ræʃənḷ)

sour (saur) *adj.* ①酸的
②乖戾的；不高興的

① = spoiled (spɔɪld)

= fermented (fə'mɛntɪd)

= bitter ('bɪtə)

= rancid ('rænsɪd)

② = disagreeable (,dɪsə'griəbḷ)

= peevish ('pivɪʃ)

= unpleasant (ʌn'plɛznt)

source (sors , sɔrs) *n.* 來源

= origin ('ɔrədʒɪn)

= beginning (bɪ'gɪnɪŋ)

= derivation (,dɛrə'veʃən)

= root (rut)

ouvenir (ˌsuvəˈnɪr , ˈsuvəˌnɪr)
紀念品

= remembrance (rɪˈmɛmbrəns)
= keepsake (ˈkipˌsek)
= memento (mɪˈmɛnto)
= relic (ˈrɛlɪk)
= token (ˈtokən)

overeign (ˈsɑvrɪn , ˈsʌv-) adj.
上的

= supreme (səˈprim)
= greatest (ˈgretɪst)
= regal (ˈrigḷ)
= royal (ˈrɔɪəl)
= imperial (ɪmˈpɪrɪəl)
= majestic (məˈdʒɛstɪk)
= ruling (ˈrulɪŋ)
= reigning (ˈrenɪŋ)
= governing (ˈgʌvənɪŋ)

sow (so) v. 散布

= scatter (ˈskætə)
= spread (sprɛd)
= disperse (dɪˈspɜs)
= distribute (dɪˈstrɪbjut)

sow (sau) n. 母豬
= *female pig*

ace (spes) n. 空間

= extent (ɪkˈstɛnt)
= expanse (ɪkˈspæns)
= measure (ˈmɛʒə)
= dimension (dəˈmɛnʃən)
= area (ˈɛrɪə , ˈerɪə)

acious (ˈspeʃəs) adj. 廣大的

= vast (væst)
= roomy (ˈrumɪ)
= widespread (ˈwaɪdˌsprɛd)
= extensive (ɪkˈstɛnsɪv)
= sweeping (ˈswipɪŋ)
= far-reaching (ˈfɑrˈritʃɪŋ)
= capacious (kəˈpeʃəs)
= commodious (kəˈmodɪəs)
= expansive (ɪkˈspænsɪv)

span (spæn) n. ① (橋樑) 架距
②短時間 ③全長

① = bridge (brɪdʒ)
= viaduct (ˈvaɪəˌdʌkt)
② = period (ˈpɪrɪəd)
= interval (ˈɪntəvḷ)
= spell (spɛl)
③ = distance (ˈdɪstəns)
= extent (ɪkˈstɛnt)
= reach (ritʃ)
= stretch (strɛtʃ)
= measure (ˈmɛʒə)
= expanse (ɪkˈspæns)

spank (spæŋk) v. 打

= slap (slæp)
= strike (straɪk)
= hit (hɪt)
= smack (smæk)

spar (spɑr) n. 拳擊

= box (bɑks)
= fight (faɪt)

spare (spɛr) ① v. 捨棄
② adj. 剩餘的 ③ adj. 瘦的

① = relinquish (rɪˈlɪŋkwɪʃ)

S

= omit (o'mɪt , ə'mɪt)
= forego (for'go , fɔr-)
= sacrifice ('sækrə͵faɪs)
= surrender (sə'rɛndə)
= yield (jild)
= *give up*
= *part with*
= *dispense with*
= *do without*
② = extra ('ɛkstrə)
= surplus ('sɝplʌs)
= remainder (rɪ'mendə)
= balance ('bæləns)
= leftover ('lɛft͵ovə)
= excess ('ɪksɛs , ɪk'sɛs)
③ = lean (lin)
= skinny ('skɪnɪ)
= thin (θɪn)
= scrawny ('skrɔnɪ)
= lanky ('læŋkɪ)
= bony ('bonɪ)

spark (spark) *n.* 火花

= flash (flæʃ)
= gleam (glim)
= glimmer ('glɪmə)

sparkle ('sparkḷ) *v.* 閃耀

= shine (ʃaɪn)
= glitter ('glɪtə)
= flash (flæʃ)
= glimmer ('glɪmə)
= shimmer ('ʃɪmə)
= twinkle ('twɪŋkḷ)
= glisten ('glɪsṇ)

sparse (spars) *adj.* 稀少的

= scanty ('skæntɪ)
= meager ('migə)
= scattered ('skætəd)
= scarce (skɛrs)
= skimpy ('skɪmpɪ)

spasm ('spæzəm) *n.* 痙攣

= twitch (twɪtʃ)
= seizure ('siʒə)
= convulsion (kən'vʌlʃən)
= fit (fɪt)

spat (spæt) *v.* 爭論

= quarrel ('kwɔrəl)
= disagree (͵dɪsə'gri)
= differ ('dɪfə)
= dispute (dɪ'spjut)
= fight (faɪt)
= squabble ('skwabḷ)
= tiff (tɪf)
= bicker ('bɪkə)

spatter ('spætə) *v. n.* 灑；濺

= sprinkle ('sprɪŋkḷ)
= speckle ('spɛkḷ)
= dot (dat)

speak (spik) *v.* 說話

= talk (tɔlk)
= say (se)
= tell (tɛl)
= express (ɪk'sprɛs)

spear (spɪr) *v.* 刺

= pierce (pɪrs)
= stab (stæb)
= puncture ('pʌŋktʃə)

= impale (ɪm'pel)

= lance (læns , lɑns)

= knife (naɪf)

ecial ('spɛʃəl) *adj.* 特別的

= unusual (ʌn'juʒuəl)

= exceptional (ɪk'sɛpʃənḷ)

= particular (pə'tɪkjələ˞)

= extraordinary (ɪk'strɔrdn̩,ɛrɪ)

= notable ('notəbḷ)

ecies ('spiʃɪz) *n.* 種類

= group (grup)

= class (klæs , klɑs)

= kind (kaɪnd)

= sort (sɔrt)

= type (taɪp)

= variety (və'raɪətɪ)

ecific (spɪ'sɪfɪk) *adj.* 明確的；
殊的

= definite ('dɛfənɪt)

= precise (prɪ'saɪs)

= particular (pə'tɪkjələ˞)

= special ('spɛʃəl)

= fixed (fɪkst)

ecimen ('spɛsəmən) *n.* 樣本

= sample ('sæmpḷ)

= representative (,rɛprɪ'zɛntətɪv)

= type (taɪp)

= example (ɪg'zæmpḷ)

eck (spɛk) *n.* 微粒

= particle ('partɪkḷ)

= iota (aɪ'otə)

= *tiny bit*

speckle ('spɛkḷ) *n.* 斑點

= spot (spat)

= mottle ('matḷ)

= mark (mark)

spectacle ('spɛktəkḷ) *n.* 景象

= sight (saɪt)

= show (ʃo)

= display (dɪ'sple)

= exhibition (,ɛksə'bɪʃən)

= pageant ('pædʒənt)

spectacular (spɛk'tækjələ˞) *adj.*
壯觀的；戲劇性的

= dramatic (drə'mætɪk)

= sensational (sɛn'seʃənḷ)

speculate ('spɛkjə,let) *v.*
①猜測 ②投機 ③思索

① = guess (gɛs)

= theorize ('θiə,raɪz)

= conjecture (kən'dʒɛktʃə˞)

② = gamble ('gæmbḷ)

= risk (rɪsk)

= chance (tʃæns)

= venture ('vɛntʃə˞)

③ = reflect (rɪ'flɛkt)

= meditate ('mɛdə,tet)

= consider (kən'sɪdə˞)

= contemplate ('kantəm,plet)

= study ('stʌdɪ)

= deliberate (dɪ'lɪbə,ret)

speedy ('spidɪ) *adj.* 迅速的

= fast (fæst , fɑst)
= rapid ('ræpɪd)
= quick (kwɪk)
= swift (swɪft)
= hasty ('hestɪ)
= fleet (flit)
= expeditious (,ɛkspɪ'dɪʃəs)

spell (spɛl) *n.* ①魔力
②一段時間

① = charm (tʃɑrm)
= fascination (,fæsn̩'eʃən)
= trance (træns , trɑns)
= *magic power*
② = time (taɪm)
= stretch (strɛtʃ)
= shift (ʃɪft)
= period ('pɪrɪəd)

spellbound ('spɛl,baʊnd) *adj.*
被迷住的

= fascinated ('fæsn̩,etɪd)
= enchanted (ɪn'tʃæntɪd)
= interested ('ɪntərɪstɪd)
= rapt (ræpt)
= enthralled (ɪn'θrɔld)
= gripped (grɪpt)
= engrossed (ɪn'grost)
= absorbed (əb'sɔrbd)
= awed (ɔd)
= charmed (tʃɑrmd)
= hypnotized ('hɪpnə,taɪzd)
= mesmerized ('mɛsmə,raɪzd)

spend (spɛnd) *v.* 花用

= use (juz)

= consume (kən'sum)
= exhaust (ɪg'zɔst)
= expend (ɪk'spɛnd)
= *pay out*
= *lay out*
= *finish off*

sphere (sfɪr) *n.* ①球體 ②範

① = ball (bɔl)
= globe (glob)
② = extent (ɪk'stɛnt)
= realm (rɛlm)
= expanse (ɪk'spæns)
= province ('prɑvɪns)
= field (fild)

spike (spaɪk) *v.* 釘

= pierce (pɪrs)
= stab (stæb)
= puncture ('pʌŋktʃə)
= impale (ɪm'pel)
= spear (spɪr)

spice (spaɪs) *n.* 調味料

= season ('sizn̩)
= flavor ('flevə)

spill (spɪl) *v.* 灑

= overflow ('ovə,flo)
= cascade (kæs'ked)
= flood (flʌd)
= pour (por , pɔr)
= spatter ('spætə)
= sprinkle ('sprɪŋkl̩)
= *run over*
= *brim over*

pin (spɪn) v. 旋轉

= turn (tɝn)
= twirl (twɝl)
= twist (twɪst)
= rotate ('rotet)
= pivot ('pɪvɪt , 'pɪvət)
= wheel (hwil)
= reel (ril)
= swirl (swɝl)

ɔinster ('spɪnstɚ) n. 老處女；
婚女子

= *old maid*
= *single woman*

ɔiral ('spaɪrəl) v. 旋轉

= coil (kɔɪl)
= twist (twɪst)
= twirl (twɝl)
= kink (kɪŋk)

ɔirit ('spɪrɪt) n. ①靈魂
性情　③精神

= soul (sol)
= heart (hɑrt)
= mind (maɪnd)
= nature ('netʃɚ)
= disposition (,dɪspə'zɪʃən)
= temper ('tɛmpɚ)
= courage ('kɝɪdʒ)
= vigor ('vɪgɚ)
= life (laɪf)
= vivacity (vaɪ'væsətɪ)

ɔiritual ('spɪrɪtʃuəl) adj.
聖的

= religious (rɪ'lɪdʒəs)
= sacred ('sekrɪd)
= holy ('holɪ)

spit (spɪt) n. 唾液

= saliva (sə'laɪvə)
= drivel ('drɪvḷ)
= dribble ('drɪbḷ)
= drool (drul)
= expectoration
　(ɪk,spɛktə'reʃən)

spiteful ('spaɪtfəl) adj. 懷恨的

= annoying (ə'nɔɪɪŋ)
= malicious (mə'lɪʃəs)
= hostile ('hɑstḷ , 'hɑstaɪl)
= vindictive (vɪn'dɪktɪv)
= mean (min)
= ornery ('ɔrnərɪ)

splash (splæʃ) v. 濺濕

= wet (wɛt)
= splatter ('splætɚ)
= sprinkle ('sprɪŋkḷ)
= spatter ('spætɚ)

splatter ('splætɚ) v. 濺濕

= splash (splæʃ)
= sprinkle ('sprɪŋkḷ)
= spatter ('spætɚ)

splendid ('splɛndɪd) adj.
華麗的

= fine (faɪn)
= excellent ('ɛkslənt)
= brilliant ('brɪljənt)

S

S

= glorious ('glorɪəs)
= magnificent (mæg'nɪfəsnt)
= grand (grænd)

splendor ('splɛndə) n. 壯麗

= pomp (pɑmp)
= glory ('glorɪ , 'glɔrɪ)
= magnificence (mæg'nɪfəsns)
= grandeur ('grændʒə)
= brilliance ('brɪljəns)
= brightness ('braɪtnɪs)
= radiance ('redɪəns)

splice (splaɪs) v. 接合

= join (dʒɔɪn)
= bind (baɪnd)
= tie (taɪ)
= connect (kə'nɛkt)
= attach (ə'tætʃ)

split (splɪt) v. 分配；劈開

= separate ('sɛpə,ret)
= divide (də'vaɪd)
= bisect (baɪ'sɛkt)
= halve (hæv)
= cleave (kliv)
= partition (par'tɪʃən)
= sever ('sɛvə)
= break (brek)
= crack (kræk)

spoil (spɔɪl) v. 損害

= damage ('dæmɪdʒ)
= injure ('ɪndʒə)
= destroy (dɪ'strɔɪ)
= botch (batʃ)

= impair (ɪm'pɛr)
= mar (mɑr)
= ruin ('ruɪn)
= upset (ʌp'sɛt)
= rot (rat)
= decay (dɪ'ke)

sponsor ('spansə) n. 贊助者

= underwriter ('ʌndə,raɪtə)
= backer ('bækə)
= financer (fə'nænsə)
= promoter (prə'motə)
= supporter (sə'portə)

spontaneous (span'tenɪəs) adj. 自然的

= instinctive (ɪn'stɪŋktɪv)
= inherent (ɪn'hɪrənt)
= natural ('nætʃərəl)
= automatic (,ɔtə'mætɪk)

spook (spuk) n. 鬼

= ghost (gost)
= specter ('spɛktə)
= apparition (,æpə'rɪʃən)
= spirit ('spɪrɪt)
= phantom ('fæntəm)

sport (sport , spɔrt) n. 遊戲；娛樂

= fun (fʌn)
= play (ple)
= amusement (ə'mjuzmənt)
= game (gem)
= contest ('kantɛst)

pot (spat) v. ①弄髒　②辨識

= stain (sten)

= mark (mark)

= discolor (dɪs'kʌlə)

= soil (sɔɪl)

= recognize ('rɛkəg,naɪz)

= know (no)

= tell (tɛl)

= distinguish (dɪ'stɪŋgwɪʃ)

= identify (aɪ'dɛntə,faɪ)

= place (ples)

= discern (dɪ'zɜn , -'sɜn)

= spy (spaɪ)

= sight (saɪt)

= *pick out*

ouse (spaʊz) n. 配偶

= mate (met)

= husband ('hʌzbənd)

= wife (waɪf)

out (spaʊt) v. 噴出

= discharge (dɪs'tʃardʒ)

= expel (ɪk'spɛl)

= spew (spju)

= eject (ɪ'dʒɛkt)

= *pour forth*

rawl (sprɔl) v. 展開

= spread (sprɛd)

= extend (ɪk'stɛnd)

= expand (ɪk'spænd)

= *stretch out*

= *fan out*

ray (spre) v. 噴灑

= sprinkle ('sprɪŋkl̩)

= spatter ('spætə)

= splash (splæʃ)

spread (sprɛd) v. ①展開
②散布

① = unfold (ʌn'fold)

= extend (ɪk'stɛnd)

= sprawl (sprɔl)

= *stretch out*

② = distribute (dɪ'strɪbjut)

= scatter ('skætə)

= disperse (dɪ'spɜs)

spree (spri) n. 遊樂；放縱

= escapade ('ɛskə,ped)

= celebration (,sɛlə'breʃən)

= fling (flɪŋ)

= whirl (hwɜl)

= lark (lark)

= *gay time*

sprig (sprɪg) n. 嫩枝

= twig (twɪg)

= branch (bræntʃ)

= limb (lɪm)

= bough (baʊ)

= shoot (ʃut)

= sprout (spraʊt)

sprightly ('spraɪtlɪ) adj. 活潑的

= lively ('laɪvlɪ)

= gay (ge)

= active ('æktɪv)

= animated ('ænə,metɪd)

S

= spirited ('spɪrɪtɪd)

= vivacious (vaɪ'veʃəs)

= spry (spraɪ)

= energetic (,ɛnəˈdʒɛtɪk)

= nimble ('nɪmbḷ)

spring (sprɪŋ) v. 跳躍

= leap (lip)

= jump (dʒʌmp)

= bounce (baʊns)

= vault (vɔlt)

= hop (hɑp)

= bound (baʊnd)

= hurdle ('hɝdḷ)

sprinkle ('sprɪŋkḷ) v. 灑

= spray (spre)

= spatter ('spætə)

= splash (splæʃ)

sprite (spraɪt) n. 小精靈

= elf (ɛlf)

= fairy ('fɛrɪ)

= goblin ('gɑblɪn)

= pixie ('pɪksɪ)

= gremlin ('grɛmlɪn)

sprout (spraʊt) v. 生長

= grow (gro)

= develop (dɪ'vɛləp)

= flourish ('flɝɪʃ)

= thrive (θraɪv)

= bud (bʌd)

= burgeon ('bɝdʒən)

= *shoot up*

spry (spraɪ) adj. 活潑的

= lively ('laɪvlɪ)

= gay (ge)

= sprightly ('spraɪtlɪ)

= active ('æktɪv)

= animated ('ænə,metɪd)

= spirited ('spɪrɪtɪd)

= vivacious (vaɪ'veʃəs)

= energetic (,ɛnəˈdʒɛtɪk)

= nimble ('nɪmbḷ)

spunk (spʌŋk) n. 勇氣

= courage ('kɝɪdʒ)

= pluck (plʌk)

= spirit ('spɪrɪt)

= nerve (nɝv)

= grit (grɪt)

= mettle ('mɛtḷ)

= *will power*

spur (spɝ) v. 刺激

= urge (ɝdʒ)

= goad (god)

= prod (prɑd)

= provoke (prə'vok)

spurn (spɝn) v. 拒絕

= scorn (skɔrn)

= reject (rɪ'dʒɛkt)

= disown (dɪs'on)

= deny (dɪ'naɪ)

= repudiate (rɪ'pjudɪ,et)

= disdain (dɪs'den)

= snub (snʌb)

= rebuff (rɪ'bʌf)

ourt (spɜt) *v.* 噴出

= flow (flo)
= gush (gʌʃ)
= spew (spju)
= expel (ɪk'spɛl)
= erupt (ɪ'rʌpt)
= jet (dʒɛt)
= spout (spaʊt)
= squirt (skwɜt)

oy (spaɪ) *v.* 看見；偵察

= see (si)
= detect (dɪ'tɛkt)
= view (vju)
= observe (əb'zɜv)
= discern (dɪ'zɜn , -'sɜn)
= sight (saɪt)
= spot (spɑt)

uabble ('skwɑbḷ) *v.* 爭論

= quarrel ('kwɔrəl)
= disagree (,dɪsə'gri)
= differ ('dɪfɚ)
= dispute (dɪ'spjut)
= fight (faɪt)
= tiff (tɪf)
= spat (spæt)
= bicker ('bɪkɚ)
= row (raʊ)

uad (skwɑd) *n.* 隊；組

= group (grup)
= unit ('junɪt)
= company ('kʌmpənɪ)
= band (bænd)

= gang (gæŋ)
= crew (kru)
= outfit ('aʊt,fɪt)
= troop (trup)
= body ('bɑdɪ)

squalid ('skwɑlɪd) *adj.* 污穢的

= filthy ('fɪlθɪ)
= degraded (dɪ'gredɪd)
= poor (pʊr)
= wretched ('rɛtʃɪd)
= shabby ('ʃæbɪ)
= sordid ('sɔrdɪd)
= slummy ('slʌmɪ)

squall (skwɔl) ① *v.* 尖叫
② *n.* 大風雪

① = cry (kraɪ)
= scream (skrim)
= wail (wel)
= howl (haʊl)
= moan (mon)
= bawl (bɔl)
= yell (jɛl)
= squeal (skwil)
② = gust (gʌst)
= gale (gel)
= blizzard ('blɪzɚd)

squander ('skwɑndɚ) *v.* 浪費

= waste (west)
= lavish ('lævɪʃ)
= misspend (mɪs'spɛnd)
= dissipate ('dɪsə,pet)
= *throw away*

S

square (skwɛr) ① *v.* 調整
② *adj.* 坦率的　③ *adj.* 保守的

① = adjust (ə'dʒʌst)
　= settle ('sɛtḷ)
　= balance ('bæləns)
　= equalize ('ikwəl͵aız)

② = just (dʒʌst)
　= fair (fɛr)
　= honest ('ɑnıst)
　= straight (stret)
　= equitable ('ɛkwıtəbḷ)

③ = old-fashioned ('old'fæʃənd)
　= corny ('kɔrnı)
　= unaware (͵ʌnə'wɛr)
　= conventional (kən'vɛnʃənḷ)

squash (skwɑʃ) *v.* 壓碎

　= crush (krʌʃ)
　= press (prɛs)
　= mash (mæʃ)
　= suppress (sə'prɛs)
　= squelch (skwɛltʃ)

squawk (skwɔk) *v.* 抱怨

　= complain (kəm'plen)
　= grumble ('grʌmbḷ)
　= mutter ('mʌtɚ)

squat (skwɑt) *v.* 蹲伏

　= crouch (krautʃ)
　= *lie low*

squeak (skwik) *v.* 尖叫

　= squeal (skwil)
　= yelp (jɛlp)

squeal (skwil) *v.* ①尖叫
②告密

① = cry (kraı)
　= squeak (skwik)
　= screech (skritʃ)
　= yell (jɛl)

② = tattle ('tætḷ)
　= *inform on*

squeeze (skwiz) *v.* 壓

　= press (prɛs)
　= crush (krʌʃ)
　= pinch (pıntʃ)
　= cram (kræm)

squirm (skwɜm) *v. n.* 蠕動

　= wriggle ('rıgḷ)
　= twist (twıst)
　= writhe (raıð)
　= wiggle ('wıgḷ)

squirt (skwɜt) *v.* 噴出

　= spew (spju)
　= spout (spaut)
　= spurt (spɜt)
　= expel (ık'spɛl)
　= jet (dʒɛt)
　= gush (gʌʃ)
　= spray (spre)
　= surge (sɜdʒ)
　= splash (splæʃ)
　= *pour forth*

stab (stæb) *v.* 刺傷

　= pierce (pırs)
　= perforate ('pɜfə͵ret)

S

= puncture ('pʌŋktʃɚ)
= impale (ɪm'pel)
= wound (wund)

:able ('stebḷ) ① *adj.* 堅固的
n. 畜舍

= steady ('stɛdɪ)
= firm (fɜm)
= unchanging (ʌn'tʃendʒɪŋ)
= steadfast ('stɛd,fæst)
= sound (saund)
= secure (sɪ'kjur)
= settled ('sɛtḷd)
= established (ə'stæblɪʃt)
= barn (bɑrn)

ack (stæk) *v. n.* 堆

= pile (paɪl)
= heap (hip)
= load (lod)

aff (stæf , stɑf) *n.* ①全體人員
奉

= group (grup)
= committee (kə'mɪtɪ)
= personnel (,pɜsṇ'ɛl)
= force (fors , fɔrs)
= crew (kru)
= gang (gæŋ)
= stick (stɪk)
= pole (pol)
= rod (rɑd)
= scepter ('sɛptɚ)

ige (stedʒ) ① *v.* 表演；安排
. 時期　③ *n.* 層　④ *n.* 舞臺

① = arrange (ə'rendʒ)
= dramatize ('dræmə,taɪz)
= present (prɪ'zɛnt)
= produce (prə,djus)
= perform (pɚ'fɔrm)
= enact (ɪn'ækt)
= *put on*
② = period ('pɪrɪəd)
= interval ('ɪntɚvḷ)
= point (pɔɪnt)
= time (taɪm)
= spell (spɛl)
③ = tier (tɪr)
= level ('lɛvḷ)
= layer ('leɚ)
= story ('storɪ)
④ = platform ('plæt,fɔrm)
= podium ('podɪəm)
= rostrum ('rɑstrəm)

stagger ('stægɚ) *v.* 搖擺

= sway (swe)
= reel (ril)
= waver ('wevɚ)
= flounder (flaundɚ)
= tumble ('tʌmbḷ)
= lurch (lɜtʃ)

stagnant ('stægnənt) *adj.*
不活潑的

= still (stɪl)
= inactive (ɪn'æktɪv)
= sluggish ('slʌgɪʃ)
= inert (ɪn'ɜt)
= static ('stætɪk)
= dormant ('dɔrmənt)

staid (sted) *adj.* 沈著的

= sensible ('sɛnsəbḷ)

= level-headed ('lɛvḷ'hɛdɪd)

= sober-minded ('sobə'maɪndɪd)

= sedate (sɪ'det)

= serious ('sɪrɪəs)

stain (sten) *n.* 污點

= spot (spɑt)

= soil (sɔɪl)

= mark (mɑrk)

= discolor (dɪs'kʌlə)

stake (stek) ① *v.* 以…爲賭注
② *n.* 柱子

① = bet (bɛt)

= wager ('wedʒə)

= gamble ('gæmbḷ)

= risk (rɪsk)

② = peg (pɛg)

= post (post)

stale (stel) *adj.* 陳舊的

= old (old)

= worn (wɔrn)

= obsolete ('ɑbsə,lit)

= musty ('mʌstɪ)

stalk (stɔk) ① *v.* 潛行 ② *n.* 莖

① = pursue (pə'su)

= hunt (hʌnt)

= chase (tʃes)

= seek (sik)

= search (sɜtʃ)

② = stem (stɛm)

stall (stɔl) ① *v.* 拖延
② *n.* 小隔間

① = delay (dɪ'le)

= procrastinate (pro'kræstə,net)

= dillydally ('dɪlɪ,dælɪ)

= dawdle ('dɔdḷ)

= block (blɑk)

= hinder ('hɪndə)

② = compartment (kəm'pɑrtmənt)

= booth (buð , buθ)

= cell (sɛl)

stalwart ('stɔlwət) *adj.*
①強壯的 ②堅毅的

① = strong (strɔŋ)

= robust (ro'bʌst)

= powerful ('pɑuəfəl)

② = brave (brev)

= courageous (kə'redʒəs)

= bold (bold)

= valiant ('væljənt)

= gallant ('gælənt)

= heroic (hɪ'ro·ɪk)

= firm (fɜm)

= potent ('potṇt)

= rugged ('rʌgɪd)

= sturdy ('stɜdɪ)

stammer ('stæmə) *n. v.* 口吃

= stutter ('stʌtə)

= falter ('fɔltə)

= stumble ('stʌmbḷ)

stamp (stæmp) *v.* ①蓋印
②踩踏

① = mark (mɑrk)

= seal (sil)

= label ('lebḷ)

= brand (brænd)

= engrave (ɪn'grev)

= print (prɪnt)

= trample ('træmpḷ)

= pound (paʊnd)

= crush (krʌʃ)

= tread (trɛd)

ampede (stæm'pid) *n. v.* 驚逃

= flight (flaɪt)

= rush (rʌʃ)

= panic ('pænɪk)

and (stænd) ① *v.* 站立
v. 忍受 ③ *v.* 持久
n. 置物臺

= rise (raɪz)

= *get up*

= endure (ɪn'djʊr)

= bear (bɛr)

= tolerate ('talə,ret)

= remain (rɪ'men)

= last (læst , last)

= continue (kən'tɪnju)

= stay (ste)

= persist (pə'zɪst)

= pedestal ('pɛdɪstḷ)

= base (bes)

= table ('tebḷ)

ndard ('stændəd) *n.* ①標準
象徵

= model ('madḷ)

= rule (rul)

= pattern ('pætən)

= criterion (kraɪ'tɪrɪən)

= ideal (aɪ'dɪəl , aɪ'dil)

② = flag (flæg)

= banner ('bænə)

= pennant ('pɛnənt)

= emblem ('ɛmbləm)

= symbol ('sɪmbḷ)

= colors ('kʌləz)

standstill ('stænd,stɪl) *n.* 停頓

= stop (stap)

= halt (hɔlt)

= pause (pɔz)

= impasse ('ɪmpæs , ɪm'pæs)

stanza ('stænzə) *n.* (詩的) 節

= verse (vɝs)

= measure ('mɛʒə)

= refrain (rɪ'fren)

staple ('stepḷ) ① *v.* 以釘書針釘
② *adj.* 最重要的

① = fasten ('fæsṇ)

= clasp (klæsp)

= attach (ə'tætʃ)

= bind (baɪnd)

= connect (kə'nɛkt)

= join (dʒɔɪn)

= link (lɪŋk)

② = important (ɪm'pɔrtṇt)

= principal ('prɪnsəpḷ)

= main (men)

star (star) ① *v.* 擔任主角
② *n.* 星星

① = headline ('hɛd,laɪn)

= excel (ɪk'sɛl)

= feature ('fitʃɚ)

② = *heavenly body*

stare (stɛr) *v.* 凝視

= gaze (gez)

= look (lʊk)

= gape (gep)

= glare (glɛr)

= gawk (gɔk)

stark (stɑrk) *adj.* 完全的

= whole (hol)

= complete (kəm'plit)

= entire (ɪn'taɪr)

= downright ('daʊn,raɪt)

= absolute ('æbsə,lut)

= full (fʊl)

= outright ('aʊt'raɪt)

start (stɑrt) *v.* ①開始 ②突動

① = begin (bɪ'gɪn)

= commence (kə'mɛns)

= *set out*

② = jerk (dʒɜk)

= jump (dʒʌmp)

= *move suddenly*

startle ('stɑrtḷ) *v.* 驚訝

= frighten ('fraɪtn̩)

= surprise (sə'praɪz)

= shock (ʃɑk)

= electrify (ɪ'lɛktrə,faɪ)

= upset (ʌp'sɛt)

= alarm (ə'lɑrm)

= unnerve (ʌn'nɜv)

starve (stɑrv) *v.* 使飢餓

= hunger ('hʌŋgɚ)

= *crave food*

state (stet) ① *v.* 陳述

② *n.* 情形 ③ *n.* 國家

① = tell (tɛl)

= express (ɪk'sprɛs)

= say (se)

= pose (poz)

= declare (dɪ'klɛr)

= assert (ə'sɜt)

= relate (rɪ'let)

= recite (rɪ'saɪt)

= report (rɪ'port)

= expound (ɪk'spaʊnd)

② = condition (kən'dɪʃən)

= position (pə'zɪʃən)

= status ('stetəs)

= situation (,sɪtʃʊ'eʃən)

= circumstance ('sɜkəm,stæns)

③ = nation ('neʃən)

stately ('stetlɪ) *adj.* 堂皇的

= grand (grænd)

= majestic (mə'dʒɛstɪk)

= dignified ('dɪgnə,faɪd)

= imposing (ɪm'pozɪŋ)

= noble ('nobḷ)

= grandiose ('grændɪ,os)

= magnificent (mæg'nɪfəsn̩t)

= splendid ('splɛndɪd)

= impressive (ɪm'prɛsɪv)

statement ('stetmənt) *n.* 陳述

= account (ə'kaʊnt)

= report (rɪ'port)
= announcement (ə'naʊnsmənt)
= proclamation (,prɑklə'meʃən)
= declaration (,dɛklə'reʃən)
= notice ('notɪs)

atic ('stætɪk) ① adj. 靜止的
n. 靜電干擾

= still (stɪl)
= inactive (ɪn'æktɪv)
= sluggish ('slʌgɪʃ)
= inert (ɪn'ɜt)
= dormant ('dɔrmənt)
= *electrical interference*

ation ('steʃən) n. ①位置
②身分

= place (ples)
= post (post)
= position (pə'zɪʃən)
= rank (ræŋk)
= standing ('stændɪŋ)
= status ('stetəs)
= post (post)

ationary ('steʃən,ɛrɪ) adj.
定的

= fixed (fɪkst)
= immovable (ɪ'muvəbḷ)
= immobile (ɪ'mobḷ)
= firm (fɝm)
= inflexible (ɪn'flɛksəbḷ)
= motionless ('moʃənlɪs)
= steady ('stɛdɪ)

ationery ('steʃən,ɛrɪ) n. 信紙

= paper ('pepɚ)
= *writing materials*

statue ('stætʃʊ) n. 雕像

= figure ('fɪgɚ , 'fɪgjɚ)
= sculpture ('skʌlptʃɚ)
= bust (bʌst)
= monument ('mɑnjəmənt)

stature ('stætʃɚ) n. 身長；身高

= height (haɪt)
= loftiness ('lɔftɪnɪs)

status ('stetəs) n. ①身分
②情形

① = standing ('stændɪŋ)
= position (pə'zɪʃən)
= station ('steʃən)
= class (klæs)
= division (də'vɪʒən)
= grade (gred)
= rank (ræŋk)
② = condition (kən'dɪʃən)
= state (stet)

statute ('stætʃʊt) n. 法規

= law (lɔ)
= ordinance ('ɔrdṇəns)
= rule (rul)
= act (ækt)
= regulation (,rɛgjə'leʃən)
= measure ('mɛʒɚ)
= decree (dɪ'kri)
= bill (bɪl)
= enactment (ɪn'æktmənt)
= charter ('tʃɑrtɚ)
= legislation (,lɛdʒɪs'leʃən)

S

staunch (stɔntʃ , stɑntʃ) *adj.*
忠誠的

= loyal ('lɔɪəl , 'lɔjəl)
= steadfast ('stɛd,fæst)
= devoted (dɪ'votɪd)
= firm (fɝm)
= reliable (rɪ'laɪəbḷ)
= dependable (dɪ'pɛndəbḷ)
= trustworthy ('trʌst,wɝðɪ)

stay (ste) *v.* ①持久 ②居留
③延緩

① = remain (rɪ'men)
= last (læst , lɑst)
= endure (ɪn'djur)
= continue (kən'tɪnju)
= persist (pə'zɪst , -'sɪst)
② = dwell (dwɛl)
= reside (rɪ'zaɪd)
= live (lɪv)
= occupy ('akjə,paɪ)
= inhabit (ɪn'hæbɪt)
③ = delay (dɪ'le)
= detain (dɪ'ten)
= retard (rɪ'tɑrd)
= stop (stɑp)
= *hold up*

steady ('stɛdɪ) *adj.* 穩定的

= constant ('kɑnstənt)
= fixed (fɪkst)
= inert (ɪn'ɝt)
= regular ('rɛgjələ)
= incessant (ɪn'sɛsṇt)
= ceaseless ('sislɪs)
= perpetual (pə'pɛtʃuəl)

steal (stil) *v.* 偷

= rob (rɑb)
= take (tek)
= thieve (θiv)
= pilfer ('pɪlfə)
= filch (fɪltʃ)

stealthy ('stɛlθɪ) *adj.* 隱密的

= secret ('sikrɪt)
= sly (slaɪ)
= sneaky ('snikɪ)
= underhanded ('ʌndə'hændɪd)
= shifty ('ʃɪftɪ)

steam (stim) ① *n.* 蒸氣
② *n.* 精力 ③ *v.* 蒸 (食物等)

① = vapor ('vepə)
= gas (gæs)
= smoke (smok)
② = power (pauə)
= energy ('ɛnədʒɪ)
= force (fors)
③ = cook (kuk)
= soften ('sɔfən)
= freshen ('frɛʃən)

steed (stid) *n.* 駿馬

= horse (hɔrs)
= stallion ('stæljən)
= nag (næg)

steep (stip) ① *v.* 浸泡
② *adj.* 陡峭的

① = soak (sok)
= drench (drɛntʃ)
= sop (sɑp)

= saturate ('sætʃə,ret)

= bathe (beð)

) = high (haɪ)

= precipitous (prɪ'sɪpətəs)

teer (stɪr) ① v. 駕駛；引導
② n. 公牛

) = guide (gaɪd)

= direct (də'rɛkt)

= drive (draɪv)

= manage ('mænɪdʒ)

= regulate ('rɛgjə,let)

= conduct (kən'dʌkt)

= handle ('hændḷ)

= lead (lid)

= head (,hɛd)

= run (rʌn)

= cattle ('kætḷ)

ep (stɛp) v. 踏足

= walk (wɔk)

= tread (trɛd)

= pace (pes)

erilize ('stɛrə,laɪz) v. 消毒

= clean (klin)

= sanitize ('sænə,taɪz)

= disinfect (,dɪsɪn'fɛkt)

= decontaminate
   (,dikən'tæmə,net)

ern (stɜn) adj. 嚴厲的

= severe (sə'vɪr)

= strict (strɪkt)

= harsh (harʃ)

= firm (fɜm)

= hard (hɑrd)

= exacting (ɪg'zæktɪŋ)

= austere (ɔ'stɪr)

= stringent ('strɪndʒənt)

stew (stju) v. ①燉 ②不安

① = cook (kʊk)

② = fume (fjum , fɪum)

= seethe (sið)

= rage (redʒ)

= rave (rev)

= rant (rænt)

= storm (stɔrm)

= fret (frɛt)

= *be angry*

stick (stɪk) v. ①刺 ②黏貼
③堅持

① = pierce (pɪrs)

= stab (stæb)

= perforate ('pɜfə,ret)

= penetrate ('pɛnə,tret)

= puncture ('pʌŋktʃ⋅)

② = fasten ('fæsṇ , 'fɑsṇ)

= attach (ə'tætʃ)

= adhere (əd'hɪr)

= cling (klɪŋ)

③ = continue (kə'tɪnju)

= persevere (,pɜsə'vɪr)

= *keep on*

stiff (stɪf) adj. ①堅硬的
②不自然的 ③費力的

① = rigid ('rɪdʒɪd)

= firm (fɜm)

= tense (tɛns)

= taut (tɔt)

= tight (taɪt)

= tough (tʌf)

= inflexible (ɪn'flɛksəbḷ)

② = formal ('fɔrmḷ)

= unnatural (ʌn'nætʃərəl)

= stilted ('stɪltɪd)

③ = hard (hɑrd)

= difficult ('dɪfəkʌlt)

= tough (tʌf)

stifle ('staɪfḷ) v. 使窒息;抑止

= stop (stɑp)

= smother ('smʌðɚ)

= suppress (sə'prɛs)

= choke (tʃok)

= suffocate ('sʌfə,ket)

stigma ('stɪgmə) n. 恥辱;瑕疵

= brand (brænd)

= blemish ('blɛmɪʃ)

= stain (sten)

= slur (slɝ)

= disgrace (dɪs'gres)

= tarnish ('tɑrnɪʃ)

still (stɪl) ① adj. 靜止的;無聲的
② adv. 更;愈;仍然

① = quiet ('kwaɪət)

= motionless ('moʃənlɪs)

= placid ('plæsɪd)

= smooth (smuð)

= untroubled (ʌn'trʌbḷd)

= tranquil ('trænkwɪl , 'træŋ-)

= noiseless ('nɔɪzlɪs)

= calm (kɑm)

= peaceful ('pisfəl)

② = yet (jɛt)

= even ('ivən)

= *until now*

= *so far*

stimulate ('stɪmjə,let) v. 刺激
鼓舞

= spur (spɝ)

= stir (stɝ)

= move (muv)

= motivate ('motə,vet)

= activate ('æktə,vet)

= rouse (rauz)

= energize ('ɛnɚ,dʒaɪz)

= invigorate (ɪn'vɪgə,ret)

= *pep up*

sting (stɪŋ) v. 刺傷;使痛苦

= pain (pen)

= inflame (ɪn'flem)

= wound (wund)

= prick (prɪk)

= distress (dɪ'strɛs)

stingy ('stɪndʒɪ) adj. 吝嗇的

= ungenerous (ʌn'dʒɛnərəs)

= miserly ('maɪzɚlɪ)

= cheap (tʃip)

= closefisted ('klos'fɪstɪd)

stink (stɪŋk) n. 臭味

= stench (stɛntʃ)

= smell (smɛl)

= odor ('odɚ)

tint (stɪnt) *n.* 指定必做的工作

= function ('fʌŋkʃən)
= assignment (ə'saɪnmənt)
= role (rol)
= work (wɜk)
= job (dʒɑb)
= chore (tʃɔr , tʃor)
= duty ('djutɪ)
= task (tæsk)

tir (stɜ) *v.* ①攪和 ②移動 ③惹起

= mix (mɪks)
= mingle ('mɪŋgl̩)
= combine (kəm'baɪn)
= jumble ('dʒʌmbl̩)
= scramble ('skræmbl̩)
= blend (blɛnd)
= merge (mɜdʒ)
= move (muv)
= budge (bʌdʒ)
= mobilize ('mobl̩,aɪz)
= excite (ɪk'saɪt)
= rouse (rauz)
= affect (ə'fɛkt)
= agitate ('ædʒə,tet)
= disquiet (dɪs'kwaɪət)
= perturb (pə'tɜb)
= trouble ('trʌbl̩)
= shake (ʃek)
= disturb (dɪs'tɜb)

itch (stɪtʃ) *v.* 縫紉

= sew (so)
= fasten ('fæsn̩ , 'fɑsn̩)
= tailor ('telə)

stock (stɑk) *v.* 供應；備置

= supply (sə'plaɪ)
= keep (kip)
= collect (kə'lɛkt)
= accumulate (ə'kjumjə,let)
= amass (ə'mæs)
= stockpile ('stɑk,paɪl)
= gather ('gæðə)
= hoard (hord)
= *store up*

stocky ('stɑkɪ) *adj.* 結實的；矮胖的

= sturdy ('stɜdɪ)
= solid ('salɪd)
= fat (fæt)
= plump (plʌmp)
= chubby ('tʃʌbɪ)
= portly ('portlɪ , 'pɔr-)
= fleshy ('flɛʃɪ)
= chunky ('tʃʌŋkɪ)
= strapping ('stræpɪŋ)

stomach ('stʌmək) ① *v.* 忍受 ② *n.* 胃

① = bear (bɛr)
= endure (ɪn'djʊr , -'dʊr)
= take (tek)
= stand (stænd)
= tolerate ('talə,ret)
② = belly ('bɛlɪ)
= abdomen ('æbdəmən , æb'do-)

stone (ston) *n.* 石

= rock (rɑk)
= pebble ('pɛbl̩)
= gem (dʒɛm)

S

stool (stul) *n.* 凳

  = seat (sit)

  = chair (tʃɛr)

stoop (stup) ① *v.* 屈身
② *n.* 門階

  ① = crouch (krautʃ)

  = squat (skwɑt)

  = *bend forward*

  ② = porch (portʃ , pɔrtʃ)

  = veranda (və'rændə)

  = platform ('plæt,fɔrm)

stop (stɑp) *v.* 使停止；阻止

  = end (ɛnd)

  = halt (hɔlt)

  = check (tʃɛk)

  = stay (ste)

  = cease (sis)

  = block (blɑk)

  = discontinue (,dɪskən'tɪnju)

  = quit (kwɪt)

  = arrest (ə'rɛst)

  = prevent (prɪ'vɛnt)

  = conclude (kən'klud)

  = terminate ('tɝmə,net)

store (stor , stɔr) ① *v.* 供給；
貯藏　② *n.* 商店

  ① = supply (sə'plaɪ)

  = stock (stɑk)

  = keep (kip)

  = collect (kə'lɛkt)

  = accumulate (ə'kjumjə,let)

  = amass (ə'mæs)

  = stockpile ('stɑk,paɪl)

  = gather ('gæðɚ)

  = hoard (hord)

  ② = shop (ʃɑp)

  = mart (mɑrt)

  = business ('bɪznɪs)

storm (stɔrm) ① *v.* 猛攻
② *v.* 狂怒　③ *n.* 風暴

  ① = attack (ə'tæk)

  = besiege (bɪ'sidʒ)

  = beset (bɪ'sɛt)

  = raid (red)

  = charge (tʃɑrdʒ)

  = assault (ə'sɔlt)

  = assail (ə'sel)

  ② = rage (redʒ)

  = rant (rænt)

  = rave (rev)

  = rampage (ræm'pedʒ)

  = seethe (sið)

  = boil (bɔɪl)

  = fume (fjum)

  = *be violent*

  ③ = tempest ('tɛmpɪst)

  = outburst ('aʊt,bɝst)

story ('storɪ) *n.* ①故事
②層；樓

  ① = tale (tel)

  = account (ə'kaʊnt)

  = chronicle ('krɑnɪkl̩)

  = yarn (jɑrn)

  = narrative ('nærətɪv)

  = anecdote ('ænɪk,dot)

  = epic ('ɛpɪk)

  = saga ('sɑgə)

= floor (flor)	= drift (drɪft)
= level ('lɛvḷ)	= stray (stre)
= tier (tɪr)	

tout (staʊt) *adj.* ①肥大的
②勇敢的

straight (stret) *adj.* ①直的
②誠實的

① = fat (fæt)
= large (lɑrdʒ)
= fleshly ('flɛʃɪ)
= plump (plʌmp)
= pudgy ('pʌdʒɪ)
= chubby ('tʃʌbɪ)
= stocky ('stɑkɪ)
= portly ('portlɪ , 'por-)
② = brave (brev)
= bold (bold)
= courageous (kə'redʒəs)
= valiant ('væljənt)
= gallant ('gælənt)
= heroic (hɪ'ro·ɪk)
= chivalrous ('ʃɪvḷrəs)

① = direct (də'rɛkt)
= unswerving (ʌn'swɜvɪŋ)
② = frank (fræŋk)
= honest ('ɑnɪst)
= upright ('ʌp,raɪt , ʌp'raɪt)
= square (skwɛr)
= sincere (sɪn'sɪr)
= open ('opən , 'opm̩)

strain (stren) ① *v.* 拉緊
② *v.* 扭傷　③ *n.* 氣質　④ *n.* 血統

tow (sto) *v.* 裝載

= pack (pæk)
= load (lod)
= store (stor , stɔr)

traddle ('strædḷ) *v.* 跨腿而站
(走、坐)

= perch (pɜtʃ)

traggle ('strægḷ) *v.* 分散

= wander ('wɑndɚ)
= ramble ('ræmbḷ)
= roam (rom)
= rove (rov)

① = stretch (strɛtʃ)
= pull (pʊl)
= extend (ɪk'stɛnd)
= tug (tʌg)
= tow (to)
② = sprain (spren)
= wrench (rɛntʃ)
= injure ('ɪndʒɚ)
= hurt (hɜt)
③ = quality ('kwɑlətɪ)
= trace (tres)
= streak (strik)
④ = race (res)
= descent (dɪ'sɛnt)

strand (strænd) ① *v.* 使束手無
策　② *n.* 繩索之股

① = abandon (ə'bændən)
= desert (dɪ'zɜt)
= leave (liv)

② = thread (θrɛd)
= string (strɪŋ)
= line (laɪn)
= cord (kɔrd)

strange (strendʒ) *adj.* 奇怪的
= unusual (ʌn'juʒʊəl)
= queer (kwɪr)
= peculiar (pɪ'kjuljɚ)
= unfamiliar (ʌnfə'mɪljɚ)
= odd (ɑd)
= curious ('kjʊrɪəs)
= eccentric (ɪk'sɛntrɪk)

strangle ('stræŋgḷ) *v.* 使窒息
= choke (tʃok)
= suffocate ('sʌfəket)
= smother ('smʌðɚ)
= asphyxiate (æs'fɪksɪ,et)

strap (stræp) ① *v.* 用皮帶綑
② *v.* 用皮帶打 ③ *n.* 皮帶
① = fasten ('fæsṇ , 'fasṇ)
= bind (baɪnd)
= tie (taɪ)
= wrap (ræp)
= lash (læʃ)
= gird (gɝd)
② = whip (hwɪp)
= beat (bit)
= thrash (θræʃ)
= spank (spæŋk)
= flog (flɑg)
③ = belt (bɛlt)

strapping ('stræpɪŋ) *adj.*
高大強壯的

= tall (tɔl)
= strong (strɔŋ)
= healthy ('hɛlθɪ)
= sturdy ('stɝdɪ)
= rugged ('rʌgɪd)
= powerful ('paʊɚfəl)
= hardy ('hardɪ)
= robust (ro'bʌst)
= vigorous ('vɪgərəs)
= athletic (æθ'lɛtɪk)
= muscular ('mʌskjəlɚ)
= brawny ('brɔnɪ)
= beefy ('bifɪ)
= well-built ('wɛl'bɪlt)

strategy ('strætədʒɪ) *n.* 戰略；
策略
= planning ('plænɪŋ)
= management ('mænɪdʒmənt)
= tactics ('tæktɪks)
= manipulation (mə,nɪpju'leʃən)
= intrigue ('ɪntrig , ɪn'trig)
= maneuvering (mə'nuvɚɪŋ)

stray (stre) *v.* 漂泊
= wander ('wandɚ)
= roam (rom)
= rove (rov)
= straggle ('strægḷ)
= gad (gæd)
= ramble ('ræmbḷ)
= drift (drɪft)
= meander (mɪ'ændɚ)

streak (strik) ① *v.* 使有條紋
② *n.* 氣質
① = mark (mɑrk)

= line (laın)

= score (skor , skɔr)

= striate ('straıet)

= stripe (straıp)

= strain (stren)

= element ('ɛləmənt)

= vein (ven)

= nature ('netʃə)

= quality ('kwɑlətı)

= characteristic (,kærıktə'rıstık)

= tendency ('tɛndənsı)

tream (strim) ① v. 流

) n. 小溪

) = flow (flo)

= pour (pɔr)

= surge (sɝdʒ)

= rush (rʌʃ)

= gush (gʌʃ)

= flood (flʌd)

) = creek (krik)

= brook (bruk)

treet (strit) n. 街道

= road (rod)

= thoroughfare ('θɝo,fɛr)

= avenue ('ævə,nju)

trength (strɛŋθ) n. 力量

= power ('pauə)

= force (fors)

= vigor ('vıgə)

= potency ('potn̩sı)

= might (maıt)

= energy ('ɛnə·dʒı)

= intensity (ın'tɛnsətı)

strenuous ('strɛnjuəs) *adj.*

①奮發的 ②費力的

① = active ('æktıv)

= energetic (,ɛnə·'dʒɛtık)

= vigorous ('vıgərəs)

= intense (ın'tɛns)

② = difficult ('dıfəkəlt)

= hard (hɑrd)

= rough (rʌf)

= rugged ('rʌgıd)

= arduous ('ɑrdʒuəs)

= laborious (lə'borıəs)

stress (strɛs) n. ①壓力 ②強調

① = force (fors)

= strain (stren)

= pressure ('prɛʃə)

= tension ('tɛnʃən)

② = emphasis ('ɛmfəsıs)

= importance (ım'pɔrtn̩s)

= accent ('æksɛnt)

= insistence (ın'sıstəns)

= urgency ('ɝdʒənsı)

stretch (strɛtʃ) v. 延伸

= extend (ık'stɛnd)

= spread (sprɛd)

= strain (stren)

= expand (ık'spænd)

= distend (dı'stɛnd)

= elongate (ı'lɔŋget)

= *draw out*

strew (stru) v. 撒布

= sprinkle ('sprıŋkl̩)

= scatter ('skætə)

S

= disperse (dɪ'spɝs)

= distribute (dɪ'strɪbjut)

strict (strɪkt) *adj.* ①嚴厲的
②詳盡的

① = harsh (harʃ)

= exact (ɪg'zækt)

= precise (prɪ'saɪs)

= rigorous ('rɪgərəs)

= severe (sə'vɪr)

= exacting (ɪg'zæktɪŋ)

= stringent ('strɪndʒənt)

= stern (stɝn)

= austere (ɔ'stɪr)

② = perfect ('pɝfɪkt)

= complete (kəm'plit)

= absolute ('æbsə,lut)

= literal ('lɪtərəl)

= exact (ɪg'zækt)

= real (ril)

= true (tru)

stride (straɪd) *n.* 步

= step (stɛp)

= pace (pes)

= walk (wɔk)

strife (straɪf) *n.* 爭論

= quarreling ('kwɔrəlɪŋ)

= fighting ('faɪtɪŋ)

= controversy ('kɑntrə,vɝsɪ)

= dispute (dɪ'spjut)

= squabble ('skwɑbl̩)

strike (straɪk) *v.* ①重擊
②背叛

① = hit (hɪt)

= knock (nɑk)

= jab (dʒæb)

= smack (smæk)

= whack (hwæk)

= bat (bæt)

= clout (klaʊt)

② = revolt (rɪ'volt)

= rebel (rɪ'bɛl)

striking ('straɪkɪŋ) *adj.* 顯著的

= attractive (ə'træktɪv)

= noticeable ('notɪsəbl̩)

= obvious ('ɑbvɪəs)

= conspicuous (kən'spɪkjʊəs)

= prominent ('prɑmənənt)

= bold (bold)

= pronounced (prə'naʊnst)

= outstanding (aʊt'stændɪŋ)

= flagrant ('flegrənt)

= glaring ('glɛrɪŋ)

string (strɪŋ) *v.* 連接

= thread (θrɛd)

= connect (kə'nɛkt)

= tie (taɪ)

= bind (baɪnd)

= *line up*

strip (strɪp) *v.* 剝去

= remove (rɪ'muv)

= uncover (ʌn'kʌvɚ)

= bare (bɛr)

= pare (pær)

= peel (pil)

tripe (straɪp) *n.* 狹長的一條

= line (laɪn)

= mark (mɑrk)

= striate ('straɪet)

trive (straɪv) *v.* 奮鬥

= struggle ('strʌgl̩)

= fight (faɪt)

= contend (kən'tɛnd)

= battle ('bætl̩)

= endeavor (ɪn'dɛvɚ)

= labor ('lebɚ)

troke (strok) ① *v.* 撫摸
② *n.* 努力　③ *n.* (疾病的)
突然發作

① = rub (rʌb)

= caress (kə'rɛs)

= massage (mə'sɑʒ)

= pet (pɛt)

② = feat (fit)

= effort ('ɛfɚt)

= act (ækt)

= deed (did)

= undertaking (ˌʌndɚ'tekɪŋ)

= attempt (ə'tɛmpt)

③ = attack (ə'tæk)

= seizure ('siʒɚ)

= convulsion (kən'vʌlʃən)

= spasm ('spæzəm)

troll (strol) *v.* 散步

= walk (wɔk)

= saunter ('sɔntɚ)

= stride (straɪd)

= strut (strʌt)

= amble ('æmbl̩)

= promenade (ˌprɑmə'ned)

strong (strɔŋ) *adj.* 強而有力的

= powerful ('paʊɚfəl)

= vigorous ('vɪgərəs)

= forceful ('fɔrsfəl)

= potent ('potn̩t)

= mighty ('maɪtɪ)

= sturdy ('stɝdɪ)

= hardy ('hɑrdɪ)

= muscular ('mʌskjəlɚ)

= brawny ('brɔnɪ)

stronghold ('strɔŋˌhold) *n.*
要塞

= bastion ('bæstʃən)

= fortification (ˌfɔrtəfə'keʃən)

structure ('strʌktʃɚ) *n.*
①建築物　②結構

① = building ('bɪldɪŋ)

= construction (kən'strʌkʃən)

= house (haʊs)

= edifice ('ɛdəfɪs)

② = form (fɔrm)

= shape (ʃep)

= figure ('fɪgɚ)

= configuration (kənˌfɪgjə'reʃən)

struggle ('strʌgl̩) *v.* ①努力
②掙扎

① = endeavor (ɪn'dɛvɚ)

= strive (straɪv)

= attempt (ə'tɛmpt)

= try (traɪ)

S

② = fight (faɪt)
= battle ('bætḷ)
= contend (kən'tɛnd)
= scuffle ('skʌfḷ)
= tussle ('tʌsḷ)

strut (strʌt) v. 昂首闊步地走
= parade (pə'red)
= swagger ('swægə)

stub (stʌb) n. 殘片
= end (ɛnd)
= tail (tel)
= tip (tɪp)

stubborn ('stʌbən) adj. 固執的
= obstinate ('abstənɪt)
= willful ('wɪlfəl)
= headstrong ('hɛd,strɔŋ)
= adamant ('ædə,mænt)
= rigid ('rɪdʒɪd)
= unyielding (ʌn'jildɪŋ)
= inflexible (ɪn'flɛksəbḷ)

stubby ('stʌbɪ) adj. 短而胖的
= stocky ('stakɪ)
= chubby ('tʃʌbɪ)
= squat (skwat)
= chunky ('tʃʌŋkɪ)
= pudgy ('pʌdʒɪ)

student ('stjudn̩t) n. 學生；學者
= pupil ('pjupḷ)
= scholar ('skalə)

studious ('stjudɪəs) adj. 好學的

= learned ('lɜnɪd)
= bookish ('bʊkɪʃ)
= educated ('ɛdʒə,ketɪd)
= scholarly ('skaləlɪ)
= cultured ('kʌltʃəd)
= profound (prə'faʊnd)
= erudite ('ɛrʊ,daɪt)
= diligent ('dɪlədʒənt)

stuff (stʌf) ① v. 填塞
② n. 物品
① = fill (fɪl)
= load (lod)
= pack (pæk)
= gorge (gɔrdʒ)
= saturate ('sætʃə,ret)
② = substance ('sʌbstəns)
= matter ('mætə)
= material (mə'tɪrɪəl)

stuffy ('stʌfɪ) adj. ①通風不良的
②拘謹的
① = close (klos)
= stifling ('staɪflɪŋ)
= airless ('ɛrlɪs)
= suffocating ('sʌfə,ketɪŋ)
= oppressive (ə'prɛsɪv)
② = pompous ('pampəs)
= prim (prɪm)
= prudish ('prudɪʃ)
= dull (dʌl)
= unimaginative
  (,ʌnɪ'mædʒɪnətɪv)
= staid (sted)
= stodgy ('stadʒɪ)
= old-fogyish ('old'fogɪʃ)
= strait-laced ('stret'lest)

tumble ('stʌmbḷ) v. 輾轉

= stagger ('stægɚ)
= flounder ('flaundɚ)
= tumble ('tʌmbḷ)
= falter ('fɔltɚ)

stump (stʌmp) ① v. 困惑
② v. 作政治性演說
③ n. 餘留的東西

① = baffle ('bæfḷ)
= perplex (pɚ'plɛks)
= confound (kən'faund)
= mystify ('mɪstə,faɪ)
= puzzle ('pʌzḷ)
② = campaign (kæm'pen)
= electioneer (ɪ,lɛkʃən'ɪr)
③ = remainder (rɪ'mendɚ)
= rest (rɛst)
= leftovers ('lɛft,ovɚz)

stun (stʌn) v. 使失去知覺

= daze (dez)
= bewilder (bɪ'wɪldɚ)
= shock (ʃɑk)
= overwhelm (,ovɚ'hwɛlm)
= numb (nʌm)
= stupefy ('stjupə,faɪ)

stunning ('stʌnɪŋ) adj.
①極美的 ②迷惑的；驚人的

① = attractive (ə'træktɪv)
= beautiful ('bjutəfəl)
= gorgeous ('gɔrdʒəs)
= ravishing ('rævɪʃɪŋ)
= glorious ('glorɪəs)
= brilliant ('brɪljənt)

= dazzling ('dæzlɪŋ)
= good-looking ('gud'lukɪŋ)
② = bewildering (bɪ'wɪldɚɪŋ)
= astounding (ə'staundɪŋ)
= shocking ('ʃɑkɪŋ)
= astonishing (ə'stɑnɪʃɪŋ)
= amazing (ə'mezɪŋ)
= surprising (sə'praɪzɪŋ)

stunt (stʌnt) ① v. 阻礙…的生長
② n. 特技

① = shorten ('ʃɔrtṇ)
= abbreviate (ə'brivɪ,et)
= abridge (ə'brɪdʒ)
= condense (kən'dɛns)
② = feat (fit)
= act (ækt)
= exploit ('ɛksplɔɪt)
= performance (pɚ'fɔrməns)

stupefy ('stjupə,faɪ) v. 使驚愕

= stun (stʌn)
= daze (dez)
= bewilder (bɪ'wɪldɚ)
= numb (nʌm)
= shock (ʃɑk)

stupendous (stju'pɛndəs) adj.
驚人的

= amazing (ə'mezɪŋ)
= marvelous ('mɑrvḷəs)
= great (gret)
= huge (hjudʒ)
= enormous (ɪ'nɔrməs)
= immense (ɪ'mɛns)
= vast (væst)

= extraordinary (ɪk'strɔrdn̩‚ɛrɪ)

= exceptional (ɪk'sɛpʃənḷ)

= remarkable (rɪ'mɑrkəbḷ)

= wonderful ('wʌndəfəl)

stupid ('stjupɪd) *adj.* 笨的

= dull (dʌl)

= unintelligent (‚ʌnɪn'tɛlədʒənt)

= dense (dɛns)

= asinine ('æsn̩‚aɪn)

= foolish ('fulɪʃ)

= silly ('sɪlɪ)

stupor ('stjupə) *n.* 昏迷

= unconsciousness
  (ʌn'kɑnʃəsnɪs)

= faint (fent)

= coma ('komə)

= swoon (swun)

= blackout ('blæk‚aʊt)

= lethargy ('lɛθədʒɪ)

= numbness ('nʌmnɪs)

sturdy ('stɜdɪ) *adj.* 強壯的；
堅固的

= strong (strɔŋ)

= firm (fɜm)

= powerful ('paʊəfəl)

= rugged ('rʌgɪd)

= hardy ('hɑrdɪ)

= robust (ro'bʌst)

= vigorous ('vɪgərəs)

= athletic (æθ'lɛtɪk)

= muscular ('mʌskjələ)

= brawny ('brɔnɪ)

= sound (saʊnd)

= stable ('stebḷ)

= well-built ('wɛl'bɪlt)

= substantial (səb'stænʃəl)

= solid ('sɑlɪd)

= durable ('djʊrəbḷ)

stutter ('stʌtə) *v.* 口吃

= stammer ('stæmə)

= hem (hɛm)

= haw (hɔ)

= falter ('fɔltə)

= hesitate ('hɛzə‚tet)

stylish ('staɪlɪʃ) *adj.* 流行的

= fashionable ('fæʃənəbḷ)

= modish ('modɪʃ)

= voguish ('vogɪʃ)

= smart (smɑrt)

= chic (ʃɪk , ʃik)

= well-dressed ('wɛl'drɛst)

= natty ('nætɪ)

= sporty ('spɔrtɪ)

= dapper ('dæpə)

subdue (səb'dju) *v.* 征服

= conquer ('kɑŋkə)

= overcome (‚ovə'kʌm)

= crush (krʌʃ)

= vanquish ('væŋkwɪʃ)

= quell (kwɛl)

= suppress (sə'prɛs)

= squelch (skwɛltʃ)

= squash (skwɑʃ)

= *put down*

subject ('ʌbdʒɪkt) *n.* 主題

= topic ('tapɪk)

= issue ('ɪʃʊ , 'ɪʃjʊ)

= problem ('prabləm)

= theme (θim)

= text (tɛkst)

= question ('kwɛstʃən)

= point (pɔɪnt)

= plot (plat)

ublime (sə'blaɪm) adj. 崇高的

= noble ('nobl̩)

= majestic (mə'dʒɛstɪk)

= grand (grænd)

= great (gret)

= distinguished (dɪ'stɪŋgwɪʃt)

= lofty ('lɔftɪ , 'laftɪ)

= prominent ('pramənənt)

= eloquent ('ɛləkwənt)

= exalted (ɪg'zɔltɪd , ɛg-)

ubmerge (səb'mɝdʒ) v.
浸入水中

= immerse (ɪ'mɝs)

= sink (sɪŋk)

= dip (dɪp)

= duck (dʌk)

= inundate ('ɪnʌndet , ɪn'ʌndet)

= dunk (dʌŋk)

ubmit (səb'mɪt) v. 屈服；投降

= yield (jild)

= surrender (sə'rɛndɚ)

= comply (kəm'plaɪ)

= obey (ə'be , o'be)

= mind (maɪnd)

= heed (hid)

subordinate (sə'bɔrdn̩ɪt) adj.
下級的；附屬的

= dependent (dɪ'pɛndənt)

= secondary ('sɛkən,dɛrɪ)

= inferior (ɪn'fɪrɪɚ)

subscribe (səb'skraɪb) v. 捐助

= contribute (kən'trɪbjut)

= support (sə'port , -'pɔrt)

= donate to

= give to

subsequent ('sʌbsɪ,kwɛnt) adj.
繼起的

= following ('faləwɪŋ)

= later ('letɚ)

= next (nɛkst)

= succeeding (sək'sidɪŋ)

= coming after

subside (səb'saɪd) v. 下降

= decrease (dɪ'kris)

= diminish (də'mɪnɪʃ)

= decline (dɪ'klaɪn)

= lessen ('lɛsn̩)

subsist (səb'sɪst) v. 生活

= live (lɪv)

= exist (ɪg'zɪst)

= survive (sɚ'vaɪv)

substance ('sʌbstəns) n. 物質；
本體

= matter ('mætɚ)

= material (mə'tɪrɪəl)

= body ('badɪ)

S

= stuff (stʌf)
= essence ('ɛsn̩s)
= gist (dʒɪst)
= content ('kɑntɛnt , kən'tɛnt)

substantial (səb'stænʃəl) *adj.*
①眞實的 ②牢固的 ③富有的

① = real (ril , 'riəl)
= actual ('æktʃuəl)
= true (tru)
= authentic (ɔ'θɛntɪk)
② = strong (strɔŋ)
= firm (fɜm)
= solid ('sɑlɪd)
= stable ('stebl̩)
= sound (saʊnd)
③ = wealthy ('wɛlθɪ)
= rich (rɪtʃ)
= prosperous ('prɑspərəs)
= affluent ('æfluənt)
= well-to-do ('wɛltə'du)

substitute ('sʌbstə,tjut) *v.* 代替

= replace (rɪ'ples)
= change (tʃendʒ)
= exchange (ɪks'tʃendʒ)
= switch (swɪtʃ)
= shift (ʃɪft)

subtle ('sʌtl̩) *adj.* ①精緻的
②狡猾的

① = delicate ('dɛləkət , -kɪt)
= thin (θɪn)
= fine (faɪn)
= faint (fent)
② = sly (slaɪ)
= crafty ('kræftɪ)

= tricky ('trɪkɪ)
= underhanded (,ʌndə'hændɪd)
= shrewd (ʃrud)
= cunning ('kʌnɪŋ)
= clever ('klɛvə)
= foxy ('fɑksɪ)

subtract (səb'trækt) *v.* 減去

= deduct (dɪ'dʌkt)
= remove (rɪ'muv)
= discount ('dɪskaʊnt , dɪs'kaʊnt)
= withdraw (wɪð'drɔ , wɪθ-)
= *take away*

successful (sək'sɛsfəl) *adj.*
成功的

= prosperous ('prɑspərəs)
= fortunate ('fɔrtʃənɪt)
= thriving ('θraɪvɪŋ)
= flourishing ('flɜɪʃɪŋ)
= victorious (vɪk'torɪəs , -rjəs)
= triumphant (traɪ'ʌmfənt)
= winning ('wɪnɪŋ)
= providential (,prɑvə'dɛnʃəl)
= booming ('bumɪŋ)
= well-off ('wɛl'ɔf)
= lucky ('lʌkɪ)

succession (sək'sɛʃən) *n.* 連續

= sequence ('sikwəns)
= order ('ɔrdə)
= progression (prə'grɛʃən)
= series ('sɪrɪz , sirɪz)

succulent ('sʌkjələnt) *adj.*
多汁的

= juicy ('dʒusɪ)

succumb ﹝ sə'kʌm ﹞ *v.* ①屈從 ②死

① = yield ﹝ jild ﹞
= submit ﹝ səb'mɪt ﹞
= acquiesce ﹝ ˌækwɪ'ɛs ﹞
= comply ﹝ kəm'plaɪ ﹞
= *give way*

② = die ﹝ daɪ ﹞
= decease ﹝ dɪ'sis ﹞
= perish ﹝ 'pɛrɪʃ ﹞
= expire ﹝ ɪk'spaɪr ﹞

suck ﹝ sʌk ﹞ *v.* 吸；吮；吸收
= drink ﹝ drɪŋk ﹞
= absorb ﹝ əb'sɔrb ﹞
= *draw in*
= *take in*

sudden ﹝ 'sʌdn̩ ﹞ *adj.* 突然的；急速的
= unexpected ﹝ ˌʌnɪk'spɛktɪd ﹞
= abrupt ﹝ ə'brʌpt ﹞
= hasty ﹝ 'hestɪ ﹞
= impulsive ﹝ ɪm'pʌlsɪv ﹞
= unforeseen ﹝ ˌʌnfor'sin ﹞
= impetuous ﹝ ɪm'pɛtʃʊəs ﹞

sue ﹝ su , sju ﹞ *v.* 起訴；控告
= prosecute ﹝ 'prɑsɪˌkjut ﹞
= litigate ﹝ 'lɪtəˌget ﹞
= *bring action against*

suffer ﹝ 'sʌfɚ ﹞ *v.* 忍受；經驗
= endure ﹝ ɪn'djʊr ﹞
= experience ﹝ ɪk'spɪrɪəns ﹞
= bear ﹝ bɛr ﹞
= stand ﹝ stænd ﹞
= undergo ﹝ ˌʌndɚ'go ﹞
= tolerate ﹝ 'tɑləˌret ﹞

sufficient ﹝ sə'fɪʃənt ﹞ *adj.* 充分的
= enough ﹝ ə'nʌf , ɪ'nʌf ﹞
= ample ﹝ 'æmpl̩ ﹞
= plenty ﹝ 'plɛntɪ ﹞
= adequate ﹝ 'ædəkwɪt ﹞
= satisfactory ﹝ ˌsætɪs'fæktərɪ ﹞

suffocate ﹝ 'sʌfəˌket ﹞ *v.* 使窒息
= smother ﹝ 'smʌðɚ ﹞
= stifle ﹝ 'staɪfl̩ ﹞
= choke ﹝ tʃok ﹞
= muffle ﹝ 'mʌfl̩ ﹞
= asphyxiate ﹝ æs'fɪksɪˌet ﹞
= suppress ﹝ sə'prɛs ﹞

suffrage ﹝ 'sʌfrɪdʒ ﹞ *n.* 投票；投票權
= vote ﹝ vot ﹞
= ballot ﹝ 'bælət ﹞
= voice ﹝ vɔɪs ﹞

suggest ﹝ səg'dʒɛst , sə'dʒɛst ﹞ *v.* 暗示；建議
= hint ﹝ hɪnt ﹞
= imply ﹝ ɪm'plaɪ ﹞
= intimate ﹝ 'ɪntəˌmet ﹞
= insinuate ﹝ ɪn'sɪnjuˌet ﹞
= advise ﹝ əd'vaɪz ﹞
= propose ﹝ prə'poz ﹞

S

suit (sut , sjut) ① *v.* 使滿意
② *v.* 適合於   ③ *n.* 一套衣服
④ *n.* 訴訟

① = satisfy ('sætɪs,faɪ)
  = *agree with*
② = fit (fɪt)
  = become (bɪ'kʌm)
③ = costume ('kɑstjum)
  = dress (drɛs)
  = habit ('hæbɪt)
④ = litigation (,lɪtə,geʃən)
  = case (kes)
  = prosecution (,prɑsɪ'kjuʃən)
  = *legal action*

suitable ('sutəbḷ , 'sju-) *adj.*
適合的

  = fitting ('fɪtɪŋ)
  = proper ('prɑpɚ)
  = timely ('taɪmlɪ)
  = favorable ('fevərəbḷ)
  = adequate ('ædəkwɪt)
  = satisfactory (,sætɪs'fæktərɪ)

sulk (sʌlk) *v. n.* 慍怒

  = fret (frɛt)
  = mope (mop)

sullen ('sʌlɪn , -ən) *adj.* 慍怒的；
鬱鬱不樂的

  = gloomy ('glumɪ)
  = dismal ('dɪzmḷ)
  = glum (glʌm)
  = moody ('mudɪ)
  = moping ('mopɪŋ)
  = morose (mo'ros , mə-)

= sulky ('sʌlkɪ)

sum (sʌm) *n.* 總數

  = total ('totḷ)
  = whole (hol)
  = entirety (ɪn'taɪrtɪ)
  = amount (ə'maunt)
  = quantity ('kwɑntətɪ)

summarize ('sʌmə,raɪz) *v.*
摘要

  = brief (brif)
  = outline ('aut,laɪn)
  = capsule ('kæpsḷ , 'kæpsjul)
  = abridge (ə'brɪdʒ)

summit ('sʌmɪt) *n.* 頂點

  = top (tɑp)
  = peak (pik)
  = crest (krɛst)
  = crown (kraun)
  = apex ('epɛks)
  = zenith ('zinɪθ)
  = acme ('ækmɪ , 'ækmi)

summon ('sʌmən) *v.* 召喚

  = call (kɔl)
  = conjure ('kandʒɚ)
  = subpoena (sə'pinə , səb'pi-)
  = *send for*

sumptuous ('sʌmptʃuəs) *adj.*
奢侈的；華麗的

  = rich (rɪtʃ)
  = magnificent (mæg'nɪfəsṇt)
  = costly ('kɔstlɪ)

= grand〔grænd〕
= grandiose〔'grændɪˌos〕
= splendid〔'splɛndɪd〕
= imposing〔ɪm'pozɪŋ〕
= impressive〔ɪm'prɛsɪv〕
= stately〔'stetlɪ〕
= majestic〔mə'dʒɛstɪk〕
= elegant〔'ɛləgənt〕
= luxurious〔lʌg'ʒurɪəs , lʌk'ʃur-〕
= elaborate〔ɪ'læbərɪt〕

undown〔'sʌnˌdaʊn〕*n.* 日落

= sunset〔'sʌnˌsɛt〕
= dusk〔dʌsk〕
= nightfall〔'naɪtˌfɔl〕
= evening〔'ivnɪŋ〕

undry〔'sʌndrɪ〕*adj.* 各式各樣的

= several〔'sɛvərəl〕
= various〔'vɛrɪəs〕
= diversified〔daɪ'vɝsəˌfaɪd , də-〕
= assorted〔ə'sɔrtɪd〕
= many〔'mɛnɪ〕

unken〔'sʌŋkən〕*adj.* ①沈下的
②凹下的

①= submerged〔səb'mɝdʒd〕
= sunk〔sʌŋk〕
②= hollow〔'halo〕
= concave〔kan'kev , 'kankev〕

unny〔'sʌnɪ〕*adj.* 歡樂的

= bright〔braɪt〕
= cheerful〔'tʃɪrfəl〕
= radiant〔'redɪənt〕
= pleasant〔'plɛzn̩t〕

sunrise〔'sʌnˌraɪz〕*n.* 黎明

= dawn〔dɔn〕
= daybreak〔'deˌbrek〕
= morning〔'mɔrnɪŋ〕

sunset〔'sʌnˌsɛt〕*n.* 日落

= sundown〔'sʌnˌdaʊn〕
= dusk〔dʌsk〕
= evening〔'ivnɪŋ〕
= nightfall〔'naɪtˌfɔl〕

superb〔su'pɝb , sə-〕*adj.*
宏偉壯麗的

= grand〔grænd〕
= stately〔'stetlɪ〕
= magnificent〔mæg'nɪfəsn̩t〕
= splendid〔'splɛndɪd〕
= excellent〔'ɛkslənt〕
= fine〔faɪn〕
= exquisite〔'ɛkskwɪzɪt , ɪk's-〕
= marvelous〔'marvləs〕
= wonderful〔'wʌndəfəl〕
= grandiose〔'grændɪˌos〕
= glorious〔'glorɪəs , 'glɔr-〕
= imposing〔ɪm'pozɪŋ〕
= impressive〔ɪm'prɛsɪv〕
= noble〔'nobl̩〕
= majestic〔mə'dʒɛstɪk〕
= sumptuous〔'sʌmptʃuəs〕
= elaborate〔ɪ'læbərɪt〕

superficial〔ˌsupə'fɪʃəl , ˌsju-〕
adj. 膚淺的；表面的

= shallow〔'ʃælo〕
= cursory〔'kɝsərɪ〕
= surface〔'sɝfɪs〕

superintendent

(ˌsuprɪnˈtɛndənt) *n.* 監督者

= supervisor (ˌsjupəˈvaɪzə)
= manager (ˈmænɪdʒə)
= director (dəˈrɛktə, daɪ-)
= foreman (ˈformən, ˈfor-)

superior (səˈpɪrɪə, su-) *adj.*
較好的；較高的

= better (ˈbɛtə)
= higher (ˈhaɪə)
= greater (ˈgretə)

supernatural (ˌsupəˈnætʃrəl)
adj. 超自然的

= spiritual (ˈspɪrɪtʃuəl)
= superhuman (ˌsupəˈhjumən,
　ˌsju-)
= ghostly (ˈgostlɪ)
= unknown (ʌnˈnon)
= mysterious (mɪsˈtɪrɪəs)
= mystical (ˈmɪstɪkl̩)

supersede (ˌsupəˈsid, ˌsju-) *v.*
代換

= displace (dɪsˈples)
= replace (rɪˈples)
= supplant (səˈplænt)
= *take the place of*

superstition (ˌsupəˈstɪʃən) *n.*
迷信

= folklore (ˈfokˌlor, -ˌlor)
= tradition (trəˈdɪʃən)
= *popular belief*
= *old wives' tale*

supervise (ˈsupəˌvaɪz) *v.* 督導

= direct (dəˈrɛkt, daɪ-)
= oversee (ˌovəˈsi)
= govern (ˈgʌvən)
= regulate (ˈrɛgjəˌlet)
= command (kəˈmænd)
= head (hɛd)
= lead (lid)
= boss (bɔs)
= administer (ədˈmɪnəstə, æd-)

supplant (səˈplænt) *v.* 代換

= supersede (ˌsupəˈsid, ˌsju-)
= replace (rɪˈples)
= displace (dɪsˈples)
= *take the place of*

supple (ˈsʌpl̩) *adj.* 柔順的；
易曲的

= bending (ˈbɛndɪŋ)
= pliable (ˈplaɪəbl̩)
= flexible (ˈflɛksəbl̩)
= plastic (ˈplæstɪk)
= elastic (ɪˈlæstɪk)
= yielding (ˈjildɪŋ)
= lithe (laɪð)
= limber (ˈlɪmbə)

supplement (ˈsʌpləˌmɛnt) *v.*
補充

= complete (kəmˈplit)
= augment (ɔgˈmɛnt)
= fortify (ˈfɔrtəˌfaɪ)
= increase (ɪnˈkris)
= reinforce (ˌriɪnˈfors)

S

application (‚sʌplɪ'keʃən) *n.*
懇求；祈禱

= prayer (prɛr , prær)
= request (rɪ'kwɛst)
= plea (pli)
= appeal (ə'pil)
= entreaty (ɪn'tritɪ)

upply (sə'plaɪ) *v.* 供給；貯藏

= furnish ('fɜnɪʃ)
= provide (prə'vaɪd)
= store (stor , stɔr)
= stock (stɑk)

upport (sə'port , -'pɔrt) *v.*
支持；幫助

= help (hɛlp)
= aid (ed)
= bolster ('bolstə)
= sustain (sə'sten)
= defend (dɪ'fɛnd)
= foster ('fɔstə , 'fɑs-)
= encourage (ɪn'kɜɪdʒ)

uppose (sə'poz) *v.* 推測；以爲

= believe (bɪ'liv)
= think (θɪŋk)
= imagine (ɪ'mædʒɪn)
= consider (kən'sɪdə)
= assume (ə'sjum)
= infer (ɪn'fɜ)
= presume (prɪ'zum)
= deduce (dɪ'djus , -'dus)

uppress (sə'prɛs) *v.* 禁止；
鎮壓

= restrain (rɪ'stren)
= repress (rɪ'prɛs)
= inhibit (ɪn'hɪbɪt)
= curb (kɜb)
= check (tʃɛk)
= arrest (ə'rɛst)
= bridle ('braɪdl̩)
= squelch (skwɛltʃ)
= stifle ('staɪfl̩)
= squash (skwɑʃ)
= subdue (səb'dju)
= restrict (rɪ'strɪkt)
= quell (kwɛl)
= limit ('lɪmɪt)
= *keep down*
= *hold back*

supreme (sə'prim , su-) *adj.*
至高的

= highest ('haɪɪst)
= greatest ('gretɪst)
= utmost ('ʌt‚most)
= uppermost ('ʌpə‚most)
= extreme (ɪk'strim)
= top (tɑp)
= maximum ('mæksəməm)
= foremost ('for‚most , 'fɔr-)
= chief (tʃif)
= paramount ('pærə‚maunt)

sure (ʃur) *adj.* 確信的

= certain ('sɜtn̩ , -ɪn)
= positive ('pɑzətɪv)
= absolute ('æbsə‚lut)
= definite ('dɛfənɪt)
= decided (dɪ'saɪdɪd)

surface ('sɝfɪs) *n.* 表面

= outside ('aut'saɪd , aut'saɪd)
= face (fes)
= exterior (ɪk'stɪrɪə)

surge (sɝdʒ) *n.* 巨浪；波濤

= wave (wev)
= gush (gʌʃ)
= flow (flo)
= mount (maunt)
= whirl (hwɝl)
= stream (strim)
= swell (swɛl)
= rush (rʌʃ)
= billow ('bɪlo)

surgery ('sɝdʒərɪ) *n.* 外科手術

= operation (ɑpə'reʃən)

surly ('sɝlɪ) *adj.* 粗暴的；陰沈的

= rude (rud)
= gruff (grʌf)
= brusque (brʌsk , brusk)
= curt (kɝt)
= harsh (harʃ)
= blunt (blʌnt)
= rough (rʌf)
= sullen ('sʌlɪn , -ən)
= moody ('mudɪ)
= bad-tempered ('bæd'tɛmpəd)

surmise (sɝ'maɪz) *v.* 臆測

= guess (gɛs)
= judge (dʒʌdʒ)
= consider (kən'sɪdə)
= regard (rɪ'gard)

= suppose (sə'poz)
= presume (prɪ'zum)
= imagine (ɪ'mædʒɪn)
= suspect (sə'spɛkt)
= infer (ɪn'fɝ)
= gather ('gæðə)
= conclude (kən'klud)
= deduce (dɪ'djus , -'dus)
= think (θɪŋk)

surmount (sə'maunt) *v.* 戰勝；凌駕

= overcome (,ovə'kʌm)
= defeat (dɪ'fit)
= *rise above*
= *triumph over*

surpass (sə'pæs , -'pɑs) *v.* 超越

= excel (ɪk'sɛl)
= exceed (ɪk'sid)
= *go beyond*

surplus ('sɝplʌs) *adj.* 剩餘的

= excess ('ɪksɛs , ɪk'sɛs)
= extra ('ɛkstrə)
= superfluous (su'pɝfluəs , sə-)
= remaining (rɪ'menɪŋ)
= spare (spɛr)
= leftover ('lɛft,ovə)
= supplementary (,sʌplə'mɛntərɪ)
= additional (ə'dɪʃənḷ)

surprise (sə'praɪz) *v.* 使驚奇

= astonish (ə'stɑnɪʃ)
= amaze (ə'mez)
= astound (ə'staund)

= bewilder (bɪ'wɪldɚ)

= dumbfound (ˌdʌm'faʊnd)

= awe (ɔ)

= *catch unaware*

urrender (sə'rɛndɚ) *v.* 投降；
棄

= yield (jild)

= relinquish (rɪ'lɪŋkwɪʃ)

= capitulate (kə'pɪtʃəˌlet)

= renounce (rɪ'naʊns)

= abandon (ə'bændən)

= forego (for'go , fɔr-)

= submit (səb'mɪt)

= *give up*

urround (sə'raʊnd) *v.* 包圍；
繞

= wrap (ræp)

= envelop (ɪn'vɛləp)

= embrace (ɪm'bres)

= encircle (ɪn'sɝkḷ)

= enclose (ɪn'kloz)

= encompass (ɪn'kʌmpəs , ɛn-)

rvey (sɚ've) *v.* ①視察
測量；評估

= examine (ɪg'zæmɪn)

= view (vju)

= scrutinize ('skrutṇˌaɪz)

= review ('rɪ'vju)

= peruse (pə'ruz)

= scan (skæn)

= study ('stʌdɪ)

= contemplate ('kɑntəmˌplet ,
kən'tɛmplet)

= observe (əb'zɝv)

② = measure ('mɛʒɚ)

= estimate ('ɛstəˌmet)

= assess (ə'sɛs)

= rate (ret)

= gauge (gedʒ)

= inspect (ɪn'spɛkt)

= appraise (ə'prez)

survive (sɚ'vaɪv) *v.* 繼續存在

= remain (rɪ'men)

= outlive (aʊt'lɪv)

= outlast (aʊt'læst , -'lɑst)

= continue (kən'tɪnju)

susceptible (sə'sɛptəbḷ) *adj.*
易受影響的

= pliant ('plaɪənt)

= suggestible (səg'dʒɛstəbḷ)

= yielding ('jildɪŋ)

= impressionable (ɪm'prɛʃənəbḷ)

= pliable ('plaɪəbḷ)

= open ('opən , 'opṃ)

suspect (sə'spɛkt) *v.* ①猜想
②懷疑

① = think (θɪŋk)

= infer (ɪn'fɝ)

= guess (gɛs)

= suppose (sə'poz)

= assume (ə'sjum)

= imagine (ɪ'mædʒɪn)

= gather ('gæðɚ)

= surmise (sɚ'maɪz)

② = doubt (daʊt)

= distrust (dɪs'trʌst)

S

= challenge ('tʃælɪndʒ)
= mistrust (mɪs'trʌst)
= dispute (dɪ'spjut)
= question ('kwɛstʃən)

suspend (sə'spɛnd) v. ①懸垂
②延緩 ③暫停

① = hang (hæŋ)
= sling (slɪŋ)
② = postpone (post'pon)
= delay (dɪ'le)
= defer (dɪ'fɝ)
= shelve (ʃɛlv)
= *hold over*
③ = interrupt (,ɪntə'rʌpt)
= break (brek)
= arrest (ə'rɛst)
= halt (hɔlt)

suspense (sə'spɛns) n. 焦慮

= anxiety (æŋ'zaɪətɪ)
= fear (fɪr)
= concern (kən'sɝn)
= agitation (,ædʒə'teʃən)
= uneasiness (ʌn'izɪnɪs)
= apprehension (,æprɪ'hɛnʃən)
= disquiet (dɪs'kwaɪət)
= distress (dɪ'strɛs)

suspicious (sə'spɪʃəs) adj.
懷疑的;可疑的

= suspecting (sə'spɛktɪŋ)
= doubtful ('dautfəl)
= questionable ('kwɛstʃənəbl)
= wary ('wɛrɪ , 'we- , 'wæ-)

sustain (sə'sten) v. 忍受;支持

= tolerate ('talə,ret)
= support (sə'port , -'pɔrt)
= bear (bɛr)
= endure (ɪn'djʊr)
= maintain (men'ten , mən-)
= suffer ('sʌfɚ)
= stand (stænd)
= abide (ə'baɪd)
= *keep up*

swagger ('swægɚ) v. 昂首闊步

= parade (pə'red)
= strut (strʌt)

swallow ('swalo) v. ①吞;吸
②輕信

① = eat (it)
= absorb (əb'sɔrb)
= devour (dɪ'vaur)
= consume (kən'sum , -'sjum)
= gulp (gʌlp)
= ingest (ɪn'dʒɛst)
② = take (tek)
= accept (ək'sɛpt , æk-)
= believe (bɪ'liv)

swamp (swamp) ① v. 淹沒
② n. 沼澤

① = sink (sɪŋk)
= flood (flʌd)
= overwhelm (,ovɚ'hwɛlm)
② = marsh (marʃ)
= bog (bag , bɔg)

swap (swap , swɔp) v. 交換

= deal (dil)

= trade〔tred〕

= exchange〔ɪks'tʃendʒ〕

= barter〔'bɑrtɚ〕

= switch〔swɪtʃ〕

warm〔swɔrm〕v. 群集

= cluster〔'klʌstɚ〕

= crowd〔kraʊd〕

= throng〔θrɔŋ〕

= collect〔kə'lɛkt〕

= meet〔mit〕

= assemble〔ə'sɛmbl̩〕

= gather〔'gæðɚ〕

wat〔swɑt〕v. 猛打

= poke〔pok〕

= jab〔dʒæb〕

= whack〔hwæk〕

= hit〔hɪt〕

= strike〔straɪk〕

= knock〔nɑk〕

way〔swe〕v. ①搖擺 ②影響

= swing〔swɪŋ〕

= reel〔ril〕

= rock〔rɑk〕

= lurch〔lɝtʃ〕

= roll〔rol〕

= toss〔tɔs〕

= pitch〔pɪtʃ〕

= influence〔'ɪnfluəns〕

= persuade〔pɚ'swed〕

= prejudice〔'prɛdʒədɪs〕

= affect〔ə'fɛkt〕

= rule〔rul〕

= move〔muv〕

= control〔kən'trol〕

swear〔swɛr〕v. ①發誓 ②詛咒

①= promise〔'prɑmɪs〕

= vow〔vaʊ〕

= vouch〔vaʊtʃ〕

②= curse〔kɝs〕

sweep〔swip〕v. ①清掃
②掠過 ③伸展

①= clean〔klin〕

= brush〔brʌʃ〕

= vacuum〔'vækjuəm〕

②= move〔muv〕

= slip〔slɪp〕

= glide〔glaɪd〕

= coast〔kost〕

= skim〔skɪm〕

= slide〔slaɪd〕

③= stretch〔strɛtʃ〕

= extend〔ɪk'stɛnd〕

= range〔rendʒ〕

sweet〔swit〕adj. ①甜的
②親切的

①= sugary〔'ʃʊgərɪ , 'ʃʊgrɪ〕

= saccharine〔'sækə,raɪn , -,rɪn〕

②= pleasant〔'plɛznt〕

= agreeable〔ə'griəbl̩〕

= lovely〔'lʌvlɪ〕

= adorable〔ə'dorəbl̩〕

= charming〔'tʃɑrmɪŋ〕

swell〔swɛl〕① v. 增大；隆起
② adj. 上等的

①= billow〔'bɪlo〕

= amplify ('æmplə,faɪ)

= magnify ('mægnə,faɪ)

= inflate (ɪn'flet)

= stretch (strɛtʃ)

= bulge (bʌldʒ)

= increase (ɪn'kris)

= gain (gen)

= expand (ɪk'spænd)

= broaden ('brɔdn̩)

= enlarge (ɪn'lardʒ)

= *grow bigger*

② = good (gud)

swelter ('swɛltə) *v.* 汗流浹背

= sweat (swɛt)

= perspire (pə'spaɪr)

= roast (rost)

swerve (swɜv) *v.* 轉向

= dodge (dadʒ)

= sidestep ('saɪd,stɛp)

= shift (ʃɪft)

= turn (tɜn)

swift (swɪft) *adj.* 迅速的

= agile ('ædʒəl , -ɪl , -aɪl)

= nimble ('nɪmbl̩)

= fast (fæst , fast)

= quick (kwɪk)

= rapid ('ræpɪd)

= hasty ('hestɪ)

= fleet (flit)

= speedy ('spidɪ)

= expeditious (,ɛkspɪ'dɪʃəs)

swim (swɪm) *v.* 漂浮;游泳

= bathe (beð)

= float (flot)

= wade (wed)

swindle ('swɪndl̩) *v.* 欺騙

= cheat (tʃit)

= gyp (dʒɪp)

= fleece (flis)

= defraud (dɪ'frɔd)

swine (swaɪn) *n.* ①豬
②鄙賤之人

① = hogs (hagz)

= pigs (pɪgz)

② = scoundrel ('skaundrəl)

= skunk (skʌŋk)

swing (swɪŋ) *v.* 搖擺

= sway (swe)

= rock (rak)

= roll (rol)

= lurch (lɜtʃ)

= reel (ril)

= fluctuate ('flʌktʃu,et)

= dangle ('dæŋgl̩)

= hang (hæŋ)

swirl (swɜl) *v.* 旋轉

= twist (twɪst)

= whirl (hwɜl)

= curl (kɜl)

= wheel (hwil)

= reel (ril)

= spin (spɪn)

switch (swɪtʃ) *v.* ①鞭打
②轉變

= whip〔hwɪp〕

= strike〔straɪk〕

= flog〔flɑg〕

= pummel〔'pʌml̩〕

= slash〔slæʃ〕

= beat〔bit〕

= thrash〔θræʃ〕

= lash〔læʃ〕

= bang〔bæŋ〕

= spank〔spæŋk〕

= strap〔stræp〕

= club〔klʌb〕

= paddle〔'pædl̩〕

= change〔tʃendʒ〕

= replace〔rɪ'ples〕

= trade〔tred〕

= swap〔swɑp , swɔp〕

= shift〔ʃɪft〕

= turn〔tɝn〕

= exchange〔ɪks'tʃendʒ〕

= substitute〔'sʌbstə,tjut〕

woon〔swun〕 v. n. 昏暈

= faint〔fent〕

woop〔swup〕 v. 猝然下降

= dive〔daɪv〕

= plunge〔plʌndʒ〕

= plummet〔'plʌmɪt〕

= drop〔drɑp〕

= pounce〔pauns〕

= fall〔fɔl〕

ord〔sɔrd , sord〕 n. 刀；劍

= knife〔naɪf〕

= blade〔bled〕

symbolize〔'sɪmbl̩,aɪz〕 v. 代表；
以符號表示

= represent〔,rɛprɪ'zɛnt〕

= typify〔'tɪpə,faɪ〕

= illustrate〔'ɪləstret〕

= *stand for*

symmetrical〔sɪ'mɛtrɪkl̩〕 adj.
對稱的

= orderly〔'ɔrdəlɪ〕

= balanced〔'bælənst〕

= regular〔'rɛgjələ〕

= even〔'ivən〕

= uniform〔'junə,fɔrm〕

= equal〔'ikwəl〕

sympathy〔'sɪmpəθɪ〕 n. 同情；
同感

= commiseration
〔kə,mɪzə'reʃən〕

= compassion〔kəm'pæʃən〕

= condolence〔kən'doləns ,
'kɑndələns〕

= pity〔'pɪtɪ〕

= sensitivity〔,sɛnsə'tɪvətɪ〕

= understanding〔,ʌndə'stændɪŋ〕

= mercy〔'mɝsɪ〕

= tolerance〔'talərəns〕

symphony〔'sɪmfənɪ〕 n. 交響樂
的音樂會

= recital〔rɪ'saɪtl̩〕

= concert〔'kɑnsɝt〕

symptom〔'sɪmptəm〕 n. 徵兆

= indication〔,ɪndə'keʃən〕

S

= omen ('omən , 'omɪn)

= token ('tokən)

= mark (mark)

= sign (saɪn)

= implication (,ɪmplɪ'keʃən)

synthetic (sɪn'θɛtɪk) *adj.*
人造的；合成的

= simulated ('sɪmjə,letɪd)

= counterfeit ('kaʊntɚfɪt)

= artificial (,artə'fɪʃəl)

= mock (mak)

= imitation (,ɪmə'teʃən)

= man-made ('mæn,med)

system ('sɪstəm) *n.* 制度；體系

= plan (plæn)

= scheme (skim)

= method ('mɛθəd)

= design (dɪ'zaɪn)

= arrangement (ə'rendʒmənt)

T

table ('tebḷ) ① *n.* 表　② *v.* 擱置

① = list (lɪst)

= chart (tʃart)

= index ('ɪndɛks)

= catalog ('kætḷ,ɔg)

= schedule ('skɛdʒul)

② = postpone (post'pon)

= delay (dɪ'le)

= shelve (ʃɛlv)

= *put off*

tablet ('tæblɪt) *n.* ①紙簿
②錠劑

① = notebook ('not,bʊk)

= pad (pæd)

② = pill (pɪl)

= capsule ('kæpsḷ , 'kæpsjul)

tack (tæk) *v.* 附加

= attach (ə'tætʃ)

= add (æd)

= join (dʒɔɪn)

= affix (ə'fɪks)

= fasten ('fæsn̩ , 'fasn̩)

= clasp (klæsp)

tackle ('tækḷ) ① *v.* 處理；從事
② *v.* 捕捉　③ *n.* 用具

① = undertake (,ʌndɚ'tek)

= attack (ə'tæk)

= *get busy*

② = seize (siz)

= *grapple with*

③ = equipment (ɪ'kwɪpmənt)

= apparatus (,æpə'rætəs)

= gear (gɪr)

= furnishings ('fɜnɪʃɪŋz)

tact (tækt) *n.* 機智；圓滑

= grace (gres)

= diplomacy (dɪ'ploməsɪ)

= taste (test)

= finesse (fə'nɛs)

= sensitivity (,sɛnsə'tɪvətɪ)

= sensibility (,sɛnsə'bɪlətɪ)

tactics ('tæktɪks) *n.* 戰術

= procedures (prə'sidʒɚz)

= operations (,apə'reʃənz)

= methods ('mɛθədz)

= strategy ('strætədʒɪ)

= maneuvers (mə'nuvəz)

g (tæg) v. ①貼標籤於
尾隨

= label ('lebḷ)

= brand (brænd)

= name (nem)

= call (kɔl)

= designate ('dɛzɪg,net)

= follow ('fɑlo)

= shadow ('ʃædo)

= pursue (pə'su)

= heel (hil)

= trail (trel)

il (tel) ① n. 尾；後部
v. 尾隨

= back (bæk)

= rear (rɪr)

= end (ɛnd)

= follow ('fɑlo)

= pursue (pə'su , -'sɪu)

= shadow ('ʃædo)

= trail (trel)

= heel (hil)

int (tent) v. 玷污

= stain (sten)

= spot (spɑt)

= spoil (spɔɪl)

= discolor (dɪs'kʌlə)

= tarnish ('tɑrnɪʃ)

= mark (mɑrk)

= soil (sɔɪl)

take (tek) v. ①捉；拿　②需要
③選擇　④拿取　⑤以為
⑥租；雇　⑦忍受

① = seize (siz)

= capture ('kæptʃə)

= get (gɛt)

= receive (rɪ'siv)

= gain (gen)

= procure (pro'kjur)

= obtain (əb'ten)

② = need (nid)

= require (rɪ'kwaɪr)

= involve (ɪn'vɑlv)

= entail (ɪn'tel , ɛn-)

③ = choose (tʃuz)

= select (sə'lɛkt)

= *pick out*

④ = bring (brɪŋ)

= carry ('kærɪ)

= convey (kən've)

⑤ = suppose (sə'poz)

= assume (ə'sjum)

= infer (ɪn'fɜ)

= understand (,ʌndə'stænd)

= gather ('gæðə)

= guess (gɛs)

⑥ = hire (haɪr)

= lease (lis)

= engage (ɪn'gedʒ)

⑦ = tolerate ('tɑlə,ret)

= endure (ɪn'djur)

= bear (bɛr)

= stand (stænd)

= suffer ('sʌfɜ)

= swallow ('swɑlo)

= stomach ('stʌmək)

T

tale (tel) *n.* ①故事　②謠言

① = story ('storı)
　= yarn (jɑrn)
　= account (ə'kaʊnt)
　= narrative ('nærətɪv)
　= epic ('ɛpɪk)
　= sage ('sɑgə)
② = falsehood ('fɔls·hʊd)
　= lie (laı)
　= untruth (ʌn'truθ)
　= fib (fɪb)

talent ('tælənt) *n.* 才能

　= ability (ə'bɪlətı)
　= skill (skɪl)
　= gift (gɪft)
　= endowment (ın'daʊmənt)
　= capability (,kepə'bɪlətı)
　= genius ('dʒinjəs)
　= capacity (kə'pæsətı)
　= forte (fort , fɔrt)
　= aptitude ('æptə,tjud , -,tud)

talk (tɔk) ① *v.* 談話　② *n.* 謠言

① = speak (spik)
　= discuss (dı'skʌs)
　= converse (kən'vɝs)
② = gossip ('gɑsəp)
　= rumor ('rumə)
　= report (rı'port)

tall (tɔl) *adj.* ①高的　②誇大的

① = high (haı)
　= big (bɪg)
　= long (lɔŋ , lɑŋ)
　= lengthy ('lɛŋkθı , -ŋθ-)
② = exaggerated (ɪg'zædʒə,retɪd)

　= magnified ('mægnə,faɪd)
　= enlarged (ın'lɑrdʒd)
　= overstated ('ovə'stetɪd)
　= excessive (ɪk'sɛsɪv)
　= extreme (ɪk'strim)

tally ('tælı) *v.* ①計算　②符合

① = count (kaʊnt)
　= score (skor , skɔr)
　= calculate ('kælkjə,let)
　= compute (kəm'pjut)
　= estimate ('ɛstə,met)
　= reckon ('rɛkən)
　= figure ('fɪgə)
　= list (lɪst)
② = agree (ə'gri)
　= correspond (,kɔrə'spɑnd)
　= coincide (,koın'saıd)
　= match (mætʃ)
　= check (tʃɛk)

tame (tem) *adj.* 馴服的；柔順

　= gentle ('dʒɛntḷ)
　= obedient (ə'bidıənt)
　= temperate ('tɛmprıt)
　= mild (maıld)
　= domesticated (də'mɛstə,ketı

tamper ('tæmpə) *v.* 干涉

　= meddle ('mɛdḷ)
　= pry (praı)
　= intrude (ın'trud)
　= interfere (,ıntə'fır)

tang (tæŋ) *n.* 味道

　= taste (test)
　= flavor ('flevə)

ngible ('tændʒəbḷ) *adj.*
確實的 ②可觸知的

= real (ril , 'rɪəl , 'riəl)
= actual ('æktʃʊəl)
= definite ('dɛfənɪt)
= substantial (səb'stænʃəl)
= concrete ('kɑnkrit , kɑn'krit)
= touchable ('tʌtʃəbḷ)

ngle ('tæŋgḷ) *v.* 使纏結

= twist (twɪst)
= confuse (kən'fjuz)
= mess (mɛs)
= complicate ('kɑmplə,ket)
= knot (nɑt)
= involve (ɪn'vɑlv)
= snarl (snɑrl)

ntalize ('tæntḷ,aɪz) *v.* 折磨

= torment (tɔr'mɛnt)
= tease (tiz)
= molest (mə'lɛst)
= bother ('bɑðə)
= harass ('hærəs , hə'ræs)
= badger ('bædʒə)
= worry ('wɜɪ)
= torture ('tɔrtʃə)
= pester ('pɛstə)

ntrum ('tæntrəm) *n.*
然大怒

= fit (fɪt)
= outburst ('aʊt,bɜst)
= scene (sin)
= rage (redʒ)
= fury ('fjʊrɪ)

= conniption (kə'nɪpʃən)
= flare-up ('flɛr,ʌp)

tap (tæp) ① *v.* 輕拍
② *n.* 水龍頭；活塞

① = rap (ræp)
= pat (pæt)
② = faucet ('fɔsɪt)
= valve (vælv)
= spigot ('spɪgət)

tape (tep) *v.* ①以帶子捆紮
②錄音

① = wrap (ræp)
= fasten ('fæsn̩ , 'fɑsn̩)
= bind (baɪnd)
= tie (taɪ)
= bandage ('bændɪdʒ)
② = record (rɪ'kɔrd)

taper ('tepə) *v.* 減少；減弱

= lessen ('lɛsn̩)
= diminish (də'mɪnɪʃ)
= contract (kən'trækt)
= narrow ('næro)

tardy ('tɑrdɪ) *adj.* 延遲的

= late (let)
= overdue ('ovə'dju)
= delayed (dɪ'led)

target ('tɑrgɪt) *n.* 目標

= object ('ɑbdʒɪkt)
= goal (gol)
= aim (em)
= end (ɛnd)

T

= mark (mɑrk)

= point (pɔɪnt)

tariff ('tærɪf) *n.* 稅

= tax (tæks)

= duty ('djutɪ)

= toll (tol)

= assessment (ə'sɛsmənt)

= levy ('lɛvɪ)

tarnish ('tɑrnɪʃ) *v.* 玷污；
失去光澤

= dull (dʌl)

= dim (dɪm)

= fade (fed)

= discolor (dɪs'kʌlə)

= stain (sten)

= soil (sɔɪl)

tarry ('tærɪ) *v.* 停留

= remain (rɪ'men)

= stay (ste)

= linger ('lɪŋgə)

= wait (wet)

= delay (dɪ'le)

= loiter ('lɔɪtə)

= dawdle ('dɔdļ)

= dillydally ('dɪlɪ,dælɪ)

tart (tɑrt) *adj.* 酸的；尖刻的

= sour (saur)

= sharp (ʃɑrp)

= bitter ('bɪtə)

= pungent ('pʌndʒənt)

task (tæsk , tɑsk) *n.* 工作；任務

= work (wɜk)

= duty ('djutɪ)

= job (dʒab)

= chore (tʃor , tʃɔr)

= stint (stɪnt)

= assignment (ə'saɪnmənt)

= function ('fʌŋkʃən)

taste (test) *v.* 品嘗；體驗

= savor ('sevə)

= sample ('sæmpḷ)

= experiment (ɪk'spɛrəmənt)

= test (tɛst)

= try (traɪ)

= experience (ɪk'spɪrɪəns)

= sense (sɛns)

= feel (fil)

tattered ('tætəd) *adj.* 破碎的；
衣衫襤褸的

= torn (torn , tɔrn)

= ragged ('rægɪd)

= shabby ('ʃæbɪ)

= shoddy ('ʃɑdɪ)

= frayed (fred)

= frazzled ('fræzļd)

= seedy ('sidɪ)

= tacky ('tækɪ)

tattle ('tætḷ) *v. n.* 閒談

= gossip ('gasəp)

= chatter ('tʃætə)

= rumor ('rumə)

= report (rɪ'port)

taunt (tɔnt) *v. n.* 笑罵

= mock (mɑk)

= jeer (dʒɪr)

= scoff (skɔf , skɑf)

= reproach (rɪ'protʃ)

aut (tɔt) *adj.* 拉緊的；緊張的

= tight (taɪt)

= tense (tɛns)

= unrelaxed (ˌʌnrɪ'lækst)

= firm (fɝm)

= stiff (stɪf)

= rigid ('rɪdʒɪd)

avern ('tævən) *n.* 旅店

= inn (ɪn)

= cabaret ('kæbəˌrɛt , ˌkæbə're)

= bar (bɑr)

= pub (pʌb)

= saloon (sə'lun)

ax (tæks) ① *v.* 使負重荷
n. 稅

= strain (stren)

= burden ('bɝdn̩)

= load (lod)

= encumber (ɪn'kʌmbə , ɛn-)

= oppress (ə'prɛs)

= duty ('djutɪ)

= tariff ('tærɪf)

= levy ('lɛvɪ)

= toll (tol)

= assessment (ə'sɛsmənt)

axi ('tæksɪ) *n.* 計程車

= cab (kæb)

ach (titʃ) *v.* 教導

= instruct (ɪn'strʌkt)

= educate ('ɛdʒəˌket , -dʒʊ-)

= show (ʃo)

= enlighten (ɪn'laɪtn̩)

= coach (kotʃ)

= tutor ('tutə , 'tju-)

= direct (də'rɛkt , daɪ-)

= guide (gaɪd)

team (tim) *n.* 組；隊

= band (bænd)

= company ('kʌmpənɪ)

= group (grup)

= party ('pɑrtɪ)

= crew (kru)

= gang (gæŋ)

tear (tɛr) *v.* 撕破

= cut (kʌt)

= sever ('sɛvə)

= split (splɪt)

= slash (slæʃ)

= slice (slaɪs)

= slit (slɪt)

= rip (rɪp)

tearful ('tɪrful , -fl̩) *adj.*
含淚的；悲傷的

= weeping ('wipɪŋ)

= sad (sæd)

= crying ('kraɪɪŋ)

= sobbing ('sɑbɪŋ)

tease (tiz) *v.* 嘲弄

= annoy (ə'nɔɪ)

= vex (vɛks)

= pester ('pɛstə)

= bother ('baðə)

= joke (dʒok)

= jest (dʒɛst)

= banter ('bæntə)

= badger ('bædʒə)

tedious ('tidɪəs , -dʒəs) *adj.*
令人生厭的

= dull (dʌl)

= dreary ('drɪrɪ , 'drɪrɪ)

= slow (slo)

= dry (draɪ)

= tiring ('taɪrɪŋ)

= boring ('borɪŋ)

= monotonous (mə'natṇəs)

= humdrum ('hʌm,drʌm)

= wearisome ('wɪrɪsəm)

teem (tim) *v.* 充滿

= flow (flo)

= abound (ə'baund)

= swarm (swɔrm)

telecast ('tɛlə,kæst , -,kɑst) *v.*
用電視廣播

= televise ('tɛlə,vaɪz)

= broadcast ('brɔd,kæst)

televise ('tɛlə,vaɪz) *v.* 以電視
播送

= telecast ('tɛlə,kæst)

= broadcast ('brɔd,kæst)

tell (tɛl) *v.* 說；告知

= say (se)

= inform (ɪn'fɔrm)

= utter ('ʌtə)

= voice (vɔɪs)

= express (ɪk'sprɛs)

= communicate (kəm'mjunə,ket)

= convey (kən've)

= impart (ɪm'pɑrt)

= state (stet)

= declare (dɪ'klɛr)

= assert (ə'sɝt)

= relate (rɪ'let)

= recite (rɪ'saɪt)

= remark (rɪ'mɑrk)

= comment ('kɑmɛnt)

= mention ('mɛnʃən)

= note (not)

temerity (tə'mɛrətɪ) *n.* 魯莽

= boldness ('boldnɪs)

= rashness ('ræʃnɪs)

= brashness ('bræʃnɪs)

= indiscretion (,ɪndɪ'skrɛʃən)

temper ('tɛmpə) *n.* 性情；趨向

= disposition (,dɪspə'zɪʃən)

= condition (kən'dɪʃən)

= nature ('netʃə)

= character ('kærɪktə , -ək-)

= constitution (,kɑnstə'tjuʃən)

= tendency ('tɛndənsɪ)

= mood (mud)

temperamental
(,tɛmprə'mɛntḷ) *adj.* 易發脾氣的

= moody ('mudɪ)

= sensitive ('sɛnsətɪv)

= touchy ('tʌtʃɪ)

= thin-skinned ('θɪn'skɪnd)

emperate ('tɛmprɪt) *adj.*
度的;溫和的

= moderate ('madərɪt)

= mild (maɪld)

= gentle ('dʒɛntḷ)

= calm (kɑm)

empest ('tɛmpɪst) *n.* 暴風雨;
亂

= storm (stɔrm)

= violence ('vaɪələns)

emporary ('tɛmpə,rɛrɪ) *adj.*
時的

= passing ('pæsɪŋ , 'pas-)

= momentary ('momən,tɛrɪ)

= transient ('trænʃənt , 'trænzɪənt)

= short-lived ('ʃɔrt'laɪvd)

empt (tɛmpt) *v.* 引誘;引起

= invite (ɪn'vaɪt)

= attract (ə'trækt)

= interest ('ɪntərɪst , 'ɪntrɪst)

= appeal (ə'pil)

= tantalize ('tæntḷ,aɪz)

= titillate ('tɪtḷ,et)

= entice (ɪn'taɪs , ɛn-)

= seduce (sɪ'djus)

= lure (lʊr)

enacious (tɪ'neʃəs) *adj.*
持的;固執的

= persevering (,pɜsə'vɪrɪŋ)

= persistent (pə'zɪstənt , -'sɪst-)

= continuing (kən'tɪnjuɪŋ)

= diligent ('dɪlədʒənt)

= steadfast ('stɛd,fæst , -fəst)

= constant ('kɑnstənt)

= unswerving (ʌn'swɜvɪŋ)

= untiring (ʌn'taɪrɪŋ)

= obstinate ('ɑbstənɪt)

= stubborn ('stʌbən)

tenant ('tɛnənt) *n.* 居住者;房客

= dweller ('dwɛlə)

= occupant ('ɑkjəpənt)

= resident ('rɛzədənt)

= inhabitant (ɪn'hæbətənt)

tend (tɛnd) *v.* ①傾向　②照料

① = incline (ɪn'klaɪn)

= lean (lin)

= bend (bɛnd)

= *be likely*

= *be apt*

② = attend (ə'tɛnd)

= administer (əd'mɪnəstə , æd-)

= help (hɛlp)

= mind (maɪnd)

= foster ('fɔstə , 'fɑs-)

= nurse (nɜs)

= serve (sɜv)

= *look after*

= *care for*

= *watch over*

tendency ('tɛndənsɪ) *n.* 傾向;
癖好

= inclination (,ɪnklə'neʃən)

T

= leaning ('linɪŋ)

= bent (bɛnt)

= proclivity (pro'klɪvətɪ)

= disposition (,dɪspə'zɪʃən)

= aptitude ('æptə,tjud , -,tud)

tender ('tɛndɚ) ① *adj.* 溫柔的
② *v.* 提出

① = soft (sɔft)

= delicate ('dɛləkət , -kɪt)

= gentle ('dʒɛntḷ)

= kind (kaɪnd)

= affectionate (ə'fɛkʃənɪt)

= loving ('lʌvɪŋ)

= sensitive ('sɛnsətɪv)

② = offer ('ɔfɚ , 'afɚ)

= present (prɪ'zɛnt)

= submit (səb'mɪt)

= extend (ɪk'stɛnd)

tense (tɛns) *adj.* 緊張的；拉緊的

= strained (strend)

= stretched ('strɛtʃt)

= tight (taɪt)

= rigid ('rɪdʒɪd)

= taut (tɔt)

tepid ('tɛpɪd) *adj.* 微溫的

= lukewarm ('luk'wɔrm)

= mild (maɪld)

term (tɝm) ① *n.* 期間
② *n.* 條件 ③ *v.* 稱呼

① = period ('pɪrɪəd , 'pir-)

= time (taɪm)

= duration (dju'reʃən)

② = condition (kən'dɪʃən)

= premise ('prɛmɪs)

③ = name (nem)

= call (kɔl)

= designate ('dɛzɪg,net)

= dub (dʌb)

= title ('taɪtḷ)

= label ('lebḷ)

= tag (tæg)

terminate ('tɝmə,net) *v.* 結束

= end (ɛnd)

= finish ('fɪnɪʃ)

= close (kloz)

= conclude (kən'klud)

= stop (stap)

= cease (sis)

= complete (kəm'plit)

terrible ('tɛrəbḷ) *adj.* 可怕的；
極壞的

= dreadful ('drɛdfəl)

= horrible ('harəbḷ)

= deplorable (dɪ'plorəbḷ ,
-'plɔr-)

= outrageous (aut'redʒəs)

= scandalous ('skændləs , -dləs

= vile (vaɪl)

= wretched ('rɛtʃɪd)

= disgustful (dɪs'gʌstfəl)

= abominable (ə'bamnəbḷ)

= detestable (dɪ'tɛstəbḷ)

= despicable ('dɛspɪkəbḷ)

= contemptible (kən'tɛmptəbḷ)

= shocking ('ʃakɪŋ)

= appalling (ə'pɔlɪŋ)

T

rrific (təˋrɪfɪk) *adj.* 極大的；
常的

= great (gret)
= superb (sυˋpɝb , sə-)
= magnificent (mægˋnɪfəsṇt)
= marvelous (ˋmɑrvḷəs)
= wonderful (ˋwʌndəfəl)
= colossal (kəˋlɑsḷ)
= tremendous (trɪˋmɛndəs)
= glorious (ˋglorɪəs ,ˋglɔr-)
= divine (dəˋvaɪn)
= sensational (sɛnˋseʃənḷ)

rrify (ˋtɛrəˏfaɪ) *v.* 使驚嚇

= frighten (ˋfraɪtṇ)
= horrify (ˋhɔrəˏfaɪ ,ˋhɑr-)
= appall (əˋpɔl)
= shock (ʃɑk)
= awe (ɔ)
= petrify (ˋpɛtrəˏfaɪ)
= paralyze (ˋpærəˏlaɪz)
= stupefy (ˋstjupəˏfaɪ)

rritory (ˋtɛrəˏtorɪ , -ˏtɔrɪ) *n.*
地；領域

= land (lænd)
= region (ˋridʒən)
= area (ˋɛrɪə ,ˋerɪə)
= zone (zon)
= place (ples)
= country (ˋkʌntrɪ)
= district (ˋdɪstrɪkt)
= section (ˋsɛkʃən)

rse (tɝs) *adj.* 簡潔的

= brief (brif)

= concise (kənˋsaɪs)
= short (ʃɔrt)
= condensed (kənˋdɛnst)
= compressed (kəmˋprɛst)
= curt (kɝt)
= succinct (səkˋsɪŋkt)
= laconic (ləˋkɑnɪk)

test (tɛst) *v.* ①檢驗 ②做試驗

① = examine (ɪgˋzæmɪn)
= question (ˋkwɛstʃən)
= quiz (kwɪz)
= grill (grɪl)
= query (ˋkwɪrɪ)
= interrogate (ɪnˋtɛrəˏget)
= cross-examine (ˋkrɔsɪgˋzæmɪn)
② = experiment (ɪkˋspɛrəmənt)
= prove (pruv)
= try (traɪ)
= verify (ˋvɛrəˏfaɪ)

testimony (ˋtɛstəˏmonɪ) *n.*
證言；宣言

= evidence (ˋɛvədəns)
= proof (pruf)
= statement (ˋstetmənt)
= declaration (ˏdɛkləˋreʃən)

testy (ˋtɛstɪ) *adj.* 暴躁的

= impatient (ɪmˋpeʃənt)
= ornery (ˋɔrnərɪ)
= mean (min)
= ugly (ˋʌglɪ)
= irritated (ˋɪrəˏtetɪd)
= cranky (ˋkræŋkɪ)
= irritable (ˋɪrətəbḷ)

T

= irascible (aɪ'ræsəbl̩ , ɪ'ræsə-)

= cross (krɔs)

text (tɛkst) *n.* 主題;正文

= thesis ('θisɪs)

= proposition (,prapə'zɪʃən)

= subject ('sʌbdʒɪkt)

= topic ('tapɪk)

= theme (θim)

= issue ('ɪʃʊ , 'ɪʃjʊ)

= point (pɔɪnt)

= problem ('prabləm , -lɛm)

= question ('kwɛstʃən)

textile ('tɛkstl̩ , -tɪl , -taɪl) *n.* 織物

= material (mə'tɪrɪəl)

= cloth (klɔθ)

= fabric ('fæbrɪk)

= goods (gʊdz)

texture ('tɛkstʃɚ) *n.* 構造;組織

= structure ('strʌktʃɚ)

= finish ('fɪnɪʃ)

= grain (gren)

= construction (kən'strʌkʃən)

= composition (,kampə'zɪʃən)

= make-up ('mek,ʌp)

thankful ('θæŋkfəl) *adj.* 感激的

= indebted (ɪn'dɛtɪd)

= grateful ('gretfəl)

= appreciative (ə'priʃɪ,etɪv)

= obliged (ə'blaɪdʒd)

thaw (θɔ) *v.* 溶化

= melt (mɛlt)

= defrost (di'frɔst)

= dissolve (dɪ'zalv)

theater ('θiətɚ , 'θɪə-) *n.* ①劇場
②戰場

① = playhouse ('ple,haʊs)

= stadium ('stedɪəm)

= hall (hɔl)

② = arena (ə'rinə)

= battlefield ('bætl̩,fild)

theft (θɛft) *n.* 盜竊行為

= stealing ('stilɪŋ)

= filching ('fɪltʃɪŋ)

= pilfering ('pɪlfɚɪŋ)

theme (θim) *n.* ①題目 ②作文
③(藝術品之)主題

① = subject ('sʌbdʒɪkt)

= topic ('tapɪk)

= text (tɛkst)

= issue ('ɪʃʊ , 'ɪʃjʊ)

= question ('kwɛstʃən)

= problem ('prabləm , -lɛm)

= proposition (,prapə'zɪʃən)

= point (pɔɪnt)

② = composition (,kampə'zɪʃən)

= paper ('pepɚ)

= article ('artɪkl̩)

= treatise ('tritɪs)

= essay ('ɛsɪ , 'ɛse)

= dissertation (,dɪsɚ'teʃən)

= discourse ('dɪskors , dɪ'skors)

= discussion (dɪ'skʌʃən)

= study ('stʌdɪ)

= thesis ('θisɪs)

= motif (mo'tif)

heory ('θiərɪ , 'θɪərɪ) *n.* 學說；
法

= hypothesis (haɪ'paθəsɪs)

= explanation (,ɛksplə'neʃən)

= inference ('ɪnfərəns)

= conception (kən'sɛpʃən)

= speculation (,spɛkjə'leʃən)

= supposition (,sʌpə'zɪʃən)

= thought (θɔt)

= view (vju)

= judgment ('dʒʌdʒmənt)

= idea (aɪ'diə , -'dɪə)

= opinion (ə'pɪnjən)

= attitude ('ætə,tjud)

= impression (ɪm'prɛʃən)

herefore ('ðɛr,for , -,fɔr) *adv.*
此

= hence (hɛns)

= consequently ('kansə,kwɛntlɪ)

= accordingly (ə'kɔrdɪŋlɪ)

= *for that reason*

hick (θɪk) *adj.* ①粗大的
稠密的　③愚笨的

= broad (brɔd)

= coarse (kors , kɔrs)

= massive ('mæsɪv)

= bulky ('bʌlkɪ)

= numerous ('njumərəs)

= teeming ('timɪŋ)

= swarming ('swɔrmɪŋ)

= crowded ('kraʊdɪd)

③ = stupid ('stjupɪd)

= dull (dʌl)

= dense (dɛns)

= asinine ('æsn̩,aɪn)

thief (θif) *n.* 賊

= robber ('rabɚ)

= pilferer ('pɪlfərɚ)

= filcher ('fɪltʃɚ)

= burglar ('bɝglɚ)

= crook (krʊk)

thin (θɪn) *adj.* ①薄的；細的
②稀少的

① = slender ('slɛndɚ)

= slim (slɪm)

= svelte (svɛlt)

= slight (slaɪt)

= frail (frel)

= skinny ('skɪnɪ)

= gaunt (gɔnt , gant)

= lean (lin)

= lanky ('læŋkɪ)

② = scanty ('skæntɪ)

= sparse (spars)

= meager ('migɚ)

think (θɪŋk) *v.* ①以為　②思索

① = believe (bɪ'liv)

= expect (ɪk'spɛkt)

= understand (,ʌndɚ'stænd)

= imagine (ɪ'mædʒɪn)

= gather ('gæðɚ)

= deem (dim)

= fancy ('fænsɪ)

= presume (prɪ'zum)

= suspect (sə'spɛkt)

= assume (ə'sjum)

= deduce (dɪ'djus , -'dus)

= conclude (kən'klud)

= guess (gɛs)

= judge (dʒʌdʒ)

= infer (ɪn'fɝ)

= suppose (sə'poz)

② = consider (kən'sɪdɚ)

= muse (mjuz)

= study ('stʌdɪ)

= reflect (rɪ'flɛkt)

= reason ('rizn̩)

= theorize ('θiə,raɪz)

= meditate ('mɛdə,tet)

= ponder ('pɑndɚ)

= deliberate (dɪ'lɪbə,ret)

= contemplate ('kɑntəm,plet)

= concentrate ('kɑnsn̩,tret , -sɛn-)

thirsty ('θɝstɪ) *adj.* ①乾燥的
②渴望的

① = dry (draɪ)

= arid ('ærɪd)

= parched (pɑrtʃt)

= dehydrated (di'haɪdretɪd)

② = desirous (dɪ'zaɪrəs)

= craving ('krevɪŋ)

= *hungering for*

thorough ('θɝo , -ə) *adj.*
完全的;徹底的

= complete (kəm'plit)

= intensive (ɪn'tɛnsɪv)

= full (fʊl)

= sweeping ('swipɪŋ)

= all-out ('ɔl'aʊt)

thoroughfare ('θɝo,fɛr) *n.*
通路;大道

= highway ('haɪ,we)

= passage ('pæsɪdʒ)

= road (rod)

= street (strit)

= avenue ('ævə,nju)

= expressway (ɪk'sprɛs,we , ɛk-)

= turnpike ('tɝn,paɪk)

= thruway ('θru,we)

= freeway ('fri,we)

= boulevard ('bulə,vard)

though (ðo) *adv.* 雖然

= however (haʊ'ɛvɚ)

= nevertheless (,nɛvɚðə'lɛs)

= notwithstanding
('nɑtwɪθ'stændɪŋ)

= *in any case*

thought (θɔt) *n.* ①意見;思想
②關注

① = thinking ('θɪŋkɪŋ)

= idea (aɪ'diə , -'dɪə)

= notion ('noʃən)

= reflection (rɪ'flɛkʃən)

= deliberation (dɪ,lɪbə'reʃən)

= consideration (kən,sɪdə'reʃən)

= reasoning ('riznɪŋ , 'riznɪŋ)

= meditation (,mɛdə'teʃən)

= contemplation
(,kɑntəm'pleʃən)

② = care (kɛr)

= attention (ə'tɛnʃən)

= concern (kən'sɜn)

= regard (rɪ'gard)

= indulgence (ɪn'dʌldʒəns)

hrash (θræʃ) v. ①打
猛烈動盪

= beat (bit)

= pound (paʊnd)

= knock (nɑk)

= rap (ræp)

= batter ('bætə)

= whip (hwɪp)

= spank (spæŋk)

= lash (læʃ)

= toss (tɔs)

= tumble ('tʌmbl̩)

= roll (rol)

= flounder ('flaʊndə)

= rock (rɑk)

= reel (ril)

= wallow ('wɑlo)

= pitch (pɪtʃ)

= *move violently*

hreaten ('θrɛtn̩) v. ①警告；
頁示 ②恐嚇；威脅

= warn (wɔrn)

= caution ('kɔʃən)

= advise (əd'vaɪs)

= admonish (əd'mɑnɪʃ)

= alert (ə'lɜt)

= forebode (for'bod , fɔr-)

= menace ('mɛnɪs)

= browbeat ('braʊ,bit)

= terrorize ('tɛrə,raɪz)

= harass (hə'ræs)

= bully ('bʊlɪ)

= intimidate (ɪn'tɪmə,det)

= bulldoze ('bʊl,doz)

threshold ('θrɛʃold , 'θrɛʃhold)
n. 門口

= doorway ('dor,we , 'dɔr-)

= portal ('portl̩ , 'pɔr-)

= gateway ('get,we)

thrifty ('θrɪftɪ) *adj.* 節儉的

= saving ('sevɪŋ)

= economical (,ikə'nɑmɪkl̩ , ɛk-)

= frugal ('frugl̩)

= prudent ('prudn̩t)

= careful ('kɛrfəl)

= sparing ('spɛrɪŋ)

= economizing (ɪ'kɑnə,maɪzɪŋ)

thrill (θrɪl) v. 因興奮顫抖；
刺激

= tingle ('tɪŋgl̩)

= excite (ɪk'saɪt)

= titillate ('tɪtl̩,et)

= delight (dɪ'laɪt)

= enrapture (ɪn'ræptʃə , ɛn-)

= enthrall (ɪn'θrɔl)

= enchant (ɪn'tʃænt)

= charm (tʃɑrm)

thrive (θraɪv) v. 繁盛；茂盛

= prosper ('prɑspə)

= sprout (spraʊt)

= develop (dɪ'vɛləp)

= increase (ɪn'kris)

= grow (gro)

T

= flourish ('flɜɪʃ)
= mushroom ('mʌʃrum , -rʊm)
= bloom (blum)
= boom (bum)

throb (θrɑb) v. 悸動；跳動

= pulsate ('pʌlset)
= palpitate ('pælpə,tet)
= pound (paʊnd)
= thump (θʌmp)
= beat (bit)

throng (θrɔŋ) v. 群集

= crowd (kraʊd)
= cluster ('klʌstə)
= assemble (ə'sɛmbḷ)
= gather ('gæðə)
= collect (kə'lɛkt)
= meet (mit)
= congregate ('kɑŋgrɪ,get)

throw (θro) v. n. 投擲

= toss (tɔs)
= sling (slɪŋ)
= cast (kæst , kɑst)
= hurl (hɜl)
= fling (flɪŋ)
= heave (hiv)
= flip (flɪp)
= pitch (pɪtʃ)
= chuck (tʃʌk)

thrust (θrʌst) v. 插入；力推；
迫使

= push (pʊʃ)
= shove (ʃʌv)

= press (prɛs)
= bear (bɛr)
= prod (prɑd)
= ram (ræm)
= drive (draɪv)
= goad (god)
= propel (prə'pɛl)

thump (θʌmp) v. 重擊；狠打

= blow (blo)
= strike (straɪk)
= pound (paʊnd)
= beat (bit)
= knock (nɑk)
= hit (hɪt)
= jab (dʒæb)
= poke (pok)
= punch (pʌntʃ)
= rap (ræp)
= bang (bæŋ)
= bat (bæt)
= clout (klaʊt)

thunderstruck ('θʌndə,strʌk
adj. 驚愕的

= flabbergasted ('flæbə,gæstɪd)
= astonished (ə'stɑnɪʃt)
= amazed (ə'mezd)
= surprised (sə'praɪzd)
= bewildered (bɪ'wɪldəd)
= astounded (ə'staʊndɪd)
= aghast (ə'gæst , ə'gɑst)
= spellbound ('spɛl,baʊnd)
= dumbfounded (,dʌm'faʊndɪd)
= awed (ɔd)

hus (ðʌs) *adv.* 因此

= therefore ('ðɛr,for , -,for)
= accordingly (ə'kɔrdɪŋlɪ)
= consequently ('kɑnsə,kwɛntlɪ)
= hence (hɛns)
= so (so)

hwart (θwɔrt) *v.* 反對；妨礙

= hinder ('hɪndə)
= frustrate ('frʌstret)
= obstruct (əb'strʌkt)
= defeat (dɪ'fit)
= hamper ('hæmpə)
= oppose (ə'poz)
= forbid (fə'bɪd)
= foil (fɔɪl)
= inhibit (ɪn'hɪbɪt)
= balk (bɔk)
= deter (dɪ'tɝ)
= spoil (spɔɪl)
= impede (ɪm'pid)
= ruin ('ruɪn)
= prevent (prɪ'vɛnt)
= prohibit (pro'hɪbɪt)

icket ('tɪkɪt) *n.* ①標籤 ②票
③候選人名單 ④違規通知單

① = label ('lebl)
= stamp (stæmp)
= sticker ('stɪkə)
= seal (sil)
= tag (tæg)
② = pass (pæs , pɑs)
= credential (krɪ'dɛnʃəl)
= voucher ('vautʃə)
= certificate (sə'tɪfəkɪt)

= token ('tokən)
③ = ballot ('bælət)
= slate (slet)
④ = summons ('sʌmənz)
= subpoena (sə'pinə , səb'pi-)
= citation (saɪ'teʃən , sɪ-)

tickle ('tɪkl) *v.* 使滿足；使愉悅

= excite (ɪk'saɪt)
= entertain (,ɛntə'ten)
= titillate ('tɪtl,et)
= delight (dɪ'laɪt)
= charm (tʃɑrm)
= amuse (ə'mjuz)
= thrill (θrɪl)

tidings ('taɪdɪŋz) *n.* 消息

= news (njuz , nuz)
= information (,ɪnfə'meʃən)
= word (wɝd)
= advice (əd'vaɪs)

tidy ('taɪdɪ) *adj.* ①整齊的
②可觀的

① = neat (nit)
= orderly ('ɔrdəlɪ)
= trim (trɪm)
= shipshape ('ʃɪp,ʃep)
= well-kept ('wɛl'kɛpt)
② = considerable (kən'sɪdərəbl)
= large (lɑrdʒ)
= sizable ('saɪzəbl)
= grand (grænd)
= big (bɪg)
= goodly ('gudlɪ)
= substantial (səb'stænʃəl)

T

tie (taɪ) *v.* 繫；綁；捆

= fasten ('fæsn̩ , 'fɑsn̩)
= bind (baɪnd)
= lash (læʃ)
= wrap (ræp)
= strap (stræp)

tier (tɪr) *n.* 一排；層；級

= story ('storɪ)
= deck (dɛk)
= layer ('leɚ)
= line (laɪn)
= level ('lɛvl̩)
= row (ro)

tight (taɪt) *adj.* ①緊的
②緊身的 ③難得到的 ④吝嗇的

① = firm (fɝm)
= rigid ('rɪdʒɪd)
= stiff (stɪf)
= tense (tɛns)
= taut (tɔt)
② = snug (snʌg)
= compact (kəm'pækt)
= close (klos)
③ = scarce (skɛrs)
= sparse (spɑrs)
= rare (rɛr)
= skimpy ('skɪmpɪ)
= *hard to get*
④ = stingy ('stɪndʒɪ)
= closefisted ('klos'fɪstɪd)
= ungenerous (ʌn'dʒɛnərəs ,
-'dʒɛnrəs)
= miserly ('maɪzɚlɪ)

till (tɪl) ① *v.* 耕種 ② *n.* 放錢處

① = cultivate ('kʌltə,vet)
= plow (plaʊ)
= work (wɝk)
② = moneybox ('mʌnɪ,bɑks)
= vault (vɔlt)
= safe (sef)
= depository (dɪ'pɑzə,torɪ ,
-,tɔrɪ)
= *cash register*
= *money drawer*

tilt (tɪlt) *v.* 傾斜

= tip (tɪp)
= slope (slop)
= slant (slænt)
= incline (ɪn'klaɪn)
= lean (lin)
= list (lɪst)

timber ('tɪmbɚ) *n.* 木材

= wood (wʊd)
= lumber ('lʌmbɚ)
= logs (lɑgz , lɔgz)

time (taɪm) *n.* ①一段時間
②時機 ③拍子

① = duration (djʊ'reʃən)
= generation (dʒɛnə'reʃən)
= term (tɝm)
= period ('pɪrɪəd , 'pɪr-)
= interval ('ɪntɚvl̩)
= era ('ɪrə , 'irə)
= age (edʒ)
= epoch ('ɛpək)
= spell (spɛl)

= occasion (ə'keʒən)

= chance (tʃæns)

= opening ('opənɪŋ , 'opnɪŋ)

= opportunity (ˌapə'tjunətɪ)

= rhythm ('rɪðəm)

= tempo ('tɛmpo)

= meter ('mitə)

= measure ('mɛʒə)

imepiece ('taɪmˌpis) *n.* 鐘;錶

= clock (klɑk)

= watch (wɑtʃ)

imetable ('taɪmˌtebḷ) *n.* 時間表

= schedule ('skɛdʒul)

= list (lɪst)

= program ('progræm)

imid ('tɪmɪd) *adj.* 膽怯的

= retiring (rɪ'taɪrɪŋ)

= shy (ʃaɪ)

= bashful ('bæʃfəl)

= meek (mik)

= coy (kɔɪ)

= demure (dɪ'mjʊr)

= sheepish ('ʃipɪʃ)

= restrained (rɪ'strend)

= reserved (rɪ'zɜvd)

= fearful ('fɪrfəl)

= cowardly ('kaʊədlɪ)

= shrinking ('ʃrɪŋkɪŋ)

inge (tɪndʒ) *v.* 染以淡色

= color ('kʌlə)

= tint (tɪnt)

= stain (sten)

= dye (daɪ)

tingle ('tɪŋgḷ) *v. n.* 刺痛

= sting (stɪŋ)

= prickle ('prɪkḷ)

tinker ('tɪŋkə) *v.* 修補

= repair (rɪ'pɛr)

= mend (mɛnd)

= condition (kən'dɪʃən)

= service ('sɜvɪs)

= fix (fɪks)

= *patch up*

tinkle ('tɪŋkḷ) *v.* 發出叮噹聲

= ring (rɪŋ)

= sound (saʊnd)

= toll (tol)

= peal (pil)

= chime (tʃaɪm)

= jingle ('dʒɪŋgḷ)

tint (tɪnt) *n.* 色彩

= tinge (tɪndʒ)

= dye (daɪ)

= stain (sten)

= shade (ʃed)

= color ('kʌlə)

tiny ('taɪnɪ) *adj.* 微小的

= small (smɔl)

= minute (mə'njut , maɪ-)

= undersized ('ʌndə'saɪzd)

= little ('lɪtḷ)

= slight (slaɪt)

= puny ('pjunɪ)

= wee (wi)

T

tip (tɪp) *n.* ①尖端 ②傾斜
③小費 ④暗示

① = end (ɛnd)
　 = extremity (ɪk'strɛmətɪ)
　 = limit ('lɪmɪt)
　 = tail (tel)
　 = point (pɔɪnt)
② = slope (slop)
　 = slant (slænt)
　 = tilt (tɪlt)
　 = list (lɪst)
　 = leaning ('linɪŋ)
　 = inclination (ˌɪnklə'neʃən)
③ = gratuity (grə'tjuətɪ)
　 = bonus ('bonəs)
　 = premium ('primɪəm)
④ = pointer ('pɔɪntɚ)
　 = advice (əd'vaɪs)
　 = warning ('wɔrnɪŋ)
　 = information (ˌɪnfɚ'meʃən)

tiptop ('tɪp'tap) *adj.* 第一流的

　 = excellent ('ɛkslənt)
　 = superior (sə'pɪrɪɚ , su-)
　 = topnotch ('tap'natʃ)
　 = high-class ('haɪ'klæs)
　 = first-rate ('fɝs'tret , 'fɝst'ret)

tired (taɪrd) *adj.* 疲倦的

　 = exhausted (ɪg'zɔstɪd , ɛg-)
　 = fatigued (fə'tigd)
　 = weak (wik)
　 = weary ('wɪrɪ , 'wirɪ)
　 = run-down ('rʌn'daʊn ,
　　 'rʌnˌdaʊn)

title ('taɪtl̩) *n.* 標題；稱號

　 = tag (tæg)
　 = caption ('kæpʃən)
　 = designation (ˌdɛzɪg'neʃən ,
　　 ˌdɛs-)
　 = headline ('hɛdˌlaɪn)
　 = name (nem)
　 = label ('lebl̩)

toast (tost) *v.* 乾杯

　 = *drink to*

together (tə'gɛðɚ) *adv.* 一起；
同時地

　 = cooperatively (ko'apəˌretɪvlɪ)
　 = collectively (kə'lɛktɪvlɪ)
　 = jointly ('dʒɔɪntlɪ)
　 = concurrently (kən'kɝəntlɪ)
　 = simultaneously (ˌsaɪml̩'tenɪəslɪ
　　 ˌsɪml̩-)

toil (tɔɪl) *v.* 辛苦工作

　 = work (wɝk)
　 = labor ('lebɚ)

token ('tokən) *n.* ①表徵
②紀念品 ③票

① = proof (pruf)
　 = sign (saɪn)
　 = symptom ('sɪmptəm)
　 = indication (ˌɪndə'keʃən)
　 = evidence ('ɛvədəns)
　 = clue (klu)
　 = mark (mark)
② = memento (mɪ'mɛnto)
　 = trophy ('trofɪ)

= remembrance (rɪ'mɛmbrəns)
= keepsake ('kip,sek)
= relic ('rɛlɪk)
= souvenir ('suvə,nɪr)
) = ticket ('tɪkɪt)
= certificate (sə'tɪfəkɪt)
= coupon ('kupɑn)
= voucher ('vaʊtʃə)
= check (tʃɛk)

olerate ('tɑlə,ret) v. 容忍

= allow (ə'laʊ)
= bear (bɛr)
= permit (pə'mɪt)
= endure (ɪn'djʊr)
= suffer ('sʌfə)
= stand (stænd)
= abide (ə'baɪd)
= accept (ək'sɛpt , æk-)

oll (tol) n. ①鐘響 ②稅；費

) = ring (rɪŋ)
= peal (pil)
= chime (tʃaɪm)
= tinkle ('tɪŋkḷ)
= jingle ('dʒɪŋgḷ)
) = charge (tʃɑrdʒ)
= dues (djuz)
= fee (fi)
= assessment (ə'sɛsmənt)
= tariff ('tærɪf)
= fare (fɛr)
= revenue ('rɛvə,nju)
= levy ('lɛvɪ)
= tithe (taɪð)
= tax (tæks)
= duty ('djutɪ)

tomb (tum) n. 墳墓

= grave (grev)
= vault (vɔlt)
= crypt (krɪpt)
= shrine (ʃraɪn)
= mausoleum (,mɔsə'liəm)

tone (ton) n. ①音調 ②風格；
品質 ③健康狀態 ④色調

① = sound (saʊnd)
= pitch (pɪtʃ)
= key (ki)
= note (not)
= intonation (,ɪnto'neʃən)
② = spirit ('spɪrɪt)
= character ('kærɪktə , -ək-)
= style (staɪl)
= nature ('netʃə)
= quality ('kwɑlətɪ)
= mood (mud)
③ = condition (kən'dɪʃən)
= vigor ('vɪgə)
= shape (ʃep)
④ = color ('kʌlə)
= shade (ʃed)
= hue (hju)
= tint (tɪnt)
= tinge (tɪndʒ)
= stain (sten)
= complexion (kəm'plɛkʃən)

tongue (tʌŋ) n. 語言

= language ('læŋgwɪdʒ)
= talk (tɔk)
= speech (spitʃ)

T

tonic ('tɑnɪk) *n.* 滋補品

= medicine ('mɛdəsn̩)

= stimulant ('stɪmjələnt)

= bracer ('bresɚ)

too (tu) *adv.* ①也；並且 ②太；過於

① = also ('ɔlso)

= besides (bɪ'saɪdz)

= furthermore ('fɜðɚ,mor , -,mɔr)

= additionally (ə'dɪʃənl̩ɪ)

= *as well*

② = very ('vɛrɪ)

= exceedingly (ɪk'sidɪŋlɪ)

= overly ('ovɚlɪ)

= excessively (ɪk'sɛsɪvlɪ)

tool (tul) *n.* 工具；器具

= gadget ('gædʒɪt)

= implement ('ɪmpləmənt)

= instrument ('ɪnstrəmənt)

= apparatus (,æpə'rætəs)

= utensil (ju'tɛnsl̩)

= device (dɪ'vaɪs)

= appliance (ə'plaɪəns)

top (tɑp) *n.* 頂；最高點

= highest ('haɪɪst)

= head (hɛd)

= acme ('ækmɪ , 'ækmi)

= apex ('epɛks)

= zenith ('zinɪθ)

= summit ('sʌmɪt)

= peak (pik)

= crown (kraʊn)

= tip (tɪp)

= maximum ('mæksəməm)

topic ('tɑpɪk) *n.* 題目

= subject ('sʌbdʒɪkt)

= theme (θim)

= question ('kwɛstʃən)

= text (tɛkst)

= problem ('prɑbləm)

= issue ('ɪʃu , 'ɪʃju)

= point (pɔɪnt)

= plot (plɑt)

topmost ('tɑp,most , -məst) *adj.* 最高的

= supreme (sə'prim , su-)

= maximum ('mæksəməm)

= highest ('haɪɪst)

= head (hɛd)

= uppermost ('ʌpɚ,most)

topple ('tɑpl̩) *v.* 傾倒；推倒

= tumble ('tʌmbl̩)

= fall (fɔl)

= overturn (,ovɚ't3n)

= sprawl (sprɔl)

= stumble ('stʌmbl̩)

topsy-turvy ('tɑpsɪ't3vɪ) *adj.* 顛倒的；混亂的

= jumbled ('dʒʌmbl̩d)

= chaotic (ke'ɑtɪk)

= confused (kən'fjuzd)

= inverted (ɪn'v3tɪd)

= reversed (rɪ'v3st)

= upside-down ('ʌp,saɪd'daʊn)

= *mixed up*

orch（tɔrtʃ）*n.* 火把

= light（laɪt）
= lantern（'læntən）
= lamp（læmp）

orment（tɔr'mɛnt）*v.* 使痛苦

= inflame（ɪn'flem）
= distress（dɪ'strɛs）
= pain（pen）
= torture（'tɔrtʃə）
= harrow（'hæro）
= agonize（'ægə,naɪz）
= irritate（'ɪrə,tet）
= trouble（'trʌbl̩）
= persecute（'pɝsɪ,kjut）
= harass（'hærəs , hə'ræs）
= heckle（'hɛkl̩）
= molest（mə'lɛst）
= badger（'bædʒə）
= bother（'baðə）
= pester（'pɛstə）
= worry（'wɝɪ）
= tease（tiz）
= plague（pleg）
= harry（'hærɪ）

ornado（tɔr'nedo）*n.* 颶風

= whirlwind（'hwɝl,wɪnd）
= gale（gel）
= hurricane（'hɝɪ,ken）
= windstorm（'wɪnd,stɔrm）
= blizzard（'blɪzəd）
= tempest（'tɛmpɪst）
= squall（skwɔl）

orrent（'tɔrənt , 'tar- ）*n.* 急流

= flood（flʌd）
= burst（bɝst）
= eruption（ɪ'rʌpʃən）
= stream（strim）
= outbreak（'aʊt,brek）
= deluge（'dɛljudʒ）

torrid（'tɔrɪd , 'tar- ）*adj.* 很熱的

= hot（hat）
= sweltering（'swɛltərɪŋ , -trɪŋ）
= burning（'bɝnɪŋ）
= scorching（'skɔrtʃɪŋ）
= blistering（'blɪstərɪŋ）
= roasting（'rostɪŋ）
= broiling（'brɔɪlɪŋ）
= scalding（'skɔldɪŋ）
= seething（'siðɪŋ）
= sizzling（'sɪzlɪŋ）

torture（'tɔrtʃə）*v.* 拷問

= pain（pen）
= distress（dɪ'strɛs）
= torment（tɔr'mɛnt）
= agonize（'ægə,naɪz）
= harrow（'hæro）
= inflame（ɪn'flem）
= persecute（'pɝsɪ,kjut）
= plague（pleg）

toss（tɔs）*v. n.* 投；擲

= throw（θro）
= cast（kæst , kɑst）
= fling（flɪŋ）
= pitch（pɪtʃ）
= hurl（hɝl）
= sling（slɪŋ）

T

= heave〔hiv〕

= chuck〔tʃʌk〕

= flip〔flɪp〕

tot〔tat〕*n.* 小孩

= child〔tʃaɪld〕

= *little one*

total〔'totḷ〕① *adj.* 完全的
② *v.* 總計

① = whole〔hol〕

  = entire〔ɪn'taɪr〕

  = complete〔kəm'plit〕

② = add〔æd〕

  = count〔kaʊnt〕

  = *sum up*

  = *figure up*

touch〔tʌtʃ〕*v.* ①觸及；觸摸
②影響 ③借

① = feel〔fil〕

  = contact〔'kantækt〕

  = finger〔'fɪŋgɚ〕

  = handle〔'hændḷ〕

  = manipulate〔mə'nɪpjə,let〕

  = graze〔grez〕

  = brush〔brʌʃ〕

  = reach〔ritʃ〕

  = scrape〔skrep〕

  = skim〔skɪm〕

② = affect〔ə'fɛkt〕

  = move〔muv〕

  = stir〔stɝ〕

  = impress〔ɪm'prɛs〕

  = strike〔straɪk〕

③ = borrow〔'baro〕

= beg〔bɛg〕

= *ask for*

touching〔'tʌtʃɪŋ〕*adj.* 動人的

= tender〔'tɛndɚ〕

= provoking〔prə'vokɪn〕

= affecting〔ə'fɛktɪŋ〕

= moving〔'muvɪŋ〕

= pathetic〔pə'θɛtɪk〕

tough〔tʌf〕*adj.* ①堅韌的
②困難的

① = hardy〔'hardɪ〕

  = strong〔strɔŋ〕

  = firm〔fɝm〕

  = sturdy〔'stɝdɪ〕

  = durable〔'djʊrəbḷ〕

② = hard〔hard〕

  = difficult〔'dɪfə,kʌlt , 'dɪfəkəlt〕

  = complicated〔'kamplə,ketɪd〕

  = obscure〔əb'skjur〕

  = unclear〔ʌn'klɪr〕

  = vague〔veg〕

tour〔tʊr〕*n. v.* 旅行

= journey〔'dʒɝnɪ〕

= travel〔'trævḷ〕

= voyage〔'vɔɪ·ɪdʒ〕

tournament〔'tɝnəmənt , 'tur-
n. 競賽

= contest〔'kantɛst〕

= tourney〔'tɝnɪ , 'turnɪ〕

= game〔gem〕

= sport〔sport , spɔrt〕

= play〔ple〕

ow（to）*v. n.* 拖；曳

= pull（pʊl）
= heave（hiv）
= haul（hɔl）
= tug（tʌg）
= draw（drɔ）
= drag（dræg）

owering（'taʊərɪŋ）*adj.* 高聳的

= huge（hjudʒ）
= lofty（'lɔftɪ , 'lɑftɪ）
= high（haɪ）
= elevated（'ɛlə,vetɪd）
= soaring（'sorɪŋ）
= immense（ɪ'mɛns）
= monumental（,mɑnjə'mɛntl̩）
= gigantic（dʒaɪ'gæntɪk）

own（taʊn）*n.* 鎮；市

= metropolis（mə'trɑplɪs）
= city（'sɪtɪ）
= municipality（,mjunɪsə'pælətɪ）

oxic（'tɑksɪk）*adj.* 有毒的

= poisonous（'pɔɪznəs）
= venomous（'vɛnəməs）
= noxious（'nɑkʃəs）
= deadly（'dɛdlɪ）
= malignant（mə'lɪgnənt）

oy（tɔɪ）*n.* 玩具

= plaything（'ple,θɪŋ）
= trinket（'trɪŋkɪt）
= bauble（'bɔbl̩）

race（tres）① *v.* 描繪
）*v.* 追蹤 ③ *n.* 微量

① = copy（'kɑpɪ）
= reproduce（,riprə'djus）
= duplicate（'djuplə,ket）
= transcribe（træn'skraɪb）
= draw（drɔ）
= sketch（skɛtʃ）
② = seek（sik）
= track（træk）
= trail（trel）
= follow（'fɑlo）
③ = bit（bɪt）
= *small amount*

trade（tred）① *v.* 交易
② *n.* 行業

① = exchange（ɪks'tʃendʒ）
= barter（'bɑrtɚ）
= bargain（'bɑrgɪn）
= deal（dil）
= switch（swɪtʃ）
= reciprocate（rɪ'sɪprə,ket）
= traffic（'træfɪk）
= swap（swɑp , swɔp）
② = vocation（vo'keʃən）
= occupation（,ɑkjə'peʃən）
= business（'bɪznɪs）
= work（wɝk）
= line（laɪn）
= calling（'kɔlɪŋ）
= profession（prə'fɛʃən）
= practice（'præktɪs）
= pursuit（pɚ'sut , -'sjut）
= career（kə'rɪr）
= craft（kræft , krɑft）

tradition（trə'dɪʃən）*n.* 傳統

= custom（'kʌstəm）

T

= usage ('jusɪdʒ)

= folklore ('fok,lor , -,lɔr)

traffic ('træfɪk) ① v. 交易
② n. 交通

① = exchange (ɪks'tʃendʒ)

= trade (tred)

= bargain ('bɑrgɪn)

= barter ('bɑrtə)

= deal (dil)

= *buy or sell*

② = *vehicle movement*

tragic ('trædʒɪk) adj. 悲慘的

= disastrous (dɪz'æstrəs , -'ɑs-)

= dreadful ('drɛdfəl)

= sad (sæd)

= catastrophic (,kætə'strɑfɪk)

= grievous ('grivəs)

trail (trel) ① v. 追蹤
② n. 小徑

① = follow ('falo)

= pursue (pə'su , -'sju)

= shadow ('ʃædo)

= heel (hil)

= tail (tel)

= track (træk)

= hunt (hʌnt)

= trace (tres)

= *go after*

= *tag along*

= *run down*

② = path (pæθ , pɑθ)

= road (rod)

= line (laɪn)

train (tren) ① v. 訓練
② n. 行;列   ③ n. 火車

① = teach (titʃ)

= rear (rɪr)

= direct (də'rɛkt , daɪ-)

= drill (drɪl)

= exercise ('ɛksə,saɪz)

= practice ('præktɪs)

= prepare (prɪ'pɛr)

= condition (kən'dɪʃən)

= cultivate ('kʌltə,vet)

= discipline ('dɪsəplɪn)

= nurture ('nɝtʃə)

= foster ('fɔstə , 'fɑs-)

= educate ('ɛdʒə,ket , -dʒu-)

= groom (grum)

= *bring up*

② = series ('sɪrɪz , 'sirɪz)

= succession (sək'sɛʃən)

= line (laɪn)

= sequence ('sikwəns)

= file (faɪl)

= string (strɪŋ)

= row (ro)

= procession (prə'sɛʃən , pro-)

= column ('kɑləm)

③ = *railroad cars*

trait (tret) n. 特性

= characteristic (,kærɪktə'rɪstɪk)

= feature ('fitʃə)

= peculiarity (pɪ,kjulɪ'ærətɪ)

= earmark ('ɪr,mɑrk)

= type (taɪp)

= quality ('kwɑlətɪ)

= property ('prɑpətɪ)

= attribute ('ætrə,bjut)

= idiosyncrasy (,ɪdɪə'sɪnkrəsɪ)

= habit ('hæbɪt)

= pattern ('pætən)

raitor ('tretə) *n.* 奸逆

= betrayer (bɪ'treə)

= informer (ɪn'fɔrmə)

= tattler ('tætlə)

= blab (blæb)

= spy (spaɪ)

= rat (ræt)

= *double crosser*

= *undercover man*

ramp (træmp) ① *v.* 徒步旅行 ② *n.* 流浪漢

① = march (martʃ)

= parade (pə'red)

= hike (haɪk)

② = vagabond ('vægə,band)

= vagrant ('vegrənt)

= hobo ('hobo)

rance (træns , trans) *n.* 狂喜；失神

= spell (spɛl)

= ecstasy ('ɛkstəsɪ)

= rapture ('ræptʃə)

= hypnosis (hɪp'nosɪs)

ranquil ('trænkwɪl , 'træŋ-) *dj.* 寧靜的

= calm (kam)

= peaceful ('pisfəl)

= quiet ('kwaɪət)

= serene (sə'rin)

= untroubled (ʌn'trʌbḷd)

transact (træns'ækt , trænz-) *v.* 辦理

= execute ('ɛksɪ,kjut)

= perform (pə'fɔrm)

= discharge (dɪs'tʃardʒ)

= dispatch (dɪ'spætʃ)

= enact (ɪn'ækt)

= *carry out*

transfer (træns'fɜ) *v.* 移轉

= deliver (dɪ'lɪvə)

= pass (pæs , pas)

= *hand over*

= *sign over*

= *change hands*

transform (træns'fɔrm) *v.* 變形

= change (tʃendʒ)

= convert (kən'vɜt)

= alter ('ɔltə)

transgress (træns'grɛs) *v.* 踰越

= overstep (,ovə'stɛp)

= trespass ('trɛspəs)

= encroach (ɪn'krotʃ)

= infringe (ɪn'frɪndʒ)

transient ('trænʃənt , -zɪənt) *adj.* 短暫的；暫時逗留的

= fleeting ('flitɪŋ)

= passing ('pæsɪŋ , 'pas-)

= migratory ('maɪgrə,torɪ , -,tɔrɪ)

= vagrant ('vegrənt)

= straying ('streɪŋ)

= drifting ('drɪftɪŋ)

= wandering ('wɑndərɪŋ)

= roaming ('romɪŋ)

= roving ('rovɪŋ)

= rambling ('ræmblɪŋ)

= meandering (mɪ'ændrɪŋ , -'ændərɪŋ)

= temporary ('tɛmpə,rɛrɪ)

= transitory ('trænsə,torɪ , -,tɔrɪ)

= short-lived ('ʃɔrt'laɪvd)

transition (træn'zɪʃən , -s'ɪʃən) *n.* 變化

= change (tʃendʒ)

= conversion (kən'vɜʃən , -ʒən)

= transformation (,trænsfə'meʃən)

= transfer ('trænsfɜ)

translate (træns'let , 'trænslet) *v.* 翻譯

= interpret (ɪn'tɜprɪt)

transmit (træns'mɪt) *v.* 傳送

= forward ('fɔrwəd)

= transfer (træns'fɜ)

= dispatch (dɪ'spætʃ)

= *send over*

= *pass along*

transplant (træns'plænt) *v.* 移植

= transfer (træns'fɜ)

= transpose (træns'poz)

= shift (ʃɪft)

= change (tʃendʒ)

= move (muv)

= reset (ri'sɛt)

transportation (,trænspə'teʃən) *n.* 輸送

= conveyance (kən'veəns)

= carrying ('kærɪŋ)

= carriage ('kærɪdʒ)

trap (træp) *n.* 陷阱

= catch (kætʃ)

= snare (snɛr)

= hook (hʊk)

trash (træʃ) *n.* 廢物

= rubbish ('rʌbɪʃ)

= rubble ('rʌbl̩)

= scrap (skræp)

= debris (də'bri , 'debri)

= litter ('lɪtə)

= junk (dʒʌŋk)

travel ('trævl̩) *v.* 旅行；移動

= journey ('dʒɜnɪ)

= go (go)

= proceed (prə'sid)

= move (muv)

= pass (pæs , pɑs)

= progress (prə'grɛs)

= traverse ('trævəs , trə'vɜs)

treacherous ('trɛtʃərəs) *adj.* 奸詐的

= deceiving (dɪ'sivɪŋ)

= unreliable (ˌʌnrɪ'laɪəbḷ)

= two-faced ('tu'fest)

= fraudulent ('frɔdʒələnt)

= shifty ('ʃɪftɪ)

= tricky ('trɪkɪ)

= underhanded ('ʌndɚ'hændɪd)

= insidious (ɪn'sɪdɪəs)

= shady ('ʃedɪ)

ead (trɛd) *v.* 步行

= walk (wɔk)

= step (stɛp)

= pace (pes)

eason ('trizṇ) *n.* 叛逆

= betrayal (bɪ'treəl)

= double-dealing ('dʌbḷ'dilɪŋ)

easure ('trɛʒɚ) ① *v.* 珍愛
n. 財富

= cherish ('tʃɛrɪʃ)

= adore (ə'dor , ə'dɔr)

= idolize ('aɪdḷˌaɪz)

= worship ('wɝʃəp)

= prize (praɪz)

= appreciate (ə'priʃɪˌet)

= *value highly*

= *hold dear*

= store (stor , stɔr)

= assets ('æsɛts)

= accumulation (əˌkjumjə'leʃən)

= collection (kə'lɛkʃən)

= funds (fʌndz)

= resources (rɪ'sorsɪz , 'risorsɪz)

= abundance (ə'bʌndəns)

= fortune ('fɔrtʃən)

= wealth (wɛlθ)

treat (trit) ① *v.* 對待
② *v.* 治療　③ *n.* 樂事

① = consider (kən'sɪdɚ)

= regard (rɪ'gard)

= handle ('hændḷ)

= *behave toward*

= *deal with*

= *think of*

② = doctor ('dɑktɚ)

= attend (ə'tɛnd)

= nurse (nɝs)

= *minister to*

③ = delight (dɪ'laɪt)

= pleasure ('plɛʒɚ)

= thrill (θrɪl)

= enjoyment (ɪn'dʒɔɪmənt)

treatise ('tritɪs) *n.* 論文

= study ('stʌdɪ)

= thesis ('θisɪs)

= article ('artɪkḷ)

= paper ('pepɚ)

= essay ('ɛsɪ , 'ɛse)

= dissertation (ˌdɪsɚ'teʃən)

= discourse ('dɪskors , dɪ'skors)

= discussion (dɪ'skʌʃən)

treaty ('tritɪ) *n.* 條約

= agreement (ə'grimənt)

= compact ('kɑmpækt)

= alliance (ə'laɪəns)

= settlement ('sɛtḷmənt)

= arrangement (ə'rendʒmənt)

T

= truce (trus)

= armistice ('ɑrməstɪs)

trek (trɛk) *n.* 旅行;移居

= travel ('trævḷ)

= journey ('dʒɜnɪ)

= voyage ('vɔɪ·ɪdʒ)

= migration (maɪ'greʃən)

tremble ('trɛmbḷ) *v.* 發抖

= shake (ʃek)

= quake (kwek)

= vibrate ('vaɪbret)

= shiver ('ʃɪvɚ)

= quiver ('kwɪvɚ)

= quaver ('kwevɚ)

= shudder ('ʃʌdɚ)

tremendous (trɪ'mɛndəs) *adj.*
①巨大的 ②驚人的

①= enormous (ɪ'nɔrməs)

= great (gret)

= huge (hjudʒ)

= immense (ɪ'mɛns)

= vast (væst , vɑst)

= titanic (taɪ'tænɪk)

= colossal (kə'lɑsḷ)

= gigantic (dʒaɪ'gæntɪk)

= giant ('dʒaɪənt)

②= superb (su'pɜb , sə-)

= exquisite ('ɛkskwɪzɪt , ɪk's-)

= magnificent (mæg'nɪfəsṇt)

= marvelous ('mɑrvḷəs)

= glorious ('gloriəs , 'glɔr-)

= divine (də'vaɪn)

= terrific (tə'rɪfɪk)

= sensational (sɛn'seʃənḷ)

tremor ('trɛmɚ) *n.* 顫抖

= trembling ('trɛmblɪŋ)

= shaking ('ʃekɪŋ)

= quiver ('kwɪvɚ)

= quake ('kwek)

= shiver ('ʃɪvɚ)

trench (trɛntʃ) *n.* 戰壕

= ditch (dɪtʃ)

= moat (mot)

= dugout ('dʌg,aʊt)

= foxhole ('fɑks,hol)

= channel ('tʃænḷ)

trend (trɛnd) *n.* 趨勢

= direction (də'rɛkʃən , daɪ-)

= course (kors , kɔrs)

= tendency ('tɛndənsɪ)

= drift (drɪft)

= current ('kɝənt)

= movement ('muvmənt)

trespass ('trɛspəs) *v.* 侵犯

= intrude (ɪn'trud)

= transgress (træns'grɛs)

= encroach (ɪn'krotʃ)

= infringe (ɪn'frɪndʒ)

= overstep (,ovɚ'stɛp)

trial ('traɪəl) *n.* ①試驗 ②苦
③審判

①= test (tɛst)

= experiment (ɪk'spɛrəmənt)

= tryout ('traɪ,aʊt)

② = trouble ('trʌbḷ)
= hardship ('hardʃɪp)
= tribulation (,trɪbjə'leʃən)
= ordeal (ɔr'dil , 'ɔrdil)

③ = *court case*

ribe (traɪb) *n.* 種族

= group (grup)
= class (klæs , klɑs)
= set (sɛt)
= kind (kaɪnd)
= people ('pipḷ)
= family ('fæməlɪ)
= sect (sɛkt)
= breed (brid)
= clan (klæn)
= folk (fok)
= culture ('kʌltʃɚ)

ibunal (trɪ'bjunḷ , traɪ-) *n.* 庭

= court (kort , kɔrt)
= forum ('forəm , 'fɔrəm)
= board (bord , bɔrd)
= council ('kaʊnsḷ)

ibute ('trɪbjut) *n.* ①貢獻 讚美之辭

= contribution (,kantrə'bjuʃən)
= donation (do'neʃən)
= subscription (səb'skrɪpʃən)
= compliment ('kampləmənt)
= praise (prez)
= glorification (,glorəfə'keʃən)
= eulogy ('julədʒɪ)
= laudation (lɔ'deʃən)

trick (trɪk) *v.* 欺騙

= deceive (dɪ'siv)
= cheat (tʃit)
= hoax (hoks)
= dupe (djup , dup)
= delude (dɪ'lud , -'lɪud)
= betray (bɪ'tre)
= fool (ful)
= hoodwink ('hʊd,wɪŋk)

trickle ('trɪkḷ) *v.* 滴流

= leak (lik)
= drip (drɪp)
= dribble ('drɪbḷ)
= drop (drɑp)

tried (traɪd) *adj.* 可信賴的

= tested ('tɛstɪd)
= proved (pruvd)

trifle ('traɪfḷ) *n.* 少量

= *small amount*
= *little bit*

trigger ('trɪgɚ) *v.* 引起；扣板機

= begin (bɪ'gɪn)
= start (start)
= fire (faɪr)
= kindle ('kɪndḷ)
= *touch off*

trim (trɪm) *v.* ①修剪 ②裝飾

① = cut (kʌt)
= shave (ʃev)

T

= pare (pɛr , pær)

= reduce (rɪ'djus)

= lower ('loɚ)

② = decorate ('dɛkə,ret)

= ornament ('ɔrnə,mɛnt)

= adorn (ə'dɔrn)

= dress (drɛs)

= garnish ('garnɪʃ)

= deck (dɛk)

= beautify ('bjutə,faɪ)

= embellish (ɪm'bɛlɪʃ)

= furbish ('fɜbɪʃ)

= tidy ('taɪdɪ)

= clean (klin)

= *fix up*

= *spruce up*

= *straighten up*

trinket ('trɪŋkɪt) *n.* 小玩意

= trifle ('traɪfḷ)

= bauble ('bɔbḷ)

= knickknack ('nɪk,næk)

= toy (tɔɪ)

= plaything ('ple,θɪŋ)

trip (trɪp) ① *v.* 絆倒
② *n.* 旅行

① = stumble ('stʌmbḷ)

= tumble ('tʌmbḷ)

= topple ('tapḷ)

= fall (fɔl)

② = journey ('dʒɜnɪ)

= voyage ('vɔɪ·ɪdʒ)

= trek (trɛk)

= tour (tur)

= expedition (,ɛkspɪ'dɪʃən)

= pilgrimage ('pɪlgrəmɪdʒ)

= excursion (ɪk'skɜʒən , -ʃən)

= jaunt (dʒɔnt , dʒant)

= junket ('dʒʌŋkɪt)

= outing ('aʊtɪŋ)

triumph ('traɪəmf) *n.* 勝利

= victory ('vɪktərɪ , 'vɪktrɪ)

= success (sək'sɛs)

= conquest ('kaŋkwɛst)

= winning ('wɪnɪŋ)

trivial ('trɪvɪəl) *adj.* 不重要的

= unimportant (,ʌnɪm'pɔrtṇt)

= petty ('pɛtɪ)

= trifling ('traɪflɪŋ)

= slight (slaɪt)

= superficial (,supɚ'fɪʃəl , ,sju-)

= shallow ('ʃælo)

= frivolous ('frɪvələs)

= light (laɪt)

= foolish ('fulɪʃ)

= silly ('sɪlɪ)

= inane (ɪn'en)

= puny ('pjunɪ)

= worthless ('wɜθlɪs)

= paltry ('pɔltrɪ)

troop (trup) *n.* 群

= group (grup)

= band (bænd)

= unit ('junɪt)

= company ('kʌmpənɪ)

= party ('partɪ)

= gang (gæŋ)

= crew (kru)
= body ('badɪ)
= bunch (bʌntʃ)
= crowd (kraʊd)
= mob (mɑb)

rophy ('trofɪ) *n.* 戰利品

= prize (praɪz)
= award (ə'wɔrd)
= laurels ('lɔrəlz , 'lɑr-)
= reward (rɪ'wɔrd)
= memento (mɪ'mɛnto)
= souvenir (ˌsuvə'nɪr , 'suvəˌnɪr)
= remembrance (rɪ'mɛmbrəns)
= keepsake ('kipˌsek)

ot (trɑt) *v.* 疾馳；疾走

= run (rʌn)
= sprint (sprɪnt)
= bound (baʊnd)
= trip (trɪp)

ouble ('trʌbḷ) *v.* 使煩惱

= distress (dɪ'strɛs)
= worry ('wɜɪ)
= disturb (dɪ'stɜb)
= agitate ('ædʒəˌtet)
= perturb (pə'tɜb)
= disquiet (dɪs'kwaɪət)
= stir (stɜ)
= bother ('bɑðə)
= upset (ʌp'sɛt)
= discomfort (dɪs'kʌmfət)
= vex (vɛks)
= plague (pleg)

oupe (trup) *n.* 班；隊；團

= band (bænd)
= company ('kʌmpənɪ)
= group (grup)
= party ('pɑrtɪ)
= gang (gæŋ)
= crew (kru)

truant ('truənt) *n.* 逃學者

= absentee (ˌæbsṇ'ti)

truce (trus) *n.* 休止；休戰

= pause (pɔz)
= rest (rɛst)
= respite ('rɛspɪt)
= break (brek)
= recess (rɪ'sɛs)
= intermission (ˌɪntə'mɪʃən)
= interruption (ˌɪntə'rʌpʃən)
= interval ('ɪntəvḷ)
= armistice ('ɑrməstɪs)
= peace (pis)

trudge (trʌdʒ) *v.* 跋涉

= plod (plɑd)
= lumber ('lʌmbə)

true (tru) *adj.* 確實的

= real ('riəl , ril , 'rɪəl)
= actual ('æktʃʊəl)
= unmistaken (ˌʌnmə'stekən)
= veritable ('vɛrətəbḷ)
= certain ('sɜtṇ , -ɪn , -ən)
= valid ('vælɪd)
= genuine ('dʒɛnjʊɪn)
= authentic (ɔ'θɛntɪk)
= natural ('nætʃərəl)

T

= legitimate (lɪ'dʒɪtəmɪt)
= right (raɪt)
= proper ('prɑpɚ)
= correct (kə'rɛkt)
= exact (ɪg'zækt)
= accurate ('ækjərɪt)
= *bona fide*

trust (trʌst) *v.* 信任

= believe (bɪ'liv)
= credit ('krɛdɪt)
= accept (ək'sɛpt , æk-)
= *rely on*
= *depend on*

try (traɪ) *v.* ①試圖 ②審問

① = attempt (ə'tɛmpt)
= test (tɛst)
= experiment (ɪk'spɛrəmənt)
= prove (pruv)
= verify ('vɛrə,faɪ)
= essay (ə'se , ɛ'se)
= undertake (,ʌndə'tek)
② = judge (dʒʌdʒ)
= prosecute ('prɑsɪ,kjut)
= hear (hɪr)

trying ('traɪɪŋ) *adj.* 難堪的

= annoying (ə'nɔɪɪŋ)
= distressing (dɪ'strɛsɪŋ)
= difficult ('dɪfə,kʌlt , 'dɪfəkəlt)
= troublesome ('trʌblsəm)
= bothersome ('bɑðəsəm)
= burdensome ('bɝdn̩səm)

tube (tjub) *n.* 管

= pipe (paɪp)
= hose (hoz)
= reed (rid)

tuck (tʌk) *v.* 摺起

= fold (fold)
= crease (kris)
= bend (bɛnd)
= gather ('gæðɚ)

tuft (tʌft) *n.* 一束

= clump (klʌmp)
= bunch ('bʌntʃ)
= cluster ('klʌstɚ)
= group (grup)

tug (tʌg) *v. n.* 拖曳

= pull (pʊl)
= jerk (dʒɝk)
= wrench (rɛntʃ)
= draw (drɔ)
= tow (to)
= haul (hɔl)
= yank (jæŋk)

tuition (tju'ɪʃən) *n.* 教學

= teaching ('titʃɪŋ)
= instruction (ɪn'strʌkʃən)
= education (,ɛdʒə'keʃən , -dʒʊ-)
= schooling ('skulɪŋ)

tumble ('tʌmbl̩) *v.* 跌落

= fall (fɔl)
= toss (tɔs)
= sprawl (sprɔl)
= topple ('tɑpl̩)

= stumble ('stʌmbḷ)

= wallow ('wɑlo)

= flounder ('flaʊndə·)

= pitch (pɪtʃ)

= plunge (plʌndʒ)

= lurch (lɝtʃ)

mult ('tjumʌlt) *n.* 喧囂

= noise (nɔɪz)

= uproar ('ʌp,ror , -,rɔr)

= disorder (dɪs'ɔrdə·)

= disturbance (dɪ'stɝbəns)

= commotion (kə'moʃən)

= turmoil ('tɝmɔɪl)

= hubbub ('hʌbʌb)

= racket ('rækɪt)

= fracas ('frekəs)

= fuss (fʌs)

= pandemonium
　(,pændɪ'monɪəm)

= turbulence ('tɝbjələns)

= excitement (ɪk'saɪtmənt)

= rumpus ('rʌmpəs)

= row (raʊ)

= to-do (tə'du)

ne (tjun) *n.* 歌曲

= melody ('mɛlədɪ)

= music ('mjuzɪk)

= harmony ('hɑrmənɪ)

= song (sɔŋ , sɑŋ)

nnel ('tʌnḷ) *n.* 隧道

= cave (kev)

= grotto ('grɑto)

= cavern ('kævə·n)

= *underground passage*

turbulent ('tɝbjələnt) *adj.*
暴亂的

= violent ('vaɪələnt)

= disorderly (dɪs'ɔrdə·lɪ , dɪz-)

= unruly (ʌn'rulɪ)

= tumultuous (tju'mʌltʃʊəs , tu-)

= storming ('stɔrmɪŋ)

= frenzied ('frɛnzɪd)

= wild (waɪld)

= blustering ('blʌstərɪŋ)

= furious ('fjʊrɪəs)

= frantic ('fræntɪk)

= excited (ɪk'saɪtɪd)

= riotous ('raɪətəs)

turf (tɝf) *n.* 草地

= grass (græs)

= sod (sɑd)

turmoil ('tɝmɔɪl) *n.* 混亂

= commotion (kə'moʃən)

= disturbance (dɪ'stɝbəns)

= tumult ('tjumʌlt)

= noise (nɔɪz)

= uproar ('ʌp,ror , -,rɔr)

= disorder (dɪs'ɔrdə·)

= hubbub ('hʌbʌb)

= racket ('rækɪt)

= fracas ('frekəs)

= fuss (fʌs)

= pandemonium
　(,pændɪ'monɪəm)

= turbulence ('tɝbjələns)

= excitement (ɪk'saɪtmənt)

= rumpus ('rʌmpəs)

T

= row (rau)

= to-do (tə'du)

turn (tɜn) v. ①旋轉 ②改變 ③變質

① = rotate ('rotet)

= pivot ('pɪvət , 'pɪvɪt)

= swivel ('swɪvḷ)

= wheel (hwil)

= twist (twɪst)

= gyrate ('dʒaɪret)

= shift (ʃɪft)

= swerve (swɜv)

= veer (vɪr)

= curve (kɜv)

= circle ('sɜkḷ)

= *go around*

② = change (tʃendʒ)

= alter ('ɔltə)

= vary ('vɛrɪ)

③ = spoil (spɔɪl)

= sour (saur)

tussle ('tʌsḷ) v. 搏鬥

= struggle ('strʌgḷ)

= wrestle ('rɛsḷ)

= scuffle ('skʌfḷ)

= contend (kən'tɛnd)

= fight (faɪt)

= battle ('bætḷ)

tutor ('tutə , 'tju-) v. 教導

= teach (titʃ)

= instruct (ɪn'strʌkt)

= coach (kotʃ)

= prime (praɪm)

= educate ('ɛdʒəˌket , -dʒu-)

= school (skul)

= enlighten (ɪn'laɪtṇ)

= direct (də'rɛkt , daɪ-)

= guide (gaɪd)

= show (ʃo)

= train (tren)

= drill (drɪl)

= prepare (prɪ'pɛr)

= condition (kən'dɪʃən)

twig (twɪg) n. 嫩枝

= branch (bræntʃ)

= limb (lɪm)

= sprig (sprɪg)

= sprout (spraut)

= shoot (ʃut)

twine (twaɪn) n. 細繩

= rope (rop)

= cord (kɔrd)

= string (strɪŋ)

twinge (twɪndʒ) n. 劇痛

= pain (pen)

= pang (pæŋ)

twinkle ('twɪŋkḷ) v. 閃爍

= sparkle ('sparkḷ)

= gleam (glim)

= glitter ('glɪtə)

= glisten ('glɪsṇ)

= glimmer ('glɪmə)

= shimmer ('ʃɪmə)

= blink (blɪŋk)

= shine (ʃaɪn)

virl (twɜl) *v.* 旋轉

= spin (spin)
= rotate ('rotet)
= whirl (hwɜl)
= turn (tɜn)
= wind (waind)
= swivel ('swivl̩)
= wheel (hwil)
= pivot ('pivət , 'pivit)
= gyrate ('dʒairet)

vist (twist) *v.* ①旋轉 ②曲解

= turn (tɜn)
= wind (waind)
= curve (kɜv)
= rotate ('rotet)
= swivel ('swivl̩)
= pivot ('pivət , 'pivit)
= wheel (hwil)
= gyrate ('dʒairet)
= circle ('sɜkl̩)
= change (tʃendʒ)
= falsify ('fɔlsə,fai)
= misrepresent (,misrepri'zent)
= distort (dis'tɔrt)
= color ('kʌlə)
= disguise (dis'gaiz)
= alter ('ɔltə)
= camouflage ('kæmə,flɑg)

vitch (twitʃ) *v. n.* 急拉

= jerk (dʒɜk)
= jiggle ('dʒigl̩)
= fidget ('fidʒit)

pe (taip) *n.* 類型

= kind (kaind)
= class (klæs , klɑs)
= group (grup)
= sort (sɔrt)
= ilk (ilk)
= variety (və'raiəti)
= species ('spiʃiz , -ʃiz)
= nature ('netʃə)
= make (mek)
= brand (brænd)
= character ('kæriktə , -ək-)
= genus ('dʒinəs)

typhoon (tai'fun) *n.* 颱風

= storm (stɔrm)
= hurricane ('hɜi,ken)
= whirlwind ('hwɜl,wind)
= cyclone ('saiklon)
= tornado (tɔr'nedo)
= twister ('twistə)

typical ('tipikl̩) *adj.* 典型的

= representative (,repri'zentətiv)
= symbolic (sim'bɑlik)
= characteristic (,kæriktə'ristik)
= distinctive (di'stiŋktiv)

tyrant ('tairənt) *n.* 暴君

= despot ('despət , -pɑt)
= oppressor (ə'presə)
= martine (,mɑrtn̩'et , 'mɑrtn̩,et)
= taskmaster ('tæsk,mæstə , -,mɑstə)
= disciplinarian (,disəplin'eriən)
= *slave driver*

U

ugly (ˈʌglɪ) *adj.* ①難看的
②脾氣壞的

① = unattractive (ˌʌnəˈtræktɪv)
  = unsightly (ʌnˈsaɪtlɪ)
  = homely (ˈhomlɪ)
  = plain (plen)
  = hideous (ˈhɪdɪəs)
② = cross (krɔs)
  = cranky (ˈkræŋkɪ)
  = disagreeable (ˌdɪsəˈgriəbḷ)
  = unpleasant (ʌnˈplɛzn̩t)
  = quarrelsome (ˈkwɔrəlsəm,
    ˈkwɑr-)
  = irritabe (ˈɪrətəbḷ)
  = testy (ˈtɛstɪ)
  = mean (min)
  = perverse (pɚˈvɝs)
  = ornery (ˈɔrnərɪ)
  = bad-tempered (ˈbædˈtɛmpɚd)

ultimate (ˈʌltəmɪt) *adj.* 最後的

  = last (læst, lɑst)
  = final (ˈfaɪnḷ)
  = terminal (ˈtɝmənḷ)
  = conclusive (kənˈklusɪv)
  = eventual (ɪˈvɛntʃʊəl)

umpire (ˈʌmpaɪr) *n.* 仲裁者

  = judge (dʒʌdʒ)
  = referee (ˌrɛfəˈri)
  = moderator (ˈmɑdəˌretɚ)
  = arbitrator (ˈɑrbəˌtretɚ)
  = mediator (ˈmidɪˌetɚ)

unable (ʌnˈebḷ) *adj.* 不能…的

  = incapable (ɪnˈkepəbḷ)
  = incompetent (ɪnˈkɑmpətənt)
  = unfit (ʌnˈfɪt)
  = unqualified (ʌnˈkwɑləˌfaɪd)

unaccountable
(ˌʌnəˈkaʊntəbḷ) *adj.* 不可解的

  = unexplainable (ˌʌnɪkˈsplenəbḷ)
  = inexplicable (ɪnˈɛksplɪkəbḷ)

unaccustomed (ˌʌnəˈkʌstəmd)
adj. 異乎尋常的

  = unusual (ʌnˈjuʒʊəl)
  = unfamiliar (ˌʌnfəˈmɪljɚ)
  = strange (strendʒ)
  = *unused to*

unanimous (juˈnænəməs) *adj.*
意見一致的

  = agreed (əˈgrid)
  = solid (ˈsɑlɪd)
  = concurrent (kənˈkɝənt)
  = *in complete accord*

unarmed (ʌnˈɑrmd) *adj.*
未武裝的

  = unprotected (ˌʌnprəˈtɛktɪd)
  = defenseless (dɪˈfɛnslɪs)
  = unshielded (ʌnˈʃildɪd)
  = unequipped (ˌʌnɪˈkwɪpt)

unassuming (ˌʌnəˈsumɪŋ,
-ˈsjum-) *adj.* 謙遜的

  = modest (ˈmɑdɪst)

= meek〔mik〕
= humble〔'hʌmbḷ〕
= unpretentious〔ˌʌnprɪ'tɛnʃəs〕
= natural〔'nætʃərəl〕
= genuine〔'dʒɛnjuɪn〕
= sincere〔sɪn'sɪr〕
= honest〔'ɑnɪst〕

nattended〔ˌʌnə'tɛndɪd〕*adj.*
無伴的

= alone〔ə'lon〕
= unaccompanied
 〔ˌʌnə'kʌmpənɪd〕

navoidable〔ˌʌnə'vɔɪdəbḷ〕
dj. 不可避免的

= inevitable〔ɪn'ɛvətəbḷ〕
= certain〔'sɝtṇ, -ɪn, -ən〕
= sure〔ʃur〕
= inescapable〔ˌɪnə'skepəbḷ〕

naware〔ˌʌnə'wɛr〕*adj.*
不知道的

= ignorant〔'ɪgnərənt〕
= unknowing〔ʌn'noɪŋ〕
= unconscious〔ʌn'kɑnʃəs〕
= unmindful〔ʌn'maɪndfəl,
 -'maɪnfəl〕
= unsuspecting〔ˌʌnsə'spɛktɪŋ〕

nbearable〔ʌn'bɛrəbḷ〕*adj.*
不堪忍受的

= intolerable〔ɪn'tɑlərəbḷ〕
= insufferable〔ɪn'sʌfrəbḷ,
 -fərə-〕

unbecoming〔ˌʌnbɪ'kʌmɪŋ〕
adj. 不合適的

= inappropriate〔ˌɪnə'propriɪt〕
= inapt〔ɪn'æpt〕
= unfit〔ʌn'fɪt〕
= unsuitable〔ʌn'sjutəbḷ, -'sut-〕
= improper〔ɪm'prɑpɚ〕
= indecent〔ɪn'disṇt〕

unbelievable〔ˌʌnbɪ'livəbḷ〕
adj. 不可信的

= incredible〔ɪn'krɛdəbḷ〕
= doubtful〔'dautfəl〕
= questionable〔'kwɛstʃənəbḷ〕
= unconvincing〔ˌʌnkən'vɪnsɪŋ〕
= suspicious〔sə'spɪʃəs〕

unbend〔ʌn'bɛnd〕*v.* 伸直；
鬆弛

= straighten〔'stretṇ〕
= relax〔rɪ'læks〕
= loosen〔'lusṇ〕
= slacken〔'slækən〕
= *ease up*
= *let up*

unbiased〔ʌn'baɪəst〕*adj.*
公平的

= impartial〔ɪm'pɑrʃəl〕
= fair〔fɛr〕
= unprejudiced〔ʌn'prɛdʒədɪst〕

unbounded〔ʌn'baundɪd〕*adj.*
未加約束的

= free〔fri〕
= unconfined〔ˌʌnkən'faɪnd〕

U

= unrestricted (ˌʌnrɪˈstrɪktɪd)

= wide-open (ˈwaɪdˈopən)

unbroken (ʌnˈbrokən) *adj.*
連續不斷的

= continuous (kənˈtɪnjuəs)

= uninterrupted (ˌʌnɪntəˈrʌptɪd)

= constant (ˈkɑnstənt)

= even (ˈivən)

= regular (ˈrɛgjələ)

= steady (ˈstɛdɪ)

= whole (hol)

= prepetual (pəˈpɛtʃuəl)

uncanny (ʌnˈkænɪ) *adj.* 奇怪的

= strange (strendʒ)

= mysterious (mɪsˈtɪrɪəs)

= weird (wɪrd)

= creepy (ˈkripɪ)

= eerie (ˈɪrɪ , ˈirɪ)

unceasing (ʌnˈsisɪŋ) *adj.*
不停的

= continual (kənˈtɪnjuəl)

= constant (ˈkɑnstənt)

= incessant (ɪnˈsɛsn̩t)

= endless (ˈɛndlɪs)

= interminable (ɪnˈtɜmɪnəbl̩)

= perpetual (pəˈpɛtʃuəl)

= everlasting (ˌɛvəˈlæstɪŋ)

uncertain (ʌnˈsɜtn̩) *adj.* 不確
定的

= doubtful (ˈdautfəl)

= unsure (ʌnˈʃur)

= speculative (ˈspɛkjəˌletɪv)

= changeable (ˈtʃendʒəbl̩)

= unpredictable (ˌʌnprɪˈdɪktəbl̩)

= insecure (ˌɪnsɪˈkjur)

= precarious (prɪˈkɛrɪəs)

unchain (ʌnˈtʃen) *v.* 釋放

= free (fri)

= release (rɪˈlis)

= unshackle (ʌnˈʃækl̩)

= extricate (ˈɛkstrɪˌket)

unchanged (ʌnˈtʃendʒd) *adj.*
未改變的

= same (sem)

= permanent (ˈpɜmənənt)

= unaltered (ʌnˈɔltəd)

= regular (ˈrɛgjələ)

= constant (ˈkɑnstənt)

uncivilized (ʌnˈsɪvl̩ˌaɪzd) *adj.*
未開化的

= barbarous (ˈbɑrbərəs)

= savage (ˈsævɪdʒ)

= bestial (ˈbɛstɪəl , ˈbɛstʃəl)

= wild (waɪld)

= brutal (ˈbrutl̩)

= unrefined (ˌʌnrɪˈfaɪnd)

= uncouth (ʌnˈkuθ)

= uncultured (ʌnˈkʌltʃəd)

unclean (ʌnˈklin) *adj.* ①骯髒的
②邪惡的

① = dirty (ˈdɜtɪ)

= filthy (ˈfɪlθɪ)

= soiled (sɔɪld)

= grimy (ˈgraɪmɪ)

= smutty ('smʌtɪ)
= slimy ('slaɪmɪ)
= polluted (pə'lutɪd)
= contaminated (kən'tæmənetɪd)
= infected (ɪn'fɛktɪd)
= evil ('ivl)
= obscene (əb'sin)
= lewd (lud , lɪud)
= foul (faʊl)
= pornographic (,pɔrnə'græfɪk)
= indecent (ɪn'disn̩t)

ncomfortable

ʌn'kʌmfətəbl̩) *adj.* 不舒適的

= distressing (dɪ'strɛsɪŋ)
= painful ('penfəl)
= disturbed (dɪs'tɜbd)
= bothered ('bɑðəd)
= troubled ('trʌbl̩d)
= upset ('ʌp'sɛt)
= uneasy (ʌn'izɪ)

ncommon (ʌn'kɑmən) *adj.*

凡的

= rare (rɛr)
= unusual (ʌn'juʒʊəl)
= unique (ju'nik)
= novel ('nɑvl̩)
= different ('dɪfərənt)
= original (ə'rɪdʒənl̩)
= scarce (skɛrs)
= infrequent (ɪn'frikwənt)

ncompromising

ʌn'kɑmprə,maɪzɪŋ) *adj.* 堅定的

= firm (fɜm)

= unyielding (ʌn'jildɪŋ)
= obstinate ('ɑbstənɪt)
= stiff (stɪf)
= rigid ('rɪdʒɪd)
= adamant ('ædə,mænt , -mənt)
= unbending (ʌn'bɛndɪŋ)
= inflexible (ɪn'flɛksəbl̩)
= strict (strɪkt)
= relentless (rɪ'lɛntlɪs)

U

unconcerned (,ʌnkən'sɜnd)
adj. 不關心的

= uninterested (ʌn'ɪntərɪstɪd)
= indifferent (ɪn'dɪfərənt)
= blasé (blɑ'ze , 'blaze)
= nonchalant ('nɑnʃələnt)
= apathetic (,æpə'θɛtɪk)
= easygoing ('izɪ'goɪŋ)

unconditional

(,ʌnkən'dɪʃənəl) *adj.* 無條件的

= unqualified (ʌn'kwɑlə,faɪd)
= absolute ('æbsə,lut)
= unlimited (ʌn'lɪmɪtɪd)
= positive ('pɑzətɪv)
= complete (kəm'plit)
= total ('totl̩)
= perfect ('pɜfɪkt)
= entire (ɪn'taɪr)
= utter ('ʌtə)
= explicit (ɪk'splɪsɪt)
= express (ɪk'sprɛs)

unconscious (ʌn'kɑnʃəs) *adj.*
①無意識的　②不覺察的

① = senseless ('sɛnslɪs)

= *out cold*

② = unaware (ˌʌnə'wɛr)

= unintentional (ˌʌnɪn'tɛnʃənl̩)

= unthinking (ʌn'θɪŋkɪŋ)

= preoccupied(pri'ɑkjəˌpaɪd)

= oblivious (ə'blɪvɪəs)

= absent-minded
  ('æbsn̩t'maɪndɪd)

U

unconstitutional

(ˌʌnkɑnstə'tjuʃənl̩) *adj.* 違憲的

= illegal (ɪ'ligl̩)

= unlawful (ʌn'lɔfəl)

= illegitimate (ˌɪlɪ'dʒɪtəmɪt)

= unauthorized (ʌn'ɔθəˌraɪzd)

uncouth (ʌn'kuθ) *adj.* 笨拙的

= awkward ('ɔkwəd)

= clumsy ('klʌmzɪ)

= crude (krud)

= ungainly (ʌn'genlɪ)

= vulgar ('vʌlgə)

= coarse (kors , kɔrs)

= gross (gros)

= rude (rud)

= crass (kræs)

= boorish ('burɪʃ)

= unrefined (ˌʌnrɪ'faɪnd)

= unpolished (ʌn'pɑlɪʃt)

= uncultured (ʌn'kʌltʃəd)

= uncivilized (ʌn'sɪvl̩ˌaɪzd)

= barbarous ('bɑrbərəs)

= common ('kɑmən)

= base (bes)

uncover (ʌn'kʌvə) *v.*
移去覆蓋物；揭發

= reveal (rɪ'vil)

= expose (ɪk'spoz)

= disclose (dɪs'kloz)

= open ('opən)

= unmask (ʌn'mæsk)

uncultivated (ʌn'kʌltəˌvetɪd)
adj. 未墾的

= wild (waɪld)

= undeveloped (ˌʌndɪ'vɛləpt)

= rough (rʌf)

= crude (krud)

= fallow ('fælo)

undaunted (ʌn'dɔntɪd) *adj.*
膽大無畏的；勇敢的

= fearless ('fɪrlɪs)

= unafraid (ˌʌnə'fred)

= daring ('dɛrɪŋ)

= bold (bold)

= brave (brev)

= courageous (kə'redʒəs)

= confident ('kɑnfədənt)

= persevering (ˌpɜsə'vɪrɪŋ)

= untiring (ʌn'taɪrɪŋ)

undecided (ˌʌndɪ'saɪdɪd) *adj.*
未決定的

= uncertain (ʌn'sɜtn̩ , -'sɜtɪn)

= unsettled (ʌn'sɛtl̩d)

= pending ('pɛndɪŋ)

= vague (veg)

= indefinite (ɪn'dɛfənɪt)

= undetermined (ˌʌndɪ't ɜmɪnd)

nder ('ʌndɚ) *adv.* 在下面

= below (bə'lo)
= beneath (bɪ'niθ)

nderfed (,ʌndɚ'fɛd) *adj.*
養不良的

= undernourished ('ʌndɚ'nɝɪʃt)
= starved (starvd)

ndergo (,ʌndɚ'go) *v.* 經歷

= experience (ɪk'spɪrɪəns)
= meet (mit)
= have (hæv)
= feel (fil)
= encounter (ɪn'kaʊntɚ)
= endure (ɪn'djʊr)
= suffer ('sʌfɚ)
= *go through*

nderhanded ('ʌndɚ'hændɪd)
j. 秘密的;卑劣的

= secret ('sikrɪt)
= sly (slaɪ)
= shifty ('ʃɪftɪ)
= surreptitious (,sɝəp'tɪʃəs)
= deceitful (dɪ'sitfəl)
= dishonest (dɪs'ɑnɪst)
= fraudulent ('frɔdʒələnt)
= crocked ('krʊkɪd)
= unscrupulous (ʌn'skrupjələs)

ndermine (,ʌndɚ'maɪn) *v.*
漸損毀

= weaken ('wikən)
= sabotage ('sæbə,tɑʒ , -tɪdʒ)

= destroy (dɪ'strɔɪ)

underneath (,ʌndɚ'niθ , -'nɪð)
prep. 在…之下

= below (bə'lo)
= beneath (bɪ'niθ)
= under ('ʌndɚ)

underrate (,ʌndɚ'ret) *v.* 低估

= minimize ('mɪnə,maɪz)
= underestimate (,ʌndɚ'ɛstə,met)
= belittle (bɪ'lɪtl̩)

understand (,ʌndɚ'stænd) *v.*
了解

= comprehend (,kɑmprɪ'hɛnd)
= follow ('falo)
= grasp (græsp)
= conceive (kən'siv)
= realize ('riə,laɪz , 'rɪə-)
= know (no)
= appreciate (ə'priʃɪ,et)

undertake (,ʌndɚ'tek) *v.*
①從事　②答應

① = try (traɪ)
= attempt (ə'tɛmpt)
= essay (ə'se , ɛ'se)
= pursue (pɚ'su , -'sɪu)
② = promise ('prɑmɪs)
= contract ('kɑntrækt)
= agree (ə'gri)

undertone ('ʌndɚ,ton) *n.* 低聲

= murmur ('mɝmɚ)
= whisper ('hwɪspɚ)

U

undesirable (ˌʌndɪ'zaɪrəbl̩)
adj. 惹人厭的；不宜的

= objectionable (əb'dʒɛkʃənəbl̩)
= disagreeable (ˌdɪsə'griəbl̩)
= unpleasant (ʌn'plɛznt)
= distasteful (dɪs'testfəl)
= offensive (ə'fɛnsɪv)
= repulsive (rɪ'pʌlsɪv)
= intolerable (ɪn'talərəbl̩)
= loathsome ('loðsəm)
= unsatisfactory
   (ˌʌnsætɪs'fæktərɪ)
= unacceptable (ˌʌnək'sɛptəbl̩)
= unsuitable (ʌn'sjutəbl̩ , -'sut-)

undisputed (ˌʌndɪ'spjutɪd) *adj.*
無疑問的

= unquestioned (ʌn'kwɛstʃənd)
= uncontested (ˌʌnkɑn'tɛstɪd)
= doubtless ('dautlɪs)
= accepted (ək'sɛptɪd , æk-)
= believed (bɪ'livd)

undisturbed (ˌʌndɪ'stɜbd) *adj.*
安靜的；未受干擾的

= untroubled (ʌn'trʌbl̩d)
= calm (kɑm)
= tranquil ('trænkwɪl , 'træŋ-)

undo (ʌn'du) *v.* ①解開
②破壞

① = unfasten (ʌn'fæsn̩)
= untie (ʌn'taɪ)
= disassemble (ˌdɪsə'sɛmbl̩)
= dismantle(dɪs'mæntl̩)
= *take apart*

② = destroy (dɪ'strɔɪ)
= spoil (spɔɪl)
= abolish (ə'balɪʃ)
= wreck (rɛk)

undress (ʌn'drɛs) *v.* 脫去

= disrobe (dɪs'rob)
= unclothe (ʌn'kloð)
= strip (strɪp)

undying (ʌn'daɪɪŋ) *adj.* 不朽的

= eternal (ɪ'tɜnl̩)
= immortal (ɪ'mɔrtl̩)
= unfading (ʌn'fedɪŋ)
= imperishable (ɪm'pɛrɪʃəbl̩)
= everlasting (ˌɛvɚ'læstɪŋ)
= indestructible (ˌɪndɪ'strʌktəbl̩)

unearth (ʌn'ɜθ) *v.* 發現；挖掘

= discover (dɪ'skʌvɚ)
= extract (ɪk'strækt)
= withdraw (wɪð'drɔ , wɪθ-)
= remove (rɪ'muv)
= uncover (ʌn'kʌvɚ)
= disclose (dɪs'kloz)
= *turn up*
= *dig up*

unearthly (ʌn'ɜθlɪ) *adj.* 怪異的

= strange (strendʒ)
= weird (wɪrd)
= ghostly ('gostlɪ)
= wild (waɪld)
= odd (ɑd)
= supernatural (ˌsupɚ'nætʃrəl)
= queer (kwɪr)

= peculiar (pɪˈkjuljə)

= spooky (ˈspukɪ)

= uncanny (ʌnˈkænɪ)

= eerie (ˈɪrɪ , ˈɪrɪ)

neasy (ʌnˈizɪ) *adj.* 不舒適的；
不安的

= restless (ˈrɛstlɪs)

= disturbed (dɪˈstɜbd)

= anxious (ˈæŋkʃəs , ˈæŋʃəs)

= uncomfortable (ʌnˈkʌmfətəbḷ)

= fidgety (ˈfɪdʒɪtɪ)

= impatient (ɪmˈpeʃənt)

= distressed (dɪˈstrɛst)

= troubled (ˈtrʌbḷd)

= bothered (ˈbɑðəd)

= agitated (ˈædʒə,tetɪd)

= perturbed (pəˈtɜbd)

nemployed (,ʌnɪmˈplɔɪd) *adj.*
失業的

= idle (ˈaɪdḷ)

= jobless (ˈdʒɑblɪs)

= unoccupied (ʌnˈɑkjə,paɪd)

= *out of work*

nending (ʌnˈɛndɪŋ) *adj.*
永遠的

= continuous (kənˈtɪnjuəs)

= endless (ˈɛndlɪs)

= eternal (ɪˈtɜnḷ)

= immortal (ɪˈmɔrtḷ)

= uninterrupted (,ʌnɪntəˈrʌptɪd)

= ceaseless (ˈsislɪs)

= incessant (ɪnˈsɛsṇt)

= interminable (ɪnˈtɜmɪnəbḷ)

= perpetual (pəˈpɛtʃuəl)

= infinite (ˈɪnfənɪt)

= everlasting (,ɛvəˈlæstɪŋ)

= permanent (ˈpɜmənənt)

unequal (ʌnˈikwəl) *adj.* 不等的

= uneven (ʌnˈivən)

= irregular (ɪˈrɛgjələ)

= disparate (ˈdɪspərɪt)

uneven (ʌnˈivən) *adj.* 不平的

= unequal (ʌnˈikwəl)

= irregular (ɪˈrɛgjələ)

= disparate (ˈdɪspərɪt)

unexpected (,ʌnɪkˈspɛktɪd) *adj.*
意外的

= unforeseen (,ʌnforˈsin)

= unanticipated (,ʌnænˈtɪsɪ,petɪd)

= chance (tʃæns)

= accidetnal (,æksəˈdɛntḷ)

= sudden (ˈsʌdṇ)

unfailing (ʌnˈfelɪŋ) *adj.*
忠實的；永久的

= faithful (ˈfeθfəl)

= loyal (ˈlɔjəl , ˈlɔɪəl)

= sure (ʃur)

= true (tru)

= constant (ˈkɑnstənt)

= reliable (rɪˈlaɪəbḷ)

= dependable (dɪˈpɛndəbḷ)

= sound (saund)

= firm (fɜm)

= secure (sɪ'kjʊr)
= stable ('stebl̩)
= substantial (səb'stænʃəl)
= steadfast ('stɛd,fæst)

unfair (ʌn'fɛr) *adj.* 不公正的

= unjust (ʌn'dʒʌst)

unfaithful (ʌn'feθfəl) *adj.*
不忠實的

= untrue (ʌn'tru)
= unloyal (ʌn'lɔjəl)
= false (fɔls)
= fickle ('fɪkl̩)

unfamiliar (,ʌnfə'mɪljɚ) *adj.*
不熟悉的

= unusual (ʌn'juʒʊəl)
= strange (strendʒ)
= uncommon (ʌn'kɑmən)
= rare (rɛr)
= unique (ju'nik)
= novel ('nɑvl̩)
= new (nju)
= different ('dɪfərənt)

unfasten (ʌn'fæsn̩) *v.* 解開；
鬆開

= undo (ʌn'du)
= loosen ('lusn̩)
= open ('opən)
= untie (ʌn'taɪ)
= unhook (ʌn'hʊk)

unfavorable (ʌn'fevrəbl̩) *adj.*
不利的

= unsatisfactory (,ʌnsætɪs'fæktrɪ
= harmful ('hɑrmfəl)
= detrimental (,dɛtrə'mɛntl̩)
= adverse (əd'vɝs , 'ædvɝs)
= contrary ('kɑntrɛrɪ)
= uncomplimentary
(,ʌnkɑmplə'mɛntərɪ)
= disapproving (,dɪsə'pruvɪŋ)

unfeeling (ʌn'filɪŋ) *adj.* 殘酷的

= cruel ('kruəl)
= heartless ('hɑrtlɪs)
= cold (kold)
= callous ('kæləs)
= hard-hearted ('hɑrd'hɑrtɪd)

unfinished (ʌn'fɪnɪʃt) *adj.*
未完成的

= incomplete (,ɪnkəm'plit)
= rough (rʌf)
= undone (ʌn'dʌn)
= crude (krud)

unfit (ʌn'fɪt) *adj.* 不適當的

= unsuitable (ʌn'sjutəbl̩)
= inappropriate (,ɪnə'proprɪɪt)
= incapable (ɪn'kepəbl̩)
= incompetent (ɪn'kɑmpətənt)
= unqualified (ʌn'kwɑlə,faɪd)

unfold (ʌn'fold) *v.* ①展開
②說明

① = reveal(rɪ'vil)
= show (ʃo)
= open ('opən)

= disclose (dɪs'kloz)
= uncover (ʌn'kʌvɚ)
= unmask (ʌn'mæsk)
= spread (sprɛd)
= unfurl (ʌn'fɝl)
② = explain (ɪk'splen)
= show (ʃo)
= clarify ('klærə,faɪ)
= demonstrate ('dɛmən,stret)
= illuminate (ɪ'lumə,net)

unforeseen (,ʌnfor'sin) *adj.*
未預料到的

= unexpected (,ʌnɪk'spɛktɪd)
= unanticipated (,ʌnæn'tɪsɪ,petɪd)
= sudden ('sʌdn̩)

unforgettable (,ʌnfɚ'gɛtəbl̩)
adj. 難忘的

= memorable ('mɛmərəbl̩)
= notable ('notəbl̩)
= noteworthy ('not,wɝðɪ)
= remarkable (rɪ'mɑrkəbl̩)
= extraordinary (ɪk'strɔrdn̩,ɛrɪ)
= exceptional (ɪk'sɛpʃənl̩)

unfortunate (ʌn'fɔrtʃənɪt) *adj.*
不幸的

= unlucky (ʌn'lʌkɪ)
= ill-fated ('ɪl'fetɪd)

unfriendly (ʌn'frɛndlɪ) *adj.*
不友善的

= unsociable (ʌn'soʃəbl̩)
= aloof (ə'luf)

= standoffish (stænd'ɔfɪʃ)
= distant ('dɪstənt)
= remote (rɪ'mot)
= cool (kul)
= uncordial (ʌn'kɔrdjəl)
= inhospitable (ɪn'hɑspɪtəbl̩)

ungainly (ʌn'genlɪ) *adj.* 笨拙的

= awkward ('ɔkwəd)
= clumsy ('klʌmzɪ)
= bungling ('bʌŋglɪŋ)
= unhandy (ʌn'hændɪ)
= ungraceful (ʌn'gresfəl)
= gawky ('gɔkɪ)

ungracious (ʌn'greʃəs) *adj.*
粗魯的

= impolite (,ɪmpə'laɪt)
= rude (rud)
= discourteous (dɪs'kɝtɪəs)
= uncivil (ʌn'sɪvl̩)
= ungallant (ʌn'gælənt)
= unkind (ʌn'kaɪnd)

ungrateful (ʌn'gretfəl) *adj.*
不知感恩的

= unappreciative (,ʌnə'priʃɪ,etɪv)
= unthankful (ʌn'θæŋkfəl)

unguarded (ʌn'gɑrdɪd) *adj.*
無保護的

= unprotected (,ʌnprə'tɛktɪd)
= defenseless (dɪ'fɛnslɪs)
= unshielded (ʌn'ʃildɪd)
= unsheltered (ʌn'ʃɛltəd)

U

unhappy (ʌnˈhæpɪ) *adj.* 憂愁的

= sad (sæd)
= sorrowful (ˈsɑrofəl)
= uncheerful (ʌnˈtʃɪrfəl)
= displeased (dɪsˈplizd)
= discontented (ˌdɪskənˈtɛntɪd)
= wretched (ˈrɛtʃɪd)
= miserable (ˈmɪzərəbļ , ˈmɪzrə-)
= dejected (dɪˈdʒɛktɪd)
= depressed (dɪˈprɛst)
= downcast (ˈdaʊnkæst)
= disheartened (dɪsˈhɑrtņd)
= despondent (dɪˈspɑndənt)
= melancholy (ˈmɛlənˌkɑlɪ)
= blue (blu)
= wistful (ˈwɪstfəl)
= unsatisfied (ʌnˈsætɪsfaɪd)

unhealthy (ʌnˈhɛlθɪ) *adj.*
不健康的

= sickly (ˈsɪklɪ)
= infirm (ɪnˈfɜm)
= unwholesome (ʌnˈholsəm)
= unsound (ʌnˈsaʊnd)
= weak (wik)
= feeble (ˈfibļ)
= frail (frel)
= ill (ɪl)
= ailing (ˈelɪŋ)
= unwell (ʌnˈwɛl)
= indisposed (ˌɪndɪˈspozd)
= run-down (ˈrʌnˈdaʊn)

unheeded (ʌnˈhidɪd) *adj.*
未加注意的

= disregarded (ˌdɪsrɪˈgɑrdɪd)
= unnoticed (ʌnˈnotɪst)
= unobserved (ˌʌnəbˈzɜvd)
= unseen (ʌnˈsin)

uniform (ˈjunəˌfɔrm)
① *adj.* 相同的　② *n.* 制服

① = even (ˈivən)
= alike (əˈlaɪk)
= unvaried (ʌnˈvɛrɪd)
= constant (ˈkɑnstənt)
= steady (ˈstɛdɪ)
= regular (ˈrɛgjələ)
= consistent (kənˈsɪstənt)
= symmetrical (sɪˈmɛtrɪkļ)
= balanced (ˈbælənst)
② = costume (ˈkɑstjum)
= outfit (ˈaʊtˌfɪt)

unify (ˈjunəˌfaɪ) *v.* 使一致

= combine (kəmˈbaɪn)
= unite (juˈnaɪt)
= consolidate (kənˈsɑləˌdet)
= join (dʒɔɪn)
= mix (mɪks)
= merge (mɜdʒ)
= blend (blɛnd)
= fuse (fjuz)

unimportant (ˌʌnɪmˈpɔrtņt)
adj. 不重要的

= insignificant (ˌɪnsɪgˈnɪfəkənt)
= trifling (ˈtraɪflɪŋ)
= inconsequential
(ˌɪnkɑnsəˈkwɛnʃəl)

= trivial ('trɪvɪəl)
= petty ('pɛtɪ)

ninhabited (,ʌnɪn'hæbɪtɪd)
j. 無人住的

= unoccupied (ʌn'ɑkjə,paɪd)
= deserted (dɪ'zɝtɪd)
= abandoned (ə'bændənd)
= vacant ('vekənt)

nnecessary (ʌn'nɛsə,sɛrɪ)
j. 不需要的

= needless ('nidlɪs)
= unessential (,ʌnə'sɛnʃəl)
= superfluous (su'pɝfluəs)
= excess ('ɪksɛs , ɪk'sɛs)
= uncalled-for (ʌn'kɔld,fɔr)

nnerve (ʌn'nɝv) *v.* 嚇壞

= upset (ʌp'sɛt)
= frighten ('fraɪtn)
= scare (skɛr)
= alarm (ə'lɑrm)
= startle ('stɑrtl)

nnoticed (ʌn'notɪst) *adj.*
注意的

= unobserved (,ʌnəb'zɝvd)
= unheeded (ʌn'hidɪd)
= unseen (ʌn'sin)

1observed (,ʌnəb'zɝvd) *adj.*
注意的

= unnoticed (ʌn'notɪst)
= unheeded (ʌn'hidɪd)
= unseen (ʌn'sin)

unoccupied (ʌn'ɑkjə,paɪd)
adj. 空的

= vacant ('vekənt)
= idle ('aɪdl)
= deserted (dɪ'zɝtɪd)
= open ('opən)
= available (ə'veləbl)
= uninhabited (,ʌnɪn'hæbɪtɪd)

unpack (ʌn'pæk) *v.* 取出

= unload (ʌn'lod)
= discharge (dɪs'tʃɑrdʒ)
= dump (dʌmp)

unpaid (ʌn'ped) *adj.* 未付的

= owing ('o·ɪŋ)
= due (dju)
= outstanding (aʊt'stændɪŋ)

unparalleled (ʌn'pærə,lɛld)
adj. 無比的

= unequaled (ʌn'ikwəld)
= matchless ('mætʃlɪs)
= unsurpassed (,ʌnsə'pæst)
= unexcelled (,ʌnɪk'sɛld)
= unbeatable (ʌn'bitəbl)
= incomparable (ɪn'kɑmpərəbl)
= extraordinary (ɪk'strɔrdn,ɛrɪ)
= exceptional (ɪk'sɛpʃənl)
= remarkable (rɪ'mɑrkəbl)

unpleasant (ʌn'plɛznt) *adj.*
不愉快的

= disagreeable (,dɪsə'griəbl)
= unsavory (ʌn'sevərɪ)
= undesirable (,ʌndɪ'zaɪrəbl)

U

= unlikable (ʌn'laɪkəbl̩)

= offensive (ə'fɛnsɪv)

= odious ('odɪəs)

= repulsive (rɪ'pʌlsɪv)

= repugnant (rɪ'pʌgnənt)

= obnoxious (əb'nakʃəs , ab-)

unpopular (ʌn'papjələ) *adj.*
不受歡迎的

= unappreciated (ˌʌnə'priʃɪ,etɪd)

= unloved (ʌn'lʌvd)

= unwanted (ʌn'wantɪd)

= unlikable (ʌn'laɪkəbl̩)

= unwelcome (ʌn'wɛlkəm)

= disliked (dɪs'laɪkt)

unprecedented
(ʌn'prɛsə,dɛntɪd) *adj.* 空前的

= unduplicated (ʌn'djuplə,ketɪd)

= uncopied (ʌn'kapɪd)

= unimitated (ʌn'ɪmə,tetɪd)

= extraordinary (ɪk'strɔrdn̩,ɛrɪ)

= exceptional (ɪk'sɛpʃən̩l)

unprepared (ˌʌnprɪ'pɛrd) *adj.*
未準備的

= unready (ʌn'rɛdɪ)

= unwary (ʌn'wɛrɪ)

unprincipled (ʌn'prɪnsəpl̩d)
adj. 無原則的；無道義的

= dishonest (dɪs'anɪst)

= crooked ('krukɪd)

= corrupt (kə'rʌpt)

= criminal ('krɪmən̩l)

= fraudulent ('frɔdʒələnt)

= unscrupulous (ʌn'skrupjələs)

unprofitable (ʌn'prafɪtəbl̩)
adj. 無益的

= unrewarding (ˌʌnrɪ'wɔrdɪŋ)

= fruitless ('frutlɪs)

unquestionable
(ʌn'kwɛstʃənəbl̩) *adj.* 確定的

= certain ('sɝtn̩)

= positive ('pazətɪv)

= undeniable (ˌʌndɪ'naɪəbl̩)

= indisputable (ˌɪndɪ'spjutəbl̩)

unravel (ʌn'rævl̩) *v.* ①解開
②闡明

① = unsnarl (ʌn'snarl)

= untwist (ʌn'twɪst)

= disentangle (ˌdɪsɪn'tæŋgl̩)

② = solve (salv)

= explain (ɪk'splen)

= answer ('ænsə)

= resolve (rɪ'zalv)

= decipher (dɪ'saɪfə)

= unriddle (ʌn'rɪdl̩)

= crack (kræk)

= decode (di'kod)

= *figure out*

unreal (ʌn'riəl , ʌn'ril) *adj.*
不真實的；空想的

= imaginary (ɪ'mædʒə,nɛrɪ)

= fanciful ('fænsɪfəl , -ful)

= fictitious (fɪk'tɪʃəs)

= counterfeit (ˈkaʊntəˌfɪt)
= make-believe (ˈmekbəˌliv)
= false (fɔls)
= mock (mɑk)
= imitation (ˌɪməˈteʃən)
= simulated (ˈsɪmjəˌletɪd)
= ungenuine (ʌnˈdʒɛnjʊɪn)
= unauthentic (ˌʌnɔˈθɛntɪk)
= artificial (ˌɑrtəˈfɪʃəl)
= synthetic (sɪnˈθɛtɪk)
= pseudo (ˈsjudo)
= fake (fek)

unreasonable (ʌnˈriznəbḷ)
adj. 不合理的;過度的

= extreme (ɪkˈstrim)
= excessive (ɪkˈsɛsɪv)
= outrageous (aʊtˈredʒəs)
= preposterous (prɪˈpɑstərəs)
= extravagant (ɪkˈstrævəgənt)
= impractical (ɪmˈpræktɪkḷ)
= illogical (ɪˈlɑdʒɪkḷ)
= senseless (ˈsɛnslɪs)
= inconsistent (ˌɪnkənˈsɪstənt)
= irrational (ɪˈræʃənḷ , ɪrˈræ-)
② = unsound (ʌnˈsaʊnd)

unrest (ʌnˈrɛst) *n.* 不安的狀態

= restlessness (ˈrɛstlɪsnɪs)
= agitation (ˌædʒəˈteʃən)
= disquiet (dɪsˈkwaɪət)
= stir (stɝ)
= disturbance (dɪˈstɝbəns)
= commotion (kəˈmoʃən)
= turmoil (ˈtɝmɔɪl)
= tumult (ˈtjumʌlt)

= excitement (ɪkˈsaɪtmənt)

unrestrained (ˌʌnrɪˈstrend)
adj. 無約束的

= unchecked (ʌnˈtʃɛkt)
= free (fri)
= uncurbed (ʌnˈkɝbd)
= uncontrolled (ˌʌnkənˈtrold)

unrivaled (ʌnˈraɪvḷd) *adj.*
無匹比的

= unmatched (ʌnˈmætʃt)
= unequaled (ʌnˈikwəld)
= incomparable (ɪnˈkɑmpərəbḷ)

unruly (ʌnˈrulɪ) *adj.* 不守法的

= disorderly (dɪsˈɔrdəlɪ)
= riotous (ˈraɪətəs)
= wild (waɪld)
= rampant (ˈræmpənt)
= lawless (ˈlɔlɪs)

unsafe (ʌnˈsef) *adj.* 不安全的

= dangerous (ˈdendʒərəs)
= unsound (ʌnˈsaʊnd)
= precarious (prɪˈkɛrɪəs)
= imperiled (ɪmˈpɛrəld)
= risky (ˈrɪskɪ)
= perilous (ˈpɛrələs)
= hazardous (ˈhæzədəs)

unsatisfactory
(ˌʌnsætɪsˈfæktrɪ)
adj. 不令人滿意的

= ungratifying (ʌnˈgrætəfaɪɪŋ)
= inadequate (ɪnˈædəkwɪt)

U

= insufficient (,ɪnsə'fɪʃənt)
= inferior (ɪn'fɪrɪɚ)
= second-rate ('sɛkənd'ret)
= low-grade ('lo'gred)

unscramble (ʌn'skræmbḷ) v.
整理;使清晰

= solve (sɑlv)
= explain (ɪk'splen)
= resolve (rɪ'zɑlv)
= decipher (dɪ'saɪfɚ)
= decode (di'kod)
= crack (kræk)
= *figure out*
= *clear up*

unscrupulous (ʌn'skrupjələs)
adj. 不謹慎的;無恥的

= dishonest (dɪs'ɑnɪst)
= unprincipled (ʌn'prɪnsəpḷd)
= unethical (ʌn'ɛθɪkḷ)
= corrupt (kə'rʌpt)
= crooked ('krʊkɪd)
= criminal ('krɪmənḷ)
= fraudulent ('frɔdʒələnt)

unseat (ʌn'sit) v. 罷免

= displace (dɪs'ples)
= dislodge (dɪs'lɑdʒ)
= depose (dɪ'poz)
= remove (rɪ'muv)
= dismiss (dɪs'mɪs)
= overthrow (,ovɚ'θro)

unseemly (ʌn'simlɪ) adj.
不適宜的

= improper (ɪm'prɑpɚ)
= unsuitable (ʌn'sjutəbḷ)
= vulgar ('vʌlgɚ)
= offensive (ə'fɛnsɪv)
= indecent (ɪn'disṇt)
= coarse (kors , kɔrs)
= crude (krud)
= objectionable (əb'dʒɛkʃənəbḷ)
= wrong (rɔŋ)
= unbecoming (,ʌnbɪ'kʌmɪŋ)

unselfish (ʌn'sɛlfɪʃ) adj.
不自私的

= generous ('dʒɛnərəs)
= liberal ('lɪbərəl)
= free (fri)
= unsparing (ʌn'spɛrɪŋ)
= lavish ('lævɪʃ)
= open-handed ('opən'hændɪd)
= bighearted ('bɪg,hartɪd)
= magnanimous
  (mæg'nænəməs)

unsettle (ʌn'sɛtḷ) v. 擾亂

= disturb (dɪ'stɝb)
= shake (ʃek)
= upset (ʌp'sɛt)
= startle ('startḷ)
= shock (ʃɑk)

unshaken (ʌn'ʃekən) adj.
堅決的

= firm (fɝm)
= resolute ('rɛzə,lut , 'rɛzḷ,jut)
= staunch (stɔntʃ , stɑntʃ)
= solid ('salɪd)

= fixed (fɪkst)

= unyielding (ʌn'jildɪŋ)

= steady ('stɛdɪ)

nsightly (ʌn'saɪtlɪ) *adj.* 難看的

= ugly ('ʌglɪ)

= unattractive (,ʌnə'træktɪv)

= homely ('homlɪ)

= plain (plen)

nskilled (ʌn'skɪld) *adj.*
不熟練的

= untrained (ʌn'trend)

= untalented (ʌn'tæləntɪd)

= inexperienced (,ɪnɪk'spɪrɪənst)

= raw (rɔ)

= green (grin)

= amateurish (,æmə'tɜʃ)

nsophisticated
ʌnsə'fɪstɪ,ketɪd) *adj.* 天眞的

= simple ('sɪmpl)

= natural ('nætʃərəl)

= artless ('ɑrtlɪs , -lɛs)

= naive (nɑ'iv)

= green (grin)

nsound (ʌn'saʊnd) *adj.*
堅固的;不健全的

= unwise (ʌn'waɪz)

= unreasonable (ʌn'riznəbl ,
  -zṇəbl)

= illogical (ɪl'lɑdʒɪkl)

= unreliable (,ʌnrɪ'laɪəbl)

= hazardous ('hæzə·dəs)

= risky ('rɪskɪ)

= unsafe (ʌn'sef)

= unsure (ʌn'ʃur)

= ill-advised ('ɪləd'vaɪzd)

unstable (ʌn'stebl) *adj.*
不穩定的

= unsteady (ʌn'stɛdɪ)

= weak (wik)

= unsound (ʌn'saʊnd)

= unreliable (,ʌnrɪ'laɪəbl)

= unsure (ʌn'ʃur)

= unsafe (ʌn'sef)

unsteady (ʌn'stɛdɪ) *adj.*
不安定的

= unstable (ʌn'stebl)

= weak (wik)

= unsound (ʌn'saʊnd)

= unreliable (,ʌnrɪ'laɪəbl)

= unsure (ʌn'ʃur)

= unsafe (ʌn'sef)

unsuccessful (,ʌnsək'sɛsfəl)
adj. 失敗的

= failing ('felɪŋ)

= unfortunate (ʌn'fɔrtʃənɪt)

= abortive (ə'bɔrtɪv)

= fruitless ('frutlɪs)

unsuitable (ʌn'sjutəbl) *adj.*
不適當的

= unfit (ʌn'fɪt)

= inappropriate (,ɪnə'proprɪɪt)

= unbecoming (,ʌnbɪ'kʌmɪŋ)

U

= improper〔ɪmˈprɑpɚ〕

= unsatisfactory〔ˌʌnsætɪsˈfæktrɪ〕

= objectionable〔əbˈdʒɛkʃənəbḷ〕

= unacceptable〔ˌʌnəkˈsɛptəbḷ〕

unthinkable〔ʌnˈθɪŋkəbḷ〕*adj.*
無法設想的

= unbelievable〔ˌʌnbɪˈlivəbḷ〕

= incredible〔ɪnˈkrɛdəbḷ〕

= impossible〔ɪmˈpɑsəbḷ〕

= inconceivable〔ˌɪnkənˈsivəbḷ〕

= absurd〔əbˈsɝd〕

= ridiculous〔rɪˈdɪkjələs〕

= preposterous〔prɪˈpɑstərəs〕

= outlandish〔aʊtˈlændɪʃ〕

= unheard-of〔ʌnˈhɝd,ɑv〕

untidy〔ʌnˈtaɪdɪ〕*adj.* 不整潔的

= neglected〔nɪˈglɛktɪd〕

= slovenly〔ˈslʌvənlɪ〕

= shabby〔ˈʃæbɪ〕

= frowzy〔ˈfraʊzɪ〕

= messy〔ˈmɛsɪ〕

= sloppy〔ˈslɑpɪ〕

= seedy〔ˈsidɪ〕

untie〔ʌnˈtaɪ〕*v.* 解開

= loosen〔ˈlusṇ〕

= unfasten〔ʌnˈfæsṇ〕

= undo〔ʌnˈdu〕

untrained〔ʌnˈtrend〕*adj.*
未受訓練的

= unskilled〔ʌnˈskɪld〕

= unprepared〔ˌʌnprɪˈpɛrd〕

= untalented〔ʌnˈtæləntɪd〕

= inexperienced〔ˌɪnɪkˈspɪrɪənst〕

= amateurish〔ˌæməˈtɝɪʃ〕

= green〔grin〕

= raw〔rɔ〕

untried〔ʌnˈtraɪd〕*adj.*
未試過的

= new〔nju〕

= unused〔ʌnˈjuzd〕

= untouched〔ʌnˈtʌtʃt〕

= unproved〔ʌnˈpruvd〕

unture〔ʌnˈtru〕*adj.* ①虛偽的
②不忠實的

① = false〔fɔls〕

= wrong〔rɔŋ〕

= faulty〔ˈfɔltɪ〕

= erroneous〔əˈronɪəs〕

= fallacious〔fəˈleʃəs〕

② = unfaithful〔ʌnˈfeθfəl〕

= disloyal〔dɪsˈlɔɪəl〕

= fickle〔ˈfɪkḷ〕

unused〔ʌnˈjuzd〕*adj.*
①未用過的 ②不習慣的

① = new〔nju〕

= fresh〔frɛʃ〕

= firsthand〔ˈfɝstˈhænd〕

= original〔əˈrɪdʒənḷ〕

= untouched〔ʌnˈtʌtʃt〕

② = unaccustomed〔ˌʌnəˈkʌstəmd〕

= *unfamiliar with*

unusual〔ʌnˈjuʒʊəl〕*adj.* 罕有

= uncommon (ʌn'kɑmən)

= rare (rɛr)

= unique (ju'nik)

= novel ('nɑvl̩)

= queer (kwɪr)

= odd (ɑd)

= different ('dɪfərənt)

= *out of the ordinary*

nveil (ʌn'vel) *v.* 揭露

= uncover (ʌn'kʌvɚ)

= disclose (dɪs'kloz)

= reveal (rɪ'vil)

= show (ʃo)

= expose (ɪk'spoz)

= open ('opən)

= divulge (də'vʌldʒ)

= unmask (ʌn'mæsk)

nwelcome (ʌn'wɛlkəm) *adj.*
受歡迎的

= unwanted (ʌn'wɑntɪd)

= uninvited (,ʌnɪn'vaɪtɪd)

nwell (ʌn'wɛl) *adj.* 病的

= ailing ('elɪŋ)

= ill (ɪl)

= sick (sɪk)

= indisposed (,ɪndɪ'spozd)

nwieldy (ʌn'wildɪ) *adj.*
重的

= unmanageable
(ʌn'mænɪdʒəbl̩)

= unhandy (ʌn'hændɪ)

= awkward ('ɔkwəd)

= clumsy ('klʌmzɪ)

= cumbersome ('kʌmbəsəm)

= bulky ('bʌlkɪ)

unwilling (ʌn'wɪlɪŋ) *adj.*
勉強的

= reluctant (rɪ'lʌktənt)

= forced (forst , fɔrst)

= involuntary (ɪn'vɑlən,tɛrɪ)

= disinclined (,dɪsɪn'klaɪnd)

unwise (ʌn'waɪz) *adj.* 不智的

= foolish ('fulɪʃ)

= unreasonable (ʌn'rizn̩əbl̩)

= unsound (ʌn'saund)

= senseless ('sɛnslɪs)

= irrational (ɪ'ræʃənl̩)

unwittingly (ʌn'wɪtɪŋlɪ) *adv.*
不經意地

= unknowingly (ʌn'noɪŋlɪ)

= unconsciously (ʌn'kɑnʃəslɪ)

= unintentionally (,ʌnɪn'tɛnʃənl̩ɪ)

= unmindfully (ʌn'maɪndfəlɪ)

unyielding (ʌn'jildɪŋ) *adj.*
不屈的

= firm (fɜm)

= stubborn ('stʌbən)

= immovable (ɪ'muvəbl̩)

= inflexible (ɪn'flɛksəbl̩)

= unpliable (ʌn'plaɪəbl̩)

= unbending (ʌn'bɛndɪŋ)

= rigid ('rɪdʒɪd)

= adamant ('ædə,mænt)

upbraid (ʌp'bred) *v.* 責備

= reprove (rɪ'pruv)

= blame (blem)

= reprimand ('rɛprə,mænd)

= scold (skold)

= rebuke (rɪ'bjuk)

= chide (tʃaɪd)

= lecture ('lɛktʃɚ)

uphold (ʌp'hold) *v.* 支持

= support (sə'port , -'port)

= confirm (kən'fɝm)

= sustain (sə'sten)

= maintain (men'ten , mən-)

= bolster ('bolstɚ)

= substantiate (səb'stænʃɪ,et)

= corroborate (kə'rabə,ret)

upkeep ('ʌp,kip) *n.* 保養;維持

= maintenance ('mentənəns)

= support (sə'port , -'port)

= backing ('bækɪŋ)

= provision (prə'vɪʒən)

upper ('ʌpɚ) *adj.* 較高的

= higher ('haɪɚ)

= superior (sə'pɪrɪɚ , su-)

= greater ('gretɚ)

upright ('ʌp,raɪt , ʌp'raɪt) *adj.*
①直立的 ②正直的

① = standing ('stændɪŋ)

= erect (ɪ'rɛkt)

= vertical ('vɝtɪkl̩)

② = honorable ('anərəbl̩)

= upstanding (ʌp'stændɪŋ)

= reputable ('rɛpjətəbl̩)

= respectable (rɪ'spɛktəbl̩)

= moral ('mɔrəl)

= law-abiding ('lɔə,baɪdɪŋ)

uplift (ʌp'lɪft) *v.* 抬高

= raise (rez)

= elevate ('ɛlə,vet)

= erect (ɪ'rɛkt)

= lift (lɪft)

= improve (ɪm'pruv)

= hoist (hɔɪst)

uprising ('ʌp,raɪzɪŋ) *n.* 叛亂

= revolt (rɪ'volt)

= rebellion (rɪ'bɛljən)

= mutiny ('mjutnɪ)

= insurrection (,ɪnsə'rɛkʃən)

= riot ('raɪət)

= revolution (,rɛvə'luʃən)

uproar ('ʌp,ror) *n.* 喧囂

= noise (nɔɪz)

= disturbance (dɪ'stɝbəns)

= commotion (kə'moʃən)

= hubbub ('hʌbʌb)

= tumult ('tjumʌlt)

= clamor ('klæmɚ)

= turmoil ('tɝmɔɪl)

= racket ('rækɪt)

= fracas ('frekəs)

= ado (ə'du)

= fuss (fʌs)

= pandemonium
(,pændɪ'monɪəm)

= rumpus ('rʌmpəs)

= row (rau)

= to-do (tə'du)

uproot (ʌp'rut) v. 將…拔起

= extract (ɪk'strækt)

= withdraw (wɪð'drɔ)

= remove (rɪ'muv)

= *pull out*

upset (ʌp'sɛt) v. ①使傾覆
②擾亂 ③打敗

① = overturn (,ovə'tɜn)

= unsettle (ʌn'sɛtḷ)

= capsize (kæp'saɪz)

= *tip over*

② = disturb (dɪ'stɜb)

= perturb (pə'tɜb)

= trouble ('trʌbḷ)

= agitate ('ædʒə,tet)

= confuse (kən'fjuz)

= shake (ʃek)

= fluster ('flʌstə)

= ruffle ('rʌfḷ)

= bother ('baðə)

= unnerve (ʌn'nɜv)

③ = overthrow (,ovə'θro)

= defeat (dɪ'fit)

= revolution (,rɛvə'luʃən)

= overwhelm (,ovə'hwɛlm)

upshot ('ʌp,ʃat) n. 結果

= conclusion (kən'kluʒən)

= result (rɪ'zʌlt)

= effect (ə'fɛkt , ɪ-)

= consequence ('kansə,kwɛns)

= outcome ('aut,kʌm)

= fruit (frut)

= development (dɪ'vɛləpmənt)

up-to-date ('ʌptə'det) adj.
最新的;當代的

= modern ('madən)

= fashionable ('fæʃənəbḷ)

= contemporary (kən'tɛmpə,rɛrɪ)

= advanced (əd'vænst)

= current ('kɜənt)

urban ('ɜbən) adj. 都市的

= metropolitan (,mɛtrə'palətn)

= civic ('sɪvɪk)

= municipal (mju'nɪsəpḷ)

= citified ('sɪtɪ,faɪd)

urge (ɜdʒ) v. 力請;驅策

= push (puʃ)

= force (fors , fɔrs)

= drive (draɪv)

= plead (plid)

= advise (əd'vaɪz)

= incite (ɪn'saɪt)

= press (prɛs)

= pressure ('prɛʃə)

= coax (koks)

= goad (god)

= prod (prad)

= spur (spɜ)

= agitate ('ædʒə,tet)

= provoke (prə'vok)

= prompt (prampt)

U

urgent ('ɝdʒənt) *adj.* 緊急的

= pressing ('prɛsɪŋ)
= important (ɪm'pɔrtṇt)
= imperative (ɪm'pɛrətɪv)
= compelling (kəm'pɛlɪŋ)
= crucial ('kruʃəl , 'krɪuʃəl)
= essential (ə'sɛnʃəl)
= vital ('vaɪtḷ)
= necessary ('nɛsə,sɛrɪ)
= moving ('muvɪŋ)
= motivating ('motə,vetɪŋ)
= driving ('draɪvɪŋ)

usage ('jusɪdʒ) *n.* 使用;用法

= method ('mɛθəd)
= practice ('præktɪs)
= way (we)
= use (jus)
= procedure (prə'sidʒɚ)
= treatment ('tritmənt)
= handling ('hændlɪŋ)

use (juz) *v.* ①使用　②利用

① = utilize ('jutḷ,aɪz)
= employ (ɪm'plɔɪ)
= practice ('præktɪs)
= exercise ('ɛksɚ,saɪz)
= handle ('hændḷ)
= manage ('mænɪdʒ)
② = exploit (ɪk'splɔɪt)
= *take advantage of*

useful ('jusfəl) *adj.* 有益的

= helpful ('hɛlpfəl)
= beneficial (,bɛnə'fɪʃəl)
= profitable ('prɑfɪtəbḷ)

= serviceable ('sɝvɪsəbḷ)
= advantageous (,ædvən'tedʒəs)
= practical ('præktɪkḷ)
= functional ('fʌŋkʃənḷ)
= handy ('hændɪ)
= valuable ('væljʊəbḷ)

useless ('juslɪs) *adj.* 無益的

= worthless ('wɝθlɪs)
= ineffectual (,ɪnə'fɛktʃʊəl)
= fruitless ('frutlɪs)

usher ('ʌʃɚ) *v.* 引導;招待

= escort (ɪ'skɔrt)
= conduct (kən'dʌkt)
= guide (gaɪd)
= lead (lid)
= squire (skwaɪr)
= chaperon ('ʃæpə,ron)
= accompany (ə'kʌmpənɪ)
= attend (ə'tɛnd)

usual ('juʒʊəl) *adj.* 通常的

= customary ('kʌstəm,ɛrɪ)
= ordinary ('ɔrdṇ,ɛrɪ , 'ɔrdnɛrɪ)
= normal ('nɔrmḷ)
= regular ('rɛgjələ)
= common ('kɑmən)
= everyday ('ɛvrɪ'de)
= typical ('tɪpɪkḷ)

usurp (ju'zɝp) *v.* 霸佔;強奪

= assume (ə'sjum)
= control (kən'trol)
= overthrow (,ovɚ'θro)
= *take over*

= *take command*

= *take charge*

= *seize command*

tensil (ju'tɛnsḷ) *n.* 儀器

= implement ('ɪmpləmənt)

= tool (tul)

= instrument ('ɪnstrəmənt)

= apparatus (,æpə'retəs , -'rætəs)

= device (dɪ'vaɪs)

= appliance (ə'plaɪəns)

tilize ('jutḷ,aɪz) *v.* 使用

= use (juz)

= employ (ɪm'plɔɪ)

tmost ('ʌt,most) *adj.* 最遠的;極端的

= greatest ('gretɪst)

= farthest ('farðɪst)

= highest ('haɪɪst)

= extreme (ɪk'strim)

= most (most)

tter ('ʌtɚ) ① *adj.* 完全的
② *v.* 說話

① = complete (kəm'plit)

= total ('totḷ)

= absolute ('æbsə,lut)

= thorough ('θɝo , -ə)

= downright ('daʊn,raɪt)

= outright ('aʊt,raɪt)

= pure (pjʊr)

= plain (plen)

= sheer (ʃɪr)

= unqualified (ʌn'kwɑlə,faɪd)

= extreme (ɪk'strim)

= positive ('pɑzətɪv)

② = speak (spik)

= express (ɪk'sprɛs)

= say (se)

= sound (saʊnd)

= voice (vɔɪs)

V

vacant ('vekənd) *adj.* 空的

= unoccupied (ʌn'ɑkjə,paɪd)

= empty ('ɛmptɪ)

= void (vɔɪd)

= barren ('bærən)

= desolate ('dɛsḷɪt)

vacation (ve'keʃən , və-) *n.* 假期

= rest (rɛst)

= holiday ('hɑlə,de)

= leave (liv)

= recess (rɪ'sɛs)

= furlough ('fɝlo)

= liberty ('lɪbɚtɪ)

= sabbatical (sə'bætɪkḷ)

vaccinate ('væksṇ,et) *v.* 接種疫苗

= inoculate (ɪn'ɑkjə,let)

= immunize ('ɪmjə,naɪz)

vacuum ('vækjʊəm)
① *adj.* 真空的 ② *v.* 打掃

① = void (vɔɪd)

② = sweep（swip）

= clean（klin）

vagabond（'vægə,bɑnd）*n.*
流浪者

= wanderer（'wɑndərə）

= tramp（træmp）

= vagrant（'vegrənt）

= hobo（'hobo）

vague（veg）*adj.* 模糊的

= unclear（ʌn'klɪr）

= indistinct（,ɪndɪ'stɪŋkt）

= indefinite（ɪn'dɛfənɪt）

= dim（dɪm）

= shadowy（'ʃædəwɪ）

= faint（fent）

= obscure（əb'skjʊr）

= blurred（blɜd）

= fuzzy（'fʌzɪ）

= hazy（'hezɪ）

= misty（'mɪstɪ）

vain（ven）*adj.* ①徒然的
②自負的

① = unsuccessful（,ʌnsək'sɛsfəl）

= ineffectual（,ɪnə'fɛktʃuəl）

= futile（'fjutḷ）

= fruitless（'frutlɪs）

② = proud（praʊd）

= conceited（kən'sitɪd）

= boastful（'bost,fəl）

= egotistical（,igə'tɪstɪkḷ）

= egocentric（,igo'sɛntrɪk）

= haughty（'hotɪ）

= lofty（'lɔftɪ , 'lɑftɪ）

= self-centered（'sɛlf'sɛntəd）

valiant（'væljənt）*adj.* 勇敢的

① = brave（brev）

= courageous（kə'redʒəs）

= bold（bold）

= gallant（'gælənt）

= heroic（hɪ'ro·ɪk）

= chivalrous（'ʃɪvḷrəs）

= daring（'dɛrɪŋ）

= dauntless（'dɔntlɪs , 'dɑnt-）

= unafraid（,ʌnə'fred）

valid（'vælɪd）*adj.* 正當的；
有效的

= sound（saʊnd）

= true（tru）

= good（gʊd）

= effective（ə'fɛktɪv）

= proven（'pruvən）

= established（ə'stæblɪʃt）

= cogent（'kodʒənt）

= legal（'ligḷ）

= lawful（'lɔfəl）

= adequate（'ædəkwɪt）

= authorized（'ɔθə,raɪzd）

= well-grounded（'wɛl'graʊndɪd）

valor（'vælə）*n.* 勇氣

= bravery（'brevərɪ）

= courage（'kɜɪdʒ）

= boldness（'boldnɪs）

= gallantry（'gæləntrɪ）

= prowess（'praʊɪs）

= heroism（'hɛro,ɪzəm）

value ('vælju) *n.* 價值

= worth (wɜθ)

= excellence ('ɛksləns)

= usefulness ('jusfəlnɪs)

= importance (ɪm'pɔrtn̩s)

= significance (sɪg'nɪfəkəns)

= weight (wet)

= merit ('mɛrɪt)

= quality ('kwɑlətɪ)

vandal ('vænd!) *n.* 破壞者

= destroyer (dɪ'strɔɪə)

= wrecker ('rɛkə)

= demolisher (dɪ'mɑlɪʃə)

vanish ('vænɪʃ) *v.* 消失

= disappear (,dɪsə'pɪr)

= fade (fed)

= perish ('pɛrɪʃ)

= *go away*

= *cease to be*

vanquish ('væŋkwɪʃ) *v.* 征服

= conquer ('kɑŋkə)

= defeat (dɪ'fit)

= overcome (,ovə'kʌm)

= subdue (səb'dju)

= crush (krʌʃ)

vapor ('vepə) *n.* 霧;蒸氣

= steam (stim)

= fog (fɑg , fɔg)

= mist (mɪst)

= gas (gæs)

= fume (fjum)

= smoke (smok)

various ('vɛrɪəs) *adj.* 多樣的

= different ('dɪfərənt)

= several ('sɛvərəl)

= many ('mɛnɪ)

= diverse (də'vɜs , daɪ-)

varnish ('vɑrnɪʃ) ① *n.* 油漆
② *v.* 掩飾

① = paint (pent)

= coat (kot)

= lacquer ('lækə)

= shellac (ʃə'læk , 'ʃɛlæk)

② = distort (dɪs'tɔrt)

= falsify ('fɔlsə,faɪ)

= misrepresent (,mɪsrɛprɪ'zɛnt)

= color ('kʌlə)

= disguise (dɪs'gaɪz)

= camouflage ('kæmə,flɑʒ)

vary ('vɛrɪ) *v.* 改變

= change (tʃendʒ)

= differ ('dɪfə)

= alter ('ɔltə)

= deviate ('divɪ,et)

vast (væst , vɑst) *adj.* 巨大的

= large (lɑrdʒ)

= immense (ɪ'mɛns)

= great (gret)

= enormous (ɪ'nɔrməs)

= huge (hjudʒ)

= stupendous (stju'pɛndəs)

= colossal (kə'lɑs!)

= monumental (,mɑnjə'mɛnt!)

= mammoth ('mæməθ)

= gigantic (dʒaɪ'gæntɪk)

V

vault (vɔlt) ① v. 跳躍
② n. 地下室 ③ n. 地下墳墓

① = jump (dʒʌmp)
= leap (lip)
= spring (sprɪŋ)
= hop (hɑp)
= bound (baʊnd)
= hurdle ('hɜdl̩)

② = storehouse ('stor,haʊs)
= compartment (kəm'pɑrtmənt)
= depository (dɪ'pɑzə,torɪ)
= safe (sef)
= coffer ('kɔfɚ)

③ = tomb (tum)
= crypt (krɪpt)
= *burial place*

veer (vɪr) v. 改變方向

= shift (ʃɪft)
= turn (tɜn)
= change (tʃendʒ)
= swerve (swɜv)

vegetation (,vɛdʒə'teʃən) n.
①植物 ②生長

① = plants (plænts)
= flora ('florə , 'flɔrə)

② = growth (groθ)

vehement ('viəmənt) adj.
猛烈的

= forceful ('forsfəl)
= violent ('vaɪələnt)
= fierce (fɪrs)
= furious ('fjʊrɪəs)
= severe (sə'vɪr)

= intense (ɪn'tɛns)
= zealous ('zɛləs)
= ardent ('ɑrdn̩t)

vehicle ('viɪkl̩ , 'viəkl̩) n.
交通工具

= carriage ('kærɪdʒ)
= conveyance (kən'veəns)

veil (vel) v. 遮掩

= cover ('kʌvɚ)
= screen (skrin)
= hide (haɪd)
= conceal (kən'sil)
= cloak (klok)
= mask (mæsk , mɑsk)
= disguise (dɪs'gaɪz)
= camouflage ('kæmə,flɑʒ)
= eclipse (ɪ'klɪps)
= obscure (əb'skjʊr)

velocity (və'lɑsətɪ) n. 速度

= speed (spid)
= quickness ('kwɪknɪs)
= swiftness ('swɪftnɪs)

vend (vɛnd) v. 售賣

= sell (sɛl)
= peddle ('pɛdl̩)

venerable ('vɛnərəbl̩) adj.
莊嚴的

= revered (rɪ'vɪrd)
= dignified ('dɪgnə,faɪd)
= stately ('stetlɪ)
= grand (grænd)

= majestic (mə'dʒɛstɪk)
= imposing (ɪm'pozɪŋ)
= important (ɪm'pɔrtn̩t)
= honorable ('ɑnərəbl̩)

ngeance ('vɛndʒəns) *n.* 報仇

= revenge (rɪ'vɛndʒ)
= retaliation (rɪ,tælɪ'eʃən)
= reprisal (rɪ'praɪzl̩)
= avengement (ə'vɛndʒmənt)

nom ('vɛnəm) *n.* ①怨恨
毒

= spite (spaɪt)
= malice ('mælɪs)
= animosity (,ænə'mɑsətɪ)
= bitterness ('bɪtənɪs)
= rancor ('ræŋkə)
= poison ('pɔɪzn̩)

nt (vɛnt) *n.* 孔；口

= hole (hol)
= opening ('opənɪŋ)
= outlet ('aʊt,lɛt)
= passage ('pæsɪdʒ)
= duct (dʌkt)

ntilate ('vɛntl̩,et) *v.* ①使通風
公開討論

= air (ɛr)
= aerate ('eə,ret)
= refresh (rɪ'frɛʃ)
= cool (kul)
= discuss (dɪ'skʌs)
= reason ('rizn̩)
= deliberate (dɪ'lɪbə,ret)

= consider (kən'sɪdə)
= treat (trit)
= study ('stʌdɪ)
= examine (ɪg'zæmɪn)
= *talk over*

venture ('vɛntʃə) *n.* 冒險

= undertaking (,ʌndə'tekɪŋ)
= enterprise ('ɛntə,praɪz)
= project ('prɑdʒɛkt)
= attempt (ə'tɛmpt)
= adventure (əd'vɛntʃə)
= experiment (ɪk'spɛrəmənt)

verbal ('vɝbl̩) *adj.* 口頭的；
言辭的

= oral ('orəl , 'ɔrəl)
= spoken ('spokən)
= uttered ('ʌtəd)
= said (sɛd)
= vocalized ('vokl̩,aɪzd)
= voiced (vɔɪst)
= pronounced (prə'naʊnst)
= sounded ('saʊndɪd)
= articulated (ɑr'tɪkjə,letɪd)
= enunciated (ɪ'nʌnsɪ,etɪd)

verdict ('vɝdɪkt) *n.* 裁決

= decision (dɪ'sɪʒən)
= judgement ('dʒʌdʒmənt)
= finding ('faɪndɪŋ)
= decree (dɪ'kri)
= determination (dɪ,tɝmə'neʃən)
= ruling ('rulɪŋ)
= pronouncement
  (prə'naʊnsmənt)

V

verge ﹝ vɝdʒ ﹞ ① v. 傾向;接近
② n. 邊

① = tend ﹝ tɛnd ﹞
  = incline ﹝ ɪn'klaɪn ﹞
  = lean ﹝ lin ﹞
  = border ﹝'bɔrdɚ﹞
② = edge ﹝ ɛdʒ ﹞
  = rim ﹝ rɪm ﹞
  = brink ﹝ brɪŋk ﹞
  = border ﹝'bɔrdɚ﹞

verify ﹝'vɛrə,faɪ﹞ v. 證實

  = confirm ﹝ kən'fɝm ﹞
  = prove ﹝ pruv ﹞
  = certify ﹝'sɝtə,faɪ﹞
  = validate ﹝'vælə,det﹞
  = substantiate ﹝ səb'stænʃɪ,et﹞
  = authenticate ﹝ ɔ'θɛntɪ,ket﹞
  = corroborate ﹝ kə'rɑbə,ret﹞
  = support ﹝ sə'port , -'pɔrt﹞
  = document ﹝'dɑkjə,mɛnt﹞
  = double-check ﹝'dʌbl'tʃɛk﹞

versatile ﹝'vɝsətl̩ , -tɪl , -taɪl﹞ adj.
多才多藝的

  = skilled ﹝ skɪld ﹞
  = talented ﹝'tæləntɪd﹞
  = competent ﹝'kɑmpətənt﹞
  = capable ﹝'kepəbl̩﹞
  = adaptable ﹝ ə'dæptəbl̩﹞
  = many-sided ﹝'mɛnɪ'saɪdɪd﹞
  = all-around ﹝'ɔlə'raʊnd﹞

verse ﹝ vɝs ﹞ n. ①詩;韻文
②詩節

① = poetry ﹝'po·ɪtrɪ , 'po·ətrɪ﹞

  = rhyme ﹝ raɪm ﹞
  = jingle ﹝'dʒɪŋgl̩﹞
② = section ﹝'sɛkʃən﹞
  = chapter ﹝'tʃæptɚ﹞
  = passage ﹝'pæsɪdʒ﹞
  = measure ﹝'mɛʒɚ﹞
  = division ﹝ də'vɪʒən﹞
  = part ﹝ pɑrt ﹞

versed ﹝ vɝst ﹞ adj. 精通的

  = experienced ﹝ ɪk'spɪrɪənst﹞
  = practiced ﹝'præktɪst﹞
  = educated ﹝'ɛdʒə,ketɪd﹞
  = skilled ﹝ skɪld ﹞

version ﹝'vɝʒən , 'vɝʃən﹞ n.
譯本;敘述

  = rendition ﹝ rɛn'dɪʃən﹞
  = account ﹝ ə'kaʊnt﹞
  = interpretation ﹝ ɪn,tɝprɪ'teʃən﹞

vertical ﹝'vɝtɪkl̩﹞ adj. 直立的
垂直的

  = standing ﹝'stændɪŋ﹞
  = upright ﹝'ʌp,raɪt﹞
  = perpendicular ﹝,pɝpən'dɪkjɚ﹞
  = erect ﹝ ɪ'rɛkt ﹞

very ﹝'vɛrɪ﹞ adv. 極;很

  = greatly ﹝'gretlɪ﹞
  = extremely ﹝ ɪk'strimlɪ﹞
  = much ﹝ mʌtʃ ﹞
  = exceedingly ﹝ ɪk'sidɪŋlɪ﹞
  = quite ﹝ kwaɪt ﹞
  = pretty ﹝'prɪtɪ﹞
  = intensely ﹝ ɪn'tɛnslɪ﹞

vessel ('vɛsḷ) *n.* ①容器 ②船

① = container (kən'tenɚ)
　 = receptacle (rɪ'sɛptəkḷ)
② = shop (ʃɪp)
　 = boat (bot)

veteran ('vɛtərən) ① *adj.* 老練的
② *n.* 退伍軍人

① = experienced (ɪk'spɪrɪənst)
　 = practiced ('præktɪst)
　 = sophisticated (sə'fɪstɪ,ketɪd)
　 = worldly-wise (wɜ˞ldlɪ'waɪz)
② = ex-soldier ('ɛks'soldʒɚ)

veto ('vito) *v.* 否認

= deny (dɪ'naɪ)
= refuse (rɪ'fjuz)

vex (vɛks) *v.* 使惱怒

= annoy (ə'nɔɪ)
= disturb (dɪ'stɜ˞b)
= trouble ('trʌbḷ)
= provoke (prə'vok)
= irk (ɜ˞k)
= irritate ('ɪrə,tet)
= aggravate ('ægrə,vet)

viaduct ('vaɪə,dʌkt) *n.* 高架橋

= bridge (brɪdʒ)
= span (spæn)

vibrate ('vaɪbret) *v.* 震動

= shake (ʃek)
= quiver ('kwɪvɚ)
= quake (kwek)
= tremble ('trɛmbḷ)

= quaver ('kwevɚ)
= wobble ('wabḷ)
= bob (bab)
= bounce (bauns)

vice (vaɪs) *n.* 罪惡；缺點

= fault (fɔlt)
= weakness ('wiknɪs)
= failing ('felɪŋ)
= foible ('fɔɪbḷ)
= shortcoming ('ʃɔrt,kʌmɪŋ)
= wrongdoing ('rɔŋ'duɪŋ)
= malpractice (mæl'præktɪs)
= sin (sɪn)
= crime (kraɪm)
= *bad habit*

vicinity (və'sɪnətɪ) *n.* ①近處
②接近

① = region ('ridʒən)
　 = area ('ɛrɪə , 'erɪə)
　 = zone (zon)
　 = territory ('tɛrə,torɪ , -,tɔrɪ)
　 = place (ples)
　 = district ('dɪstrɪkt)
　 = quarter ('kwɔrtɚ)
　 = section ('sɛkʃən)
　 = neighborhood ('nebɚ,hud)
② = nearness ('nɪrnɪs)
　 = closeness ('klosnɪs)
　 = proximity (prak'sɪmətɪ)

vicious ('vɪʃəs) *adj.* 邪惡的

= evil ('ivḷ)
= wicked ('wɪkɪd)
= spiteful ('spaɪtfʊl)

V

= malicious (mə'lıʃəs)
= bad (bæd)
= naughty ('nɔtɪ)
= wrong (rɔŋ)
= sinful ('sɪnfəl)
= base (bes)
= low (lo)
= vile (vaɪl)
= cruel ('kruəl)
= ruthless ('ruθlıs)
= brutal ('brutḷ)
= barbarous ('barbərəs)
= savage ('sævɪdʒ)
= inhumane (ˌɪnhju'men)
= ferocious (fə'roʃəs , fɪ-)

victim ('vıktım) *n.* 受害者

= prey (pre)
= dupe (djup)
= loser ('luzɚ)
= underdog ('ʌndɚ'dɔg)
= sufferer ('sʌfərɚ)

victory ('vıktərı , 'vıktrı) *n.*
勝利

= success (sək'sɛs)
= triumph ('traɪəmf , -mpf)
= conquest ('kaŋkwɛst)
= winning ('wɪnɪŋ)
= knockout ('nak,aʊt)
= win (wɪn)

vie (vaɪ) *v.* 競爭

= compete (kəm'pit)
= rival ('raɪvḷ)
= match (mætʃ)
= *compare with*

view (vju) ① *v.* 觀看
② *n.* 意見；看法

① = see (si)
= sight (saɪt)
= behold (bɪ'hold)
= observe (əb'zɝv)
= watch (watʃ)
= perceive (pɚ'siv)
= regard (rɪ'gard)
= *look at*
② = opinion (ə'pɪnjən)
= belief (bɪ'lif)
= attitude ('ætə,tjud)
= sentiment ('sɛntəmənt)
= feeling ('filɪŋ)
= impression (ɪm'prɛʃən)
= notion ('noʃən)
= idea (aɪ'diə , -'dɪə)
= thought (θɔt)
= conception (kən'sɛpʃən)
= theory ('θiərɪ , 'θɪə-)
= judgment ('dʒʌdʒmənt)
= outlook ('aʊt,lʊk)

vigilant ('vıdʒələnt) *adj.* 警戒[

= watchful ('watʃfəl)
= alert (ə'lɝt)
= cautious ('kɔʃəs)
= careful ('kɛrfəl)
= wide-awake ('waɪdə'wek)

vigorous ('vıgərəs) *adj.*
精力充沛的

= strong (strɔŋ)
= energetic (ˌɛnɚ'dʒɛtɪk)
= potent ('potṇt)

= powerful ('pauəfəl)

= mighty ('maɪtɪ)

= forceful ('forsfəl)

= rugged ('rʌgɪd)

= hearty ('hartɪ)

= robust (ro'bʌst)

= dynamic (daɪ'næmɪk)

= intense (ɪn'tɛns)

= lively ('laɪvlɪ)

= active ('æktɪv)

= animated ('ænə,metɪd)

= spirited ('spɪrɪtɪd)

= vivacious (vaɪ'veʃəs , vɪ-)

ile (vaɪl) *adj.* 低劣的；可恥的

= foul (faul)

= disgusting (dɪs'gʌstɪŋ)

= bad (bæd)

= terrible ('tɛrəbḷ)

= dreadful ('drɛdfəl)

= horrible ('harəbḷ)

= deplorable (dɪ'plorəbḷ)

= outrageous (aut'redʒəs)

= wretched ('rɛtʃɪd)

= base (bes)

= odious ('odɪəs)

= obnoxious (əb'nakʃəs , ab-)

= abominable (ə'bamnəbḷ)

= detestable (dɪ'tɛstəbḷ)

= despicable ('dɛspɪkəbḷ)

= contemptible (kən'tɛmptəbḷ)

llain ('vɪlən) *n.* 惡徒

= rescal ('ræskḷ)

= scoundrel ('skaundrəl)

= rogue (rog)

= knave (nev)

= scamp (skæmp)

= devil ('dɛvḷ)

vim (vɪm) *n.* 力量；活力

= force (fors , fɔrs)

= energy ('ɛnədʒɪ)

= vigor ('vɪgə)

= verve (vɜv)

= punch (pʌntʃ)

= dash (dæʃ)

= drive (draɪv)

= snap (snæp)

vindicate ('vɪndə,ket) *v.* 辯明；證明

= justify ('dʒʌstə,faɪ)

= uphold (ʌp'hold)

= pardon ('pardṇ)

= excuse (ɪk'skjuz)

= acquit (ə'kwɪt)

= forgive (fə'gɪv)

= *defend successfully*

vindictive (vɪn'dɪktɪv) *adj.* 報復的

= revengeful (rɪ'vɛndʒfḷ)

= avenging(ə'vɛndʒɪŋ)

violate ('vaɪə,let) *v.* 違反

= break (brek)

= trespass ('trɛspəs)

= infringe (ɪn'frɪndʒ)

violence ('vaɪələns) *n.* 猛烈；暴力

= anger ('æŋgə)

V

= rage (redʒ)

= passion ('pæʃən)

= fury ('fjʊrɪ)

= force (fors , fɔrs)

= intensity (ɪn'tɛnsətɪ)

= vehemence ('viəməns , 'vɪhɪməns)

virgin ('vɝdʒɪn) *adj.* 純潔的

= pure (pjʊr)

= spotless ('spɑtlɪs)

= unused (ʌn'juzd)

= new (nju)

= firsthand ('fɝst'hænd)

= original (ə'rɪdʒənḷ)

= fresh (frɛʃ)

= green (grin)

virtual ('vɝtʃʊəl) *adj.* 實際上的

= real ('riəl , ril)

= actual ('æktʃʊəl)

= basic ('besɪk)

= essential (ə'sɛnʃəl)

= fundamental (,fʌndə'mɛntḷ)

virtuous ('vɝtʃʊəs) *adj.* 善良的

= good (gʊd)

= moral ('mɔrəl)

= righteous ('raɪtʃəs)

= angelic (æn'dʒɛlɪk)

= saintly ('sentlɪ)

= chaste (tʃest)

= pure (pjʊr)

= innocent ('ɪnəsṇt)

= faultless ('fɔltlɪs)

= sinless ('sɪnlɪs)

visible ('vɪzəbḷ) *adj.* 可見的；明顯的

= apparent (ə'pærənt , ə'pɛ-)

= manifest ('mænə,fɛst)

= noticeable ('notɪsəbḷ)

= open (opən)

= exposed (ɪk'spozd)

= perceptible (pə'sɛptəbḷ)

= evident ('ɛvədənt)

= obvious ('ɑbvɪəs)

= plain (plen)

= clear (klɪr)

vision ('vɪʒən) *n.* ①視力；觀察力　②幻影

① = sight (saɪt)

= perception (pə'sɛpʃən)

② = apparition (,æpə'rɪʃen)

= image ('ɪmɪdʒ)

= illusion (ɪ'ljuʒən)

= phantom ('fæntəm)

= fantasy ('fæntəsɪ , -zɪ)

= dream (drim)

= specter ('spɛktə)

= ghost (gost)

visit ('vɪzɪt) *v.* 訪問

= attend (ə'tɛnd)

= *go to*

= *drop in*

= *call on*

vista ('vɪstə) *n.* 景色

= view (vju)

= scene (sin)

= sight (saɪt)

= outlook ('aʊt,lʊk)
= perspective (pə'spɛktɪv)
= scenery ('sinərɪ)

ital ('vaɪtḷ) *adj.* ①極重要的
②有生命的

① = necessary ('nɛsə,sɛrɪ)
= important (ɪm'pɔrtṇt)
= essential (ə'sɛnʃəl)
= fundamental (,fʌndə'mɛntḷ)
= needed ('nidɪd)
= required (rɪ'kwaɪrd)
② = living ('lɪvɪŋ)
= alive (ə'laɪv)
= animate ('ænəmɪt)

itality (vaɪ'tælətɪ) *n.* 活力

= strength (strɛŋθ)
= vigor ('vɪgə)
= might (maɪt)
= potency ('potṇsɪ)
= power ('paʊə)
= energy ('ɛnədʒɪ)
= stamina ('stæmənə)

vacious (vaɪ've∫əs) *adj.*
活潑的

= lively ('laɪvlɪ)
= sprightly ('spraɪtlɪ)
= animated ('ænə,metɪd)
= gay (ge)
= spirited ('spɪrɪtɪd)
= exuberant (ɪg'zjubərənt)
= active ('æktɪv)
= spry (spraɪ)
= brisk (brɪsk)

= dynamic (daɪ'næmɪk)
= energetic (,ɛnə'dʒɛtɪk)

vivid ('vɪvɪd) *adj.* 活潑的

= bright (braɪt)
= brilliant ('brɪljənt)
= strong (strɔŋ)
= clear (klɪr)
= distinct (dɪ'stɪŋkt)
= splendid ('splɛndɪd)
= flamboyant (flæm'bɔɪənt)
= glaring ('glɛrɪŋ)
= dazzling ('dæzlɪŋ)
= rich (rɪt∫)
= colorful ('kʌlə-fəl)

vocal ('vokḷ) *adj.* 口頭的；
有聲的

= spoken ('spokən)
= uttered ('ʌtəd)
= said (sɛd)
= voiced (vɔɪst)
= pronounced (prə'naʊnst)
= sounded ('saʊndɪd)
= oral ('orəl , 'ɔrəl)
= verbal ('vɝbḷ)
= enunciated (ɪ'nʌnsɪ,etɪd)
= articulated (ɑr'tɪkjə,letɪd)

vocation (vo'ke∫ən) *n.* 職業

= occupation (,ɑkjə'pe∫ən)
= business ('bɪznɪs)
= profession (prə'fɛ∫ən)
= trade (tred)
= line (laɪn)
= work (wɝk)

V

= calling ('kɔlɪŋ)
= craft (kræft , krɑft)

vociferous (vo'sɪfərəs) *adj.*
嘈雜的

= noisy ('nɔɪzɪ)
= loud (laud)
= shouting ('ʃautɪŋ)
= clamoring ('klæmərɪŋ)
= boisterous ('bɔɪstərəs)
= blatant ('bletn̩t)

vogue (vog) *n.* 時尚;流行

= fashion ('fæʃən)
= style (staɪl)
= mode (mod)
= popularity (,pɑpjə'lærətɪ)

voice (vɔɪs) *v.* 發表;說出

= express (ɪk'sprɛs)
= utter ('ʌtə)
= verbalize ('vɜbl̩,aɪz)
= say (se)
= articulate (ɑr'tɪkjə,let)
= enunciate (ɪ'nʌnsɪ,et)
= pronounce (prə'nauns)
= tell (tɛl)
= communicate (kə'mjunə,ket)

void (vɔɪd) *adj.* ①空的;空缺的
②無效的

① = empty ('ɛmptɪ)
= vacant ('vekənt)
= bare (bɛr)
= blank (blæŋk)
= barren ('bærən)

= desolate ('dɛsl̩ɪt)
= unoccupied (ʌn'akjə,paɪd)
= deserted (dɪ'zɜtɪd)
= open ('opən)
= available (ə'veləbl̩)
② = invalid (ɪn'vælɪd)

volume ('valjəm) *n.* ①容量;
數量 ②書冊

① = amount (ə'maunt)
= quantity ('kwantətɪ)
= capacity (kə'pæsətɪ)
= content (kən'tɛnt)
= proportion (prə'porʃən ,
-'pɔr-)
= measure ('mɛʒə)
= extent (ɪk'stɛnt)
② = book (buk)
= publication (,pʌblɪ'keʃən)
= work (wɜk)
= writing ('raɪtɪŋ)

voluminous (və'lumənəs) *adj.*
大的;多的

= generous ('dʒɛnərəs)
= ample ('æmpl̩)
= bulky ('bʌlkɪ)
= extensive (ɪk'stɛnsɪv)

volunteer (,valən'tɪr) *v.* 自願

= offer ('ɔfə , 'afə)
= *come forward*

vomit ('vamɪt) *v.* 噴出;嘔吐

= retch (rɛtʃ)
= heave (hiv)

= regurgitate (ri'gɜdʒə,tet)

= spew (spju)

= *throw up*

voracious (vo'reʃəs) *adj.*
貪婪的

= ravenous ('rævənəs)

= greedy ('gridɪ)

= piggish ('pɪgɪʃ)

= hoggish ('hɑgɪʃ)

= gluttonous ('glʌtn̩əs)

vote (vot) *n.* 選舉

= ballot ('bælət)

= choice (tʃɔɪs)

= voice (vɔɪs)

= poll (pol)

= designation (,dɛzɪg'neʃən)

= referendum (,rɛfə'rɛndəm)

= decision (dɪ'sɪʒən)

= determination (dɪ,tɜmə'neʃən)

= selection (sə'lɛkʃən)

vouch (vautʃ) *v.* 擔保

= testify ('tɛstə,faɪ)

= swear (swɛr)

= assure (ə'ʃur)

= promise ('prɑmɪs)

= pledge (plɛdʒ)

= vow (vau)

= guarantee (,gærən'ti)

= *bear witness*

vow (vau) *v.* 發誓

= swear (swɛr)

= promise ('prɑmɪs)

= assure (ə'ʃur)

= guarantee (,gærən'ti)

= pledge (plɛdʒ)

= vouch (vautʃ)

voyage ('vɔɪ·ɪdʒ) *v.* 航行

= journey ('dʒɜnɪ)

= travel ('trævl̩)

= sail (sel)

= navigate ('nævə,get)

= cruise (kruz)

vulgar ('vʌlgɚ) *adj.* 粗俗的

= coarse (kors , kɔrs)

= common ('kɑmən)

= unrefined (,ʌnrɪ'faɪnd)

= indecent (ɪn'disn̩t)

= improper (ɪm'prɑpɚ)

= offensive (ə'fɛnsɪv)

= crude (krud)

= crass (kræs)

= obscene (əb'sin)

= uncouth (ʌn'kuθ)

= foul (faul)

= filthy ('fɪlθɪ)

= nasty ('næstɪ)

vulnerable ('ʌnlnərəbl̩) *adj.*
易受傷害的

= sensitive ('sɛnsətɪv)

= exposed (ɪk'spozd)

= open ('opən)

= susceptible (sə'sɛptəbl̩)

= unprotected (,ʌnprə'tɛktɪd)

= defenseless (dɪ'fɛnslɪs)

V

vying (ˈvaɪɪŋ) *adj.* 競爭的

= rival (ˈraɪvl̩)

= competitive (kəmˈpɛtətɪv)

W

wad (wɑd) *n.* 小塊

= chunk (tʃʌŋk)

= hunk (hʌŋk)

= lump (lʌmp)

= mass (mæs)

wag (wæg) *v. n.* 搖擺

= bob (bɑb)

= flap (flæp)

= flutter (ˈflʌtɚ)

= sway (swe)

= swing (swɪŋ)

= wave (wev)

= wobble (ˈwɑbl̩)

wage (wedʒ) ① *n.* 工資
② *v.* 從事

①= compensation (ˌkɑmpənˈseʃən)

= pay (pe)

= payment (ˈpemənt)

= remuneration (rɪˌmjunəˈreʃən)

= salary (ˈsælərɪ)

②= conduct (kənˈdʌkt)

= follow (ˈfɑlo)

= practice (ˈpræktɪs)

= pursue (pəˈsu, -ˈsju)

= exercise (ˈɛksɚˌsaɪz)

= *carry on*

= *engage in*

wager (ˈwedʒɚ) *v.* 打賭

= bet (bɛt)

= gamble (ˈgæmbl̩)

= hazard (ˈhæzɚd)

= stake (stek)

wagon (ˈwægən) *n.* 貨車

= carriage (ˈkærɪdʒ)

= vehicle (ˈviɪkl̩, ˈviəkl̩)

waif (wef) *n.* 流浪者

= gamin (ˈgæmɪn)

= stray (stre)

= vagabond (ˈvægəˌbɑnd)

wail (wel) *v.* 哭泣

= bawl (bɔl)

= cry (kraɪ)

= howl (haʊl)

= moan (mon)

= scream (skrim)

= screech (skritʃ)

= shriek (ʃrik)

= squeal (skwil)

wait (wet) *v.* 等候；延緩

= defer (dɪˈfɝ)

= delay (dɪˈle)

= linger (ˈlɪŋgɚ)

= postpone (postˈpon)

= procrastinate (proˈkræstəˌnet)

= shelve (ʃɛlv)

= stay (ste)

= table (ˈtebl̩)

= tarry (ˈtærɪ)

= *put off*

wake (wek) v. 醒來

= arise (ə'raɪz)
= arouse (ə'rauz)
= awake (ə'wek)
= rouse (rauz)
= stir (stɜ)
= *get up*

walk (wɔk) v. 行走

= ambulate ('æmbjə,let)
= hike (haɪk)
= pace (pes)
= step (stɛp)
= stroll (strol)
= tread (trɛd)

wallet ('walɪt) n. 皮包

= billfold ('bɪl,fold)
= purse (pɝs)

wallop ('waləp) v. 痛打

= bat (bæt)
= beat (bit)
= clout (klaut)
= crack (kræk)
= flog (flag)
= hit (hɪt)
= jab (dʒæb)
= knock (nak)
= lick (lɪk)
= rap (ræp)
= slug (slʌg)
= smack (smæk)
= spank (spæŋk)
= strike (straɪk)
= thrash (θræʃ)

= whack (hwæk)
= whip (hwɪp)

wallow ('walo) v. 打滾;（船）顛簸而行

= flounder ('flaundə)
= lurch (lɝtʃ)
= pitch (pɪtʃ)
= reel (ril)
= rock (rak)
= roll (rol)
= sway (swe)
= swing (swɪŋ)
= toss (tɔs)
= tumble ('tʌmbl̩)

wan (wan) adj. 蒼白的

= ashen ('æʃən)
= bloodless ('blʌdlɪs)
= colorless ('kʌlə-lɪs)
= faint (fent)
= ghastly ('gæstlɪ , 'gast-)
= haggard ('hægəd)
= pale (pel)
= pallid ('pælɪd)
= pasty ('pæstɪ)
= sallow ('sælo)
= weak (wik)

wand (wand) n. 棍;棒

= rod (rad)
= scepter ('sɛptə)
= staff (stæf , staf)

wander ('wandə) v. 徘徊

= drift (drɪft)
= gad (gæd)

W

= meander (mɪ'ændə)
= ramble ('ræmbḷ)
= roam (rom)
= rove (rov)
= stray (stre)

wane (wen) v. 減弱

= abate (ə'bet)
= decline (dɪ'klaɪn)
= decrease (dɪ'kris)
= diminish (də'mɪnɪʃ)
= lessen ('lɛsṇ)
= recede (rɪ'sid)
= reduce (rɪ'djus)
= subside (səb'saɪd)

want (wɑnt) v. ①要；欲 ②缺少

① = desire (dɪ'zaɪr)
= fancy ('fænsɪ)
= like (laɪk)
= *long for*
= *wish for*
② = lack (læk)
= need (nid)
= require (rɪ'kwaɪr)

wanton ('wɑntən) adj. ①任性的；胡亂的 ②淫蕩的

① = careless ('kɛrlɪs)
= erratic (ə'rætɪk)
= hasty ('hestɪ)
= impetuous (ɪm'pɛtʃʊəs)
= reckless ('rɛklɪs)
= uncontrolled (ˌʌnkən'trold)
= unreasonable (ʌn'riznəbḷ)

= wayward ('wewəd)
= whimsical ('hwɪmzɪkḷ)
= wild (waɪld)
② = immoral (ɪ'mɔrəl)
= loose (lus)
= unchaste (ʌn'tʃest)

war (wɔr) n. 戰爭

= battle ('bætḷ)
= campaign (kæm'pen)
= clash (klæʃ)
= combat ('kɑmbæt , 'kʌm-)
= conflict ('kɑnflɪkt)
= encounter (ɪn'kaʊntə)
= engagement (ɪn'gedʒmənt)
= fight (faɪt)
= hostilities (hɑs'tɪlətɪz)
= strife (straɪf)
= struggle ('strʌgḷ)

warehouse ('wɛrˌhaʊs) n. 倉庫

= depository (dɪ'pɑzəˌtorɪ)
= depot ('dipo , 'dɛpo)
= storehouse ('storˌhaʊs)

warm (wɔrm) adj. ①暖的 ②熱誠的

① = hot (hɑt)
= tepid ('tɛpɪd)
② = congenial (kən'dʒinjəl)
= cordial ('kɔrdʒəl)
= enthusiastic (ɪnˌθjuzɪ'æstɪk)
= friendly ('frɛndlɪ)

warn (wɔrn) v. ①通知；警告 ②威脅

= advise (əd'vaız)

= alert (ə'lɜt)

= caution ('kɔʃən)

= forebode (for'bod , fɔr-)

= inform (ın'fɔrm)

= notify ('notə,faı)

= *give notice*

= menace ('mɛnıs)

= threaten ('θrɛtn̩)

arp (wɔrp) *v.* 使彎曲

= bend (bɛnd)

= contort (kən'tɔrt)

= distort (dıs'tɔrt)

= twist (twıst)

arrant ('wɔrənt) *n.* ①權利
證明

= authority (ə'θɔrətı)

= authorization (,ɔθərə'zeʃən)

= certificate (sə'tıfəkıt)

= justification (,dʒʌstəfə'keʃən)

= mandate ('mændet)

= reason ('rizn̩)

= right (raıt)

= sanction ('sæŋkʃən)

= voucher ('vautʃə)

= writ (rıt)

= assurance (ə'ʃurəns)

= guarantee (,gærən'ti)

= oath (oθ)

= pledge (plɛdʒ)

= promise ('pramıs)

= vow (vau)

= word (wɜd)

warrior ('wɔrıə , 'wɑ-) *n.* 戰士

= fighter ('faıtə)

= soldier ('soldʒə)

wary ('werı , 'wærı) *adj.* 小心的

= careful ('kɛrfəl)

= cautious ('kɔʃəs)

= distrustful (dıs'trʌstfəl)

= guarded ('gɑrdıd)

= suspicious (sə'spıʃəs)

wash (waʃ , wɔʃ) *v.* 洗

= bathe (beð)

= clean (klin)

= launder ('lɔndə , 'lɑn-)

= rinse (rıns)

= scour (skaur)

= scrub (skrʌb)

waste (west) ① *v.* 浪費
② *n.* 廢物

① = consume (kən'sum , -'sjum)

= exhaust (ıg'zɔst , ɛg-)

= spend (spɛnd)

= squander ('skwɑndə)

= *use up*

② = dregs (drɛgz)

= garbage ('gɑrbıdʒ)

= refuse ('rɛfjus)

= rubbish ('rʌbıʃ)

= scraps (skræps)

watch (watʃ) *v.* ①看　②照顧

① = observe (əb'zɜv)

= regard (rı'gɑrd)

W

= view〔vju〕

= *look at*

② = guard〔gɑrd〕

= mind〔maɪnd〕

= protect〔prə'tɛkt〕

= shield〔ʃild〕

= tend〔tɛnd〕

= *care for*

waterway〔'wɔtə,we〕*n.* 水道

= canal〔kə'næl〕

= channel〔'tʃænl〕

= passageway〔'pæsɪdʒ,we〕

= river〔'rɪvə〕

wave〔wev〕*v.* ①揮動
②做手勢

① = flap〔flæp〕

= flutter〔'flʌtə〕

= move〔muv〕

= sway〔swe〕

= swing〔swɪŋ〕

② = gesture〔'dʒɛstʃə〕

= signal〔'sɪgnl̩〕

wax〔wæks〕*v.* ①增大
②塗以蠟

① = develop〔dɪ'vɛləp〕

= enlarge〔ɪn'lɑrdʒ〕

= flourish〔'flɝɪʃ〕

= gain〔gen〕

= grow〔gro〕

= heighten〔'haɪtn̩〕

= increase〔ɪn'kris〕

= intensify〔ɪn'tɛnsə,faɪ〕

= rise〔raɪz〕

= sprout〔spraʊt〕

= swell〔swɛl〕

② = burnish〔'bɝnɪʃ〕

= furbish〔'fɝbɪʃ〕

= glaze〔glez〕

= polish〔'pɑlɪʃ〕

= shine〔ʃaɪn〕

way〔we〕*n.* ①方式 ②手段
③方面；點 ④方向 ⑤路程
⑥習性

① = custom〔'kʌstəm〕

= fashion〔'fæʃən〕

= manner〔'mænə〕

= mode〔mod〕

= practice〔'præktɪs〕

= style〔staɪl〕

= usage〔'jusɪdʒ〕

② = means〔minz〕

= method〔'mɛθəd〕

= procedure〔prə'sidʒə〕

= process〔'prɑsɛs , 'prosɛs〕

③ = detail〔'ditel〕

= feature〔'fitʃə〕

= point〔pɔɪnt〕

= respect〔rɪ'spɛkt〕

④ = course〔kors , kɔrs〕

= direction〔də'rɛkʃen , daɪ-〕

= line〔laɪn〕

⑤ = distance〔'dɪstəns〕

= extent〔ɪk'stɛnt〕

= length〔lɛŋθ , lɛŋkθ〕

= reach〔ritʃ〕

= remoteness〔rɪ'motnɪs〕

⑥ = character〔'kærɪktə〕

= constitution〔,kɑnstə'tjuʃən〕

= disposition (ˌdɪspəˈzɪʃən)

= humor (ˈhjumɚ , ˈju-)

= mood (mud)

= nature (ˈnetʃɚ)

= temperament (ˈtɛmprəmənt , -pərə-)

= will (wɪl)

waylay (ˌweˈle) v. 半路埋伏

= ambush (ˈæmbuʃ)

= attack (əˈtæk)

= *lie in wait*

wayward (ˈwewɚd) adj.
①任性的 ②不規則的

① = contrary (ˈkɑntrɛrɪ)

= difficult (ˈdɪfəkəlt , klt)

= disobedient (ˌdɪsəˈbidɪənt)

= immoral (ɪˈmɔrəl , ɪmˈmɔrəl)

= lawless (ˈlɔlɪs)

= loose (lus)

= perverse (pɚˈvɝs)

= troublesome (ˈtrʌbl̩səm)

= undisciplined (ʌnˈdɪsəˌplɪnd)

= wanton (ˈwɑntən)

② = changeable (ˈtʃendʒəbl̩)

= erratic (əˈrætɪk)

= irregular (ɪˈrɛgjəlɚ)

= unsettled (ʌnˈsɛtl̩d)

= unsteady (ʌnˈstɛdɪ)

= wavering (ˈwevərɪŋ)

weak (wik) adj. 衰弱的

= debilitated (dɪˈbɪləˌtetɪd)

= feeble (ˈfibl̩)

= fragile (ˈfrædʒəl)

= impotent (ˈɪmpətənt)

= powerless (ˈpaʊɚlɪs)

wealth (wɛlθ) n. 財富

= abundance (əˈbʌndəns)

= affluence (ˈæfluəns)

= assets (ˈæsɛts)

= fortune (ˈfɔrtʃən)

= opulence (ˈɑpjələns)

= possessions (pəˈzɛʃənz)

= prosperity (prɑsˈpɛrətɪ)

= resources (rɪˈsorsɪz)

= riches (ˈrɪtʃɪz)

= treasure (ˈtrɛʒɚ)

wean (win) v. 使戒絕

= cure (kjur)

= *break of*

= *turn away from*

weapon (ˈwɛpən) n. 武器

= arms (ɑrmz)

= munition (mjuˈnɪʃən)

wear (wɛr) v. ①穿上 ②耗損

① = don (dɑn)

= *dress in*

= *have on*

② = corrode (kəˈrod)

= decay (dɪˈke)

= deteriorate (dɪˈtɪrɪəˌret)

weary (ˈwɪrɪ , ˈwɪrɪ) adj. 疲倦的

= faint (fent)

= fatigued (fəˈtigd)

= lethargic (lɪˈθɑrdʒɪk)

W

= listless ('lıstlıs)
= sluggish ('slʌgıʃ)
= tired (taırd)
= weak (wik)

weather ('wɛðɚ) *n.* 天氣

= climate ('klaımıt)
= *the elements*

weave (wiv) *v.* 編織

= braid (bred)
= intertwine (,ıntɚ'twaın)
= lace (les)

wed (wɛd) *v.* 嫁給

= join (dʒɔın)
= marry ('mærı)
= unite (ju'naıt)

wedge (wɛdʒ) *v.* 擠進

= jam (dʒæm)
= lodge (lɑdʒ)
= push (puʃ)
= squeeze (skwiz)

wedlock ('wɛdlɑk) *n.* 婚姻

= marriage ('mærıdʒ)
= matrimony ('mætrə,monı)

weep (wip) *v.* 哭泣

= bawl (bɔl)
= blubber ('blʌbɚ)
= cry (kraı)
= snivel ('snıvl̩)
= sob (sab)

= *shed tears*

weigh (we) *v.* 估量

= appraise (ə'prez)
= assess (ə'sɛs)
= estimate ('ɛstə,met)
= gauge (gedʒ)
= measure ('mɛʒɚ)
= rate (ret)
= *size up*

weighty ('wetı) *adj.* ①重的
②累人的 ③重要的

① = heavy ('hɛvı)
= hefty ('hɛftı)
② = burdensome ('bɝdn̩səm)
= onerous ('ɑnərəs)
= oppressive (ə'prɛsıv)
③ = effective (ə'fɛktıv)
= important (ım'pɔrtn̩t)
= influential (,ınflu'ɛnʃəl)
= powerful ('pauɚfəl)
= serious ('sırıəs)

weird (wırd) *adj.* 奇異的

= creepy ('kripı)
= eerie ('ırı , 'ırı)
= fantastic (fæn'tæstık)
= ghostly ('gostlı)
= mysterious (mıs'tırıəs)
= odd (ad)
= peculiar (pı'kjuljɚ)
= queer (kwır)
= spooky ('spukı)
= strange (strendʒ)

W

welcome ('wɛlkəm) v. 歡迎

= greet (grit)

= receive (rɪ'siv)

weld (wɛld) v. 熔接

= bind (baɪnd)

= cement (sə'mɛnt)

= join (dʒɔɪn)

= solder ('sadə)

= unite (ju'naɪt)

welfare ('wɛl,fɛr , -,fær) n. 福利

= advantage (əd'væntɪdʒ)

= behalf (bɪ'hæf)

= benefit ('bɛnəfɪt)

= comfort ('kʌmfət)

= good (gʊd)

= interest ('ɪntərɪst , 'ɪntrɪst)

= prosperity (pras'pɛrətɪ)

= success (sək'sɛs)

= well-being ('wɛl'biɪŋ)

welt (wɛlt) n. 傷痕

= sore (sor , sɔr)

= swelling ('swɛlɪŋ)

whack (hwæk) v. 重擊

= bat (bæt)

= blow (blo)

= clout (klaʊt)

= crack (kræk)

= hit (hɪt)

= jab (dʒæb)

= slug (slʌg)

= smack (smæk)

= strike (straɪk)

wharf (hwɔrf) n. 碼頭

= dock (dak)

= harbor ('harbə)

= pier (pɪr)

= port (port , pɔrt)

wheedle ('hwidl̩) v. 勸誘；阿諛

= coax (koks)

= goad (god)

= persuade (pə'swed)

= press (prɛs)

= prod (prad)

= urge (ɝdʒ)

whet (hwɛt) v. 磨；使興奮

= edge (ɛdʒ)

= intensify (ɪn'tɛnsə,faɪ)

= sharpen ('ʃarpən)

= stimulate ('stɪmjə,let)

whether ('hwɛðə) conj. 是否

= if (ɪf)

= provided (prə'vaɪdɪd)

whiff (hwɪf) n. 一陣氣味

= fume (fjum)

= odor ('odə)

= smell (smɛl)

= scent (sɛnt)

whim (hwɪm) n. 奇想

= caprice (kə'pris)

= fad (fæd)

= fancy ('fænsɪ)

= notion ('noʃən)

= phase (fez)

W

whimper (ˈhwɪmpɚ) v. 啜泣

= cry (kraɪ)

= whine (hwaɪn)

whine (hwaɪn) v. 哭訴

= cry (kraɪ)

= whimper (ˈhwɪmpɚ)

whip (hwɪp) v. 鞭打

= beat (bit)

= flog (flɑg)

= lace (les)

= lash (læʃ)

= paddle (ˈpædḷ)

= pummel (ˈpʌmḷ)

= spank (spæŋk)

= strap (stræp)

= strike (straɪk)

= thrash (θræʃ)

whirl (hwɝl) v. 迴旋

= pivot (ˈpɪvət)

= reel (ril)

= rotate (ˈrotet)

= spin (spɪn)

= swirl (swɝl)

= turn (tɝn)

= twirl (ˈtwɝl)

= wheel (hwil)

whisk (hwɪsk) v. ①掃
②迅速拿走

① = brush (brʌʃ)

= sweep (swip)

② = hasten (ˈhesn̩)

= hurry (ˈhɝɪ)

= rush (rʌʃ)

= speed (spid)

whisper (ˈhwɪspɚ) v. n. 低語；
耳語

= mumble (ˈmʌmbḷ)

= murmur (ˈmɝmɚ)

= mutter (ˈmʌtɚ)

whole (hol) adj. 完全的

= complete (kəmˈplit)

= entire (ɪnˈtaɪr)

= one (wʌn)

= solid (ˈsɑlɪd)

= total (ˈtotḷ)

= undivided (ˌʌndəˈvaɪdɪd)

wholehearted (ˈholˈhɑrtɪd)
adj. 熱烈的

= cordial (ˈkɔrdʒəl)

= earnest (ˈɝnɪst , -əst)

= gracious (ˈgreʃəs)

= hearty (ˈhɑrtɪ)

= sincere (sɪnˈsɪr)

wholesome (ˈholsəm) adj.
有益（健康）的

= beneficial (ˌbɛnəˈfɪʃəl)

= healthful (ˈhɛlθfəl)

= salutary (ˈsæljəˌtɛrɪ)

= sound (saʊnd)

wicked (ˈwɪkɪd) adj. ①邪惡的
②不愉快的

① = bad (bæd)

= base (bes)

= evil ('ivl̩)

= low (lo)

= naughty ('nɔtɪ)

= sinful ('sɪnfəl)

= vicious ('vɪʃəs)

= vile (vaɪl)

= wrong (rɔŋ)

= difficult ('dɪfəkəlt)

= hard (hɑrd)

= rough (rʌf)

= rugged ('rʌgɪd)

= severe (sə'vɪr)

= tough (tʌf)

= unpleasant (ʌn'plɛzn̩t)

ide (waɪd) *adj.* 寬廣的

= ample ('æmpl̩)

= broad (brɔd)

= expansive (ɪk'spænsɪv)

= extensive (ɪk'stɛnsɪv)

= roomy ('rumɪ)

= spacious ('speʃəs)

ield (wild) *v.* 揮舞;使用

= employ (ɪm'plɔɪ)

= handle ('hændl̩)

= hold (hold)

= manage ('mænɪdʒ)

= manipulate (mə'nɪpjə,let)

= use (juz)

= wave (wev)

ife (waɪf) *n.* 妻子

= mate (met)

= spouse (spaʊz)

= *married woman*

wig (wɪg) *n.* 假髮

= hairpiece ('hɛr,pis)

= toupee (tu'pe , -'pi)

wiggle ('wɪgl̩) *v. n.* 扭動;搖動

= fidget ('fɪdʒɪt)

= jerk (dʒɝk)

= squirm (skwɝm)

= twist (twɪst)

= twitch (twɪtʃ)

= wriggle ('rɪgl̩)

= writhe (raɪð)

wild (waɪld) *adj.* ①野蠻的
②狂暴的

① = barbarous ('bɑrbərəs)

= bestial ('bɛstɪəl , 'bɛstʃəl)

= brutal ('brutl̩)

= fierce (fɪrs)

= ferocious (fə'roʃəs , fɪ-)

= rampant ('ræmpənt)

= savage ('sævɪdʒ)

= unchecked (ʌn'tʃɛkt)

= uncivilized (ʌn'sɪvl̩,aɪzd)

= unrestrained (,ʌnrɪ'strend)

= untamed (ʌn'temd)

= violent ('vaɪələnt)

② = crazy ('krezɪ)

= delirious (dɪ'lɪrɪəs)

= frantic ('fræntɪk)

= frenzied ('frɛnzɪd)

= furious ('fjʊrɪəs)

= hysterical (hɪs'tɛrɪkl̩)

= impetuous (ɪm'pɛtʃʊəs)

= mad (mæd)

= overwrought ('ovɚ'rɔt)

W

= rabid ('ræbɪd)
= rash (ræʃ)
= reckless ('rɛklɪs)
= wanton ('wɑntən)

wilderness ('wɪldə‧nɪs) *n.* 荒野

= wasteland ('west‧lænd)

will (wɪl) *n.* ①願望 ②目的；
決心 ③遺囑

① = desire (dɪ'zaɪr)
= fancy ('fænsɪ)
= hope (hop)
= inclination (‧ɪnklə'neʃən)
= pleasure ('plɛʒə)
= urge (ɝdʒ)
= volition (vo'lɪʃən)
= wish (wɪʃ)

② = choice (tʃɔɪs)
= contemplation
  (‧kɑntəm'pleʃən)
= decision (dɪ'sɪʒən)
= design (dɪ'zaɪn)
= determination (dɪ‧tɝmə'neʃən)
= election (ɪ'lɛkʃən)
= intention (ɪn'tɛnʃən)
= plan (plæn)
= purpose ('pɝpəs)
= resolution (‧rɛzə'ljuʃən)
= resolve (rɪ'zɑlv)
= selection (sə'lɛkʃən)

③ = bequest (bɪ'kwɛst)
= legacy ('lɛgəsɪ)
= testament ('tɛstəmənt)

willful ('wɪlfəl) *adj.* ①固執的
②有意的

① = adamant ('ædə‧mænt)
= bullheaded ('bʊl'hɛdɪd)
= firm (fɝm)
= headstrong ('hɛd‧strɔŋ)
= obstinate ('ɑbstənɪt)
= stubborn ('stʌbən)
= uncompromising
  (ʌn'kɑmprə‧maɪzɪŋ)

② = calculated ('kælkjə‧letɪd)
= conscious ('kɑnʃəs)
= deliberate (dɪ'lɪbərɪt)
= designed (dɪ'zaɪnd)
= intended (ɪn'tɛndɪd)
= intentional (ɪn'tɛnʃənḷ)
= meant (mɛnt)
= purposeful ('pɝpəsfʊl)
= voluntary ('vɑlən‧tɛrɪ)

willing ('wɪlɪŋ) *adj.* 情願的

= agreeable (ə'griəbḷ)
= compliant (kəm'plaɪənt)
= consenting (kən'sɛntɪŋ)
= eager ('igə)
= inclined (ɪn'klaɪnd)
= ready ('rɛdɪ)

wilt (wɪlt) *v.* 枯萎

= deteriorate (dɪ'tɪrɪə‧ret)
= droop (drup)
= fade (fed)
= languish ('læŋgwɪʃ)
= pine (paɪn)
= shrivel ('ʃrɪvḷ)
= wither ('wɪðə)
= *dry up*

ily ('waɪlɪ) *adj.* 狡詐的

= artful ('ɑrtfəl)
= canny ('kænɪ)
= clever ('klɛvɚ)
= crafty ('kræftɪ , 'krɑftɪ)
= cunning ('kʌnɪŋ)
= foxy ('fɑksɪ)
= shrewd (ʃrud)
= shifty ('ʃɪftɪ)
= slippery ('slɪpərɪ)
= sly (slaɪ)
= smooth (smuð)
= tricky ('trɪkɪ)

in (wɪn) *v.* 獲得；贏得

= capture ('kæptʃɚ)
= carry ('kærɪ)
= gain (gen)
= prevail (prɪ'vel)
= succeed (sək'sid)
= triumph ('traɪəmf , -mpf)
= *be victorious*

ince (wɪns) *v.* 畏縮

= cringe (krɪndʒ)
= flinch (flɪntʃ)
= recoil (rɪ'kɔɪl)
= shrink (ʃrɪŋk)
= *draw back*

wind (wɪnd) *n.* ①風 ②呼吸

= air (ɛr)
= breeze (briz)
= draft (dræft)
= gust (gʌst)
= breath (brɛθ)

= respiration (ˌrɛspə'reʃən)

2. wind (waɪnd) *v.* 蜿蜒

= bend (bɛnd)
= coil (kɔɪl)
= pivot ('pɪvət)
= roll (rol)
= spiral ('spaɪrəl)
= swivel ('swɪvḷ)
= turn (tɜn)
= twist (twɪst)

wink (wɪŋk) *v.* 眨眼

= blink (blɪŋk)
= squint (skwɪnt)

winning ('wɪnɪŋ) *adj.* 迷人的

= alluring (ə'ljʊrɪŋ)
= appealing (ə'pilɪŋ)
= attractive (ə'træktɪv)
= bewitching (bɪ'wɪtʃɪŋ)
= captivating ('kæptɪˌvetɪŋ)
= charming ('tʃɑrmɪŋ)
= delightful (dɪ'laɪtfəl)
= enchanting (ɪn'tʃæntɪŋ)
= enthralling (ɪn'θrɔlɪŋ)
= enticing (ɪn'taɪsɪŋ , ɛn-)
= fascinating ('fæsṇˌetɪŋ)
= fetching ('fɛtʃɪŋ)
= interesting ('ɪntərɪstɪŋ , 'ɪntrɪstɪŋ)
= intriguing (ɪn'trigɪŋ)
= inviting (ɪn'vaɪtɪŋ)
= lovely ('lʌvlɪ)
= provocative (prə'vɑkətɪv)
= tantalizing ('tæntəˌlaɪzɪŋ)

W

wipe (waɪp) v. 擦去

= rub (rʌb)

= stroke (strok)

wire (waɪr) ① n. 電報
② v. 綁起　③ v. 裝電線

① = cable ('kebḷ)

= telegraph ('tɛlə,græf)

② = bind (baɪnd)

= fasten ('fæsṇ , 'fɑsṇ)

= tie (taɪ)

③ = electrify (ɪ'lɛktrə,faɪ)

wiry ('waɪrɪ) adj. ①瘦長而結
實的　②剛硬的

① = lean (lin)

= stringy ('strɪŋɪ)

② = athletic (æθ'lɛtɪk)

= brawny ('brɔnɪ)

= muscular ('mʌskjələ)

= strong (strɔŋ)

= tough (tʌf)

wise (waɪz) adj. 明智的

= bright (braɪt)

= cultured ('kʌltʃəd)

= educated ('ɛdʒə,ketɪd , -dʒʊ-)

= knowing ('noɪŋ)

= knowledgeable ('nɑlɪdʒəbḷ ,
'nɑlɛdʒ-)

= learned ('lɜnɪd)

= profound (prə'faʊnd)

= sage (sedʒ)

= smart (smart)

= scholarly ('skɑləlɪ)

wish (wɪʃ) v. 想要；希望

= desire (dɪ'zaɪr)

= fancy ('fænsɪ)

= like (laɪk)

= request (rɪ'kwɛst)

= want (wɑnt)

= *long for*

wistful ('wɪstfəl) adj. 渴望的

= desirous (dɪ'zaɪrəs)

= hankering ('hæŋkərɪŋ)

= homesick ('hom,sɪk)

= longing ('lɔŋɪŋ , 'lɑŋ-)

= melancholy ('mɛlən'kɑlɪ)

= nostalgic (nɑ'stældʒɪk)

= pensive ('pɛnsɪv)

= pining ('paɪnɪŋ)

= yearning ('jɜnɪŋ)

wit (wɪt) n. 智力；機智

= humor ('hjumə)

= intelligence (ɪn'tɛlədʒəns)

= sense (sɛns)

= understanding (,ʌndə'stændɪŋ

witch (wɪtʃ) n. 女巫

= hag (hæg)

= shrew (ʃru)

= sorceress ('sɔrsərɪs)

= vixen ('vɪksṇ)

withdraw (wɪð'drɔ , wɪθ-) v.
①撤回　②移去

① = abandon (ə'bændən)

= quit (kwɪt)

W

= recede (rɪ'sid)

= retire (rɪ'taɪr)

= retreat (rɪ'trit)

= reverse (rɪ'vɝs)

= vacate ('veket)

= *fall back*

= deduct (dɪ'dʌkt)

= extract (ɪk'strækt)

= remove (rɪ'muv)

= subtract (səb'trækt)

ither ('wɪðɚ) *v.* 凋謝

= deteriorate (dɪ'tɪrɪə,ret)

= droop (drup)

= fade (fed)

= languish ('læŋgwɪʃ)

= pine (paɪn)

= shrink (ʃrɪŋk)

= shrivel ('ʃrɪvl̩)

= wane (wen)

= wilt (wɪlt)

= *dry up*

ithhold (wɪð'hold) *v.* ①克制
②拒絕

= keep (kip)

= preserve (prɪ'zɝv)

= reserve (rɪ'zɝv)

= save (sev)

= deny (dɪ'naɪ)

= disallow (,dɪsə'lau)

= refuse (rɪ'fjuz)

ithin (wɪð'ɪn) *prep.* 在…之內

= in (ɪn)

= inside (ɪn'saɪd)

without (wɪð'aut) *prep.* 沒有；
無

= lacking ('lækɪŋ)

= less (lɛs)

= minus ('maɪnəs)

= wanting ('wɑntɪŋ)

withstand (wɪθ'stænd) *v.*
抵抗

= endure (ɪn'djur)

= oppose (ə'poz)

= repel (rɪ'pɛl)

= resist (rɪ'zɪst)

witness ('wɪtnɪs) *v.* ①證明
②目擊

① = swear (swɛr)

= testify ('tɛstə,faɪ)

= vouch (vautʃ)

② = behold (bɪ'hold)

= discern (dɪ'zɝn , -'sɝn)

= glimpse (glɪmps)

= observe (əb'zɝv)

= perceive (pɚ'siv)

= see (si)

= sight (saɪt)

= spy (spaɪ)

= view (vju)

witty ('wɪtɪ) *adj.* 詼諧的

= amusing (ə'mjuzɪŋ)

= clever ('klɛvɚ)

= droll (drol)

= funny ('fʌnɪ)

= humorous ('hjumərəs)

= whimsical ('hwɪmzɪkl̩)

W

wizard (ˈwɪzəd) *n.* ①巫師 ②專家

① = conjuror (ˈkʌndʒərə)
= sorcerer (ˈsɔrsərə)

② = expert (ˈɛkspɜt)
= genius (ˈdʒinjəs)
= master (ˈmæstə, ˈma-)

wobbly (ˈwɑblɪ) *adj.* 不穩定的

= rickety (ˈrɪkətɪ)
= shaky (ˈʃekɪ)
= trembling (ˈtrɛmblɪŋ)
= unsteady (ʌnˈstɛdɪ)
= wavering (ˈwevərɪŋ)

woe (wo) *n.* 悲痛

= agony (ˈægənɪ)
= anguish (ˈæŋgwɪʃ)
= desolation (ˌdɛsḷˈeʃən)
= distress (dɪˈstrɛs)
= grief (grif)
= heartache (ˈhɑrtˌek)
= misery (ˈmɪzərɪ)
= oppression (əˈprɛʃən)
= sorrow (ˈsɑro)
= trouble (ˈtrʌbḷ)

woman (ˈwʊmən) *n.* 女性

= female (ˈfimel)
= lady (ˈledɪ)
= matron (ˈmetrən)

wonder (ˈwʌndə) *v.* ①感到驚奇 ②想知道

① = gape (gep)
= marvel (ˈmɑrvḷ)

= stare (stɛr)

② = doubt (daʊt)
= question (ˈkwɛstʃən)
= *be uncertain*

wonderful (ˈwʌndəfəl) *adj.* 令人驚奇的

= astonishing (əˈstɑnɪʃɪŋ)
= exceptional (ɪkˈsɛpʃənḷ)
= extraordinary (ɪkˈstrɔrdṇˌɛrɪ)
= fabulous (ˈfæbjələs)
= incredible (ɪnˈkrɛdəbḷ)
= magnificent (mægˈnɪfəsṇt)
= marvelous (ˈmɑrvləs)
= miraculous (məˈrækjələs)
= remarkable (rɪˈmɑrkəbḷ)
= splendid (ˈsplɛndɪd)
= striking (ˈstraɪkɪŋ)
= superb (sʊˈpɜb, sə-)

woo (wu) *v.* 求取；追求

= court (kort, kɔrt)
= pursue (pəˈsu, -ˈsju)
= *bid for*

woods (wʊdz) *n.* 森林

= bush (bʊʃ)
= forest (ˈfɔrɪst, ˈfɑr-)

word (wɜd) *v.* 說出

= communicate (kəˈmjunəˌket)
= express (ɪkˈsprɛs)
= phrase (frez)
= put (pʊt)
= say (se)
= tell (tɛl)
= voice (vɔɪs)

W

ork (wɜk) *v.* ①工作 ②使用

= accomplish (ə'kɑmplıʃ)
= achieve (ə'tʃiv)
= busy ('bɪzɪ)
= effect (ə'fɛkt , ı- , ɛ-)
= employ (ım'plɔı)
= engage (ın'gedʒ)
= labor ('lebɚ)
= make (mek)
= occupy ('ɑkjə,paı)
= toil (tɔıl)
= conduct (kən'dʌkt)
= handle ('hændḷ)
= manage ('mænıdʒ)
= maneuver (mə'nuvɚ)
= manipulate (mə'nıpjə,let)
= operate ('ɑpə,ret)
= run (rʌn)

orkout ('wɜk,aʊt) *n.* ①練習
②測驗

= drill (drıl)
= exercise ('ɛksɚ,saız)
= practice ('præktıs)
= rehearsal (rı'hɜsḷ)
= test (tɛst)
= trial ('traıəl)
= tryout ('traı,aʊt)
= *dry run*

orld (wɜld) *n.* 世界

= earth (ɜθ)
= globe (glob)
= universe ('junə,vɜs)

orn (wɔrn) *adj.* ①破舊的
②疲倦的

①= damaged ('dæmıdʒd)
= impaired (ım'pɛrd)
= old (old)
= ragged ('rægıd)
= secondhand ('sɛkənd'hænd)
= used (juzd)
②= faint (fent)
= fatigued (fə'tigd)
= tired (taırd)
= weak (wik)
= wearied ('wırıd)

worry ('wɜı) *v.* 使煩惱

= badger ('bædʒɚ)
= bother ('bɑðɚ)
= harass ('hærəs , hə'ræs)
= harry ('hærı)
= molest (mə'lɛst)
= plague (pleg)
= torment (tɔr'mɛnt)
= trouble ('trʌbḷ)
= vex (vɛks)

worse (wɜs) *adj.* 更差的；
惡化的

= aggravated ('ægrə,vetıd)
= deteriorated (dı'tırıə,retıd)
= impaired (ım'pɛrd)

worship ('wɜʃəp) *v.* 崇拜；尊敬

= admire (əd'maır)
= adore (ə'dor , ə'dɔr)
= awe (ɔ)
= cherish ('tʃɛrıʃ)
= esteem (ə'stim)
= honor ('ɑnɚ)
= idolize ('aıdḷ,aız)

W

= respect (rɪ'spɛkt)

= revere (rɪ'vɪr)

worth (wɝθ) *n.* 價值

= benefit ('bɛnəfɪt)

= importance (ɪm'pɔrtəns)

= merit ('mɛrɪt)

= significance (sɪg'nɪfəkəns)

= usefulness ('jusfəlnɪs)

= value ('vælju)

= weight (wet)

wound (wund) *v.* ①傷害
②激怒

① = bruise (bruz)

= damage ('dæmɪdʒ)

= harm (hɑrm)

= hurt (hɝt)

= injure ('ɪndʒɚ)

② = grieve (griv)

= infuriate (ɪn'fjʊrɪ,et)

= irritate ('ɪrə,tet)

= madden ('mædn̩)

= offend (ə'fɛnd)

= pain (pen)

= provoke (prə'vok)

= sting (stɪŋ)

wrangle ('ræŋgl̩) *v.* 爭吵

= argue ('ɑrgju)

= bicker ('bɪkɚ)

= contend (kən'tɛnd)

= differ ('dɪfɚ)

= disagree (,dɪsə'gri)

= dispute (dɪ'spjut)

= quarrel ('kwɔrəl , 'kwɑr-)

= row (rau)

= spat (spæt)

= squabble ('skwɑbl̩)

wrap (ræp) *v.* 包；裹

= bind (baɪnd)

= cover ('kʌvɚ)

= encompass (ɪn'kʌmpəs , ɛn-)

= envelop (ɪn'vɛləp)

= sheathe (ʃɪð)

= surround (sə'raʊnd)

wrath (ræθ , rɑθ) *n.* 憤怒

= anger ('æŋgɚ)

= ire (aɪr)

= rage (redʒ)

wreath (riθ) *n.* 花圈

= coronet ('kɔrənɪt)

= festoon (fɛs'tun)

= garland ('gɑrlənd)

wreck (rɛk) *v.* 破壞；毀壞

= demolish (dɪ'mɑlɪʃ)

= destroy (dɪ'strɔɪ)

= devastate ('dɛvəs,tet)

= dismantle (dɪs'mæntl̩)

= ravage ('rævɪdʒ)

= ruin ('ruɪn)

wrench (rɛntʃ) *v.* ①猛扭
②扭傷

① = jerk (dʒɝk)

= pull (pʊl)

= twist (twɪst)

= wrest (rɛst)

W

= wring〔rɪŋ〕
= yank〔jæŋk〕
② = hurt〔hɝt〕
= injure〔'ɪndʒɚ〕
= sprain〔spren〕
= strain〔stren〕

wrestle〔'rɛsl̩〕v. 奮鬥

= battle〔'bætl̩〕
= fight〔faɪt〕
= struggle〔'strʌgl̩〕
= tussle〔'tʌsl̩〕

wretch〔rɛtʃ〕n. ①不幸的人
②卑鄙的人

① = beggar〔'bɛgɚ〕
= derelict〔'dɛrə,lɪkt〕
= sufferer〔'sʌfərɚ〕
= *poor devil*
② = knave〔nev〕
= rogue〔rog〕
= scoundrel〔'skaʊndrəl〕
= shrew〔ʃru〕
= villain〔'vɪlən〕

wriggle〔'rɪgl̩〕v. 轉動

= squirm〔skwɝm〕
= turn〔tɝn〕
= twist〔twɪst〕
= wiggle〔'wɪgl̩〕
= writhe〔raɪð〕

wring〔rɪŋ〕v. 扭；絞

= squeeze〔skwiz〕
= twist〔twɪst〕
= wrest〔rɛst〕
= *press out*

wrinkle〔'rɪŋkl̩〕v. ①起皺
②變老；變衰弱

① = corrugate〔'kɔrə,get〕
= crease〔kris〕
= crinkle〔'krɪŋkl̩〕
= fold〔fold〕
= furrow〔'fɝo〕
= pucker〔'pʌkɚ〕
= ridge〔rɪdʒ〕
② = age〔edʒ〕
= decline〔dɪ'klaɪn〕
= decrease〔dɪ'kris〕
= *grow old*

writ〔rɪt〕n. 命令

= notice〔'notɪs〕
= order〔'ɔrdɚ〕
= warrant〔'wɔrənt , 'wɑ- 〕

write〔raɪt〕v. 書寫

= inscribe〔ɪn'skraɪb〕
= mark〔mɑrk〕
= note〔not〕
= pen〔pɛn〕
= post〔post〕
= record〔rɪ'kɔrd〕
= scribe〔skraɪb〕

writhe〔raɪð〕v. ①轉動
②受苦

① = squirm〔skwɝm〕
= turn〔tɝn〕
= twist〔twɪst〕
= wiggle〔'wɪgl̩〕
② = ache〔ek〕
= agonize〔'ægə,naɪz〕

W

= anguish ('æŋgwɪʃ)
= hurt (hɜt)
= moan (mon)
= suffer ('sʌfɚ)
= wince (wɪns)

wrong (rɔŋ) *adj.* ①錯的
②邪惡的

① = false (fɔls)
= improper (ɪm'prapɚ)
= incorrect (,ɪnkə'rɛkt)
= mistaken (mə'stekən)
= unfit (ʌn'fɪt)
= unsuitable (ʌn'sjutəb!)
= untrue (ʌn'tru)
② = bad (bæd)
= evil ('iv!)
= ill (ɪl)

wry (raɪ) *adj.* 扭歪的

= askew (ə'skju)
= contorted (kən'tɔrtɪd)
= crooked ('krʊkɪd)
= distorted (dɪs'tɔrtɪd)
= twisted ('twɪstɪd)

X

x-ray ('ɛks're) *n.* X 光照片

= photograph ('fotə,græf)

Y

yacht (jɑt) *n.* 遊艇

= boat (bot)

yank (jæŋk) *v. n.* 猛扭；猛拉

= draw (drɔ)
= haul (hɔl)
= heave (hiv)
= jerk (dʒɜk)
= pull (pʊl)
= tug (tʌg)
= wrench (rɛntʃ)
= wrest (rɛst)

yap (jæp) *v.* 吠

= bark (bɑrk)
= howl (haʊl)
= yelp (jɛlp)

yard (jɑrd) *n.* ①庭院 ②碼

① = confine ('kɑnfaɪn)
= court (kort , kɔrt)
= enclosure (ɪn'kloʒɚ)
= pen (pɛn)
② = *three feet*

yarn (jɑrn) *n.* ①毛線 ②故事

① = thread (θrɛd)
= wool (wʊl)
② = account (ə'kaʊnt)
= anecdote ('ænɪk,dot)
= narrative ('nærətɪv)
= spiel (spil)
= story ('storɪ)
= tale (tel)

yearn (jɜn) *v.* 渴望

= crave (krev)
= desire (dɪ'zaɪr)

= *long for*

= *hope for*

= *pine for*

= *wish for*

yell (jɛl) *v.* 呼喊

= bawl (bɔl)

= bellow ('bɛlo , -lə)

= call (kɔl)

= howl (haʊl)

= roar (ror , rɔr)

= scream (skrim)

= shriek (ʃrik)

= shout (ʃaʊt)

= squall (skwɔl)

= wail (wel)

= whoop (hup , hwup)

= *cry out*

yelp (jɛlp) *v.* 吠叫

= bark (bɑrk)

= howl (haʊl)

= yap (jæp)

yield (jild) *v.* ①生產　②放棄

① = bear (bɛr)

= furnish ('fɝnɪʃ)

= give (gɪv)

= grant (grænt)

= produce (prə'djus)

= provide (prə'vaɪd)

= supply (sə'plaɪ)

② = forego (for'go , fɔr-)

= relinquish (rɪ'lɪŋkwɪʃ)

= sacrifice ('sækrə,faɪs , -,faɪz)

= surrender (sə'rɛndɚ)

= waive (wev)

= *give up*

= *part with*

yoke (jok) *n.* 牛軛

= bridle ('braɪdl̩)

= harness ('hɑrnɪs)

= shackle ('ʃækl̩)

young (jʌŋ) *adj.* 年輕的

= juvenile ('dʒuvənl̩ , -,naɪl)

= youthful ('juθfəl)

youngster ('jʌŋstɚ) *n.* 少年

= child (tʃaɪld)

= kid (kɪd)

= minor ('maɪnɚ)

= youth (juθ)

Y

youthful ('juθfəl) *adj.* 年輕的

= callow ('kælə , 'kælo)

= childish ('tʃaɪldɪʃ)

= fresh (frɛʃ)

= juvenile ('dʒuvənl̩ , -,naɪl)

= kiddish ('kɪdɪʃ)

= young (jʌŋ)

yowl (jaʊl) *v.* 號叫

= cry (kraɪ)

= howl (haʊl)

= scream (skrim)

= shriek (ʃrik)

= wail (wel)

= whoop (hup , hwup)

= yell (jɛl)

Z

zany ('zenɪ) *adj.* 小丑的；
愚蠢的

= clownish ('klaunɪʃ)

= comical ('kɑmɪkḷ)

= crazy ('krezɪ)

= foolish ('fulɪʃ)

= scatterbrained ('skætəˌbrend)

= silly ('sɪlɪ)

zeal (zil) *n.* 熱心

= ardor ('ɑrdə)

= eagerness ('igənɪs)

= enthusiasm (ɪn'θjuzɪˌæzəm)

= fervor ('fɝvə)

= passion ('pæʃən)

= sincerity (sɪn'sɛrətɪ)

zenith ('zinɪθ) *n.* 天頂；頂點

= acme ('ækmɪ , 'ækmi)

= apex ('epɛks)

= crest (krɛst)

= crown (kraun)

= peak (pik)

= pinnacle ('pɪnəkḷ)

= summit ('sʌmɪt)

= top (tɑp)

= tip (tɪp)

zero ('zɪro) *n.* 零

= naught (nɔt)

= nil (nɪl)

= none (nʌn)

= nothing ('nʌθɪŋ)

zest (zɛst) *n.* 風味；趣味

= delight (dɪ'laɪt)

= eagerness ('igənɪs)

= enjoyment (ɪn'dʒɔɪmənt)

= gusto ('gʌsto)

= pleasure ('plɛʒə)

= relish ('rɛlɪʃ)

= satisfaction (ˌsætɪs'fækʃən)

= savor ('sevə)

zone (zon) *n.* 區域

= area ('ɛrɪə , 'e-)

= compartment (kəm'pɑrtmənt)

= department (dɪ'pɑrtmənt)

= district ('dɪstrɪkt)

= division (də'vɪʒən)

= neighborhood ('nebəˌhud)

= part (pɑrt)

= place (ples)

= quarter ('kwɔrtə)

= region ('ridʒən)

= territory ('tɛrəˌtorɪ , -ˌtɔrɪ)

= section ('sɛkʃən)

= vicinity (və'sɪnətɪ)

zoo (zu) *n.* 動物園

= menagerie (mə'nædʒərɪ ,
  -'næʒ-)

= *animal enclosure*

zoom (zum) *v.* 嗡嗡作響地移動

= fly (flaɪ)

= speed (spid)

= whiz (hwɪz)

= zip (zɪp)

「一口氣背同義字」
以3字為一組，9字為一回。

「一口氣背同義字」

是以一個劇情，9個句子，

背100多個單字。

背同義字有助於演講。

背同義字有助於閱讀。